A MAGIC OF TWILIGHT

"Farrell weaves the lives of his characters into an enthralling mix of politics, religion, magic, love, and betrayal—allowing a novel of Imperial conquest and the questions of faith to remain a tapestry of very personal stories." —bestselling author Tanya Huff

"Moving gracefully between the intrigues of palaces and slums, *A Magic Of Twilight* is fast-paced yet intricate, a delight for readers of both military and political fiction."

—bestselling author Jane Lindskold

". . . gorgeously detailed setting and intriguing characters. Then there's the tangled knot, knitted up of at least seven different kinds of treachery . . . a fantasy novel to settle down with for a nice, long time . . . Farrell's world-building is, as always, impressive: intricate and well-thought out . . . a vivid rich story of treachery, hope, faith, and snarled loyalties as complex as the city that houses them."

—Charlene Brusso in BLACK GATE

". . . a wondrous tale of intrigue, adventure, the collision of politics and religion, and the triumph of personal virtue over fear and doubt. . . . The craft of world-building has rarely been put on display so ingeniously." —Drew Bittner in SFREVU

"Considerable charm and appeal. . . . It's always refreshing to read a fantasy where neither side in a conflict has much of a moral edge on the other, and the cast of characters are an enjoyable mix of the sympathetic, the villainous and the ambiguous." —KIRKUS REVIEWS

"Farrell easily wields an immense cast of characters. . . . Readers who appreciate intricate world building, intrigue, and action will immerse themselves effortlessly into this rich and complex story."

—PUBLISHERS WEEKLY

"Lust, hate, envy, greed and pride—if there was a sacrilege to savor or a commandment to break, the schemers in this tale grabbed it with gusto. Farrell . . . swept me away on a thoroughly enjoyable ride."

—John R. Alden in the CLEVELAND PLAIN DEALER

". . . a fantasy epic steeped in Machiavellian politics in a Renaissance world that should appeal to fans of the genre while providing an entertaining and addicting read . . . skillfully realized and balances well the needs of world-building, characterization and plot. . . . The strength of *A Magic of Twilight* resides in politics. . . . The portrayal of these Machiavellian politics rivals writers like Robert Jordan at their best, even approaching the skill of George R. R. Martin. . . ."

". . . the skillful multiple-pers[...]
an engaging mix of schemes, [...]
ant surprise, and one which d[...]

*Coming in March from DAW Books

S. L. FARRELL

A Magic of Twilight

A Novel in *The Nessantico Cycle*

DAW BOOKS, INC.
DONALD A. WOLLHEIM, FOUNDER
375 Hudson Street, New York, NY 10014

ELIZABETH R. WOLLHEIM
SHEILA E. GILBERT
PUBLISHERS
www.dawbooks.com

First Paperback Printing, February 2009
1   2   3   4   5   6   7   8   9   10

DAW TRADEMARK REGISTERED
U.S. PAT. AND TM. OFF AND FOREIGN COUNTRIES
—MARCA REGISTRADA
HECHO EN U.S.A.

PRINTED IN THE U.S.A.

Acknowledgments

I read several books for inspiration and reference in writing this book (and I read them for pleasure as well, since I enjoy reading historical texts; it's a character flaw, I know . . .). Since this is a work set entirely in a fictional, imagined world, it doesn't particularly reflect any one period or place in our own history but I have instead borrowed freely from several. For those interested in those historical texts that sparked my own imagination, some of them old and some relatively new, I'd like to list them here, in the order in which I read them:

A Nervous Splendor: Vienna 1888/1889 by Frederic Morton. Little, Brown, 1979

The House of Medici: Its Rise and Fall by Christopher Hibbert. Perennial / Harper Collins, 2003

Athénaïs: The Life of Louis XIV's Mistress, the Real Queen of France by Lisa Hilton. Back Bay Books / Little, Brown & Company, 2002

The Serpent and the Moon: Two Rivals for the Love of a Renaissance King by Her Royal Highness, Princess Michael of Kent. Simon & Schuster, Inc., 2004

Seven Ages of Paris by Alistair Horne. Vintage Books (Random House), 2004

The Seashell on the Mountaintop by Alan Cutler. Plume (Penguin), 2003

Love & Death in Renaissance Italy by Thomas V. Cohen. University of Chicago Press, 2004

The God Delusion by Richard Dawkins. Houghton Mifflin, 2006

*   *   *

A trip to France also served as inspiration for much of this book. In particular, the Loire Valley region, with its chateaux and lovely countryside, sparked several ideas, as did our days in Paris. I would like to recommend that anyone going to France see the Loire Valley and spend time exploring not only the chateaux, but the small villages in the surrounding countryside such as Azay le Rideau or Villaines les-Rochers. Nessantico is not specifically France, but many details are drawn from our experiences there. Hopefully they have enriched the book.

Many thanks, as always, to my agent Merrilee Heifetz of Writers House, who has been my partner-in-writing for many years now—without her, none of this would have been possible.

I also want to express my gratitude to Sheila Gilbert, editor extraordinaire, who has nurtured my books and never allowed me to make them any less than the best I can manage. For each of my books that Sheila has edited, her input has produced an "Aha!" moment (or two or three) that has made the novel richer. This book is no different. Thanks, Sheila!

My appreciation to Justin Scott, who proofed the final manuscript and gave me several pages of corrections. Thanks!

And thanks also to Karen who reminded me that twilight is better than dusk!

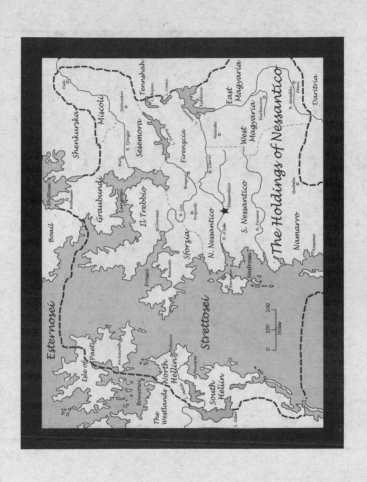

The Holdings of Nessantico

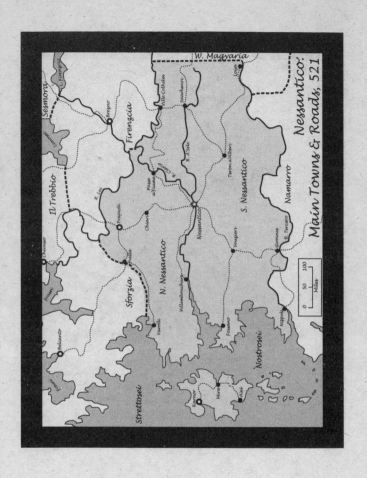

Nessantico: Main Towns & Roads, 521

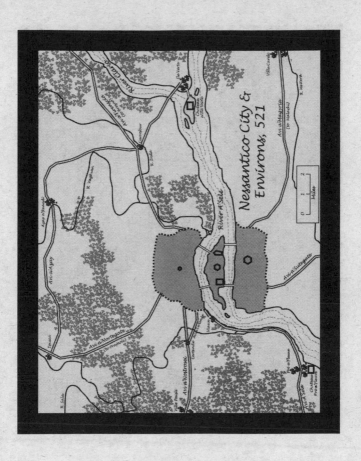

Nessantico City & Environs, 521

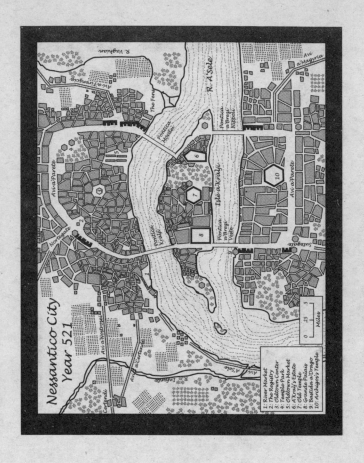

Nessantico City
Year 521

1: River Market
2: The Registry
3: Oldtown Center
4: Temple Park
5: Oldtown Market
6: A'Kralj's Estate
7: Old Temple
8: Grande Palaüs
9: Pontica de Batisse
10: Archigos' Temple

0   .25   .5
Miles

Table of Contents

Prelude: Nessantico

IF A CITY CAN HAVE A GENDER, Nessantico was female.

She began life as a jewel in the glittering, slow waters of the River A'Sele. She was an island city in infancy, connected to land by massive stone bridges and connected by the A'Sele to the sea that nourished her with trade goods. The A'Sele bustled with ship-borne commerce from its convergence with the River Clario to the river's wide, protected mouth in the Nostrosei, all of the largesse passing through Nessantico. As the influence of the tribal chieftains who first settled Nessantico began to grow, so did the city, spreading out from the island to the banks on either side.

By the time the rulers of Nessantico began to call themselves Kraljiki and Kraljica, by the time they extended their rule beyond the city's borders, she had grown into a vital young woman, swathed and armored in great walls that were never breached by any invader, her armies sweeping over the villages, towns, and city-states around her. Irresistibly strong, she was also seductive: the city where the Kralji held their illustrious courts, where the ambassadors of a hundred lands came to beg and bargain and bluster, where ships from foreign lands of the Strettosei and the Rhittosei brought their goods and treasure, where a dozen cultures melded to form a stronger alloy, where the magical gifts of a dozen gods were displayed and sought after.

Over the decades and the slow centuries—as the

country which took its name from her became yet more influential; as the Kralji became de facto rulers not only of Nessantico but of Il Trebbio, then Firenzcia, Magyaria, and more; as the Holdings spread out in all directions even across the Strettosei to the shores of the Westlands; as the Faith of Concénzia subsumed and forcibly converted the majority of the other religions and lesser gods within the Holdings, Nessantico—the city, the woman— allowed herself to relax and enjoy her reputation. Always strong even as the borders of the Holdings ebbed and flowed under the effects of war and commerce, always magnificent even as tastes and styles changed, always seductive and desirable no matter what other exotic lands and places might come into brief fashion, she spread steadily beyond the walls that had once confined her, gathering to herself all that was intellectual, all that was rich, all that was powerful. Her standard of deep blue and rich gold fluttered from the towers, and the lights of the téni glistened like star-jewels in the night.

There was no city in the known world that could rival her.

But there were many who envied her.

BEGINNINGS

Ana cu'Seranta
Karl ci'Vliomani
Marguerite ca'Ludovici
Ana cu'Seranta
Dhosti ca'Millac

Ana cu'Seranta

ANA KNELT DOWN alongside the bed, smiling determinedly at the motionless, unresponsive body under the white linen sheet. She took the woman's hands: clammy and limp, the loose skin netted with fine wrinkles. "Matarh," Ana whispered, then spoke her name, since Ana thought she sometimes responded better to that. "Abini, I'm here."

Eyelids fluttered but did not open, and Abini's fingers twitched once in Ana's hand but failed to clasp hers in return. "It's nearly First Call," Ana continued, "and I've come to pray with you, Matarh." The wind-horns sounded plaintively from the Old Temple dome at the same moment, muffled by distance and blurred with echoes from the intervening buildings. Ana glanced up; beyond the curtains, the sun glazed the rooftops of the city. "Do you hear the horns, Matarh? Listen to them, and I'll pray for both of us."

Ana placed her matarh's hands together just under her throat, then clasped her own hands to forehead. She tried to pray, but her mind refused to calm itself. The comforting routine of the morning prayers was diluted with memories: of U'Téni cu'Dosteau's rebukes, of her fading memories of the time before the Southern Fever left her matarh helpless and unresponsive, of the happier times before Ana had to bear the guilt of what she did nearly every morning just to keep her matarh alive. "Forgive me, Cénzi," she said, as she always did, wondering whether He heard, wondering when He would punish her for her impertinence—because that was what the Divolonté, the code of rules governing the Concénzia Faith, insisted must inevitably happen. Cénzi was a stern God, and He would insist that Ana pay for her impertinence in subverting His intentions. "Forgive me…"

She wondered whether she spoke to Cénzi or to her matarh.

She began to chant, the words coming unbidden: guttural nonsense syllables that were not the rigid forms U'Téni cu'Dosteau taught her. Her hands moved with the chant, as if she were dancing with her fingers alone. Even before Vatarh had sent her to the Old Temple to become an acolyte, even before she'd begun to learn how to channel the power of Ilmodo, she'd been able to do this.

And even then, she'd known it was something she needed to hide.

She'd listened to the téni thundering their admonitions from the High Lectern enough to realize that. U'Téni cu'Dosteau, the Instruttorei a'Acolyte, was just as blunt and direct: "A téni does not thwart Cénzi's Will unpunished…" or "To use the Ilmodo for your own desires is forbidden…" or "The Divolonté is clear on this. Read it, and if the harshness of it gives you chills, it should."

Ana told herself that she wasn't using the Ilmodo for herself, but for her matarh. She told herself that if it were truly Cénzi's Will that Abini die, well, Cénzi certainly had the power to make that happen no matter what small efforts she might produce to keep her alive. She told herself that if Cénzi had not wanted her to do this, He would not have given her the Gift so early.

Somehow, it never quite convinced. She suspected that Cénzi had already chosen her punishment. She already knew His displeasure.

She shaped the Ilmodo now, quickly. She could feel the cold power of what the téni called the Second World rising between her moving hands, and her chant and the patterns she formed sent tendrils of energy surging toward her matarh. As the Ilmodo touched the prone body, Ana felt the familiar shock of connection. There was a hint of her matarh's consciousness lost somewhere far below, and she felt that if she wished, she might, she *might* be able to pull her entirely back.

But that would have been truly wrong, and it would be too obvious. So, as she had done for the last few years, she used just a touch of the Ilmodo, enough to ensure that her matarh would not sink any further away from life, enough for her to know that Abini would live for another few days longer.

And she let the Ilmodo go. She stopped her chanting, her hands dropped to her sides. The guilt—as always—surged over her like the spring flood of the River A'Sele, and with it came the payment for using the Ilmodo: a muscular exhaustion as severe as if she had been up all day laboring at some impossible physical task—once more, she would be fighting an insistent compulsion to sleep as she listened to U'Téni cu'Dosteau's lectures. She clasped hands to forehead again and prayed for Cénzi's understanding and forgiveness.

"Ana? Are you with your matarh?"

She heard her vatarh open the door to the bedroom. *So quickly, Cénzi?* she asked. *Is this what I must bear for what I do?* Ana bit her lip and squeezed her eyes shut, refusing to let herself cry.

"I know your presence comforts your matarh," her vatarh said softly, coming up behind her. Tomas cu'Seranta had a voice that purred and growled, and once she'd loved to hear him talk. She would curl up in his lap and ask him to tell her a story, anything, just so she could lay her head against his broad chest and listen to the rumble of his deep voice.

Once . . .

She felt his hand on her shoulder, stroking the soft fabric of her tashta where it gathered. The hand followed the curve of her spine from neck to the middle of her back. His hand slid along the curve of her hip. She closed her eyes, hearing him half-kneel alongside her. "I miss her, too," he whispered. "I don't know what I'd do if I were to lose you, too, my little bird." She wouldn't look at him, but she felt him as a warmth along her side, and now his hand slid along the tashta's folds to where the cloth swelled over her breasts. His fingers cupped her.

She stood abruptly, and his hand dropped away. He was looking down at the floor, not at her nor at Abini. "I have to leave for class, Vatarh," Ana said. "U'Téni cu'Dosteau said we must be there early today . . ."

~

Karl ci'Vliomani

"CAN YOU IMAGINE this in summer?" Mika ce'Gilan whispered, leaning close to Karl. His long, aquiline nose wrinkled dramatically. "I smell more sweat than perfume."

Karl could only nod in agreement. The Kraljica's Throne Room was crowded with supplicants. It was the second Cénzidi of the month, the day that the Kraljica accepted all supplicants—at least all those who managed to reach her in the few turns of the glass she sat on the Sun Throne. The long hall was stuffed as tightly as sweetfruit in a crate with people dressed in their best finery. The room sweltered; Karl could feel beads of perspiration gathered at his brow and running freely down his spine to soak the cloth of the bashta he wore. *"It's what all the ca'-and-cu' are wearing this season,"* the tailor had declared, but Karl could see nothing at all similar in the cut of the bashtas and tashtas nearest him. He suspected that it was last year's fashion at best, and that those staring appraisingly at him were snickering behind their fluttering, ornate fans. He also noted that he and Mika stood in their own little open space, as if those with ca' or cu' in front of their name would be contaminated if they came too close. He touched the pendant around his neck nervously—a seashell that looked as if it had been carved of stone, the plain gray rock polished from usage.

At the front of the room, the Sun Throne gleamed beneath the Kraljica Marguerite ca'Ludovici: the ruler of Nessantico and the Holdings, the great Généra a'Pace, the Wielder of the Iron Staff, the Matarh a'Dominion, who would in a few months be celebrating the Jubilee of the fiftieth year of her reign: the longest reign yet of any Kralji. Most of the people now living in the Holdings had known no other ruler. The seat of the Kralji was carved from a single massive crystal, enchanted by the first Archigos Siwel ca'Elad over three centuries ago in a way that no téni had since been able to duplicate. When someone wearing the Ring of the Kralji sat in its hard, glittering embrace, the Sun Throne gleamed a pale yellow. Karl knew there were persistent whispers that the radiance had actually vanished long ago; now, skeptics insisted, the interior light was created at need by special téni sent by the Archigos whenever the Kraljica appeared publicly on the Sun Throne. It was certainly true, given accounts written during Archigos Siwel's lifetime of how the throne had "shone like a true sun, blinding all with its radiance," that the Sun Throne must have paled considerably in the intervening centuries. In full daylight, its glow could barely be seen. The swaying chandeliers overhead were decidedly necessary: even though it was nearly Second Call, the tall windows of the Throne Room were too narrow to allow much of the light to enter.

It was also true that Karl would have been able to duplicate that glow himself, had he dared to do such a thing here.

"Vajiki Tomas cu'Seranta!" Renard, the Kraljica's

ancient and wizened aide, called out the name in a wavering voice, reading from a scroll in his hand. The murmur of voices in the room went momentarily quiet. Karl saw someone moving toward the Sun Throne in response, a middle-aged man who bowed low as he approached, and Karl scowled and sighed at the same time.

"I told you that you should have slipped Renard a siqil or two," Mika stage-whispered. "He's not going to call us forward."

"I'm the Envoy a'Paeti a'Numetodo," Karl answered. "How can he ignore us?"

"For the same reasons that the Kraljica ignored the Marque of Paeti that you sent her when you requested a private audience. She's tied too tightly to the Concénzia Faith; she doesn't want to contaminate herself by acknowledging heretics."

"You're a pessimist, Mika."

"I'm a realist," Mika retorted. "'I would remind you that I have been here in Nessantico for far longer than you, my friend, and I know these people all too well. I think we're lucky to have even been allowed in the hall—it's only your pretty title that got us past Renard. Look over there to the side. You see that man staring our way? The one in black? You can't miss him—he has a silver nose."

Karl lifted up on his toes, scanning the room in the direction in which Mika had nodded. The man stood against the wall, too casually posed. When he noticed Karl's gaze, the mustachioed lips under the metallic nose twisted in what might have been an amused smirk. He nodded faintly in Karl's direction. "That's Commandant ca'Rudka of the Garde Kralji," Mika continued. "If either of us appear to be even halfway threatening, we'll be in the Bastida faster than a fly to a dead horse. So don't make any sudden gestures."

"I think you're being paranoid."

Mika sniffed. "Things are different in the west away from Nessantico," he said. "I'll tell you what. I'll wager you dinner tonight that we don't meet the Kraljica today."

"Done," Karl said.

Three turns of the glass later, the Kraljica rose and everyone bowed as she left the room. Karl had yet to be called forward for his audience.

"I'm terrifically hungry," Mika commented as those in attendance filed from the Throne Room. "How about you?"

~

Marguerite ca'Ludovici

THE RECEPTION—as it did every month—left Marguerite exhausted and irritated. Renard, her aide, waved away the cluster of servants who had accompanied them from the Throne Room. When the door closed behind them, his stiff, proper stance finally relaxed. "Here, Margu," Renard said as he handed her a glass of cool water freshened with slices of yellow fruit. His use of her familiar name pleased her—in this place, where no one else could hear. "I know your throat is parched."

"And my rear is sore, as well," Marguerite answered. She handed him her cane. "The cushion did nothing against that damned crystal."

"We can't have that, can we?" He chuckled. "I'll see that it's replaced with a more appropriate covering." He proffered the water again, and this time she took it. She let herself sink gratefully into one of the well-padded chairs in the private reception room. The windows were opened slightly though the air still held much of winter's nip, and the fire roaring in its hearth was welcome.

Marguerite sighed. "I'm sorry, Renard. It's my duty and I shouldn't complain."

"You are the Kraljica," he told her. "You can do whatever you'd like."

She smiled at that. Renard cu'Bellona had been with her for the bulk of her five decades as Kraljica. Marguerite might be Kraljica, but it was Renard who scheduled her life and made certain that the days ran smoothly. Brought into her service as a page at age five, he had been simply Renard Bellona, with not even a lowly ce' before his family name, but he had shown his loyalty and intelligence and progressed over the years to his current position.

Then she had not been the "Généra a'Pace" but the "Spada Terribile," the Awful Sword, who brought the Outer Lands into the Holdings by negotiation when she could, and with the Garde Civile, her armies, and simple brute force when she could not. She had been young then, energetic, and full of anger at the way her vatarh had been treated as Kraljiki. She had vowed that the ca'-and-cu' would never call her "weak," that the chevarittai of the Holdings would never call her "cowardly." None of them would ever call her "fool" . . . not and keep their lives.

". . . Marguerite?" Renard was saying.

"I'm sorry," she told him. "You were saying?"

"I was asking if you wished to know the evening's appointments."

"Will it matter?" she asked, and they smiled at each other.

"The Archigos Dhosti is bringing his niece Safina to meet you at dinner," Renard told her. "I have asked the A'Kralj to be there as well, so he might have a chance to talk with her."

"And will he attend?"

Renard shrugged. "The A'Kralj pleaded other commitments. But if you sent word to him . . ."

Marguerite shook her head. "No. If my son can't be bothered to meet the women I suggest as good matches, then Justi will have to be satisfied when I choose a wife for him."

Renard nodded, his face carefully neutral.

It was a full decade after her husband died that she finally took Renard into her bed. The seduction was unplanned but seemed entirely natural. They had become more than servant and mistress over the years. In private, they had long been friends, and Renard had no family of his own. "I can't ever offer you more," she told him that night. "I know," he'd answered, with that gentle lifting of his lips that she loved to see. "The Kraljica might need to use marriage as a tool. I understand. I do . . ."

". . . and also the planning committee for your Jubilee Celebration would like to go over their tentative arrangements with you to see if they meet your approval," Renard was saying. "I've told them that you might have time tonight following your dinner with the Archigos, but I can delay them until tomorrow if you'd like."

Marguerite waved a hand. "No, that's fine. Let them come. I'll listen and nod my head as long as they haven't done anything enormously stupid."

Renard nodded. He touched her shoulder softly, almost a caress. Even here, alone, he was careful of the boundaries between them. "Then I'll send word to the committee to be prepared. And . . ." He stopped. Pressed his lips together. "There is a letter from Hïrzgin Greta, brought by private courier. I took the liberty of decoding it for you."

"Bring it here." She didn't ask what her niece, married to the impetuous Jan ca'Vörl, the Hïrzg of Firenzcia, had said; she could see from Renard's suddenly-clouded face that it was not good news. She unfolded the paper Renard handed her and read the underlined words. She shook her head and let the paper drop. "Thirty Numetodo publicly executed in Brezno . . . A'Téni ca'Cellibrecca goes too far, and the Hïrzg encourages him. Does the Archigos know?" she asked.

"I suspect the news will have reached him through his

own sources," Renard said. "I will draft a strongly-worded letter to Hïrzg ca'Vörl from you. I'm sure the Archigos will be doing the same for A'Téni ca'Cellibrecca."

"I'm certain of that," Marguerite replied. "And I'm sure the families of the slain Numetodo will be very pleased with a strongly-worded letter."

~

Ana cu'Seranta

"NO!" U'Téni cu'Dosteau's thin oak pointing rod hissed through the air and rapped once on Ana's moving hands. "Not that way. Pay attention, Ana. You need to create a better pattern. Wider. Larger."

Her knuckles ached from the blow, but she wouldn't give him the satisfaction of stopping. But the instructor's reprimand sent Ana into momentary silence as she glared at the elderly téni, her voice faltering in the midst of the chant she and the other acolytes were reciting. The words were not in her own language, but in the téni-speech that could shape the Ilmodo, and were difficult enough to remember without cu'Dosteau's scoldings. With the stumble, she felt the Ilmodo—the gift of Cénzi, the energy which fed the téni-spells—begin to slip away from her control. She grasped for the Ilmodo with her mind; as she did, odd new words came to her, words that she knew not at all but which somehow felt right for the task, the same words that would come to her when she was with her matarh. The sounds of the words was similar to téni-speech, but the accent was subtly different. She whispered them, not wanting U'Téni cu'Dosteau to hear how she had changed his chant, and let her hands fall back into the spell-pattern.

Wider. Larger. U'Téni cu'Dosteau treated them like

children just learning their letters. In the acolyte's hall, he acted as if he had a ca' in front of his name instead of a cu', even with the acolytes whose family names *did* begin with ca', even with Safina ca'Millac, the niece of the Archigos. Cu'Dosteau acted as if *he* were the Archigos of Concénzia himself. The joke among the acolytes was that cu'Dosteau had enchanted his head so that he could see behind him. He certainly seemed to miss nothing that happened, especially where Ana was concerned. He seemed to be always watching her, especially now as they all approached the time when they would either be given their Marques to become a téni, or receive the dreaded Note of Severance.

Wider. Larger. U'Téni cu'Dosteau was wrong. Ana could sense it. She could nearly see the Ilmodo snaking around her body, and she knew that if instead she tightened the hand-pattern, if she made it smaller rather than larger, she could shape the Ilmodo more carefully.

The task was simple enough: U'Téni cu'Dosteau had brought the class down to the basement of the Archigos' Temple, where several e'téni of the temple had set a huge coal fire ablaze in the furnace. The class was to use the Ilmodo to smother it—it was a task that they might have to perform if they were eventually assigned to be one of the many fire-téni, who had more than once saved the city from burning down, especially in the crowded Oldtown district. The class finished their chant just as Ana caught up with them, their final gestures causing the flames to shudder and dim, although the coals still gleamed mockingly. Ana finished her spell a breath afterward, her hands moving in a quick, subtle gesture that changed the outline of the Ilmodo, focusing it.

Air rushed away from the remaining blue flames and they went out with an audible *whoomp,* the noise so loud that all of them took an involuntary step back as a hot breeze laden with the smell of coal ash moved past them and fluttered the green robes of the e'téni. Cu'Dosteau alone didn't seem to react. He remained standing near

Ana, the tip of his pointing rod on the stone-flagged floor and his hands cupped over the handle, his téni-robes looking more brown than green in the sudden dimness of the room. He stared at Ana with dark, speculative eyes from under the hair-rimmed cave of his brow. She lowered her head so that she didn't have to meet his gaze. The weariness that always came from using the Ilmodo made her want to do nothing more than sink to the floor entirely, especially after her use of it this morning with her matarh. A few of the acolytes already had done so, drained by their effort.

Using the Ilmodo always came with a cost. Cénzi made the téni pay for His gift. It was the first lesson they had all learned, three years ago now.

"This is why most of you will not receive a Marque from the Archigos," cu'Dosteau commented as the e'téni began to chant and the coals reignited—it wouldn't do for the Archigos to be cold in his dressing chambers. In the renewed flames, cu'Dosteau's shadow shuddered on the wall nearest Ana. "A single experienced fire-téni would have been able to douse those flames alone—a necessary skill, or half the houses in the city might have burned to the foundations by now. Yet it took the whole *group* of you, and you very nearly didn't accomplish it. You had ample time to review the proper patterns and the correct chant-words, and yet several of you were stumbling over them." He tapped a long forefinger to his right ear. "I listen, and I see. And I'm not impressed today. Some of you—" He hesitated, and Ana glanced up to find him looking at her before his gaze swept over the rest of the acolytes. "—seem to feel that the Ilmodo will come to you no matter how you wave your hands about. I assure you that would be a mistake. Vajica cu'Seranta, might you agree with that statement?"

Ana's head came up. She heard Safina ca'Millac snicker, then go abruptly silent as cu'Dosteau cast her a baleful glance. "Yes, U'Téni," Ana answered quickly. "I'm sure you're right."

Cu'Dosteau sniffed, as if amused. "That's enough for today," he told them. "We're already late for the Archigos' service. I know you're all tired from using the Ilmodo, even as poorly as you did, but see if you can manage to stay awake until after the Admonition. Then go home and sleep. Tomorrow I expect to see evidence that you have actual brains inside those skulls, as unlikely as that appears at the moment."

~

Dhosti ca'Millac

THERE WERE FEW PEOPLE other than U'Téni cu'Dosteau's class in the main nave of the temple: two or three of the ca'-and-cu' families in their fashionable bashtas and tashtas, several dozen ce', ci', or unranked citizens hanging farther back in the shadows of the vaulted interior. Archigos Dhosti ca'Millac climbed the small set of stairs placed judiciously behind the High Lectern that stood in front of the quire; even when he stood on the top step, his balding head—adorned with a gold circlet with a riven globe—barely topped the wooden structure. Those below him saw mostly the hairless summit of his head.

Dhosti had once been a lowly street performer, a dwarf gymnast in a traveling circus in the desert wastes in southern Namarro, with no denotation of status before his name at all. But a young téni happened to attend one of the traveling circus' performances and had seen in the misshapen young man's startling performances of strength and agility the fact that Dhosti was tapping, unconsciously and poorly, the power that those of Concénzia called "Ilmodo," the unseen energy the téni shaped through their deep faith and ritualized chants.

Dhosti Millac, as he was known then, was brought to the nearest temple and converted to the Faith—easy in the Holdings, where Concénzia was the state religion, and anyone who wished to become cu' or ca' must be one of the Faithful. The promise glimpsed in Dhosti by that téni—none other than U'Téni cu'Dosteau himself, then a humble e'téni—was found to be greater than anyone expected. Over the course of several decades, the dwarf had risen through the ranks from e'téni to his installation as Archigos eighteen years ago.

Eighteen years as Archigos. Dhosti felt each of those years tenfold. Not too long from now, someone else would take the globe of Cénzi from his dead hands and wear the green-and-white robes. Those around Dhosti were constantly reminding him of his mortality, reminding him that he had yet to designate someone to be the next Archigos, reminding him that far too many of the a'téni—those téni just under Dhosti, who controlled the largest cities of the Holdings—didn't agree with Dhosti's views and found him "soft." They wanted the Concénzia Faith to wield its power and strength, they felt that the proper response to heretical statements was not discussion and negotiation, but the measures outlined in the harsh Commandments of the Divolonté.

Dhosti sighed, as much from the exertion of climbing the steps as from his thoughts.

He looked over the worn, polished oak of the High Lectern toward the small congregation gathered below him. He nodded faintly to U'Téni cu'Dosteau and also to his niece Safina, there in the midst of the acolytes, and began his Admonition.

"We of Concénzia know that the Toustour is the word of Cénzi, given to us so that we would understand Him. To guide us along the right path, our predecessors within the Faith created a companion to the scrolls of the Toustour, the Divolonté, and for long years, they have both served us. But we should always remember that while the Toustour was inspired by Vucta through Her son

Cénzi, and while the Divolonté in turn was inspired by the Toustour, the Divolonté comes from *our* minds: the minds of frail people, not from Vucta or Cénzi or even the Moitidi who in turn created us. Just as the Moitidi which came from Cénzi were imperfect, so too are we. Even more so. In fact, we of the Faith must constantly look to the Divolonté we have made, and change it in response to the world in which we find ourselves . . ."

It was an old Admonition, one that Dhosti had proclaimed so often that it required no thought on his part, and—he could see from the nodding heads before him—that those who came to the temple no longer even heard it when he spoke. He saw U'Teni cu'Dosteau put his hand over his mouth to cover a small, injudicious yawn.

You bore even yourself, old man. Dhosti wondered whether this was what Cénzi had intended for him: a long, slow, and sleepy decline from the vigor of his younger years. He wondered if this was why he'd fought so hard to become Archigos.

Half a turn of the glass later, he ended the Admonition and gave Cénzi's Blessing to the congregation. They left the temple gratefully, the acolytes especially, half-running from before the High Lectern as soon as they were dismissed. Dhosti moved slowly across the quire toward the vestry, his head bent down because of his curved spine. Kenne, his secretary and an o'téni despite his relative youth, took Dhosti's arm, helping him from the dais. "Archigos," Kenne whispered urgently. "There is news."

Dhosti raised bristling white eyebrows as he regarded Kenne's somber face. "Not good news, then. The Kraljica?"

"The Kraljica is fine. The news comes from Brezno."

"Ah. What has A'Téni ca'Cellibrecca done?"

Dhosti could see from Kenne's plain, round face that the guess had hit close to the mark. But Kenne's next words nearly sent him staggering to the carpeted tiles.

"A'Téni ca'Cellibrecca and Hïrzg ca'Vörl have captured and executed several Numetodo in Brezno Square."

"He dares . . ." Dhosti sputtered. The téni attendants at the vestry entrance looked at him quizzically, and he waved them away. They scattered as Kenne helped Dhosti into the vestry and closed the door. Dhosti sat in the nearest chair and looked up at Kenne. His heart pounded against the cage of his ribs, and his breath was tight. His weariness had vanished, and he felt a burning in his stomach as if he'd just taken a glass of firebrew. "Tell me," he said to Kenne. "Tell me what you know."

Kenne nodded. "The report is from O'Téni ci'Narsa, who is the Hïrzgin's personal téni. He says that A'Téni ca'Cellibrecca had confessions taken from the captives in the Bastida Brezno first. Evidently many of the Numetodo, when they were paraded out, could barely walk. They were displayed to the crowds while the charges were read and sentences given. At least five of the prisoners were drawn before their heads were taken. The crowd was much amused, according to ci'Narsa." The téni swallowed hard; Dhosti could see him imagining the scene. "The bodies were gibbeted on the square as a warning to any other Numetodo in the city, and the Hïrzg and A'Téni ca'Cellibrecca both made speeches to the crowds. There were at least thirty killed, from the report that came here."

He could see the bodies. In their black iron cages, their skeletal faces stared at him. "I did this," Dhosti said quietly.

"Archigos?"

"I did this," Dhosti repeated. "A'Téni ca'Cellibrecca has made no secret that he opposes my feelings toward the Numetodo, but now he goes beyond words to actions. It is my fault: I have been asleep here. If I were a stronger Archigos, he would not have dared."

"You can't blame yourself for A'Téni ca'Cellibrecca's actions, Archigos. Only he is responsible."

Dhosti nodded, wanting to believe Kenne, and knowing he could not. He could see the dead in Brezno Square, and all of them seemed to be looking directly at him. *My fault* . . .

This was Cénzi's warning. This was Cénzi telling him that he had been drifting, that if he continued to drift, far worse than this would happen.

My fault . . .

He promised Cénzi that the sign would not be forgotten. He began to breathe again, but the blaze inside him remained. "Draft a letter to ca'Cellibrecca," he told Kenne. "Make it clear to him that I am not pleased by this. And tell him that I expect him to come to Nessantico for the Kraljica's Jubilee, and that we will talk further then."

"I will do that," Kenne answered. "Here, let me help you with your robes, and I will send for one of the e'téni to accompany you to your apartments. You can rest there until I bring you the draft."

"No," Dhosti told him. "We will work on this together. In my office. I've been resting too long, Kenne. It's time to wake up once more."

HARBINGERS

Ana cu'Seranta
Marguerite ca'Ludovici
Ana cu'Seranta
Mahri
Ana cu'Seranta
Karl ci'Vliomani
Sergei ca'Rudka
Ana cu'Seranta

Ana cu'Seranta

BECAUSE IT WAS the month of the Kraljica's Jubilee, the fiftieth anniversary of her rule, the sky was a perfection of deepest azure, decorated tastefully with pillows of white clouds. Because it was the month of the Kraljica's Jubilee, spring deigned to arrive a few weeks early: flowers bloomed in a determined barrage of unadulterated hues from the boxes below nearly every window and in the dozens of great and small public gardens of Nessantico. Because it was the month of the Kraljica's Jubilee, the sun, which until the last week had been a pale apparition easily overcome by the cold winds and snow off the Strettosei, girded its celestial loins and beamed renewed warmth down on the city. Because it was the month of the Kraljica's Jubilee, the days were full of ceremonies and rituals, all of which were occasions for those whose family names were prefaced with a ca' or cu' to attend and be seen, to mingle and gossip and at least pretend that they were universally joyous at this milestone in the current Kraljica's long reign over the Holdings.

Because it was the month of the Kraljica's Jubilee, nothing would be allowed to mar the perfection.

Ana cu'Seranta made certain that she wore yellow for her afternoon's appointment at the temple, since the Kraljica had appointed the trumpet flower with its sun-tinted petals as the official flower of the celebration, and one never knew when the Kraljica might deign to take her carriage for a turn around the

Avi a'Parete. Besides, yellow enhanced the golden-brown tones of her skin and contrasted nicely with the nightfall black of her hair. When the Kraljica had declared the trumpet flower as her symbol, there'd been an immediate rush on the last harvest's stock of sapnuts, from which the richest golden dyes were derived. Sapnut-dyed cloth had become difficult to find and expensive to buy, but when the invitation had come from the Archigos' own office requesting Ana to view the Archigos' afternoon blessing, Ana's vatarh had managed to find a small bolt at Oldtown Market.

"No, Vatarh, you don't need to do that."

"But it's what I want, Ana," he'd said to her. "You're going to see the Archigos, and I want you to look beautiful."

He'd reached out to her then, and she'd turned quickly away. She kept her face averted until he dropped his hand back to his side. When he returned that afternoon, he'd given the bolt to the upstairs servant Sala, not to Ana. He'd left the house again without another word.

The hue of the cloth was perhaps more subdued than the optimum, the dye diluted or mixed with less expensive dyes, but the shade was acceptable. Ana had fashioned a robelike tashta from the cloth, the folds drawn tight just under her bosom and then falling free to the sandals on her feet, a Magyarian fashion that had been adopted for the last several years in Nessantico.

"They're here, Vajica Ana. They've sent an open carriage for you." Tari, one of the two remaining lower-floor servants, was bowing at the door to Ana's dressing room. "It's being driven by a téni," she added. Ana glanced a final time at the mirror, waving off Sala, who was wielding a brush as she arranged Ana's hair and tied it with ribbons.

"Tell them I'll be down directly," Ana told Tari, who inclined her head once more. They could hear her footsteps on the stairs.

"An open carriage," Sala said quietly. Sala had been Ana's wet nurse, and had stayed on in the family's employ to become an upper-floor servant. She still seemed to consider Ana her special charge, and had stayed on even as the family's fortunes had declined and the staff that had formerly kept the house was reduced. "The Archigos wants you to be seen. As you should be."

"Or he wants the wind to tangle my hair," Ana replied, and managed to laugh despite her nervousness. "In any case, it's not the Archigos I'll be meeting, just one of the lesser téni."

"But they're going to give you your Marque, then," Sala said. "They wouldn't be sending for you if you hadn't passed. You're to be a téni yourself."

Ana didn't dare to hope that was true; she wasn't going to think it. If anything, she feared that she'd be given worse than a Note. *"We've learned how you've abused your gift. We know what you've done with your matarh . . ."* If that was why she'd been summoned, she would not be returning here, not as a whole person.

She shuddered. "Are you cold?" Sala asked. "I can get a shawl . . ."

"No. I'm fine." *It can't be that. Please, Cénzi, don't let it be that. They wouldn't have sent a carriage to take me to the Bastida, certainly. Maybe Sala's right. . . .*

She forced the image away. Ana desired her Marque more than she could admit—because of the work and tears; because of the expense to her family; because of the way the wealthier acolytes had treated her, or the way the téni who staffed the school had done nothing but criticize her. Three years ago, there had been over seventy students accepted in her class; only twenty remained in the final year. Three of the twenty of her class had received their Marques on Cénzidi last week, giving them the rank of e'téni and placing them in the service of the Concénzia Faith. The gossip among the acolytes was that the rest had received their Notes of Severance, though none of them admitted such—Ana feared the way her vatarh would respond if she were given a Note. It would be worse than anything he'd done yet.

"Don't expect more than a bare few of you to receive the Marque," U'Téni cu'Dosteau, in charge of the acolytes, had told them when they'd started their studies. *"Of the seventy here, it will be five at most, and likely fewer. The majority of you will leave early and receive neither Marque nor Note. For those of you who manage to stay, nearly all of you will fail to go any further in your instruction with the Ilmodo."*

Ana had heard nothing from the temple or U'Téni cu'Dosteau. Still, if impossibly Sala was right, Ana could leave this house and forge her own life.

That was what she wanted most of all. To be away from here.

To be away from Vatarh. No matter how guilty it might make her feel for abandoning Matarh.

"Thank you, Sala," Ana said, moving her head away from Sala's brush. "If you brush it any more, you'll pull the hair right from my head. I should be back to take evening supper to Matarh, and I'm still planning on attending the lighting ceremony tonight with her and Vatarh, so make certain her carry-chair is ready and the help hired for the evening."

Ana walked slowly from her rooms to the main stairs, forcing herself to keep a leisurely pace even though she wanted nothing more than to hurry. Tari was at the front doors with an acolyte in pale green robes, the broken-world crest of the Archigos on the boy's left shoulder. He lowered his head as Ana came down the steps, lifting his eyes up to her only after she stopped before him, but there was no subservience in his eyes, only a penetrating regard. She'd seen that attitude before, many times. His unconscious bearing told her that he was probably the younger son of one of the ca'-and-cu' families placed into the temple's service, too new to Concénzia to be someone she would know by sight. She wondered whether he noticed how few servants there were in their house, or how the hall needed to be repainted and that there were cobwebs in the high corners, wondered whether he knew that she had once been like him. Whatever he might be thinking, it never reached his impassive face.

"If you'd follow me, Vajica ..." he said, gesturing to the carriage waiting on the street.

She followed behind him, into the air that still held a faint kiss of winter in its embrace despite the sun. She shivered and wished, briefly, that she'd brought the shawl Sala had offered with her, though that would have spoiled the effect of the tashta. She could see a few of their neighbors standing outside in their front gardens, pointedly not staring at the carriage adorned with an ornate gold-and-enamel fractured globe, the sign of Cénzi and the Concénzia Faith. She lifted her hand to them; they nodded back, as if happening to notice her and the carriage for the first time. "Why, good morning, Vajica Ana. How is your matarh today? When does Vajiki cu'Seranta return from Prajnoli ... ?"

"Matarh is still very weak from the Fever and still can't talk or move on her own, but she is beginning to recover, thank you for asking. We expect Vatarh back later today or this evening," she answered as the acolyte opened the door of the carriage for her and helped her inside, then closed the door and took his place standing on the step outside. The driver was indeed one of the téni, and as he turned to nod to Ana, she glanced at the doubled white slashes on the shoulders of his green, cowled robes. "E'Téni," she said, addressing him by the rank denoted by the slashes, the lowest of the téni positions. "I'm ready."

He nodded again, turning. She heard him muttering softly—the sibilant chanting that she'd heard many times over the years, his hands gestured—and the wheels of the carriage began to turn in response to the incantation. They moved off onto the street.

The carriage proceeded at the stately pace of a person

walking energetically, with the acolyte ringing a small
bell occasionally to warn the pedestrians: out from the
Rue Maitré-Albert onto the wide, landscaped expanse
of the Avi a'Parete at the Sutegate. Two immense stone
heads of past Kralji flanked the city gates there, rotating
slowly so that they always faced the sun; below each of
the sculptures, in an open room carved from the pillars
of the ancient city wall, was an e'téni whose task it was to
chant the spell that allowed the heads to turn—quickly
exhausted by their task, each would be relieved on the
turn of the glass with a new e'téni.

Ana had always wondered if one day she might be
there, chanting as the stone groaned and grumbled overhead on its daily rotation.

Just past midday, the Avi was crowded: throngs of
strolling couples and families near the central, tree-lined
divider; buyers gathered around the stalls set up against
the government buildings to the north side of the boulevard; crowds moving past the street entertainers on the
south side; the occasional carriages, all of those horse-
drawn except for hers. Most were moving slowly in the
direction of the Archigos' temple, the sextet of domes
radiant in the sunlight. Ana sat in the carriage, trying to
pretend that she didn't notice the attention she was receiving. The sun glinting from the fractured globe mounted
by the door, the lack of horses, the téni chanting on the
driver's seat, the tenor clatter of the acolyte's bell—all
brought eyes around to their carriage. Some stared—
mostly those of the lower classes—but the families in
their finery would only wave, as if it were altogether a
common occurrence that one of the Concenzia's téni-
driven carriages was sent out to convey someone. Ana
could see them peering squint-eyed even as they inclined their heads politely, and she could nearly hear the
whispered conversations as she passed.

"Is that one of the ca'Faromi daughters? Or one of
the Kraljica's grandnieces? Perhaps Safina ca'Millac, the
Archigos' niece; I hear she's a favorite for the A'Kralj's

hand. What? Abini cu'Seranta's daughter? Truly? Oh, yes, I've seen her before; wasn't she at the A'Kralj's Winter Ball? Why, her family is just barely cu', I hear. My cousin is on the Gardes a'Liste, and he says that the family might become just ci'Seranta next year. What is she doing being taken to the temple, I wonder?"

Ana wondered herself, and hope and fear battled inside her.

~

Marguerite ca'Ludovici

THERE WAS A KNOCK, then the door slowly opened. "Kraljica? The painter ci'Recroix is here . . ."

Marguerite—Kraljica Marguerite I of Nessantico, born of the royal ca'Ludovici line which had produced the Kralji for the last century and a half—looked away from her son and nodded to the hall servant whose head peered from behind the massive doors of her outer parlor. "Set the water clock," she told the servant. "When it empties, bring Vajiki ci'Recroix to me here." He touched clasped hands to forehead, glanced quickly at the Kraljica's son, and vanished, the door clicking shut behind him.

Her son—the A'Kralj Justi, who might one day, upon her death, become the Kraljiki Justi III—had not moved. Usually the Kraljica's parlor was crowded with supplicants, courtiers, and chevarittai: the ca'-and-cu' of Nessantico. Today, they were alone. Justi was standing before a painting set on an easel near the west wall, bathed in sunlight. The A'Kralj's appearance was regal: a gray-flecked beard carefully trimmed in the current fashion, like a thin band glued to his chin; straight hair combed and oiled and arranged to minimize the alarming thinness at the crown of his skull; a long nose, deep-set dark eyes, and a nearly geometrically squared and jutting jaw, all features he'd inherited from his long-dead father. The resemblance still made Marguerite occasionally startle when she looked at him. His body, molded by days spent hunting in the saddle, was that of an aging warrior—in his youth, the A'Kralj had ridden in the Garde Civile along with the other chevarittai of Nessantico. Despite the long decades of order under the Kraljica, despite her popular title as "Généra a'Pace," the Creator of Peace, there were still the occasional border skirmishes and squabbles, and Justi fancied himself quite the military man. Marguerite, who had seen the reports from the Garde Civile, had an entirely different opinion of her son's prowess.

Justi's head canted slowly as he regarded the painting.

"This is truly marvelous, Matarh," he said. His voice belied his appearance; it was reedy and unfortunately high. That was another trait he'd inherited from his long-dead father. *"He's a handsome thing to look at,"* Marguerite's own matarh had said long decades ago when she'd informed her daughter that a marriage had been arranged for her. *"Just keep him from talking too much, or he'll completely destroy the illusion . . ."* She wondered if other matarhs elsewhere said the same of Justi to their daughters.

"I'd heard that this ci'Recroix was the master among masters," Justi continued, "but this . . ." He reached out with a thin index finger that stopped just short of the surface of the canvas. "I feel that if I touched the figures I would feel warm flesh and not cold brush strokes. It's easy to see how some say that he uses sorcery to create his paintings." He paced in front of the canvas. "Look, their eyes seem to follow me. I almost expect their heads to move."

She had to agree with him that the painting was superbly crafted, so lifelike as to be startling. Three strides long, half that high, caught in an exquisite, filigreed gold frame as wide as two hands, the painting depicted a peasant family: a couple with their two daughters and a son. The wife and husband, dressed in stained linen with plain overcoats, sat behind a rough-hewn table laden with a simple dinner, a cloth dusted with bread crumbs covering the planks. An infant daughter sat on the matarh's lap, a son on the vatarh's, while a female toddler played with a puppy underneath the table. Marguerite had seen paintings that appeared realistic from a distance, but the ci'Recroix ... No matter how closely she approached it, no matter how she leaned in and peered at the surface, nowhere could she see the mark of a brush. The only texture was that of the canvas on which the pigments rested: it was as if the painting were indeed a window into another world. More details within the scene revealed themselves as you came closer and closer, until the varnished surface of the painting itself stopped you. Marguerite knew (because she had looked) that if you examined the wimple on the matarh's head, that you could not only see the texture of the blue cloth and how it had been wrapped and folded, but you could also note where a rent had been repaired and sewn shut with thread of a slightly different hue. You could see how she was just beginning to glance down at her daughter in her lap, her attention beginning to move away from the viewer as her daughter's hand clutched at the hem of her blouse. The way the blouse bunched around the infant's pudgy, fragile fingers, the acne scars dimpling the young matarh's cheeks ...

This was a true moment frozen and captured. It was difficult to be in the same room as this painting and not have it dominate your attention, not demand that you stare at it in hopeless fascination and examine its endless wealth of detail, to be drawn into its spell.

Sorcery indeed.

"Yes, Justi," Marguerite said impatiently. "I can see why you would have recommended ci'Recroix to me. He certainly has talent, even if the rumors about him are dis-

turbing." Neither the painting nor the painter were why
she'd asked Justi to come to her. She wanted to tell him
what she'd just learned: Hïrzg Jan ca'Vörl of Firenzcia,
alone of all the leaders of the countries that made up the
Holdings, had declined Marguerite's invitation to her
Jubilee Celebration: a decided breach of etiquette, certainly, and knowing ca'Vörl, a deliberate affront. More
worrisome, he had placed the Firenzcian army on maneuvers at the same time—not near the eastern borders by
Tennshah, but close to the River Clario and Nessantico.
She'd already sent a sharply-worded communiqué to
Greta ca'Vörl, her niece and the Hïrzgin of Firenzcia. She
knew Greta would pass along her displeasure to her husband. After the incident with the Numetodo in Brezno,
two months ago now, this was a disturbing development.

And there was the other, pressing matter that seemed to
be an eternal subject between the two of them. But Justi,
as was his wont, seemed uninterested in state affairs and
politics. He was already talking before she'd finished.

"Indeed, Matarh. I can't wait to see what he does. It
will be a fine official portrait for your Jubilee—"

"Justi," Marguerite interrupted sharply, and her son's
chiseled, handsome jaw shut with an abrupt snap of
strong white teeth—good teeth were another, and luck-
ier, family trait. "There will be another announcement
before the end of the Jubilee."

"What, Matarh?" he asked, but she knew that he had
guessed, knew from the way his lips twisted below the
crisp black line of his mustache. Her son might be pam-
pered, indolent, and perhaps somewhat dissolute, but he
was not stupid.

"It's been seven years now since Hannah died," she
said. "It's time. Time for you to marry again." His features scrunched as if he'd bitten into a sour marshberry,
but she ignored the look. She'd seen it too many times.
"Marriage is a stronger and more permanent weapon
than a sword," she told him.

A barely-stifled sigh escaped him. "I know, Matarh.

You've said that often enough. I thought of having the aphorism engraved on my saber." He sniffed, looking away from her and back to the painting.

"Then show me you understand," she answered tartly, pressing her own lips together in annoyance at his tone.

"Do I have a choice?" he asked, but didn't give her a chance to answer. "I take it you have candidates in mind? Someone appropriately connected, no doubt. Someone whose children might actually live."

Marguerite sucked in her breath. "It wasn't your wife's fault that your children died. Why, little Henri was five and thriving when the Red Pox took him, and poor Margu . . ." Her eyes filled with tears, as they often did when she thought of the granddaughter who'd been her namesake. Hannah might have been of the fertile ca'Mazzak line, whose descendants governed Sesemora, but she'd not had the luck of her matarh, who had nine children survive into adulthood. No, Marguerite was fairly certain that the fault lay in the ca'Ludovici seed. In Justi. Stout and plain herself, Hannah had nonetheless performed her spousal obligations, giving birth to eight children over the decade of her marriage to Justi, but only two of those had survived past the second year: Henri, the eighth and last, whose long and difficult birth Hannah had survived by less than a month; and Marguerite, secondborn, who had been eleven and the Kraljica's favorite when the horse drawing her carriage had bolted unexpectedly and the careening vehicle had struck a tree. Marguerite herself had nursed the terribly injured girl and the Archigos had sent over—surreptitiously, since such a thing was heresy and specifically forbidden by the Divolonté—a téni skilled with healing chants, but still little Margu had not survived the night.

Marguerite had gone to the stables afterward and killed the horse herself.

"I know, Matarh," Justi said. "It was Cénzi's will that they died. And what is the Kraljica's will, which is second only to Cénzi's? Who am I to marry, some cowled waif from Magyaria? Someone of those half-wild families from Hellin? Which of the provinces are causing problems? Have them send their daughters for your inspection so they may be subdued by marriage. Once more, rather than out-warring your adversaries, you will out-marry them. Tell me—who have you picked?"

"I don't appreciate your sarcasm, Justi."

"I'm certain you don't. And I'm certain that I care about your appreciation as much as you care about my feelings concerning this. When are *you* marrying, Matarh? How long has Vatarh been dead now? Twenty-three years? Twenty-four? What has kept *you* from marrying all these years?"

For a moment, Marguerite feared that Justi knew about Renard, but the slackness in his face told her that it was simple irritation in his voice. "You know why I don't marry."

"Yes, I know. 'The sword in the scabbard still threatens . . .' I've heard that one often enough, too." Justi gave a sigh. His hands lifted and dropped back to his sides. "So who is it to be, Matarh? When will you make the grand announcement of my engagement, and when do I get to at least see a painting of this person?"

"I've selected no one as yet," Marguerite told him. "I thought that perhaps you would like some input in this as the A'Kralj." She saw the new grimace and could nearly hear the thought that no doubt accompanied it: *You became Kraljica at eighteen, Matarh; I'm forty-seven and still the A'Kralj, still waiting patiently for you to die.* . . . "But I do have a few prospects you should consider. The ca'Mulliae family, for instance, might be a good choice given their connections with the northern provinces, especially with the Numetodo heresy spreading there. Or even someone with a strong connection to the Faith, such as the Archigos' niece Safina, who you've already met a few times."

She was trying to placate him, knowing how strongly he believed in the tenets of Concénzia, but she saw that

Justi was either no longer listening or disinterested. He was studying ci'Recroix's painting as if answers might be hidden there. "You may make the decision, Justi, if that's what you want," she continued. "Find someone who appeals to you or not, as you prefer. Find someone who will understand that they need to look away from your . . . indiscretions with half the *grandes horizontales* of Nessantico. All I require is that the person you choose also provide us some political advantage and you an heir or two, and that you make your decision by the end of my Jubilee. Otherwise, I *will* make the announcement for you. Do we understand each other?"

Justi sniffed, his nose almost touching the painting. "Yes, Matarh," he answered. "Perfectly. As always." As he spoke, there was a quiet knock on the doors. Justi straightened, taking a long breath, as Marguerite scowled at him. "And perfectly timed as well. Matarh, I'll leave you."

"There is more I need to discuss with you, Justi."

"I've no doubt of that. But it will have to wait. Your painter awaits."

Justi started toward the door. "Justi," Marguerite called out and he stopped. "I am your Matarh and you are my son, my only child. I am also the Kraljica, and you are the A'Kralj. You will always be my son. As to the other . . . some of your cousins would love nothing better than to see me change my decision as to my heir. And I can."

Justi didn't reply, but went to the door and opened it. Marguerite caught a glimpse of a tall man standing just outside: black robe, black hair, black beard, black pupils—a fragment of night walking in the daylight. Justi nodded to the man, who clasped hands to forehead as he bowed. "Vajiki ci'Recroix," Justi said. "I must say I admire your talent very much. The Kraljica is waiting just inside. I hope you can capture all the complexities she hides so well. . . ."

~

Ana cu'Seranta

AS THEY APPROACHED the temple, the crowds
became more dense and the acolyte's bell ringing
was a constant din too near Ana's ear for comfort. For the
month of the Kraljica's Jubilee, the population of Nessantico swelled with tourists and visitors hoping to meet the
Kraljica and mingle with the ca'-and-cu'. Every day, the
Archigos emerged from the temple to bless the crowds
promptly at Second Call, then proceeded along the Avi
a'Parete and over the River A'Sele via the Pontica a'Brezi
Nippoli. There, at the Old Temple on the Isle A'Kralji, he
offered up prayers of thanksgiving for the Kraljica's continued health.

Near the temple plaza, a line of Garde Kralji, the city
guards, held back the crowds from the doors through
which the Archigos would appear. The gardai's brass-
tipped staffs jutted above the heads of the onlookers
like the posts of a fence, and Ana could glimpse the
midnight blue of their uniforms through the less somber
colors of those waiting for the Archigos to appear. The
acolyte standing at the door to Ana's carriage produced
a whistle from under his robes and blew a piercing note.
The gardai responded, opening a gap in the crowd for
the carriage to pass through. They rode into the plaza, the
wheels of the carriage chattering against the marble flags
set there, the téni-driver's chant ending as the carriage
came to a halt to the east of the main doors. The acolyte
hopped down from his perch and opened the door, as-
sisting Ana to the ground.

"Who am I supposed to see?" she asked the acolyte,

glancing around. She saw no one obviously waiting for them. "U'Téni cu'Dosteau?"

"Wait here," the acolyte answered. "That's all I was told. After the Archigos' blessing . . ."

The great wind-horns, one in each of the six domes of the temple, sounded at that moment: low, sonorous notes that throbbed and moaned like giants in distress, the wail clawing at the stones of the buildings bordering the plaza and driving clouds of pigeons up from the rooftops. The crowd went silent under the assault, pressing clasped hands to foreheads as the huge temple doors— carved into intertwined trees—swung open. Ana made the same gesture of obeisance alongside the carriage. A phalanx of acolyte celebrants in simple white robes emerged first, each with an incense brazier clanking and swaying on the end of brass chains, the fragrant smoke curling and drifting in the slight breeze. As they entered the sunlight they began to sing, their melodious, youthful voices dancing with the intricate harmonies of Darkmavis' well-known hymn "Cénzi Eternal". A dozen green-robed a'téni of the Archigos' Council followed them—the highest of the téni, elderly men and women blinking at the assault of daylight after the dimness within the temple's basilica. Then, finally, came the Archigos' open carriage, wrought in the shape of Cénzi's fractured globe, the blue of the seas a pure lapis lazuli, the green and gold of the continents a matrix of emeralds and gold, the crack that rent the world bright with tiny bloodred rubies. A téni chanted alongside each of the four wheels of the carriage and the wheels turned in response, while the green-robed Archigos himself stood atop the globe, pressing his own clasped hands to forehead as if he were no more than any of the people in the crowd. Four acolytes in white robes carried long poles, over which was draped an awning of gold-and-green silk, sheltering the Archigos from the elements.

Archigos Dhosti ca'Millac, despite his standing as head of the Concénzia Faith, hardly cut a magnificent

figure. The dwarf was old—nearly as old as the Kraljica
herself. His liver-spotted scalp was bordered by a short
hedge of white hair just above the ears and low around
the back of his skull. His already-shrunken stature was
further diminished by the bowing of his spine, which
forced his chin down onto his chest, and the arms which
emerged from the short, wide sleeves of his stately robes
were thin, wobbling with loose, wrinkled skin. Yet the
eyes were alert and bright, and the mouth smiled.

Ana smiled in return, just seeing him; she had never
been this close to the Archigos before, not even in the
Temple during ceremonies. It was probably just coincidence, but he seemed to notice her as well, nodding once
in her direction before turning back to the crowds. He
lifted his hands, his voice—no doubt strengthened by his
mastery of the Ilmodo—beginning to call the traditional
blessing of Cénzi on the throngs.

Ana heard the disturbance before she saw it: another
voice striving against that of the Archigos. Turning her
head from the Archigos toward the crowd, she caught a
glimpse of someone standing in the midst of the kneeling throngs. The gardai saw the man at the same moment
and began to move toward him, but they were already
too late. The stranger—she saw a ruddy complexion and
hair the color of summer straw—moved his hands in a
pushing motion and the gardai between him and the
Archigos went down as if struck by an invisible fist, as
well as those in a circle around him.

The acolyte next to Ana sucked in his breath; the téni
in the driver's seat of her carriage grunted in alarm.
The crowd was shouting now: "A Numetodo . . . ! The
Archigos . . . !" Ana couldn't hear the magic-chanting
of the man, but his mouth still moved and a blue-white,
sputtering glow had swallowed his right hand. Ana had
seen similar effects, had performed them imperfectly
herself, for that matter. She knew the set of words that
could conjure up the heat of the air, could concentrate

it into a ball—but the Numetodo performed the spell faster than any téni, with just a few words. . . .

The gardai the man had struck down were starting to stagger up, but she knew none of them could reach him quickly enough to prevent the attack. Ana knew that the Archigos had seen the disturbance as well, but when she glanced at him he was still smiling, his hands still raised in blessing even though he'd stopped speaking. Otherwise, he had not reacted.

The Numetodo—he had to be one of that shadowy group; who else would dare to do something like this?— swung his arm in a throwing motion and the spitting glare in his hand arced toward the Archigos.

Ana, almost without realizing, had begun whispering a chant herself, and as the glow hissed in the air toward the Archigos—who still smiled—she cupped her hands before her and brought them together. The ball of blue fire fizzled, sputtered, and vanished long before it reached the Archigos. The Numetodo, standing stupefied in the plaza as his attack failed, went down under a rush of the Garde Kralji. She saw his capture as she staggered with the release of her spell and the inevitable weariness surged over her. For a moment, there was darkness at the edges of her vision and she thought she might faint entirely away, but the shadow passed, leaving her with only an immense fatigue.

The disturbance was over almost as quickly as it had begun, the Garde Kralji reforming their line as the attacker was hustled away from the plaza into one of the nearest buildings with his hands bound and his mouth gagged, as the Archigos—who seemed entirely unshaken and unperturbed by the incident—raised his voice over the noise of the crowd to finish the blessing. He gestured to the Garde Kralji, making obvious his intention to continue the procession, and the gardai formed an opening in the crowd for the Archigos to pass through in his carriage.

The Archigos looked at Ana and gestured to her.

For a breath, she thought she'd been mistaken, until the téni-driver spoke in a harsh, awed whisper. "Go *on*, Vajica. The Archigos asks for you." She forced herself to ignore the desire to do nothing more than lie down and close her eyes as the inevitable weariness of spell-casting washed over her. Hesitantly, her legs aching, she walked toward the carriage, glancing somewhat nervously at the a'téni who stared at her as she approached.

She went to one knee alongside the globe and bowed her head, giving the Archigos the sign of Cénzi.

"Get up, Vajica. Please," she heard the Archigos say, his voice amused. "And come up here with me. I'd like to speak with my new protector." She heard a few of the a'téni behind her snicker at that, and her face reddened. But the Archigos was extending a stubby arm toward her and one of the carriage-téni had opened a door in Cénzi's globe for her, revealing a set of short stairs that led to the platform on which the Archigos stood under his canopy of silk. She climbed up to him, going to a knee again as she reached the platform. Kneeling, she was as tall as the Archigos. She took the hand he extended to her and touched her lips to his palm. She felt him lifting her up and she rose. "Can you stand?" he whispered to her.

"For a bit," she answered.

"Then you should sit." He pulled down a seat built into the compartment of the carriage. "It's just as well, after all. Otherwise, you'd have to stand there," he told her, and she noticed that the platform to the Archigos' left was several inches lower. "Appearances," he told her with a gentle smile, and she gratefully sank down onto the hard wooden seat, her head no longer higher than his. "I see that you've learned how to reverse an incantation as well as to create one, Vajica cu'Seranta. Strange, I didn't think that was something that was generally taught to acolytes. Nor, I think, does U'Téni cu'Dosteau know of counter-spells that can be cast quite so quickly."

Ana felt her cheeks flush again, but the fatigue made her response slow. "Archigos, I—"

He waved off her protest with a gentle laugh. "I was never in any real danger. The Numetodo haven't the faith to truly use the Ilmodo. His attack would never have reached me, even if you'd done nothing, not with the a'téni here. And I have my own defenses if they'd failed." His grin tempered what might have been a rebuke.

"I'm sorry for my presumption," she told him. "I should have realized . . ."

"There's no need to apologize, Vajica. You've only shown me that what I was told about you was correct. Now, ride with me so we can talk—no matter what happens, it's important that the schedule isn't interrupted, after all. It's all about appearances."

What does he mean, 'what I was told about you . . .'? Again, the Archigos' quick, genuine smile made Ana relax and cooled the flush in her cheeks. The téni alongside the carriage were chanting, the silk awning above them flapping in the breeze as the acolytes holding it began to move and the carriage rolled smoothly and slowly forward. The a'téni filed behind the carriage and behind them the u' and o'téni, and finally the acolyte choir, while the gardai with their long staffs moved into formation on either side of the street and the procession turned out from the plaza onto the Avi a'Parete. The Archigos waved to the crowds lining the boulevard even as he continued to speak to Ana. "Surely you wondered why I would ask to meet with you."

"*You* asked, Archigos?" she managed to blurt out. "I thought . . ."

"I know what you thought," Archigos ca'Millac answered. "You were wrong."

~

Mahri

HE LURKED AT THE FRINGES of the crowd, as he always did. Watching, as he always did.

Even in the warmth of the sun, Mahri wrapped himself in several layers, his clothing rent with great tears and the hems all tattered, the patterns on the cloth smeared with filth and blackened where they dragged the ground. His hood was up, so that his scarred and ravaged face could only be glimpsed: the empty socket of his left eye, the smashed nose laying on the right cheek, the gaping darkness between his remaining teeth, the shiny white tracks of burns over the left side of his face, pulling and twisting at the flesh. Those who glanced at his face always quickly looked away—except sometimes the children who would point and stare.

"That's just Mahri," the parents would tell them, pulling the children away with a brief glance at Mahri himself, talking as if Mahri weren't there, as if he couldn't see or hear them. Sometimes, they might toss a bronze d'folia in his direction in compensation for their son's or daughter's rudeness. He'd stare at the tiny coin on the pavement, not deigning to pick it up. Perhaps for that reason, or perhaps for others, he was sometimes called "Mad Mahri."

He generally didn't attend the Archigos' blessing, but he'd heard the rumors flowing through the nether regions of Nessantico; he'd seen the whispers of possibilities in his vision-bowl, and so he'd come. The Numetodo had been stupid, so stupid that Mahri decided that the clumsy assassination attempt must have been carried out entirely through the man's own foolish impulse. Certainly Envoy ci'Vliomani wouldn't have condoned this. No, this person had to be a rogue within the Numetodo, and one that the Envoy would quickly renounce if only to save his own flesh. Mahri watched the Garde Kralji hustle the man roughly away, shoving him through the door of a neighboring government building. He shook his head; whoever the Numetodo was—and he was not one of those Mahri recognized, probably someone new to the city—he was destined for a slow, painful end.

But what interested Mahri more than the doomed would-be assassin was the young woman the Archigos brought into his carriage afterward. Mahri had seen her téni-driven carriage near Sutegate and he'd wondered who the Archigos had sent for, so he'd followed her to the temple. He'd seen that it was her defense that had foiled the attack. He knew enough about the techniques of Ilmodo use by the téni that the speed and power with which the woman reacted had widened his remaining eye and made him scratch at the ruined skin of his chin.

Now he knew why an image of a young woman had haunted the vision-bowl.

This one . . . this one would bear watching. Obviously the Archigos felt the same, for the woman stayed with him as the téni around the dwarf's carriage began their chants and the carriage made its turn onto the Avi in its slow procession toward the Old Temple amid the renewed clamor of the wind-horns atop the temple domes and the cheers of the crowds—doubly pleased that their beloved religious leader had escaped unharmed.

As the crowds closed in around the Archigos, Mahri watched them go, unsurprised that the Archigos would keep to his routine despite the attack. After all, ritual was important in Nessantico. The city was bound and fettered and choked with ritual, as ancient and unyielding as the walls that had once enclosed it. The carriage passed within a few dozen strides of where Mahri lurked at the corner of an apartment building.

He stared not only at the Archigos, but at the woman who sat alongside him, looking uncomfortable at the attention, her face weary.

Mahri would watch this young woman. He would know who she was.

Mahri slunk back deeper into the shadows between the buildings. Silent, a shadow himself, he slid away from the Avi and the noise, finding his own hidden path through the city.

~

Ana cu'Seranta

"YOU'RE BEGINNING TO RECOVER?" the Archigos asked, and Ana nodded. The Archigos had said nothing to her for several minutes, allowing her to gather herself. The fatigue was receding and she no longer felt as if she needed to sleep, though a deep ache still lingered in her muscles.

"I'm feeling much better now," she told him. "Thank you."

"So tell me, Vajica cu'Seranta, do you know why I wanted to speak with you?"

Ana shook her head vigorously at the Archigos' question. "Certainly not, Archigos. In fact, I thought . . ." She shook her head again.

The sound of the wind-horns faded as they moved away from the temple, but the crowds still hailed the Archigos as they passed, their clasped hands tight against their foreheads. The acolytes were still singing, another of Darkmavis' compositions. The Archigos nodded to the people lining the Avi as they approached the Pontica a'Brezi Nippoli. He raised his hand in greeting even as he spoke with Ana, not looking at her though she had the impression that he knew the expressions that twisted her lips and lowered her eyebrows. "Go on," he said quietly.

"I thought that, if anything, I would hear only from U'Téni cu'Dosteau," Ana continued. "As often as he corrected me or told me that I wasn't trying hard enough or wasn't paying close enough attention in his classes, I thought that he would give me a Note of Severance. I knew all the Marques had already been signed. . . ." The Archigos had turned completely away from her, and she wondered whether she'd offended him. "I'm sorry, Archigos. I'm chattering on and I shouldn't speak so about U'Téni cu'Dosteau, who was entirely correct in his attitude toward me. I wasn't a good enough student for him, I'm afraid."

"I have indeed signed the Marques that the Acolytes' Council gave me," the Archigos said. He waved to the crowds. He smiled. The sun danced on the silken field over his head. He didn't look at her at all. "Your name wasn't on any of them."

Ana nodded in acceptance, not able to speak. Despite having steeled herself for the inevitability of her failure, the intensity of the disappointment that washed over her then told her how stubbornly she'd been grasping to hope that she was wrong. *Three years . . . three years and all the solas that my family paid to Concénzia for the privilege, money Vatarh really didn't have, money they'd begged and borrowed . . . Three years, and now Vatarh will be angry, and that will be worst of all. . . .*

She'd told herself that she wouldn't cry, though she'd done so many nights in private since she'd heard about the Marques, but until the note she dreaded came from U'Téni cu'Dosteau she could dry the tears and pretend that she had confidence, at least during the day. The Archigos' words made her eyes burn and caused the boulevard around them to waver before her as if it were under the waters of the A'Sele. She could feel the moisture on her cheeks and dabbed at it with her sleeve angrily, hating that she would cry before the Archigos, that her pride was so overweening that she couldn't accept the fate Cénzi had set before her with due humility, that her faith was so fragile and her fear so great.

She hoped that the Archigos didn't know about what she'd done with her matarh. If so, she was entirely lost.

Ana realized that the Archigos was looking at her, and she wiped at her eyes again. "You should know that it was U'Téni cu'Dosteau who came to me after I was given this year's Marques," the Archigos said softly. "He wanted to talk to me privately. About you, Vajica cu'Seranta. Do you have an idea of what he said?"

Ana shook her head, mute. Hope lifted its head again, battered and bloodied, but fear caught it in a stranglehold and bore it down. "I won't tell you all," the Archigos continued. "It's enough for you to know that U'Téni cu'Dosteau insisted that the Acolytes' Council had made a mistake, that they'd looked too much at the family names and too little at the students themselves and U'Téni cu'Dosteau's evaluations. He told me that he had a student who sometimes created her own spells with the Ilmodo rather than those of her instructor's. A student who used the Ilmodo for fire or earth or air or water, when most students found a strength in only one of those. A student who could quote the Toustour and seemed a devout follower of the Divolonté, even though there were whispers among her fellow students regarding Numetodo tendencies. A student with a natural talent who didn't quite know how to harness or control it—who started a terrible fire, he said, in the Acolytes' Dining Hall one night, then put it out before the fire-téni could come."

"It was an accident—" Ana began, but the Archigos glanced at her, his hand raised.

"I was impressed by the force of the u'téni's argument, especially after he reminded me that sometimes Cénzi manifests even in the most common of frames. As the Toustour says—"

" 'Even the humblest can be raised, even the lowest exalted.' " She provided the quote without thinking.

He laughed then, indicating his own stunted body with a hand. "Even the lowest," he repeated. "Vajica cu'Seranta, do you still desire to accept a Marque? Are you willing to join the Order of Téni if asked?"

"Oh, yes!" she answered in a rush. The affirmation burst from her in a near shout and a laugh that shook tears again from her eyes. She thought the carriage must be shaking with the surge of joy the words had unleashed. "Certainly, Archigos."

"Good," the Archigos said. He chuckled at her unrestrained joy. "Then I'll have your Marque prepared and signed. You'll no longer be Vajica; you'll be O'Téni Ana cu'Seranta."

He spoke the title slowly and clearly. He was still looking at her, his head—too large for the small body—tilted to one side as if waiting for the question she wanted to ask. His silence gave her the courage to speak. "I must have misheard you, Archigos. I thought . . . thought you said *o'téni.*"

"Do I speak so poorly?" he said with a chuckle. "U'Téni cu'Dosteau was . . . well, he was quite persuasive, and after what I witnessed . . . I think that we have more than enough e'ténis already. U'Téni cu'Dosteau believed you were already well past the ability expected from an e'téni, and I would agree with him. In fact, you will be attached to my personal staff, O'Téni. Is that acceptable to you?"

She had no words. She could only nod, a helpless grin on her face.

"I'll take that as acceptance, then," the Archigos said. He sighed, turning away from her to raise his hands again to the crowds. "O'Téni, look behind the carriage. Look at the faces you see there."

Ana glanced down and behind. The a'téni immediately behind the carriage stared back at her, nearly all their gazes lifted toward the carriage. One face in particular snagged her attention. She knew him: Orlandi ca'Cellibrecca, A'Téni of Brezno, Téte of the Guardians, and the man who had arrested dozens of Numetodo last Cénzi's Day in Brezno, tried them for forbidden use of the Ilmodo, then had the prisoners executed in the temple square before cheering throngs—his face was turned to her, and his stare was intense and appraising.

"You see them?" the Archigos said softly. "They're all wondering why you're standing up here with me, wondering what they've missed and how critical it will be to their own power. They're wondering how it is that an inexperienced acolyte could manage a counter-spell that quickly and remain standing afterward. They're wondering, honestly, if they could have done the same. They're trying to figure out how to turn this to their advantage, and whether they should make an overture to you as soon as they can, just in case. When they're dismissed at the Old Temple, they'll be scattering to their offices and apartments, whispering hurried instructions to their own underlings, trying to find out everything they can about you, hoping to uncover something they can use. One thing you should understand is that in the world you're entering, 'trust,' 'loyalty,' and 'friendship' are all concepts that are liquid and mutable. But then, that's something I suspect you already know."

Ana shivered. Except for A'Téni ca'Cellibrecca's stern and dour face, most of the faces of the a'téni smiled blandly up at her, as if they were pleased with what they saw; one or two even nodded as they made eye contact, their smiles widening. A few of them, looking away, were frowning as if lost in thought. Ana turned quickly back to the Archigos, and his face was also appraising. She wondered how much he knew. *If Sala or Tari have whispered to the téni, or if Vatarh has said something . . .*

But the Archigos chuckled again. "As soon as we finish this tiresome routine, I'll sign your Marque in the Old Temple," he said. "Tonight, after the Lighting of the Avi, you'll be anointed before your family, in Cénzi's

Chapel in the Archigos' Temple." Pudgy, splayed fingers touched her shoulder softly and she forced herself not to flinch away from his touch, a touch that reminded her too much of her vatarh's hand. *"Shh, Ana. . . . You know how much I love you. Don't pull away, my little bird. . . ."*

"You've been gifted by Cénzi Himself, Ana," the Archigos said so softly that she could barely hear him over the crowd. "It's rare, that blessing, and sometimes the hardest thing is realizing everything that Cénzi demands of us in return for the gift." His fingers tightened on her shoulder, and she frowned as the lines deepened in his face. He leaned in closely, so that she could see herself in the dark pupils of his eyes. "The greater the gift, the greater the cost," he whispered. "You will learn that, O'Téni. I'm afraid you will learn that well."

~

Karl ci'Vliomani

"**D**HASPI CE'COENI was a damned fool. Now we need to make sure his foolishness doesn't hurt the rest of us and my mission."

Karl chopped his arms through the turgid air of the basement as if he were slicing a sword through the man's neck—a gesture, he realized, that was probably prophetic for the captured ce'Coeni. He spoke in Paeti, the language of the island he called home, a language he was certain few would understand here even if they could overhear it. Mika ce'Gilan, there with Karl, sank back into the plentiful shadows lurking in the corners. The basement room was a shabby area stinking of old stone and mold. The only light was from a trio of candles guttering in their stand on a wobbly table, thin, greasy trails of smoke twining upward from the flames, shifting as the wind from Karl's gesture made them waver and sputter. Above, they could hear muffled conversation and the creaking of floorboards under heavy feet: the room was below a tavern in the twisting streets of the Oldtown. Even at midday, there were patrons drinking and eating there.

"Ce'Coeni didn't know *me,*" Mika said, his own Paeti colored with the more guttural accents of Graubundi. "He can't betray anyone beyond the lower cell that recruited him. He had no contact with you as Envoy, so we're isolated from him. The damage will be minimal. He was just a rogue, Karl. A stupid rogue."

"I wish I were that confident." Karl grimaced. He rubbed his shell pendant between his fingers as he stalked back and forth in front of the small table, too agitated to sit. "The téni preach against us even if the Archigos is less vocal than most, the Kraljica still refuses to meet us directly, and we know how closely the Kraljica's people are watching me. Now the talk is going to be—again—about how dangerous and violent we are, and there are going to be those telling the Kraljica that the Numetodo can't be tolerated any longer. A'Téni ca'Cellibrecca will be calling for the Archigos to do what he did in Brezno, or worse. We can tell them the truth, but the truth isn't what they want to hear. You can bet that Commandant ca'Rudka is already in the cell where they've put poor ce'Coeni, and after the commandant's through with him, ce'Coeni will be happy to sign any confession that ca'Rudka puts in front of him, just to stop the pain."

Even in the wan candlelight, Karl could see that Mika's face was pale. He stopped his pacing and let the pendant swing back around his neck on its silver chain as he leaned on the table with both hands.

"I'm not about to kill the messenger, my friend," he told Mika, and that brought a quick smile. "I'm glad you came as quickly as you did. There's nothing we can do about anything that's happened. It was incredibly stupid and it's going to cause us problems, but it's done." The words, intended for Mika, also managed to staunch the anger inside him. He was starting to think again, at least, instead of only reacting. He took a long breath. "All right. We need to minimize the damage. I want you to draft a statement for me to send to the Kraljica, denying that the attack on the Archigos was part of a Numetodo plot or that ce'Coeni was anything but a deranged man with a personal grudge against the Concénzia Faith and the Archigos. Deny that we've ever met with him or know him at all. You know what to say. Ask again if I can meet with her; she won't agree, especially now, but I might get a meeting with ca'Rudka and be able to garner some idea of how he intends to react. The Archigos, I'm sure, will be making light of the attack, especially given that no one was hurt—he'll use it as an example of how weak the Numetodo are against the truly faithful, but you know that everyone's going to be talking about it for a few days. We need to make certain that this doesn't happen again, so get the word flowing down to the others through the usual channels."

Mika nodded. "I'll get a draft to you by this evening."

"Good. We can finish it then and I'll sign it. . . ." Karl closed his eyes momentarily, shaking his head. "Tell me about this woman who stopped ce'Coeni."

"I don't know who she is yet, but we'll find out. I know she arrived in one of the Concénzia carriages, but she's not a téni that we know and wasn't dressed as one. Afterward, the Archigos brought her into his own carriage; she rode with him to the Old Temple."

"That could be gratitude, or worse—it could all have been planned," Karl said. "Is it possible ce'Coeni was working both sides, that the Archigos planned this to bolster his standing? That would explain how this strange woman was able to counter the spell so rapidly, and also why ce'Coeni would be so stupid as to try to attack the Archigos in the first place. We need to find out if that's a possibility, and who this woman is. She could be important to us."

"It's already being done." Mika pushed his chair back from the table and stood up as Karl straightened. "Though I don't believe that ce'Coeni was anything but a rash idiot. As to the woman, from the description I had, she used a counter-chant. She took out Dhaspi's spell a second after he launched it, and before any of the a'téni around the Archigos had a chance to react."

Karl's right eyebrow lifted, wrinkling his forehead. "That's an accurate account?"

"I believe my source, yes."

"Then we *really* need to find out more. Téni spells take time—they can't create them *that* quickly. I'll work on this myself. You get word going through the cells. See if ce'Coeni could be a Concénzia infiltrator; I'll see what I can discover about this mysterious young woman. Meet me back here after Third Call."

Mika inclined his head slightly. He went up the wooden steps to the door. Karl heard the sound of voices as momentary light bathed the rough wooden planks. Then the shadows settled around him again. He waited there for several minutes, fingers prowling his beard as a dozen contentious thoughts tried to crowd each other in his head. Finally, uneasy and troubled, he bent down to blow out the candles.

Shrouded in blackness, he felt his way to the stairs.

~

Sergei ca'Rudka

THE BASTIDA A'DRAGO, the fortress of the dragon, was a dreary, ancient building set on the south bank of the A'Sele. The Bastida had once served to guard the city from attack from the west: one wall of the structure was formed from the ancient city wall itself just where the A'Sele curved south; another plunged from a five-story tower into the waters of the river. The edifice was named because during its building the bones of a huge dragon had been uncovered there, a fire-serpent turned to stone by some unknown magic. The creature's flesh was gone, but the great skeleton was unmistakably that of a once-living and mythical beast. The fierce, needle-toothed and polished head of the creature still loomed above the entranceway of the Bastida like a nightmare sculpture, set there by the order of Kraljiki Selida II, who had ruled the city at the time.

The Bastida was no longer a fortress, just as the few remaining sections of the city wall no longer protected Nessantico but had been overrun and mostly consumed by the spreading town. Instead, its walls weeping with moisture and covered by black moss, the fortress had long ago been transformed into a gloomy prison where those deemed to be enemies of Nessantico resided, often for the remainder of their lives. Levo ca'Niomi, who had reigned for three short and violent days as Kraljiki, had been the first prisoner held in the Bastida, nearly a hundred and fifty years before. He languished there for nearly half his life, writing the poetry that would gain him an immortality that his brief coup never

accomplished. More recently, the Kraljica's first cousin
Marcus ca'Gerodi had been imprisoned for having fi-
nanced the attempted assassination of Marguerite prior
to her coronation. Luckily for Marcus, he had not been
gifted with Marguerite's longevity, or perhaps the dank
atmosphere of the Bastida had infected him; he had died
there six years later from a fever.

Sergei ca'Rudka, Commandant of the Garde Kralji,
Chevaritt of Nessantico, an a'offizier in the Garde Civile, had never liked the Bastida. He liked it less since
the Kraljica had placed it under his control.

Sergei was certain that the poor fool who had tried
to attack the Archigos would not be one of those remembered for his interment in the Bastida. Rather, he
would be one of the far more numerous enemies of the
state who entered these gates and were immediately
forgotten.

The gardai around the massive oaken gates of the
Bastida jerked to attention as Sergei approached from
the Pontica a'Brezi Veste. He gave them only the barest nod, glancing up—as he always did—to the stone-
trapped head of Selida's dragon that snarled down on
him. The dark shapes of house martins fluttered from
where they'd nested under the crenellated summits
of the towers on either side of the gate, but as Sergei
watched, one of the birds darted out from the creature's
open mouth. A barred door at the foot of the left tower
opened, and the Capitaine of the Bastida emerged, a
graybeard whose pasty skin betrayed long hours in darkness. The capitaine had once been the sole authority in
the Bastida; now, by order of the Kraljica, he reported to
Sergei. Neither one of them liked that fact. "Commandant ca'Rudka, we've been waiting for you."

Sergei was still looking up at the dragon's mouth.
He pointed as the martin darted back into the dragon's
mouth and another left. "Do you know what's wrong
with that, Capitaine ci'Doulor?"

The man stepped out from the door, blinking in the

sunlight. He stared at the dragon. He rarely looked at Sergei; when he did, like many people, his gaze was snared by the gleaming silver nose that replaced the one of flesh Sergei had lost in a duel. "Commandant?"

"I love the freedom that the martins portray," Sergei told him. He smiled, gesturing at them. "Look at them, the way they dart and flit, the way they fly with the gift of wings Cénzi has given them. There are times I envy them and wish I could do the same. I would give up much if I could see the city as they do and move effortlessly from one rooftop to another."

Ci'Doulor nodded, though his face was puzzled under the grizzled beard. "I . . . I suppose I understand what you're saying, Commandant," he said.

"Do you?" Sergei asked, more sharply, the smile gone to ice on his lips. A martin emerged from the dragon's mouth again and fluttered off. "That dragon's head is the symbol of the Bastida, of its power and strength and terror. What message do you think it sends when those we bring here see birds nesting in that mouth, Capitaine? Do you think your prisoners feel terror as they pass underneath, or do you see a sign of hope that we're impotent, that they might pass through the Bastida's clutches as easily as that martin?"

The capitaine blinked heavily. "I'd never thought of it before, Commandant."

"Indeed," Sergei answered. "I see that." He took a step toward the capitaine, close enough that he could smell the garlic the man had eaten with his eggs that morning. His voice was loud enough that the gardai around the gate could still hear him. "Signs and symbols are potent things, Capitaine. Why, if I hung someone from a gibbet there below the dragon, someone who—let us say—didn't understand how important symbols are, I believe that seeing that body twisting in its cage would send a powerful message to those who work here. In fact, the more important that person, the more powerful that message would be, don't you think?"

Capitaine ci'Doulor visibly shuddered. His throat pulsed under the beard as he swallowed. He was staring at Sergei now, at his own warped reflection in the polished surface of Sergei's silver nose. "I'll see that the nest is removed, Commandant, and you may be assured that no birds will roost there again."

The smile widened. Sergei reached out and patted ci'Doulor's cheek as if he were a child Sergei was correcting. "I'm certain you will," he said. "Now, I'd like to see this Numetodo."

Sergei followed ci'Doulor into the Bastida. The door shut solidly behind them, a garda locking it after them. Musty air enclosed them and Sergei paused, waiting for his eyes to adjust to a dimness made only darker by the small barred windows set in walls as thick as a man holding out both arms. Ci'Doulor led him down a long hall and into the main tower, then down a winding stone staircase. Moisture pooled on foot-worn steps furred with moss on the edges where no one walked. From the barred doors of the landings, Sergei could hear the sounds of other prisoners: coughs, moans, someone calling out distantly. They came to a landing well below river level with one of the gardai standing at careful attention. The man opened the door and stepped aside.

They entered a square, compact room, the garda entering with them. Chains clattered: a man shackled to rings on the far wall stirred, his hands bound tightly to the wall so he couldn't move them to create one of the Numetodo spells, his mouth gagged with a metal cage that trapped his tongue. Sergei could see that the would-be assassin had been beaten. His face was puffy and discolored inside the bars of the face-cage, one eye was swollen shut, and a trail of dried blood drooled from one nostril. He'd soiled himself at some point—his torn hosiery was discolored and wet, and the smell of urine and feces was strong. "Capitaine," he said. "Has this man been mistreated?"

"No, Commandant," ci'Doulor answered quickly. The

garda, behind him, sniffed in seeming amusement. "It was the citizenry who did this in retaliation. Why, our Garde Kralji had tremendous difficulty even getting him away from the mob after the attack on the Archigos."

Sergei knew that to be a lie; the gardai assigned to the Archigos had subdued the man immediately after the attack and hurried him away before the crowd was even certain what had happened. "The people do love the Archigos," Sergei said, more to the prisoner than to ci'Doulor. "And hate those who would try to harm him." He stepped closer to the prisoner, taking a kerchief from his pocket and dusting the seat of a scarred, three-legged stool near the prisoner. The man moved his head inside the cage, watching Sergei with his one good eye. "If I remove the tongue-gag, will you promise to speak no spells, Vajiki?" Sergei asked, leaning toward him.

The man nodded. His gaze was not on Sergei's eyes, but the gleaming metal nose. Sergei reached around the man's head and loosed the leather straps that held the device in place. The man gagged as the metal spring holding down his tongue was removed.

"What's your name?" Sergei asked.

"Dhaspi ce'Coeni." The man's voice was pain-filled and hoarse, and the syllables—unsurprisingly—held the accent of the north provinces.

"You're a Numetodo?" A hesitant nod. "And who sent you to harm the Archigos? Was it Envoy ci'Vliomani, perhaps?"

"No!" The denial was quick. The man's undamaged eye went wide, and the chains clanked dully against stone. "I . . . I've never met Envoy ci'Vliomani. Never. What I did, I did alone. That is the truth."

Now it was Sergei who nodded. "I believe you," he said soothingly, watching his sympathetic tone leech the tension from the man's face. He sat there for several seconds, just gazing at the man. Finally he stood, going over to a small niche in the wall. From it, he took a brass bar, as thick around as a man's fist and perhaps two fists

high, and satisfyingly massive and heavy. Both ends of
the bar were polished and slightly flattened, as if they'd
been battered many times. "I love history," he said to the
prisoner. "Did you know that?"

The man's gaze was on the bar in Sergei's hand now.
He shook his head hesitantly. "Of course you don't," Sergei continued. "But it's the truth. I do. History teaches us
so much, Vajiki ce'Coeni—it's from understanding what
has happened in the past that we can best see the dan-
gers of the future. Now this piece of metal . . ." He put his
index finger into a large hole bored through the middle
of the bar; only the tip of his finger emerged. "There was
once a large bell in this very tower. The bell enclosure is
still there at the top of the tower; you may have seen it
when they brought you here, though I doubt you were
much in the mood to notice such things. The bell was
to be rung if there was a threat to the city so that the
citizenry would be warned and react. Now, the bell itself
has long ago been removed and melted down—I believe
that the statue of Henri VI in Oldtown was cast from the
metal of the bell; you might have seen it. But this . . ."
Sergei hefted the bar again. "This was the bell's clapper. You see, a rope went through the hole here, knotted
above and underneath to keep it at the right height, then
the remainder of the rope dropped down to the floor of
the tower so that someone could ring the bell at need.
And it *was* rung, five times all told, the last being when
the Hellinians sent their fleet of warships up the A'Sele
to attack the city back in Maria III's reign." He took his
finger from the hole and hefted the clapper in his hand.
"So I look at this and I have to marvel at the history I'm
holding, Vajiki, at the fact that this very piece of metal
has been part of so much of what has happened here. It
has protected us before, and—this is the part that's cru-
cial to you, Vajiki ce'Coeni—it continues to do so."

Sergei went back to the niche. From it, he took a short
length of oak, rounded by a lathe at one end. He fitted
the rounded end into the hole of the clapper, transform-

ing the metal bar into the sinister head of a hammer. He nodded to the garda, who came forward and unlocked the fetters from the prisoner's left hand. "I require your hand, Vajika. Please place it on the stool, like this." He held out his own hand, palm upward, with the little finger extended out and the rest of the fingers curled in. The prisoner shook his head, sobbing now, and the garda took ce'Coeni's hand and forced it down on the stool's seat. Ce'Coeni curled his fingers into an impotent fist. "I need only your little finger, Vajiki," Sergei told him. "Otherwise, the pain will be . . . far worse." Sergei moved alongside the stool, looking down at the prisoner. "I need to know, Vajiki ce'Coeni, the names of the Numetodo with whom you were involved here in Nessantico."

"I don't know any other Numetodo," the man gasped. He tried to move his hand back, but though the chains rattled, the garda held it fast.

"Ah," Sergei said. "You see, I believed you when you told me that you acted alone, because I don't think even the Numetodo would be so foolish as to send a lone person on such a futile mission as yours. But I don't believe you now. I can see the lie in your eyes, Vajiki. I can hear it in your voice and smell it in the fear that comes from you. And I've learned over the years that there is truth in pain." He touched his finger to his false nose, and saw ce'Coeni's eyes follow the gesture. He hefted the hammer made by the bell clapper and looked down at the stool where ce'Coeni's hand was still fisted. "What will it be, Vajiki? Your entire hand, or just the little finger?"

The man sobbed. The smell of urine became stronger. "You can't . . ."

"To the contrary," Sergei told him, his voice soft and sympathetic. "I will, not out of desire, but because I must. Because it's my task to keep this city, the Kraljica, and the Archigos safe."

"No, no, you don't have to do this," the man said desperately, his voice rushed. "I'll tell you the names. I met once with an older man named Boli and another one my age whose name was Grotji. I don't know their family names, Commandant; they never told me. I met them in a tavern in Oldtown. I could show you where, could describe them for you—"

Sergei was still looking at the hand on the stool. "The finger or the hand, Vajiki?"

"But I've told you everything I know, Commandant. That is the truth."

Sergei said nothing. He lifted the hammer, bending his elbow. With a whimper, ce'Coeni extended his little finger.

Sergei brought the hammer down with a grunt: hard, fast, and sudden. The blow crushed bone and flesh, tendon and muscle. Blood spattered from beneath the brass. A shrill scream tore from ce'Coeni's throat, a high-pitched screech that echoed from the stones and Sergei's ears before it faded away into a wailing sob. Sergei was always surprised by the sheer volume the human throat could produce.

He lifted the hammer; the man's finger was flattened and destroyed, nearly torn in half near the second joint. He heard the capitaine's intake of breath hiss behind him.

"There's truth in pain," Sergei said again to the man. The garda had released ce'Coeni's hand, and the prisoner cradled it to his chest, rocking back and forth on the floor of the cell as he wept. "I'm very sorry, Vajiki, but I'm afraid I need to be certain there isn't anything else you have to tell us. . . ."

Sergei remained, asking questions until only the thumb of ce'Coini's ruined hand remained untouched. Then he wiped the bloodied and gore-spattered end of the hammer on the prisoner's clothing, and pulled the handle from the clapper with some effort. He placed the metal bar and handle back in their niche. Nodding to the garda, he and Capitaine ci'Doulor left the cell.

"He knows nothing of any use," he said to the capitaine as they ascended the stairs.

"He named Envoy ci'Vliomani, there at the last," ci'Doulor said. "Isn't that what you wanted, Commandant?"

"He would have named his own matarh then," Sergei answered. "I wanted the truth, and the truth is that he was a fool acting alone. We have two first names, almost certainly false, and a tavern in Oldtown that was probably chosen at random. I'll send out the Garde Kralji and see if they can find these men from the descriptions he gave us. But I don't have much hope. I'll speak with the Kraljica and the Archigos and tell them what we've learned."

"And the prisoner, Commandant?"

Sergei shrugged. "Have him sign a confession. Leave the paper blank so we can fill in what we might require later. Then execute him for his crime. A quick and painless death, Capitaine. He deserves that much. Afterward, cut off the hands and pull out the tongue, as required for Numetodo, then gibbet the body from the Pontica Kralji so that all of Oldtown can see it."

"I'll see to it."

"And to the birds?"

"The birds?" the capitaine said in puzzlement, then: "Ah, yes. In the dragon's mouth. Yes, Commandant. I'll see to that also."

"Good." They reached the top of the stairs. Sergei turned, and the capitaine brought his hands to his forehead in salute. "It's been a productive day, then. You have your tasks to attend to, Capitaine. I can find my own way out."

~

Ana cu'Seranta

THE TÉNI-LIGHTS OF NESSANTICO were famous throughout the Holdings. It was the Night
Circle that people often spoke of when they reminisced
about their visit to the capital city. As the sun faded behind the bend of the A'Sele, as the western sky deepened to purple and the first stars appeared, a procession
of dozens of e'téni clothed in yellow-hemmed robes
filed from each of the several temples of the city. Ana
watched with her family, Sala (tending to her matarh),
and the other onlookers as one group of light-téni left
the Archigos' Temple, proceeding east and west along
both sides of the Avi a'Parete as they passed the gates.
The e'téni each went to one of the tall, black iron poles
erected several strides apart along the boulevard. There
they paused, chanting and performing intricate motions
of hands and fingers as the wind-horns blew a mournful
dissonance from the towers. Finally the e'téni lifted their
hands high, fingers spread wide open, and the yellow-
glass globes high atop the poles flared and illuminated
as if a tiny sun had been born inside them. The e-téni
clapped their hands once and moved to the next light
poles, repeating the spell. Around the entire long loop
of the Avi a'Parete and the Four Bridges, the daily ceremony was repeated until all the lamps were lighted and
the boulevard that encircled the inner city was ablaze
with pools of false day.

"When I was at Montbataille, I swear I could look to
the south and west from the high slopes and see Nessantico at night, miles and miles and miles away, like

a necklace of stars fallen to the ground and glittering there." Ana's vatarh Tomas smiled at her, his arm slipping around her shoulders and pulling her tight to his side. Ana forced herself to return the smile and to remain in his embrace though she ached to pull away. *No more. Not after tonight* . . . "Seeing the lights always made me think of you and your matarh, safe there. And I wondered if one day it might not be you in the procession every night, lighting the lamps. You always played at being a téni, even when you were just a child—do you remember that? And now . . ." His smile transformed into a grin tainted with greed. She knew his thoughts: *an o'teni could command a dowry of her own for the family.* . . . "They won't waste an o'téni to just light the Avi, will they?"

Ana shook her head, starting to pull away, but Tomas hugged her tightly again as the e'téni moved on to the next lamps and the crowd that had gathered to watch the procession began to thin. She felt his fingers cup the side of her breast, but before she could react, his arm slipped from her. Tomas crouched down in front of Ana's matarh, seated in her carry-chair. Her matarh's eyes were open, but they saw nothing and tracked no one. He put his hands on hers, folded on her lap. "We're proud of our Ana, aren't we, Abi?"

The woman didn't reply. She rarely spoke anymore, and when she did, no one could understand her. Her eyes seemed to search for something past his shoulder. Another of the coughing spasms struck her and she hunched over, the cough rumbling and liquid in her lungs. Tomas took a kerchief from the pocket of his bashta and dabbed at the mucus around her mouth.

I will need to help her again tomorrow. "Vatarh? We should be going to the temple," Ana said.

Tomas stood slowly and nodded to the quartet of hired servants with them; they took up the poles of the carry-chair once more. They proceeded across the street into the plaza where, just this morning, everything in Ana's life had changed. A female acolyte was waiting there, approaching them as they crossed the Avi. Ana recognized her: Savi cu'Varisi, one of the current third-years who—unlike Ana when she'd been there—had been plucked by the téni from the common rabble of the acolytes and given special tasks at the temple. Even though Ana was the senior student, in their few encounters Savi had treated Ana as she might have some merchant's apprentice. Tonight, Savi seemed subservient and overawed by her task. She kept her head down, refusing to meet Ana's gaze.

"This way, O'Téni cu'Seranta," Savi said. She stumbled over the title, and her face reddened. "The Archigos is awaiting you and your family."

" 'O'Teni cu'Seranta.' " Tomas chuckled as the acolyte led them toward a side door of the temple. "That has a wonderful sound, doesn't it, Ana?"

"Yes, Vatarh," Ana admitted, watching Sala as she turned and started to walk toward the temple, wishing he sounded more pleased for her and less for himself. "But I don't know if I'll ever get used to it."

"Oh, you will. And more. I'm certain of it. One day soon it will be U'Téni ca'Seranta. This is Cénzi's will; this is our reward for the trials He sent us. I always knew it would come."

Ana nodded at her vatarh's confidence, though she knew that Tomas' certainty was new and fragile. True, Cénzi had sent trials enough to their family: the deaths of her two younger siblings to Red Pox six years before, followed closely by the loss of Ana's older brother Louis the next year, serving with the Garde Civile in one of the border skirmishes with Tennshah. Then Vatarh, a mid-level bureaucrat within the Department of Provincial Commerce, had been assigned to the town of Montbataille only to have his position eliminated within six months. Since then, he had held a variety of positions within the Nessantico government, each of them of less status and lower compensation as Abi and Tomas were forced to squander their savings and rely on the largesse of the cu'Seranta relatives to avoid the shame of becoming ci'Seranta or worse.

Ana thought the nadir had come four years ago when Abi had been stricken. That had seemed the final blow. Her apprenticeship to the Concénzia Faith had been her vatarh's desperate attempt to salvage something from the unrelenting downward spiral of the family's fortunes.

The healers had all said that her matarh would die, and Ana had watched her fail. When Ana was little, she had often put her hands on her matarh's temples when she complained of headaches, and there were always words in her mind that she could say, words that would take away the pain. *You always played at being a téni. . . .* She had, and Ana knew now that it was the early manifestation of her Gift, an instinctive use of the Ilmodo.

It was also wrong. The Divolonté, the laws and regulations of Concénzia, explicitly said so. "To heal with the Ilmodo is to thwart the will of Cénzi," the téni thundered in their Admonitions from the High Lectern in the temple. Ana, always devout, had stopped as soon as she realized what she was doing.

But . . .

She couldn't watch her matarh die. After the last healer Vatarh had hired left in defeat, Ana finally put her hands on her matarh again and spoke the words that came—carefully, tentatively, letting the Ilmodo ease the pain, letting Ana bring her back from the death spiral she was in, but not all the way back: because that would be too visible and too dangerous. Ana parceled out the relief, feeling guilty both for her misuse of the Ilmodo and because she didn't use it as fully as she might.

Then came the true shame. The worst of it all. Her vatarh . . . First it was just words and hugs, then he came to her for the more intimate comforts that Abi had once given him. Too young and too immature and too trusting, Ana had endured his long, careful seduction, knowing

that if she told anyone, the shame would destroy the
family utterly, that it would be her matarh who would
suffer most of all. . . .

"O'Téni? Through here . . ." Savi had led them to a
set of gilded wooden doors. The panels were carved
with a representation of Cénzi's ascension to the Second World—the elongated figure of the god being lifted
up toward the clouds while below an immense fissure
yawned in the globe below, where Cénzi had fallen in his
struggle with the Moitidi, His children. Ana stroked the
polished wood as Savi pulled open the doors. Beyond
was a small, simple chapel which might have held fifty
people at the most, lit by candles set in silver candelabra
swaying on chains from the high ceiling. Ana could smell
incense burning in a brazier, then motion caught her eye
near the altar covered with fine damask at the far end
of the chapel. The Archigos stepped up onto the altar
dais, supported by a young male o'téni who towered
over him. The Archigos gestured to them as Savi closed
the chapel door, remaining behind in the corridor. Ana
glanced around; there was no one else in the chapel.

"Are you disappointed, O'Téni?" the Archigos asked,
his voice reverberating from the stone surfaces around
them. "I know that the official ceremony was better at-
tended with all the families and all the a'téni. . . ."

"No, Archigos," Ana answered. She remembered
A'Téni ca'Cellibrecca's stern, unforgiving face staring at
her, and the way the others had looked at her as if she
were a puzzle they had to solve. She was pleased none
of them were there now. "I'm sorry. I'm . . . very happy
tonight."

"Then please come forward and sit—there are chairs
for all of you here in front. This is your vatarh and
matarh?"

"Yes, Archigos." Ana introduced her parents, Tomas
going forward to kneel before the Archigos with clasped
hands, playing—as he always did—the devout follower.

The Archigos came forward to put his own gnarled and small hands around her vatarh's.

"I thank you for sending us your daughter," the Archigos said. "Vajiki cu'Seranta, I've arranged for the Concénzia treasury to transfer five thousand solas to your family's account against Ana's future services to the Faith. I assume that will be sufficient?" Ana could see Vatarh's eyebrows lift and his mouth drop. She sucked in her own breath in surprise as well—the families of the acolytes in her class had been given a tenth of that sum.

"Oh, yes, Archigos. That is quite . . ." Tomas stopped. She wondered what he'd intended to say. His mouth closed and he swallowed. ". . .adequate for the moment," he finished. Ana could see him toting up accounts in his head.

The Archigos had noticed the internal greed as well, Ana realized. He favored her vatarh with a dismissive smile. "One of my clerks will be outside when you leave, Vajiki," the Archigos said. "She will have papers for you to sign that will complete the transfer. You'll note that you will also be giving up the family's right to either select or approve a husband for Ana: she now belongs to Concénzia and can make her own choice freely. You will have no voice in that, nor will you receive any further dowry for her."

Her vatarh frowned at that. "Archigos, we had expected to advance the family through Ana's marriage."

"Then perhaps a thousand solas will suffice, if you prefer to retain those rights. It doesn't matter to me. My secretary, O'Téni Kenne ci'Fionta, is right here." The Archigos nodded to the téni who was standing next to him. "Kenne, would you be so kind as to tell the clerks to make that change in the contract. . . ."

Vatarh's eyes widened again and he hurried to answer as the o'téni bowed and started down the aisle of the chapel. "No, Archigos," he answered. "I think the agreement will be sufficient as is."

"Ah," the Archigos said. Kenne, with a slight smile, returned to the Archigos' side. To Ana, the Archigos seemed to be smothering laughter. "Then let us begin . . ."

The ceremony was brief. Afterward, O'Téni ci'Fionta handed the Archigos the green robes that would be Ana's attire from this time forward. The Archigos uttered a blessing over the robes, then handed one set to Ana. "If you would put this on," he said. "You may go behind the screens there at the side of the altar."

The robes felt strange against her skin; softer than she'd expected from the times U'Téni cu'Dosteau's robes had brushed against her. She touched the slashes at the shoulders of the robe: yes, they were those of an o'téni, and on the left shoulder was sewn the broken-globe crest of the Archigos. Taking off her tashta and putting on the robes, she realized that she was also severing herself from her old life and putting on a new one. She would not be returning to her family's home this evening, but retiring to a new apartment here in the temple complex.

I'm finally gone, Vatarh, and you can't touch me anymore. . . .

She came out from behind the screen, holding her yellow tashta folded in her arms. Sala, beaming, hurried forward to take it from her. Her vatarh nodded his approval, tears glistening unashamedly in his eyes—she wondered whether he was truly proud of her, or only saddened by what was being taken from him. Her matarh stared blankly ahead, as if transfixed by candle glints from the gold-threaded robes of the Archigos.

"Ah . . ." the Archigos breathed. "Now you look the proper téni. Vajiki cu'Seranta, I wonder if you would allow me a few minutes alone with your daughter. My clerk, as I said, is waiting outside to take care of the fund transfer while you wait. Your servants should go with you, but I would like Vajica cu'Seranta to remain."

Anna's vatarh looked startled, but he brought his

hands to his forehead and motioned to Sala and the other servants. The Archigos waited, silent, until the chapel doors had closed again behind them. Then he turned to Ana.

"I deliberately brought you here, to this chapel and without any of the a'téni about. Your matarh, her illness is grave. The Southern Fever, isn't it? She was incredibly fortunate to survive at all. I've only rarely heard of anyone recovering who has been affected that badly. I remember all the funerals years ago when the Fever was at its height here in the city."

He was staring at her, as was O'Téni ci'Fionta. "It was Cénzi's Will that Matarh lived, Archigos," she said, and the lie felt like pins stabbing her throat

"No doubt," the Archigos said. "And *your* will, also."

"Archigos?" Ana started.

Faintly, the dwarf smiled. "There's no one here but the four of us, Ana. No a'téni listening, no ears here that shouldn't hear what you might say, no prying eyes watching." Ana couldn't stop her gaze from going to the young o'téni. The Archigos' smiled widened slightly. "Kenne ci'Fionta is someone I trust implicitly, so you must also." He paused. "You no doubt prayed for your matarh's life."

"Of course, Archigos. Every day."

"And Cénzi answered your prayers? Or was it something else?" the Archigos prompted, and Ana's face colored helplessly. "You lie badly, O'Téni," the Archigos said. He stepped from the dais and put his hand on her matarh's arm. At the touch, the woman stirred, turning her head slightly but still staring off vacantly. "Your innocence and naïveté is very fetching, Ana, but we'll need to work on that. Tell me the rest, and tell me the truth now. Did you use the Gift of Cénzi to thwart Cénizi's Will for your matarh? Did you do what you knew was forbidden for the téni by the Divolonté? Tell me the truth, here where you can."

Ana saw the joyous evening and her triumph beginning

to collapse around her. She wondered how she would be able to tell Vatarh how it had gone so badly so quickly. She could imagine his face going slack, his shoulders slumping and his will shattering inside him . . . and the foul anger and abuse that would follow. "Matarh was *dying*. Archigos," Ana said, looking down at her matarh unmoving in her carry-chair. "That would have killed Vatarh, too, after all that had happened to us. So I . . . I . . . Just the smallest help . . . Just enough that . . ." She couldn't finish, her voice choking. Her hands lifted. Fell back to her sides.

"You know the punishment for this sin? You know the Divolonté?"

Ana clasped her hands behind her back. She could barely speak. "Yes, Archigos." *Cénzi has given me His own punishment to bear for what I did. If I'd let her die, then Vatarh might have married someone else, and he might have left me alone.*

"Look at me. Quote the Divolonté for me; you've certainly heard it often enough in your studies."

She forced herself to look down into his face: stern now, the wrinkles holding his ancient eyes drawn harshly in his skin. Her voice was little more than a whisper. " 'The sinner has abused Cénzi's Gift and shown that she no longer trusts in Cénzi's judgment; therefore—' " She stopped.

"Finish it," the Archigos told her.

" 'Therefore, strike her hands from her body and her tongue from her mouth so that she may never use the Gift again.' " Ana took a long breath.

"You put yourself above Cénzi?" the Archigos asked.

"No, Archigos," Ana protested. "I truly don't. But I watched her suffering, watched my vatarh suffer with her. . . ."

"Does your vatarh know what you did? Does anyone?"

"No, Archigos. At least, I don't think so. I was always alone with her when I tried. I made certain of that."

The Archigos nodded. His hand was still on her matarh's arm. "You didn't do all you could for her, did you?"

Ana shook her head. "I was afraid. I knew Cénzi would be angry, and I was also afraid that everyone would notice—"

"Do it now," the Archigos said, interrupting her. At her look of shock, his stern face relaxed. "The gift of healing is the rarest tendency, the most easily abused, and the most dangerous to the person using it, which is why it's proscribed. It's also why I made certain that the only other person here tonight was someone I could trust. Your hands and tongue are safe for now, Ana. Show me. Show me Cénzi's Gift. Use it as you wanted to use it. Go on," he said as she hesitated.

Ana took a long breath. She could feel the Archigos staring at her as she closed her eyes and brought her hands together. As she been taught, she reached deep into her inner self as she prayed to Cénzi to show her the way, and again the path to the Ilmodo opened up before her, sparking purple and red in her mind. Her hands were moving, not in the patterns that U'Téni cu'Dosteau had laboriously taught the acolytes but in her own unconscious manner, the way she *knew* they must go to shape this particular Gift. She could feel it now, a warmth between her still-moving hands, a glow that penetrated her eyelids and sent blood-tinted, pulsing streaks chasing themselves before her.

Before, she'd stopped at this point, just as the energy began to be felt, and applied it to her matarh. This time she allowed it to continue to flow around her, gathering it. She chanted: words she didn't know, in a language that wasn't hers. A calmness filled Ana as her hands stopped moving, as she cupped Cénzi's Gift in her hands.

She opened her eyes. Her matarh was staring at the brilliance she held between them. "This is for you, Matarh," Ana whispered. "Cénzi has sent it to you." With that, she bent forward and placed her hands on her matarh's shoulder. The brilliance darted out, striking her matarh and seeming to sink into her.

As Ana touched her matarh, she felt again the wild, black heat in the older woman: patches of it in her head, around her heart, in her lungs. It paled where the Ilmodo touched it, and this time, *this* time Ana let the power flow freely, let it cover the illness. She could *feel* it through her hands: as if Ana herself had the Fever, as if it could crawl out from her matarh into herself. She pushed it back, back into the maelstrom of the Ilmodo, and the heat rose so intensely that she thought her hands would be burned.

She lifted her hands away from her matarh, unable to hold the power any longer.

Abini jerked in her seat, a shuddering intake of breath as if she were a drowning person gasping for air. Her eyes went wide, and she gave a long, low wail that held no words at all. She sank back, her eyes closing . . . and when they opened again, her pupils were clear, and she looked at the Archigos and O'Téni Kenne alongside him, then at Ana in her green robes.

"Ana? I feel as if I've been away for a long time . . . I'm so tired, and I don't remember . . . Why are you dressed that way, child, like a téni? And so much older . . ."

Ana's breath caught in a sob. She felt too weary to stand, and sank down alongside the carry-chair, gathering the woman in her arms. She looked at her own hands, marveling that they weren't burned to the bone. "Matarh . . ." The doors to the chapel pushed opened suddenly and her vatarh strode in, looking concerned. The servants peered around the opening. Ana glanced at him; her matarh turned in her carry-chair and laughed.

"Tomas!"

"Abi?" he said. He gaped, almost comically, caught in a half-stride. "Abi, is that *you* I heard?"

"Indeed it was," the Archigos answered him, moving between Tomas and Ana as Kenne lifted Ana to her feet, his hands supporting her as she swayed, exhausted.

"Cénzi has moved here tonight, Vajiki, in honor of your daughter's anointment. We have witnessed a special blessing."

Ana heard the Archigos' last words as if they were coming from a great distance. She thought she saw her vatarh rushing to them, but the shadows in the chapel were growing darker and the candlelight could not hold them back. The darkness whirled around her, a night-storm. She pushed at it with her hands, but the blackness filled her mouth and her eyes and bore her away.

MOVEMENTS

Marguerite ca'Ludovici
Justi ca'Mazzak
Ana cu'Seranta
Karl ci'Vliomani
Ana cu'Seranta
Jan ca'Vörl
Orlandi ca'Cellibrecca

Marguerite ca'Ludovici

"**K**RALJICA?"

"When I'm eighteen, I'll be Kraljiki just like you became Kraljica," Justi said, smiling at her as she held him. She laughed.

"Is that what you want, Justi? That means I only have twelve more years to live." She pouted dramatically, and Justi's eyes widened and his mouth dropped open. The courtiers gathered around them laughed.

"Oh, no, Matarh," Justi said, the words tumbling out all in a rush. "I want you to live forever and ever!"

"Kraljica?"

The Throne Room smelled of oils. When Renard's voice came, Marguerite found herself startled—she'd nearly fallen into a trance as the painter ci'Recroix first sketched her likeness on the canvas and began applying the underpainting. She was startled to see darkness outside the windows of the West Reception Chamber, and to find the room lit by a dozen candelabra and the eternal glow of the Sun Throne.

Several of the courtiers were standing well to the back of the room—banished there because ci'Recroix had said that he could not work with gawkers looking over his shoulder—and talking softly among themselves while servants bustled about. How long had she been sitting there? Had she ordered the candles lit? It seemed bare minutes ago that Third Call had sounded.

"Yes?" she asked Renard, blinking at him standing before her with hands on forehead—here, in public, always the correct image of an aide. Renard glanced over at the painter. Ci'Recroix straightened by the canvas set at the foot of Marguerite's dais, stirring his brush in a jar of turpentine. Pale colors swirled around the fine sable hairs. The strange, dark box of a mechanism he'd used to sketch her initial likeness, the device he'd called a "miroire a'scéne," was draped in black cloth on the floor nearby.

"Kraljica, the Commandant ca'Rudka is here with his report."

"Ah!" Marguerite blinked. She felt somnolent and lethargic, and shook her head to clear it. She wondered whether she'd been sleeping, and if anyone had noticed. "Send him up. Vajiki ci'Recroix, I'm afraid that our session is over for today."

The painter bowed and pressed his paint-stained hands to his forehead, leaving behind a smudge of vermilion. "As you wish, Kraljica. When should I return? Tomorrow afternoon, perhaps? The lighting I want to capture on your face is that of the late day—the light looks so dramatic on your face, coupled with the Sun Throne behind you. . . ."

"That will be fine—Renard, make certain there are a few turns of the glass in my schedule for Vajiki ci'Recroix before Third Call. And please clear the room so that the commandant and I have some privacy; I will meet with the court afterward in the Red Hall for supper." As Renard bowed and went to the courtiers, as the painter began to gather up his oils and brushes, Marguerite rose from the crystalline seat. The light in the Sun Throne dimmed and faded, making the room seem dark as the courtiers noisily filed out of the room. "I would like to see what you've done," she told the artist.

Ci'Recroix was visibly startled by the request. He dropped the brushes he was holding on the small table next to the easel and quickly draped a white sheet over the canvas. "You cannot, Kraljica."

"I *cannot?*" Her head tilted slightly to one side with the word, and an eyebrow lifted.

"Well ... I would strongly *prefer* that you do not, Kraljica," ci'Recroix quickly amended, with another pressing of hands to forehead. He picked up the brushes again and began to place them in a case. "I've only just made my sketch and begun to place the undertones on the canvas. You would be more pleased if you could wait until I have something substantial to show you. It's the way I work with my subjects; I want to surprise them with an image of themselves, as if they were looking into a mirror, but this . . ." He waved his hand at the hidden canvas. "This would only disappoint you at the moment, I'm afraid. So if it would please the Kraljica, I beg you not to look. In fact, perhaps it would be best if I took it with me. . . ."

His face seemed so comically distressed that she nearly laughed. "I'll manage to contain my curiosity for the time being, Vajiki," she told him, then did laugh at the relief that softened the hard lines of his thin face. "Leave your canvas here; no one will disturb it."

A knock came on the doors at the far end of the room. "Enter," Marguerite said; the door opened and Commandant ca'Rudka strode into the room, walking quickly toward them, his bootsteps loud on the tiled floor. His sharp eyes flickered over to ci'Recroix even as he quickly touched hands to forehead yet again; the painter stared openly at the man's silver nose.

"Kraljica," the commandant said. "You'd do well to open your windows. The stench of the oils . . ." He strode to the windows nearest the dais and pushed them open. Fresh, cold air wafted in and the Kraljica shivered, but the breeze did seem to clear her head.

"Thank you, Sergei," she said. "Vajiki ci'Recroix, if you have everything . . ."

The man nearly jumped, still watching ca'Rudka. He grabbed the case of brushes under his left arm and took up the valise that held the jars of mixed paints in the same hand, then picked up the miroire a'scéne by a handle; it seemed rather heavy, judging by the way ci'Recroix leaned to one side while holding it. "Forgive me, Kraljica. I'll see . . . uh . . ." He hesitated.

"Renard cu'Bellona. My aide," she reminded him.

"Renard cu'Bellona. Yes. That was the name. Remember, Kraljica, you shouldn't look. Umm . . . tomorrow, then." He started to bring hands to forehead, remembered that he was holding something in each hand, and set them down again to salute her. Then he picked up case, valise, and miroire a'scéne and lurched toward the doors, grunting with the effort. He knocked on one of the doors with a foot; the hall garda opened them and he went out. The garda saluted the Kraljica and closed the doors again.

"That is a very strange man," ca'Rudka said. He was staring after the painter.

"But a talented one, from what I've seen." She glanced at the draped painting on its easel. "You've questioned the assassin, Sergei?"

Ca'Rudka nodded. He looked at his hands as if making certain that they were clean. "Yes." He told her, briefly, what had happened during the interrogation at the Bastida—leaving out, Marguerite suspected, some of the more brutal details. She did not press him for them.

"So this ce'Coeni was a rogue," she said when he'd finished. "Nothing more. He may have been in the Numetodo faction, but you're satisfied he was acting on his own, not on their orders?"

"That's my conclusion, Kraljica. Yes."

"I assume you have a signed confession."

He smiled at that. "Indeed. One that you may . . ." He paused. ". . . use as you wish."

"Did he name Envoy ci'Vliomani as the instigator?"

Sergei shrugged. "Only if you wish it to be so."

Marguerite sniffed. Her fingers trailed along the hem of the cloth over her painting. "At this point, I don't know what would be to our best advantage," Marguerite answered. "The confession can remain blank for now, until we know better. Envoy ci'Vliomani has sent over an urgent request to meet with me, along with an official statement denying any connection with the attempt on the Archigos' life."

"That's not surprising. He's no doubt shaking in his Paetian boots at this, knowing that it's only going to inflame the anti-Numetodo sentiments in the city. You've refused, just to make him worry some more?"

A smile: Sergei knew her well. Sometimes too well. "Yes. I thought perhaps you should talk with him first. Then, if you think I should, I can meet with the man. He's been very patient thus far."

"Indeed he has. I'll make the arrangements. You heard how the Archigos was saved?"

"Yes. An acolyte's spell: a girl from the cu'Seranta family. I also understand that the Archigos will giving her a Marque in gratitude."

"He already has," Sergei told her. "The Archigos made the girl an o'téni and placed her on his private staff." Marguerite glanced again at the windows and the darkness beyond, seeing the bright lights shimmering along the Avi a'Parete. How long had she been sitting there, half-asleep? That was unlike her. "Kraljica, my contacts among the téni tell me that she reacted more like an experienced téni than a raw acolyte; in fact, some of them think what she did may have been against the Divolonté. There are some . . . rumors among the téni also—that the girl's mother was suffering from Southern Fever and that after years in a weak dream-state, she's suddenly recovered completely. The talk is that a healing might have been performed."

Marguerite's eyebrows sought her forehead with that. "Then I'll need to meet her and the Archigos, won't I? But that can wait until tomorrow, surely."

"As the Kraljica wishes. Do you want me to brief the A'Kralj?"

Marguerite shrugged. "If you can find him at this time of night. My son is often . . . out." She didn't need to say more; it had, after all, been Sergei who alerted her to Justi's nocturnal wanderings and what they implied. For the moment, her son's dalliances could be tolerated, but Marguerite knew that she would have to do something to disengage him, and soon.

She had done it several times before, after all.

"If that's the case, then I will see the A'Kralj in the morning. If the Kraljica will excuse me . . . ?"

Marguerite gestured dismissal, and Sergei saluted and strode quickly to the door. She watched him leave, standing next to the easel. She waited, her breathing slow, taking in the scent of oiled pigments and dust, looking down at the little table set next to the painting, speckled with a thousand colors. The breeze from the window touched the cloth masking the portrait and rippled the candle flames, and the swaying of cloth and light seemed to mock her.

She lifted the covering.

~

Justi ca'Mazzak

THE A'KRALJ MOVED through the Oldtown night unnoticed.

Or at least he hoped so.

It was difficult to conceal his identity. The fine and expensive clothing he normally wore could be exchanged—and had been—for a plain, rough bashta that a tradesman might wear. He'd scrubbed away the scent of perfumes and ointments and let the smoke from the choked flue of a tavern hearth coil around him until he smelled of soot and ashes. He'd mussed his hair; he'd been careful not to

use the cultured accents of the ca'-and-cu', but instead
the broad intonation of the lower classes. Still, his voice
was distinctly high-pitched, which he knew was a cause
of occasional jest when people talked of him. There was
no disguising the squared jaw under the band of well-
trimmed beard: the jaw his vatarh and great-vatarh had
possessed also, and which was prominent in portraits of
them. He could stoop, but it was still difficult to disguise
the way he towered over most people, or to hide the
trim muscularity of his body. He kept a cowl pulled over
his head, he leaned heavily on a short walking stick, and
he spoke as little as possible.

He enjoyed nights like this. He enjoyed the anonym-
ity; he enjoyed the escape from the constricting duties
of the Kraljica's court; he enjoyed being simply "Justi"
and not "the A'Kralj." As A'Kralj, he was bound to his
matarh's whims and her rules.

When he was Kraljiki, all that would change. Then
Nessantico would dance to his call. The empire would
awaken from its long decades of slumbering under his
matarh and the current Archigos and his predecessors
and realize its true potential.

Soon enough . . .

Oldtown, despite the intimation of the name, wasn't
the oldest settling within Nessantico. That honor went to
the Isle A'Kralji, where the Kraljica's Grande Palais, the
Old Temple, and A'Kralj's own estate all were situated.
But the original dwellings on the Isle had long ago been
razed to make room for those far more magnificent
buildings and the lavish, manicured grounds on which
they stood. Oldtown and the narrow, twisting streets on
the north bank of the A'Sele had been the shores onto
which the growing city on the Isle had spilled four centuries ago, and Oldtown had changed little in the last
few hundred years. Many of the buildings dated back
that far. Oldtown clasped its dark past to its bosom and
refused to let it go. Mysteries lurked down claustrophobic alleyways, murder and intrigue in the shadows. Its

shops contained anything the human heart might desire, if you knew where to find it and could afford it; its taverns were loud and boisterous with the alcohol-buoyed glee of the common folk; its streets swarmed with life in all its glory and all its disgust.

If you can't find what you desire in Oldtown, it doesn't exist. It was an old maxim in Nessantico.

Justi had found love in Oldtown, and it was toward love that he hurried, every night that he could find the time to steal away from those around him.

"Pardon, Vajiki. Might you have a d'folia to spare for someone to buy a loaf of bread?" The voice came from the black mouth of an alley, accompanied by the scent of rotting teeth. Here in the bowels of the city near Oldtown Center, well away from the téni-lights of the Avi a'Parete, what illumination there was came mostly from the open windows of taverns and brothels, fitful and dim. Wedges of darkness shifted and Justi saw the man there. He knew him, also: the beggar known as Mad Mahri. *Where foul things happen, you'll see Mad Mahri.* It was another saying within the city. The man seemed to be ubiquitous, wandering everywhere through the city, and present often enough at critical events in the city that Commandant ca'Rudka himself had questioned the man. It was rumored that Mahri had acquired at least some of the scars on his body then.

Justi rummaged in the pocket of his cloak; his fingers plucked a small coin from among the others there. He brought his hand out.

"Here," he said to the beggar. He kept his voice deliberately low, growling the words and disguising his natural high tenor. "Buy yourself bread or a tankard. I don't care which."

A hand flashed out and caught the coin as Justi flipped it toward the man. "Thank you, Vajiki," he said. "And in return, let me give you something."

"I want nothing from you, Mahri." Justi took a step

away from the man, his right hand straying to the knife he had hidden under his cloak.

Mahri seemed to chuckle. "Ah, Mahri's no threat to you, Vajiki. Not tonight. But you *do* want something from me. You simply don't realize it. Isn't that the way it happens too often? We don't know what it is we need until it's taken from us, or until we receive it." His voice changed: it became a breath, a hoarse, urgent whisper. "I know who you are. I know what you want. I know what you're searching for, and what you've found."

Justi exhaled mockingly, a half-laugh. "I'm supposed to listen to the wisdom of a half-wit who doesn't even have a d'folia to buy bread?"

A hiss sounded in the darkness. "You wait for your matarh to die. You yearn for it, and you fear it at the same time. And you lie in the bed of a woman who belongs to another man, and who is her vatarh's pawn."

Justi sucked in his breath. His eyes narrowed. He forgot to lower the pitch of his voice, and his reply was shrill. "Why are you accosting me? What is it you want? All I need to do is call for the utilino . . ."

"What I want you'll eventually give me," Mahri answered. "I came to tell you this: I know the painted face is also a funeral mask. It will soon be your time, as it should be."

The words sent a chill through Justi. "What does that mean? Do you offer nothing but riddles?" Justi demanded. Mahri was sinking back into the mouth of the alley, back into darkness. "Wait." He took a step toward the beggar, but faint candlelight glinted on something arcing toward him, and Justi stepped back, ducking reflexively. He felt something strike his chest, then fall to the cobbled street with a faint clink. He glanced down. The d'folia he'd given Mahri lay there, his own face in profile on the coin. "Mahri!"

Mahri's voice called back to him, already distant. "The Concénzia believe that everything was put into the world for Cénzi's purpose, A'Kralj. Discovering what that purpose might be is the real task of life. If you abandon the path your eyes show you, you'll never know truth."

"Mahri!" Justi called again.

No answer came from the night. The man was gone. Justi glanced down at the coin.

"A problem, Vajiki? Is there something I can do for you?" Sudden light made the bronze d'folia shimmer on the paving stones. Justi jerked his head back up. Where the street intersected another lane, a man in the brocaded uniform of an utilino stood holding up a spell-lit lamp with the reflector aimed toward Justi, who shielded his face from the glare. The utilino were e-téni placed in service of the Garde Kralji: their job was to patrol the streets and put down any trouble they might find, or aid any citizen who needed their help. The utilino's nightstaff was still looped to his belt, but the man placed his lamp on the cobbles and held his copper whistle close to his lips. Justi thought he saw the man's free hand already moving in the shape of a spell.

"No," Justi answered. He cleared his throat, tried to bring his voice down. "No problem at all, Utilino. I've just dropped something while on my way. I've found it now."

The man nodded. He let the whistle drop on its chain to his chest and picked up his lamp again. "Very good." The reflector clicked and the light focused on Justi went soft and diffuse, but the utilino paused there, still watching. Justi wondered whether the téni had recognized him. He shrugged his cloak around his shoulders and pulled the cowl up so that his face was in shadow to the utilino. He stepped on the d'folia as he walked past the man, feeling the utilino's appraising stare on his back.

Justi hurried now, turning left, then right, then left again, moving past the knots of people outside tavern doors or walking down the street, keeping the cowl close to his face as he passed the glowing lantern of another utilino on her rounds, then striding quickly down a deserted lane where the houses seemed to lean toward each other from either side of the street as if weary. He went to a door painted a light blue that seemed pale gray in the night. He pushed it open; inside, a young woman turned from stirring the fire in a shabby but clean room. "Ah, Vajiki," the woman said, though Justi knew that she knew well who he was and his true title. "We wondered . . . My lady's upstairs, waiting for you . . ."

She took the cloak he handed her silently and placed it on a hook next to another. He went up the stairs and knocked on the door at the landing before pushing the door open. Candles glowed about the room, touching with gold the tapestries on the wall. Naked nymphs and rampant satyrs cavorted there in woven fields, entwined in dozens of inventive embraces. The only furniture in the room was a canopied bed with two nightstands.

A room such as one of the *grandes horizontales* he'd known kept—blatantly sexual, blatantly inviting. The similarity secretly amused him. Francesca would be appalled if he mentioned the comparison to her.

The draperies of the bed were moved aside by a delicate hand as Justi entered. He could glimpse the woman lying there, her hair unbound and spread over the pillow. "I'm sorry to be late, Francesca. I . . ." The memory of Mahri's strange admonitions made him shiver. "I had an encounter on the way here."

She frowned, her face at once concerned. She tossed aside the blankets; through the gauze of her gown he saw the hint of darkness at the joining of her legs and the shadows of her breasts. "Dearest, you look as if you just walked through a ghost." Her eyes were large with pupils the color of newly-turned, rich soil.

Justi forced himself to smile. "It's nothing," he told her. "Nothing. Not when I'm here with you again."

He closed the door as she came to him in a miasma of perfume. He embraced her, she pulled his head down to her, pressing soft and gentle lips to his, and he would forget everything else for a few hours. . . .

~

Ana cu'Seranta

THE SUN WAS DANCING on her eyelids.
Ana blinked and raised her hand to shade herself from the glare. She glimpsed lacy cuffs and felt the warmth of a thick blanket over her. She raised her head: she was in a room she'd never seen before, large and richly decorated with a single door. On the wall opposite the foot of her bed was an ornate fireplace within whose hearth Ana could have easily stood upright, and to her left white curtains billowed inward with a breeze from a balcony. The night robe she wore was not one of hers. The door opened and a head peered in: a young woman, the white, loose cap of a house servant futilely attempting to contain her red curls. "Oh," she said. "You're awake, O'Téni."

The door closed, only to open again before Ana could move from the bed. Two more servants entered: a middle-aged, stout woman and a younger woman who from their shared features must have been the older woman's daughter. The daughter bore a tray with a silver teapot and plates of fruit and bread; the matarh hurried over to the bed. "Stay there, O'Téni. Here, let me put this tray up over you. Now, a few pillows behind your head . . ." A moment later, the tray was placed before Ana as she sat up against the headboard. A sumptuous breakfast steamed in front of her, fragrant, and she realized that she was famished.

"Where am I?" Ana asked, and the servants chuckled in unison. They had the same laugh, also.

"The Archigos said you'd probably be confused when

you woke," the older woman said. "You're in your own apartments, across the plaza from the temple." The daughter went to a chest across the room and pulled underclothing and a green robe from the drawers, placing them gently over the foot of the bed. The older woman fluffed the pillows around her, then went to the balcony doors, pulling back the curtains. Ana could glimpse the domes of the Archigos' Temple behind her. "Are you feeling better, O'Téni? Go on, eat the toast before it gets cold, and here, let me pour you some of this wonderful tea; it comes all the way from Quibela in the province of Namarro. The Archigos, he said that Cénzi touched you after your appointment and that's why you were so exhausted, and we were to let him know when you woke. I've already sent Beida to tell him."

Ana half-listened to the woman's prattling as she sipped the tea (which was indeed wonderful, flavored with spices that flirted coyly with her tongue) and ate the bread and fruit before her. She learned that the woman was Sunna and the other one, who was indeed her daughter, was Watha, and that Watha was betrothed to a minor sergeant of the Garde Kralji, "but he's on the Commandant ca'Rudka's staff, and very visible to the commandant"; that they came from Sesemora and their family name was Hathiga, currently without any prefix of rank though the Archigos had promised them that they would become ce'Hathiga in the Rolls next year; that they'd been in the Archigos' employ for the last six years and were now attached to Ana's apartments.

By the time she'd learned all this, she'd eaten her breakfast, performed her morning ablutions, and allowed the servants to help her dress. Beida knocked on the door as she finished. "The Archigos is in the reception room, O'Téni," she said with a quick pressing of hands to forehead. "He said to come in as soon as you're ready."

The reception room was, like the bedroom, lavish and large, with its own balcony and fireplace, set with a desk, leather sofa, and plush matching chairs. The Archigos was standing out on the balcony, so small that for a moment Ana thought he might be a child. Then he turned and she saw the ancient face, the stunted arms, the bowed legs and bent spine. "Good morning to you, O'Teni Ana," he said. "Please, come out here. . . ."

She came to stand alongside him. The morning was cool, a breeze ruffling the folds of the soft, grass-colored robes she wore and bringing them the scent of wood fire from the breakfast hearths of the city. She was looking down to the courtyard of the temple from four stories up—the top floor. Directly across, seemingly nearly at eye level, the golden domes of the temple itself reflected sunlight back to the sky. As she looked, watching the people below scurrying about their business, the wind-horns sounded First Call. Automatically, Ana went to a knee and bowed her head; she felt the Archigos do the same alongside her. She silently mouthed the morning prayers: as the wind-horns continued to call, the strident sound carrying the burden of the city's prayers skyward to Cénzi and the other gods. As the last notes died, Ana rose again. The Archigos held out his small hand toward her. "If you would . . ." She helped him rise, the dwarf groaning as his knee cracked once in protest. "Old joints," he said. "I wonder if you could cure them."

With the words, the events of the evening before came back to Ana: *Matarh, the spell of healing, the darkness closing around her . . .* "My matarh . . ."

He smiled up at her, his lips caught in folds. "She is doing quite well, from what I understand. I sent Kenne to your family's house this morning to inquire after her, knowing you'd ask. He was told that she slept easily last night, that her cough had vanished, and she is conversing with your vatarh and the house servants as if nothing had ever happened. It would appear that a minor miracle has occurred, eh?" One eyebrow raised as he glanced at Ana. "She also doesn't remember what happened in the temple last night—which is just as well. I would suggest that you don't remember it, either."

"Archigos, what I did . . ." She wasn't certain what she wanted to say.

"Is something that will remain between the two of us, because it must," he answered for her. "Let's go inside; the air is holding a bit of the old winter this morning."

He held aside the balcony's sheer curtains for her. Inside the apartment, Watha had started a small fire in the hearth. She smiled at them, then left the room, closing the doors behind her. "Your servants are all three excellent people," the Archigos said. "Discrcet. Prudent. Closemouthed about what they see and hear. They will do whatever you ask of them." His mouth twisted and his gaze wandered to the flames in the hearth. "As long as what you ask doesn't conflict with *my* instructions to them, of course," he added. She could sense the layers of meaning underneath his words. She felt her stomach twist.

"Archigos, what happened to me last night?"

His gaze returned to her and he smiled again. He took a seat on one of the sofas and motioned to her to sit across from him. "What happened was what I expected to happen. You can't touch Cénzi that closely and not have consequences. You know that."

"I've felt weariness before; all of us did while U'Téni cu'Dosteau was teaching us the chants. But not like that. Never anything so . . . exhausting."

"You'd never gone that deep before," the Archigos answered. " 'The greater the Gift, the greater the cost.' I've already said that once to you. It's an old cliché, but there is often truth buried in platitudes. The war-téni know that weariness; their spells have that same kind of power. You could easily be a war-téni, if that's what you wanted."

"My spell . . ." She bit her lip for a moment, wondering what to say. "My spell was wrong. It violated the Divolonté. I thwarted Cénzi's Will."

"Did you? Do you believe Cénzi is so weak that you could bend His will to your whim? Do you think He couldn't stop you if He wished? There's nothing wrong with what you did. You have a rare skill; it would be thwarting Cénzi's will for you *not* to use it."

Ana's eyes widened: what the Archigos said was heretical; it went against all the railing of the téni in their Admonitions. "Archigos, the precepts of the Toustour and the Divolonté teach us that the Gift is never to be used that way." It was what U'Téni cu'Dosteau had taught her, it was what she had always been told.

"Sometimes what the Faith teaches is wrong."

The statement snapped Ana's mouth shut. The Archigos smiled, as if the expression he saw on her face amused him. "Oh, I'd deny it if you ever said that I spoke those words, Ana," he told her. "And I'd never say them in public. Not even the Archigos can spout heresy without consequences; some of the a'téni are waiting for just that opportunity. A'Téni ca'Cellibrecca especially would love an excuse to wrest the title away from me. Nor can you perform such feats without consequences; that's why you must be very careful henceforth with what you do."

The smile vanished, and there was something in his face that made Ana sit back hard against the seat of her chair. "After all," he continued, "if I told ca'Cellibrecca what you did last night, why, he'd have no choice but to send you to the Bastida. An acolyte made an o'téni by the Archigos ... why, they'd wonder if you hadn't used your skills to place a charm on me, and if you hadn't arranged the attempted assassination for your own purposes. And believe me, in the Bastida you *would* tell them whatever they wanted to hear." The smile returned then, but utterly failed to comfort her. "You see, O'Téni Ana, we must trust each other not to reveal the secrets we know."

The Archigos pushed himself forward on the sofa, then let his short legs slip to the ground and stood. He walked over to Ana and put his hand on her knee as she sat, stunned. She could feel the heat of his skin through the cloth of her robe.

It felt the way her vatarh's hand felt. She shuddered. She clasped her legs tightly together under her robes.

"We are coming on dangerous times," he said. "The general populace, they don't realize it yet. The people only see the prosperity and the celebrations for the Kraljica's fiftieth. They fail to notice the storm clouds gathering on the horizon or hear the grumbling underneath the cheers. Dangerous times. *I* didn't realize, until almost too late."

The Archigos' hand lifted from her knee. She pulled back quickly; she saw the Archigos' lips tighten as his hand dropped back to his side. His ancient lips parted softly and he sighed.

"Ah. So that's the way it was. I wondered, when I saw how your vatarh was with you. I'm sorry."

Ana felt the heat of embarrassment on her face. "Archigos . . ."

He shook his head. "No. Say nothing. We all have demons in the night that we must struggle with. I have mine, too. I didn't intend to make you think that I . . ." His hand brushed hers, but he shook his head and brought his hand back. He took a breath and stepped away from her. "You'll have to trust me, Ana, because in the days to come you'll have to choose sides," he said. His voice was carefully neutral. "In the trials that I suspect are on us, those with strength and influence must take their stand. I hope you can choose wisely." Then the smile came again, and all the reserve was gone from his voice. "As I chose you. Ana, I have been asleep. Since . . . I don't know when, but for years now. While I've been sleeping, those who don't think of Concénzia as I do have risen, slow step by slow step, until I find they are all around me. A'Téni ca'Cellibrecca, yes, but he has several allies among the a'téni. A few months ago, I think I awoke again. . . ."

He took a breath. Ana remained silent, sitting motionless, not knowing what to say or how to react. She felt lost, as if she'd wandered away from everything familiar to her in the world. The Archigos went to the hearth and held his hands out, warming them. Without a word, Beida came in with an overcloak and helped the Archigos put it on; Ana realized she must have been watching and listening the whole time. Shrugging the cloak around his shoulders, the Archigos turned and smiled back at Ana. "You should rest and finish recovering, O'Téni," he said. "I'll send someone to fetch you just before Second Call; you'll walk in the procession today with the rest of my staff. After the blessing at Old Temple, you and I will go to see the Kraljica. She sent word that she would like to meet you. Beida, if you'll be so kind as to show me out . . ."

With that, he left. As the door closed behind him, Ana touched the hand the Archigos had touched. Her own fingers felt cold on her skin.

∽

Karl ci'Vliomani

THE LAST NOTES of First Call drifted away. Karl watched ca'Rudka lift his head and rise from his bended knee, his clasped hands dropping from his forehead. "No prayer at all, Envoy ci'Vliomani?" ca'Rudka asked. Karl thought the man's smile seemed more a mocking leer, and the gleaming metallic nose was impossible to ignore. "I thought the Numetodo were still believers in *something,* even if they've abandoned the Concénzia Faith."

"We do believe, Commandant," Karl answered. "We believe in logic, in proofs that we can see and touch and feel. We believe that if the gods do exist, then the way to understand them is through the abilities they've given us: reason and logic. What better way to worship them than to use all the qualities we have?"

" '... *if* the gods do exist.' " Ca'Rudka inclined his head, looking upward as if tasting the words on his tongue. "I have no doubt as to Cénzi's existence, Envoy ci'Vliomani, nor do I need anything but my faith to *understand* Him." The commandant smiled at Karl. "But we're not here to discuss theology, are we?"

The response to Karl's request to meet with the Kraljica had come not long after the Lighting of the Avi: not from the Kraljica herself, but from her aide Renard cu'Bellona. The Kraljica would regrettably be unable to meet with Envoy ci'Vliomani, but Commandant ca'Rudka would be available to address his concerns. It was, honestly, more than Karl had expected. He'd arrived at the Grande Palais before First Call, as the note had requested, and been ushered into one of the lower reception rooms in the East Wing, where tea and breakfast had been laid out on a small table with two servants standing patiently behind it, and where Commandant ca'Rudka entered a few marks of the glass later, just as the wind-horns announced First Call.

Ca'Rudka went to the table. One of the several attendants hovering around the edges of the room poured the commandant's tea, stirring a bit of honey into the fragrant brew. He took one of the pastries and bit into it, seeming to savor the taste with closed eyes before taking a sip of the tea. "Something for you, Envoy? The pastry chef the Kraljica retains is truly excellent. You really must have one of the tarts. Here ..." He pointed to the tarts, and another attendant quickly placed one on a plate.

Ca'Rudka passed Karl the small plate with the inlaid Kraljica's crest obscured by the pastry. "We'll eat on the patio," ca'Rudka told the servants. "Bring the envoy his tea, give us an assortment of the pastries, and leave us."

As the servants scurried about the table, ca'Rudka escorted Karl from the room out to a raised stone patio that emptied into the palace's formal gardens. Several workers moved through the grounds, trimming the bushes and pruning the flowers. "Take a seat, please, Envoy," ca'Rudka said, gesturing to two chairs facing the garden with a small, cloisonné-topped table placed between them. Karl sat; the commandant took the other chair; the servants came in with tea and pastries and vanished again. "I enjoy watching the gardens this time of day," ca'Rudka said.

"They're quite beautiful, I would agree, Commandant."

"Indeed. But what I enjoy seeing are the gardeners at their work. You see, Envoy, all the order and loveliness you see there in front of you has a cost. Did you know that the Kraljica employs over a hundred workers for the palais grounds alone, just here on the Isle? If you take into account all the rest of the property she owns, her chateaux and houses throughout the Holdings, then there are a thousand and more. They maintain the beauty you and I see, and to do that, they must ruthlessly rid the garden of anything that is rotting or diseased, or that threatens the setting."

Karl allowed himself a small smile, glancing at the commandant, who was looking not at the garden but at Karl. The commandant's eyes flicked over the stone-shell necklace around his neck, then back up to his face. "So you see yourself as a simple grounds worker, Commandant?" Karl asked him. "And we Numetodo are weeds threatening the flower of Nessantico? I suppose you believe that A'Téni ca'Cellibrecca is but the Gardener of Brezno."

Ca'Rudka chuckled; Karl found the sound to be sinister. "I knew my crude analogy wouldn't escape you, Envoy. Yes, in fact, I do sometimes think of myself as in charge of the garden that is this city, as the Kraljica is in charge of the much greater garden that is the Holdings, as the a'téni and the Archigos are responsible for the flowering of the faithful. As to the Numetodo . . ." Ca'Rudka set his tea down on the stand; the cup chattered on the plate. "You're the Envoy. You're the one sent here to speak to the Kraljica on their behalf."

"Commandant, the attack on the Archigos yesterday was not part of some Numetodo plot. It was the act of a single madman, who unfortunately does seem to have had Numetodo connections but whom I've never personally met. My credentials from the government of the Isle of Paeti . . ."

Ca'Rudka waved him silent. "Your credentials are in order. I know; I checked them myself, months ago. If they weren't, we wouldn't be talking; well, at least not in this manner." He rose from his chair and Karl stood with him. "Come, Envoy, let's walk while we discuss this."

He led Karl from the patio into the gardens. As they strolled the graveled walkways, the commandant pointed out some of the blooms and arrangements. The commandant seemed to have a wide knowledge of horticulture, certainly more than Karl, who could name only the most common of the flowers here in Nessantico. The conversation, to Karl's frustration, never seemed to come back to the Numetodo and the attempted assassination of the Archigos, but he forced himself to patience. Ca'Rudka, Karl had learned in his few months here, was—like the Kraljica herself—a person who did things in his own time. Like a handsome but dangerous beast of prey, he had to be watched carefully. They'd been walking for some time when ca'Rudka stopped. He crouched down near the path's manicured edge. He pointed to a small plant there, its saw-toothed and purplish leaves just overhanging the edge of the walkway. "Weed or flower?" he asked Karl.

"I don't know, Commandant."

"It's difficult to tell, isn't it? Right now there's no sign of a bloom, yet it could burst into triumphant color a week from now, or spread out to infest the entire area." The commandant plunged his fingers into the soft earth around the plant, pulling it out of the ground with its roots intact. "You, my man!" he called to the nearest of the garden workers, who came running over at the summons. "Take this and put it in a small pot for me." The man took the plant in cupped hands and hurried off.

"Dhaspi ce'Coeni has been executed," ca'Rudka said without preamble as he wiped dirt from his hands. His dark eyes seemed to probe Karl's face.

He forced himself to show nothing. "That's as I expected, Commandant. Nessantico is well known throughout the Holdings for its . . ." He allowed himself the slightest of hesitations. ". . . quick justice," he finished.

Muscles pulled at the corners of ca'Rudka's mouth. "It *was* justice, Envoy," he answered. "And more. For attacking the Archigos, ce'Coeni's life was forfeit, even if he'd tried to use a sword or arrow. But worse, his weapon was the Ilmodo, which is Cénzi's Gift alone and which is forbidden by both Holdings law and the Concénzia Divolonté to anyone but the téni."

"It wasn't the Ilmodo, Commandant," Karl said. "It was what we call the *Scáth Cumhacht*."

"Call it whatever you like," ca'Rudka answered. "That's only semantics." Ca'Rudka continued to stare, unblinking even in the bright sun. Karl found the man's gaze disconcerting, but he couldn't look away. "I should tell you that ce'Coeni signed a full confession before he died."

"And that was of his own free will, no doubt."

"I understand your skepticism, Envoy, but it happens often enough. Some criminals wish to ease their souls by admitting their guilt before they go to meet Cénzi's soul-weigher. I find it difficult to believe that ce'Coeni was acting entirely alone, Envoy. I suspect there were other Numetodo involved."

"Am I to be arrested, then, Commandant? Did his confession name me as an accomplice? If so, I appreciate that you brought me here before taking me to the Bastida so I could sign my own confession for you."

The gardener approached, and the commandant turned away for a moment to take the small clay pot from him. "Here," ca'Rudka said to Karl, handing him the pot. Karl accepted the plant, and ca'Rudka reached toward him to stroke the leaves with a forefinger. "A garden can accept many plants: if they prove their own beauty, if they provide the right accents for the gardener's taste, and if they can safely coexist with all the other plants. So—weed or flower, Envoy? Which is it, I wonder? Take care of that plant, water it and give it sun, and you'll learn."

"But you already know which it is, do you not, Commandant?"

Ca'Rudka's eyes glittered. He smiled again, with a flash of teeth. "I do indeed, Envoy. But you don't, and that's what you need to decide, isn't it?"

~

Ana cu'Seranta

WHEN THEY WERE USHERED into the Kralji-ca's presence by Renard, the Kraljica was seated on the Sun Throne. There were perhaps three or four dozen other people in the long Hall of the Throne, gathered near the doors: chevarittai, cousins, diplomats, supplicants, courtiers; all waiting for their tightly scheduled moments with the Kraljica, to be seen in her company, to ask for favors or promote their pet causes. Their various conversations —Ana overheard a circle of young women talking about what they would wear to the *Gschnas*, the False World Ball that would take place in the coming week—died momentarily as she followed the Archigos into the hall and they all turned to look. The Kraljica herself was separated from the ca'-and-cu' by several strides, with a painter daubing his brush on a canvas before her, though none of the courtiers were close enough to see the painting well. There was an odd black box on a table next to the painter.

"That will be all for now, Vajiki ci'Recroix," the Kraljica said, her voice sounding sleepy and tired as Renard closed the doors behind Ana and the Archigos. Everyone stared at the newcomers. Ana felt herself being examined, weighed and measured in their gazes. "If you would leave us . . ." the Kraljica said to the room, and the courtiers bowed and murmured and left the room in a fluttering of bright finery. "Archigos Dhosti," they said, nodding politely to the dwarf as they passed. "Good evening, O'Téni. So pleased to meet you, O'Téni," they said to Ana, and they also smiled to her. She could see annoyance behind some of the expressions despite the careful social masks—irritation at the schedule and routine being disrupted, at their own appointments being set back or perhaps lost entirely. But Ana smiled back, as was expected, and her smile meant as much as theirs.

The painter had spread a linen sheet over the canvas so that the work was hidden. Then he, too, turned, and his gaze went to the Archigos and then to Ana. He held Ana too long in his regard for her comfort, as if she were a scene he was considering sketching, before he began bustling about cleaning up his pigments and brushes. As he did so, the Kraljica pushed herself up from the chair and gestured to them as she walked to the balcony of the room. She moved like an ancient, Ana noticed, with her back bowed much like the Archigos'. She took small, careful, shuffling steps.

"You're not feeling well, Kraljica?" the Archigos asked with obvious concern in his voice as they went out into the sunshine. Below them, in the courtyard, the gardens were bright with colors set in orderly squares and rows.

"My joints are all a bother today, Dhosti; I suspect it will be raining tomorrow, the way they're aching. And I've been sitting too long and talking to too many sycophants." She grimaced, taking a cushioned seat on the balcony. Inside, they could hear the painter gathering up his case and leaving, the sound of his boot soles loud on the tile. "Please, Dhosti, I know your aches and pains are easily as bad as mine. Please sit."

She gestured to another chair, and the Archigos sat. The Kraljica made no such offer to Ana. She remained standing, trying to appear composed and calm as the Kraljica gazed openly at her, with lips pressed together into an appraising moue. Ana kept her eyes properly lowered but glanced at the Kraljica's face through her lashes, a face she'd glimpsed only from a great distance on those occasions when the Kraljica appeared in public. She wore a gown of dark blue silk liberally embroidered with pearls, an emerald set at the center of the high bodice; her hands, arthritic in appearance and pale, lay unmoving in her lap. Her throat was covered by lace, but underneath the thin fabric Ana could see loose skin hanging under the chin. Her pure white hair was trapped in a comb inlaid with abalone and more pearls. Her mouth, puckered in reflection, was set in a spiderweb of wrinkles, but the eyes—a thin, watery, and delicate blue—were gentler than Ana had expected, lending mute credence to the Kraljica's popular title as "Généra a'Pace." For the last three decades the delicate fabric of alliances she'd spun had kept the various provinces and factions within the Holdings from erupting into open hostilities. There'd been the inevitable skirmishes and attacks, but open warfare had been avoided. To Ana, the Kraljica seemed impossibly regal, and Ana kept her hands clasped together in front of her to stop their nervous trembling at being in her presence.

"How has your sleep been, Dhosti?"

"As it is always, Kraljica. I'm too often ... *visited* during the night. That hasn't changed. The herbs from the healer you sent me helped for a bit, but lately . . ." He shrugged.

"I'm sorry to hear that." Then the Kraljica's gaze was on Ana again. "She's so *young,* Dhosti."

Ana saw the Archigos shrug in the corner of her vision. "We forget, Kraljica. They all look too young to us now. But when I was her age, I was also already a téni. When you were her age, you took the throne and married. She's adept with Ilmodo, that's what matters. A natural talent, as strong as I was at her age."

"I understand her matarh was . . ." The Kraljica hesitated, and she lifted her chin, still staring at Ana. ". . . blessed by Cénzi when you anointed her."

The Archigos smiled at that. "Your sources are very good, Kraljica."

"They're also concerned."

"I know which of the a'téni to watch, Kraljica."

A nod. "You know, of course, that the Archigos' life was never in real danger, not from that fool Numetodo."

Ana started, realizing belatedly that the Kraljica was addressing her, not the Archigos. She cleared her throat, bringing her hands to her forehead. "I didn't think about it at all, Kraljica," she said. "There wasn't time to think."

"The Archigos has given you a great honor, making you an o'téni. I hope you prove worthy of it."

The Archigos shifted in his seat and Ana glanced quickly over to him. She could still feel the way he'd touched her knee this morning, as if she were a piece of art or a bottle of fine wine he'd purchased—in that sense, it had been different than when her vatarh touched her. The Archigos hadn't touched her since, but the memory clung to her and colored the smile she gave the Kraljica. "I will try, Kraljica. Whatever Cénzi wills, will be." The aphorism from the Toustour was all she could think to say. She felt as if she were drowning here, lost in innuendo and hidden meanings.

"You'll need to do better than rely on clichés," the

Kraljica said sharply, then grimaced. "Forgive me, O'Téni; I forget how new you are to your station, and that you don't realize what is expected of you. When in private, I prefer directness and blunt honesty from my advisers. In private, I expect you to tell me what you truly think and believe. You can save polite evasions for when other ears can hear them."

The criticism reminded her of what U'Téni cu'Dosteau had told her, back when she'd been accepted as an aco-lyte. *"You have no idea what you've put yourself into. If you did, you wouldn't be standing in front of me with that meaningless smile pasted to your lips. I know who you are and what you are, Vajica cu'Seranta. Unless you're more than I believe you to be, you'll be broken and gone in a few months. You'll go sniveling back to your fam-ily...."* But her resolve hadn't broken and she hadn't left; now, years later, she was here.

"You shouldn't apologize, Kraljica," Ana said. "You're right to criticize me. I realize that I know far too little. But I also know that I can learn what I need to under-stand, and I can learn it quickly. This is what I wanted—this is *more* than I'd dared to want—for me and for my family. I intend to do all I must to prove myself worthy of the great honor that's been given me."

The Kraljica gave a quick laugh that ended in a cough. "Nicely said, at least." She patted her mouth with a linen kerchief. "You trust her, Dhosti?" the Kraljica asked the Archigos.

"She knows where her loyalty needs to be," the Arch-igos answered. "Don't you, O'Téni cu'Seranta?"

Ana forced herself to smile. The Kraljica might in-dicate that she wanted directness, but Ana wasn't yet prepared to leave herself that vulnerable. The events of yesterday had swept her up into a whirlwind, and until she found solid ground again, she was going to continue to act as society had always told her she should. She knew from her vatarh, from her matarh, from her great-vatarh and -matarh, from her peers: the cu' lived always

on the precipice of society, looking for a path upward
to the ca' but always aware that it was easier to slide
downward than to climb. She also understood the fist
concealed in the velvet glove of the Archigos' words. "I
do, Archigos," she answered. "I serve Cénzi, and I serve
Nessantico."

That, at least, seemed to mollify the Kraljica. "So what
type of téni are you?" she asked. "Did the Archigos save
you from having to light the Avi a'Parete every night
for the rest of your life, or from stopping the city from
burning down, or from driving one of his carriages, or—
Cénzi forbid—from purifying the sewage or some other
téni task? Are you fire, water, air, earth?"

"She could do any of them," the Archigos said. "She
could easily be a war-téni or more."

The Kraljica sniffed. "Impress me, then," she said. She
waved an indulgent hand toward Ana.

Ana resisted the impulse to scowl angrily at the Archigos for putting her in this position. She thought madly,
trying to decide what to do or what the Kraljica might
consider "impressive." *You'll need to help me, Cénzi...*
She closed her eyes with the prayer, and the words
evoked the Ilmodo. She felt it swirling around her, the
path to the Second World yawning open, snarled energy
caught in strands of violent orange and soothing blues,
waiting for her to shape them, to use them....

She didn't know what birthed the decision. Perhaps
it was the draped canvas she could glimpse through the
balcony doors. There had been other paintings all along
the corridors down which she and the Archigos had just
walked: the Kraljica as a girl, as a young woman, as a
newlywed, as a mother, as a mature woman. Ana had
been most struck by a painting of the Kraljica on her
coronation. The expression on the new Kraljica's face
had struck Ana as perfect: she could see both resolve
and uncertainty fighting there, as Ana imagined she
might have felt herself on being handed such awesome
responsibilities at a young age.

She heard the chant change, felt her hands moving, as if Cénzi Himself had taken them. She sculpted the Ilmodo. . . .

The Kraljica gasped audibly, and Ana opened her eyes.

Standing at the edge of the balcony, leaning against the polished stone railing a few strides from Ana as if she were gazing out into the gardens, was the Kraljica— young, wearing her coronation robes, the signet ring of the Kralji heavy on the index finger of her right hand. She turned to the three of them and smiled. "Fifty years," she said, and it was the Kraljica's voice, soft with youth. "I would never have imagined it." She smiled again . . .

. . . and the strands fell apart in Ana's mind, too difficult to hold in their complexity. The weariness of the Ilmodo came over her then, and she put her hand on the railing to keep her balance.

The Kraljica was still staring at where the image of her earlier self had stood. "I'd forgotten: how I looked, how I sounded . . ." Her voice trembled, then she pressed her lips together momentarily. "I've never seen a téni do this. Dhosti? Could you?"

The Archigos was also staring, but at Ana. She could feel his appraisal. "No," he said. "I couldn't. At least not easily. The girl makes up spells rather than using ones taught to her."

"No wonder A'Téni ca'Cellibrecca is muttering about the Divolonté and the Numetodo with her," the Kraljica said.

Ana shook her head. "It's Cénzi's Gift," she insisted. "It's *not* against what He wants. It can't be."

The Kraljica seemed to chuckle, nearly silently. "What you think might not matter, O'Téni, if ca'Cellibrecca gains any more power in the Concord A'Téni. But it's obvious that you'd be utterly wasted as a light-téni." She exhaled deeply, looking again at the spot where the illusion had stood. "Let's talk," she said, "because I find that I'm growing concerned at what I hear from both outside and inside our borders. . . ."

~

Jan ca'Vörl

JAN GLANCED DOWN the ranks of soldiers as his
carriage passed by, their right hands fisted and raised
in salute, their faces grim and serious. Most of them were
young, but there were grizzled sergeants here and there
whose scarred faces remembered the eastern campaigns
on the plains of Tennshah and the glorious victory at
Lake Cresci, where the Firenzcian army had nearly been
destroyed before turning the tide.

The near-disaster at Lake Cresci had been the fault
of the a'téni of Brezno at the time, who had sent but a
quarter of the war-téni that Hïrzg Karin, Jan's vatarh,
had requested to support the ground troops with their
magic. The campaign had nearly been lost in that final
battle before Jan and the Chevarittai of the Red Lancers had broken through to storm the Escarpment of the
Falls and send the T'Sha's turbaned troops fleeing back
to the Great Eastern River.

Jan had sustained his own first battle wounds there,
protecting the lamented Starkkapitän ca'Gradki of the
Lancers. With that battle, he'd demonstrated to his vatarh the Hïrzg that his second child—the one who was
hardly the favorite, the one that he invariably denigrated
and mocked and derided—was a far braver and more
decisive leader than his first son Ludwig, who the Hïrzg
had named as heir. Jan had taken more territory from
Tennshah than his vatarh could have hoped—before
Kraljica Marguerite insisted that the borders be restored
to what they'd been before the war, and given another
one of her seemingly endless grandnieces to the T'Sha

to seal the vile treaty that wasted what had been gained through the lives of hundreds of Firenzcian troops.

That memory of that treachery galled, still, two full decades later, bringing stinging bile to Jan's throat. The Kraljica had stolen Jan's victory, his victory over both Tennshah and over his brother Ludwig. She had squandered the proof that Jan was more fit to be the next Hïrzg than the simpering, vain fool Vatarh obviously preferred. Had both Ludwig and Hïrzg Karin not succumbed to the Southern Fever within a few months of each other—five years ago now—Jan would never have taken the throne of Brezno.

Yes, the memory still galled. But Jan ignored it and saluted the troops from his seat open to the air, nodding now and then to those with the star of Tennshah pinned to their uniforms.

Several large tents had been set at one end of the field, and the carriage pulled up there. Servants rushed forward: to take the reins of the horses, to open the door of the carriage, to set a stool on the ground, to take his hand as he dismounted, to relieve him of his sword and his military overcoat, to hand him his walking stick, and to offer refreshments and drinks which he waved aside.

Markell, his aide, was there directing the staff. "Your Hïrzgin and daughter are within, my Hïrzg."

Jan followed Markell between the twin rows of bowing servants and court followers and into the welcome shade of the tents. The tents had been arranged so as to mimic the Palais a'Brezno, the "rooms" curtained off, carpets laid over the grass and furniture set along the "walls" as if they had sat there for years. He allowed himself to be escorted down canvas-lined corridors to where another servant held aside a flap painted to resemble a wooden door. Inside the room—a separate tent—he could see his eleven-year-old daughter Allesandra playing with a set of toy soldiers on a table, while the Hïrzgin Greta, grandniece of the Kraljica, rose with her ladies-in-waiting from the circle of seats where they'd been chatting. Greta was heavily pregnant with their third child—Jan had performed his duties as husband every month or so, grudgingly, but Greta had remained stubbornly barren since Allesandra's birth until this unexpected, late pregnancy. Greta was helped to her feet by Mara cu'Paile, one of her attendants; as Jan nodded to their courtesies, he caught Mara's eye and her smile in return.

"Please, sit and take up your conversation, Hïrzgin, Vajica," he said. Greta had lowered her own gaze, as if afraid to look to see where the Hïrzg had put his true attention. The relationship between Vajica cu'Paile and the Hïrzg was something that any close observer of the court could see but that no one—not Greta, not Mara's own husband, nor any of the inner circle of the court— would dare to mention aloud.

But Jan's interest was focused now on the blonde-haired child standing with her maidservant, who had survived the outbreak of Southern Fever that had taken her older brother six months ago. Jan had wept bitterly at Toma's funeral, but if Cénzi must take one of his two children, it was better that it was Toma. He had been too much his matarh's child, or perhaps too much like Jan's brother Ludwig: weak both physically and mentally. His daughter, however, was molded from the true ca'Belgradin line, the line of the Hïrzgs. . . .

It was the second child of the ca'Belgradin line that was always the strongest. His vatarh should have realized that.

"How is my Allesandra today?" Jan asked. He crouched down and opened his arms. Allesandra smiled and rushed toward him to be gathered up, giggling and kissing his stubbled cheeks.

"I received your present, Vatarh," she said.

"And do you like it?"

She nodded solemnly. "I do, very much. Would you like to see?" She took Jan's hand and led him to the table (the maidservant stepping shyly aside), where tiny golden figures of soldiers were arrayed over a varnished field. "Look, Vatarh, I had Meghan tie beetles to the supply wagons to pull them, but they don't do a very good job of going where I want them to go. I have to keep them in place with this." Allesandra plucked a knitting needle from the table and used it to nudge the glossy green carapace of an insect laced by the hindmost legs to its silken traces.

"You've done nicely. I'm certain you'll train your beetles well, and they will bring the supplies safely to your army," Jan told her. He took one of the figures from the table: no larger than the top of his little finger, the figure was delicately carved and cast. "I'll have to send the artisan a small sum in appreciation since you like the soldiers so much, won't I? See, this is one of the Red Lancers—down to the lacing on his boots." He placed the figure down again. "But you should move your archers back behind your war-téni, Allesandra. They're too near the front ranks, where they can be easily overrun by the enemy chevarittai."

Allesandra frowned. "That's what Georgi said, too, the offizier you sent."

"Then he knows what he's doing. Did you like him?"

Allesandra nodded. "He was nice. And very patient."

"I'll tell him you said so, and I'll make sure he gives you more lessons."

"Hïrzg, she is only a child," Greta chided him softly from her chair. Jan looked over; Mara was standing just behind the Hïrzgin, her green eyes on his. "I don't know why you told that o'offizier to teach her battle tactics. She doesn't need to know this."

Jan looked away from Mara to the far-less pleasant face of Greta. "If she is to be Hïrzgin after me, she does," Jan answered firmly. "Firenzcia always needs leaders who can also be starkkapitän at need."

"Firenzcia is part of the Holdings, and the Holdings are at peace," Greta said placidly. "Firenzcia needs a leader, yes, but not another starkkapitän. The threat to

us isn't from soldiers, but from dangerous beliefs that
pull the people away from the correct path Cénzi has
given us." Her hands, folded over the mound of her
stomach, now made the sign of Cénzi on her forehead.
She was plain and unhandsome, her straight hair an
unremarkable brown, her jaw slightly too square and
protruding: that damned family trait. Jan could see that
in another few decades, if she survived her pregnancies,
she would look much like the Kraljica or, worse, like the
A'Kralj. She already, for Jan's taste, sounded too much
like the old hag Marguerite. "We should not be practicing war; we should be preparing for the Kraljica's Jubilee in Nessantico."

"There will be time for that after the maneuvers."

"Yes," Greta said, her voice just shy of mockery. "You
have to play with your own toy soldiers."

"Nessantico is a doddering old woman, just like the
Kraljica, Hïrzgin, and it is only the army of Firenzcia
that keeps her safe," he told Greta. "And only stupid and
useless people think otherwise." The ladies-in-waiting,
all but Mara, sucked in their breath and pretended to be
engaged in their own whispered conversations. Jan gestured toward Allesandra's table. "If Firenzcia weren't
the strong right arm of Nessantico, then Nessantico
would be nothing. Unless you think the effete chevarittai of the Garde Civile can protect you."

"The Kraljica is the Généra a'Pace. She has brought
peace to the Holdings. You talk like a Numetodo railing against Concénzia." The rebuke was gently spoken,
almost an apology, and she brought her hands to her
forehead at the mention of the Faith. But the chiding
tone was still there, and it would be there again, and
again, and again, until the constant touch of it burned
like witchfire. That was her way.

He hated the woman. He hated that his vatarh had
been so cowed as to agree to the Kraljica's "wish" that
the two of them marry.

"The Kraljica has put the Holdings to sleep," Jan retorted, "and I talk like a realist, Hïrzgin. That's all. A good general—a good leader—must make certain his sword is sharp and his skills well-practiced for when the need is there. And it *will* be there. War always comes. Inevitably."

"There is such a thing as Truth, my dear husband, and Truth comes from faith—faith in Concénzia and faith in the Kraljica." Greta shook her head, a disagreement so slight as to be nearly invisible. "Truth does not change. It remains the same. Eternal."

"Much like our argument, dear wife," Jan answered, with no warmth in his voice at all. Greta's hands pressed together hard enough to pull the color from them, and he thought he saw the faintest glimpse of annoyance in her eyes. He smiled, but the smile was for Mara, whose eyes glittered in silent amusement behind Greta.

"Look, Vatarh," Allesandra interrupted before Greta could gather herself for another rejoinder. "See, I moved the archers . . ."

Jan looked down at the table. Allesandra had altered the ranks of soldiers. They were set now as he might have set them himself before a battle. He noticed especially the lancers set to either flank, where they could wait for the right moment to enter the battle, and a vanguard was set well ahead of the main force to draw the enemy's attack and force them to show their hand. He grinned and patted Allesandra's soft curls. "Well done, my dearest one. Perfect. Each piece has its own part to play in the whole. Just remember, a good Hïrzgin would never move without knowing what is set against her. You must know when to bow, and when to take up arms. Knowing which battles you can win and which you cannot is what separates the great leader from a mediocre one."

"Then you must be a great leader, Vatarh," Allesandra answered. He heard Mara's soft, encouraging laughter (but not Greta's) as his daughter spoke, though he kept his attention on his daughter's large, earnest eyes.

"I try, darling one. But history will be the one to judge that, I'm afraid." He patted her head again. "I find that I'm more tired than I expected from my journey," he announced. "I will retire to my own chamber and take supper there shortly."

"I will join you, then," Greta said, but Jan was already shaking his head.

"No, my dear wife. I think tonight I prefer to dine in private." Above and behind Greta, Mara gave him the slightest of nods. "After I've eaten and rested for a time, I will come and see what entertainments you've arranged for the evening. If you'll excuse me . . ."

Greta and her ladies rose once more, and the servants hurried to open the canvas panel that served as a door. Markell was waiting just outside, and Jan clapped his arm around the man's shoulder. Markell had been Jan's companion since childhood, raised with him to become his aide, his bodyguard, and most trusted confidant. "A certain lady will be coming to my apartments in an hour," Jan said quietly. If any of the servants nearby could hear, they knew enough to not indicate it. "See that she's escorted there discreetly."

"Certainly, my Hïrzg." Markell inclined his head. "I'll attend to it personally."

"Good. Tomorrow we will watch the maneuvers and begin our *other* preparations. Make certain that the Hïrzgin understands that Allesandra is also to attend, despite the protests she'll undoubtedly make." As Markell nodded again, Jan stretched. "It feels good to finally be *doing* something," he said. "Our message was sent?"

"It was, Hïrzg, and should have been received by now."

"Excellent." Jan allowed himself a smile. *Then you must be a great leader, Vatarh.* He would know. Soon enough. "Markell, I have the sense that this will be a good year for Firenzcia. A very good year indeed."

~

Orlandi ca'Cellibrecca

" . . . **T**HE FAMILY IS BURDENED with debt. Vajiki cu'Seranta has borrowed heavily, not only from his wife's family, but from his own cu'Barith relatives. The family would almost certainly have been named ci' in the next Roll, except that the giving of a Marque to the daughter saved them. At least that's what my contacts in the Gardes a'Liste tell me. Now, though . . ."

"The Archigos saved them." Orlandi snorted derisively. *The Dwarf Mockery . . . He should never have been Archigos. . . .* "Five thousand solas will keep them safely cu' as well as pay back the family's debts. And I'm certain the new o'téni has quite an adequate salary herself. She will keep the family cu'. She might even make them ca' one day."

Carlo cu'Belli's eyebrows sought to join his receding hairline. "It's true that the Archigos gave them five thousand solas for this new o'téni's Marque?"

"Indeed." Orlandi—A'Teni of the city of Brezno, Téte of the Guardians of the Faith, and nearly elected Archigos himself during the concordance that had instead chosen Dhosti ca'Millac—let the heavy curtain drop, cutting off his view of the village of Ile Verte across the river. He was staying in the Chateau a'Ile Verte, on its island at the confluence of the Rivers Clario and A'Sele, a day's journey upriver from Nessantico. The chateau was owned by the Kraljica herself, but she had given Orlandi use of the estate while he was in Nessantico for the Jubilee celebrations.

He found that arrangement far more satisfactory than taking an apartment within the Old Temple complex; he had his eyes and ears within the Faith's vast bureaucracy in the city, and the air was better here: close enough to reach Nessantico at need, far enough away that he himself could not be easily observed, though he was certain that both the Archigos and the Kraljica had a spy or two on the house staff reporting back to them—in fact, he was certain that was why the Kraljica had offered the chateau to him even when he knew that she was displeased with his purge of the Numetodo in Brezno. Perhaps, when he became Archigos, he would take the Chateau a'Ile Verte as a small part of his spoils; it would make an excellent summer residence to escape the stifling air of the Nessantico summers.

But for the moment, there was only cu'Belli in the room with him: Carlo, who had been for several years now Orlandi's eyes and ears in Nessantico, an importer/exporter with his own network of informers within the business community of Nessantico. Carlo was seated at a table with a platter of venison and potatoes and a flagon of good red Brezno Temple wine, his plate and glass full for the third time now.

"Five thousand solas to the family . . ." cu'Belli repeated, his eyes lifted to the frescoed ceiling as if totting up invisible figures there. He waved a fork whose silver tines held a chunk of dripping meat. If Orlandi knew the man at all, he was trying to figure out how he might acquire some of Vajiki cu'Seranta's newfound wealth. "She must be truly unusual. What did the téni in charge of the acolytes say?" He placed the meat in his mouth and chewed contentedly and loudly.

"Very little of any help," Orlandi answered brusquely. *Especially since U'Téni cu'Dosteau is the Archigos' friend, and hardly sympathetic with our cause. That damned dwarf . . .* Orlandi cleared his throat. One of cu'Belli's faults was his tendency to ask questions as if he and Orlandi were somehow, impossibly, peers. "And this is not what I brought you here to discuss, in any case."

Cu'Belli accepted the rebuke with a shrug, swallowing and taking a sip of the wine. "My apologies, of course, A'Téni. I just wonder if perhaps Vajiki cu'Seranta will be pleased with his payment from the Archigos. The family's debts, from what I understand, are substantial, and there will be far less than five thousand solas remaining after they're paid. Along with that, the family servants who have been dismissed over the last few years tell me that Vajiki cu'Seranta was in his daughter's bedchamber at . . . odd times. We may be able to exploit that and his greed, and make him pliable to our needs."

Orlandi's lips curled into a near-snarl at cu'Belli's use of the plural possessive. "*My* needs," he said, "go well beyond the cu'Seranta family. You're a crude man, Carlo, and you think crudely. You'd use a hammer when a pinprick would do. It may be that I'll look to Vajiki cu'Seranta later, but for now, I'm far more interested in what you have to tell me about your trip to Firenzcia. I expected a packet . . ."

"Ah, that . . ." Cu'Belli put the fork down on the plate with a clatter that made Orlandi's eyes narrow. The man rummaged in a large leather pouch hanging from his chair. "While I was in Brezno arranging for a shipment of snowstout hides—and I must say, A'Teni, that they are beautiful hides and wonderfully soft and thick. Three of them would make a most attractive overcloak for you, and I would of course give you a generous discount—a messenger gave this to me for you." He held up a small bundle wrapped in plain brown paper and tied with twine. "I couldn't help but feel that there was a large seal on the envelope underneath." He favored Orlandi with a conspiratorial smile. "While I was there, I heard that Hïrzg ca'Vörl has been making overtures to the Numetodo provinces against the Hïrzgin's strong advice. It would seem that the Hïrzg has stronger ambitions than simply being related by marriage to the Kraljica. Maybe the Faith has something more substantial to offer him than a few Numetodo gibbeted in Brezno?"

Orlandi snatched the packet from cu'Belli, who snickered. "Have you been sufficiently refreshed, Carlo? If so, then I'll direct my aide to give you payment for three snowstout hides, and to make arrangements for you to broker the sale of this season's Brezno Temple wines."

Cu'Belli took a sip of the wine on the table. "If all the bottles are as excellent as this one, I will secure you the best prices in the Holdings. You anticipate a good harvest?"

"We pray for it," Orlandi answered. "As you should pray for continued good fortune, Vajiki."

"Always, A'Téni. You know that I'm a devout follower of Concénzia." He ostentatiously pressed clasped hands to forehead before pushing his chair back from the table. "A pleasure doing business with you, A'Téni, as always. May Cénzi keep you well, my friend."

Business is indeed all it is. Orlandi smiled at cu'Belli as he left the room, but it was only a practiced and meaningless movement of his lips. *And perhaps it's time I look for a better, more grateful, and less talkative partner.*

As the door closed, Orlandi placed the packet on the table. With the knife cu'Belli had been using to cut the meat, he sliced the twine, then pulled apart the paper wrapper. He had little doubt that cu'Belli had already done the same, but the seal on the thick white envelope below seemed intact, the Hïrzg's monogram—a "V" composed of twin inclined swords wrapped in garlands of ivy—pressed deeply into the red wax. Orlandi doubted that cu'Belli had the courage or the skill to have taken off and reattached the seal, but it hardly mattered. The letter inside the envelope was written in a fair hand, but the words were unintelligible: coded.

Orlandi seated himself at the table, pushing aside cu'Belli's plate and goblet, and spread out the paper. From a drawer under the table, he took a bottle of ink and a stylus; from a pocket in his vestments, he withdrew a disk composed of two dials of thin board, one slightly smaller than the other, both inscribed along their edges with the letters of the alphabet, though the sequence of the inner dial was scrambled. He looked again at the Hïrzg's message—the number of letters in the first word told him how many steps to advance the inner dial, as well as the number to advance it for each succeeding word in the actual message. Hïrzg ca'Vörl had an identical disk.

Laboriously, Orlandi decoded the message, turning the inner dial with each word and writing down the decoded snippets. By the time he finished, he was smiling.

Taking the letter, he rose from the table and went to the fireplace on the far wall, where he fed the missive to the flames one sheet at a time. After the last sheet curled into ash, he returned to the window, gazing out beyond the rooftops of Ile Verte to where—a hundred and more miles beyond—the Hïrzg arrayed his army in Firenzcia.

When I'm the Archigos . . .

The pieces were all in place, and Orlandi was seated on both sides of the board moving them. It didn't matter who won this game: Justi ca'Mazzak might become Kraljiki (and perhaps he would even be Justi ca'Cellibrecca at that point . . .), or perhaps Hïrzg Jan might sit on the Sun Throne on the Isle A'Kralji with the Ring of the Kralji on his finger. Orlandi didn't care—either way, he would depose the dwarf and the Concord A'Téni would name him Archigos even if the dwarf had named a successor. He would have the title that should have been his all along. The dwarf was of weak faith and had far too much sympathy for those whose beliefs differed from the correct interpretation of the Toustour, and for those who would bend the laws of the Divolonté. Orlandi was furious at how ca'Millac could tolerate an "envoy" from the Numetodo in his own city; Orlandi had shown in Brezno what a genuine Archigos' response should have been to those who mocked Cénzi and Concénzia. The Numetodo disgusted him. They believed in no gods. Worse, they believed that they could do what was forbidden in the Divolonté and use the Ilmodo without the Faith, without training from Concénzia, without the blessing of the Archigos. They believed that it was not *faith* that was necessary, but only reason. They were the true enemies. They would destroy Concénzia, and in doing that they would also destroy Nessantico and the Holdings. Their use of the Second World's power mocked Cénzi. Their souls were already doomed; Orlandi would also doom their bodies.

Cénzi was on Orlandi's side. He could feel the strength Cénzi lent him, stronger each day.

He lifted his clasped hands to his forehead. He prayed, and he thought, and he imagined.

When I'm the Archigos. . . .

ENCOUNTERS

Ana cu'Seranta
Karl ci'Vliomani
Dhosti ca'Millac
Ana cu'Seranta
Jan ca'Vörl
Ana cu'Seranta
Karl ci'Vliomani

Ana cu'Seranta

"IT'S SO GOOD to see you, Vaji . . . I mean, O'Téni Ana." Sala blushed, her head down. "After we heard about what you did for the Archigos, and how he rewarded you . . . well, we were so happy for you. You look very good in the green, I must say."

"Thank you, Sala," Ana said. She glanced around the entranceway. The walls of the house had been freshly painted; she could smell the oils. A cabinet of carved wood with blue glass stood in what had been an empty corner, two huge ceramic pots frothed with greenery and flowers on either side of the doors, and she glimpsed a woman she didn't recognize in servant's drab clothing in the kitchen hallway. "How is Matarh? Is she still . . . ?"

"Oh, she's nearly recovered, though still a bit weak. She's in the garden out back. Would you like me to run and fetch her for you?"

"No, I'll go back there myself in a moment. I just wanted to retrieve a few things from my rooms." She took a few more steps into the house. The stairs had been carpeted with a runner that looked Magyarian, with diagonal patterns of orange and green. The air was aromatic with a spicy incense.

"I'll go tell her to expect you, then. Wait until you see the garden. Vajiki cu'Seranta has brought in all sorts of workers in the last several days, though sometimes they seem to be everywhere underfoot. . . ." Sala bowed, and gestured at the stairs. "We have three new servants for the house, including a woman who's taken over the cooking duties from Tari. But your rooms have been left just as they were. I wouldn't let anyone in there. I told them they weren't to be touched until you'd been here."

"Thank you, Sala. I appreciate that."

Again, a shy blush and a duck of the head. "I'll go tell your matarh now." She rushed away. Ana went up the stairs, marveling at the touch of the banisters, which seemed freshly varnished and polished. The house had been so drab and shabby for the last several years, and now . . .

"I thought I heard your voice."

Ana's hand tightened on the railing at the top of the stairs. "Vatarh. I thought you'd be . . . gone at this time of day." She turned. He was standing at the bottom of the flight, a smile on his face: the forced smile he always wore around her. He bounded swiftly up the steps, the smile fixed, the fine bashta he wore flowing around him. Ana found herself backing away, looking from side to side. Everything was different—the hallway that had once been bare was crowded with furniture. Her shin collided with the side of a plush chair. *We all have demons in the night . . ."* She heard the Archigos' voice, and she took in a breath, drawing herself up as her vatarh reached the top of the stairs, his hands extended toward her as if he expected her to come to him.

"I've quit my job, since I expect to be offered a better one by the Kraljica soon," he was saying to her. "You see all I've done here already? For *you,* Ana. So you could be proud of our family again. So you and I—"

"I've been paid for, Vatarh," she said, interrupting him. "You don't own me anymore. I owe you nothing."

"Ana!" He recoiled as if in horror. "You make me sound like a monster. You know how much you mean to me. I . . . I love you, my little bird. You know that. All this . . ." He was walking toward her again, the smile returning tentatively. "They're just *things.* I would rather have you here still with us, Ana. With me."

"I came to get my belongings from my rooms, Vatarh. That's all."

"Then let me help you."

"I don't need your help." She turned away, rushing to her room and closing the door behind her. She stood there, letting her heartbeat slow and her breath sink back into her lungs. Finally, she pushed away from the door, moving from the antechamber into her old bedroom. She went to a chest at the foot of the bed, pulling out a few clothes and a wooden box that held a few mementos.

She heard the click of the outer door. "Sala?" she called out, but she knew who it was, knew from the sound of the breathing and the heaviness of the tread on the carpets. "Get out of here, Vatarh," she told him, rising. He was standing in the door of her bedroom, filling it. His expression was at once sad and eager.

She realized that she'd dropped the clothes and the box and clasped her hands together before her. She'd prayed in this room before, after the other times he'd come to her, masked in night and shielded by a daughter's respect for her vatarh, when he'd held her and told her how frightened he was for Matarh and how much he missed her and how difficult times were for their family, how all they had was each other and how they had to help each other and how she could help him now. And the embraces changed with his breathing, and then, finally one night, when even her tears didn't stop him, his hands slipping under her nightclothes . . .

And afterward, after her vatarh's tears and apologies and explanations, after he'd left her in the darkness, and she'd allowed her own tears to come while she'd prayed. She had prayed as she shaped Cénzi's Gift and used it inside herself even though she knew that to be wrong—if Cénzi desired more punishment for her, then she should have allowed the possible consequences to happen.

But she couldn't, not when she had the power to prevent them.

As she had the power now . . .

She prayed now, chanting the words of Ilmodo-speech, and as she spoke she felt the Second World open with her plea to Cénzi. She stopped the chant long enough to reply. "I gave you Matarh back, Vatarh, and the Archigos has paid you handsomely—far more than any dowry you could have received for me. Stay away from me."

"Ana . . ." He took a step toward her, his lips twitching with a faint smile under his mustache. "You don't understand. What we did, you and I . . . It was your fault as much as mine."

His words sent white-hot fury surging through her. "*My* fault?" she shouted at him. "It wasn't me who came into my room at night. It wasn't me who touched . . ."

Her vatarh's eyes widened at her vehemence. "Ana, listen. I'm sorry. You need to understand—"

She was chanting, not listening to him at all. The Ilmodo opened to her, and she took it. Light shimmered between her clasped hands, so intense that it passed through and illuminated her skin, the shadows of bones dark against orange-red flesh. Knife-edged shadows surged and flowed around the room. She could see him looking at her hands, could see his throat pulse as he did so. Holding the Ilmodo, fully formed, she could speak again. "I do understand, Vatarh. I'm the only one who can. And I'm telling you to stay away. For your own good, stay away from me."

"You're my daughter. You'll always be my daughter," he answered. "What we did . . . I did . . . well, we shouldn't have. I was wrong, terribly wrong, and I've already asked you to forgive me. To forget it." Each sentence was another step. He was close enough that he could touch her now. He was watching her face, only her face. Her prayers were already answered; she held Cénzi's power in her hands and it ached to be released, screaming so loudly in her blood that its pounding rhythm nearly drowned out her vatarh's words. If he touched her, if his hands moved toward her . . .

They did. His fingers stroked her cheek, touched the tears that she hadn't realized were there.

"No," she said, very quietly. "You don't touch me. You don't ever touch me again." She opened her hands.

The concussion hammered at her chest, the roar deafened her, the burst of light sent her vision tumbling away. Faintly, she thought she heard her vatarh scream.

Her head spun and she thought she might lose consciousness. She fought to stand upright, blinking to clear away the blotches of purple afterimages. Her vatarh lay crumpled against the wall near the door, the plaster cracked around him. Ana wondered whether she might have killed him, but his chest rose and his eyes opened even as she looked at him: she'd flung the spell aside at the last moment.

It was her bed, the bed where she'd borne his suffocating weight on top of her, that had taken the direct force of the spell's impact; it lay shattered, black, and nearly unrecognizable, the bedposts splintered. All the furniture in the room was overturned and damaged, the wall where the headboard had rested broken all the way through the mortared stones to reveal the sunlight outside. Shards of mirrored glass glittered in the wreckage near where her dresser had stood; her vatarh's cheek trailed blood where a flying piece had cut him.

Sala came running in, stopping at the doorway to look in horror at the wreckage of the room, at Ana's vatarh slumped dazedly on the floor. "O'Téni Ana . . . what . . . ?" Ana forced herself to stay upright though the edges of her vision were closing in. *Just get to the carriage. That's all you have to do, then you can let go.*

"Tell Matarh I can't stay, Sala," Ana said. "Let her know that I'll send a carriage for her tomorrow after Second Call so we can talk. So I can explain." She looked at her vatarh, his eyelids fluttering as he groaned and stirred. "I won't come back while you're here, Vatarh.

I won't ever see you again willingly. If you ever try, you won't survive the attempt."

Ana reached down to the floor for her clothes and the memento box and picked them up, clutching them to her. Then she walked past the dumbstruck Sala and out of the house. She managed to make it to the carriage waiting outside before the darkness closed around her.

~

Karl ci'Vliomani

THE STENCH MADE Karl's stomach lurch hard enough that he could taste the garlic from the pasta he'd eaten a few turns of the glass ago. Here on the banks of the A'Sele near the Pontica Kralji, the open sewers of Oldtown and—across the river—those of the Isle A'Kralji emptied into the water. Adding to the noxious smells were the slaughterhouses, tanneries, and dyers which clogged the riverbank all the way to the River Market, each of them dumping their own wastes in the water.

The air was foul, and the rocks along the riverbank and the piers of the Pontica Kralji were snagged with wriggling trailers of slime and filth. Karl could see the skeletal, rotting carcass of a pig in the water a few arm's lengths from them, the eyeless and lipless skull leering at him.

"No one drinks from the A'Sele anymore, at least not here in the city, and not anywhere close to Nessantico downriver," Mika said, as if he'd overheard Karl's thoughts. "The old folk will talk about how in their own grandparents' time the A'Sele ran clean and sweet, and you could dip a cup in and quench your thirst, but not anymore. That's why everyone goes to the fountains for their water, or they drink only wine or ale, and they don't eat any fish unless they were caught east of the Fens."

His gaze went up then to the ramparts of the Pontica Kralji, the longest of the bridges over the A'Sele. They'd both seen the small, black iron cage that had been suspended from a post there, and the corpse that was stuffed inside it: Dhaspi ce'Coeni's body. The chain groaned and protested as the cage swung in the breeze. The crows had found the display quickly; there was a crowd of them pecking at Dhaspi's remains through the bars. They could see people passing over the bridge stopping to look at the gibbeted body. Two painted signs had been attached to the cage. *Assassin,* one said. *Numetodo* was written on the other. Ce'Coeni's hands were nailed to that sign, and there was a bare nail above the hands where his tongue had once been—the crows had taken that.

"Poor stupid bastard," Karl muttered.

They both looked away, deliberately. Mika picked up a stone from the mud and tossed it into the river, where it splashed brownly and vanished, then looked at his hand, grimaced, and wiped it on his cloak. Mika was wearing a perfumed cloth over his nose and mouth; Karl wished he'd taken the same precaution. "I doubt the river's been truly clean for centuries, not with Nessantico straddling it forever," Mika said. "I heard that the Kraljica had swans brought in for the Jubilee all the way from Sforzia. She thought they'd look nice swimming around the Isle A'Kralji. They took one look at the A'Sele, sniffed in disgust, and took off for home."

Karl grunted at the image. "I can believe that," he told Mika. "Right now, I'm tempted to do the same."

"I've been here for, oh, almost seven years now, Karl. They can make the city look brilliant and wonderful with their téni-lights, with their dances and their clothes and their great buildings. They can make certain that the Avi a'Parete is swept and clean so the ca'-and-cu' can promenade and be seen; they can build temples and palaces that prick the very clouds with their towers, but they can't hide this. Look over there ..." Mika pointed to the nearest slaughterhouse where Karl glimpsed cloth the color of spring grass through the twilight of an open door. "Do you see the téni? There are dozens and dozens of e'téni assigned—probably as punishment, I'd think—to cleanse the filth from the sewers and the slaughterhouses with their Ilmodo skills, but it's not anywhere near enough. It would take an army of them working all day, every day, to keep up with the garbage this city spews out, and the place grows bigger each year. Cénzi knows what Nessantico would be like without the téni—and each year there are more people for the téni to clean up after. I don't even want to imagine Nessantico a generation forward." Mika lifted his kerchief and spat on the ground. "Even the Kraljica must shit and piss, and it smells no better than mine or yours."

Karl laughed despite the filth, despite the grim reminder on the Pontica above them. "Now there's an image I don't care to retain."

Mika sniffed and pressed his kerchief against his nose. "It's true, still. All those grand ca'-and-cu' sit and look at Oldtown from their lovely houses on the Isle or South Bank and grumble about how disgusting and filthy it is, but they're no different. Even the grandest chateau has its privies."

"If you're going to start spouting clichés, then let's do it where we can drink and eat as well. Where's this Mahri? I thought he asked to meet us?"

"I'm here." With the word, a portion of the stained Pontica seemed to detach itself from an arched support, and Mahri stepped out from the shadows under the bridge, directly under Dhaspi's gibbet. Karl shivered at the sight of the man's ravaged face under the black cowl, hoping that Mahri didn't notice the quick revulsion.

"You live up to your reputation," Karl said.

"And what is that?" The man's voice was as broken

as his face, a hissing and grumbling issuing from a mis-shapen maw. If the expression on his twisted lips was a smile, it couldn't be read; the raw and exposed socket of the missing left eye seemed to glare. The breath from his mouth smelled nearly as bad as the riverbank itself.

"That you're a ghost who appears anywhere there's trouble."

That seemed to amuse Mahri. He turned his head, glancing back and up over his shoulder at the caged body surrounded by crows. Something approaching a cackle emanated from his mouth, and a thick tongue prowled the edges of his few teeth as he looked back to them. "Ah, the Numetodo are indeed trouble, aren't they, Envoy?"

"That's not our intention," Karl said. "Why did you want to meet with me, Mahri? You told Mika it was important." Karl had been reluctant to agree to the rendezvous, but Mika had persisted. *"They may call him Mad Mahri, but I've also heard them say that Mahri knows things that no one else knows, that nothing happens here without his somehow knowing about it first. It may be a waste of time, but . . ."*

Again, the cackle. "Ah, so impatient. That's not a good quality for someone trying to gain the Kraljica's sympathy. Patience is a virtue she possesses in abundance, and one she expects from those who petition her. I would expect that someone trying to negotiate with her must understand that."

Karl pushed down the rising annoyance. He saw Mika glance at him and shrug. "I'll remember that advice," he said. "It's true enough, considering how long I've been here." He waited, his boots squelching noisily in the mud as he shifted his weight. Mahri waited also, until frustration at the man's silence threatened to make Karl snort in derision and stalk away. He was ready to do exactly that when Mahri spoke again.

"I came to offer an alliance."

"An alliance?" Karl couldn't keep the scornful chuckle from his voice. "I'm afraid that I wasn't aware that you represented anyone."

Mahri lifted a single shoulder. "You mean to say that you can't imagine an alliance with a common beggar? I see the Numetodo aren't so much different from the ca'-and-cu', Envoy. I hear the same disdain and scorn in your voice that I hear from those who worship Cénzi."

Karl glanced at Mika, who rolled his eyes. Again, he took a breath and pushed down his irritation. "I'm sorry for that, Mahri. You're right, and I would ask you not to judge all Numetodo by my poor example." He could hear Mika snicker under his breath.

"Ah, now *that* is spoken more like a diplomat, even if you mean nothing of it. Good." The beggar pulled his tattered clothing around himself as if cold; on one hand, Karl glimpsed a thick silver seal ring. The insignia carved in it was unfamiliar, and it was certainly not a ring a beggar would wear. *He stole it or found it. He'll have sold it by evening for a drink.* "Those I represent have some of the same interests as the Numetodo, Vajiki. We, too, see the world changing, and we want to ensure that we have a place in it."

"And who is it that you . . . represent?" Karl couldn't avoid the hesitation, nor the faint smile that accompanied it.

"I'm not prepared to reveal that yet."

"That makes it difficult for me to assess whether this proposed alliance between us would be advantageous."

"I'm prepared to make it worthwhile to you. What I can offer you now is knowledge. Other than the ca'Ludovici line, which of the ca' families is most dangerous to you?"

Karl felt the scowl that tightened the muscles of his face. "That doesn't require any thought at all," Karl answered. "It's the ca'Cellibrecca family, with A'Téni Orlandi ca'Cellibrecca the worst among them. No Numetodo is going to forget what he did in Brezno; the skeletons are still gibbeted on the town walls."

"A'Téni Orlandi's daughter Francesca, here in Nessantico, holds her vatarh's beliefs just as strongly," Mahri said.

"If that's the knowledge you have to offer, then I'm afraid I have to tell you that we're well aware of that. I've met the woman at the court. She's made it quite clear where she stands, as has her husband U'Téni Estraven in his admonitions from the High Lectern. Estraven comes from the ca'Seurfoi family, after all, and his vatarh is Commandant of the Garde Brezno—the blood of the Numetodo killed there are on the commandant's hands as well as those of A'Téni ca'Cellibrecca and Hïrzg Jan."

Mahri was nodding. "Do you *know* this, Envoy? From what I hear, there's no love between Estraven and Francesca. Their relationship is simply what it was intended to be—a political marriage: A'Teni ca'Cellibrecca's reward to his commandant's family for long and loyal service. That's all. But Francesca *is* in love, Envoy. She is the A'Kralj's paramour."

The announcement sent a lightning bolt shock coursing through Karl. If the A'Kralj was indeed making Estraven ca'Cellibrecca a cuckold, and if the A'Kralj shared Francesca's beliefs as well as her bed . . .

Karl shivered. He could imagine a dozen scenarios of what might happen, and none were pleasant. For the Numetodo, they could each make Brezno seem like a summer's dance as soon as Justi took the Sun Throne as Kraljiki.

"Cénzi's balls," Mika cursed softly, and Karl knew his friend's thoughts had traveled along the same lines as his own.

"You can prove this?" Karl asked, though his heart knew that Mahri had spoken the truth. He could feel it in the dread that burned in his stomach. He could hear it in the groan of the gibbet's chains.

"If I do, will I have your ear, Envoy ci'Vliomani? Will you want to talk further with me?"

A glance at Mika. A quick nod. "Yes."

"Good," Mahri answered. His hand came from under his clothing again, this time with a scrap of grimy paper on which Karl could see a scribbled address. "Be here tonight, an hour after Third Call. I'll meet you there. Just you. Alone."

With that, Mahri turned and began walking back toward the Pontica. He stopped halfway and looked back at them. "What you smell here is the true odor of the city," he said. "Without the perfumes and the grand houses, the jewelry and the clothing. This is the city stripped of its pretensions. And we all, eventually, end up like your friend above us." Mahri pointed, and Karl and Mika followed the gesture to the cage holding Dhaspi's body.

When they looked down again, Mahri was gone.

~

Dhosti ca'Millac

CLAWED FEET CLICKED on the tiled floor; a hissing, malevolent breath scented the air with the foul odor of carrion, and the heat from the creature's body made him sweat. Dhosti's eyes opened in the darkness. He could feel the demon creeping closer to him as he lay there, but he couldn't move. The muscles in his body were locked and frozen. Sweat beaded his forehead as he felt the long, taloned hands of the beast clutch at the covers. Then the bed shifted as the thing slowly crawled up the short length of his body. The creature hissed and burbled and chuckled. Dhosti heard and felt it more than he saw it, but there were two flaring red points of light in the room: the beast's eyes. The creature climbed over him until it was sitting perched on his chest, as heavy as a chest of lead ingots and growing heavier, pressing down

*on him until he couldn't breathe, until his rib cage threat-
ened to burst and the bed's frame to collapse under the
demon's massive weight. "Cénzi sent me," the creature
spat as Dhosti struggled to pull air into his lungs. "He
sent me to punish you . . ."*

"Archigos, A'Téni ca'Cellibrecca is in the outer chamber. Archigos?"

Dhosti started and blinked. The pressure on his chest
eased as the memory of the nightmare faded. His stubby
hands were clenched atop the papers on his desk. The
bright colors of his invitation to the Gschnas glittered between his fists. He took a breath and unclenched them;
the joints ached and protested. "Thank you, Kenne.
Give me a few minutes, then send the a'téni in. Oh, and
Kenne . . . wait long enough to annoy the man, would
you?"

Kenne grinned at that. "With much pleasure, Archigos."

As Kenne closed the door, Dhosti groaned as he
stretched and stood up on the stool in front of his chair.
His entire body was sore, and flames seemed to shoot
from his curved upper spine as he tried to straighten. The
effort barely lifted his chin above his chest. "Once, you
could have flung yourself into a double somersault from
the desk and landed on your feet." He shook his head
as the thought stirred memories of his days as a performer: the crowds, the applause, the sheer joyful vigor
of those moments of seeming flight. "And you didn't talk
to yourself then, either. . . ." He stepped carefully down
from the stool, supporting himself with a hand on the
desk, and took his cane in his hand. He hobbled painfully to the ornate throne on a dais at the other end of
the long room. A few hard chairs faced it from the floor.
He glanced up at the fractured globe of Cénzi carved in
the wooden back of the throne, at the varnished, contorted bodies of the Moitidi clustered around the globe.
"Cénzi sent me. He sent me to punish you . . ."

"You didn't have to bother," he told the memory. "I'm

punished enough in this old body. You could at least let me sleep."

Groaning, he pulled himself up onto the dais and then onto the padded seat. Like his desk chair, the back of the throne had been modified by a local carpenter to accommodate his bowed spine; Dhosti sighed as he sat back in its comfortable embrace. The chair itself had served as the throne for every Archigos for three hundred years now, since the time of Archigos Kalima III. Although there was little of Kalima's throne left, pieces of the original wood were always incorporated into the throne as it was refurbished or altered for each new Archigos. He sat on long history. Dhosti found himself nearly dozing again when Kenne's knock finally came at the door and A'Téni ca'Cellibrecca entered in a swirl of green robes trimmed with intricate arabesques of golden thread.

"Orlandi, please come in and sit," he said, waving a stunted arm at the seats in front of the throne. "I trust that Kenne has given you something to drink or eat while you were waiting? Kenne, if you'd see that we're not disturbed . . ."

Ca'Cellibrecca grunted a monosyllabic reply as Kenne nodded and closed the door. He clasped his hands on his staff and raised it to his forehead, but his obeisance wasn't to Dhosti but to the globe of Cénzi above him. "I've heard what your new pet o'téni did this morning," the man said without preamble as he brought his hands down and the door closed. He sat, the joints of the chair groaning under him. Double chins wobbled as he spoke. Where Dhosti seemed to be shrinking into himself as he aged, ca'Cellibrecca was growing larger. Everything about him was ponderous, his stentorian manner of speaking no less than his girth. "Seems she used the Ilmodo to put a rather large hole in the wall of her vatarh's house. Given some of the other rumors I've heard, I wonder if you haven't chosen to give your Marque to someone best suited to be a war-téni. Here in Nessantico, she seems to be a wild sword."

"No one was seriously injured, Orlandi."

"Not this time. But I understand her vatarh was injured, and the neighbors are understandably terrified. What of next time?"

"There will be no next time. It's over."

"Can you guarantee that, Dhosti? Let's talk frankly here, at least. When O'Téni cu'Seranta's matarh suddenly recovers from Southern Fever into full health, I have to wonder whether it was Cénzi's Will or someone who has ignored the Divolonté."

"Are you making an accusation, Orlandi? I was there, after all. Should I call a Council of Examination together so I can give them my witness?"

Ca'Cellibrecca gave the slightest shake of his head; his eyes, already masked under the weight of their eyelids, narrowed to slits. "Not at the moment."

"Then why are you telling me this?"

Dhosti thought he saw the flicker of a smile on ca'Cellibrecca's lips. The man's hands spread wide before coming back to rest in his green-clothed lap. "You know me, Dhosti. I follow the Divolonté. Always. Strictly. I expect those to whom I attend to do the same."

"I know," Dhosti answered quietly. "Your devotion has been quite . . . visible."

Again, the smile came and his eyes widened slightly. "I do what is necessary. The Archigos should as well."

"Then perhaps it's fortunate that the Concord A'Teni named me Archigos and not you."

The smile vanished. The eyes slitted again. In his lap, the a'téni's fingers tightened into his palms. " 'Tell your enemy that he offends you before you strike, for he may not understand what it is he does,' " he quoted.

"I know the quote," Dhosti said, nodding. He pretended nonchalance, but the tea he'd had this morning burned again in his throat. His spine ached even against the padded throne back, but he knew if he moved, he would groan at the pain it would cause, and he didn't want ca'Cellibrecca to hear that. He forced himself to remain still. Dhosti knew that he could not afford to make the mistake of underestimating ca'Cellibrecca's influence among the other a'téni. If the man was going to quote that verse of the Divolonté to him, then Dhosti needed to make certain that he still had the support he believed he had. "Let me finish it for you. '. . . but if he does not change afterward, then make your blow quick and strong, and don't hold back your fury.' It's come to that? Do I offend you so greatly, Orlandi?"

"It's not *me* you offend but the entire Faith, Dhosti. I've made no secret of my feelings on that, and I tell it to your face now. Cénzi blessed you and brought you to your position. I've seen how well you used to craft the Ilmodo and I know that, at least at one time, Cénzi smiled on you. I've even admitted how much I admire your intellect and your skill. But in this time especially, when Concénzia needs to remain with the Toustour and the Divolonté, I see you falling away from those tenets or ignoring them. You've become soft, Dhosti."

"We believe the same things. We simply interpret the Divolonté differently, Orlandi. That's all. The Toustour is the word of Cénzi and we agree on that; the Divolonté, however, is only a set of laws fallible people have created to interpret the path the Toustour shows us."

Ca'Cellibrecca's head was shaking before Dhosti had finished. "No," he answered before Dhosti's voice had even faded. "There are no *interpretations* of the Divolonté any more than there are of the Toustour. There is only the *truth,* right there in the words Cénzi has given us. You convinced the Kraljica that she could coddle the Numetodo and even listen to their entreaties when they, in fact, threaten everything we believe in—that was bad enough. And now you allow this protégée of yours to flaunt the Divolonté as well. I tell you, Archigos, that your arrogance is visible and I'm not the only one who sees it.

While you have been sitting there doing nothing, there are those within Concénzia who are less patient and more faithful, and we have more power than you think."

Dhosti again feigned nonchalance. He suspected it fooled neither of them. "What is it that you want me to do?"

"What you should have done all along. The Kraljica listens to you. Advise her that this tolerance of the Numetodo must stop. Tell her to use the laws that are already in place that she ignores. Stop giving audiences and diplomatic privileges to the delegates the Numetodo sent to Nessantico from Paeti or Graubundi. Send this grotesque 'Envoy' ci'Vliomani away, or better yet, toss him in the Bastida. The Numetodo threaten our society and all that we believe, and their presence will tear the Holdings and the Concénzia Faith apart. The Numetodo are a pestilence. One doesn't rid oneself of a swarm of rats by inviting them into your house. You capture them and you eliminate them."

The man's words sent a shudder through Dhosti's contorted body. "You sound so certain of yourself, Orlandi."

"I am. As you should be. I pray to Cénzi every day for His guidance. And I'm not alone, Archigos. Talk to A'Téni ca'Xana of Malacki, A'Téni ca'Miccord of Kishkoros, A'Téni ca'Seiffel of Karnmor. Do you want me to keep going, Dhosti? You know I can."

This is my fault. Dhosti sighed. *I was sleeping here too long, and I've let this poison fester until it may be too late to stop it. Cénzi, forgive me. I was a poor servant to You.* "Then you must do what you must do, Orlandi. Summon a Council of Examination against me if you can get the votes of enough of the a'téni. That's also in the Divolonté."

Orlandi rose from his chair. Again he clasped hands over his staff and lifted it toward the throne. "I've done what I needed to do, Archigos. I've given you my warning, and I hope you can reflect on it, pray to Cénzi for guidance, and change. I see you leading the Faith to the very precipice, and it's not only my inclination but my solemn duty to do all and everything I can to change that course."

"I consider myself adequately warned, A'Téni."

"Good." Ca'Cellibrecca began to turn to leave, then hesitated. "We've never been friends, Archigos. Neither one of us would pretend that. But I want you to understand that I only want what is best for Concénzia. That's my sole concern."

"As it's mine," Dhosti answered.

A nod. Heavily, ca'Cellibrecca made his way to the door and tapped on it with the head of his staff. Kenne opened the doors, glancing sympathetically toward Dhosti as the a'téni passed him. "Can I get you anything, Archigos?"

Dhosti shook his head and Kenne closed the doors again.

"Cénzi sent me. He sent me to punish you . . ." He could feel the crushing weight of the demon on his chest and he could not take a breath. "I don't care. Take me," he said aloud to Cénzi, to the demon, but the weight was already lifting and he could breathe again.

"Tell me that I'm right," he said to the air. "Is that too much to ask?"

But there was no answer.

~

Ana cu'Seranta

"MATARH! I'm so glad you've come."
Abini—her eyes wide as she looked all around her—entered the reception room of Ana's apartment behind Watha, who nodded to Ana and shut

the door again. Ana took her matarh's hand, led her to the soft brocade of the couch before the fire, and sat beside her. "You're looking so well, the way I remember you. I've missed you so much, Matarh. Do you remember?—while you were sick, I used to come to see you every morning before I had to go to the Old Temple for classes. We prayed together, and I'd talk to you. Do you remember that at all?"

Abini was shaking her head, either in answer to Ana or because of what she saw around her. "Ana, this is all yours . . . ?"

"Yes," Ana told her. "The Archigos gave this apartment to me. And it's yours as well, Matarh, if you ever want to stay here with me."

That brought Abini's gaze back to Ana with a quick, sharp movement of her head. "Why?" she asked. "Why would I want to stay here, Ana? Is that why—" She closed her mouth abruptly.

Ana sighed, taking her matarh's hands again. "What happened yesterday with Vatarh was a mistake, Matarh. I let myself get too angry, and I shouldn't have."

"How could you possibly become so angry with your vatarh that you would use the Ilmodo against him?"

Ana shook her head. She had spent the night restlessly, unable to sleep, wondering what she should say to her matarh. In the end, after much reflection and prayer, she had decided to say nothing. *Perhaps Vatarh will change now that Matarh's well again. Maybe he will be the person I used to love. Perhaps he was right and we should both forget what happened.* The decision still didn't feel right; it left a burning in her stomach, but to confess . . .

Ana took a long breath. "We argued, Matarh. Why doesn't matter. Let's not talk about it. Let's enjoy our time together, now that we can once again." Ana rose quickly from the couch, not wanting her matarh to see what was in her face. "I'll ask Sunna to brew some tea, and she makes wonderful sweet biscuits."

"Not talk about it? You nearly destroyed our—my—house, Ana, and the gossip from the neighbors—" She stopped again, putting her hands to her lips, and Ana sank down beside her again.

"Matarh, you've been sick so long. I was terribly afraid that I was going to lose you." *So much so that I made certain I wouldn't, even against the rules of the Faith.* But that was something she couldn't say, either. "Please. You're better now, and that's what's important. We have so much to talk about. Have you started going out yet? I'm certain that I could get you an invitation to the Gschnas: at the Grande Palais, Matarh. Would you like that? The Gschnas at the Palais itself, instead of some old hall filled with ci' and ce'."

"Why were you arguing with your vatarh?" Abini persisted. "I heard you, all the way in the garden."

"Matarh . . ." *I don't want to say it. I don't know how to even begin.*

"Tell me."

Ana looked at her matarh's face, saw the suspicion in it. She could feel her lower lip trembling, could feel the tears burning in her eyes. Her matarh's features swam before her, and she wiped angrily at the betrayal of her eyes. "Please, Matarh . . ."

"Tell me," she repeated.

And so she did. Slowly. Haltingly. Feeling the shame and the guilt and the pain all over again. Her matarh sat there, listening, her head shaking more with each word until Abini finally spread her hands wide apart angrily and rose from the couch. "No!" her matarh shouted, the word echoing in the room. "You're making this up. You're lying. Your vatarh wouldn't do that, Ana. Not Tomas. I don't believe it and I won't hear it. I won't. It's . . . it's *evil*. Tomas is a good man and he's done all he could to provide for us, even with everything that Cénzi gave us to bear. How can you be so cruel to make those accusations—do you know the sacrifices Tomas made to get you accepted as an acolyte, to pay for all your instruction so you could wear those green robes and live in this luxury? Where is your gratitude, child? Oh, why did Cénzi bring me back to this . . . ?"

She began to sob, uncontrollably, and Ana, crying in sympathy and her own pain, went to her, trying to take her matarh in her arms and accomplish with an embrace what she could not do with words. But Abini recoiled, pushing her away with an inarticulate cry and a wild, angry gaze. She ran from the room as Sunna opened the door. The servant watched Abini rush past her and down the hall toward the outer doors.

"O'Téni?"

Ana forced herself to speak through the tears that choked her throat. "Go with her," she said to Sunna. "Make certain she gets home safely."

~

Jan ca'Vörl

"WILL HE DIE QUICKLY, Vatarh?" Allesandra asked.

"I don't know, Allesandra. Probably."

Alongside Jan, the Hïrzgin stirred. "This is not something our daughter needs to see, my Hïrzg," Greta said. One hand rubbed the swelling arc of her belly. The Hïrzg and Hïrzgin, accompanied by several members of the court, stood on a viewing platform erected just outside the tent-palace. Starkkapitän Ahren Ca'Staunton, commander of the Firenzcian army, and U'Téni Semini cu'Kohnle, head of the war-téni, were at Jan's left hand. Mara stood discreetly to his right on the other side of Greta, just slightly behind the Hïrzgin so that she could make eye contact with Jan without Greta noticing, though Jan was certain that their occasional exchanges of smiles didn't escape the rest of the court.

Below them, in the meadow lined by the army's tent-city, a soldier, stripped to the waist with his back and chest displaying the bloodied stripes of a flogging, was bound with his arms behind him to a large post. A line of six archers had been placed facing him, an o'offizier to their side; the remainder of the troops stood in silent ranks around the meadow. Markell stood near the post, overseeing the proceedings. Allesandra's maidservant Naniaj started forward to take the girl away, but Jan shook his head and raised a finger. The woman stopped in mid-step.

"She's only eleven. She's too young," the Hïrzgin insisted again, making Jan scowl. Everything Greta said made him frown. Just the sound of her thin voice or the sight of her plain, long face with its forward-canted ca'Ludovici jaw or the prominent reminder of her fecundity was enough to make him grind his teeth. She knew her duty as wife, and performed it as if it were exactly that—and no more often than she must. The lack of regular intimacy between them hardly bothered Jan, nor did it prevent him from seeking that intimacy elsewhere, as a few bastard children scattered around Firenzcia testified. Perhaps Mara might end up producing another, if the midwife's potions failed to work. "Please, my Hïrzg, let Naniaj take her inside . . ."

"Vatarh, if I'm to lead the army one day as Hïrzgin, then I need to understand this," Allesandra pleaded. Jan laughed, a roar of delight and amusement that spread out from him to Mara, to the Starkkapitän and U'Téni cu'Kohnle, then to the other courtiers like the ripples from a stone dropped in a pond. He stroked her hair, pressing her to his side possessively. Only the Hïrzgin was frowning. Mara's gaze twinkled at him over Greta's shoulder as the Hïrzgin glared at him.

"You see, wife," he said. "The child knows what she must learn. She stays."

"Hïrzg . . ." Greta began, but Jan glanced at her sharply.

"I said she will stay," he repeated, the words sharp and cutting this time. "If you don't care to witness this yourself in your condition, Hïrzgin, it would frankly please us very much if you removed yourself." Greta's mouth closed at that, her teeth clacking together as she turned away from him and waddled away from the platform. Mara gave the barest of nods to Jan, and then moved to follow the Hïrzgin with the rest of her whispering, reluctant entourage. He heard Allesandra chuckle once, softly.

Below, the man was firmly lashed to the post, and Markell and the o'offizier with him stepped well back. Markell gestured; the archers placed arrows to bowstrings and drew them back with a creaking of leather and wood. The bound man moaned. "What did he do, Vatarh?" Allesandra asked.

"He's a Numetodo," Jan told her. "And he was stupidly vocal about his beliefs. Belief in Cénzi and the rewards that await the brave when they die are what sustains our troops, my darling. Without their faith, they will have no hope, and this fool tried to take that away from them with his words. I want them all to see what happens to those without faith." At Jan's left side, U'Téni cu'Kohnle nodded sternly in agreement with his words.

"Why are there six archers there, Vatarh? Wouldn't just one be able to kill him?"

"All six will let loose their arrows at the starkkapitän's command," Jan told her patiently. "That way, each of the archers can believe that it wasn't their arrow that took the life of a fellow soldier. It helps them—it's difficult for a soldier to kill one of their own, even when that person has betrayed them and his oaths."

Allesandra nodded solemnly at that. "I understand, Vatarh."

"Hïrzg, we're ready," Markell called up to Jan.

"Excellent," Jan said. He stepped forward with

Allesandra. He raised his voice, speaking loudly so that the bound man could hear him. "Would you pray now?" he asked the man, whose head was turned up toward them. His pupils were large, frightened and bloodshot. Blood drooled from his mouth and nostrils. "Would you plead for Cénzi to save you? Would you ask that His hand move through mine?"

The man's thick tongue slid over bruised lips. Sudden hope filled those desperate eyes. "Yes," he managed to say, the voice barely audible. "I do pray, Hïrzg. I'm . . . so sorry. I was wrong . . . I renounce it all . . ."

"What do you think, Allesandra?" Jan asked his daughter, who was pressed to the railing of the platform, standing on tiptoes so that she could look down over the top. She looked up at him.

"I think a person in his position would say whatever they need to say to save themselves, Vatarh," she answered.

Jan laughed again. "Indeed. They most certainly would." He called out to the court, to the soldiers watching. "Did you hear that?" he proclaimed. "Wisdom comes from the young." He waved to the starkkapitän. "You may proceed, Starkkapitän ca'Staunton," he said.

The Numetodo moaned and shrieked. He cursed and thrashed uselessly against the ropes holding him. Starkkapitän ca'Staunton gave the sign of Cénzi to Jan, then to U'Téni cu'Kohnle, and stepped forward. He lifted his arm and the sextet of archers pulled their bows back to full draw, the leather-wrapped wood creaking ominously. His hand dropped as the Numetodo screamed and the bows sang. The Numetodo's scream was cut off abruptly with the solid, dull stutter of arrowheads impacting flesh.

Jan saw Allesandra stare as the man slumped against the post, six arrows piercing his body, blood running down from the new wounds to join that of the crusted old ones from his flogging. She stared at the patterns of the blood, at the rounded ball of the man's head. The man's mouth yawned open.

The offiziers barked orders to the troops and they began to file away. Several men hurried forward to cut the executed man down and take away the body. Markell spoke briefly to the group of archers, clapping each of them on the back.

U'Téni cu'Kohnle nodded silently, as if the death of the Numetodo had particularly pleased him.

"I think, Vatarh," Allesandra said very quietly, as the courtiers chattered excitedly around and behind Jan, "that all the soldiers and the court will remember this very well. I know I will." He looked down at her, and the expression on her face was what he'd hoped to see. There was a pleased contemplation there, her head nodding faintly as if in satisfaction at a well-accomplished task. "I don't think they will listen to the Numetodo anymore, Vatarh. They'll only listen to you . . . and to A'Téni Orlandi, too."

He snorted at that, and U'Téni cu'Kohnle glanced over to them before he went to join Starkkapitän ca'Staunton. Jan had not let his daughter witness A'Téni ca'Cellibrecca's reprisals against the Numetodo in Brezno, but she'd known about them, peppering him and the others with insistent questions. And, like the rest of them, she had seen the bodies gibbeted on the walls afterward; there had been no way to prevent that. "Yes. I think it will have that effect."

"When A'Téni Orlandi is Archigos, will you divorce Matarh?"

"You wouldn't want me to take your matarh away from you, would you?"

Allesandra seemed to ignore the question. Her gaze left him, looking down once again at the soldiers disposing of the mess on the grounds. The courtiers had moved politely away from the conversation, pretending that they weren't trying to listen as they engaged in their own conversations. "I like Mara, Vatarh. She's very nice to me, better than Maṭarh is, but you won't marry her, will you, Vatarh? I think you should marry someone more important, who will help you get what you want."

"And what would you know of Mara?" he asked her.

She gave him a look of exaggerated scorn, her mouth pursed, her head shaking so that the soft curls around her cheeks swayed. "I'm eleven and I'm not *stupid,* Vatarh. And I don't have to pretend I don't see things, like Matarh does."

Jan hugged her to him, and her arms clasped around his waist. He bent down and kissed the top of her head. "I love you, my dear. You'll be a fine Hïrzgin when the time comes."

She turned her face up to smile at him. "I know," she said. "You will teach me, Vatarh, and I'll learn everything from you. You'll see."

He kissed her again.

"I'm looking forward to going to Nessantico for the Kraljica's Jubilee, Vatarh," she said. "I've always wanted to see Nessantico."

Jan smiled at that. "Oh, we'll be going there, Allesandra," he answered. "Soon enough."

~

Ana cu'Seranta

"YOUR PROBLEM, Ana, is that your abilities make you too visible."

"I'm sorry, Archigos."

The dwarf chuckled. "I didn't say that to reprimand you. Simply being with me makes you visible, also, and doing what I ask you to do also makes you visible. Most often, it's not possible for a person to hide their power. You *shouldn't* hide it. I'm telling you this so that you know: those people who are against me or against the Kraljica will perceive you in the same light they cast on me. You need to be aware of that fact, and prepare for it."

"I . . . I think I understand, Archigos."

In truth, she wasn't entirely certain what he was warning her against. They were in a téni-driven closed coach, traveling toward the Pontica a'Brezi Veste and the Grande Palais on the Isle A'Kralji, the coach's springs complaining metallically as they bounced over the cobbles on the bridge's approach. The Archigos sat on velvet cushions across from her; she huddled against the side of the coach. The last few days had not gone well: the incident with her vatarh, then the visit with her matarh, which had left her emotionally drained. Her servants Beida, Sunna, and Watha had all been solicitous and comforting, but she also suspected that everything that was said or done in her apartments was being reported back to the Archigos. As if he'd overheard her thoughts, the Archigos took a long breath through his nose and smiled at her.

"Your matarh . . . She understood what you told her?"

"No," Ana answered. "She doesn't want to believe me."

"Give her time," the Archigos said. "She heard what you said, even if she doesn't want to admit it. She'll be thinking it over and she'll be asking questions of those around her; she may already realize it's true. She'll listen. She'll believe. In time."

The Archigos' figure swam in Ana's suddenly-starting tears, and she turned her head away from him, pretending to look out the window of the carriage. She heard the rustle of cloth, then felt the dwarf's hand touch hers. She drew her hand back with a hiss, and his withdrew. Neither of them said anything else for the duration of the trip.

Renard escorted them to the Kraljica's inner apartments rather than to the Hall of the Sun Throne, passing through the knotted clusters of courtiers and supplicants.

Ana could feel their appraising glances on her even as they bowed and brought clenched hands to their foreheads, but they were quickly past them as Renard conducted them down a long hall to where a duo of servants waited to open the doors for them.

The Kraljica was in the outer chamber, holding up a cloth draped over a canvas set on an easel. She let the cloth drop as they entered and Renard announced them. "How well has ci'Recroix captured you, Kraljica?" the Archigos asked. "May we see?"

"No." The refusal came perhaps too loudly and quickly, and the Kraljica frowned. "I'm sorry, Dhosti. That sounded harsh. It's just that ci'Recroix doesn't want anyone looking at the painting yet. It's not done. But I figure that since it's me he's portraying, I have some privileges."

"Of course you do, Marguerite," the Archigos answered. Ana saw that his glance went to the jars of paints, oils, and pigments on the table near the canvas, the jar of brushes and the smell in the room, and then to a large painting of a peasant family hung over the massive fireplace in the room. Ana found herself startled, looking at the painting: it was as if she were staring through a window into a cottage room. The figures seemed nearly alive, so vivid that she expected them to breathe and talk. "I thought ci'Recroix was painting you in the Hall."

"I haven't been feeling well lately, I'm afraid, and so he's been working in here." The Kraljica walked across the room toward the fire crackling in the hearth, and Ana saw the slow caution in her steps, the way her body stooped visibly, and the heaviness with which she leaned on the filigreed, silver-chased ebony cane she carried— not the way she'd appeared even a few days ago. She had shriveled, she was collapsing in on herself. She coughed, and the cough was full of liquid. Her face was pale, the skin of her arms so translucent that Ana could see the tracery of veins underneath. She seemed to have aged suddenly, the years she had held back so well for so long crashing down on her. Her voice trembled. The Kraljica stared up at the painting over the hearth, standing before the fire as if she were absorbing its heat. "I'll be fine by the Gschnas. You're coming, of course?" she said to the Archigos, turning with evident reluctance away from her examination of the painting. "And you, Ana? Have you been to the Gschnas Ball before?"

"Never to the one here in the palace, Kraljica," Ana told her. "We've always gone to one of the other halls when we've gone at all. Once, though, four years ago, the A'Kralj made an appearance where my family was celebrating. I remember that."

"I should introduce the two of you," the Kraljica said. She cocked her head in Ana's direction. "In fact, I'll make certain of it."

"Don't go making plans for her, Kraljica," the Archigos said. "Ana's still getting used to being one of the téni. I chose her for the Faith and I don't want you planning to steal her from me for your own purposes."

The Kraljica sniffed at that as Ana felt her cheeks redden. "I'll do what's best for the Holdings, no matter what you might say." Again, she glanced at Ana. "Dhosti, let's talk. Ana will wait here; Renard, you'll get her whatever she'd like. This business with Hïrzg ca'Vörl is troubling me. I wish I were more certain of his intentions. . . ."

With a final glance at the painting on the wall, Marguerite shuffled away from the fire toward a set of doors on the far wall. Ana caught a glimpse of another room beyond, with velveted red wallpaper, heavy sconces, and heavier furniture. The Archigos lifted a shoulder to Ana and followed.

"O'Téni?" Ana turned at Renard's voice. He seemed nearly as old as the Kraljica, and the years seemed to have sucked him as dry as a length of smoked meat. He picked up a chair sitting next to the painter's jar-littered desk and placed it between the hearth and the doors through which the Archigos and the Kraljica had vanished. "You'll be most comfortable if you sit exactly there," he said, with an odd emphasis in his voice. The chair he'd taken looked neither particularly comfortable nor well-placed; it certainly was less appealing than the cushioned, padded leather chair set before the fire. "Please sit *here*, O'Téni cu'Seranta," he said again. "I'll bring you tea and something to eat." With that, he gave her the sign of Cénzi accompanied by a slight bow and left the room.

Ana hesitated. She glanced from the painting on the wall, where the family seemed to stare back at her, to the draped canvas. The painting, she knew, must be one of ci'Recroix's, and that made her all the more tempted to lift the cover from the portrait of the Kraljica, to see what was there.

Ana touched the drapery, letting the paint-stained folds move between her fingers, but remembering the Kraljica's admonition, she didn't lift it. Instead, she went to the chair Renard had placed against the wall, and realized immediately why he'd placed it there. Through the wall, she could hear the voices from the room beyond, faint and muffled, but understandable if she remained still and quiet.

"What's all this about ca'Cellibrecca?" the Kraljica was saying. "I expect you to take care of your own house, Dhosti. I've enough trouble with my own concerns with the damned Hïrzg. I don't need to worry about Concénzia as well."

"I think both issues are intertwined," the Archigos answered. "As A'Téni of Brezno, ca'Cellibrecca speaks to Firenzcia, and I know that he has had ongoing communications with the Hïrzg. One of my contacts in ca'Cellibrecca's staff at Ile Verte was able to see one of those communiqués and send a partial copy to me—the letter was in code. I have people working on deciphering it, but the very fact that ca'Cellibrecca would see a necessity for such subterfuge speaks volumes. Marguerite, I believe that A'Téni ca'Cellibrecca and the Hïrzg have already formed an alliance. I know what ca'Cellibrecca wants—what he did in Brezno had the cooperation of the Hïrzg, and he makes no apology for it. As to the Hïrzg and why he would ally with ca'Cellibrecca, well, you know what the Hïrzg might desire."

Ana could almost hear the Kraljica's frown. "I'm afraid you're right, Dhosti. Greta . . . the Hïrzgin . . . tells me that much of Firenzcia's army is 'on maneuvers' south of Brezno near the River Clario, and the Hïrzg has called down most of the divisions that were stationed on the Tennshah border. Still, the maneuvers are scheduled to end in a handful of days—the Hïrzgin assures me that she is confident that despite the Hïrzg's statements, she and Hïrzg Jan will be in Nessantico for the final week of the Jubilee. She says she is insisting on it. That's why the maneuvers were set near the Clario—so they could travel down the river afterward."

"Convenient," the Archigos said. "For river travel, or to send the army into Nessantico."

"You don't really think . . . ?" There was silence for a few moments, then Ana heard the Kraljica's voice again. "Perhaps you're simply too suspicious, Dhosti. The Holdings have always depended on Firenzcia's troops as necessary support for the Garde Civile and the chevarittai, and we expect the Hïrzg to keep them in readiness. And before you start lecturing me again, I know my history. Hïrzg Falwin's Insurrection was long ago, and only the Hïrzg's own personal division took part in that; the bulk of the Firenzcian troops remained loyal to Kraljiki Henri and refused to fight for the Hïrzg. It would be no different now; I don't think the troops would fight against the Garde Civile, nor do I believe that the Hïrzg's war-téni would obey ca'Cellibrecca's orders over yours."

There was a long pause before the Archigos responded. "I hope you're right. Marguerite, I've learned that the same go-between ca'Cellibrecca employed with Hirzg ca'Vörl has also met with your son. And—you've often told me to speak frankly in private with you, and so I hope you forgive me—the A'Kralj has made no secret of his own attitude toward the Numetodo. And he's becoming increasingly impatient to sit on the Sun Throne."

Ana heard the Kraljica's intake of breath, like an angry teakettle, but it was interrupted as Renard knocked on the door of the outer chamber, and he and two servants entered to place tea and and cakes and tarts on the table near the fire. "Your chair is . . . comfortable?" Renard asked Ana, with a faint smile.

"Perfectly," Ana told him. "And well-placed."

"I thought it might be." The man's rheum-glazed eyes flicked over to the draped portrait of the Kraljica as if he were checking to see if the covering had been disturbed. He evidently realized she'd seen his attention. "I worry about the Kraljica," he said. "This painter demands too much of her time, and she's not been well since he started his work. Yet she indulges him . . ." He stopped, brushing imaginary lint from his sleeves. "But that doesn't concern you, and I shouldn't have mentioned it. Have some tea, O'Téni. And the cakes are delicious."

Renard clapped his hands, and the servants finished placing the trays and vanished. Renard gave Ana another bow and followed them. Ana hadn't eaten since before Second Call: her stomach rumbled at the sight of the desserts and the tea smelled delicious, and the draped painting still beckoned to her, but she didn't move, not wanting to miss the conversation in the next room.

". . . you know," the Kraljica was saying. "My son will do as I tell him to do."

"While you're alive, he will." Ana's eyes widened with the Archigos' blunt statement.

"You go too far, Dhosti." Annoyance sharpened the words.

"To the contrary, Marguerite. Look at me. Any day, Cénzi could call me to Him. That's simply reality. Ana— she's the future, as is A'Kralj Justi." Ana sat up in the chair at the mention of her name, pressing her head back against the wall. "You and I . . . We're the present, ready to become the past all too soon. We both have been perhaps too comfortable in our positions for the last many years, and we both have enemies who are willing to rush Cénzi's call."

"Three decades, Dhosti. It's been thirty years and more since the last time the Garde Civile had to fight more than a border skirmish or a minor uprising."

"And that's your legacy as the Généra a'Pace, and the sobriquet is well-deserved. People will call this time the Age of Marguerite, and future generations will always look back on it with longing. But the time is short for your age. Not even you can defy Cénzi and time."

"Justi could continue it." The Archigos said nothing. The silence loomed like a thunderhead. "He can," the Kraljica said at last. "He will."

"I hope so, Kraljica. I sincerely pray that you're right."

"And your new protégée?" the Kraljica said. "At least Justi was brought up to be Kraljiki. He's been groomed for it for decades. That one's just a pup, unproven and inexperienced. And potentially dangerous, from what I hear. You think she can continue *your* legacy, Dhosti?"

"I don't know," Ana heard the Archigos answer. She could feel her stomach burning, and the heat in her face. "I'd hoped that I'd have time to find out for certain."

"She'll break like an untempered sword."

"She might. Or not."

Ana heard footsteps in the room, and she lurched upright guiltily and stood in front of the fireplace as if she'd been there all along studying ci'Recroix's painting. The door remained closed. The rustic mother in the painting above the mantel smiled sadly at her. Ana could see the imperfections in her face, the pockmarks on her cheeks, the lines that besieged the corners of her mouth, the smudge of soot on her forehead. Ana forced herself to look away from the painting. She glanced at the door to the other room, which remained closed. She walked slowly toward the canvas on its easel. Again, she touched the cloth and this time let her fingers close around the folds.

She lifted it.

And nearly dropped it again.

She was staring into the Kraljica's face and the woman was gazing back. The painting was obviously unfinished, but already it was startling. The face, in particular, seemed perfectly three-dimensional and rounded, so realistic in its portrayal that Ana felt herself reaching forward with an index finger to touch the surface of the canvas.

With the touch, she dropped the covering with a gasp.

In the instant her fingertip grazed the canvas, she thought she'd felt warmth like that of a living face, and she would have sworn that she heard a voice, a distant call just on the edge of recognition. But all the sensations were gone as swiftly as they had come. Ana took several steps back from the painting, cradling her hand to her green robes and staring at the telltale hint of pigment on her forefinger.

The door opened, and the Archigos and Kraljica emerged. ". . . understand each other," the Kraljica was saying. *The paint is still drying; that's why it was warm. And I heard the Kraljica's voice as they approached the door* . . . Ana smiled at them: as if she'd been waiting patiently, as if she'd overheard nothing they'd said.

"Renard's brought some refreshments," she said to them. "Would either of you care for tea?"

~

Karl ci'Vliomani

"HSST! Here—quickly!"
         Karl had come to the address on the note
Mahri had given him—a street that was barely more
than an alleyway in the snarled depths of Oldtown.
Only a few people were about, none of them near him.
Mahri's voice came from a shadowed archway. His hand
beckoned from the slit of the door. Karl moved toward
the door, and it opened wide enough to allow him entry
before closing again.

   He could smell the beggar as his eyes struggled to
adjust to the darkness: mildew, soiled clothing, rotting
teeth. Then he heard the click of the door shutting, and
light flooded the room. Mahri spoke a word that Karl
did not understand, and light streamed from Mahri's
hand: in his cupped palm, a glass orb gleamed with light
so bright that Karl shielded his eyes. The light itself was
intense, but it illuminated only a globe around them; the
rest of the room was dark, and the light—impossibly—
cast no shadows. In the harsh, bluish illumination Karl
could see Mahri's face, the torn, ravaged, and scarred
landscape that the cowl usually masked. He took a step
backward, away from Mahri and outside the globe of
light, and night returned, shot through with afterimages of remembered glare. The effect was startling. He
couldn't see Mahri at all, nor the globe of light. They
were . . . gone. He stepped forward again to where
Mahri had been standing . . . and sunlight dawned once
more, caught in Mahri's hand.

   Karl shook his head, stunned. The quickness of the

spell didn't startle him; that was a Numetodo trick, after
all, one that the téni couldn't match with their slow
chants. But the spell itself . . . "That's . . . Well, that's truly
marvelous, Mahri. You're a téni, then, or were once?"

Mahri laughed at that, a dry and strangled chuckling.
"No. Not a téni."

Karl frowned. "A Numetodo? If so, then—"

Mahri interrupted Karl before he could finish the
statement. "Could you do this, Envoy, you or any Numetodo you know?"

"No," Karl admitted. "My own skills are . . . more limited. I've still much to learn before I would claim to have
mastered the Scáth Cumhacht. But I've known a few
who, back in Paeti . . ." He stopped. "No, I don't think
they could have done that, either."

Mahri nodded. "I'm not Numetodo. But let us say that
I have sympathy for your cause. And one doesn't *master*
the Ilmodo or the Scáth Cumhacht or whatever you wish
to call it. It always, in the end, masters you." From outside, there was the sound of carriage wheels and hooves
on cobblestones. Mahri tightened his fingers around the
globe, and the light it cast dimmed appreciably. "Follow
me," Mahri told Karl. "Stay close to me or you'll lose the
light—the stairs are steep and narrow."

Staying close to the man's back, Karl shuffled behind
Mahri to an archway, then along a short corridor. The interior of the building was shabby and rundown, with walls
broken and rat-holed. He heard the slithering of the creatures in the walls as they passed. At the end of the corridor was a staircase, as steep and narrow as Mahri had
advertised; they ascended, then turned into a room directly above the one he'd entered on the ground floor. A
feral cat streaked along the wall and out a window as they
came in. Mahri extinguished the light entirely, thrusting
the globe somewhere in his tattered robes. "Come here,
Envoy," he said.

In the dim light from the quartered moon, Karl could
see Mahri beckoning to him from alongside a window

with the shutters half-open. A chair was set just to one side, where someone could watch the street but not be noticed. Karl went to the window and glanced down. A covered, four-person carriage had stopped on the street below at the house next to theirs. Two lanterns mounted on the sides pooled light on the street. The driver had dismounted from his seat and gone to the carriage doors. "Vajica Francesca ca'Cellibrecca—you would know her face?" Karl nodded. "Then watch. You'll only have a moment."

The driver opened the carriage doors, and Karl leaned forward, squinting into the night. "That's not her," he said as the driver helped down a woman, plainly dressed, and thinner and decidedly shorter than Vajica ca'Cellibrecca, but the woman immediately turned back to the carriage, and he realized she was a servant. Another woman, with an ornate feathered hat and a fur draped around her shoulders, took the driver's hand and descended from the carriage. As she reached the street and the two women began to hurry toward the door of the house next door, she lifted her face up to the buildings and the dim light of the carriage lamps slid over her features.

"Yes. That's the Vajica," Karl said.

"I know," Mahri answered. "Now get comfortable and wait a bit. The A'Kralj will come."

Karl watched the women enter the house as the carriage that had brought them drove off again, then turned back toward the beggar. "How soon . . ." he began, then realized that he was talking to no one. Mahri wasn't in the room.

"Mahri?" There was no answer. Karl sighed, sat in the chair by the window and waited.

There was little to watch. The lane, off the main streets, had little traffic, locals walking from their apartments to unknown destinations or appointments, or returning with a sack of greens or a long loaf of bread. Very occasionally, a hired carriage would pass, but none

stopped. He could smell woodsmoke nearby and heard
the whistle of an utilino shrilling alarm and saw a wan
glow on the bottoms of the clouds from a few blocks
away. He hoped the fire-téni were close by to put out
the blaze—Oldtown feared fire more than anything.
Some time later, the glow subsided; maybe half a turn
of the glass, maybe more: the fire-téni had arrived and
snuffed out the blaze. Karl was nearly ready to give up
his vigil when he saw a man dressed in a dark cloak hurrying down the street. Something about the man's gait
and bearing struck him; when the man stopped across
from the house, he pushed the cowl back from his head.
There was no mistaking the thrusting chin nor the fine
features of his face—Karl had seen them in paintings
and glimpsed them a few times at public ceremonies in
the city: it was the A'Kralj. Karl leaned forward to watch
him go to the door of the house. He didn't knock—the
door opened as he approached and he went in.

"They meet three times a week." Karl jumped at the
sound of Mahri's voice, turning to see the man standing
a bare stride from him. "Always the same days, always
the same time, always for the same length of time. The
A'Kralj has his matarh's habit of punctuality and ritual.
One might suspect that the A'Kralj performs the same
acts in the same way each time as well. Nessantico runs
on routine, after all."

"You might warn a person before you sneak up on
them."

"And spoil the mystery?" Karl thought a grim smile
creased Mahri's scarred, distorted mouth, but it might
have been a trick of the shadows. "If I were you, I'd
be wondering what Nessantico might be like if A'Téni
ca'Cellibrecca became Archigos and the A'Kralj was
suddenly Kraljiki Justi III."

"I don't have to wonder," Karl told him. He rose from
the chair.

"You should. There are worse options."

"Such as?"

"What if it weren't Kraljiki Justi who ruled Nessantico, but someone who had once been Hïrzg? Brezno is ca'Cellibrecca's seat of power, after all."

"Then why would ca'Cellibrecca's daughter be tying herself to the A'Kralj?"

"An intelligent man makes plans for every possible scenario. Whatever you may think of A'Téni ca'Cellibrecca, don't make the mistake of thinking him or Hïrzg Jan stupid."

"And *your* plans, Mahri? What might they be?" Karl glanced out of the window toward the street again, empty now except for an utilino strolling south toward Oldtown Center. "I'll grant that you're more than you seem and I won't make the mistake of mocking you again. But I still don't know what you have to offer me—or what I might offer you. I'm here representing what's at best a loose coalition of minor kinglets whose lands are smaller than some of the Kraljica's personal estates, all huddled just outside the Holding's current borders. I don't control an army; I don't even have much influence on those to whom I report. I'm a minor dignitary who hasn't yet managed to steal even a moment of the Kraljica's time despite persistent efforts and—I must say—some substantial bribes."

"You've neglected to mention that you sit at the top of a network of Numetodo here in the city and throughout the Holdings. You control Mika ce'Gilan, who in turn is part of the top cell here in the city. I've been watching him for some time now. The unfortunate ce'Coeni was just a member of one of the lower cells—the one you know as Boli's cell, wasn't it—though I'm certain that he wasn't acting on your orders."

His training allowed Karl to show nothing to Mahri of what he was thinking. *How does he know all this? I have to tell Mika that we have a bad leak in our organization . . .* "You're constructing a conspiracy by the Numetodo where there's nothing, Mahri," Karl said. "I'm sure Commandant ca'Rudka would be impressed by your analysis, but I'm not. We Numetodo can't even agree on what we believe ourselves, much less cooperate well enough to organize. We have people who still have some lingering belief in Cénzi, however different from the Concénzia; we have those who worship some of the Moitidi in various forms; we have others who believe that there may be no gods at all, that everything in the world can be explained without the need for a god's intervention. We'd like the freedom to search for our own truths without being persecuted by the Concénzia Faith or the Kraljica's minions. We're not a threat to the Holdings or Concénzia as long as they're not a threat to us. Beyond that, I don't care who rules the Holdings. That's all I'm here to ask for, and I'm just what I appear to be. Nothing more."

"So am I," Mahri answered blandly. "As much as you."

Karl decided to ignore that. "If the A'Kralj worries you, then why not kill him? You know where he is and from what I've seen, you'd have no problem getting to him. Get rid of the man."

"Death doesn't kill beliefs," Mahri said. "It only gives those beliefs more strength. A philosophy is not a person—if it's a truly vital way of thinking, the death of its founder only feeds its growth. That's the mistake ca'Cellibrecca and Hïrzg Jan would make. It would be a shame if the Numetodo did the same."

"Then what kills a belief, if not the death of those who believe?"

Mahri didn't answer. Under the shadowed cowl, the man's single eye stared back at Karl. "Ah, that is the question, isn't it?"

GSCHNAS

Ana cu'Seranta
Karl ci'Vliomani
Sergei ca'Rudka
Dhosti ca'Millac
Justi ca'Mazzak
Ana cu'Seranta

Ana cu'Seranta

"**H**AVE YOU A COSTUME yet for the Gschnas, Ana?" Kenne asked.

Ana shrugged. She glanced past Kenne, seated at his paper-strewn desk, to the open door of the Archigos' reception room, where she could see Archigos Dhosti and three of the a'téni: Joca ca'Sevini of Chivasso, Alain ca'Fountaine of Belcanto, and Colin ca'Cille of An Uaimth. Also in the room was a tall and rather handsome man she didn't recognize. All five of them were in the midst of what appeared to be an energetic discussion. "Beida and Watha tell me that they have something put together for me, but they won't show it to me yet. What about you?"

Kenne shook his head. "Not going. The Archigos has me working here tomorrow evening." He tapped the nearest pile of paper. "Going through reports from Firenzcia."

Ana felt a guilty blush creep up her neck from the high collar of her green robes. "I'm sorry," she said. "If I'd known, I'd have told the Archigos to have you accompany him instead of me."

Kenne chuckled at that. "Do you think you're *not* going to be working? Believe me, you will be, and far more visibly than me. No, I'm quite content with my lot, Ana. Besides, you're the new celebrity and he has to show you off."

Her blush heightened and Kenne laughed again. "And before you go apologizing for that, too," he continued, "let me tell you that I'm not even slightly jealous. I'm happy where I am, where I can pass along any difficult problems to the Archigos or the a'téni." He must have noticed her gaze drifting, for he glanced over his own shoulder to the open door. "Envoy Karl ci'Vliomani is with them," he said.

That made Ana's eyebrows rise. "The Numetodo?"

Kenne nodded. "For a heretic, he's on the attractive side, don't you think? He speaks very well also. I've always found the Paeti accent enchanting." Ana's eyebrows lifted even higher on her forehead, and Kenne grinned at her. "I'm just telling you what I'm thinking. I'll wager you'll feel the same way."

Ana decided not to answer, but she continued to stare at the man. "Why is he here?"

"The Archigos asked to see him. I think the Archigos wanted to allay fears that what happened in Brezno would be repeated here. He wanted the envoy to know that not all the a'téni have the same opinion as A'Téni ca'Cellibrecca. Ah, here they come."

The group was moving toward the door. Ana caught a hint of the envoy's speech, colored—as Kenne had intimated—with a strong accent and a pleasing, sonorous baritone. The man had a voice any téni at the High Lectern would envy. ". . . pleased to have been able to speak to you, Archigos, A'Téni. I would appreciate it, too, Archigos, if you could speak to the Kraljica on my behalf. I would be most grateful for the chance to meet with her and directly address any concerns she might have."

"Perhaps after the Jubilee is over, Envoy," the Archigos answered.

The envoy smiled—he had a pleasant smile, one that seemed genuine and guileless. Lines creased around his eyes and the corners of his mouth, well-worn and telling Ana that the expression was one comfortable and familiar for him. She found herself staring at his features, imagining what he might be thinking, trying to visualize him performing the forbidden Numetodo magic or denying the existence of Cénzi. This was the enemy, yet it was far easier to have imagined heretical thoughts being reflected in a twisted, ugly visage, not this. Not this. "Ah, yes," the envoy said, and his green eyes sparkled in the téni-light from Kenne's desk lamp. "The Kraljica should have her much-deserved celebration first. After the Jubilee, then—and I'm in your debt, Archigos. I can see myself out...."

With that, he turned to go. His gaze swept momentarily to Ana with the movement, and he smiled and nodded faintly to her before he began to walk away.

"Ah, Ana," Archigos Dhosti said. "I'm glad you're here. I'd like to introduce you formally to A'Ténis ca'Sevini, ca'Fountaine, and ca'Cille."

Ana tore her gaze from the envoy, walking briskly down the corridor away from Kenne's desk. Kenne was smiling at her; she ignored him. "Certainly, Archigos," she said.

"Look!" Ana pointed and laughed with delight.

Outside the Grande Palais, the shrubbery had been placed upside down, their greenery half-buried in the earth and bare roots curling like gnarled fingers toward the cloudless night sky. Téni-lighted globes were set inside the nest of roots, surrounded by colored glass so that multicolored root-shadows crisscrossed the grounds. The grass had been painted a white that gleamed eerily, as if the moonlight illuminating the city had been poured out on the land, while the fountains set between the wings of the Grande Palais bubbled water that was jet black and opaque. Ornate, brightly-colored birds from the jungles of Namarro and South Hellin, their wings clipped and bound, strutted and preened over the skeletal grass while several well-groomed and jeweled-collared dogs, looking rather startled and uncertain of their fate, were suspended by ebon strings from cables strung between the palace roofs, so it appeared that they were treading air.

It was the festival of Gschnas, when reality was set topsy-turvy and nothing was as it seemed to be.

The Archigos nodded and grinned at Ana's excitement. "This is the Kraljica's favorite celebration," he said. He was seated across from her, but instead of the usual green robes of the téni, he wore the shrouds of a corpse, and his face was hidden behind a porcelain skull mask. The eyes behind the open sockets of the face startled Ana every time she glimpsed them in the dim carriage.

Ana, with the help of Beida and Watha, was dressed as a young male chevaritt, her breasts bound tightly (and rather uncomfortably, she had to admit) under a frilled bashta decorated with medallions, a wooden sword girt to a wide leather belt, and leather boots that reached her knees. Her hair was pulled severely back and braided like one of the Garde Civile, and a floppy cap with a long feather teetered jauntily on her head. *"You look quite the handsome creature," Beida had said, stepping back after they were finished dressing her. "Why, you may have to fend off some of the ca'-and-cu' women who are looking for a husband." She'd giggled at the thought.*

The carriage stopped, and a footman—dressed, Ana recognized with a start, in the very outfit that the A'Kralj Justi had worn for his official portrait, and with a golden crown encircling his head—opened the door for them. Ana peered around at the fantasy landscape, at the dark fountains and bright grass, at the spidery cracks and fissures that had been painted in the walls of the palais, so that it appeared the building had been shaken and broken in an earthquake and the Grande Palais was a ruin in a lost land.

As she stepped from the carriage, Ana heard sudden discordant and strange music, and saw a trio next to the main doors. The dulcimer player was striking her instrument with the hammer held in her bare feet while she reclined on the ground; the tambour player had set his drum on a stand in front of him and was bouncing three metal balls onto the stretched goatskin while juggling them—and keeping surprisingly good time, Ana had to admit. The man with the sacbut seemed to be playing with the mouthpiece of his device lodged in his nether regions; Ana decided she didn't want to know how he was producing a sound. She grimaced at the distressing *blat* of his instrument.

"They're not very good," Ana said to the Archigos. His skull face peered up at her.

"The marvel," he said, "is that they can play at all, isn't it?" She heard muffled laughter behind his mask.

They handed their invitations to the attendant—wearing a goat's head and mittens that looked like a goat's feet—who promptly announced them by reading their names backward—"Callim'ac Itsohd Sogihcra dna Atnares'uc Ana Inét'o"—impressing Ana with his facility. Inside the ballroom, the ca'-and-cu' milled in interweaving knots of conversation. For a moment, Ana was overwhelmed at the sight of the upper society of Nessantico in all their grand finery and elaborate costumes. At the far end of the hall, an orchestra was playing—properly this time, though they were seated high above the crowd in the frame of a gigantic crystalline figure, his massive outstretched hands the seats for the musicians, his flesh a carapace of colored glasses, his bones white stone. A thousand candles blazed everywhere in the statue's frame, and twin fires blazed in the sockets of his skull. Red liquid poured from his open mouth and splashed into a pool in which the giant knelt, as if praying.

Before the strange figure, the crowd swayed and glittered and preened, their intermingled conversations nearly overwhelming the musicians. They danced in pairs and circles and lines; they gathered around the periphery of the dance floor to talk—and many of them were staring at Ana and the Archigos standing by the door. Ana began to feel intimidated and a bit frightened, sweat beading on her forehead under the powder she wore, but the Archigos took her arm. "Remember," he whispered to her, "most of them are just as uncertain as you are, maybe more so. They've just had more practice hiding it. You are O'Téni cu'Seranta, and you arrived with the Archigos. That puts you above nearly everyone you see."

"I'm not used to that." Her voice cracked, barely above a whisper as she leaned toward him, his head only level with her elbows.

"*Get* used to it," he whispered. "And learn to use it to your advantage. Come. Let's go down . . ."

She linked her hand to his arm. They went down the stairs together, into the whispering sea of faces and costumes.

"O'Teni . . ." she heard from a dozen directions as they reached the floor, and she nodded politely to the greetings. A waiter dressed as an ape offered her a glass; she took it and sipped sweetened, chilled wine. She stayed close to the Archigos, following him as he made his way through the crowds, away from the dancers and into the relative quiet of one of the alcoves.

"Archigos," she heard a voice call. "I must say that it takes a certain bravery to wear grave shrouds. I would be too afraid to dress that way, thinking that I was tempting fate."

A trio of shadows detached themselves from near a fireplace along the wall, where cold green flames leaped up from a pool of water set in the hearth—most likely created by another téni-spell. Ana's eyes widened: in the uncertain light of the water-flames, one of them appeared to be a muscular and bare-breasted woman walking on her hands, but as they approached, she realized that what she'd thought was skin was not flesh at all, but cloth bound tightly to a frame and painted to look realistic, that the "woman's" head was bewigged and waxen, and that a man's features peered from just above the frozen skirt, his hands encased in shoes and his feet clad in hosiery that looked like hands. Ana shivered: the sight was not pleasant.

A genuine woman stood next to the man, dressed all in colorful feathers that frothed around her attractive face and accentuated her figure, with equally flamboyant wings sprouting from her back. The third person was an older man, heavier and double-chinned, and wearing a simple peasant's costume, with his face artfully streaked with black paint that must have been intended to represent dirt.

He was smiling at them, and Ana recognized him suddenly: A'Téni Orlandi ca'Cellibrecca. "And my guess is that this must be O'Téni cu'Seranta," ca'Cellibrecca said, and Ana realized it was his voice that had spoken a moment ago.

"A'Téni ca'Cellibrecca," the Archigos said. "I appreciate your concern for me, and I hope that your rags don't presage a loss of your own fortune. Death, at least, is over and done with. Poverty lingers." Ca'Cellibrecca sniffed as the Archigos waved a hand toward Ana. "I suppose I should be giving everyone a formal introduction. A'Téni ca'Cellibrecca, this is indeed O'Téni Ana cu'Seranta."

Ca'Cellibrecca bowed his head and gave the sign of Cénzi; Ana did the same, bending a bit lower with her bow as etiquette demanded. "I was there when you intervened with the assassin, O'Téni," ca'Cellibrecca said. "Very impressive, I must say. You've been well-Gifted by Cénzi, if all the rumors are true." His smile seemed as cold and false as the flames in the fireplace. There was a predatory look in his eyes, as if he were a snake looking at a mouse in front of him. Ana found herself wanting to look away, and forced herself to lift her chin and return his smile.

"Rumors tend to become exaggerated with each telling," she said. "I wouldn't believe them, A'Téni."

"Ah, and modest, too," ca'Cellibrecca said. "I'm

pleased to meet you in person at last; the Archigos has
sadly kept you away from me, though I know he must
have had good reasons to do so. And I forget myself.
O'Téni cu'Seranta, I would like to introduce my daughter, Francesca, and her husband, Estraven, who serves
here in Nessantico as U'Téni of the Old Temple on the
Isle A'Kralji. No doubt you've heard some of his Admonitions, since I know your family occasionally attends
services there." The two bowed and gave the sign—
Estraven doing so awkwardly with his shoe-clad hands;
Ana noticed that Francesca favored her husband with
an odd look of mingled amusement and disgust.

A clot of people entered the alcove and stood near
the fireplace, looking at the watery fire and holding their
hands in the leaping, bright flames. Their laughter took
Ana's eyes toward them; one of them, a slim man dressed
in the robes of a téni and wearing a simple black domino
mask, nodded to her and she looked away again.

"The Kraljica has outdone herself this year,"
ca'Cellibrecca was saying. "This is a very impressive
Gschnas, one we'll no doubt remember. She and the
A'Kralj should be making their entrance soon, and I understand the Kraljica's new portrait is to be unveiled at
midnight. Have you seen it yet?"

"I've not had that pleasure," the Archigos told him.
"The painter ci'Recroix has insisted that it remained
covered until tonight. But I've seen other of his works,
and they are most impressive—the figures look as if they
could walk out of the very canvas."

"Then I will truly be looking forward to seeing what
he has done with our Kraljica. I wonder if she'll dress
again as the Spirit of Nessantico for the ball? That was
an impressive costume she wore last year."

"She has told me that tonight she will be Vucta, the Great
Night Herself," the Archigos answered. "She has had several of our more creative e'téni working with her."

"I'm certain that she will outdo herself once more,"
ca'Cellibrecca responded. He turned back to Ana then,

looking her up and down slowly and obviously, as if appraising her. He spoke to the Archigos as he did so. "Have you given any more thought to our last conversation, Archigos?"

"I have given it all the reflection that it required, A'Téni," the Archigos answered, and that brought ca'Cellibrecca's gaze back to the dwarf.

"Indeed," the man said. "Then I'd love to speak further with you. If you'd excuse us? O'Teni cu'Seranta, Francesca . . ."

The Archigos nodded to Ana as ca'Cellibrecca ushered him away. U'Téni Estraven was obviously fuming at ca'Cellibrecca's disregard of him, his face suffused above the hem of the dress. "Francesca, I really think . . ." he began, and stopped as the woman raised her hand.

"Not here, Estraven. Please." Her tone was imperious and sharp, the u'téni's mouth snapped shut in response. Francesca favored Ana with a smile. "I apologize, O'Téni," she said. "If you'll be so kind as to excuse my husband. So pleased to meet you, and I hope you enjoy the Gschnas tonight. Perhaps we can talk later; I'd love to have a chance to get to know you better. Vatarh has said so much about you."

"Yes," Ana said. "Of course, Vajica, U'Téni. Later."

Francesca smiled, bowed, and gave the sign of Cénzi, her husband doing the same a moment later. Ana returned the gesture. Before the couple had gone four steps, she heard Estraven start in again. "I won't be treated this way, Francesca. Your vatarh . . ."

"They make a pleasant couple, don't you think?"

~

Karl ci'Vliomani

KARL ATTACHED HIMSELF to a group that was moving in the direction of the alcove into which the Archigos had disappeared with his companion. As Karl laughed and joked with them around the water-fire, he watched the Archigos, who was conversing with A'Téni ca'Cellibrecca, his daughter, and her husband. He realized, with a start, that the person with the Archigos was not a young man in a rather too-gaudy outfit, but a somewhat plain-faced woman dressed as a man—and with the realization, he thought he knew who she might be. If she *was* the cu'Seranta woman, she looked oddly familiar to him as well, though he couldn't remember where he might have seen her before. Once, she looked over at him, making eye contact, and he nodded back. She glanced quickly away, as if embarrassed at being caught staring at him.

He began moving closer: as the Archigos and ca'Cellibrecca left the group, as Francesca ca'Cellibrecca and her husband also departed, obviously arguing with each other.

"They make a pleasant couple, don't you think?" he said. "An argument against purely political marriages. And that costume U'Teni ca'Cellibrecca is wearing . . ." He *tsked* loudly, shaking his head.

She turned, startled. He inclined his head to her. He could see puzzlement cross her face at the bow he made, unaccompanied by the customary sign of Cénzi, then her mouth opened in a soft breath and her eyes widened slightly. She took in his costume, her eyes narrowing. "Envoy ci'Vliomani?"

He laughed. "I've been found out," he answered. "I see I have more of a reputation than I might like. And you have the advantage of me."

He thought he saw the ghost of a nod, but she didn't give him her name. She seemed strangely quiet, not like most of the ca'-and'cu' he'd met, most of whom seemed anxious to dominate every conversation. "You've chosen an odd costume, Envoy," she said, with a gentle remonstrance underneath the words.

He brushed a hand over the green cloth of his téni's robes. "I was going for irony. But I suspect I may have succeeded only in achieving poor taste."

He watched her struggle not to smile, then allow herself to show her amusement. He found himself smiling in return. "Oh, you could have made a worse choice, as I think U'Téni Estraven might tell you," she answered. There was bright laughter in her voice, and the comment suggested that her opinion of the ca'Cellibrecca family was no higher than his own. He thought she was going to say nothing more, that she wouldn't ever give her name and confirm his suspicion. Her gaze wandered past him to the other room as the orchestra lurched into a gavotte and dancers filled the floor. She seemed enthralled and terribly uncomfortable all at the same time. He found the combination intriguing.

"I'm O'Téni Ana cu'Seranta," she told him, and her gaze returned to him. She had eyes the color of long-steeped tea. Her head was tilted slightly, as if she were trying to decide how she should feel about him. "Just so we're properly introduced. I saw you the other day, Envoy, when you were at the Archigos' Temple."

He realized then why she had seemed familiar. "Ah, the téni who was outside the room when we left, the one with the Archigos' secretary. So you're the Archigos' new protégée, and not just another handsome vajiki and chevaritt." His smile widened, then he shook his head. Compared to most of the women at the Gschnas, she was unremarkable and ordinary in appearance, yet Karl found a compelling earnestness about her that made him want to linger. *You've been too long away. Now what would Kaitlin think, you thinking about her like that?* "I owe you both an apology and my gratitude, O'Téni."

"Apology? Gratitude? I don't understand, Envoy. We've never really met. How is it that you need to either apologize to or thank me?" Puzzlement crossed her face under the foppish, silly hat.

"It was you who saved the Archigos' life last week. And it was, unfortunately, a Numetodo who was the would-be assassin. I apologize on behalf of all the Numetodo for that action—we're not murderers or insurrectionists, no matter what the popular opinion might be. And I owe you my gratitude for intervening: because had you not, I'm afraid I would be in a cell in the Bastida or worse, and not standing here speaking with you."

Her lips pressed together and her cheeks were touched with a hint of color. "Am I supposed to be flattered by that?"

"Are you?"

"No." Her answer came quickly and without any leavening. *Yes, she's honest to a fault. In that, she's much like Kaitlin.* Her head tilted a bit further; she crossed her arms, her weight on one leg. "I'd also suspect that it's no accident that we're speaking now, and that I really didn't need to introduce myself. Would I be wrong?"

He thought of a pleasant lie, of coming up with one of a dozen plausible excuses to have initiated the conversation with her, but he decided instead to respond to her with the same honesty. "I was watching A'Téni ca'Cellibrecca and the Archigos," he told her. "You can imagine how I might find their conversation interesting, or that I would want to know who A'Téni ca'Cellibrecca is having conversations with, given what happened in Brezno a few months ago. And you might also imagine that I pay attention to what happens within Concénzia—and that I would know of you as a result. As to why I would introduce myself to you . . ."

He rubbed a hand through his hair, his shoulders lifting under the green cloth. "Well, I'm not quite sure that I know the answer to that. It was a whim, truthfully. I saw your face when you were talking to Vajica ca'Cellibrecca, and I thought perhaps . . ."

An eyebrow lifted as he hesitated. "You thought perhaps you might use me as a way to get to the Archigos?"

And she has a bite when she wants to . . . He spread his hands wide. "If I admit that, will you at least admire my honesty and keep talking to me?"

"Talking to a Numetodo, even if he is the Envoy of Paeti?" The response was less harsh than it might have been.

"We're not all monsters who cause milk to sour, eat children, and lace the city wells with poison. Very few of us actually do that."

The barest hint of a smile touched her lips. "And what do the rest of you do?"

This time, it was his turn to tilt his head and regard her. "We search for explanations." She said nothing. She waited, silent, as the gavotte ended and another dance began. He reached into his pocket. "Have you ever been to the hills east of your city?" he asked her. "I'm told that there, embedded high up on the cliffs and days from the sea by even the swiftest boat, you can find seashells made of rock. Here, look . . ." He brought his hand from the pocket. In his palm was a closed clam shell, formed in pale gray stone. "We have these in Paeti, too. I brought a few of them with me when I left to remind me of my home." He pulled out the necklace he wore under the green robes so she could see it. "Our rock-shells have a different shape than those here, but we also find them in the mountains, far from the ocean, and they're different than the shells in our sea. But look at it . . ." He held out the shell to her. "Go on. Take it. Look at it. It's perfectly formed, little different than what might wash up on the shore. Yet there are no seas in the mountains, and rocks don't live and breathe and reproduce, as clams do."

She took the stony shell in her fingers, turning it over in front of her and running her fingertips over the thick ridges of the shell before handing it back to him. "I've seen these before," she said. "The Toustour tells us that the earth is alive and that it pulses with forces. Those forces are the very ones Cénzi used to create the world. In the Final Admonition of the Toustour, it says that the interior of the world is filled with 'lapidifying juices, wet exhalations, and subterranean vapors.' All the shapes in rock that mimic life are formed by those."

"Why?" Karl asked. "Why do these forces make shapes that look natural?"

She blinked at the question, startled. "Why? There's no 'why' necessary, Vajiki. It's written in the Toustour. One doesn't question Cénzi's reasons; one accepts them."

"I know a learned man—Stenonis, his name is—who lives in Wolhusen, Graubundi. He claims that these shells are incredibly ancient, that they form when shells are buried in the silt and sand of the sea floor, and then more and more layers fall on top of it until they're buried deeply. He says that the shells are actually dissolved away and what you're holding is an impression they left behind: like a sculptor's mold, filled with the minerals dissolved in the water, while the soil and sand compress them so tightly they turn to stone."

"And then the water sprites who live under the sea quarry the rock and carry it up into the mountains at night when no one is watching?"

Karl grinned and chuckled. "I must say that was kinder than the reaction I usually get. No, according to Stenonis' theory, the mountaintops where the rocks are found were once at the bottom of the sea. Upheavals in the world have raised the land in some places and lowered it in others. And I know your next objection, too: why doesn't this great cataclysm show up in any of our histories? Stenonis says that the world is untold millions of years old, and these risings and fallings took place long before any people were there to witness them."

She was already shaking her head. "That's not possible. Archigos Pellin I studied the Toustour, and he determined that Vucta created the world between ten and twelve thousand years ago. Are you telling me you believe this Stenonis and not the Toustour, which is the sacred word of Cénzi?"

Karl shrugged. "I think there's an elegance to Stenonis' theory. I believe much of what we attribute to Cénzi and Vucta and the Moitidi may have more ... *natural* causes."

"Like the Ilmodo?" she asked. "Or whatever it is you call it."

He nodded. "The Scáth Cumhacht. I could show you," he said. "If your mind isn't sealed shut with what the téni have taught you."

"I think I'll decline your invitation, Envoy," she answered. "I'm not easily duped by the tricks of street magicians. My faith is stronger than that." She moved away from him, with a backward glance, going to the marble railing that separated the alcove from the main hall. She looked down at the lines of dancers, knotting and unknotting in the intricate patterns of the Cooper's Dance. When she looked up he was leaning against the rail beside her, and he looked more at her than at the dancers. The corners of her lips were turned up unconsciously, her eyes were wide, and she leaned forward as she stared.

"Would you care to dance, O'Téni?" he asked.

"With a Numetodo?" She glanced at him, but the smile widened. "What would they say?"

"They would say that you'd chosen a particularly ungraceful partner, but one who at least attacks the movements with energy and enthusiasm. They would say, 'She must be taking pity on him ...' "

Now she did laugh. "Surely it's not as bad as that?"

"Oh, it's far, far worse," he said, and extended his arm to her. "May I demonstrate?"

He thought she'd take his arm, but instead she stepped back. "I'm still not certain of your intentions, Envoy." He could see the uncertainty still in her face, and he suspected that it was more than his intentions that worried her. She glanced around, as if looking for the Archigos.

"In my country, they say that there is truth in music, that no one can lie while they're dancing. Ask me your questions out on the floor, and I must tell the truth in response. Think of the information you could bring to the Archigos as a result."

That brought a faint smile to her lips. "I don't think the Archigos would care to see one of his o'téni dancing with the Numetodo Envoy."

"But the Kraljica herself sent me an invitation to this Gschnas. Are you saying she made a mistake?" The young woman shook her head. As she started to speak, Karl brought his finger to his lips. "No, I won't listen to any more arguments. Here's the bargain. I'll tell the Archigos you were attempting to convert me, and that as a result I now find myself sorely tempted to abandon my heretical ways. That should earn you the Archigos' gratitude."

"I'm certain achieving your conversion wouldn't be that easy."

"How will you know unless you try, O'Téni? Or is that answer also in the Toustour?"

She looked around again, but the Archigos was nowhere to be seen. She laughed, if a bit nervously, and laced her arm in his. They went down the steps toward the dancers.

~

Sergei ca'Rudka

TO ONE SIDE of the hall, a massive apple tree
seemed to be growing from the wall, with sparkling
juice flowing freely from the ripe apples on its branches
into a small rocky pool below. Attendants dressed as
squirrels handed out mugs which the attendees could fill
from the tree. Sergei shook his head as he was offered
a mug, and brushed his hands against the overhanging
leaves—the stiff silk was amazingly realistic, and he
wondered how long it had taken to sew the thousands
of them on the false tree. He glanced up at a large knot
in the bole of the tree and nodded: there, he knew, behind a mesh of black fabric, a pair of eyes were carefully watching the Gschnas for any signs of trouble. So
far, the evening had been without incident, but with the
Kraljica and the A'Kralj about to make their entrance,
Sergei preferred to scan the hall himself.

He wore a hawk's head mask that concealed his silver
nose, but otherwise his athletic figure was dressed only
in simple black, and though all real weapons were forbidden in the hall, he wore his own sword at his side.

He moved easily through the crowds, who tended to
part before him in any case, with a glance at the fierce
hawk's beak and the glittering eyes behind it. He nodded
to the ca'-and-cu' who guessed at his identity with a tight
smile under the mask, but he didn't linger for conversation. He saw the Archigos and Λ'Téni ca'Cellibrecca in
conversation in one of the private alcoves and moved
on. He saw other, more intimate trysts in the shadows of

the hall and passed them by also. He had nearly made a circuit of the entire ball when he stopped.

There was something wrong about the man: the manner in which he regarded the crowd; the frayed edges of the jester's costume that he wore; the fact that his cape didn't seem to move as freely as it should; the predatory gesture of rubbing his fingertips together as he started to move toward a knot of people in conversation near the kneeling glass statue holding the musicians. Sergei watched the man seem to accidentally bump against one of the men there, and apologize profusely before moving away again.

Sergei sidled up behind the jester. "I'm impressed," he said.

The man turned, startled. He looked as if he were about to run, but Sergei waggled a forefinger in front of the man's face. The jester stared at it, as if transfixed. "You've a very smooth touch," he told the man "Chevaritt ca'Nephri never noticed, but I did."

"What . . ." The man stopped, licked his lips. His body was tensed, as if he were about to bolt. "What are you talking about, Vajiki?"

"I'm talking about Chevaritt ca'Nephri's purse that is now in there," Sergei said, pointing to the man's cape. "And I wouldn't try to run. Look around you—do you see the three men in hawk masks approaching us?" The man's gaze flickered over the crowd, his mouth open. "Yes, I see that you do. If you go quietly, it will be better for you. If you were to make a scene and disturb the revelry, well, I would be very . . . irritated. And I would make certain that my irritation was assuaged back in the Bastida."

The man's shoulders sagged. "Vajiki, please . . . All I wanted was to get a little money for my family. To buy some food. The children . . ."

"I'm certain your motives were pure," Sergei told him softly, almost sympathetically. "But the law is also clear. Take him," he said to the guards who had come up alongside. "Chevaritt ca'Nephri's purse is in the lining of his cape—please make certain it's immediately returned to him—the chevaritt is a good friend of the A'Kralj, after all. You'll find other purses there as well; hold them until you can locate the owners."

With that, Sergei turned as the man was escorted quietly from the hall. He allowed himself a small smile as he regarded the hall once again. The orchestra was playing the Cooper's Dance, one of his favorite of Darkmavis' songs, and he watched the dancers for a bit. A couple, late onto the floor, caught his eye. One of them was dressed as a fashionable young man but was obviously a woman; the other, dressed as a téni ... his gait, his bearing were familiar. Sergei strolled slowly toward them down one side of the dance floor, watching. The attention they were paying to each other was a more subtle and sensual dance than the one to which they moved. He sniffed once through his silver nose in quiet amusement, realizing who was wearing the téni's robes.

The man certainly was brazen. He admired that in an enemy.

When the dance ended and the two paused at the edge of the floor, he came up to them.

"Have you been tending to your plant, Envoy?" he asked the téni. "Has it bloomed for you yet?"

He'd expected more of a reaction, but the man only smiled. "Commandant. As you can see, I've discovered a flower all on my own." He indicated the woman next to him. "O'Téni Ana cu'Seranta, this is Commandant Sergei ca'Rudka, whose name I'm sure you've heard."

"You flatter me, Envoy ci'Vliomani," Sergei said, smiling politely. He bowed and gave the sign of Cénzi to the woman, whose gaze kept moving from one of them to the other. "O'Téni, I don't believe we've formally met, though I certainly know of you. It seems that you're as much a protector of the Archigos as I am of the Kraljica."

"The Archigos doesn't need my protection, I'm afraid," the o'téni replied. "He's quite capable on his own."

Sergei nodded. "I hope your family home has been

repaired satisfactorily, O'Téni. An unfortunate accident. It was fortunate no one was seriously injured."

The polite smile she was wearing froze on her lips. He saw ci'Vliomani glance strangely at her. "Yes, I'm sure Vatarh would agree with you, Commandant."

"I wouldn't trouble myself with it much, O'Téni," Sergei said. "Mistakes will happen; the important thing is to learn from them and to not repeat them." He glanced from her to ci'Vliomani. "Envoy, I trust you're not here to make a mistake yourself."

"I'm here to enjoy myself, Commandant, like everyone else. And to have a chance to glimpse the Kraljica, who invited me."

"Ah. The Kraljica. I'm certain you know that her time is extremely limited and her schedule for the evening already made. I would hate to have to . . . disengage someone who tried to approach her without her express permission."

"You worry too much, Commandant. I'm certain that O'Téni cu'Seranta would stop me if I attempted anything that would make me look foolish."

Sergei smiled thinly. "Yet somehow she didn't stop you from dancing, Vajiki."

The Numetodo put on a face of exaggerated hurt, placing his hand over his chest. "Commandant, you wound me to the quick. Why, we of the Isle of Paeti are renowned for our grace and form, as I'm sure you know. If I missed a step or two, it was because the musicians don't know how to play properly."

"I'm certain that's the case," Sergei answered. He bowed and gave the sign of Cénzi once more. "O'Téni, it was a pleasure to meet you. Now I can understand how both the Archigos and the Kraljica were impressed by you. But if you'll excuse me, I have duties to which I must attend."

He bowed once more and left them. Within three steps, his hand had come up to stroke his chin under the hawk's mask. This would bear watching. Cu'Seranta had already shown herself to be both powerful and erratic, and if the Archigos trusted her, Sergei did not, especially if—as he suspected—she were vulnerable to romance. The Numetodo wouldn't be above using that to his own advantage.

Yes. Sergei would watch. And wait.

Then, at the right time, he would stoop like a hawk and strike.

"Commandant?" One of Renard's young aides came hurrying up to him. "The Kraljica is asking if everything is ready."

"Is the painting in place for the presentation?" The boy nodded. "Then, yes," Sergei told the page. "You may tell Renard that we're ready."

The boy hurried away as Sergei walked unhurriedly to his post near the stairs to the inner apartments. As he reached them, the trumpets blared a fanfare.

~

Dhosti ca'Millac

IT TOOK FAR TOO long to disengage himself from ca'Cellibrecca. They fenced verbally, using the same ancient, hoary arguments and the same weary answers. Dhosti suspected they both could have written down the exchange beforehand and have missed nothing of import. Ca'Cellibrecca prattled on about the Toustour and the Divolonté and how the Faith must not tolerate dissent, and how the Archigos' "lenience" was tearing down the foundations on which the Concénzia Faith had been built. Dhosti had stopped listening after the first few sentences, his back aching from standing so long, and ca'Cellibrecca had left with his usual imprecations and thinly veiled threats.

And now he'd come back out to find Ana dancing
with ci'Vliomani. He hoped that ca'Cellibrecca didn't
notice, but he was certain that even if the a'téni failed to
see it himself, the news would come to him very quickly.
Dhosti frowned and his fingers tightened on the railing
of the alcove: the commandant had stopped to speak
with Ana and the Numetodo. *You can't be with her all
the time, and she must make her own choices. In the end, it
is all Cénzi's Will.* He would have to marry her off soon,
he decided. That would cure her of any romantic ideal-
ism. Like the Kraljica, he knew that marriage could be
as potent a weapon as any sword, if carefully arranged,
and he suspected that Ana could be an exceedingly potent sword.

Leaning heavily on his walking stick, Dhosti made his
way down the stairs, nodding to the ca'-and-cu' that he
passed, exchanging a few words with those he knew by
name and face. It took him several minutes to reach the
main floor. He could see Ana and ci'Vliomani having
an energetic discussion. "Come," he said to Ana, glancing once sharply at ci'Vliomani. "We should be at the
stairs for the Kraljica's entrance. Envoy, if you'll pardon
us . . ."

Ana glanced back at ci'Vliomani as Dhosti took
her arm, but she followed him. They'd just reached the
stairs—the commandant nodding to them from the far
side—as a fanfare rattled the walls of the room. A flock
of white doves exploded from the balconies in a flurry
of soft wings as pieces of shredded, bright paper fluttered down in a slow rain. The candles in the Kneeling
Man went out, all at once, followed by all the téni-lights
around the hall. The only spot of illumination was at the
top of the main stairway. There, an apparition stood.

She seemed to be clothed entirely in light: fierce reds
and oranges and shimmering bright ultramarine swirled
around her in a whirlwind of color, masking all of her
body but the face. And the face . . . It was the Kraljica, yes,
Dhosti knew, but it was the Kraljica transformed. Each

strand of her white hair was a sun, and the light seemed to radiate from deep within her. Her eyes blazed.

She lifted her hands, and rays of purest yellow shot from her fingertips. The crowd cooed appreciatively, bursting into applause.

Dhosti could hear the soft murmuring of the téni hidden at the top of the stairs as they chanted, releasing the light display, but that was unheard by the crowd farther back.

Then the lights returned, the musicians began playing once again, and the Kraljica descended the stairs. Her costume glowed, softer now but difficult to look at directly—it was as if she were clothed in the flicker of sight at the edge of an eye: when Dhosti tried to capture an image, it blurred and was gone. Her hair still gleamed, but more softly now, like stars in a night sky. Her eyes glistened like those of a cat caught in firelight.

He took her hands, and they were simply the ancient hands of the Kraljica. He looked at her face, and he saw weariness and deep, eroded lines there. "Kraljica," he said. "You were magnificent. Your entrance will be the talk of the evening. Nessantico has seen nothing like it. It was as if Vucta walked again on the earth, just as I've imagined Her."

"Your téni did the work," she told him. "Thank you for sending them to me." Her voice quavered, so soft that he found himself leaning forward to listen. "Dhosti, I'm so very tired. Tell O'Téni Ana I would like to take her arm and lean on her, if she doesn't mind." Then, for a moment, her old voice returned. "Besides, Ana's accompaniment would send a message to A'Téni ca'Cellibrecca, wouldn't it?"

Dhosti smiled at that. "Certainly, Kraljica. Ana . . ." He gestured to her to come forward. "The Kraljica's not feeling well," he whispered to her. "She needs your arm."

Ana glanced at the Kraljica with concern, bowing her head to give the sign, then moved to the Kraljica's side. "I'd be honored, Kraljica," she said. The young woman's arm sparked as it contacted the eddies of light wrapping the Kraljica, and Ana grimaced. "The Ilmodo is a bit cold," she said aloud.

"It's damned frigid," the Kraljica answered. "My blood has turned to ice. But come, let's do what we must do so I can get back to my apartments. We need to move on so that Justi can be announced." With that, the Kraljica gave the nearest onlookers a practiced smile and stepped forward into the crowd, the commandant to her left and Dhosti to her right just behind her.

"Kraljica, what a magnificent Gschnas . . ."

". . . the best I've ever seen . . ."

". . . what a wonderful tribute to your Jubilee . . ."

As the Kraljica nodded and smiled and waved to the well-wishers among the ca'-and-cu' who gathered around her, Dhosti leaned closer to the commandant. "The Kraljica doesn't look well to me, Sergei. Just these last several days . . ."

"I share your concern, Archigos. Renard's talked to her attendants and nurses; they all say the same." The commandant's forehead creased above the hawk's mask. He didn't look at the Archigos, but at the crowd of the elite pressing around the Kraljica and Ana. "At her age, one never knows, but this sudden decline . . . I've wondered about the possibility of poison."

"Is that possible?"

A shrug. "I don't know yet. But I will." The commandant almost smiled at that, an expression that caused Dhosti to shiver as if snow were blowing down his bent spine. "Renard tried to convince her not to come down tonight, to let the A'Kralj represent her, but she refused."

"That, at least, hasn't changed," Dhosti said. He saw A'Téni ca'Cellibrecca moving toward the Kraljica with his daughter and marriage-son in tow. Behind them, the trumpets blew their fanfare again, and all turned to the stairs to see the A'Kralj make his entrance. Following his matarh's lead, he was dressed as a mythological figure from the Toustour: Misfal, the first of the Moitidi breathed into existence by Cénzi. The A'Kralj's costume was chosen perfectly for his athletic figure: dark, close-fitting leather trousers and vest, a shirt painted with marbled veins, his mirrored mask gleaming and studded with polished stones, and a floor-length cape that, like the Kraljica's clothing, was alive with silver-and-blue color, as if a waterfall were cascading from him. As he stood there, he rose slowly into the air as white clouds fumed from the floor below him before rolling heavily down the stairs. The A'Kralj remained suspended, his hands lifted as if in benediction, before he descended slowly to the floor once more.

The applause that greeted his performance was enthusiastic, if carefully less long in duration than that which had greeted the Kraljica.

As the A'Kralj descended the stairs, the Kraljica, as was customary, came forward to greet him, still supporting herself on Ana's arm. The A'Kralj, at the bottom of the steps, bowed and gave the sign of Cénzi to Dhosti, who returned the gesture, then Dhosti watched the Kraljica grasp her son's hand, and place his other hand on Ana's. Her voice was too faint for him to hear as she inclined toward her son, but he assumed that she was introducing Ana to the A'Kralj, and that made Dhosti suspect that the Kraljica's insistence that Ana help her wasn't entirely an accident. He wasn't certain how he felt about that; he knew it certainly wouldn't please his niece Safina, who had often been mentioned as a possible match for Justi. Safina, though, had already shown that she had not inherited Dhosti's skill with the Ilmodo; he doubted that Safina would ever rise above her current status as e'téni, and that made her less than a good fit for the A'Kralj.

Justi nodded to his matarh, smiled his polished and perfect smile, and moved away, slicing through the throngs directly toward A'Téni ca'Cellibrecca and his daughter and son-in law, and there he entered into an animated discussion.

"The A'Kralj keeps his own counsel," Sergei said alongside Dhosti. "And his own affairs." Sergei pointed his chin toward Francesca, whose hand lightly drifted down the A'Kralj's arm. It was the intimacy of the gesture that caught Dhosti's attention; he noticed that it also caught the attention of Estraven, whose face darkened and scowled above the hem of his costume dress.

"Truly?" Dhosti whispered to Sergei.

The commandant nodded.

"Does the Kraljica know?"

"I think she suspects. But not through me."

"I thought that was part of your job, to give the Kraljica the information she needs."

The commandant smiled. "It's my job to know as much as possible about *everything* that happens here in the city, Archigos. And it's my job to give the Kraljica information that requires her action or that would affect her adversely. I know far more than I tell the Kraljica," he said, and his eyes locked on Dhosti's. "Far more. But I keep it to myself until the proper time. Or I tell others, who may know better than I when the proper time might be. I trust you take my meaning."

Dhosti nodded. "I will bear that in mind," he said.

"I'm sure you will," Sergei answered. "Especially if the Kraljica or you has a thought toward marrying the church to the state."

Justi ca'Mazzak

IT WAS THE APPLAUSE tha seemed to lift him up, rather than the chants of the téni hidden behind him. The acclaim of the ca'-and-cu' drowned out their chanting, and he closed his eyes as he spread his hands wide. He stood on warm air, suspended in the ovation. Too soon, though, he was standing on the stairway's landing once again, and he walked slowly down the stairs toward the crowds.

Very soon, when he came to the ca'-and-cu' it would be as Kraljiki, and the applause and the attention would be his alone. He would not have to share it with his matarh.

But for the moment he had to smile, had to bow to the dwarf who, without realizing it, was likely in his last days as Archigos; had to reach for Matarh's hand in supplication: smiling, always smiling, even as he glanced quizzically at the young man—no, it was a young woman, he decided suddenly—who was on the arm of the Kraljica.

The woman was *supporting* his matarh, he realized suddenly. He almost smiled.

His matarh took his hand in hers. It was cold and trembling, that hand, with skin spotted and wrinkled. She reached for his other hand and placed it over the young woman's. "Justi," she said. "This is O'Téni Ana cu'Seranta . . . you know, the one who saved the Archigos from the Numetodo assassin." Her voice quavered, and was so weak he could barely hear it. She looked decidedly *old* tonight. She looked ill.

"So *this* is the one I've heard so much about," Justi said. "It's a delight to meet you, O'Téni."

She couldn't give him the full curtsy that etiquette demanded while on the Kraljica's arm, but she bowed her head, muttering more to the floor than to him. "Thank you, A'Kralj," she answered. "Your costume . . . was quite impressive."

He nodded quickly, ignoring the nicety. "Matarh, should you be out here? If you'd like to retire, I'd be happy to . . ."

"No." For a moment, her voice had its honed edge and imperiousness. "I'm fine. I am thinking, Justi, that you and O'Téni Ana should dance later."

"I'm certain we can find the time for that, Matarh," he answered. *So is this the one you've chosen, Matarh?* he wanted to ask. *You could at least have chosen someone less plain.* "But if you'll excuse me for the moment . . ."

His matarh's eyes widened at his brusqueness, but he strode quickly away before she could gather herself to comment. He'd glimpsed Francesca through the crowd, standing next to her vatarh, and he moved toward her. "A'Téni ca'Cellibrecca," he said, accepting the older man's bow. "It's good to see you again, and I must say that the simplicity of your costume is refreshing." He gestured at his own costume ruefully. "I feel a bit too . . . conspicuous."

"The A'Kralj is always conspicuous," ca'Cellibrecca answered, "as he should be. And it will be more so in the future." He stopped, glancing pointedly in the direction of the Kraljica and the Archigos. "You already know my daughter, and her husband . . ."

"Yes, of course. Vajica, U'Teni, how are the two of you this evening?" He could not quite keep the amusement from his face at the sight of Francesca's husband, whose already-rouged cheeks flared even more over the edge of the ridiculous costume he wore—that he knew Francesca had chosen for Estraven; she'd laughed about it the last time she and Justi were together. Justi wondered how much the man knew or suspected—not that it mattered. Ca'Cellibrecca had already promised that the marriage would be annulled as soon as he was Archigos, and that U'Téni Estraven would be placated with another wife—Allesandra, the daughter of the Hïrzg of Firenzcia, had been mentioned. Justi took Francesca's hand. "You shame the other women here, Vajica," he said to her. "They have no chance of competing." Her gaze stayed on him as she smiled.

"You honor me, A'Kralj," she murmured.

"A'Kralj," A'Téni ca'Cellibrecca said, "we must talk later. I have some news I would like to relate to you. Perhaps after the unveiling of the Kraljica's portrait?"

Justi smiled at that. *After the unveiling, there may be no need for words.* "I would be pleased to do so, A'Téni." He glanced upward, where a star seemed to be descending from the ceiling, in a new fanfare of krumhorns and trumpets. A space was cleared beneath the lowering brilliance, and servants hurried forward with chairs. Justi could see the Archigos and his matarh being seated, and one of Renard's aides was moving earnestly in his direction. "If you'll excuse me, A'Téni. It is the duty of the A'Kralj to be submissively at the Kraljica's side at these moments, I'm afraid."

Ca'Cellibrecca bowed slightly, and Justi released Francesca's hand, squeezing it gently beforehand so that she smiled. He moved quickly to the center of the hall, where the star pulsed and radiated, so bright that he had to shade his eyes. Renard, standing next to O'Téni cu'Seranta just behind the high back of the Kraljica's chair, gestured to the empty chair to the right, its back just slightly lower than either that of the Kraljica or the Archigos. The star sent harsh shadows dancing madly behind the spectators. As Justi slid into his seat, the star flared in the colors of Nessantico's standard: alternating blue and gold. Then it went dark, and the crowd gasped, blinking and trying to adjust their sight to what seemed to be sudden night. Justi closed his own eyes, purple-and-yellow afterimages chasing themselves behind his eyelids. When he opened them again, a tall rectangle draped in black cloth stood before them, caught in a white glow from téni-lit lamps set near it.

"Where's that damned painter?" Justi heard Renard whisper harshly behind his seat. "He's supposed to *be* here . . ." He heard an attendant patter off. Justi smiled inwardly. The crowd was beginning to mutter restlessly as the draped painting remained unrevealed. "Matarh," Justi said, leaning over to her. "I think Vajiki ci'Recroix suffers from a sudden modesty regarding his painting skills. Perhaps O'Téni cu'Seranta might take his duties . . ." He glanced at the young woman and smiled.

"Yes. Ana, if you would . . ."

The O'Téni bowed. He heard her take a deep, nervous breath as she moved around the chairs and out into the glare. She went to the draped painting, made a deep bow with the sign of Cénzi to the seated trio, then pulled the silken cloth from the painting.

The room was a large, massed inhalation. Even Justi found himself drawing in breath. The painting . . .

It was magnificent. There was no other word for it. Ci'Recroix's brush had snared the Kraljica as if in the midst of turning toward the viewer. The figure seated on the Sun Throne was captured larger than life-size. The lighting was chiaroscuro, her features illuminated from the side, each hair on her head and each fold in her face visible. The mouth was slightly open and one hand was lifting from her lap, as if she were beckoning to someone and about to speak to them.

The painting seemed almost to writhe in place, so lifelike and realistic that Justi could almost believe his matarh could step from the frame of the picture and onto the tiles of the hall.

The applause began as a smattering, then quickly became a tidal wave of appreciation that swept over the hall, deafening and tremendous. People pressed forward to see better . . .

And the Kraljica, next to Justi, gave a strangled cry. He looked over to see her fall.

~

Ana cu'Seranta

"MATARH, I think Vajiki ci'Recroix suffers from a sudden modesty regarding his painting skills. Perhaps o'Téni cu'Seranta might take his duties . . ." The A'Kralj glanced over the back of his chair toward her and smiled. It was a polished, artificial smile, and it held no warmth. Ana found herself recoiling from it.

"Yes. Ana, if you would," she heard the Kraljica say, and she wanted to refuse but then the Archigos nodded, his gaze solemn, and she forced herself to bow in agreement. She could feel the stares of the crowd on her as she moved into the brilliant pool of light around the painting. Her breath was caught high in her throat; she thought she might faint, but she forced herself to take a deep, long breath. She saw Envoy ci'Vliomani standing well behind the Kraljica, Archigos, and A'Kralj, at the railing of the half-landing at the edge of the hall. He lifted a hand to her, shaking his head. She wondered at that as she performed the deep curtsy that etiquette required. She put her hand on the soft cloth that draped the canvas.

She tugged, and the shroud fell away like a dark cloud. Ana gasped. She would have sworn that she saw the image underneath *shift* in that instant, as if the figure had been startled at the sudden movement, that its eyes stared at her own for an instant before turning away to look at the three people seated before it.

She heard the crowd gasp at the same time . . . and she felt . . . she felt . . .

Ana wasn't sure what it was. The sense was like a

winter river rushing through her as she stood there next to the painting, a river that flowed from the Kraljica in her chair toward the painting itself, a cold so intense that it burned, and the invisible waters were loud with a wail that was the voice of the Kraljica herself.

Ana saw the Kraljica start to rise in her chair, her face distraught and terrified, then just as suddenly she crumpled and fell forward. Her head made a terrible hollow sound as it struck the tiles. Her dress, still alive with téni-illumination, pooled around her.

For a moment, everything was frozen in tableau. Ana could see them all: The A'Kralj, motionless except for his head turned toward his matarh; the Archigos lurching forward in his chair, his stubby feet dangling; Renard, behind the Kraljica's chair, his hand reaching helplessly and far too late for her; the commandant's face stern and terrifying, glaring at the crowd as if searching for someone; Envoy ci'Vliomani, at the rear of the crowd, turning away. Then everything moved again. Renard shoved the throne-chair aside and rushed toward the Kraljica as the A'Kralj slid to his knees beside her; the Archigos pushed away from his seat, a chant on his lips; the commandant drew his sword as the crowd pushed inward; Karl ci'Vliomani vanished in the sea of movement.

Ana rushed away from the painting herself to huddle next to the Kraljica.

"Back!" she heard the commandant shout. "Everyone move back!" But they were still pressing forward, drawn by the commotion, and the Archigos lifted his hand, still chanting. She felt the ripple of power flow outward from him, a shimmering of air that pushed past her without touching but then hardened into a wall that shoved back at the crowd, holding them.

The A'Kralj had lifted his matarh in his arms; Ana could see her breathing, gasping as he pushed himself up, and she felt relief—*she isn't dead*. "Renard!" the A'Kralj shouted. "Call for the healer. Bring him to the

Kraljica's rooms. Now!" Renard bowed and hurried off. "Archigos . . ."

"I will clear the way," the Archigos said, and Ana felt the invisible wall shift. A path began to open before them. She could hear the commandant shouting orders to his staff, and the crowd roar was deafening. "Ana, come with us."

She followed the Archigos, going ahead of the A'Kralj. They moved quickly from the hall, out a side door and across a corridor to another door. Servants scurried ahead of them. The door opened into a staircase and they went up a quick two flights, and Ana found herself finally in the corridors of the Kraljica's private apartment. More servants appeared, opening the doors and ushering them into the Kraljica's bedchamber, where the A'Kralj laid the Kraljica down on her bed. "Matarh," he said, "can you hear me?"

A faint nod. The Kraljica's eyes flickered open, showing mostly the whites of her eyes traced with red veins. "I felt . . . my heart was tearing out of me . . . my head splitting . . ." Her voice was a husk, barely audible. "So tired . . ."

"Where's that healer?" the A'Kralj said, his voice loud and his face flushed. He went to the door. "Renard!" he shouted.

"A'Kralj," the Archigos said. His voice was weary and trembling, but Justi spun around, his eyes blazing. "The commandant will need you downstairs, to reassure the guests."

The A'Kralj glanced at the bed. "If my matarh is in danger . . ."

"She's resting now," the Archigos said, soothingly. "You have your duty to perform. The ca'-and-cu' will be in an uproar, and they need your leadership at this moment. Your matarh needs it."

Ana saw the A'Kralj's lips press together. The flush in his face lessened, though his gaze stayed on the bed. "Yes," he said. "But . . ."

"Let me care for her," the Archigos said. "We will handle this. There's nothing you can do here, but downstairs there is. The commandant will need orders from you as the A'Kralj—and as the acting Kraljiki for as long as the Kraljica remains incapacitated. I will send for you immediately if there is any change here."

The A'Kralj nodded. He rushed out the door. The Archigos looked at the servants who were in the room, getting bedding, pouring water, uncovering the banked fire in the hearth. An e'téni on the palais staff chanted to put light in a lamp; another started the blades of a fan circulating to move the stale air. "Leave us," the Archigos said to all of them. "Now." They bowed and hurried from the room, closing the door behind them.

The Archigos was staring down at the still figure on the bed, at the frail chest rising and falling shallowly.

"Archigos," Ana said. The man glanced over at her, and the severe look in his eyes frightened her. "When the painting was uncovered, I felt something . . ."

"We don't have time for this," the Archigos told her. "Renard might come here, or the A'Kralj might return. Come here, Ana. Stand by the bed."

She knew what he wanted of her. "Archigos, I shouldn't . . . The Divolonté . . ."

"I rule Concénzia, child, and I know what the Divolonté says and I know it was written by the a'téni and not by Cénzi Himself. I also believe that Cénzi does not gift people needlessly. Now—do what you can for her, and do it quickly. Go on; we're alone here."

Ana approached the bed. She looked down at the Kraljica, so pale in her resplendent costume. She seemed nearly dead already, her breath so shallow that it barely touched her chest, her cheeks hollow and sunken. "You know what to do," the Archigos said. "Pray to Cénzi, Ana."

She did. She took a long, shuddering breath. She closed her eyes and took one of the Kraljica's hands in her own. The chant came to her, unbidden, rising from the place that she thought of as the core of her belief, far inside her. Her lips moved with the words that shaped the power that emerged with them, the Ilmodo. Her hands lifted from the Kraljica's, molding the growing power. She formed the Ilmodo so that it could coil from her heart into her hands, and from there into the Kraljica. It was warm, this power, like a liquid sun, and when it touched the old woman on the bed, Ana found herself caught in the Kraljica's mind, also. She could hear her, crying and weeping in an interior darkness. She let more of the Ilmodo rush from her so that it entered the Kraljica ...

... but this was not as it was before. Then, the Ilmodo had filled Ana's matarh as if she had been a empty vessel, moving through her like blood. The cup of her matarh's body had held the Ilmodo like a goblet, and it had strengthened her.

But that didn't happen with the Kraljica. The Ilmodo moved into her and out again as if she were a bowl with a hole bored through the bottom, and Ana could feel the Kraljica's life force rushing through that same hole, draining away from her. The flow was compelling; Ana found herself falling with it, unbidden, caught in the white-foamed rush that went into and through the Kraljica—and she knew where it was taking her even as she fought to hold herself back. The Ilmodo was being torn from her, away and down, down to the hall far below where the painting stood. The spell within the painting sucked greedily at her, clawed at her, ripped the Ilmodo's energy away. She fought against the incantation, pulling herself back and concentrating on the Kraljica, on the connection that bound her to the painting. She struggled to control the Ilmodo, to use it to close the rent in the Kraljica's spirit and seal it off. The resistance was terrible; it was as if she were physically struggling with someone, someone easily as strong as her and bent on taking her down.

Ana gasped. She felt as if she were shouting her chant

into a gale, but for a moment she felt that she was winning. Her Ilmodo brightened, and she could hear the Kraljica's voice—*I'm here, Ana ... I feel you ...*—but then she was tossed aside before she could reach for that voice. Tossed aside and out.

She was back in the room, holding the Kraljica's hand. Her hair was damp with perspiration; she was breathing as heavily as if she'd run here from the Archigos' Temple. She could feel the weariness gathering, the payment for her spell.

"Archigos ..."

"I know," he said. "I felt it. The Ilmodo moving."

Ana nodded. "The Kraljica ... It's the painting that's killing her. I think this ci'Recroix somehow ..." She didn't finish the thought as the Archigos nodded.

"I suspect we'll find that Vajiki ci'Recroix has left the city in a hurry," he said.

"I should have known, Archigos," Ana said. She forced herself to stay awake against the compulsion to give in to the exhaustion. "When we were here last, I looked at the painting. I thought I felt something like a téni-spell then within it, but I thought it was how the painter made his figures so true. I thought it was something he did unconsciously, without even knowing he was doing it, like I did with healing headaches as a child. I should have told you. If I had, perhaps ..." She stopped, her hand over her mouth. "I've slowed it, but I don't think I can heal her. There must be someone else, some other way ..."

"I doubt it," the Archigos answered. He stirred and started toward the door, the graveclothes he wore fluttering as he moved. "I'll call the commandant and have him take the painting and bring it here. If we burn it, perhaps ..."

"No!" Ana interrupted. She panted from the effort of the shout, the weariness calling to her to succumb. "She's bound to the painting. If you destroy the painting, you destroy *her*."

"You're certain of that, Ana?"

Ana shook her head. Her breath wheezed from her lungs. "I can't be certain. But I felt the connection. Too much of the Kraljica is already there, captured. Sever the bond between her and the painting, and she will have nothing left."

The room was darkening around the Archigos. Ana saw him as if he were standing at the end of a long tunnel, outlined in aching light. "All I could do was lessen the draining from the Kraljica to the spell in the painting," she continued, "but I couldn't close it completely. Even if I could, I think we need to keep the connection open so that perhaps we could bring her back." The explanation took all of her breath. "It's like she's bleeding from a wound, Archigos, only inside."

Ana moved her gaze from the Archigos back to the Kraljica; the turning of her head made her nauseous and disoriented: like a child who'd been twirling around and around, then suddenly stops. The room tilted and she staggered. "Ana!" she heard the Archigos call as she clutched at a post of the Kraljica's bed, but his voice seemed to come from somewhere far outside, and now the room was spinning in earthquake madness and the fire in the hearth erupted from its bed, and the heat and the flames and the sound bore her down and carried her away.

MANEUVERS

Jan ca'Vörl
Ana cu'Seranta
Karl ci'Vliomani
Edouard ci'Recroix
Ana cu'Seranta
Mahri
Ana cu'Seranta

Jan ca'Vörl

" . . . **Y**OU ALWAYS HAVE to be aware of your ground. Having to charge uphill is a tremendous disadvantage."

"Though we had to do exactly that at Lake Cresci on the Escarpment," Jan interjected. "It was a tremendous slog, but the tactic worked because they weren't expecting it of us."

O'Offizier ci'Arndt seemed to levitate to his feet and salute at the appearance of the Hïrzg, with Vajica Mara accompanying him. Allesandra jumped from her seat at the table where her toy soldiers were set and rushed to Jan. "Vatarh! Georgi has been teaching me. He says I'd make an excellent Starkkapitän." The young offizier blushed at that, still holding his salute.

"Take your ease, O'Offizier," Jan told him. "I appreciate the time you're taking with Allesandra, and she enjoys your company."

"Thank you, Hïrzg. She learns quickly, truly."

Jan smiled at him. The young man—he couldn't be much more than twenty—was good-looking enough, and he could see the proprietary way Allesandra regarded him. He wondered if he'd be well-advised to send the o'offizier away soon; sometimes, Allesandra acted distressingly older than her actual age, and there was no way that a ci', no matter how good an offizier he might be, would be a suitable infatuation for the Hïrzg's daughter.

Mara was looking at him, too, and that amused Jan.

"You may go, O'Offizier," he told ci'Arndt. "I'll relieve you here."

The young man saluted again and left the tent. Jan sat next to Allesandra and glanced up at Mara. "You should probably be returning to the Hïrzgin, Mara," he said. "There are proprieties we still need to observe." He took her hand and kissed her upturned palm.

Mara smiled at him and at Allesandra. "I understand, my Hïrzg," she said as she curtsied. She left the tent in a flurry of perfume and swaying, brightly-colored cloth.

"Mara is much nicer than Matarh," Allesandra ventured as Jan watched Mara depart, his gaze leaving her reluctantly.

"I can understand how you would feel that way, Allesandra," Jan told her, returning his attention to her. He glanced at the soldiers in their array on the table, tousling his daughter's hair idly. "Allesandra, I would like to talk to you."

"You sound so serious, Vatarh."

"I am," he told her. He went to the opening of the tent and glanced out—Markell had placed guards just far enough away to be out of earshot, and Jan smiled. The sunlight would betray anyone who tried to sneak up close enough to the rear to listen. He went back inside and sat again. "Allesandra, you were right when you said that I shouldn't marry Mara, even if I could. She is . . ." He stopped, choosing his words carefully. ". . . someone whose company I enjoy, but she is not my equal, nor yours, nor even your matarh's. She gives me what she can, and in turn I can give her some little favors now and then. I know you understand. She and I are . . ." He paused, and Allesandra hurried into the gap with a smile.

"Like me and Georgi, Vatarh?"

Jan laughed aloud at that. "You're too perceptive, my little bird," he said. "Allesandra, even if your brother Toma had survived the Southern Fever, I think you would be the one I named as my heir."

Allesandra grinned, though there was sadness lurking there. She pushed back at the curls around her forehead. "I do miss Toma, Vatarh."

"I do too," Jan told her. "Very much. But I look at you—" he glanced again at the miniature armies laid out on the table, at the placement of the archers and war-téni, the infantry and the chevarittai "—and I know that you, more than Toma ever did, think as I do. And you're growing older faster than I can believe, my darling. So . . . I need to speak to you as Hïrzg to A'Hïrzg, because things will happen very soon."

"What things?" Her round face twisted, as if she wasn't certain whether she should be pleased or upset.

"Nothing I can tell you yet, though you'll know when they happen." He plucked one of the soldiers from the table: an infantryman with his sword raised in mid-strike. "If your enemy were looking for a threat coming from another direction, and you were the starkkapitän with your army placed ready to move, what do you think your Georgi would tell you to do?"

"He would say to attack quickly, before they could react," Allesandra answered, and Jan chuckled again.

"He would be right," Jan said. "That is exactly what I would do." He set the soldier back down on the table. "Exactly."

~

Ana cu'Seranta

ANA RUBBED THE PAPER between her fingers. A small package had come to her apartments the morning after the terrible events of the Gschnas, the seal on the stiff wrapping paper still attached, with a clamshell insignia pressed into the red wax. Inside the tiny box had been a stone clamshell like the one Vajiki ci'Vliomani had shown her the night before, only this one was suspended from a fine silver chain.

Also inside was the folded note she held now. Despite her sadness, she'd smiled momentarily, remembering the ball and Envoy ci'Vliomani, their conversation and their dancing, but the pleasure of the memory was obliterated the next moment by guilt. How could she feel anything but sadness from the Gschnas after what had happened to the Kraljica? Still . . .

She wondered whether someone had opened the package: she could have done it herself easily with a touch of the Ilmodo magic. She wondered whether Arch-igos Dhosti had seen the short message:

You must know that I had nothing to do with what happened last night. That is the truth. If you would like to know more, meet me at Oldtown Center just after the lamps have been lit. Wear the shell over your clothing. The best way to learn the truth is by seeing it with your own eyes. After what happened at the Gschnas, there may be very little time.

There had been no signature.

Ana wasn't certain what she should feel or what she should do. A note from the Numetodo Envoy, offering to meet . . . Would the Archigos expect her to tell him about this? For that matter, if he did already know and she remained silent, then what might he think?

She crumpled the note and the box and flung them into the fireplace, watching the edges turn brown and then erupt into flame. She picked up the shell on its chain and twirled it in front of her. She thought of putting it in one of the drawers in her desk, or perhaps hiding it among her clothing. She examined the shell, the grooves so well-defined in the stone, as if they had been sculpted. She lifted the chain and placed it around her neck. She glanced in the mirror as she touched the shell, and then placed it under her robes. No, it wasn't obvious there. "Watha," she called, "has the Archigos arrived yet?"

Watha entered, bowing and giving Ana the sign of Cénzi. "He should be here any moment, O'Téni," she said. Ana saw her eyes flicker over the table and around the room—looking for the box, she was certain. The woman licked her lips as if she were about to speak, then evidently thought better of it. "I'll send Tari out to watch for the carriage," she said at last.

"Thank you, Watha." The woman bowed again and left the room. Ana touched the shell again under the folds of her robe as she looked in the mirror. A plain, weary face stared back at her, with brown circles under the eyes. She remembered nothing of last night beyond her attempt to heal the Kraljica. All the events of the Gschnas were overlaid with a sense of unreality, as if it were something that had happened to another Ana. The payment for her use of the Ilmodo had been severe; her body still ached and the weariness touched her limbs despite a long sleep; it was already nearly noon and she felt as if she'd slept only moments.

"The Kraljica . . ." she'd asked through cracked, dry *lips as soon as she'd awakened. Watha had been there, sitting on the chair at the foot of her bed. "Is she . . ."*

"The Archigos sent a messenger around earlier, O'Téni," she'd answered. *"He said that the Kraljica is unchanged, and to tell you that you'll be seeing her midday. He'll send a carriage. We were all terribly worried when we heard what happened, O'Téni, especially after what nearly happened with the Archigos."*

Ana sighed, looking in the mirror. She knew that the Archigos intended her to use the Ilmodo once again today on the Kraljica, and she wasn't certain she could do that, not as drained as she was. And if she did, then how would she feel when the lamps were lit around the city. Would she even be awake?

She touched the shell under her robes once more. Ana had certainly felt attraction before, certainly, though that affection had rarely been returned—it seemed to be reserved for prettier women than her.

But Vajiki ci'Vliomani . . . Karl . . .

It could all be pretense, her mirror image seemed to be telling her with the frown she saw. *He's a Numetodo; you're an o'téni. What you felt could be pretext, all one-sided yet again, so that he has a door into the Faith. He could be intending to corrupt you. Be careful. Be very careful.*

"I will be," she said to the mirror.

"O'Téni?" a voice questioned from the door, and she started, turning her head to see Sunna there. "What were you saying?"

"Nothing," she said. "Is the carriage here?"

"Yes," Sunna said. "I told the téni to let the Archigos know that you'll be right down."

The Archigos said little beyond the required greeting until the téni driver closed the carriage door and began his chant to start the vehicle rolling through the streets. The carriage lurched over the cobbles as it turned onto the Avi a'Parete, people on the street bowing and giving the sign of Cénzi as they passed, their faces solemn. Ana knew what the gossip of the city must be like. The Archigos sighed deeply. "I was able to learn something last night," he said. "Do you remember ci'Recroix's painting in the Kraljica's parlor? The one of the family?"

"Yes, Archigos. It's a very enchanting painting that makes me want to keep staring at it. The woman with the baby . . . I half expect to hear the infant suckling."

"The family he portrayed is dead. Every one of them," the Archigos told her. "They died, I'm told, within a day after the painting was completed, of some tragic and unknown disease. Strangely, that seems to be the case with several of the subjects of ci'Recroix's paintings over the last four or five years, though not before: the person whose portrait he captured suddenly and unexpectedly died. A series of tragic coincidences, which didn't come to light since ci'Recroix never accepted a commission in the same city twice."

Ana's chest felt as if someone were sitting on it. "I don't think it's coincidence, Archigos."

The dwarf sniffed. "Neither do I, Ana. Neither do I. I think ci'Recroix has been . . . practicing."

"But why, and for his own reasons or for someone else's?"

"That I don't know, but I will find out. I have my suspicions, however."

"The Numetodo?" Ana asked hesitantly, thinking of the note she'd received. She was afraid to even glance at the Archigos, afraid that he would see what she was hiding.

She felt more than saw the Archigos shrug. "Possibly, but I doubt that. The Kraljica is more likely to be sympathetic to the Numetodo than the A'Kralj, after all. Why, do you know something about them that would lead you to suspect them? I saw you with Envoy ci'Vliomani last night."

He was watching her. She could feel his gaze on her, and she stared out the window of the carriage rather than look at him. *If he knows about the note, if he's read it, then I should tell him now so he knows that I won't keep secrets from him. . . .*

She knew she should open herself to him, but even as she started to speak, another inner voice objected. *If you tell him and he knew nothing, he won't let you go. He'll make certain that Envoy ci'Vliomani is kept far away from you, and you'll never know if anything he's said or anything you might have felt is true. . . .* "No," she said to the window. "I was only speculating, that's all. You're right, of course, Archigos. Envoy ci'Vliomani told me that he was looking forward to meeting the Kraljica, and I believe he was sincere in that." She forced herself to turn back to the Archigos. There was nothing in his wizened face that suggested he might be disappointed in her or that she had failed a test set her. "If not the Numetodo, then who?" she asked.

The Archigos only shook his head. "I won't say. Not without more proof—proof that I fully expect is forthcoming. I've told Commandant ca'Rudka what I've learned, and he has started his own investigation. The commandant has . . ." The Archigos pressed his lips together momentarily. ". . . sources and ways of gaining information I do not."

Ana shivered, remembering the man and the sense of unspoken menace that exuded from him. She could imagine the ways to which the Archigos referred. "And the Kraljica?" she asked. "How is she this morning?"

The Archigos shook his head. "No better. Somewhat worse, perhaps. Renard wasn't optimistic. She's remained unconscious since the incident, and no one can rouse her."

"Archigos, I don't know if I can. Last night drained me so deeply."

He reached out with his small, malformed hand and patted hers. "I won't ask you to do anything you don't feel you can do, Ana. The choice is yours—yours and Cénzi's."

"And if she dies?"

The Archigos looked at her sharply, then frowned. "If she dies, Ana, then I fear for Nessantico. I truly do."

~

Karl ci'Vliomani

"IF SHE DIES, we're doomed. Utterly doomed."

"It's not that dire, Mika," Karl answered. The tavern was cold despite the roaring fire in the large stone hearth near their table. The walls were laced with shadows and smoke, and the inn smelled of soot and ash from the poor ventilation of the flue. Despite the noon sun outside, the shuttered windows kept the tavern in perpetual dusk. The ale in the tankard in front of him was sour and too infused with hops for Karl's taste. He longed for the malty, dark, and thick stouts and porters of home. Beyond the tankard, Mika looked frightened and worried, leaning forward to whisper harshly across the table.

"No? Did your dancing with the Archigos' new toy go so well? You mean to say that you don't foresee bodies hanging from gibbets here in Nessantico when the A'Kralj becomes the Kraljiki? Well, I do, Karl. I see them very clearly, and I see your face and mine on two of the bodies."

"This wasn't our fault. We both know that."

"Right. That will be a great comfort to my surviving relations, I'm sure. I'll make sure it's carved on my gravestone: *It wasn't his fault.*" With a disgusted growl, Mika sat back in his chair and downed his beer in one long gulp. "And you invited your toy to the meeting tonight?"

"Mika." Now Karl leaned forward over the scarred, grimy tabletop. "I'm going to ask you just once, politely, not to refer to O'Téni cu'Seranta that way. I won't ask you a second time."

Mike started to retort, then swallowed whatever he'd intended to say. His gaze drifted away from Karl. "I'm sorry," Mika said. "I'm terrified by what's happened, Karl. I have family here in the city; you don't. It's not just what they'd do to me; it's what would happen to them."

"That's why it's all the more important that we meet with O'Téni cu'Seranta. The Archigos isn't A'Téni ca'Cellibrecca, and maybe she can make the Archigos hear us. I came here to plead the case for tolerance with the Kraljica; if she's gone, then I'll go to Concénzia again and—"

Karl stopped. The door to the tavern opened, flooding the room with light. There were growls and curses from the patrons until the figure outlined there shut the door again. Karl had shaded his eyes, though it hadn't helped much: wild splotches of color chased each other over his field of vision, and he thought he saw, impossibly, a glint of metal in the middle of the man's face. Through the welter of afterimages, the figure looked around, then fixed on them, striding up to their table.

"Cénzi's balls," Mika cursed, his chair scraping and falling backward as he rose, his hand going to the knife on his belt. There was an answering ring of steel as the figure drew a sword from his scabbard. Even before Karl could react, Mika was pressed back to the wall with the point at his throat. In the attacker's other hand, a knife blade flashed, pointed at Karl.

The intruder's nose was silver.

Ca'Rudka clucked twice scoldingly at Karl, who started to speak as his hand lifted. "I really wouldn't do that," he said, and the point of his sword pressed harder against Mika's throat, dimpling the skin. Mika lifted his chin, his mouth open, his eyes wide and frightened. "He'll be dead before you can finish, Envoy. I'm faster than your spell, I promise you."

"Commandant," Karl said, swallowing the release word that was in his own throat and forcing himself to remain still. The point of ca'Rudka's knife gleamed a few inches from his chest; his sword remained at Mika's throat. The pressure of the unreleased spell made Karl grimace. His head pounded. "I apologize for my friend. Here in Oldtown, a little paranoia is a survival tactic, as I'm sure you realize." There was a commotion at the door; he heard several other people enter and the sound of their drawn weapons, but he didn't dare look away. He thought he glimpsed blue and gold in his peripheral vision. "Commandant?"

The tip of ca'Rudka's sword withdrew slightly, leaving behind a mark that drooled blood. Mika touched his fingertip to the tiny wound and looked at the smear of red, his eyes still saucered.

"Mika." Karl caught his friend's gaze and nodded his head toward the chair he'd overturned. "Sit down, and don't move your hands—either to your knife or to make a spell. Commandant, will you take a chair with us? Can I order you a pint of ale? The local brew isn't quite up to the Isle's standards, but . . ." Slowly, deliberately, Karl sat back down in his own chair. He put his hands on the table where ca'Rudka could see them.

He saw ca'Rudka's tight-lipped smile through his clearing vision. The commandant was still watching Mika, though now he lowered the knife that had threatened Karl. After a breath, the tip of his thin saber dropped and he sheathed both weapons. He waved to the men at the door—Garde Kralji—and they bowed and retreated, though they left the door open. No one in the tavern objected this time.

Ca'Rudka took a chair from the nearest table and turned it backward before he sat—Karl realized suddenly that it was a fighter's move: there was no back to block him if he decided to stand and retreat suddenly or to draw his sword again, and the chair itself would be easy to pick up as a defensive shield. Across the table, Mika sat gingerly, rubbing at the wound on his neck. "Too early in the day for ale," ca'Rudka answered easily, as if conversing with old friends. "It's not good for digestion."

"Nor would be sitting in a cell in the Bastida, I suspect," Karl answered. "Is that where I'm bound, Commandant?"

"Have you done something deserving of such punishment, Envoy?" Ca'Rudka folded his arms on the chair's back and leaned forward, the smile still playing on his lips. "Or perhaps you hired someone to do it for you?"

"I had nothing to do with the Kraljica's collapse, Commandant. Nothing. Nor did any Numetodo. This is not what any of us wanted. Quite the opposite."

Ca'Rudka stared at him for a breath, silent. At last, he gave a faint nod. "Yet the Archigos tells me that the Kraljica was attacked with a spell, Envoy, and not a spell like those the téni use. The rumors I hear of the Numetodo . . ."

". . . are much exaggerated," Karl told him. "You just saw that demonstrated a moment ago, Commandant. If we were as powerful as people seem to believe, we would have burned your body to a cinder in the instant you drew your sword or turned you into a clucking chicken. Or we'd have hidden our presence so well that you wouldn't have known where we sat drinking. Seeing that I could do none of those things, then I doubt that I have the ability to harm the Kraljica."

"This is my city, Envoy. It's my business to know certain people within it and where I might find them. But let's not be disingenuous. We both know that the Numetodo play with the Ilmodo, despite the interdiction against such meddling in the Divolonté. Or are you claiming that the Numetodo attack on the Archigos was just a parlor trick?"

"Everyone also saw how easily a mere acolyte turned that fool's spell, Commandant. If I'd used the Scáth Cumhacht at the Gschnas, I would have been seen and heard doing so and the Archigos or A'Téni ca'Cellibrecca or any of the other dozens of téni there would have noticed it, don't you think? And if we had the ability to plant a triggered spell that powerful, I assure you I wouldn't have made myself so visible in the crowd."

"No, I doubt you would have," ca'Rudka answered. "Which is why you're not headed for the Bastida already. But I think you understand why I would need to ask, and to watch your face as you answered." The smile tightened and faded. Karl could see his distorted reflection in the polished nostrils of the commandant's nose. "I consider myself a good judge of character, Envoy. I find that I like you. I do. You're unfortunate in your choice of companions—" that with a glance at Mika, "—and your loyalties are suspect, but I like you. I'd hate to see you, well, *suffer* for your choices."

"I would say we are in agreement with that final sentiment, Commandant. So how might I avoid that?"

Ca'Rudka's hand curled and lifted. Drifted down

again. "It may be that you can't, Envoy. So much is in flux at the moment. I'm only a tool in the hand of the Kraljica, after all—or the Kraljiki, should the A'Kralj take the throne—and I do what they ask me to do."

"Even if innocents are hurt."

The smile returned. "I find that, like those who give me my orders, I don't really care whether a few innocents suffer as long as Nessantico herself is protected."

"The way innocents were butchered in Brezno?" Mika interjected. "Did their blood and their torment protect Nessantico? Are the Holdings and Concénzia better for the display of their tortured bodies?"

Ca'Rudka didn't answer, only flicked his gaze over to Mika for a moment before returning his attention to Karl. "I would suggest, Envoy, that you leave Nessantico now. Your diplomatic mission is over at this point. Leave as soon as you can. Today." With an abrupt and lithe movement, ca'Rudka stood, one hand on the hilt of his sword.

"I can't," Karl told him. "I have my own orders that I have to fulfill. You can understand that, Commandant."

A nod. "I can. Then I've done all I can do for you, Envoy. I can't protect you. The rest is in the hands of Cénzi."

"That's something else we'll have to disagree upon," Karl answered.

This time, ca'Rudka's smile seemed almost genuine. He nodded again, deeper this time, and turned. He left the tavern, closing the door behind him. Slowly, as false darkness settled around the patrons once more, the sound of conversations swirled through the smoke-tinged air. "So the man with the silver nose rather likes you," Mika said. "How interesting."

Karl was still staring at the door. He could still feel the tension in his body, a vibration so strong that he wondered it wasn't audible. Mika rubbed at his wounded throat.

"Shut up, Mika," Karl said. "Or next time I'll just let him run you through."

~

Edouard ci'Recroix

EDOUARD SAT PERCHED on a rock on the banks of the A'Sele not far downriver from Pré a'Fleuve. *Leave Nessantico by the Avi a'Firenzcia,* his contact had told him. *But then follow the flow of the A'Sele. I will meet you on the day after Gschnas where we first met, on the river below the chateau, once we know that you've done your part.*

Edouard had followed the instructions, abandoning his horse at a small village, then stealing a small boat to take him down the River Vaghian to the A'Sele, where he traveled once more through Nessantico, passing under the Pontica Mordei and the Pontica Kralji in the night before leaving the walls behind for the last time.

Now he sat on the bank with his sketchbook open on his lap and a stick of charcoal in his hand. A dove sat on the branch of a willow bending to the water near him, and he quickly sketched the outlines of the bird and the tree. The drawing came easily—and as the charcoal flowed around the shadows of the bird, he closed his eyes, whispering the words that opened that place deep within himself, the place the old téni had shown him. . . .

"The Numetodo . . ." the ancient had told him, his voice blurred by the few teeth still left in his gums and the phlegm in his throat. But that face: Edouard had come across the man in a run-down inn far from any of the cities, and he'd been fascinated by the lines, by the great hooked nose and the complexity of the channels running from the corner of his eyes and his mouth, the strands of white hair wisping from the spotted scalp. There was great

beauty in the man's ugliness, and Edouard was striving to capture it in his painting. "They almost have it right. I discovered it myself. It's not faith in Cénzi that controls the Ilmodo. No . . ." The man had shaken his head. "I was once an o'téni. Did you know that? I was in the service of the temple in Chivasso, and I found out the truth of things before I'd even heard of the Numetodo." The man spit on the floor, a huge splotch of mucus that darkened the sawdust on the boards of the floor. He went silent then, for so long that Edouard had wondered whether he was asleep with his eyes open.

"What's this truth?" he'd asked the old man at last. "What happened?"

"There was a girl there," he said. "Arial, her name was. Just a ce', one of the servants there in the Temple. But she had a fair face and a full figure, and we became lovers. It was wrong, but we didn't care. I learned that her family was from Boail and—like them—she didn't believe in Cénzi at all. They worshiped some minor Moitidi, who they were convinced was the only god, She would watch me use the Ilmodo—it was my task to light the temple every night—and she'd ask me to show her how I did it. I told her what I'd always been told myself: that it was impossible, that to use the Ilmodo required much training and a deep faith, that it wasn't something that those not blessed by Cénzi could do, that the sorcerers and witches who claimed to be able to use magic were liars and abominations who had been seduced by the Moitidi who survived Cénzi's purge. She nodded and said she understood, but she was listening to me and watching me, and one night I saw her. She was using the Chant of Light, and there was cold fire between her hands as she spoke, and I knew then, even as I called for the a'téni, even as I betrayed her, that what I been taught was wrong. There were those who could shape the Ilmodo without believing in Cénzi, and that . . . that shook the very foundations of my faith and tore them down."

He went silent again for a time, then licked his lips

and began again. "They cut off her hands and took out her tongue as the Divolonté requires, so that she could never use the Ilmodo again. I watched as they tortured her, trying to convince myself that I'd done what Cénzi had wanted me to do, but my faith ... my faith was already shaken, already failing. But every night, I could still light the temple, even though the words to Cénzi meant nothing to me, even though I doubted my faith and my beliefs. I told myself that Cénzi was showing His mercy, that He wanted me to come back to Him and that was why I could still shape the Ilmodo, but my faith continued to fail, until I found I didn't believe at all. I left, finally, because I couldn't stand the hypocrisy and the lies I spoke every day. I left, and Cénzi has punished me ever since."

The man's voice was a bare whisper when he said that, and he glanced at the canvas before Edouard. "You've the Gift," the old man had said. He touched Edouard's head, then his hands. "You're using the Ilmodo even though you don't know it. It flows from you out onto the canvas. Not many can do that."

"Show me what you showed Arial," Edouard had said suddenly. "Show me the truth."

The ancient had protested and argued, but in the end he'd agreed. He'd taught Eduoard how to open the place inside so that he could feel the Ilmodo, and Edouard in turn had learned that his Gift was indeed special. The old téni was dead when Edouard left, but the painting, the old man's portrait ... It was the best painting he'd ever done. The face that stared out from the canvas was so genuine, so compelling ...

The old man was dead, but it was not the last time that Edouard would see him or hear him. Oh, no, not the last time at all.

Edouard let the Ilmodo flow uninterrupted: out from his fingers, through the charcoal stick to the paper, and from there radiating out to the bird. He could see the bird in his mind, snared in the radiance of the Ilmodo.

He could feel its heart fluttering and its shivering body, and he let that pass through him onto the paper.

He heard the soft fall of the bird onto the grass, and opened his eyes to see its perfect form captured on the paper.

"It's gorgeous, as I would expect." He heard the voice from behind him, the man's approach masked by the sound of the breezes in the willows and the rush of the A'Sele.

"Vajiki," Edouard said, placing the sketchpad on the grass next to the bird. "I was beginning to wonder if you would come."

"Exactly as promised," the man said. Edouard didn't know his name; he'd first approached Edouard when he was painting a commissioned portrait in a chateau near Prajnoli. Even his face was common and unremarkable, his hair a nondescript brown, though the eyes had irises of the most saturated grass-green. But the money he'd offered had staggered Edouard—enough that Edouard would never have to touch a brush again, not unless it was what he wanted.

Maybe then they'll leave me alone: the voices of those I've taken . . .

He hoped it would be true. They haunted him at night—the faces of those he'd painted, those he'd killed. They came in his nightmares, tormenting him. They were still alive, all of them, alive in his head.

He didn't know who the man worked for, nor how they had discovered the "gift" he bore—though he wondered if it weren't Chevaritt ca'Nephri, since it was his chateau that overlooked the river nearby. Whoever it was, Edouard didn't know how they'd arranged to have him paint the Kraljica. He knew very little beyond the fact that his purse was far heavier when the green-eyed man had left, and that it would be much heavier again today.

That was enough to know.

"You have my final payment?" he asked the man.

"The Kraljica's not dead," the man answered.

Edouard shook his head. "That's not possible. I finished the painting. I tied her spirit to it."

"She's been stricken, but she lingers," the man said. "That's not what you promised, Vajiki. It's not what was wanted by my employer."

Edouard was still shaking his head. There was no explanation for it, and he was frightened. Panic surged through him as he tried to fashion an excuse. "Sometimes . . . sometimes it takes a few days, Vajiki. Perhaps a week, even. But she *will* die; they always die." He licked his lips, staring at the man's eyes of spring grass and hoping he saw belief there. It wouldn't matter once he was paid. He could disappear forever then, and even if the Kraljica somehow lived . . . He forced his voice to sound angry. "You still owe me the solas you promised. Where are they?"

"I have them," the man said. "You're certain she'll die?"

Edouard poked the body of the bird with the toe of his boot. "Yes. I'm certain."

The man nodded, staring down at the bird and the sketch. "Then let's give you your reward. I have a horse right over here." He waved a hand toward a path leading to a stand of trees farther up the bank, and Edouard stooped to pick up his sketchbook. The man gestured again, and Edouard stepped in front of him.

Edouard heard the sound, but failed to understand its significance until it was too late. He had a moment to contemplate the strange feeling as the blade entered his body from behind and thrust entirely through him. Strangely, there was very little pain. He stood there, impaled, staring at the blood marbling the steel of the long blade that emerged from just under his rib cage. He tried to breathe, and coughed instead, and blood sprayed from his mouth. The blade was withdrawn in a sudden, ripping movement and he fell to his knees.

The world seemed to move as if underwater. He could

see the fluttering pages of his sketchbook as it fell from his hands. He could hear the birds in the trees and the crystalline water and even the hush of the clouds sliding across the sky. The colors were impossibly bright and unreal, as if painted with pigments mixed by Cénzi Himself.

The weapon sliced at him again, a blow to the side of the neck this time, and he toppled. He fell to the ground, eyes open, and the grass was an emerald like the man's eyes and a ruby river flowed between the blades. He could see the dove's body, only a stride away, and he reached out his hand to touch it, but his arm refused to move.

Something golden—a shell?—flashed in front of him, and he felt his head lifted and a cold chain placed around his ruined neck.

"Here's your reward, painter," the man's voice said, and there was laughter in the gathering darkness, the laughter of all those he'd painted, and their faces came to him and carried him far away as he tried in vain to scream.

~

Ana cu'Seranta

THE KRALJICA was a husk wrapped in white linen. For a moment, Ana wasn't certain she was breathing at all, but then her breath stuttered and the folds of the linen lifted with a breath. A sour odor hung in the air despite perfumed candles that provided the only light in the draped and shuttered room. Renard ushered them into the room, obviously weary from having stood vigil over the Kraljica during the night. A healer was there with his assortment of medicines and instruments, and a trio of servants were emptying bedpans, keeping the fire lit in the hearth, or changing the leeches placed on the Kraljica's body under the direction of the healer.

The Archigos ordered them all out of the room except Renard. As the servants slid away with low bows and the healer packed up his implements with obvious irritation, the Archigos placed a comforting hand on Renard's arm. "You've been up all night?" Renard nodded. "How is she?"

"No better," Renard said. "After you and O'Téni cu'Seranta visited her—" this with a swift, appreciative glance at Ana; she smiled in return despite her own weariness, "—she seemed to rally, but then slowly slipped back. I fear . . ." His lower lip trembled and he closed his mouth. He wiped at an eye with his sleeve. "I've served the Kraljica for nearly thirty years, since I was a young man myself."

"And you've served her well," the Archigos said. "You have been her crutch and her support, Renard. Don't give up hope yet. Cénzi may still hear our prayers."

Renard nodded, but Ana could see the despair etched in the lines of his face. "Leave us with her again," the Archigos said to him, "so that we might pray with her. In the meantime, get a bit of sleep. You'll be no good to her if you're exhausted."

"I will try," Renard said. He looked back at the bed and gave a long sigh before moving toward the door. As he came near Ana, he stopped for a moment. "Thank you for your efforts, O'Téni," he said quietly. "May Cénzi bless you."

He bowed and clasped his hands to his forehead. He left the room, leaving them alone with the Kraljica's erratic breath.

"He knows," Ana said.

"He's hardly a stupid man. And he loves the Kraljica." He was standing beside her and his fingers brushed her hand. She jerked her hand away. His eyes regarded her with what she thought might be pity, but he didn't touch her again. "He suspects, but he doesn't *know,* Ana," he said. "And he'll say nothing to anyone, no matter what the Divolonté states. Nor will I."

She wasn't certain that she believed this. She wasn't certain she trusted any of them. Ana could imagine the Archigos betraying her to save himself, and she rubbed her hands. *They would cut them off, and take your tongue as well. . . .* She shuddered.

"Ana . . . ? Are you all right?"

Ana blinked. The Archigos was staring at her. "I know you're tired, but this may be our last chance to save her," he said. His voice was rushed and quiet, and she realized that the Archigos was frightened himself—afraid of what might happen to him if the Kraljica died and the A'Kralj became Kraljiki. In that moment, she glimpsed how fragile was the Archigos' hold on his position in the church, and thus how precarious her own situation, tied to his standing, was in turn. The realization made her stomach turn uneasily.

She nodded to the Archigos and went to the side of the bed, looking down at the white, drawn face of the Kraljica: her cheeks sunken, her skin draped loosely over her skull. She looked half a corpse already. *She doesn't deserve this. If Cénzi gave you this ability, then He didn't intend for you to ignore it.*

Ana clasped hands to forehead for a moment, taking deep breaths. Then she opened her hands wide and let them move in the pattern she felt in her head, and she spoke the words that Cénzi sent her.

Eyes still closed, she shaped the power of the Ilmodo and let it rush into the Kraljica. Faintly, she heard a gasp from the old woman on the bed. "Ana . . ." she heard the woman say aloud, and the word echoed in her mind as well. *Ana . . . The painting calls me and I can't resist.* The stream of the Ilmodo cascaded from Ana into the Kraljica and back out through that terrible rent in the Kraljica's very being, the awful wound nearly as wide now as it was last night. Ana found herself in the Kraljica and in

the painting at the same time—the painting where most
of the Kraljica's awareness seemed to reside now. The
body on the bed was largely an empty shell.

Ana found herself marveling again at the spell that
had done this: no téni could enchant an object this way.
A téni could place a nonburning glow within a lamp
that would remain for several turns of the glass, but to
do so required the proper chanting and hand motions,
which must be performed at the time the spell was cast.
But there had been no one chanting to ensorcell the
painting—the spell had been cast with Ana's pull of
the cover: instantaneously, without words of prayer or
gestures.

Ana had no idea how that had been accomplished,
and it made her wonder again if ci'Recroix had been
Numetodo. The rumors she had heard about how they
twisted the Ilmodo . . .

But she couldn't think of that now. She could not
spare the distractions.

Ana reshaped the Ilmodo, wrapping it around the
Kraljica and trying to pull the woman back into her body
and away from the painting, but the spell within the painting resisted, tearing at the Ilmodo and shredding it so that
it couldn't hold the Kraljica. Where her spell touched that
within the painting, it was as if claws raked her body, dragging deep furrows that tore muscles and ripped ligaments
from bones. Ana screamed with the pain, not knowing if
she did so aloud. She could *feel* the spell, could glimpse
how it had been shaped and constructed . . . and there was
nothing of Cénzi in it: She could not feel Him in it at all.

The shell on its chain under her robes seemed to be
glowing white-hot, burning her skin.

Ana pulled at the Kraljica desperately, dragging the
old woman's awareness back toward her body as much
as she could and trying to close off that awful hole
within her once more. Slowly, it began to heal itself, but
the effort cost Ana. She screamed again, her body and
her mind aching from the exertion . . .

... and she could hold the Ilmodo no more. It slipped from her, and she was back in the Kraljica's room, on her knees on the carpeted floor, her body soaked in perspiration, the front of her téni-robes stained with vomit, her hands curled and as stiff as if she'd been outside unprotected for hours in winter.

"I tried..." she managed to husk out to the Archigos, who was kneeling alongside her. She looked at him, stricken. "I did all I could, and I almost... almost..."

And that was all she remembered for a time.

~

Mahri

THE ROOM WAS CHILLY even in the late afternoon sun, but Mahri hardly noticed. He was staring at a shallow, battered pan set on the wobbly table in front of him, in which he could see the distorted reflection of his own ravaged face. He heard the teapot over the fire in the hearth begin to sing, and he went to it. Wrapping the sleeve of his ragged clothing around the handle of the pot, he lifted it from the crane and poured the steaming water into the basin, then sprinkled leaves from a leather pouch on his belt into the water. He sat back.

"Show me," he said softly, and the steam above the basin writhed and twisted and coalesced. There, in the mist, was a shimmering image: the figure of the A'Kralj, his jutting chin unmistakable even if he hadn't been dressed in his usual finery, and seated across a small table from him, the Vajica Francesca ca'Cellibrecca. "A'Kralj," the woman said, a bit too loudly and forced, obviously for the benefit of someone else within earshot. "You do us a great honor by coming here, and I know my husband will be displeased that he missed you. We were both so shocked by your matarh's collapse at the Gschnas. How is she?"

"No better, I'm afraid, Vajica," Mahri heard the A'Kralj answer. His hand moved on the table, sliding a few inches toward the woman's. He glanced away to his right, as if looking at Mahri, and his eyebrows lifted slightly. The Vajica glanced that way also.

"Cassie, would you go to the kitchen and see if Falla still has those cakes from the morning? A'Kralj, some tea also perhaps? Cassie, have Falla make some new tea as well, and bring it here."

"Yes, Vajica," Mahri heard a faint voice answer, and there were footsteps and the sound of a door closing from the steam-wrapped scene before him. With the sound, the A'Kralj reached across the table to take the woman's hand. He started to rise, as if he were about to embrace and kiss her, but she shook her head slightly.

"Not here," she said in a whisper. "Too many eyes. But we can speak openly, for a moment anyway. The Kraljica?"

"She's dying," he said. "If I could keep that dwarf Archigos and that ugly cow of a téni of his away from her, she'd be dead already. I think he's using the Ilmodo on her, or cu'Seranta is."

"I'll make certain that my vatarh knows," the woman said. "I'm certain that he'd be interested in that." She shook her head. "Such a strange, sudden thing. Vatarh thinks that the Numetodo had a hand in it."

"No," the A'Kralj answered. "They didn't, though I certainly don't mind if they pay the price for it." He smiled, his chin jutting out even further. Mahri heard the slow intake of breath through the Vajica's nostrils and saw the rising of her eyebrows.

"Justi . . ."

The smile grew larger. "Matarh was always insisting that it was time for me to think of heirs and marriage. I will be Kraljiki soon—and I find that I'm now thinking of exactly those two things. Are you, Francesca my love?"

The woman seemed to be looking for escape—left, then right. "Of course, Justi. Of course. But this is so quick. All the careful plans we were making with my vatarh . . ."

". . . weren't necessary," he answered. "I made my own plans, and I have followed them through. I think Matarh's portrait should go in the West Hall, where she can see the Kralji's throne and see me sitting there with you beside me, don't you think?"

There was a soft knock at the door and the click of the latch. The A'Kralj sat back, releasing Francesca's hand. Her smile was a frozen gash on her face. "But, of course, I came to ask U'Téni Estraven if he would perform a special ceremony for Matarh," the A'Kralj said smoothly, as if continuing an interrupted conversation, as Mahri saw the servant approach the table and place a silver tray with tea and cakes between the two before curtsying and backing quickly away. "It would mean so much to her."

"Certainly," Francesca answered. She blinked, reflexively moving to serve him tea. "I will mention it to Estraven." The water in the basin was cooling, and the scene above it was fading, the figures going transparent and their voices failing. "I know he would be most willing . . ."

They were gone, suddenly, and the bowl was simply a bowl of lukewarm water. Mahri sighed. Rising, he put the teapot back on the crane. He picked up the bowl reverently and went to the window, tossing the water out onto the Oldtown alleyway below. He took the bowl back to the table and sat once again, waiting for the teapot to boil. When it did, he poured more water into the bowl and once more dusted the steaming water with the infusion from his pouch.

"Show me," he said again, and this time the scene that formed was a different place, and new figures appeared. . . .

~

Ana cu'Seranta

"YOU CAN'T GO OUT, O'Téni," Watha insisted. "You're not strong enough. The Archigos said you must rest. He was very emphatic about that."

"The Archigos isn't me and doesn't know how I feel," Ana insisted. She shrugged off the hands that attempted to hold her back on the bed and swung her feet down to the floor. She stood. The room threatened to tilt under her, but she took a long breath that stopped the movement. "I need clothes," she said. "Not my téni-robes. A tashta, perhaps, or something else."

Watha's eyes seemed about to burst from her skull. "I can't—"

"You will," Ana insisted. "And you'll do it now. I'll also need a carriage."

The young woman seemed terrified. Her matarh, Sunna, came in a moment later, and Ana repeated her request. Sunna conferred with Watha, who left the room with a terrified glance at Ana. Sunna muttered to herself as she rummaged—far too slowly—through trunks and closets to find clothing for Ana. Ana heard the outer door to her apartment open and close before Watha returned to help her matarh; Ana decided that Beida had been sent to inform the Archigos. By the time she'd dressed, the outer door opened again and Beida entered the bedchamber to announce that a carriage was at the door for Ana's use.

Ana left the apartment, refusing the offer of a quick dinner from Watha, and Sunna's insistence that someone from the household should accompany her. She wondered if she were being entirely foolish, since the walk down to the carriage exhausted her and she half-stumbled into the seat as the téni-driver held the door open for her. "Your destination, O'Téni?" the young man asked. It was the same driver who had picked her up from her house that day that seemed so long ago now; she knew that he would tell the Archigos everything. He was staring at her, at her lack of green robes.

"Cooper Street, one block from Oldtown Center," she said to him. He nodded and closed the door. She felt the carriage sway as he took his seat and heard the beginning of his chant as the wheels began to turn. She leaned back against the cushions, her hand touching the shell under her tashta.

You shouldn't be doing this. You're already exhausted and need to rest. The Archigos will be upset, and thus you risk not only yourself but your family's well-being. Worse, you endanger your very soul. . . .

She ignored the nagging voice and closed her eyes, feeling the lurch of the carriage and the sound of the wheels as it passed along the Avi a'Parete.

"We're here, O'Téni," the e'téni's voice said through the leather flap between the carriage and his seat, seemingly only a few moments later, and Ana realized that she'd fallen asleep during the trip. She lifted the curtain at the side of the carriage. They were parked on a street lined with shops, with a tumult of people moving around them. Poking her head out the window, Ana looked around. It was dusk, the sun already gone though the sky was still deep blue and the first stars had yet to appear. Farther up the street, she could glimpse the wide expanse of Oldtown Center, where lamps set on ornate posts around the circumference of the Center waited for the spells of the light-téni to set them ablaze.

Oldtown Center had, a few centuries ago, been the social nexus of Nessantico, a function now given over to the square around the Archigos' Temple and the newer and grander buildings on the southern bank of the A'Sele. The memory of Oldtown Center's past was preserved in the tall, ancient buildings that flanked it and in the fountain in the middle with its stained bronze statue of Selida II, posed far larger than life with his war-spear and shield and the writhing body of a subdued Magyarian chieftain raising his hands in mute supplication at his feet: at its height, Oldtown Center had been known as Victory Square.

Now, the buildings that had once housed the offices of the Kralji's government and the grand apartments of the wealthy were run-down, tired, and ancient. The offices were now street-level shops, the grand residences had been broken up into myriad tiny apartments above the shops teeming with the households of ci' and ce' and even unranked families. There was still a vitality to Oldtown Center, but it was unrefined and raw, just as strong as it had always been but gone darker and potentially more dangerous.

"O'Téni," the driver called through the flap, his voice audibly tired from the exertion of the drive. "Where did you want to go?"

"This is fine," she told him. She glanced out again at the signs over the doors. "Just there—Finson the Herbalist. They have a tea infusion that my matarh always made, and I thought it might help the Kraljica." She opened the door and stepped out before the driver could dismount. "Wait here for me," she told him. He was only a black silhouette against the ultramarine sky. "I shouldn't be long. Stay here."

She hurried away even as she heard him protest; she was fairly certain that his instructions from the Archigos were to remain with her. She rushed into the shop, a bell chiming as she opened the door. The herbalist—an older man with white eyebrows that curled over deep-set eyes, glanced up from a table near the rear of the store. The store smelled of herbs and the multitude of lit candles holding back the murk. "What can I do for you, Vajica?" he asked, coming forward to a counter adorned with glass jars stuffed with dried leaves.

Ana placed a siqil on the counter, the the silver profile of the Kraljica on the coin glimmering in the candlelight. "You have a rear door?" Ana asked, her fingers still on the coin.

He was staring at the siqil—more money than he would see in a week's sales. "Yes, Vajica. Just past there." He pointed to the darkness at the back of the store without taking his eyes from the coin. "Here, I'll show you. . . ."

Ana shook her head. "I'll find it," she said. "Thank you." She lifted her fingers from the coin and hurried around the counter. The smell of herbs was nearly over-powering, but she found the door and found herself in a narrow alleyway where the stench was more human and far less pleasant. To her right, an opening beckoned, leading to another of the warren of streets around the Center. Faintly, she thought she heard the bell chime on the herbalist's front door. She pulled the shell necklace from under her clothing and half-ran down the alley and out into the street, letting the rush of the crowds carry her. She circled around Oldtown Center for a time, moving around it and away from where she'd left the carriage—always looking around her to see if she saw the driver, avoiding the neighborhood utilinos with their staffs, lanterns, and whistles in case they'd been in-structed to watch for her—until she heard the chant of the light-téni at their work.

Then she walked into Oldtown Center itself.

The open space was busy, but quickly looking around, Ana saw no one who seemed to be searching for her. No one seemed to notice her at all. She wondered what the driver was doing; whether he was frantically looking for her or whether he'd returned to the Archigos with the admission that he'd lost his charge. In the sky above, the first stars were twinkling, and a group of six e'téni were moving slowly from lamp to lamp, each in turn erupting into cold, bright flame. The crowd—many of them in for-eign clothing—cheered with each lamp, giving the sign

of Cénzi and following the téni around the perimeter,
then to the quartet of lamps around the fountain.

As Ana lurked on the edge of the crowds well away
from the téni, she felt someone brush against her side.
"O'Téni cu'Seranta?"

She started, taking a quick step away from the man,
who raised his hands as if to show he had no weapon.
He was no one she knew, dressed in nondescript, plain
clothing. "Who are you?"

"My name is Mika," he said. "The rest of my name
you don't need. Envoy ci'Vliomani asked me to escort
you to where he's waiting. He said to tell you that the
shell is one from the Isle of Paeti, and that he hopes you
found it interesting. Will you follow me?"

He started to walk away from the fountain and the
crowds, to the west. He didn't look back. Ana watched
him for several strides, until there were several people
between them. Biting her lip between her teeth, she followed at last, quickening her steps and weaving among
the passersby until she was at his elbow. He didn't speak,
only moved out from the center into the narrow streets
leading away and into Oldtown itself. "Where are you
taking me?" she asked at last.

He shook his head without looking at her. "Nowhere
you would know," he answered. He stopped then, turning to her. "If that frightens you, then you're free to
return to Oldtown Center. I'm sure the téni would be
happy to escort you back to one of the temples. I told
Karl you wouldn't come."

"Then you were wrong."

He seemed amused at that. He shrugged and started
walking again.

They walked for some time, following streets that
twisted and turned until Ana was thoroughly lost. Twice,
he ushered her into the mouth of an alleyway or into the
shadows between two houses as an utilino passed. They
circled around a block where fire-téni were putting out a
smoldering house fire. For the most part, the people they

passed seemed to be intent on their own business, which in most cases was provided by the numerous taverns.

Oldtown was not an area she knew well; like most South Bank families, hers had rarely ventured over the ponticas to the North Bank except to visit Oldtown Center or the River Markets. Even when they had come here, they kept to the main streets on those excursions, never venturing too far away from the Avi a'Parete. By the time Mika stopped before a door with peeling strips of blue paint clinging stubbornly to the wood, Ana was no longer even certain which way the river lay, and full night had fallen heavily over the claustrophobic streets. Here, there were no bright téni-lights, only dim candles in windows punctuating the darkness—this seemed another city entirely. Mika rapped twice on the door, then a single sharp knock. A small peephole opened and Ana saw an eye peering out. The door opened just wide enough to admit them. Mika entered, and Ana—more hesitantly, with the opening words of a defensive chant on her lips and her hands ready to make the proper motions—followed.

She found herself in a dim foyer. Directly in front of her, steps led up to a second floor and a hallway led farther into the building; a curtained archway hid a room to the right. She could heard voices from somewhere close by. "Where is Envoy ci'Vliomani?" she demanded of Mika, but she was answered from the room to her right.

"Here." Karl ci'Vliomani moved the curtains aside and stepped from the room. He smiled and bowed to her, his hands remaining at his sides. "Thank you, Mika. We'll meet you upstairs," he said, and gestured to the room behind him. "Would you come in, O'Téni? It's hardly as grand as the Kraljica's Palais, but it will have to do." He smiled at her. "I'm pleased to see you again. Truly. That shell looks far better on you than it did on me." He smiled again; despite herself, Ana found herself returning the smile. The tension within her eased; she could feel her shoulders relax as she walked through the curtains he held aside for her.

"Water? Wine? Some cakes?" He gestured to a small table in the center of the room holding a refreshment tray.

Her stomach growled, but she shook her head. There were two windows, both heavily curtained. There was a fire in the hearth, but most of the light in the room came from a large glass ball that glowed a strange blue-white. Ana put her hands toward the globe: colder than the room by far. As cold as Ilmodo fire. "I want nothing right now, Vajiki," she said.

"Here, at least, you could call me Karl." He smiled again. "If you'd like."

She'd wondered whether she'd feel that strange pull again, that attraction. Now she knew that she did. *You can't trust that. You don't know him.* "Karl," she said, looking up from the frigid glow. "Then here, at least, you may call me Ana."

He bowed again. "I want to apologize for the subterfuge," he said as she glanced down once more at the light. "I assumed you wouldn't want the Archigos to know where you were tonight, and I know *I* certainly don't, especially after what's happened with the Kraljica. I can assure you that you weren't followed." She heard his voice change, his voice at once serious and sympathetic. "How is the Kraljica, Ana? We've heard nothing since the Gschnas but what the news-criers have said."

"I'm surprised you care." She placed a hand on the globe; the shadow of it covered the wall behind her. "For all I know, the Numetodo were responsible."

"If you truly thought we had anything to do with that, you wouldn't be here." The remonstrance was gentle. "We might be at odds with the Kraljica and Concénzia, but we would much rather have the Kraljica on the throne than her son."

"Is that why I'm here, then—you think I'll provide you with a sympathetic voice within the Faith? I'm afraid you overestimate my influence, Envoy."

"Karl," he corrected. "I think you're here because you're curious, and I asked you because . . ." He stopped. He walked to the globe, put his own hand on it, and shadows leaped. Ana removed her hand quickly. ". . . because I feel that we share a common interest."

"And what is that?"

"You want to understand how the world works, as do I." His hand slid caressingly over the round curve of the globe. "Like how one can use the Scáth Cumhacht, the Ilmodo, even in ways that your Divolonté says it shouldn't or even can't be used. You understand that, don't you?"

Ana felt her stomach lurch. She told herself it was the lateness, the exertions with the Kraljica, and the fact that she'd eaten nothing for some hours. He must have seen it also, for his hand was no longer on the globe but under her elbow, and his face was concerned. "O'Téni? Do you need to sit down?"

"I'm fine," she told him, forcing a smile. "Just tired. I've . . . had very little sleep in the last few days."

"I understand. The Kraljica." His hand had not left her arm, and she didn't want to pull away from his touch. "I was doubly sorry that happened as it did. I . . . I enjoyed talking with you, and our dance. And I would not wish the Kraljica harm." His hand did leave her then, and he frowned. "I apologize, Ana. I presume."

You don't need to apologize. I appreciate your concern, more than I should. But she didn't speak her thoughts. "What is it you wanted to show me, Karl? We don't have much time. The Archigos . . ."

"Will be frantically looking for you, no doubt." He nodded. "You're right. Come with me, then. We'll go upstairs to the hall. Things will have started by now."

The foyer was empty when he pushed aside the curtain, and she followed him up the stairs. The sound of talking grew louder, until she could make out individual voices in the mix. The stairs entered out onto a balcony that circled the floor below, lit brightly by the same cold light that had been in the globe downstairs. "Here, Ana,"

Karl said. He was standing at the railing to the balcony, behind a scrim of thin, dark fabric. "Those below can't see you if you stand behind this, but you'll be able to see them well enough." As she started forward, he raised a hand. "You understand the trust I'm showing you, Ana? You'll see the faces of the Numetodo who live in Nessantico, and that's knowledge that the Archigos, A'Téni ca'Cellibrecca, and Commandant ca'Rudka would find extremely interesting. You will literally hold these people's lives in your hands. I must have your promise now that you won't reveal what you see here."

"How do you know my promise is good?"

A momentary smile. "That's the same objection Mika gave me. I'll tell you what I told him: I look at you, and I know. Swear it," he said. "Swear it on Cénzi's name."

"I thought Numetodo didn't believe in Cénzi."

"I don't," he answered. "But you do."

You came here because you wanted to know. The knowledge is there, waiting. "I'll say nothing of what I see here," she told him. "On Cénzi's name, I give you my word."

He nodded. He beckoned her forward.

The room below was large and open. There were perhaps thirty people below, most of them seated before a small raised dais where Mika stood. She recognized none of them. "So few?" Ana whispered.

"You'd think from the threat that A'Téni ca'Cellibrecca says we are that there would be hundreds of us, wouldn't you?" Karl answered. "I wish that were the case. There are others who couldn't be here tonight, but not many. Not in Nessantico herself. Watch, though, and you'll see what the Numetodo can do."

"... tonight will be her first time," Mika was saying. "Her name within the group is Varina. Please make her feel welcome." There was a smattering of applause as a young woman came up on the stage. "Be kind, now," Mika said to the others as the girl stood there. "Go on, Varina. Demonstrate what you've learned to do."

Varina nodded. She took a long breath, closing her eyes. She began to chant: a phrase that wasn't in the Ilmodo language Ana had been taught, though it had affinities— the same cadences and guttural vowels, and she thought she recognized a word or two pronounced strangely. Still, these weren't the calls to Cénzi that were a part of every chant she'd been taught. Varina's hands moved with the chant, and Ana saw the beginnings of light forming around them. As Varina continued her chant, the glow strengthened until it was a fitful, small ball of light resting now on the upturned palm of her left hand. She ended the chant with a deep sigh. The ball of light sputtered and failed.

There was applause again from the onlookers. Varina nodded, then her eyes rolled backward in her head and she collapsed to the floor of the dais. She tried to stand again and failed. Mika gestured and two of the Numetodo came forward; they helped her to a chair. Another brought her water. Someone placed a dampened cloth over her forehead.

"You don't seem impressed, Ana," Karl said as Mika took the stage again.

"How long did it take her to learn that?" Ana asked.

"Mika started working with her around the time of the first winter snow," Karl answered. "It takes time."

"I could do that, and better, the first day U'Téni Dosteau began teaching us," Ana said. "So could nearly everyone in my class. Even in the Toustour there are stories of witches and sorcerers who could use the Ilmodo, however badly. The Moitidi, they are always trying to taunt Cénzi, to defy Him, and they allow the Ilmodo to be tainted despite Cénzi's wishes."

Karl was shaking his head. "Varina called on neither Cénzi, nor any of the Moitidi," he responded. "There are no gods or demigods involved at all. Only a certain set of words and hand motions: something anyone could be taught. But you're right—you téni do learn to shape the Ilmodo faster than us, and Varina has little skill as yet. But watch. Watch."

Mika was speaking again. "It's important that we understand the Scáth Cumhacht and how to contain and shape it," he was saying. "But as I've been telling you, it's also vital to learn how to store the power of the Scáth Cumhacht so it can be used quickly. That's where those of Concénzia are lacking." He glanced quickly at the scrim along the balcony, then back to the audience. "Look there," he said, pointing to an unlit lamp set on a table at the end of the room.

He spoke a single word and thrust his hand in the direction of the lamp. The word was concussive, as if someone had struck a great, invisible drum. Ana nearly jumped backward with the sound. No human voice alone could have made that sound. At the same moment, the lamp flared—as bright as that of the téni-lamps, though the color was greenish. The watchers applauded, but Mika raised his hand to quiet them. He spoke another drum-beat word and gestured again. The lamp flared once more, but this time not with light but enormous heat, as if a roaring furnace gaped there. The heat was intense, so much so that Ana brought an arm up to shield her face. She thought that in another moment, the walls and curtains around the room would erupt into flame. Mika spoke a final word, and the heat and light both vanished as if they had never been there.

There was no applause this time. There was only a relieved silence. "That," Mika said, "is what you need to learn. That is what we will teach you when you're ready."

Ana's hands were white-knuckled on the railing of the balcony. "He gave no chant, made no hand patterns, just a single word and gesture . . ." She looked down again at Mika. He was smiling and walking about the dais; the shaping of what he called the Scáth Cumhacht seemed to have affected him not at all. Ana looked back at Karl. "He's not tired from the spell-casting?"

"He performed the incantations hours beforehand, and then rested from his exertions." Karl told her.

"We're doing nothing different than what you téni do, Ana—handling the Ilmodo is a great effort and it costs the person who does it. But Mika made his payment several turns of the glass ago. He needed to speak only a release word for the energy he was holding. They don't teach you that in your classes, do they?"

"*You* can do that?"

Karl nodded. "I was <u>one</u> of those who taught Mika." He paused, tilting his head. "And I could teach you. Or does your Faith insist that such a thing can't be done?"

Ana stared down at the gathering, where Mika was talking to several of the Numetodo. The spells Mika had formed—they were nothing that she hadn't seen U'Téni Dosteau show the acolytes, that she couldn't do herself. She could do more, in fact—as she knew from her confrontation with her vatarh or the illusion she'd cast for the Kraljica—and the war-téni devised enormously destructive spells. But they all required time and effort; they all required the chants and the patterns of the hands; they all had to be cast immediately afterward, and they cost the shaper in weariness and pain. U'Téni Dosteau had been amazed by Ana's quickness at shaping the Ilmodo, the rapid casting of power that had protected the Archigos.

But this . . . A single word, a single gesture . . .

Not even the a'téni can do that, nor the war-téni. And if I did it, they would say it is the work of the Moitidi. They would take my hands and my tongue. . . .

"You téni shape the Ilmodo with your Faith," Karl was saying, but she had trouble concentrating on what he said. "I don't deny that. I don't deny that you of the Concénzia, especially the war-téni, can create spells more powerful than any Numetodo, but you've had long centuries to learn the ways of the Ilmodo. We learn more with each passing year. But I want you to think beyond just the shaping of the Ilmodo to the implications, Ana."

He glanced down at the shell around her neck, and

Ana put her hand over the ridged shape. "You explain the shapes of shells and fish in the stones in terms of the Toustour," Karl continued, "but we look for other explanations—explanations that can be proved or disproved through examination. I don't know for certain yet, but I suspect that we'll learn that the shells of the mountains were once indeed shells within the sea. The explanation makes at least as much sense as the creation story of the Toustour, and it doesn't require gods, only natural forces within the earth. And if the Scáth Cumhacht, your Ilmodo, can be reached and shaped by those without faith, if we Numetodo can even learn to do things that the téni can't do, then perhaps the Scáth Cumhacht also has nothing to do with faith and belief at all. You have to at least acknowledge the possibility, Ana. You've seen it here tonight with your own eyes."

Her hand tightened around the shell until she felt the edges press into her flesh. She shook her head in mute denial, but his words crashed and thundered inside her. *Not true, not true . . .* The denial shattered and reformed.

"Ana?"

She could barely breathe. The atmosphere seemed thick and heavy. "I have to leave," she said. "I have to go now."

His lips tightened. His face was grim. "Your promise, Ana?"

"I gave you my word, Envoy. I won't break it," she told him. "Now, please, I want to leave."

He nodded. "I'll escort you back to Oldtown Center," he said.

ENDINGS

Jan ca'Vörl
Ana cu'Seranta
Orlandi ca'Cellibrecca
Sergei ca'Rudka
Estraven ca'Cellibrecca
Ana cu'Seranta
Jan ca'Vörl
Karl ci'Vliomani

Jan ca'Vörl

"ALLESANDRA," JAN CALLED. "Come here to your vatarh."

The girl pulled away from the servant holding her hand and the knot of women around the Hïrzgin as they emerged from the Hïrzg's tent-palace. Her feet raised pouts of dust from the torn ground as she came up to Jan. Starkkapitän ca'Staunton, U'Teni cu'Kohnle, and Jan's aide Markell were standing with Jan in the slanted, foggy rays of early morning. They all smiled politely as the girl hugged him around the waist. "Good morning, Vatarh," she said. "It's a good day to move the army, I think."

Jan grinned and embraced his daughter tightly, allowing himself an additional taste of satisfaction at the sour look on his wife's face. He had told Greta the night before that they would not be going to Nessantico for the Jubilee, and her howls of outrage had kept many of the courtiers awake. Markell and cu'Kohnle nodded in satisfaction at seeing daughter and vatarh embrace, but Starkkapitän ca'Staunton's face mirrored that of the Hïrzgin. "You see," he told ca'Staunton, "my daughter has a fine military mind. All I get from you, Starkkapitän, are excuses. *She*, at least, isn't afraid to advance."

"My Hïrzg," ca'Staunton said, a trace of careful arrogance in his voice, "it's not fear. Any of the chevarittai, the offiziers, or our soldiers would lay down their lives for you—and many have, for you or for Hïrzg Karin before you. But to move toward Nessantico's borders

during the Kraljica's Jubilee, even as an exercise . . ."
Shoulders lifted under the sash of his rank. Medals
clashed. "We risk misinterpretation. As I've said, if we
marched instead toward Tennshah, the Kraljica could
protest not at all, and the longer march would provide
ample opportunities for formation exercises, especially
once we reached the eastern plains."

Jan glanced at the Hïrzgin again, who had paused with
her entourage carefully out of earshot. He watched her
face as she chatted with her attendants, though his attention now drifted toward Mara, standing beside the
Hïrzgin. He'd spent most of the night with her after the
Hïrzgin's outburst had finally faded. Mara's face was
turned slightly toward the Hïrzg rather than to the Hïrzgin, and she nodded to him.

"Have we not always been the mighty sword in
the hand of Nessantico, the spear that the Kralji send
against their enemies?" Markell was asking Starkkapitän ca'Staunton. "Don't we have the need—nay, the
obligation—to exercise that arm, lest it become weak
and slow? U'Téni cu'Kohnle—" Markell pointed to the
war-téni "—was instrumental in the success of A'Téni
ca'Cellibrecca against the Numetodo in Brezno. He understands what is at stake. I begin to wonder who you
serve first, Starkkapitän: the Kraljica or our Hïrzg."

Starkkapitän ca'Staunton glared at Markell. "I serve the
Hïrzg, of course," he snapped. "But I still say that moving
the army so close to Nessantico's border is an unnecessary
provocation when we could as easily turn east."

"Starkkapitän," Allesandra said, "aren't you the
Hïrzg's strong right arm?"

Ca'Staunton appeared startled, though whether it
was at the question itself or from being addressed so
presumptuously by an adolescent, Jan could not tell.
"Indeed, I suppose that is what I—and our army—
represent, A'Hïrzg Allesandra," the starkkapitän replied, a bit stiffly and with a glance at Jan, as if looking
for his approval.

"If my right arm refused to obey me, I would chop it off myself," Allesandra told him. She smiled innocently as she said it. "What good is an arm that thinks it owns the body?"

Jan broke into laughter at that, with Markell and cu'Kohnle following a moment later. The starkkapitän's face flushed, and his mouth opened silently. "There, you see, Starkkapitän?" Jan said. "We have wisdom from the young A'Hïrzg. Maybe I will make her Starkkapitän—what do you think?"

The man's cheeks were as ruddy as if the winter wind had scrubbed them raw, and his mouth had tightened into a thin line. He bowed his head to Jan. "The Hïrzg may certainly do as he wishes," ca'Staunton answered. His hands were clenched at his sides, and his medals rang with his movement. "I have served you, the late A'Hïrzg Ludwig, and your vatarh all my life. If that no longer means anything to you, my Hïrzg . . ."

"Look at me, Starkkapitän," Jan interrupted, and ca'Staunton's eyes came up. "I am grateful for your long service, and you have proven your worth a dozen times over during your career. That is why I have listened to you at all this morning, and that is why I tell you now that we *will* take the army west."

"Then I will inform the a'offiziers," ca'Staunton said. There was still fury in his gaze, but it was banked now. He bowed again, to Jan, to Markell, and to Allesandra, then turned to leave.

"Starkkapitän," Jan called to him, and ca'Staunton turned back. "Prepare them as if we were truly going into battle. I want them as ready as they were when we fought in Tennshah."

The man's eyes widened then, and Jan saw the realization there. "Yes, my Hïrzg. They'll be ready."

"Good. Then go, and make preparations. I expect us to be on the move by Second Call."

Another bow, and ca'Staunton strode quickly away. "And I will inform the war-téni," cu'Kohnle said. His eyes narrowed. "If I may say, my Hïrzg, I look forward to this. Cénzi will bless you." He made his bow and followed ca'Staunton.

"Can I ride with you, too, Vatarh?" Allesandra asked, tugging at his bashta. "I can ride very well now."

"I'm afraid not," he told her. "You'll be going back to Brezno with the Hïrzgin."

"Vatarh!" Allesandra stamped her foot, though the grass rendered the protest silent. "If I'm going to lead the army one day, I need to learn."

"And you will," Jan told her, tousling her hair affectionately. "But not today. Not yet. I want you in Brezno, and I want you to write to me every day. Tell me what the Hïrzgin is doing and who's she talking to. That's your job."

"Isn't that what Mara does for you?" Allesandra asked, and Jan laughed again as Markell grinned.

"I need your eyes there," he told her, not answering her question. "Remember, I want to hear from you each and every day. Markell will tell you how to send me private messages before you leave today. Now—what I need you to do is go back to your matarh. Don't tell her anything we've talked about. Not yet; I will tell her myself in a few minutes, after I finish talking with Markell. Go on now."

"I don't want to," she said. "I want to stay here with you. I want to listen."

"Allesandra, you are my heart," Jan said to her. "Just like Starkkapitän ca'Staunton is my right arm. And I don't want to have to rip out my own heart because it won't obey me."

"That's not fair, Vatarh." She pouted dramatically

"No, it's not," he said, smiling. "But it's still necessary. Go on, now. Be the A'Hïrzg, not my daughter."

Allesandra sighed loudly, then finally stood on her toes as Jan bent down to give her a kiss. "I'll write every day," she whispered to him, hugging him with her arms around his neck. "And I'll tell you everything." With that, she released him and ran back to the knot of women near the tents.

"My Hïrzg?" Markell said. "Should I send a message to A'Téni ca'Cellibrecca, to make him aware of your intentions?"

Jan watched Mara bend down to take Allesandra in her arms; she smiled over the little girl's shoulder to Jan. The Hïrzgin's mouth tightened so that even from this distance, Jan could see the lines folding in her plain, flattened face. "Yes," Jan said to Markell. "Tell the a'téni that it's time for him to make his choice: either for me, or for the A'Kralj. Tell him he can no longer play both sides. He must make his choice now. Tell him that I hear his daughter will be looking for a new husband soon, and that I'll be looking for a wife." Jan clapped Markell on the shoulder. "When we reach the border, Markell, the Kraljica will realize that the might of the Holdings is Firenzcia. She will negotiate, as she always has, rather than risk war—and the terms will make me the A'Kralj, not her son. From what I've heard, that may even please her. And if not . . ." He shrugged. "Then may Cénzi have mercy on her in the afterlife."

~

Ana cu'Seranta

SHE HAD EXPECTED that the Archigos would be waiting at her apartments when she returned from Oldtown. He was not. There was, in fact, only silence from him the next day, a day in which she performed her duties in the Archigos' Temple without seeing him, a day in which the Kraljica lingered—according to all the rumors—on the edge of death, a day in which she found that she could not stop thinking of what she had seen. The Numetodo haunted her dreams and skulked like shadows in her waking thoughts.

She'd returned changed, and she knew it. She wondered how everyone else could not see it as well.

On the morning of the following day, a note came from the Archigos: he would meet her at the Kraljica's Palais immediately. The carriage was already waiting for her; the Archigos was not in it, but the driver was the same e'téni who had taken her to Oldtown. He glared at her accusingly as he opened the carriage door.

At the palace, Renard was waiting to escort her to the Kraljica's chambers. "How is she?" Ana whispered as they walked. The mood in the palais was somber; the servants Ana glimpsed hurried about their tasks, silent and frowning. Renard shook his head.

"I pray, O'Téni, as does the Archigos, but I fear that Cénzi calls her too strongly."

The hall servants opened the door to the Kraljica's chambers as they approached. "The Archigos said for you to go in directly to her bedroom. I'll wait here," Renard said. Ana nodded, and the old man took her hands before she could move away. "If you can help," he said, "the healers with their potions and leeches have been able to do nothing, but you . . . you were able to keep her alive. I know that it is what she would want, and Cénzi will forgive you."

He released her hands and turned away before she could respond, leaving Ana alone. The Archigos' voice called to her from the bedroom. "Ana? Come here . . ."

The bedroom looked the same as she'd last seen it, all but the Kraljica. Her face was a pale skull draped with parchment above the covers, strands of white hair clinging to it stubbornly. She looked already dead, her eyes and cheeks sunken.

"She's nearly gone," the Archigos said. He was seated alongside the bed, looking like a wizened child in the tall chair with his legs dangling below the robes of his office, clad in white stockings and slippers. She looked for accusation in his face and saw nothing there but grief.

"I'm sorry, Archigos." She came to the other side of the bed and looked down at the Kraljica. "I can't help her. Not anymore."

"Try," he said. The single word was an order. The deep sadness in his face had been erased. He looked across the bed to Ana, his eyebrows raised angrily.

"Archigos, I *have* tried. You know that. And the Divolonté . . ."

He cut her off, lifting himself nearly off the seat with his hands. "You will try again," he repeated. "I brought you into the Faith from obscurity; I have raised you up. I've protected you. I have given you and your family all that they have. I know where you went the other night and I've said nothing. I've protected you from enemies you don't even know you have, Ana. You *will* try." She started to protest, but his voice softened. "The Kraljica has been my support and my dearest friend for decades, and that she's stricken is not Cénzi's plan but someone else's. I know what I ask of you, and I know the Divolonté. Try. One more time."

The Kraljica's mouth opened slightly in a sour breath. Ana nodded. "I'll try," she told the Archigos. She closed her eyes, drawing in a long, calming breath, trying not to think of the exhaustion and pain that were going to follow.

The words of the chant sounded false in her ears. She kept thinking of what she'd seen with the Numetodo. *"Perhaps the Ilmodo also has nothing to do with faith and belief at all . . ."* She called to Cénzi . . . but there was no answer. Not this time. The words were empty and her hands swept only through air, not into the cold, unseen stream of the Ilmodo. Frightened, she opened her eyes to see the Archigos watching her. He seemed not to notice that her spell was vacant, his face expectant and hopeful.

Cénzi, what have I done? Have You abandoned me?

She stopped chanting. She let her hands fall to her side. "Archigos," she said. "I'm sorry. I can do nothing for her."

He nodded as if it was what he'd expected to hear, and Ana realized that he misunderstood her, that he believed she had already tried and failed. She started to tell him the truth but could not think of a way to do that without betraying her promise to Karl. *I saw another side of the Ilmodo, and Cénzi has taken away my Gift because I doubted.* The Archigos would take away her Marque and send her away. He would demand that Vatarh return the solas he'd been given in payment for her service. Her family would be disgraced and she would be the cause of it all.

The Kraljica would die, and she would bear the blame.

"Thank you for the effort, Ana," the Archigos was saying. "I knew it was her time, but I didn't want . . ." He stopped. She saw the grief wash again over his face as he looked down at the Kraljica. "Stay here with me. Pray with me."

Ana nodded. She brought a chair over to the side of the bed and sat across from him. His eyes were closed and his lips were moving. A faint glow emanated from his hands; he was calling the Ilmodo reflexively, unconsciously. Ana found herself mute. She watched the Archigos, but she could not bring herself to pray. Her thoughts were chaotic: a nightmare mix of fright at what would happen to her, of images from the Numetodo's heretical use of the Ilmodo, of what she'd been taught of téni who had lost their faith and found themselves punished by Cénzi, never to be able to use the Ilmodo again.

"Archigos," she said softly, almost a whisper. "Let me try again, one more time . . ." The dwarf's eyes opened, the glow faded from his hands. He nodded to her, silently.

Please, Cénzi. I shouldn't have doubted You . . . She began the chant again, trying to open the way to Cénzi and the Second World. There was no immediate response, no sense of the cold power of the Ilmodo, and she thought that once more she'd failed. She continued to chant the words, to move her hands, as if by sheer determination she could wrench open a path . . . and she began to feel the Ilmodo close to her once more, and she took the power and shaped it, moving its frigid waves over the comatose Kraljica.

Again she felt the emptiness there, how the frayed thread of life in her body led irrevocably back to the painting elsewhere in the palais. She wrapped the Ilmodo around that thread, began to tug at it delicately. Slowly, slowly, she started to pull the Kraljica back once more. Ana nearly sobbed with the relief and effort. *Thank you, Cénzi. Thank you* . . .

She could do this, she could bring the Kraljica back yet again even if she could not fully heal her. She could—

—but a strange nausea passed over Ana, a sudden disorientation. It was as if someone had shaken the world. For a moment she thought that it was the tremor of an earthquake . . . and she realized that the thread holding the Kraljica to her body was—impossibly—broken.

"No!" Ana screamed. The spell dissolved, the Second World vanished, the Ilmodo fled from her.

The Kraljica's mouth was open, but her chest was still. Her hair, only a few seconds ago brushed and arranged, was mussed, as if in her last moment she had thrashed and struggled. The Archigos stood, and Renard, from his station along the wall, called through the door for the healer, in a choked voice. The healer entered, glanced at the body and held a silvered glass to the Kraljica's nostrils.

He shook his head.

The Archigos began the prayer of the dead as Renard sobbed, and the servants fled the room. Ana sobbed with him, and wondered whether she was weeping for the Kraljica or because Cénzi had snatched her away from Ana, as if in punishment.

Before the Archigos had finished his prayer, the wind-horns in the temples began to call throughout the city.

~

Orlandi ca'Cellibrecca

ORLANDI FELT PHYSICALLY ILL, as he had since he'd deciphered the message from the Hïrzg. *The ground trembles under the feet of soldiers, the Hïrzg would have a new wife, and the Kraljica will submit. The time has come. Choose.*

Everything had gone utterly wrong since the Gschnas. Orlandi had anticipated playing the Hïrzg against the A'Kralj for several months yet, time in which he could gauge which one would ultimately make the best ally. But now ... the Hïrzg, ever impetuous and dangerous, was forcing his hand. He'd underestimated both men and their willingness to follow a slower, more circumspect path. The Hïrzg was pushing his army forward in blatant threat, and if Francesca's suspicion was true, then the A'Kralj had been the one responsible for the Kraljica's death.

The A'Kralj a matricide: unfortunately, such abominations were hardly unknown in the lineage of the Kralji.

But the Kraljica *was* dead and the A'Kralj *would* be crowned Kraljiki, and Justi had already informed Orlandi that he wished Francesca as his bride. The Hïrzg was as yet unaware of the Kraljica's death, and Orlandi must be the one to tell him before the news reached him some other way, or the Hïrzg would perceive that Orlandi had already made his choice. When the Hïrzg received that confirmation, Orlandi was certain the Hïrzg would not hesitate at all.

He would send the army forward over the border, hoping to take the Sun Throne himself.

That was the most frightening thought of all. Orlandi had thought of himself as the master, moving the pieces in the game, but the pieces had asserted their own wills.

Choose. You must choose.

The Archigos had given Orlandi an office in the Temple so that he wouldn't need to return to Ile Verte in the wake of the Kraljica's sudden illness. Orlandi went to his knees on the carpet, groaning with the effort as his joints protested, bending over until he huddled there with his back bowed, his forehead on the woolen nap. He prayed, as if he were a simple e'téni in the service of the temple. *Cénzi, I beg You to help me now. Show me Your will. Tell me how I can accomplish Your work . . .* He prayed, not knowing how long he stayed there, reciting from the praise-poems he loved so much in the Toustour. *It is Your task that I do here. Not mine. Guide me, for I am too blind and too confused to see the way. . . .*

After a time, he rose slowly, sore and stiff. He wiped at his eyes. He'd heard no clear answer to his prayers, but he knew one thing: whether the A'Kralj or the Hïrzg eventually sat on the throne, that person would need a proper wife who gave them a political tie they could use: And Orlandi could—he must—provide that.

Orlandi went to the door and spoke to the e'téni stationed there. "Find someone to fetch the courier from Firenzcia and send him to me; I have a note for him to deliver to the Hïrzg. Then go yourself to U'Téni Estraven ca'Cellibrecca at the Old Temple—inform him that he is to come here immediately. Do you understand?" The e'téni—a young woman who looked to be no more than sixteen and fresh from her studies as an acolyte—nodded with wide eyes. She hesitated, and he waved an impatient hand at her. "Go," he said, and she fled, without even giving him the sign of Cénzi.

Orlandi returned to his desk, pulling the cipher disk from a pocket in his vestments. He took a piece of vellum from the drawer and unstoppered the inkwell. He wrote slowly and carefully, dusting the manuscript with sand and blowing it off before folding it. He took a candle and a stick of red wax and sealed the letter, pressing his ring into a cooling pool of wax the size of a bronze folia. He put the letter in an envelope, addressed it to the Hïrzg, and also sealed that.

By the time he'd finished, the rider had arrived. He handed the man the envelope. "The Hïrzg *must* have this in his hand in two days," he told the man. "It's vital and I don't care how many horses you have to kill to get it to him. Do you understand me?" The rider nodded. Estraven was outside as Orlandi opened the door to usher out the courier.

"A'Téni," Estraven said, bowing and giving the sign of Cénzi as the courier hurried away. "You asked for me?"

"I did," Orlandi told him. "Come in. Sit, Estraven. There's wine and water on the desk; please, refresh yourself."

He watched while Estraven poured himself a glass of wine. "Sorry it took so long to get here, A'Téni; when your e'téni came to tell me, I was just finishing the Second Call passages for the celebrants, and I had to speak to the choirmaster regarding the evening services and the ceremony for the Kraljica. I came as soon as I could."

Orlandi waved his hand. "The needs of the Faith come first," he said. "In a sense, that's why I've sent for you. I need you—because I can trust you to keep the Faith's business private."

His marriage-son's face took on a faint blush of pride. "Indeed you can, A'Téni. What do you need of me?"

"I want you to go to Brezno, Estraven," he said. "Quickly. I want you to leave tomorrow morning."

Estraven's smile collapsed. The wine shuddered in his glass. "To Brezno? With the Kraljica's funeral in a week?

I thought you had left U'Téni cu'Kohnle in charge of Brezno and Firenzcia. A'Téni, what of my charge here?—all the services, my obligations . . . I couldn't possibly . . ."

"You can. You will," Orlandi said firmly, and that closed Estraven's mouth. "I will make arrangements for your obligations to be covered. U'Téni cu'Kohnle is with the Hïrzg and away from Brezno, and I need someone in that city for the next month or two. I need you there soon, *especially* with the loss of the Kraljica. I can't leave Nessantico myself, not with the funeral."

"What . . ." Estraven stopped, licking his lips. He took a sip of the wine. He seemed to be recovering himself. "This is all so sudden. I'm sorry, A'Téni, if I seemed flustered, but this comes so unexpectedly. Certainly, I'll do whatever you ask, as I always have. What do you require me to do in Brezno?"

"I will send you written instructions this afternoon, Estraven, for you to open once you reach the temple in Brezno. I will also send word to U'Téni cu'Kohnle about your temporary assignment. In the meantime, I want you to get yourself ready to leave at daybreak."

Estraven set the wine down, rising. "I'll begin, then," he said. He tapped his clean-shaven chin with a finger. "I should send word to Francesca that we'll be leaving—or have you done that already, A'Téni? She'll need to get the household together."

"Francesca will be staying here," Orlandi told him, and he enjoyed the blink that Estraven gave in response. "You'll be traveling with Vajiki Carlo cu'Belli and those in his employ. He's a trader who travels frequently through the Holdings, and he has served me as well for the last several years. I will send along two of the téni from my own staff to act as your aides and coordinate things for you once you reach Brezno; your personal staff should remain here since they know the routines for the Old Temple. Vajiki cu'Belli has been an associate of mine for some time, and I have every confidence in him, despite what you'll find are his some-what coarse ways. His loyalty is unquestioned."

"Of course, A'Téni. Is there more I should know?"

"Not now," Orlandi told him. He came over to him, taking the man's hands in his own and patting them. "Estraven, I'm giving you this task because I know how committed you are to the Faith, and how well you've always served me. I rewarded you with Francesca's hand because of your faith. Now I ask you to trust me once again."

"Of course, A'Téni." The bravado was back in Estraven's voice, his ego adequately stroked. "I won't fail you."

"I know you won't," Orlandi answered. He released Estraven's hands and went to one of the windows, pulling aside the curtain to look down at the temple square. "Now, you should go. You don't have much time."

Orlandi didn't bother to watch Estraven's bow. He'd send word immediately to cu'Belli and let the man know what needed to be done. And he would have a late dinner with Francesca, alone, so they could talk.

Choose. He would choose. He must. But he would delay the choice until he could be certain which of the two major pieces on the board were the stronger: the A'Kralj or the Hïrzg.

He wondered how Francesca would react to the news.

~

Sergei ca'Rudka

"COMMANDANT, the body is over here."

Sergei walked over to where a man gestured. His companion, O'Offizier ce'Falla, offered a silken handkerchief soaked in perfume, but Sergei waved it away. He walked through the high meadow grass to the bank of the A'Sele. He could see the body, like a black hummock in the grass, a few strides from the sullen green currents of the river. The scent of corruption already hung around the corpse, and black flies lifted in shrill irritation as he approached. A quartet of peasants stood close by, looking uneasy and half-frightened. Sergei smiled at them, though he could see them staring at his face. At the gleam of his nose.

"You did as you should, and I am here to give you the Kraljica's thanks," he told them. They ducked their heads at that and gave the sign of Cénzi. "You will each also be given a half-siqil reward. The o'offizier will take care of that . . ." He nodded to ce'Falla, who quickly ushered the now-smiling peasants aside as Sergei crouched down next to the body.

The corpse lay faceup on the ground. The scavengers had been at it, but even though the face was nearly gone, Sergei knew from the black clothing and the lanky body that it was ci'Recroix, even if the dew-ruined sketchbook a few feet away weren't already a mute witness. "Did the peasants steal anything, Vajiki?" Sergei asked the man who had remained behind: Remy ce'Nimoni, a retainer employed by Chevaritt Bella ca'Nephri, who owned the chateau and the land on which it resided, and who was, as Sergei knew, also one of the A'Kralj's good companions.

Sergei had found that he instinctively didn't care for ce'Nimoni. There was an air of smugness about him, and he'd caught the man smiling strangely as they conversed on the way from the chateau to where the body had been found. Nor did the retainer's startlingly green eyes want to rest on Sergei's face. His answers to Sergei's questions had been too quick and too pat, as if he'd given every possibility too much thought, or someone had coached him well.

That suspicion was not a path Sergei cared to tread. Chevaritt ca'Nephri was far too close to the A'Kralj for that to be comfortable.

"Steal anything? I don't think so, Commandant,"

ce'Nimoni answered now. "They saw the body and the blood, and with the dark clothing they were afraid it was a sorcerer or worse, and they came running back to the chateau. I searched all of them afterward and found nothing. Then I placed guards here until you could be summoned—they kept away most of the beasts, but . . ." He waved a hand at the corpse, and again there was that odd flash of a smile and his glance at the body was almost possessive. "Not all, as you can see. The dogs and wolves are less afraid of a dead body than us, and very persistent."

"Wild beasts know an opportunity when they see it," Sergei answered. "If you'll excuse me, Vajiki, I would like to examine the body. Alone."

Ce'Nimoni bowed. "As you wish, Commandant. I'll be at the trail with the horses."

Sergei leaned closer to the body as the man strode away. His flesh wrinkled above the bridge of his false nose at the smell, but the stench was no worse than the lower cells of the Bastida, where sewage and corruption mingled with the odor of chained, desperate men. He could see blood crusted on the man's blouse, though the animals had chewed away most of the stained cloth and ripped open the stomach to get to the man's entrails—it would be difficult to determine whether ci'Recroix had been wounded there first. The cut at the neck, though . . . even with the animal gnawings and the maggots wriggling deep in the wound, it was apparent that a blade had made that cut.

So the man had been murdered. Sergei had expected that to be the case as soon as news had come of the body found near Pré a'Fleuve. Disappointing: Sergei would have liked the opportunity to find out what ci'Recroix knew: the slow, careful, and painful interrogations that the Bastida could provide. Sergei was certain that the person who had hired ci'Recroix had been afraid of exactly that.

He hadn't yet touched the body. A chain glittered

dully around the torn neck; Sergei leaned closer. His gloved fingers brushed aside the ripped cloak. A pendant hung on the man's chest: a dark seashell, a shell carved of stone.

He wondered only for a second before the answer of where he'd seen a similar pendant came to him. He reached down and pulled the pendant away; the fine chain broke against the weight of the skull. Sergei grimaced and placed the shell in his pocket.

"How very clumsy, Vajiki ci'Recroix," he told the corpse. "Could a man of your great talent truly be that stupid?"

As if in answer, a beetle clambered from the corpse's open mouth. Sergei smiled grimly.

Moving away from the body, he stooped to pick up the sketchbook, glancing at a few of the pages, and staring at the final sketch there—a bird drawn in charcoal that looked as if it were solid enough to fly away from the page—before closing it. He put the sketchbook under an arm. Standing, he stared down at the body again for several breaths. Finally, he gave the sign of Cénzi over the remains, then went up from the bank to the narrow lane that led to the chateau. The retainer ce'Nimoni waited there with ce'Falla, as well as Sergei's gray stallion and their own horses; the peasants were gone.

"We're done here, O'Offizier," he said to ce'Falla. He put the sketchbook into a pouch of his saddle. "We'll ride now. I have work to do back in Nessantico."

Ce'Nimoni frowned, brows lowering over meadow-bright eyes. "Commandant, the body . . .?"

"Bury it, burn it, let it rot—whatever Chevaritt ca'Nephri bids you to do with it. I don't care. I've learned all I can from it." With that, Sergei hoisted himself astride the gray, who nickered nervously and flared his nostrils as if the smell on Sergei's clothes bothered him. Sergei pulled at the reins and leaned forward to pat the gray's neck to calm him. "You did well," he told ce'Nimoni. "When the Gardes a'Liste looks at the Roll of names

next, I know they will consider your service here. I will
convey your cooperation and your quick intervention
here to Chevaritt ca'Nephri, and the Kraljiki."

The retainer bowed and clasped hands to forehead.
Again, Sergei caught a glimpse of that self-satisfied grin
on the man's face. *And I may yet see if I can find an excuse to give you a tour of the Bastida,* he added silently.

Then he gestured to O'Offizier ce'Falla, and they rode
east and north toward Nessantico.

~

Estraven ca'Cellibrecca

"CU'BELLI! Where are you?"
There was no answer. Estraven stared at the
trio of gray, lichen-spotted plinths leaning against each
other a stone's throw from the Avi a'Firenzcia, the road
bordering the River Clario. In the misting drizzle, they
appeared particularly dark and foreboding, as if they'd
been set down by the Moitidi's children in the First Age.
"Cénzi's piss," Estraven muttered and slapped the reins
of his horse, then quickly gave the sign of Cénzi and whispered a quick prayer for forgiveness at his blasphemy.
His horse shook its soggy mane and nickered, the ears
flicking as if it had heard something. Estraven shifted
anxiously in his saddle. "Cu'Belli!" he called again.

Their little troupe—Estraven, the trader cu'Belli, two
e'téni from A'Téni ca'Cellibrecca's staff, and four men
whose job it was to handle the pack animals cu'Belli
brought with him—had crossed the border yesterday
into Firenzcia, passing through the guard station set up
across the Avi at the border town of Ville Colhelm. They
were three days from Nessantico, and Estraven was
regretting ever having agreed to his marriage-vatarh's

request. At the least, A'Téni ca'Cellibrecca could have allowed him to bring his own staff, but the A'Téni had insisted that they remain behind at the temple on the Isle A'Kralji so they could attend to the Kraljica's funeral ceremonies.

"When you get to Brezno, my own people will be waiting for you," ca'Cellibrecca had said. "As I told you, cu'Belli is a crude man in many ways, but he's also a loyal one. He'll make certain that you're comfortable, if only because that's what he'll want himself."

Estraven had to agree with his marriage-vatarh's assessment of "crude." The man was certainly that. His vision of "comfortable" seemed to consist mostly of whether the inn's kegs were full of good ale and that the barmaids were comely and seducible. He'd drunk and whored the night away in each village they'd stayed in. Estraven had stayed in his room in disgust, forcing the e-téni to do the same, spending his time writing letters to Francesca and to his o'téni aides at the Old Temple back in Nessantico.

It would all be worth it one day. One day he would be A'Téni ca'Cellibrecca himself, stationed in one of the great cities of the Holdings. He would work with his marriage-vatarh, who would be Archigos Orlandi, and together they would create a Concénzia Faith stronger than it had ever been, unassailable and more powerful even than the Kralji and the rulers of the other lands of the Holdings. They would be the founders of a new order firmly rooted in the words of the Toustour and the law of the Divolonté.

A better world than this one. Which wasn't at the moment hard for Estraven to believe at all. Nearly any world would be better than this one. Estraven's clothes were soaked, and he was fairly certain he'd picked up a horrible infestation of lice from one of those lonely beds.

They'd spent the previous night at one of Ville Colhelm's many inns, with cu'Belli imperiously telling the innkeeper that "A'Téni ca'Cellibrecca of Brezno will pay for your best rooms." In the morning, one of the chambermaids had delivered a note from cu'Belli. *Business to conduct. Will meet you at standing stones beyond the village midmorning.* Estraven wondered just what business cu'Belli might be conducting that was so urgent and what her name might be, but the maid knew nothing beyond the fact that "the fat Vajiki and his companions had left not long after dawn, along with the two téni. Without any sleep at all, Vajiki. They were up all night, in the tavern and . . ." She'd blushed then, smiling and closing her mouth on the rest of the tale. "They said to tell you to wait for them at the stones. The stableboy can tell you where they are."

Now it seemed cu'Belli's "business" had kept him longer than expected. The sun was hidden behind scudding clouds and the fine rain misted Estraven's woolen cloak, but it was midmorning. Had to be. Estraven glanced in annoyance at the zenith, blinking into the drops of rain. He sneezed. "Damn the man," he said.

Estraven gave the sign of Cénzi, then began to whisper a quick chant, his hands moving in the wet air: a warming chant. He felt the surge of blessed heat wash over him as he finished the spell and he sighed gratefully—one of the quicker and more useful of the little chants that any téni was taught to do, and one most téni tried to work surreptitiously when trapped in long ceremonies on cold winter mornings in the temples, especially since the spell taxed its caster very little. At least he wouldn't catch his death of illness out here in the cursed weather.

He thought he heard the snap of a branch from the trees beyond the standing stones, and he straightened in his saddle, turning his head. "Cu'Belli?" he called. "Come, man. We've wasted half the day already. We're still a good two days' ride from Brezno."

This time an answer came in the sinister *thwang* of bowstrings.

Estraven grunted in surprise and shock as an arrow

whistled past his left ear; an instant later he fell backward from his horse's saddle as a trio of feathered shafts
sprouted from his cloak: two in his chest, the other in his
right shoulder, the shock of their impact sending him to
the ground. Spattered with mud, blinking in the rainfall,
he looked down at the arrows in surprise, confused by
their impossible appearance, touching the dark feathers
of their fletching even as he saw the blood beginning to
spread out from the wounds. He tried to rise, managing
to struggle up on his knees. Strangely, he felt little pain,
only a great tightness in his chest.

This was a dream. This was a sign from Cénzi. This
wasn't real. It couldn't be real.

"I'm here as promised, U'Téni," Estraven heard
cu'Belli's voice call out, and the portly man stepped
from behind one of the moss-flecked stones. His quartet of companions were with him, and they held bows
with new arrows nocked to the strings. There was another man with him as well, dressed in the uniform of
Firenzcia's army.

"Treachery!" Estraven tried to call, but his voice was
garbled and he spat blood. "Help!" He started to chant,
tried to force his hands to move in a new spell, one that
would smash cu'Belli and gain him time to get back on
his horse and ride away, but cu'Belli gestured quickly
and the bows came up and the bowstrings sang their
note of death, and Estraven was slammed backward
again into the rain and into the mud of Firenzcia and
into whatever afterlife awaited him.

~

Ana cu'Seranta

SHE TRIED TO REFUSE to see him. She'd feigned sickness that morning so she wouldn't have to attend the opening of the Archigos' Temple at First Call, and so she wouldn't need to chant with the others and light the temple's lamps. When the Archigos had come to her apartment, she'd sent Watha out to tell him that she could not see him now, but she'd returned with a pleased, grim smile. "The Archigos waits for you in the outer reception room, O'Téni," she'd said. "He said that you will dress and meet him for breakfast. Beida is already serving him tea."

She'd dressed, and gone to him. There had been no choice. Now, after the formal, empty greetings, after sitting there watching the Archigos drink his tea and eat his biscuits, the smell of them making her own stomach grumble in protest, the Archigos had pushed away the tray with his breakfast and leaned forward with his elbows on the table.

"I am going to suggest to our new Kraljiki that you would make an excellent wife for him."

It was a statement that had shocked Ana to her core, and now he stared at her as the discomfort colored her face. She could not breathe for a moment; her hands pressed against her heart as she sat back in her chair across from him. Underneath her robes she could feel the stone shell Karl had given her. It gave her no comfort.

"That is not what I want, Archigos," she said. "You have no right to use me that way, no matter what you paid my parents." A sullen, liquid fire burned high in her throat and her temples pulsed with the beat of her heart. She could feel her hands trembling as she placed them on the table. "Even if the A'Kralj would agree to it, I will not."

The Archigos nodded, as if her response was what he had expected. "I understand your reluctance, Ana. I do. But you will learn, sooner than I did, perhaps, that the higher you ascend in life, the higher are the payments expected of you. Certainly the Kraljica expected such of her nieces and nephews, and of the A'Kralj himself. She knew what a weapon the right marriage could be. She had already broached this possibility to me, the day after she first met you—when, you should know, my own niece Safina had been considered for the same position. So I don't suggest this lightly; this alliance could be more important now that the Kraljica is gone. The A'Kralj will be the Kraljiki, and he is unduly influenced by A'Téni ca'Cellibrecca. Without some countering influence, Justi's ascension to the Sun Throne could cause changes in Concénzia—changes that would undo all that I and Kraljica Marguerite tried to accomplish."

He sighed, lifting a hand and letting it fall again. The tea shivered in his cup; the biscuits jumped on their plate. "There's another matter also. The army of Firenzcia is gathering too near the border for anyone's comfort. I think now is indeed the time for action, or it may be too late. Justi is not who I would want as Kraljiki, but he is still a better option than Jan ca'Vörl. Would it be so bad, Ana, to be the Kraljiki's wife? Do you have other and better prospects? Your Numetodo from the Gschnas, perhaps? I know you went to see Envoy ci'Vliomani the other day, Ana—" he raised his hand against Ana's burgeoning protest, "—and I want you to know that I don't care—as long as your curiosity doesn't get in the way of your faith or your duty."

It has already become an obstacle to my faith. It killed the Kraljica . . . But she would not say that. The Archigos seemed to take her silence as consent, and continued to speak. "Cénzi has given you an extraordinary Gift, Ana. Cénzi would expect you to *use* that Gift as well, Ana, and all that Gift has given you. Surely you see that."

He said it without the question mark, as if it were an obvious conclusion, and at the same moment, a realization came to Ana. "You intended all along to connect me to the A'Kralj," she said. The accusation made the Archigos smile.

"Yes," he said simply. "Very nearly."

"The Kraljica . . . ?"

"She agreed, once she'd met you and once I'd told her about you. We had hoped to introduce the two of you formally at the Gschnas, but . . ." The Archigos' mouth twisted. "It is still what she would want," he continued. "Even more so now. With the Kraljica gone, we must tie together the new Kraljiki and the Concénzia Faith—not with ca'Cellibrecca and his movement, but with our own faction."

Our own faction . . . The Archigos said it casually, and Ana shook her head mutely. *Not ours. Not now* . . .

After the Kraljica's death, she had been unable find the Ilmodo again. Cénzi had abandoned her for her lack of faith, for her betrayal of Him with the Numetodo. She had tried. She had attempted the simplest spells, the ones she had been able to do since she'd been a child, and they crumbled in her hands. She wouldn't be able to keep her failures secret for long: how she avoided using the Ilmodo, how weak her spells were, how she could barely manage to conjure up light or heat from the energy with which Cénzi filled the air. She couldn't hide the decay of her skills for long; no téni could, not when the rituals and ceremonies of the Faith required their daily use. Someone would mention their suspicions to the Archigos, and he would come to her and demand that she show him whether the rumors were true. . . .

"That's all I was for you from the beginning, Archigos?" she demanded, trying to disguise her fear with bluster. "A way to bring the A'Kralj closer to you? You're no different than Vatarh; you'd use me in the same way, only with another man."

The Archigos managed to look hurt. "My intention, and the Kraljica's, was to keep the Faith strong in a changing world. We need to look forward, Ana. Ca'Cellibrecca would return us to the dark. The world changes, Ana, whether we like it or not, and the Faith must learn to change with it—that's not something ca'Cellibrecca is willing to do. Our ships go ever farther out into the world. One day, perhaps even in your lifetime, they will have touched the shores of every land. As the Holdings reaches out into new territory and finds new peoples, we also find the rich beauty of Vucta and Cénzi's creation, a richness we never suspected before."

"The Numetodo, Archigos? Are they part of this richness?"

He cocked his head to one side as he stared at her. "They could be, if they would only acknowledge that their Scáth Cumhacht is actually the Ilmodo and that it derives from Cénzi. There are other ways of bringing people to the truth than through violence, torture, and imprisonment—certainly that's what the Kraljica believed, and why she was able to rule so well for so long. The more Nessantico draws from the knowledge of those she rules, the stronger she becomes. I don't look to exclude the Numetodo or to ignore what they might have to teach us, as long as they can be brought to understand the truth of the Toustour. I thought, Ana, that we might share that outlook in the same way that we share a deep faith in Cénzi."

"I do share that," Ana answered. *Then why did you doubt Him?* She shook her head. Her fears and confusion roiled in her head, boiling, and she could not snatch at them long enough to examine them. "It's just . . . Archigos, I can't . . ."

"You can. You will. If it's what Cénzi decrees." He waved a diminutive hand at her. When it dropped again to the table, china and silver clattered once more. "It

may be, Ana, that the new Kraljiki is already too well
snared by ca'Cellibrecca—I may have made a horrible
mistake, allowing them to become close. I saw all this
over the last several years and I did nothing. The rumors I've heard of ca'Cellibrecca's daughter . . ." He
shrugged. "If that is the case, then we will have to find
a new tactic. But if Justi *is* willing to listen, if he will
look to how his matarh governed the Holdings so well,
then he'll realize how well served he would be aligning himself with us. Marriage can tie together even two
enemies, who then discover they must work together.
And we are not the Kraljiki's enemy, Ana; ultimately,
we are on the same side. As to love . . ." He reached out
as if to touch Ana's hand; she drew back. The Archigos
shrugged. "Well, that's never been a necessity in a political marriage, has it?"

He paused, and Ana remained silent, still seated on
the other side of the table and staring past the Archigos
to the windows of her apartment without seeing any of
the day outside. The Archigos pushed himself off his
chair, giving her the sign of Cénzi. "You know I'm right,"
he said. "And you know your place, I trust."

"I know where you have placed me, yes, Archigos."
She could not move. She felt bound to the chair in which
she sat, caught in cords she could not see.

He gave her a strange, twisted smile, and nodded.

~

Jan ca'Vörl

"WE FOUND HER in the baggage train, my
Hïrzg, raiding the stores." The offizier standing before Jan looked embarrassed by his tale. He stood
well back, obviously uncertain how Jan would react.

Markell, seated at the traveling desk with a sheaf of reports before him, stifled a chuckle as Jan frowned.

Allesandra stood trembling before Jan, hands clasped behind her back, her head bowed. "What do have to say for yourself?" he barked at his daughter. "You disobeyed me. What is your matarh thinking now? She must be frantic."

"I left Matarh a note," Allesandra said to the floor. "And I told Naniaj that she had to pretend as long as she could. Maybe Matarh thinks I'm still with them—she never comes to my carriage unless she has to."

Markell snorted. Jan glanced at him, shaking his head. "How long have you been gone?"

"Two days, Vatarh. I left the first night, so that I could find the army again."

"You rode back alone in the night, unprotected? You snuck through our rear guards?"

She gave him the ghost of a nod. "I climbed into one of the wagons. There was plenty of food there, Vatarh."

"Those are the army's supplies, food for our soldiers. Do you know what the punishment is for someone who steals from those wagons?"

She shook her head. He could see her shoulders beginning to shake with subdued tears. "We cut off their hands," he told her harshly, "for they are no better than our enemies."

Allesandra clutched her hands tightly to her stomach, but she did not cry. She lifted her face to Jan, and he had to force himself not to take her in his arms and hug her. "I wanted to be with *you*, Vatarh," she said. "I wanted to learn to command an army. I wanted to learn to be a Hïrzgin you would be proud of. I didn't . . . I didn't eat very much."

Her face was so penitent and sorrowful that he could not keep up the pretense any longer. He knelt down and opened his arms, and she ran to him. She broke into heaving sobs against his shoulder. "It's a good thing you are the A'Hïrzg," he whispered to her, "because that means everything here also belongs to you."

"You can't send me back now, Vatarh," she said fiercely, sniffing. "I won't go. I won't."

Jan looked at Markell over her shoulder. Markell shook his head. "This isn't a place for a child, Allesandra."

"I'm not a child. I'm the A'Hïrzg. This is where I should be, with my vatarh the Hïrzg, and besides, Matarh is days away and you will protect me and I will learn ever so much from you, and Georgi could continue to teach me . . ."

Behind her, Markell busied himself with the reports.

"It will be dangerous," Jan said. "There may be fighting, Allesandra."

"Then teach me how to use a sword as you do, Vatarh, or have Georgi do it. I'll learn fast. I will."

Jan hugged her again. He sighed. "Markell," Jan said. "Take a note to send to the Hïrzgin with our fastest rider. Tell her that Allesandra is with her vatarh and safe, and that she will remain with me for the time being."

Allesandra squealed happily. "Thank you, Vatarh. I'll be good, I promise. Where is my sword? You promised."

"No sword," he told her. He unlaced the belt around his waist and and pulled from it a soiled leather scabbard holding a double-bladed knife with a jeweled hilt. He displayed it to her. "This is a knife Hïrzg Karin, your great-vatarh, gave me when I was about your age." He didn't tell her that it was one of the few things the Hïrzg ever gave Jan, or that the same day he'd given Ludwig, little more than a year older, a full suit of armor and a sword. "I give it to you now, and I'll show you how to use it. For now, though, keep it in a pocket of your tashta."

Allesandra took the knife and clutched it as if it were the most precious gift he could have given her. "Thank you, Vatarh," she said. "Thank you so much. I will learn. I will learn everything you have to teach me."

"You will," Jan said, almost sadly, "whether it's what you want to learn or not. Markell, summon O'Offizier ci'Arndt. We have an additional assignment for him."

~
Karl ci'Vliomani

"I DIDN'T EXPECT TO SEE YOU so soon, Ana," he said. "In fact, I wondered . . . well, no matter. I'm truly glad for the chance to speak with you again." He smiled at her, taking her hands in his. He thought she would pull away immediately; she did not, and he let his hands linger. He enjoyed the touch, enjoyed looking at her face, at the eyes that stared into his. *You can't, Karl. You can't. There's Kaitlin, waiting for you back in Paeti. . . .* He released her hand with a quick, uncertain smile and went to the window, glancing down at the téni-driven carriage waiting in the street below. "I'm surprised you'd be so open about meeting me, Ana, I have to admit. But I'm glad you came."

He saw her face relax slightly at that, but the determination in her face remaincd. "I'm tired of everything being hidden. I don't *want* to hide anything," she told him, and there was heat and anger in her voice that seemed to emanate from somewhere else. "But you need to know that I've kept my promise to you from the other night, and I'll continue to keep it."

"I know you will," he told her, "or I wouldn't have made the invitation in the first place. I knew when I saw you . . ." He stopped, shaking his head. He gestured to a chair without saying more. "Would you sit? I could have someone bring up refreshments . . ." She shook her head, and he could see the agitation in her: in the way she paced the room, in the shine that touched her eyes, in her quick breath. She went to the fire and held her hands out to the flames. He could see her trembling, and he came to her, touching her gently on the shoulder. "Ana, what's troubling you? What's happened?"

She gave an odd bark of a laugh that turned into a choked sob, turning to him. "Everything." She spread her arms wide, her téni's robes flaring with the motion as if she were giving Cénzi's Blessing. A single tear tracked its way down her cheek, and she brushed at it. "I've lost my ability," she told him. "The Gift I had. Since you showed me what the Numetodo do . . . I can't . . ."

She began to cry fully then. He watched her, wanting to go to her but not daring to, until the pain and sorrow in her made him take a step, then another. She made no resistance when he folded her into his arms. She leaned into his embrace, burying her face into his shoulder. He held her silently, one hand stroking her hair. He pressed his lips into the fragrance of her hair, touching his lips to the strands. She felt . . .

She felt as if she belonged there. Guilt tore through him for the thought.

After a few moments, she sniffed and pushed away; he released her as she wiped at her eyes with her sleeve. "I'm sorry," she said. "I . . . we . . . I shouldn't have. This isn't what I came here for."

He wanted to embrace her again. Her sorrow and distress pulled at him. *Fool. You can't afford this. Think of what you're here for. What about Kaitlin, who said she would always wait for you, always be faithful, and you told her the same. . . .* He forced himself to remain where he was. He tried to think of Kaitlin, but he found that he couldn't remember her face; it was hazy in his memory, a ghost that seemed to belong to another person's past. *You've been away for a year and more already; you haven't heard from Kaitlin in months and months. She may have found someone else. . . .*

Ana was here, though. *She's your enemy. She's a tool you intended to use.* But the reminder didn't convince, not when he saw her this way. Not when she pulled at him the way she did.

"What do you mean, you lost your gift?" he asked.

Haltingly, she told him. "I noticed when . . ." She stopped, pressed her lips together, and he realized that she was holding something back from him. "I noticed the next time I tried to use the Ilmodo. I couldn't. I called to Cénzi, but He wouldn't come, wouldn't let me shape the Ilmodo as I used to. I felt like an apprentice again, stumbling through the simplest spell." She looked at him, and he thought he saw both accusation and hope in her eyes. "Did *you* do it, Envoy?" she asked. "An enchantment, a Numetodo spell . . . ?"

He shook his head. "No," he told her softly. "I wouldn't do that to you, Ana. I don't expect you to believe that, but it's the truth. Even if I could manage that—and I can't—I wouldn't have done that to you. No, I'm afraid you did this to yourself."

That sounded cruel even to his ears, and he brought a hand up both against her protest and in apology. "Ana, let me explain. With the Numetodo, everyone finds their own individual path to the Scáth Cumhacht. Each of us uses a slightly different technique, our own words and gestures. That's where we're different. You téni use your faith to open the Second World; we use a standard routine, one that we must discover ourselves, no different than an herbalist who mixes the ingredients of her potions in the same quantities each time so that the effects are always the same. Your faith . . ." He shook his head. "I think it's just another formula. A routine. What you saw, well, it shook that faith, and so . . ."

"No!" she shouted at him. "Stop. I know what you're saying, and I don't believe it. I still believe. I do. Cénzi is punishing me."

"I told you the other night that I could show you our path," Karl said. "I still could. Your gift isn't gone, Ana. It's still there—and it doesn't matter whether you believe in Cénzi or not. It's still there." He took a stride toward her, taking her hands in his. She didn't resist, didn't pull away. He could see that she wanted to believe him. He brought her to him. Their faces were close. So close. *Kaitlin* . . . "I can show you, Ana. I will."

As he said the words, he heard the creaking of the door behind them. Ana's eyes widened and her gaze shifted. "How touching," a voice said drolly, and as Karl started to turn, releasing Ana's hands so his own were free, the voice *tsked* in caution. "Now, Envoy ci'Vliomani, what did I tell you the last time we met? There's no need for violence here."

Commandant ca'Rudka stood at the door, his sword still in its scabbard and a sardonic grin on his face. In the hall beyond, Karl could see the woman who owned the building cowering against the far wall with her keys in her hand, and two gardai in the uniform of the Bastida, both holding crossbows with bolts nocked and ready. Ca'Rudka motioned to the two, and they lowered their bows slightly. "O'Téni cu'Seranta," he said, bowing slightly and giving her the sign of Cénzi. "Your driver said you would be here. Evidently the envoy's dancing at the Gschnas impressed you more than the Archigos believed."

Ana's face, when Karl glanced at her, was pale, all the color gone from her cheeks. "Commandant," she said. She took a breath, drawing herself up. "The Vajiki and I have been discussing religion. I had hopes of making him see the error of the Numetodo."

"Indeed, that's a noble exercise," ca'Rudka said. He entered the room, the two gardai following, closing the door on the landlady's curious face. "But somehow I doubt that the Vajiki is convinced of the greatness of Cénzi and the Faith." He went over to the sill of the window, where Karl had set the plant the commandant had given him. Ca'Rudka touched a fingertip to the soil, then looked at the black earth clinging there. "Damp," he said. "I'm impressed, Vajiki." He looked at the plant. "But I'm afraid it's only a common weed after all. You're wasting your efforts."

"Why are you here, Commandant?" Karl asked. He

could feel the tension gnawing at his belly. *This is what Mika feared. It's begun . . .* He knew it, knew by the way the commandant glanced around the room, knew from the careful stares of the gardai whose weapons never quite moved away from him. "If it's a social call, as you can see, I'm otherwise engaged."

"Unfortunately, I'm here in my official capacity," ca'Rudka answered. "Vajiki ci'Vliomani, I regret to inform you that you are under arrest. Now, you will give O'Offizier ce'Falla your hands . . . Unfortunately, we can't risk you using the Ilmodo. Please don't move, Vajiki, nor you, O'Téni, until the o'offizier is done." The garda moved forward quickly as the other kept his crossbow carefully aimed at Karl's chest. Karl held out his hands, and ce'Falla confined them in metal cuffs. He saw another device on the man's belt: a contraption with straps and a gag. He shuddered, knowing that would be next.

"What is it I've supposedly done, Commandant? Am I allowed to know that?"

"Certainly," ca'Rudka answered. He reached into a pouch on his belt, withdrawing a length of chain. On the end dangled a stone shell.

"This was found around the painter ci'Recroix's neck when his body was discovered. Does it seem familiar to you, Vajiki?" Ca'Rudka looked at Karl's chest, where a similar symbol rested. "You needn't answer; I see that it does."

Karl glanced at Ana, who was standing with her hand on her breast. Karl suspected he knew what she hid there under her robes, and he shook his head at her warningly as ca'Rudka followed his gaze.

"I'm sorry, O'Téni," ca'Rudka said to Ana, "but I'm afraid Vajiki ci'Vliomani is under arrest for plotting the assassination of the Kraljica."

REPERCUSSIONS

Ana cu'Seranta
Orlandi ca'Cellibrecca
Karl ci'Vliomani
Sergei ca'Rudka
Mahri
Ana cu'Seranta

Ana cu'Seranta

SHE KEPT HEARING what Karl had said as the
commandant led him away. She clung to the words
in desperation. *"Trust yourself, Ana. No matter what they
say to you, no matter what they do, trust yourself and what
you feel in your heart. That will give you back everything
you've lost."*

Then the carriage door closed as it hurried off toward
the Bastida. The commandant had escorted her back to
her quarters, a silent ride in his private carriage. "I'm
sorry, O'Téni," he'd said finally when he'd walked her to
the sheltered back entrance of the building, away from
curious eyes. "We all have our duties to perform, as I'm
sure you know."

She rushed into the apartment, closing the door to
her bedroom and refusing to let any of the servants in
to attend to her. She didn't cry; she felt beyond tears.
Outside, the world bloomed with spring, but inside her,
everything was snared in the desolation of winter. She
sat, silent, watching the flames dance in the hearth. She
couldn't tell whether she had no thoughts at all, or so
many that she could not hear them for the uproar they
made.

That night, the Archigos summoned her to a private
viewing for the a'téni of the Kraljica's body. Watha
handed her the robes the Archigos had sent over: not
the traditional green, but off-white: the color of bone,
the color of death. She put them on dully, without feeling them. At the temple, Kenne, also robed in that sad

white, brought her to the Archigos. The dwarf asked nothing; he only looked at her with sorrow, as if disappointed. "Come," he said. "Let us say our good-byes to Marguerite."

She walked with him. A river of bone white flowed through the doors up to the flat, polished granite stone that was the altar of Cénzi. The body of the Kraljica lay there, resting on cushions of brilliant yellow with trumpet flowers arranged around her. Her face was already covered by a gold-plated death mask sculpted in her likeness. Her hair, brushed and perfect, was caught in the ornate hairpin of abalone and pearls that Ana had seen the first time she met the Kraljica, and the scent of incense and perfume hung heavily about her. The iron rod of Henri VI lay cradled in her left hand; in her right hand, the palm upturned, was the signet ring of the Kralji. Around the Stone of Cénzi, wreaths had been laid, and from the forest of greenery and ribbons rose seven candelabra of crystal from the mountains of Sesemora, each with téni-light globes so furiously alight so that the Kraljica seemed to recline in the radiance of the sun.

Seeing the Kraljica so still, composed, and masked, Ana finally did cry. Unashamed, she let the tears flow as she knelt in front of the bier, her head bowed. She didn't care that the Archigos, the gathered a'téni, and ca'Cellibrecca and all the others were watching and making their own judgments.

It was my fault. I should have been able to save you, Kraljica, but I had betrayed Cénzi. . . .

But she did not pray. She didn't think Cénzi would listen to her.

The Archigos touched her shoulder in sympathy, though he had said nothing to her as they left beyond the necessary talk: no rebukes, no accusations. She was certain that he knew she'd been with Karl when he'd been arrested. The commandant would have told him, and Watha or Sunna or Beida must have whispered to him about how distraught she was when she returned.

"Tomorrow," the Archigos told her and the rest of his staff as they left the temple, "the doors of the Archigos' Temple on the South Bank will open at dawn, so that the A'Kralj and all the Kraljica's nephews and nieces may have their first official viewing. You'll accompany me there, Ana—the rest of you will be taking your shifts this evening and tonight in attendance to the Kraljica at the temple. After the A'Kralj has paid his respects to his matarh, there will be the day-long procession of the ca'-and-cu'—again, you'll be required to take shifts in attendance while the ca'-and-cu' file through. Kenne, I'm placing you in charge of the scheduling. Ana, you'll be needed again for the funeral carriage's procession at midnight around the Avi a'Parete; you'll accompany me in my carriage. Is that understood?"

She and the other téni of his staff nodded.

Ana stared at the lamps of the city as she walked back to her apartments, and she gazed from her windows that looked west, trying to see if she could pick out the Bastida among the clustering of rooftops. She could not.

That morning, after a sleepless night, Watha brought the news that all the Numetodo within Nessantico had been rounded up, that squads of the Garde Kralji, on the A'Kralj's orders, had entered Oldtown while she and the Archigos had been at the temple, taking all those suspected to be Numetodo into custody. The Bastida, it was rumored, was full of them.

This was for the safety of Nessantico during the Kraljica's funeral, the A'Kralj had declared, according to Watha. No Numetodo would be allowed to mar the elaborate, ritualized display of grief and affection for their fallen ruler. They would remain in the Bastida during the three days of official mourning, after which the new Kraljiki would make a ruling regarding them.

While Ana waited in the Archigos' outer room with Kenne and the other téni of his staff, she could hear them whispering the gossip and rumors, each of the statements wilder and more unlikely than the next:

". . . I've been told in confidence that it was a Numetodo servant who poisoned the Kraljica. Yes, I'm certain; my sister's husband works in the palace and they
all know it there . . ."

". . . my vatarh told me that the Numetodo were planning to steal the Kraljica's body and hold it for ransom.
That's why the commandant is so upset . . ."

". . . No, they wanted the Kraljica's body to desecrate
it in a bizarre rite of theirs. I've heard that from four
people who would know . . ."

". . . what happened was that the Numetodo were
caught using their sorcery to poison the entire drinking water system of the city. Several people have already died from it in Oldtown. That's why they've been
rounded up . . ."

". . . I've heard that the Numetodo are rising up in all
the cities of the Holdings in celebration of the Kraljica's
death, the bastards. Why, in Belcanto, they were running
through the streets singing . . ."

Ana could not listen to their chatter; she saw Karl's
face in each of the rumors.

The Archigos came out at last, leaning heavily on his
staff of office, and as Ana and the others descended the
stairs from his apartments, she could detect nothing in
his glances to her. She wondered at that. She wanted to
ask him what he was thinking; she wanted to tell him
that she'd rather he screamed his anger than to have this
silence between them, but there was no time. They came
out onto the square outside the temple just as the A'Kralj
was being helped from his carriage, accompanied by the
commandant and several of the city guards. The early
morning sun illuminated an orderly chaos—the a'téni
all moving their own people into position for the formal
procession; the press of onlookers past the ring of guards;
the ca'-and-cu' families awaiting their moment to view
the body of the Kraljica.

"Ah, A'Kralj ca'Mazzak," the Archigos said as the

A'Kralj approached, the quartet of Garde Kralji with him pushing aside those citizens and téni between the A'Kralj and the Archigos. The A'Kralj wore a white, silken bashta over which hung a heavy cloak brocaded in gold filigree. Against the white, his dark beard and hair stood out in harsh contrast, the jaw jutting forward characteristically. Around his neck was a golden chain from which depended a pendant set with ambergris and a yellow diamond. His fingers were bare of rings, but Ana knew that later this night, before the public procession, he would take the signet ring from his matarh's hand and place it on his own finger. Renard walked alongside him, carrying the A'Kralj's gilded mourning mask should it be needed. The mask was to allow the A'Kralj privacy in his grief, but to Ana, the A'Kralj seemed more exuberant than sorrowful.

The commandant, accompanying the A'Kralj, nodded faintly to Ana. She shivered and gave no sign that she noticed. The Archigos gestured, and his retinue bowed as one and gave the A'Kralj the sign of Cénzi.

"A'Kralj, I am so sorry for your loss, but I know you will follow her and take Nessantico to heights beyond even her dreams," the Archigos said as they rose from their bows. He looked like a wizened child against the athletic bulk of the A'Kralj.

"Thank you, Archigos," the A'Kralj answered in his high, nasal voice. It sounded like an adolescent's. "I know Matarh appreciated your long service and devotion to her, and I look forward to the same service from you."

The Archigos bowed again at that, though Ana knew that he heard the same lack of conviction in the A'Kralj's words—ritualistic, too polite, and ultimately meaningless. The man's deep-set eyes flickered across Ana's face, and she thought his lips tightened with the glance. The Archigos seemed to notice as well, for he motioned to Ana to step forward. "You remember O'Téni Ana cu'Seranta?"

he said. "I spoke of her to you the other day, as we were discussing the arrangements for the funeral."

"Matarh introduced us at the Gschnas, Archigos," he said. He held out his hand and she took it. His eyes appraised her; she could almost hear the calculations inside his head. "Yes, I remember her, and I remember our talk, Archigos. Good to meet you again, O'Téni. I only wish it were in better circumstances."

She realized that they were both waiting for her to speak. "As do I," she answered belatedly. "We all mourn your loss, A'Kralj. It's a tragedy for the entire Holdings."

Words vacant of true feeling, she knew. Like herself.

He nodded. "Indeed," he said. He sniffed—a concession to congestion rather than grief, Ana thought—and looked her up and down once more. "The Archigos speaks highly of you, O'Téni, and my matarh did as well, when she was alive. They both seem to feel that you've been particularly blessed by Cénzi, and that it would be ..." He paused, as if considering his next words. "... advantageous for me to know you better. I have always found that listening to the advice of those I trust is a good tactic, so I intend to do exactly that. Very soon. I trust you'll be amenable as well? A luncheon in the palais perhaps, the day after tomorrow—Gostidi?"

Ana lowered her head. She could see no way to refuse politely. "Certainly, A'Kralj," she answered. "It would be my pleasure, assuming my duties to the Archigos do not interfere."

"I'm positive the Archigos will make certain they do not," he answered, and Ana could hear the Archigos grunt his assent, though she would not glance at him. "I'll tell Renard to arrange it, then."

"Arrange what?" a voice interrupted, and Ana lifted her head to see A'Téni ca'Cellibrecca and his daughter standing just behind the A'Kralj. The a'téni was smiling, but the expression on his daughter's face was far less friendly.

"I was arranging to take luncheon with O'Téni cu'Seranta on Gostidi," the A'Kralj said to ca'Cellibrecca.

"Gostidi?" ca'Cellibrecca asked. He pursed his lips over his doubled chin and tapped a forefinger on his cheek. "I must remind the A'Kralj—as the Archigos should know, too—that he has the Ceremony of the Kralji that morning, and he and I were planning to discuss the disposition of the Numetodo in the Bastida afterward, and both will take some time."

"I assume that I will still find sufficient time to eat, A'Téni," the A'Kralj remarked. "Or would you deny the new Kraljiki his sustenance?"

"Of course not," ca'Cellibrecca answered quickly. The expression on his face soured. "In fact, I could join you, and I'm certain Francesca would be willing as well. I hope to have some news from her husband by Mizzkdi or Gostidi, and . . ."

"I think not," the A'Kralj interrupted. "While the company of you and Vajica ca'Cellibrecca would be most agreeable, I would like to speak with the O'Téni more privately." Ca'Cellibrecca's mouth remained open for a moment as if he would say more. The A'Kralj raised his eyebrows, and ca'Cellibrecca bowed his head. His daughter's dark eyes were reproachful as they stared at the A'Kralj, but he stared blandly back at her.

For a moment, the tableau held. Ana thought of ca'Cellibrecca and what he'd done to the Numetodo in Brezno, and she imagined Karl in the a'téni's hands. From the roiling inside her, a flame of anger sent searing heat. She lifted her chin. "I would like to talk to the new Kraljiki regarding the Numetodo as well," Ana said. "I think the Kraljiki needs to make his decision as well-informed as possible."

The Archigos coughed as if startled. With the comment, both A'Téni ca'Cellibrecca and his daughter swiveled their heads to stare at Ana. She could feel the heat

of their gazes and didn't dare look at them. Instead, she
kept her eyes on the A'Kralj, who laughed, suddenly and
surprisingly. "There, you see, A'Téni? O'Téni cu'Seranta
is not the quiet, obedient mouse you think she is, and
judging by the look on the Archigos' face, she has surprised him as well. I'm beginning to look forward to our
luncheon, O'Téni, to see what other surprises you might
have for me."

With that, the A'Kralj took a long breath and looked
toward the temple. "And now I must pay my respects.
Archigos, are you ready to lead us to my matarh? Vajica
ca'Cellibrecca, would you do me the favor of accompanying me? Renard, my mask, if you please . . ."

As Renard tied on the mask, Francesca placed her arm
inside the A'Kralj's proffered elbow with a venomous
glance at Ana. The Archigos also looked up at her before
gesturing to A'Téni ca'Cellibrecca. The processional line
of téni began to move, haltingly, behind the Archigos'
slow progress. His staff clattered on the polished flagstones of the court, and Ana walked carefully alongside
him, aware of the gazes burrowing into her back.

~

Orlandi ca'Cellibrecca

FRANCESCA GLANCED BACK to him as they
entered the temple. Orlandi could see from her face
that she was distressed and upset, but there was nothing
he could do for her other than to frown sympathetically
and nod in the direction of the A'Kralj, to whose arm
she clung. *Pay attention to him. Be with him,* he said with
that glance. *It's what you need to do right now. He asked
you to accompany him and that's a great public honor.
We've lost nothing yet. . . .*

He'd believed that the A'Kralj was firmly under his control through Francesca. This morning had shown him the error of that belief. The lesson sent doubt careening through Orlandi's head. He was like one of the street jugglers along the Avi, with far too many balls in the air around him, each moving in its own pattern. There was the Hïrzg, already marching toward Nessantico's border, as dangerous to handle as glowing coals. Orlandi had yet to hear from cu'Belli about Estraven's fate, despite having told the man to immediately send a rider back. And now the Archigos appeared to have placed his own pawn directly in Francesca's path, and the A'Kralj had not allowed Orlandi to sweep it aside.

He must continue to juggle. He could not put anything down safely yet.

He prayed as he walked, but his prayer was not for the Kraljica whose body they approached slowly. The procession was lengthy: the Archigos, followed by the A'Kralj, then the half-dozen or so a'téni who, like Orlandi, had come to the city for the Jubilee, then the Kraljica's many direct relatives—all walking between the lines of white-robed téni who had been in attendance of the Kraljica's body since it had arrived here, walking in the téni-lit glory of the temple.

Cénzi, I have done everything for Your glory, for Your purposes. Show me, Your servant, that I have not lost Your favor . . . Orlandi prayed, and he looked past the A'Kralj to the damned dwarf and his ugly whore, and his stomach burned.

I deserve the staff and the crown. I deserve to be Archigos; I should have been Archigos instead of him. I am the true keeper of the Divolonté, the true guardian of the Faith. The Divolonté and the Ilmodo and the téni hold together the very fabric of Nessantico, and I protect it for You against Your enemies who would tear it apart . . .

As they entered the temple, the choirmaster in his loft moved his hands and the choir began to sing: Darkmavis' "Requiem for a Kraljiki." The mournful harmonies swirled and circled, reverberating along the temple's length, amplified and shaped by the téni choirmaster's spell, the delicate melody sliding from tenors to baritones to sopranos and back again, the cadence of the basses relentless underneath. Orlandi watched the Archigos turn to his whore and whisper, and he saw her hands move in the pattern of light-making. Yet the motions were hesitant, and he saw her fumble and start over, and when the light blossomed between her hands it was weak and pale compared to that of the other téni standing in prayer along either side of the main aisle.

Orlandi found his eyes narrowing. *Is this your sign, Cénzi? Have you answered me that quickly?* The o'téni had danced with that foul Numetodo during the Gschnas, after all—and now she wanted to speak to the A'Kralj about the Numetodo the commandant had taken prisoner. No doubt her viewpoint would be conciliatory and weak, mirroring that of the Archigos. She lacked the power of the true Faith no matter how much Cénzi had gifted her. Orlandi was certain that she misused her Gift as well—it certainly was the simplest explanation of why she would have seen the Kraljica so often during her final illness: under the dwarf's direction, she had been using the Ilmodo against the laws of the Divolonté to try to heal the Kraljica. That certainly made sense for ca'Millac, since it was the Kraljica's support that had helped maintain him as Archigos.

But perhaps . . . perhaps there was more here, something he was missing. Could Cénzi have withdrawn his Gift from cu'Seranta? There, the dwarf frowned at his o'téni, and she released the poor spell entirely. Her hands went dark and empty. He saw her whisper to the Archigos apologetically, no doubt pleading weariness if the dark, pouched flesh under her eyes were any sign.

Orlandi made a mental note to speak to the commandant. Perhaps the man knew something, though he was the Kraljica's man, not Orlandi's . . .

The A'Kralj had reached his matarh's body, the Archigos and O'Téni cu'Seranta moving to one side. The Kraljica's face remained covered with her death mask: painted, closed eyelids and mouth, her hair frothing white around the gold. The A'Kralj stood at his matarh's right hand with Francesca still at his side, gazing down on her. As Orlandi watched, the A'Kralj's hand reached out and stroked not her hand but the staff of the Kralji, which would be in his own hand tomorrow morning. Orlandi bowed his head and closed his eyes as the procession halted to let the A'Kralj have his time with his matarh, Francesca moving politely to one side to allow the A'Kralj his privacy, but Orlandi doubted that the man prayed. Rather, he was probably thinking of tomorrow, when he would be declared Kraljiki, when he would sit on the Sun Throne, bathed in the radiance of his position.

You must choose . . .

Perhaps the Hïrzg would indeed be his best choice. Jan ca'Vörl would certainly be a strong Kraljiki, and his sympathies were definitely in line with Orlandi's, and Orlandi already had in hand the proposal from the Hïrzg for Francesca's hand to cement their alliance. While the A'Kralj might be Francesca's lover, while he intimated that such a marriage would interest him, he'd also announced no formal engagement. If the A'Kralj was going to assert himself, if he was going to consider scorning Francesca for that plain whore of the dwarf's who was no better than one of the *grandes horizontales,* then perhaps . . .

Orlandi sighed. His temples ached, and he wanted nothing more than to sink into his heated tub with minted balm on his forehead. But that wouldn't happen for some time yet, not until all the Kraljica's interminable relatives had had their moment with the Kraljica.

The A'Kralj finally stirred, lifting his head and making the sign of Cénzi over his matarh. He leaned forward and gave her a ceremonial final kiss, their masks clinking metallically as they touched. The Archigos waddled forward as Francesca took the A'Kralj's arm once more. The Archigos blessed the A'Kralj, his voice loud in the temple. Orlandi thought the dwarf looked ridiculous, like a wrinkled toddler talking to an adult—not only would Orlandi be an Archigos as the needs of the Faith demanded, he would *look* the part as well. He would not be a mockery of the position like this one.

Soon enough, if it is Your will . . .

The A'Kralj, as the choir's dirge swelled again, strode regally away with Francesca at his side and the Archigos and O'Téni cu'Seranta and his staff behind. They left the temple by the side door, and faintly Orlandi could hear the crowds packed into the temple square acknowledge the A'Kralj.

Orlandi came forward himself, and he and the other a'téni arranged themselves around the body. With satisfaction, Orlandi noted that none of the a'téni challenged his right to stand at the Kraljica's head. The a'téni . . . the majority of them would stand with him, he was certain, when the time came. A Concord A'Téni would vote to depose the hated dwarf ca'Millac when Orlandi brought charges, and then they would elevate him to Archigos . . .

The first of the Kraljica's too-numerous nephews and nieces came forward with his family, the line stretching well into the rear of the temple, and Orlandi sighed again.

As the mourners slowly moved past, he contented himself with thoughts of what he would do once he was Archigos, when this was *his* temple. . . .

~

Karl ci'Vliomani

THE NOON SUN spilled golden on the walls of the Bastida, but seemed to avoid actually touching the dark, grimy stones. Karl stood on a ledge high in the tower, protected only by a flimsy strip of open wooden rail. From his vantage point looking east, he could see the gilded domes of the Archigos' Temple. Between the rooftops of the intervening buildings, he glimpsed the massive crowd around the temple as the city waited for the Kraljica to begin her slow, final procession around the ring of the Avi a'Parete: at dusk as the lamps of Nessantico were lit.

"I hope you weren't considering jumping, Vajiki. Now that would be a shame—though a few of this room's inhabitants have been, ah, disappointed enough in our hospitality to prefer death to confinement."

Karl glanced back over his shoulder into the small, gloomy cell in which he'd been placed, furnished with a rude chair and desk and a tiny bed of straw ticking. The metal door hung open. He saw the commandant half-seated on the desk with one leg up, the other on the floor. The man wore his dress uniform, boots polished and gleaming. Behind him, in the corridor past the bars, Karl could see two gardai leaning against the stone walls. A torch guttered in its holder between them. "Though that wasn't the case with Chevaritt ca'Gafeldi, as I recall," ca'Rudka said to Karl. "His mind became addled after a few months here, and he insisted that he was able to turn into a dove and fly away. He looked rather silly, flapping his arms all the way down."

The gardai in the corridor chuckled. Karl said nothing—he *could* say nothing, not with the cloth-covered metal band that held down his tongue, bound with straps and locked around his head. The chains binding his hands tightly together rattled as he turned fully, though he remained standing on the balcony.

"You should be honored," ca'Rudka continued, speaking as if they were having a casual conversation over dinner. "This was originally Levo ca'Niomi's cell, centuries ago. It was thought the lovely view was proper punishment for ca'Niomi—to be able to look out at the city he ruled for three blessedly short days, and to know that he would never walk there again as a free man. He was also a stubborn man; he lived here for thirty years, writing the poetry that would finally overshadow his cruelty. I understand that the Kraljiki who put him here had ca'Niomi displayed on the anniversary of his deposing every year. They chained him, entirely naked, to the balcony so everyone who passed by on the Avi could look up and see him: an object lesson of what happens to those who overstep their place. If you look, I think you can still see the brackets for the chains there on the stones."

Karl glanced at the rusted loops of metal set at the ledge's end just before the long fall to the courtyard below where the dragon's head glared at the Bastida's gates, and he shivered. He swallowed with difficulty around the tongue gag. "More recently, the Kraljica had her cousin Marcus ca'Gerodi put here for treason, early in her reign," ca'Rudka said, "but he was neither as long-lived or stubborn as ca'Niomi, nor as artistic. We never had any poetry from poor ca'Gerodi."

Ca'Rudka sighed, standing. "One-sided conversations are boring, I'm afraid. For both of us. I believe you to be a man of honor, Envoy ci'Vliomani. I would accept your pledge not to use any of your Numetodo tricks and remove your silencer. Your hands, I'm afraid, will have to remain bound, but we could at least talk. Do I have your word?"

Karl nodded as he stepped back into the dank room, unable to keep the gratitude from his eyes. "If you would turn around, Envoy . . ." As Karl complied, he heard the jangle of keys, and a *click* that reverberated through the straps bound tight to his skull. A moment later, ca'Rudka slid the horrid device from Karl's mouth. Karl sighed gratefully, stretching his jaw and swallowing to rid his mouth of the taste of metal and foul cloth. "I know it's uncomfortable," the commandant said. "But it's a less, shall we say, *final* option than cutting off your hands and removing your tongue."

The man managed to say it with a smile, as if they were sharing a joke. Again, the gardai in the corridor chuckled softly. Karl struggled to keep the shock from his face, but the broadening smile on ca'Rudka's face made him suspect he'd not been successful.

"It's a preferable alternative, Commandant," Karl told him. His jaw ached with the movement, and his words were slurred. "I'll grant you that. Though we Numetodo aren't the threat to Nessantico that you believe us to be."

"Ah. You think I'm a monster."

Karl shook his head. "A monster would have already done those things to me. A monster wouldn't have . . ." He glanced at the gardai in the corridor and lowered his voice to a whisper. ". . . tried to warn me to leave the city."

Another smile. "Ah, yes. A man of discretion, even in these circumstances. You see, I do like you, Envoy. I liked you from the time we talked in the Kraljica's gardens. It's rare to find people who are honest about what they believe, and rarer still when they persist in the face of persecution."

"I didn't kill the Kraljica, Commandant. I had nothing to do with it."

"I believe that completely," ca'Rudka said. "I truly do."

"Then let me go."

"What I believe has little impact on what I'm required to do, Envoy," the man answered. "Tell me, did you know that painter ci'Recroix?"

"I saw him once or twice, walking in the city," Karl answered. "I knew he was painting the Kraljica's portrait, but so did everyone else."

"Was he a Numetodo?"

Karl shook his head vigorously. "I would have known that, Commandant. The man was very recognizable, and someone of his reputation . . . Well, I would have heard of him even before I came to Nessantico were he one of us. I didn't. Why do you ask about the painter? If you think that he had something to do with the Kraljica's death, then why am I here?"

"The A'Kralj ordered your arrest, as well as that of all the Numetodo in the city."

Karl found his breath caught in his throat. "All . . ."

The commandant nodded. "Those we suspect, in any case. They're here in the Bastida, though not . . ." He let his gaze wander around the tiny, dour room. ". . . in such palatial conditions as you. All silenced and bound, though—until the Kraljiki tells me what I'm to do."

Karl grimaced. In the manacles, his fists clenched. "Given that the Kraljiki has already made it clear that he favors ca'Cellibrecca over the Archigos, then we'll see Brezno repeated, and worse. Will you enjoy that, Commandant? It will be your duty to direct the maimings and executions, after all."

Ca'Rudka made no answer at first. His eyebrows lifted slightly. "If it comes to that, Envoy ci'Vliomani," he said finally, "I promise you that your end will be quick."

Karl could not keep the bitterness from his voice. "That gives me great solace."

If ca'Rudka heard the sarcasm in Karl's voice, he didn't respond to it. "You Numetodo don't understand what it is to obey," he answered. Ca'Rudka said it without heat, without any apparent passion at all. "You believe what you each please. You're like wild horses. Despite any power you might have, you're useless because you don't understand the bridle and the bit." The commandant moved to the window of the cell, looking out toward the city. "It's obedience to a higher authority that created everything you see out there, Envoy. All of it. All of Nessantico, all of the greater Holdings. Without obedience—to Cénzi, to the Divolonté, to the laws of the Kralji, to the rules of society—there's nothing but chaos."

"Were you born here, Commandant? In the city, I mean?"

The man glanced back over his shoulder at Karl. "I was," he said.

"You've never been elsewhere?"

"I served in the Garde Civile when I was young. I saw war along the frontier of East Magyaria, when the Cabasan of Daritria crossed the Gereshki with his army in violation of the Treaty of Otavi." He touched his silver nose. "I lost my real one there, in a stupid quarrel with one of our own men. Afterward, I came back here a chevaritt, with a recommendation from my superiors, and joined the Garde Kralji."

"You've never been to the western borders? Never crossed the Strettosei to Hellin or the Isle of Paeti?" Ca'Rudka shook his head. "If you had," Karl continued, "you might understand. Ah, the Isle . . . There's not a greener, more lush and more varied country in the world. And there, Commandant, where a dozen cultures have come and gone, we understand that 'different' isn't a synonym for 'wrong.' There are many ways to learning the truth of how the world works, Commandant. The Concénzia Faith is just one. It's just not *the* one, not the *only* way. I have seen things . . ." He stopped, shaking his head. The motion rattled the chains around his hands and caused the guards to glance into the cell again. "You would probably have me flayed for telling you," he said.

Ca'Rudka had turned back into the room, leaning against the wall by the balcony. "If I wanted to flay you, Vajiki, I would have already done it, and for less provocation. Tell me."

Karl licked his lips. "My parents lived on the eastern coast of the Isle. They were of the Faith, and they brought me up to believe in Cénzi. They read the Toustour to me; they followed the precepts of the Divolonté. When I became a young man, though, I had the wanderlust and I traveled with a company of traders beyond the Isle to what you call the Westlands, past the green mountains on the borders of Hellin. That trip opened my eyes and my mind. There, out in a flat plain of grasses that stretched like a waving ocean from horizon to horizon, I saw a city that could have easily held three Nessanticos, grand and glorious, with enormous buildings like stepped mountains on top of which their priests held their ceremonies, with buildings of cut stone that gleamed in the sun, while canals glittered with sweet water alongside avenues wider than the Avi. The people there wore clothing of a fabric I'd never seen before, bright and smooth to the touch, a cloth that let the breezes flow through to keep you cool in the heat. And at night—Commandant, the city glowed with magefire brighter than the Avi. They used your Ilmodo, too, though they didn't call it either 'Ilmodo' or 'Scáth Cumhacht,' nor did they worship Cénzi, who they considered just another god among many. But they could shape the Second World as well as any of the téni. That, Commandant, is when my own faith began to waver."

"Perhaps it was a test," ca'Rudka answered without emotion. "One that you failed."

"That's what the téni on the Isle told me later." Karl shrugged. "The traders I traveled with said that there were even greater cities, farther west and south, all the way to the shore of the Western Sea two hundred days' or more march from where we were. They said that they were part of an empire larger, richer, and more powerful than the Holdings. I don't necessarily believe those stories—I know as well as you that travelers' tales grow with each telling, and that it's our nature to make ourselves sound more like great adventurers than simple tourists. But this city . . . I saw it with these eyes, and I've never seen its like anywhere else. I *know* this, Commandant: there are more mysteries in this world than the Concénzia Faith will allow you to believe."

Ca'Rudka smiled indulgently at the long speech. "Sometimes, to young eyes, the small looks larger than it is. I would think that if such a great empire exists beyond the Hellin Mountains, we would have met its armies or at least its envoys when we came to the Hellins. I may not have been there myself, but I met the Governor of the Hellins when he was last in Nessantico, and he said that the natives there were little more than savages."

"He sees them with the wrong eyes, then," Karl answered. "Like looking through the stained glass of the temple, he doesn't see the true colors beyond."

"And you do? I find that rather arrogant, Envoy ci'Vliomani. It surprises me to find that quality in you."

"We all have colored glass through which we view the world, Commandant," Karl answered. "Our society and our upbringing and our experiences place the glass before us, with the Numetodo no less than the Concénzia Faith. I don't deny that. But I think we Numetodo have more shades of color from which to choose and that, as a result, we are closer to the truth."

Ca'Rudka laughed again, though this time the guards remained quiet. "You are a fascinating creature, Envoy ci'Vliomani." He took a long breath. "I enjoy listening to you, and no doubt we'll have ample opportunity to continue our conversation. But for now . . ." He picked up the silencer from the table, its metal buckles jangling. The taste of foul leather filled Karl's mouth, just seeing it.

"Commandant, I will give you my word . . ."

"And I would accept it," ca'Rudka answered before Karl finished. The silencer swayed in his hand. "The Kraljiki will want a confession from the Kraljica's assassin. Are you prepared to give that to him, Envoy?"

"I can't confess to what I didn't do," Karl answered, and ca'Rudka smiled at that, with the indulgent expression of an adult listening to a young child.

"Can't?" he said. "I'm afraid that happens all the time here in the Bastida, Envoy. I think you might be surprised what a person would be willing to admit under the right encouragement. Why, give me six lines written by the hand of the most honest man, and I could find something in them to have him hanged."

Karl's breath vanished. He felt suddenly cold. "Open your mouth, Envoy," ca'Rudka said. "I promise you that I'll be back tomorrow, and each day until the Kraljiki tells me what I must do with you, and as long as you give me your word, I'll take the silencer from you so we can talk more. I will cherish those times, truly. Now . . . I need you to open your mouth, or I will have the gardai come in and put on the silencer in their own fashion. Which would you prefer?"

There was nothing but despair in Karl's heart now. He knew he would die here, and he knew that there was nothing he could do except make that death as painless as possible. Karl opened his mouth and allowed ca'Rudka to buckle the device to his head. He felt tears forming as ca'Rudka stepped behind him to tighten the straps, and he forced them back, blinking hard.

Sergei ca'Rudka

"COMMANDANT, I wish to see Karl ci'Vliomani."
Sergei straightened the inkwell on his desk, arranging the quills in their holder. Then he looked again at the young woman in front of him, wearing the green robes of the téni. "I find that I'm surprised you would make such a request, O'Téni cu'Seranta, especially given that you were with the Numetodo when I arrested him." He raised his eyebrows. "I doubt that the Archigos would be pleased to find you here after that coincidence."

"As it turns out, I'm here on the Archigos' business." The slight hesitation and the way she averted her eyes before she spoke was enough to tell Sergei that she wasn't telling the truth—lies in all their shades and forms were something he knew intimately, and the o'téni was hardly a facile liar.

"I see," he answered. He rubbed the cold metal of his nose. "The stamina of our Archigos never fails to amaze me, especially on a day such as today, when there must a hundred details to which he must attend for the Kraljica's funeral and for the procession this evening. You have a letter for me, perhaps, outlining this 'business' on which he has sent you?" She shook her head. Her gaze wandered somewhere past him, to the bare stone walls behind. "Ah, I see. An unfortunate gaffe on his part. The Archigos must understand after all his years here in Nessantico how the gears of the Holdings are milled from paper and greased with ink. But perhaps if

you could tell me about this . . ." He paused deliberately.
". . . business."

His hands were folded on his desk and she stared at
them. Perhaps she was expecting to see blood there.
She hadn't prepared the lie; she startled with the last
word, like a dove surprised on a windowsill. "I . . . the
Archigos . . . we know Envoy ci'Vliomani had wished to
meet the Kraljica . . . and . . . and . . ."

"O'Téni." Sergei lifted a hand and she lapsed into
a flushed silence. "We needn't pretend. Not here. The
Bastida is not a place for posturing. The two of you are
lovers?"

The flush crept higher on her neck. "No," she said
quickly. That was the truth, he could tell, though he
could guess the rest: ci'Vliomani was attractive enough,
intelligent enough, and given her unremarkable features and the rank of her family before her recent el-
evation, he doubted that she had been much pursued
by suitors in the past. He could imagine the attraction
ci'Vliomani might have for her; he could also imagine that she would be an easy mark for a seduction, if
ci'Vliomani had wanted to use her. He'd glimpsed her
fear for ci'Vliomani's fate in the apartment when he'd
arrested the man, heard it in the urgent whispers they'd
exchanged as he took ci'Vliomani away. If they weren't
lovers, there was still a bond between them. He hoped,
for her sake, that the bond ran both ways.

She was attracted to the lure of the foreign, the alien,
the forbidden. He knew that. He felt it himself. He understood. So he smiled at the young woman.

"No," he repeated, just to watch the flush bloom again
in her cheeks. "Then what is your interest in him?"

"He . . ." She swallowed. Her eyes found his face and
wandered away again. Then she took a long breath
in through her nose and stared hard at him. "He is a
friend. I don't believe that those who possess a true
faith have anything to fear from learning about other
ways. We won't bring the Numetodo back to the Faith

through torment and death, Commandant. We will bring them back through understanding."

She spoke with such passion and earnestness that Sergei leaned back in his chair and patted his hands together softly. "Bravo, O'Téni. Well said—though that doesn't appear to be a position most of the a'téni or the A'Kralj would take, nor even the Archigos himself. And unfortunately . . ." He spread his hands wide. ". . . those are the masters I serve."

He could see the fear in her face, could nearly taste it in the air, sweet. "Envoy ci'Vliomani . . . is he . . ."

"He is bound and silenced, as he must be so that he doesn't misuse the Ilmodo. But otherwise, he is well-treated and in good health." He saw her relax slightly. "Thus far," he added, and the pallid fear returned to her. "You understand that I can make no promises."

"If it would be possible . . . if I could see him, Commandant . . ." She licked at dry lips. "I would be grateful, and perhaps such a favor could be returned to you."

"You offer me a bribe, O'Téni?" he asked, smiling to gentle the blow.

She said nothing. Did nothing.

He nodded, finally. "You will be part of the Kraljica's final procession this evening?" She nodded in mute answer. "As I will be. Afterward, I could perhaps accompany you when you take your leave. The Archigos would understand that I might have questions for you regarding Envoy ci'Vliomani. If I happened to escort you here, neither the Archigos nor the A'Kralj would be surprised, and perhaps I might be persuaded to let you see Envoy ci'Vliomani for a few moments. As a . . . favor."

"I would be in your debt, Commandant."

"Yes," he answered solemnly. "You would indeed, O'Téni cu'Seranta." He saw the way she drew back a step with his statement, and the furtive, reflexive manner in which she tightened her robes around her. The sight gave him a small satisfaction. "Tonight, then."

She nodded and drew the hood over her head. As she reached the door, he called out to her. "We both believe Envoy ci'Vliomani is innocent, O'Téni. But what we believe may be of no matter."

~

Mahri

THE MASSIVE TWIN HEADS of two ancient Kraljiki, set on either side of Nortegate, gleamed eerily with téni-fire. At night, their features were illuminated from within the hollow stone so that they appeared almost demonic, but rather than facing out as they usually did, glaring at any potential invaders, the e'téni tending them had used the power of the Ilmodo to turn the heavy sculptures inward so that the great, scowling visages glared eastward: toward the oncoming procession of the Kraljica as it paraded slowly along the gleaming Avi a'Parete toward the Pontica Kralji and the Isle A'Kralj, where the final ceremony would be held. They seemed angry, perhaps furious that the Kraljica had been taken from the city in the midst of the celebration of her Jubilee.

The procession coiled along the Avi like a thick, gilded snake caught in the famous téni-lights of the city, which gleamed in doubled brilliance tonight. First came a phalanx of the Garde Kralji in their dress uniforms, led by Commandant ca'Rudka. Their stern, forbidding faces cleared the crowds from the Avi, pushing any errant pedestrians back into the onlookers who lined the Avi and clogged the openings to the side streets. More of the Garde Kralji, in standard uniform and bearing pole arms, marched slowly on either side of the Avi, herding the crowds and watching for any signs of disturbance.

Given the reputation of the Garde Kralji for cruelty and thoroughness, it was hardly surprising that there were none.

Then came the chevarittai of the city, astride their horses and in their field armor, polished and gleaming. In the midst of them was a lone, riderless white horse, shielded by their lances and their swords. The chevarittai paraded by, grim-faced and solemn, the hooves of their destriers loud on the cobblestones of the Avi.

Then came the Sun Throne from which the Kraljica had ruled for her five decades, floating effortlessly above the stones through the effort of several chanting téni who paced with it, the eternal light inside the crystalline facets alive and gleaming a sober, sullen ultramarine, as if the throne itself understood the import of the moment. Two dozen court musicians paced behind the throne, dressed in bone-white, their horns and pipes inflicting an endless dirge on the onlookers that echoed belatedly from the buildings on either side. The Archigos' carriage followed the musicians at a judicious distance from the cacophony, bearing the Archigos as well as several of the older (and less mobile) a'téni currently in residence in Nessantico, A'Téni ca'Cellibrecca among them.

Behind the Archigos was a long double line of green-robed a'téni and u'téni, all of them chanting, their hands moving in the patterns of spells. In the air above them flickered images of the Kraljica as she had been when she was alive: not solid illusions, but wispy ghosts shimmering in the air, far larger than life and looming over the mourners in the street below.

The Kraljica's carriage was next. She had been placed in a glass coffin, and a quartet of chanting téni stood at each corner, molding the Ilmodo so that the carriage itself could not be seen and the Kraljica's coffin appeared to float in a golden, smoky glow that smelled of trumpet flowers and anise, and from which came the sound of high voices singing a choral lament. A shower of trumpet

flower petals rained from the cloud under the coffin,
carpeting the Avi and those in the front ranks of the onlookers in fragrant yellow.

The A'Kralj's carriage wheels crushed the trumpet
flower petals underneath. Directly behind his matarh's
coffin and flanked by a stern border of Garde Kralji, all
of whom stared intently at the onlookers, the A'Kralj sat
alone and solemn, wrapped in thick furs, his face covered with a golden mourning mask on the cheeks of
which were set twin, tear-shaped rubies, though his fingers were conspicuously bare of ornamentation. His carriage was not téni-driven, but pulled by a trio of horses
in a four-horse harness.

Finally, the ca'-and-cu' families themselves followed in
careful order of their social rank, dressed in ostentatious
white and with heads respectfully bowed. A squadron of
the Garde Civile from the local garrison protected them
from the commoners who closed in after the procession
passed, filling the Avi again.

All of Nessantico, it seemed, had turned out to watch
the Kraljica's final procession around the ring of the Avi:
young, old, from the ca' all the way down to the ce' and
the unregistered. Many of them held lighted candles, so
that it seemed that the stars had fallen from the sky to
land here. For the vast majority of them, the Kraljica
had been the only ruler of Nessantico they'd known, all
their lives. As Kralji went, hers had been a quiet reign,
especially for the last few decades. Now they watched
her last promenade through the city that had been her
home, and they wondered what the future might bring.

Mahri wondered that as well. He watched from the
inner side of the avenue, near the flanks of the Registry
building. Even among the packed crowds in Oldtown,
Mahri was left in his own space. The masses of people
around him sighed but left him alone, a dark mote in the
téni-lit brilliance of the funeral procession.

Mahri had watched the slow, solemn procession pass
the Pontica a'Brezi Nippoli some time ago, and he had

hurried through the maze of Oldtown to see it again here at Nortegate. He had wanted to make certain of something.

As the dirge of the court musicians began to fade, the Archigos' carriage passed into Nortegate Square. Alongside the Archigos' carriage walked several of his staff, among them O'Téni cu'Seranta. It was her that Mahri leaned forward to see.

He'd prepared the spell before he'd come here, after images of O'Téni cu'Seranta dominated several of the auguries he'd performed. He spoke a guttural word (causing those nearest him to glance over at the strange sound), and made a motion as if shooing away a persistent fly. He could see the X'in Ka—what the téni called the Ilmodo and the Numetodo called Scáth Cumhacht—twisting in response, though he knew the movement was invisible to anyone else there. That was his gift, that he could see it: tendrils of energy, like the wavering of sunlight above a still lake, wrapped around the Archigos' carriage. No one there reacted. But O'Téni cu'Seranta . . .

Her head was down as if praying. He thought for a moment that nothing would happen, then he saw her glance up, slowly, though her eyes were bright and suspicious and her fingers reflexively curled as if she wanted to make a warding. It was enough; he released the spell, let it evaporate as if it had never been there. Her reaction had been sluggish; he'd hoped for a more immediate and stronger response, but it was possible she had been lost in her prayers for the Kraljica and her grief, distracted by the noise and the crowds.

But she *had* felt him. She was able to sense the very movements of the X'in Ka, not simply manipulate it. He knew that much; it was more than the Numetodo ci'Vliomani could do. She was still glancing around, as if searching for the source of the energy she had felt. He pushed back into the shadows of the Registry so she wouldn't see him.

Perhaps it could be her. Perhaps. If circumstance

didn't interfere. If the gods smiled. If he was interpreting the images in the augury-bowl correctly. If he wasn't simply wrong ...

There were too many ifs ...

But perhaps ...

The Archigos' carriage and O'Téni cu'Seranta had passed him now, moving on toward the Pontica Kralji and the final ceremony. The sculptured heads flanking the Nortegate swiveled as the Kraljica passed, their fiery gazes tracking the carriage that held her body. The coffin still floated in its golden cloud—the téni creating the illusion replaced as the effort of the spell became too exhausting. The four there now were not the four Mahri had seen when the procession passed the Pontica a'Breze Nippoli, and already he could sense the weakness in the X'in Ka—they were flagging and would soon be relieved themselves.

The téni were so weak.

The heads stared at the Kraljica and also caught Mahri in their fiery scowl, as if they were chastising him for his arrogance. He turned his back to them, striding away from the Avi and ignoring the comments of the crowd as he pushed through them. A block south of the Avi, the crowds had vanished and the sound of chanting and music faded, replaced by the familiar clamor of Oldtown.

If he reached the Pontica Kralji before the Kraljica's procession, he could cross over to the Isle and watch the passing of the Kraljica into history.

He wondered how quickly the new Kraljiki might follow her.

~

Ana cu'Seranta

THE TOWER STANK of mold and urine and fear, and the torches set in their sconces accentuated the darkness rather than banishing it. The long climb left the muscles in her legs aching, but she wasn't going to give the commandant the satisfaction of her pain.

Ana's heart sank when Karl turned at the sound of footsteps outside his cell and she saw his chained hands and the awful device clamped around his head. The commandant nodded to the garda outside the door, who took the keys from his belt and opened the cell door. "You may go eat your supper, E'Garda," ca'Rudka said, inclining his head toward the spiral stone staircase. The man saluted and hurried away. The commandant stepped aside and gestured to Ana to enter; he followed behind her.

"Envoy ci'Vliomani, I've brought someone to see you. I assume I have your word as before not to use the Ilmodo?"

A nod. The commandant moved behind Karl and took the silencer from his head. Karl grimaced and drew his sleeve over his saliva-slick mouth. "You shouldn't have come," he said to Ana, and she thought for a moment that he was truly angry. "But I'm glad you did," he added. "I could see the flames of the Kraljica's pyre from here." He nodded toward the open shutters of the balcony, where flickering yellow still touched the stones. "You were there?"

Ana nodded. "I watched the A'Kralj take the scepter and ring from her hands. The Archigos lit the pyre with the Ilmodo. The heat was almost too much to bear. I've never felt a fire so intense . . ." She stopped, realizing that she was talking only to keep away the silence. She heard the clatter of metal against metal and saw the commandant holding a set of heavy cuffs, the thick rings of metal opened.

"I would leave the two of you alone to talk," he said, "but I'd be failing in my duty if I did so without making certain you can't use the Ilmodo, O'Téni cu'Seranta."

"I will give you my word, Commandant," Ana told him. She was looking more at the manacles than at him.

"And I would take it, except that if you *were* to break your word and help the envoy to escape, then I would be the one sitting in this cell. As I've already told the Envoy, I know the Bastida all too well, and I have made enemies in my career who would no doubt take great delight in my pain. That's not a chance I'm willing to take. So . . ." He smiled, jingling the manacles. "I will accept your word, O'Téni, but I will also have your hands bound while you're here so that I *know* your word will be kept. I'll give you *my* word that I'll return in a turn of the glass to release you. That is, if my word is something you're willing to accept. . . ."

He raised his eyebrows, proffering the manacles. Reluctantly, Ana extended her hands to him. The steel was lined with leather, with dark stains that Ana tried to ignore. The shackles pinched her skin as the commandant pressed the halves around her wrists and locked them together. The harsh click of the lock sent panic rushing through her: he could keep her here; he could take her to one of the cells in the Bastida and do whatever he wished to her—torture her, rape her, kill her.

He must have sensed her growing panic. He stepped back. "My word is law here, O'Téni, and I don't make promises that I won't keep," he told her. "One turn of the glass, and I will take these away from you."

Ana nodded. The commandant glanced from her to

Karl. "And I trust your word as well, Envoy," he said. With that, he left the cell, locking the door behind him. They heard his footsteps on the stairs.

"Ana," Karl said, bringing her gaze away from the locked and barred door. "I had nothing to do with the Kraljica's death. Nothing. I swear to you."

"I believe you," she told him. "Only Cénzi knows why, but I do."

"How are you? Does the Archigos know you were with me when I was arrested?"

"The commandant told him, I'm certain. He seems mostly, I don't know, disappointed. Dejected. But he has more important issues."

"And you? Have you been able to find the Scáth Cumhacht, the Ilmodo, as you did before?"

She could only shake her head, not trusting her voice. "I'm sorry," he told her. She felt his bound hands touch hers. Their fingers linked. "I wish I could show you," he said quietly. "I wish I could teach you."

"I wish that, too," she told him. His head bent toward her. His lips brushed her hair, her forehead. She remembered her vatarh doing the same to her: at night, in the darkness. With her vatarh, she had trembled and turned her face away. With him, she had endured the embrace and the touch. With him, she had felt nothing but ice and fear.

It was not what she felt now. She lifted up her face to meet Karl's. She felt the trembling of her lips against his as they touched. She closed her eyes, feeling only the kiss. Only the kiss.

She drew away from him. "Ana?" he asked.

"Don't say anything," she told him. Her hands still held his. She leaned her head against his shoulder. She felt him start to move to put his arms around her, but there was only the clanking of chains and a muttered curse. "It's all fallen apart," she said. "Everything I thought I had. Everything I might have wanted."

"I'm so sorry, Ana."

"Don't be. It's not your fault. It's mine. I . . . I lost my faith."

"I did once, too," he told her, his breath warm on her ear. "And I found a new one. A better one."

"I glad you could," she told him. "I can't."

He stepped back from her then, though he would not let go of her hands. Iron clinked unmusically in response. "You have to have faith in yourself first," he told her, and she made a scoffing noise as she turned her head. The yellow light of the Kraljica's funeral prowled the stones of the tower. She released his hands and went to the opening to the balcony. Vertigo swept over her momentarily as she looked at the shelf of stone and the long fall below. She clung to the side of the balcony, staring out rather than down. The Avi was a circlet of glowing pearls around the city, and the waters of the A'Sele glittered and reflected the téni-lights. The Kraljica's—no, the Kraljiki's—palais on the Isle was brilliant, all the windows alive with téni-lights or candelabras, and the gilded roofs of the temples shimmered in their own radiance. Between the Old Temple and the palais, the embers of the Kraljica's pyre still threw tongues of flame and whirling sparks at the stars.

Out there, the téni worked: keeping Nessantico alive and vital. Nessantico held back the night, refusing to allow it dominion. *Like your faith once did for you,* she thought.

"It's pretty, isn't it?" Karl said behind her. She nodded.

"My vatarh . . ." She started to tell him about how he'd said he could see the city at night from afar, and stopped herself. She didn't want to talk about her va-tarh. He was dead, as far as she was concerned. "Tell me about you," she told him. "Tell me more about the Numetodo. Please. Let's sit here, where we can look out at the city . . ." She asked him because she didn't want to think, didn't want to talk. She only wanted to sit next to him, to feel his warmth on her side, and listen to his voice. The words didn't matter, only his presence.

She wondered if he realized that.

They sat, and he talked, and she half-listened, her own thoughts crashing against themselves in her head so loudly that they nearly drowned out his voice.

BONDS

Jan ca'Vörl
Ana cu'Seranta
Dhosti ca'Millac
Orlandi ca'Cellibrecca
Ana cu'Seranta
Mahri
Karl ci'Vliomani
Ana cu'Seranta

Jan ca'Vörl

FROM THE WOODED crown of the rise, the army spread out along the valley like a horde of black ants on the march. Dust enveloped them in a tan, hazy cloak as they trudged along the rutted, boot-stamped dirt of the Avi a'Firenzcia. The western horizon promised rain, and their banners hung limp in a breezeless air, stained with the same tan that caked the boots of the foot soldiers and packed the hooves of the cheverittai's horses. Faintly, Jan could hear the sound of the drummers beating cadence.

Jan watched as a single rider broke off from the main force and galloped toward the ridge where he, Starkkapitän ca'Staunton, Allesandra, and Markell were watching. Markell gestured to one of the starkkapitän's offiziers, standing with their own horses judiciously downhill from the group above. An offizier saluted and mounted, intercepting the rider; they exchanged words and a packet. The offizier gestured back up the hill. "Your pardon, my Hïrzg," Markell said. Nudging the side of his horse with his bootheels, he rode down and spoke for a few minutes with the rider before returning to the ridge.

"Word has come from Nessantico, my Hïrzg," Markell said as he came abreast of Jan. Markell frowned as he handed Jan a leather courier's pouch. "There's a letter from A'Téni ca'Cellibrecca inside."

"And?" Jan asked.

The frown deepened. "The rider tells me that the

Kraljica is dead," Markell answered. "Assassinated. Justi ca'Mazzak has been installed as the new Kraljiki."

Jan felt himself sitting up in his saddle at the words. *That's not possible,* he wanted to rail at Markell. *It must be a mistake.* Jan stared out at his army, the army used so often by the Kralji when they wanted a rebellion crushed or a territory conquered, the army that the Garde Civile believed they rather than the Hïrzg commanded. The army that was intended to force the Kraljica's hand, a hand that was now dead and still.

"Vatarh? What's the matter?" Allesandra asked him. He ignored her.

"Assassinated by whom?" he growled at Markell.

"The gossip is that it was a Numetodo, according to the rider," Markell said. "Kraljiki Justi has ordered the arrest of all Numetodo in the city."

Jan clenched his jaw, staring at the pouch in his gloved hand. He opened it, glanced at the letter with A'Téni ca'Cellibrecca's seal on it, still intact. A suspicion began to form. *All I did for him, all the planning . . .* "Stark-kapitän," he told ca'Staunton, waiting patient and silent with his face carefully arranged to show nothing, "we will make camp here for the day. Have your men prepare my tent. Find that rider; if he hasn't spread word yet about the Kraljica, make certain that it stays that way. This is news I need to contemplate, and I don't need rumors spreading though the ranks."

Ca'Staunton saluted and rode off, calling to his offiziers. He barked orders to them and they scattered, dust rising in a line from their horses' hooves as they galloped toward the main force of the army.

Two turns of the glass later, Jan called Markell to his tent. When the man entered, he went to Allesandra, playing with her soldiers, and hugged her quickly. "Go outside for awhile," he told her. "Find your Georgi or get some food."

"I want to stay, Vatarh. I want to listen."

"No." The single, firm word made her close her lips

tightly. She gave Jan an ironic bow like a common offizier and left the tent. Watching the tent flap close behind her, Jan picked up the sheaf of parchments from his travel desk and tossed it toward Markell. "Ca'Cellibrecca is going to get his balls squeezed in a vise of his own making if he isn't careful. When he does, I am going to enjoy hearing him squeal like the pig he is."

"Hïrzg?"

Jan waved a hand. "The man plays both sides, Markell. He had us get rid of his daughter's inconvenient husband so she'd be free for marriage, and we went along with him. Now the woman's free, yes, but she's also free to marry the Kraljiki."

Markell blinked. "To have the Kraljiki married to . . ." He stopped.

Jan nodded. "Yes, my friend," he said dryly. "You see it, too. A Kraljiki married to the Archigos' daughter would be a perfect marriage of secular and religious power. And there just happens to be an unmarried Kraljiki." He pointed to the paper in Markell's hands. "With her husband dead, ca'Cellibrecca's daughter is now conveniently available for Justi. And the new Kraljiki will certainly be looking to marry soon to consolidate his position. Serendipitous, don't you think?" Jan leaned back in his chair. "Kraljiki Justi ca'Cellibrecca. I'm sure A'Téni ca'Cellibrecca thinks that would be an excellent name. In fact, it makes me suspect that our Orlandi was the one behind the murder of the Kraljica, though of course he talks about nothing but the Numetodo in his letter, and how they must be exterminated. It's wonderful to have such a convenient, politically-expedient excuse as the Numetodo. He also tells us that 'it's urgent that we abandon our present course for the time being.' He says our plans must now wait 'until we have a chance to fully examine the implications of the current situation.' Though, of course, he's now stuck in Nessantico for the duration and doesn't know when he'll return to Brezno. The cunning bastard . . ."

Rising from his chair, Jan snatched the letter back from Markell's hand and scanned it again, his nostrils flaring. He tossed the parchment into the small warming stove in the center of the tent and watched the edges curl, darken, and finally burst into flame. "I begin to believe that A'Téni ca'Cellibrecca always considered us a secondary strategy, something to use if his plot to kill the Kraljica failed and he couldn't manipulate Marguerite's poor excuse for a son. Now everything's fallen in place for him. All that remains is for our army to stand down and he has everything he wants. The next news from Nessantico will tell us how that dwarf ca'Millac has died and ca'Cellibrecca has been installed as the new Archigos, and that the Kraljiki has married Francesca. As Archigos, he would hold the threat of withdrawing the Faith's support from Firenzcia if I don't submit—and U'Téni cu'Kohnle, who served with ca'Cellibrecca, just happens to be our chief war-téni."

"Cu'Kohnle is Firenzcian, unlike ca'Cellibrecca," Markell said. "His loyalty is to you more than A'Téni ca'Cellibrecca."

"Maybe," Jan grunted. "But when the A'Téni is Archigos Orlandi, that may change. The new Kraljiki will also insist that I stay married to that pious cow Greta. No doubt the news has reached Brezno by now; I'll wager she's on her knees praying to Cénzi in gratitude for her deliverance. I wonder if she and ca'Cellibrecca weren't plotting this all along."

Jan paced the small perimeter of the tent and sat again. Outside, he could hear the sounds of the encampment: low talk, a burst of laughter, the clatter and bustle as food was prepared. Markell waited patiently, warming his hands over the coals where ca'Cellibrecca's paper was now ash.

"Vatarh?" It was Allesandra, standing at the tent flap. She let it drop behind her. "Vatarh, you told me that a good general must know which battles he can win and which he cannot. Is this one you can win?"

He stared at her, shaking his head. "You were listening?"

"You told me to go outside and find Georgi. I looked and I didn't see him. You didn't tell me not to listen."

Markell raised his eyebrows. Jan sighed. "So you've listened and you know. In that case, what do you think?"

"In all the stories you've ever told me, and in all the ones Georgi knows, the Hïrzg never gives up. I think A'Téni ca'Cellibrecca doesn't know those stories, or he didn't listen to them very well."

Jan laughed, and Markell joined in. "The wisdom of a child," Jan said. He nodded, and applauded softly. "This has been a battle without armies," he told her, "as it has been since we started this course. But we have an army with us. If we turn back now, we lose the advantage of the field."

"My Hïrzg?" Markell asked.

"Justi has the title. That's all. He has nothing else yet. And ca'Cellibrecca isn't yet the Archigos. We're only two days from the border and a fortnight to the gates of Nessantico itself. Ca'Cellibrecca advises us to wait—but he has the interests of Orlandi ca'Cellibrecca in mind, not the Hïrzg of Firenzcia. As my daughter has just said, he doesn't know the stories of Firenzcia."

Jan saw the ghost of a smile press against Markell's thin lips. "Should I inform the starkkapitän that we will continue our advance in the morning?"

"Tell him that I intend to pay a personal visit to the new Kraljiki," Jan told him. "And send U'Téni cu'Kohnle in; I need to know where his loyalties truly lie."

"As you wish, my Hïrzg," Markell answered with a quick bow. He opened the flaps of the tent, and Jan heard him speak quickly to one of the gardai, and then the rattle of armor as the man strode quickly away.

"A good general doesn't hedge," Jan said to Allesandra. "And he doesn't hesitate because the winds have changed. He uses them, instead."

~

Ana cu'Seranta

"LET ME TAKE YOUR CLOAK, O'Téni Ana. They say the weather will change soon."

"Where's Vatarh?" Ana asked Sala. The maidservant shook her head.

"He's not here, O'Téni Ana," she answered. "He's away in Prajnoli on business. He's away almost all the time, ever since . . ." She hesitated, and Ana saw a blush creep from her neck to her cheeks.

"I understand," she told the girl. "Don't worry about it, Sala. Matarh?"

"She's expecting you, in the sun room. I'll announce that you're here."

"Don't bother. I'll go on back and surprise her."

The house no longer seemed familiar to her at all—it had changed even more since she'd last been here. The smell of fresh plaster and paint hung in the foyer, an odor like guilt. The hallway beyond the front door was now a pale blue instead of the yellow she remembered, and when she reached the archway into the sun room, it was no longer draped with black as it had been when her matarh was sick but was now filled with flowers and plants, and there was a young male servant she didn't know there with Tari. And the woman, standing with her back to Ana and tending to a pot of blue-and-white-petaled skyblooms . . .

Ana felt her breath catch. After the argument they'd had the last time they met, Ana had been surprised when her matarh had sent Ana a request to visit. *Please, Cénzi, don't let her still hate me. . . .*

"O'Téni Ana!" Tari exclaimed, seeing her, and the woman turned from the skyblooms.

"Ana. I'm glad you came." Matarh smiled gently, and Ana felt the tension within her dissolve with the greeting. Abini set down the small trowel and spread her arms. Ana went to her, letting herself fall into the embrace, her matarh's arms snug around her. Ana found herself crying, all unbidden; her matarh continued to hold her tightly. "Hush, child. Hush . . ."

Ana sniffed and wiped at the betraying tears, pulling away slightly. Tari and the young man were pointedly looking away from them. "You've engaged some new help," she said.

"That's Jacques, who works around the house and on the grounds, and we have a new cook as well, who makes the most wonderful soups. They were both recommended to me by Vajica cu'Meredi—do you remember her? She's used to call on us before . . ." For a moment the old pain crossed her matarh's face. ". . . when your brothers were still alive and before I became sick. She's made several calls to our house since you received your Marque. All this . . ." Her matarh pressed her lips together, fine wrinkles gathering. "All this is because of you, Ana. Everyone knows how the Archigos chose you personally, and that you tended to the poor Kraljica . . ." She stopped then. "Tari, why don't you have Cook make Ana something? Jacques, if you'd tend to the bushes in the rear garden . . ."

They ducked their heads and left. Abini continued to hold Ana. "You look so sad," she said. "Is something wrong?"

Ana could only nod. She didn't trust her voice.

"Is it the Kraljica? Her death was a shock to us all, and now there's that horrible news come from Firenzcia about poor U'Téni Estraven ca'Cellibrecca being murdered; I used to enjoy his Admonitions. I hope they kill every last Numetodo in the city for what they did."

The image of Karl, bound and silenced in the tower

of the Bastida, came to her. So did the memory of seeing him, of his brief single kiss . . . "Matarh," Ana interrupted. "Stop. Please."

Abini's eyes widened, and Ana kissed her cheek to
soften the impact of the words. "I should have come to
see you sooner, Matarh," she said. "I wanted to. But . . ."
I couldn't, because I was afraid he *would be here. I
couldn't because of what we said to each other the last
time. . . .*

There was pain in her matarh's eyes. "Ana, I thought
about what you told me, and for a long time I was
angry."

"Angry with *me,* Matarh?"

Abini was shaking her head. She'd let go of Ana's
arms and returned her attention to the skyblooms. Her
fingers fluffed the petals idly. "Tomas told me about
what happened the time you came here, when . . ." She
stopped, sighing. "Tomas told me that he said something
to you that made you angry, and there was an accident.
He said the Ilmodo is so strong in you, which is why the
Archigos chose you, and that you couldn't control it."

"No, Matarh. That's not why. Vatarh—"

"Hush, daughter!" Abini said sharply, turning back
to her. Her eyes were wide again. Her fingers touched
Ana's mouth, trembling. "Don't say anything, Ana.
Please. Tomas . . . he could have left me after I became
sick, but he didn't. No matter what you think of him, no
matter what . . ." She paused, her lips pressing together
before she began again. "He's not a horrible man. He's
flawed, yes, but he lost his sons and thought he had lost
a wife, and the struggle he had to keep our family as
cu' . . . In his heart, I truly believe he didn't intend to
hurt anyone, Ana."

"And that forgives him?" Ana could not keep the
anger from her voice. "That makes everything all right
for you?"

"No," she answered. Her gaze grew hard. "It doesn't.
It's why . . . it's why he's not here anymore. He may never

be here again." She brought Ana to her once more; Ana resisted for a moment, then let herself fall stiffly into the embrace. "I confronted him, Ana. I told him what you said. He denied it at first, but he . . . he couldn't look at me." She looked away herself, blinking away tears, then hugged Ana tightly again. "I know, and I'm terribly sorry for what he did to you, but I don't want to talk about this, Ana. Not now when I finally have you here." Abini's voice whispered in her ear. "Let's talk about you. Tell me how things are for you."

Talking about Vatarh is talking about me, she wanted to say to her matarh. *He is part of why I am the way I am.* But she could not. She sighed. *You've kept it inside this long. If that's the price you must pay to have Matarh back, pay it. Pay it and be grateful.*

She didn't know what to say. Too many things pushed at her, but she was afraid to talk of Karl, and if she could not speak of Vatarh . . . "I'm having luncheon with Kraljiki Justi tomorrow," she said finally. "The Archigos, he feels that I—" She stopped as Tari entered the room again, placing a tray down on a low table. Fragrant steam wafted from two bowls there; wine purpled twin goblets. Tari bowed at the two of them and left. Abini gestured toward the chairs.

"Sit," Abini said. "Let's talk as we eat." As they sat, as Ana took a spoonful of the soup, Abini looked at her curiously. "The Kraljiki will be looking for a wife," she said. "It's what everyone is talking about. Even Vajica cu'Meredi mentioned it . . . and you. You're in much of the gossip I hear now, Ana."

"It's not what I would want, Matarh," Ana said. She set the spoon down; it clattered too loudly on the porcelain.

Abini smiled sadly. "Ana. When did you ever believe that marriage is what someone who is ca'-and-cu' might 'want' it to be?" she asked gently. "We're not the un-ranked, who can marry whomever they want because it doesn't matter. Love isn't a necessary element for a marriage, Ana; you know that. Love comes later, if it comes at all. If Cénzi Wills it."

"Did it come for you, Matarh?"

The smile vanished. "No," she answered. "I always respected your vatarh, and he always respected me." The frown deepened. "At least until my illness. Until what he did with you."

"Why did you marry him? You've never told me."

"I never told you because you were too young at first, then the Southern Fever took me away when I might have sat with you and explained how things are for a young woman." She smiled again. "But now I can tell you. His family came to my vatarh and matarh. They offered a substantial wedding price; the cu'Seranta name was considered to be on the rise; your great-vatarh even thought that the Gardes a'Liste might name us ca' once, though that turned out to be a vain hope after Vatarh died, only two years after my marriage. Still, Tomas kept the requirements of our contract. Our marriage was what it needed to be. But did we come to love each other?" Her head moved from side to side. She stared at her soup. "No."

"Did you ever love someone?"

Abini's smile returned, faint and tentative. "You did," Ana said, and the realization made her suddenly feel one with her matarh. "You loved someone. And did you give in to it?" she asked.

Abini glanced out toward the grounds. "Yes," she said, so quietly that Ana leaned forward to hear her. "Once."

"Who? Tell me, Matarh. Who was it, and did you . . . ?"

"You can never tell your vatarh."

Ana sniffed. "That's an easy promise. I don't intend to ever see him again."

Abini's face colored, and Ana didn't know if it was because of her remark or because of the memory of her matarh's indiscretion. "I won't tell you who it was—you would know the name. But . . ." Abini leaned back in her chair. Her eyes closed. Her mouth opened slightly.

"What caught me first was the *smell* of him: sweetnut perfume. The perfume smelled so different on him, and then I turned to look, and he was looking right at me. I remember that best of all—the shock of our gazes meeting that first time. I was much younger then, of course, and I'd recovered my figure after Estravi's birth." Her eyes opened. "Do you hate me, knowing that I was married already, that I was already a matarh?"

Ana shook her head. "No, Matarh. I don't hate you. I understand."

A nod. Abini's eyes closed again. "We didn't say anything to each other, not that first time. But I found that our paths kept crossing, as if Cénzi Himself were throwing us together, and your vatarh was gone all the time with his duties, and so . . . well, we began to talk. His own wife had died the year before in childbirth, and the child hadn't survived the year. We talked about that, and other things, and . . ."

She paused. Ana could see her matarh's eyes fluttering under the closed lids, and a smile ghosted across her lips with the memories. "I loved the sound of his voice," Abini continued, "and the way he always kept his eyes on mine when we talked. He listened, he truly *listened* to me as Tomas never did. And his touch: it was so soft. So gentle. Being with him was how I had hoped things would be with Tomas."

A sigh escaped her. She sat up, her eyes open once more. "What happened then?" Ana asked. "Did Vatarh . . . ?"

Abini shook her head. "No, he never found out. It ended because it had to. We were together for a few years, whenever we could manage, but he . . . his birth family had prospects for him. We finally had to end it, or rather *I* had to end it—to give his new wife the chance she deserved. If we had continued, our relationship would have always been a wall between him and his wife, and I knew her also. She was young, and she liked him and I knew she wanted him to love her, and I . . . well, I just couldn't."

"He married her?"

The nod was so slight that Ana wasn't certain she saw it. "Seeing him . . . seeing him around the city, it was hard for both of us, I think. But I hope, I hope he came to love her. I know she loves him, loves him still."

"Matarh . . ."

Abini reached across the table and touched Ana's hand. "You are now in the family of the Faith, Ana, and you must do as the Faith wishes. Whatever happens, it will be Cénzi's Will. Remember that." Ana felt Abini's eyes searching hers. "You already have a lover, darling? Is that why you're upset?"

"No," she said , then corrected herself. "Maybe. I don't know. It's all so confusing."

"Tell me. Who is it?"

"I . . . I can't, Matarh. I'm sorry. I can't. I wish I could."

Abini nodded. "Ana, if you would marry, then you must give your husband a chance. The respect between you may blossom into more, and you have to give it the opportunity. But if it doesn't . . . You might find someone with whom you *can* share that part, if you're careful and discreet. People in Nessantico *will* look the other way, if you don't force them to stare at it. I know."

Her fingers tightened around Ana's. They said nothing. Finally, Abini released Ana's hand and sat back once more.

"I've been talking and your soup is sitting there," she said. "You really should give it a taste before it goes cold."

Dhosti ca'Millac

THE PACKET CAME the morning of Gostidi: the morning of Estraven's funeral service, a gloomy day mirrored in the clouds that promised rain. Kenne, who had brought the envelope, glanced at the banked fire in the hearth. "It's a cold morning, Archigos," he said. "Would you like me to send an e'téni to attend to the fire?"

"Thank you, Kenne, but no," Dhosti told him. "A little discomfort I can offer up to Cénzi, eh? If you would, make certain that the staff is ready to go to the Old Temple as soon as I come down. Oh, and Ana should be on her way here. Bring her up as soon as she arrives."

Kenne nodded and gave the sign of Cénzi before he left the room, closing the doors behind him. Dhosti looked again at the stiff, creamy paper of the envelope in his hand, at the ornate handwriting that addressed it to him, and the insignia pressed into the red wax of the seal: a trumpet flower. The Kraljica's flower. The seal was intact—Dhosti made certain of that before he opened the envelope and took out the folded parchment leaves inside. He shivered in his robes as he moved to the windows where the light was slightly better. The letter was signed by Greta ca'Vörl and the tiny, careful handwriting was hers—or an excellent imitation of the example that the Kraljica had given to him. Dhosti made a small, sure pattern with his left hand, closing his eyes and calling out a short spell at the same time. He felt the Ilmodo rise within him and he released it toward the paper. In the lower left corner of the first page, where there had been nothing before, five small trumpet flowers glowed yellow, gradually fading back to invisibility.

Dhosti began to read slowly, paying attention only to every fifth word.

Archigos: I write to you as the Kraljica had told me I should if I ever learned that she was dead. The news I must relay is not good. The Hïrzg has taken the army, and I believe that he may be intending to threaten Nessantico. He is plotting with ca'Cellibrecca. You are in danger. If I learn more, I will write you again, but I am watched closely in Brezno. Be careful.

Dhosti sighed. Someone knocked at the door and he folded the papers. "Enter," he said. The door opened, and Kenne let Ana slip through before closing the doors behind her. She bowed, more deeply than she needed to, and he smiled, though it did nothing to erase the frown she wore. "Good morning, Ana," he said. "You're ready?"

"For U'Téni ca'Cellibrecca's funeral?" she asked. "Yes."

"And for the Kraljiki's luncheon afterward?"

Her shoulders lifted and fell. "How should I prepare for that, Archigos?"

"I don't know, quite honestly, but I thought we might discuss possibilities." He shivered again. "It's terribly cold this morning. Could you start the fire for me, Ana?" He saw her glance at the hearth, then reach for the tools to the side to poke at the coals. "Not with those," he told her. "With the Ilmodo."

She stared at him, almost as cold as the draft that billowed the curtains behind him. He could see her considering a reply, then she turned her head to the side. "I don't know that I can do that," she said.

He nodded, pleased with the honesty. He walked past her to the fire and threw the letter onto the coals. It curled, blackened and smoked before finally igniting. They both watched it. He turned back to Ana.

"Give me your hands," he said. She hesitated, drawing

back a half step. "I'm not going to hurt you, Ana," he told her. "I'm not your vatarh."

She grimaced, but she held out her hands and he took them in his own wrinkled and small ones, marveling at the smoothness of her skin against his own. *You are an old man, and you haven't much time . . .* He shoved the thought aside and opened his mind to the Ilmodo, his lips mouthing a hushed sequence of words. He let go of her, his hands shaping the air between them. The Ilmodo rose again, much stronger this time, and he let the energy wrap about her extended hands. When it glowed bright, he took her hands once again, both their hands caught in the bath of Cénzi's power. He let his attention drift out from himself, down from his hands and into hers. His eyes closed, he gazed outward with the illumination of the Ilmodo. The light reflected from the pool within her soul, and he found himself filled with mild jealousy at what he saw there.

He released her hands. The light faded. He felt himself dizzy suddenly, and he seated himself on the nearest chair. "So tiring," he said. "The Ilmodo becomes easier to shape as you age, but the demands on the body are worse." Ana was watching him, but her hands were still held out. She seemed to notice it belatedly, dropping them to her sides.

"I felt you," she said. "Like you were looking at me from the inside."

"I was," Dhosti answered. "And I can tell you that Cénzi hasn't taken His power from you, even if you've lost the path to find it. He has indeed blessed you, Ana. And His blessing remains. It is there. Still."

She had caught her upper lip in her teeth as he spoke, and he saw moisture gathering at the corners of her eyes. "Archigos—"

He raised his hand wearily, slumping back against the cushions of the chair. "Say nothing," he said. "I know. I know you went to see Envoy ci'Vliomani after the Gschnas. I know you were with him when he was arrested, and that you went to see him at the Bastida. You are perhaps lovers. Ca'Rudka has told me."

"We're not lovers," she said quickly, then dropped her head again. "Not . . ."

"Not yet," he finished for her. "You find yourself drawn to him?"

She nodded.

"He's handsome enough, charming enough, and intelligent enough," Dhosti said. "I was impressed by him the few times I met him, and the Numetodo chose well when they sent him to represent them to the Kraljica, even if he never had the chance to plead his case to her. I'm also told that he is betrothed to a woman back on the Isle of Paeti. Did he tell you that?"

Her eyes widened.

"I thought perhaps he had left out that bit of information," the Archigos continued. "Her name is Kaitlin Mallaghan; beyond that I know nothing about her; after all, she doesn't even have a ranked name, so it's obvious who would gain the advantage from any marriage between them. But that name might be enough for you, eh?—to mention to Envoy ci'Vliomani when you see him next." He stopped and pulled a chair alongside around so that it faced him. He patted the cushions. "Sit, Ana. You look pale."

She obeyed, moving as if he'd struck her. "Do you think . . ." She swallowed hard. ". . . that the envoy killed the Kraljica?"

Dhosti shook his head. "No, I don't, no matter what ca'Cellibrecca says or what Numetodo trinket was found on ci'Recroix's body. I don't believe that any more than I believe U'Téni Estraven ca'Cellibrecca was also killed by Numetodo, as A'Téni ca'Cellibrecca is claiming."

She took a long breath; he could see that she wanted to believe him. "Then who?"

Now it was Dhosti who shrugged. "I don't know. I do know that I find it *convenient* that ca'Cellibrecca's daughter would be without a husband just at the time that the Kraljiki takes the throne without a wife. I know that Justi and ca'Cellibrecca have views in common when it comes to the Faith and the Divolonté." She was looking away, as if lost in her own thoughts. "Ana," he said sharply, and her head turned back to him. "You're caught in the middle of this, whether you like it or not, and the choices you make now are going to be important: for you, for the Faith, and for Nessantico. You have to realize this. I need you here with me."

"I didn't want to be part of it."

"I know you didn't, but it was Cénzi's decision to give you this burden, and you must carry it."

"How?" she asked. "How, when even the simplest spells are hard for me?"

"The gift is still with you, Ana. Regain your faith, and the rest will return."

"The Numetodo . . . I *saw* them, Archigos. They can do things with the Ilmodo that we can't, not with all our belief. They create their spells beforehand, and cast them later with a single word and gesture; none of us can do that. Ka—Envoy ci'Vliomani told me he could show me how, that *anyone* who can find the Second World could do it. He said using the Ilmodo has nothing to do with faith or with Cénzi at all. I saw them cast spells, Archigos, without calling on Cénzi at all."

"And you wondered how Cénzi could allow that, didn't you? And afterward, what happened?"

She ducked her head again. She gave the sign of Cénzi, an involuntary motion. "Since then, I haven't been able to use the Ilmodo. Not as I once did."

He reached over to her; she didn't flinch this time as he touched her cheek, her neck. "Look at me, Ana," he said, his fingers under her chin as if she were a child, and her head slowly lifted. "I've seen this before, with other téni who came into contact with the Numetodo and also found their belief shaken. This is nothing new, and it's nothing permanent. Now you know what happens when faith falters. It's a test that Cénzi has set to you. Cénzi has done this so you see His power, and so you return to Him even stronger than before. That's all that's required of you: you must truly believe in Him."

"But the Numetodo don't believe in Cénzi at all, and what I saw . . . None of them had any téni-training . . ."

"Trickery and misdirection," he told her. "I know. I was once in a circus, and I saw 'magic' there, too." He closed his eyes and spoke a harsh, sibilant word, lifting his fisted hand at the same time. He opened his eyes and his fist; there, dangling from his fingers, was a fine silver chain from which hung a shell of stone.

Ana gasped, her hand at the collar of her robes as if searching for something hidden underneath. "Trickery," Dhosti told her again. "And hands that have been trained to deceive. I took your necklace, yes, but not with magic and not with the Ilmodo. It's amazing how you never really lose the skill. You shouldn't believe your eyes so much, Ana, but your soul." He held out the chain to her, letting the chain pour into her palm over the shell. "That's not a symbol that a téni should wear. Let me give you a better one."

He reached around his own neck and removed the broken-globe pendant he wore, cast in gold and set with jewels. He offered it to her. "Keep the shell the Envoy gave you," he told her. "Let it remind you of what you saw with the Numetodo. But wear this instead, close to your heart."

"I can't," she whispered.

"I insist."

She closed her hand around the stone shell, then placed the chain in the pocket of her robe. She took the pendant with Cénzi's symbol from Dhosti and placed it around her neck. The globe gleamed on green cloth in the valley between her breasts.

Dhosti smiled. "Now, that looks far better on you than on me," he said. He sighed. "Now, let's talk about your luncheon with the Kraljiki. There's something you should tell him—it will be a gift from you to him. We don't have much time. . . ."

~

Orlandi ca'Cellibrecca

"THOSE WHO WOULD bring down the Concénzia Faith are utterly without bounds and without remorse, and they would bring down Nessantico
herself," Orlandi thundered from the High Lectern of
the Old Temple: Estraven's temple. The téni who had
served U'Téni Estraven were there, solemn in their
green robes in the front rows, and the ca'-and-cu' who
had come to the service were arrayed in their finery behind them. Francesca sat with the family to Orlandi's
left, all of them in white mourning, Francesca's face covered with a heavy veil so that her features were hidden.
The Archigos was there as well, seated with his whore in
the balcony to the right. Orlandi glared up at the dwarf,
his thick, graying eyebrows lowered.

Orlandi gestured again at the casket before the altar
where Estraven ca'Cellibrecca lay, the coffin closed because of the deteriorated condition of the body. "Look
there," Orlandi railed. His voice was in fine form this
morning, blessed by Cénzi in this significant moment,
roaring low like deep thunder throughout the temple.
"The enemies of the state and of the Faith have struck
down another of our finest, the husband of my own
daughter, someone who may have one day worn the
robes of the Archigos."

There hadn't been a chance of that, Orlandi knew. Estraven had been a competent follower, but that was all.
Still, Orlandi saw ca'Millac's lips purse at the comment,
and that was pleasure enough. Orlandi gathered himself,
drawing in a long breath. *Help me with this, Cénzi. Help*

me to make them understand Your will. "It should be obvious to anyone with true faith that we have tolerated those who mock Cénzi long enough. It should be obvious to anyone with true faith that the *only* course we have is to destroy them before they destroy us. The Divolonté says it: 'When threatened, protect yourself and *do not fear to use the sword,* for Cénzi alone will judge those who are sent to Him.' Well, we know who struck down Estraven. We know, yet they go unpunished. I say that it is time for such tolerance to end. I say that it is time that we follow the Divolonté that is derived from Cénzi's law. I say it is time for the Faith to show its full strength and its full fury. I say we find those who scorn us and we *strike!*"

With the last word, he lifted his hand high and brought it down again hard, striking the lectern with his fist. The sound of the blow echoed through the Old Temple, and he heard the susurration of assent roll through the audience. It took all his will to resist looking up at the Archigos with a smile of triumph. Now he leaned forward on the lectern and lowered his voice; he saw the congregation lean forward to hear him.

"Listen," he said to them in a near-whisper. "Listen." He paused, holding a hand to his ear. "If we listen to our hearts and our prayers, we will hear Estraven ca'Cellibrecca and Kraljica Marguerite, both of them calling to us from the arms of Cénzi and Vucta. Listen: they call out with the voices of all those who have been murdered over the years. They cry for justice. And we must . . ." He paused, looking from the congregation to the casket, to Francesca and the family, and back again to the people crowding the Old Temple. He let his voice roar once more. "We *must* listen to their pleas and give Estraven and Kraljica Marguerite what they ask for. If we do nothing, if we refuse to hear them, then it will be Cénzi's wrath that we will face next. *I will not let that happen.* This must be the task for all of us: *do not let that happen.*"

There was no applause, not here in the sacred space below the painted vault, but he knew they yearned to shout and clap their hands. He could *feel* it. Orlandi pressed his lips together, looking at them and nodding once, slowly. Then he left the lectern, and the u'téni leading the service called out the recitatives as the choir began to sing from the loft.

Orlandi took his seat next to Francesca. He took her hand into his lap.

"You should have seen the Archigos, Vatarh," Francesca whispered to him, leaning on his shoulder. "I thought the man was going to collapse right there, his face was so red."

"If only that were truly Cénzi's Will," Orlandi told her. The choir's lament masked their voices. He patted her hand. "It will have to be enough that Cénzi has called Estraven back to Him. That will suffice."

"Was he called, Vatarh, or was he sent?" He glanced at Francesca, at the strange sound of her voice, but the funeral veil obscured her features. For a moment, he wondered, then her fingers pressed against his. He leaned back, closing his eyes and singing along with the choir.

After the service, as Estraven's body was placed on a white-draped carriage to be taken to the crematorium for its final dissolution, the Archigos approached them, bypassing the long line of ca'-and-cu' prepared to pay their respects to the new widow. Low, fast clouds drizzled rain as they emerged from the Old Temple and hoods and scarves had come up, but the Archigos' head was bare, his bald scalp gleaming with the moisture. It had also turned colder, as if the spring had decided to retreat back to winter, and his breath was a cloud around him. His staff remained behind in the shelter of the temple alcove, and the whore was not among them. That made Orlandi scowl under the blue-and-gold canopy held up by four of his e'téni—today was Gostidi, and cu'Seranta would no doubt be hurrying to meet the Kraljiki. He would need to go to the palace himself, as soon as he could politely escape.

"Vajica ca'Cellibrecca," the Archigos said to Francesca, also protected under Orlandi's canopy. She bowed her head and gave him the sign of Cénzi, as etiquette required. "My prayers go out to you, and for your husband. O'Téni cu'Seranta asked me to extend her sympathy as well—unfortunately, she had to rush away for her luncheon with the Kraljiki. We will miss U'Téni Estraven here in Nessantico." Then the Archigos cocked his head to look up at Orlandi. "His loss is a great tragedy for the Faith," he said. "But we shouldn't let that lead us into rash actions, especially in times like these."

"You believe defending our Faith is rash, Archigos?" Orlandi said it loudly enough that heads turned toward them. The e'téni holding the cloth over them struggled to pretend that they weren't listening.

The Archigos smiled placidly. "By no means, Orlandi," he answered. "Such a tragedy and a coincidence, though, Estraven being assassinated only a few days after the Kraljica. I hope you're feeling no guilt for having dispatched him to Brezno." The dwarf's smile widened slightly, as if he were amused at his choice of words. Then his face fell back into serious lines. "And a horrible loss for you, Vajica, in these troubled and uncertain times. I do remain certain, though, that Cénzi will cause the truth to emerge, and—as your vatarh said so eloquently—those responsible will be brought to justice."

With that, the dwarf gave them the sign of Cénzi and waddled away back toward his staff, seemingly uncaring of the rain that beat down on him. Orlandi glared after him.

"Cénzi will send that horrid little man to the soul shredders," Orlandi said, not caring that the e'téni would hear. "He is a disgrace to the title, and Cénzi will call him to task for the damage he has done to the Faith."

"That may be, but he's not foolish, Vatarh. Don't make the mistake of underestimating him." Francesca shivered. "It's cold, Vatarh, and I'm feeling truly ill."

"I'm sorry, my dear," he told Francesca, then gestured

to the e'téni on Estraven's hearse. "My daughter's grief is about to overcome her," he said to the well-wishers. "If you will forgive us . . ."

There were murmured assents and calls of condolences. No one objected to the curtailment of niceties, not in this weather. "You spoke the truth in your Admonition, A'Téni," one of the ca' called out from the crowd, gesturing with his fist to the sky. "It's time that we punish the Numetodo for what they've done. We should see their bodies hanging from the bridges of the A'Sele." There were shouts of agreement and more fists, and ca'Cellibrecca saw the Archigos staring back at them from the cluster of his staff.

"They *will* pay," he answered them loudly. "Cénzi has promised me that, and I won't fail Him."

They shouted, clamoring. At the entrance to the Old Temple, the Archigos grimaced and began walking away quickly with his staff gathered around him, hiding the little man from view.

As Orlandi bowed and gave the sign of Cénzi to the crowd, the e'téni began chanting and the wheels of the funeral carriage began to turn. The congregation dispersed with more calls of support and sympathy, leaving the family to their slow, ritual walk behind the carriage.

The rain pattered angrily on the cloth above them, and Orlandi glanced up. "The Moitidi's tears," Orlandi said. *I know, Cénzi,* he prayed. *I know You are angry that we coddle those who deny You, and I promise You that I will do Your will. Thank You for showing me the way. Thank you for permitting the sacrifice of this one man to save many. I won't fail You.*

"Vatarh?"

"Estraven's death was not in vain," he told Francesca. "Cénzi will make certain of it." He took her hand. "I know this," he said to her. "I know it."

~

Ana cu'Seranta

THE RAIN POUNDED at the walls and drummed
on the ceiling, but inside the room in the Grande
Palais, the roar of the great fireplace held the cold at
bay while servants bustled in to burden the table with
offerings. "Here, O'Téni," the new Kraljiki said. "This is
spiced icefruit from Graubundi; you really must try it."
Ana still wasn't used to the voice, a boy's voice housed
in a man's body. She smiled at him from across the small
table draped with fine linen and placed near the fire,
overpowered by the vastness of the room beyond. Their
voices echoed despite the heavy curtains pulled back
from the tall, leaded-glass windows, the padded chairs,
and the hypnotically-patterned rugs.

He seemed to notice her glances around the room,
already far different from what she remembered of the
palais in her visits with the Kraljica. He took a large gulp
of the wine before him and gestured to the room with
the glass. "Matarh's taste was rather staid, old-fashioned,
and, well, boring, I must admit. I find that I prefer more
visual stimulation. The Holdings, after all, are drawn
from many nations and many cultures, and we should
enjoy them all, don't you think?"

"I would agree, Kraljiki, that we can find much of interest in other ways if we bother to look, even with beliefs we might consider antithetical to our own views."

He set down the glass. "Ah, well-spoken. So you might
even find something worthwhile in the beliefs, say, of the
Numetodo?"

"I do. In fact, I know."

He glanced down to where the Archigos' gift lay on her robes, then back to her face. "Isn't that a heretical belief for a téni to hold? A'Téni ca'Cellibrecca, for instance, would never say such a thing."

"A'Téni ca'Cellibrecca, like your matarh, is rather more staid, old-fashioned, and boring than me, Kraljiki," Ana answered, hoping she had judged the man correctly. The Kraljiki peered at her for a moment with his dark eyes, and she wondered whether she had miscalculated, but then he leaned his head back and unleashed a shrill laugh. She saw the servant bringing in a tureen of stew raise his eyebrows at the sudden sound.

"Indeed," the Kraljiki said. "And please, while we are here alone, could we simply be Justi and Ana? The formality is so . . ." He smiled at her. ". . . staid."

His matarh was regal and aware of her position, always, and because of that some people thought Marguerite was somewhat cold and distant," the Archigos had told her. *"Those who believed that of her were mistaken. The Kraljiki is her opposite. He can be disarmingly charming and open, but those who believe those qualities define him are also mistaken. Justi uses those attributes only when he wants something. It's the charm of a snake, and just as dangerous."* Ana remembered the warning. She smiled back at him. "If it pleases you to do so, then yes, Justi."

"Thank you, Ana," he replied. "You see, isn't that better already?" He nodded to her. In the light of the candelabra set in the middle of the table, his eyes glittered like smoky glass. "So . . . you truly believe the Numetodo aren't the evil creatures the Divolonté says they must be?"

"Neither the Toustour or the Divolonté say anything directly about the Numetodo at all," she replied carefully. "They're too new in the world. So any interpretation from Toustour or Divolonté is exactly that: interpretation, not fact."

"Again, that's not what A'Téni ca' Cellibrecca would

say. In fact, Ana, he would say that I should not be listening at all to someone who is known to consort with the Numetodo."

Ana felt her face color—she knew that he would know, but it didn't make his statement of the fact any less a shock. "I know Envoy ci'Vliomani personally, yes," she answered. "And it's because I *do* know him that I also know he was not responsible for the death of your matarh, Kraljiki."

"Justi," he corrected her. "And is that what you know, or is it your *interpretation*?"

She forced herself to smile at the word. "Only Cénzi *knows*," she told him. "But, yes, I'm confident in what I say."

"You would wager your life against that, Ana?" He said it with the same odd smile, leaning forward. Ana took a slow breath.

"The Kraljiki always holds my life in his hands," she said. "And I trust his judgment to do what is best for Nessantico and Concénzia, just as I trust my belief in the innocence of Envoy ci'Vliomani."

He chuckled, leaning back slightly and taking another sip of wine. "That was well-spoken also. I'm beginning to suspect that my matarh may have been entirely right about you, Ana." He reached across the table to where her hand lay on the linen. She forced herself not to move as his hands closed over hers. His grip was strong. "We might make a fine team, the two of us. Don't you think so?"

She forced another smile to her face, hoping that none of them seemed false. Her stomach tightened; she felt a knot of tension forming deep within her. "You flatter me, Justi," she said.

Fingers pressed on hers. "No," he said seriously. "I don't. False flattery isn't something I indulge in. Ever." His fingers pressed on hers. "For instance, I won't insult either one of us by telling you how beautiful you are. Matarh used marriage the way another Kralji might have used the

Garde Civile—as a weapon. The protégée of the Archigos, a person who has been well-blessed by Cénzi, a person of intelligence . . . that could become a good weapon for me, as I could be for you in return, with people like A'Téni ca'Cellibrecca. That's what I'm saying, Ana. I understand how one would be willing to do whatever must be done to attain a goal. I sympathize with that."

She saw the door to the room open behind the Kraljiki as he spoke and Renard entered to stand discreetly a few strides from the table, just within Justi's peripheral vision. Justi held Ana's gaze for a moment, then glanced over at Renard with obvious annoyance. "Yes?" His hand didn't leave Ana's; Renard very pointedly did not look away from Justi's face.

"I'm sorry to interrupt, Kraljiki, but A'Téni ca'Cellibrecca is here and he is . . . *very* insistent that he must speak with you immediately."

Justi was looking at Ana when he replied. The mention of ca'Cellibrecca reminded her of what the Archigos had told her, and she wanted to blurt it out. Justi kept his gaze on her face as he spoke to Renard. "No doubt he is." He waved his free hand toward the man, still not looking at him. "Tell the a'téni that I again extend my condolences to him on the loss of U'Téni Estraven, and I'm sure that it is the grief of his loss and not blatant rudeness that would cause him to think that I have forgotten that I'm scheduled to meet with him shortly. I will be with him when I have finished my luncheon. No sooner. Is that clear, Renard?"

"As crystalline as the Sun Throne, my Kraljiki," Renard answered. Ana thought there might have been the barest glimpse of a smile on the aide's face. "It will be my pleasure to convey your message to the a'téni." Renard bowed to the Kraljiki, then gave Ana the sign of Cénzi. He left quickly, snapping his fingers at the gardai to open the doors as he approached. As the door clicked shut behind Renard, Justi's fingers tightened again on her hand.

"When Renard mentioned ca'Cellibrecca, you nearly started to speak."

"You're very perceptive, Justi. I have news to give you, Kraljiki. From the Archigos."

Justi nodded. "When I meet with him after our luncheon, A'Téni ca'Cellibrecca will be counseling me to do here in Nessantico as he did in Brezno," he said. "He wants the Numetodo in the Bastida tortured until they confess their crimes, then he would see them mutilated, executed publicly, and displayed as a warning. He will be most insistent in this, and he will give me persuasive arguments from both the Toustour and Divolonté, both of which he knows I hold in the greatest regard. He will appeal to my faith and to my duty as Kraljiki."

Ana started to interrupt, but Justi lifted a finger and she swallowed her words. "My faith is genuine, Ana," he continued. "I have very little sympathy for the Numetodo. My sense of duty to Nessantico is also strong; I believe my matarh did the Holdings a disservice with her neglect of the Garde Civile and the chevarittai—we are not as strong as we should be, and we have given too much strength to Firenzcia as a result. Now ... ca'Cellibrecca, as I said, will appeal to my role as Protector of the Holdings and my own security. The fact that O'Téni cu'Seranta doesn't believe in the Numetodo's guilt will hold little weight for him. Your belief would hold no weight at all if Orlandi were to discover that you knew Envoy ci'Vliomani, or that you'd actually been with him when he was arrested. I also know that Orlandi offers me another marriage-weapon I could use: his own daughter, the new widow ca'Cellibrecca. Like any good swordsman, I prefer to practice with my weapon and know it very well before I use it in battle."

His gaze would not release her. The smile was gone now, and his hand felt as if it weighed as much as the Sun Throne itself. "I'm a much stronger and more independent person than A'Téni ca'Cellibrecca believes me to be. He thinks I am still the A'Kralj, bound to Matarh's will. He's wrong; I'm more like Matarh herself, even if she didn't see it. I would have no difficulty telling A'Téni ca'Cellibrecca that I will release the Numetodo entirely, or perhaps choose a single one of them, the least of them, to act as a symbol for all and let all the rest go, including Envoy ci'Vliomani. That's what you want, isn't it, Ana?—you don't have to answer. I see it in your face. I can do that, Ana. I *will* do that: *if* it would seem to be in my best interests."

He withdrew his hand, suddenly, and she felt chill air on her skin. "So—what is the news from the Archigos?"

Ana couldn't answer immediately. She took a breath, pretended to sip her wine while she absorbed what Justi was saying. "The Archigos . . . He received a letter, Kraljiki, from your cousin the Hïrzgin. She believes that Hïrzg Jan intends to bring his army into Nessantico. She believes that he and A'Téni ca'Cellibrecca are conspiring to take the Sun Throne from you."

Justi's eyes did widen at that. "I can believe that the Hïrzg would be foolish enough—Jan ca'Vörl's a half-barbarian and not known for the subtlety of his strategy. I'd enjoy seeing him rot in the Bastida. But it's more difficult to think that ca'Cellibrecca is willing to be part of such an alliance when the cost of failure is so high. The Archigos genuinely believes this to be true?"

Ana shrugged. "He knows that the Hïrzgin believes it to be true."

"Then I will have to make my own investigation. And quickly. The Hïrzg and ca'Cellibrecca both overstep themselves if they think I'm so easily cowed." He nodded, as if to himself. He said nothing for a few moments, scowling. Then, abruptly, he smiled again. "In any event, that news means that A'Téni ca'Cellibrecca won't have a decision from me this afternoon. In fact, I will make him wait quite a bit longer while I set some things in motion. I'm sorry that the a'téni has seen fit to interrupt our luncheon, Ana. I would make it up to you: if you would come by tonight for a late supper, in my private chambers?

If you would do that, then I'll make ca'Cellibrecca wait some days for his answer on the Numetodo."

She knew what he asked; she knew what he threatened. *"He will try to trap you, Ana,"* the Archigos had said. *"You have to remember this: there are no decisions without consequences, and the more critical the decision, the harsher those consequences will be. In the circles in which the Kraljiki operates, there are also no rewards that come without payment. In that, it is like our use of the Ilmodo: the spells give us power, but we must always pay for them."* She could feel the bars enclosing her. For a moment, the memory of Vatarh's face looming over her rose in her mind, and she shivered. The hand that the Kraljiki had held was fisted on the damask. The smell of the food before her made her ill.

He was waiting for her answer, a single eyebrow lifted, his prominent chin thrust forward. "I have services with the Archigos at Third Call, Kraljiki . . ."

He would not let her finish. He pounced, like a cat on a mouse skulking along a wall. "Then I will expect you immediately afterward." It was not a question. "I will have a carriage waiting at the Archigos' Temple for you."

She nodded. The fist in her stomach clenched tighter.

"Good." He gestured to the servants against the wall. "I have to leave you, Ana—your news demands attention. Please, take your time and finish your lunch, Ana. Leisurely, and with the knowledge that A'Téni ca'Cellibrecca will be fuming more with every bite, thinking about the two of us together—that will add a lovely spice to the dishes, don't you think?"

~

Mahri

THE RAIN HAD SENT the residents of Nessantico scurrying from doorway to doorway while scowling at the sky, and left the streets devoid of all traffic but the occasional hire-carriage with a miserable driver hunched over in his oilcloth greatcoat. However, the weather bothered Mahri very little. The cold drizzle soaked the dark rags that swaddled his scarred body, but the moisture felt soothing on his ravaged flesh. He walked unhurriedly along the banks of the River A'Sele near the Bastida, and paused as he approached the Avi a'Parete and the Pontica a'Brezi Veste. He could see the tower where Karl ci'Vliomani was held rising glumly above the walls girdling the prison, walls that had once been part of the ancient city wall that Nessantico had long outgrown. Mahri had chosen this spot carefully, where he could see the tower easily and yet there would be few passersby to interfere or notice him; the rain would only help.

He slumped down on the wet grassy slope of the riverbank. He could smell the water—the foul scent of filth, human sewage, and rotting fish. He grimaced and tried to put the odor out of his mind. He pulled an oiled paper scroll from a pocket of his robe and placed it on his lap. He stared at the tower and began to chant, his hands and fingers dancing an intricate gavotte before him.

He closed his eyes.

He felt himself drifting as he if were no longer attached to his body, though he could sense the mental cord that tied him to the body, stretching as he floated

away and growing more taut and resistant with distance.
The sensation was disconcerting, and for a moment nausea threatened to send him tumbling back into his body,
but he forced his awareness to continue flowing outward.
He could see the tower coming closer; he rose above the
crumbling top of the wall and up, up to the open balcony
where he'd seen the Numetodo and into the darkness
beyond. The connection to his body was nearly at its ex-
treme distance; he had to fight mentally to stay, to not
go tumbling backward toward his abandoned body. He
could see a form seated at the crude table in the center
of the cell, his head enclosed in a strange contraption,
his hands chained tightly together: the envoy. He was
staring directly at Mahri, his eyes wide as if he were staring at a ghost—which, Mahri knew, was somewhat the
case. Mahri had seen others do this spell before; he'd
seen the translucent outline of the person that resulted:
incorporeal, untouchable, spectral. And fragile. Mahri
knew he had little time.

Ci'Vliomani grunted something that the mouthpiece
forced between his lips rendered unintelligible; Mahri
lifted a finger to lips in warning. He forced himself to
slide forward to the door against the growing resistance
of his body, feeling the chill of the metal as he passed
through it entirely. Beyond, a garda snored, leaning
against the wall with his eyes closed. Mahri spoke a
word and gestured; the man slumped to the floor, the
snoring intensifying. Mahri let his body pull him backward into the cell, forcing his awareness to stop within
the cell once again, though he could feel himself desperately yearning to return.

"I don't have time, Envoy ci'Vliomani," he said. He
could hear his voice as if he were speaking through a
long tube, whispering and hollow. "They intend to kill
you as an example to all Numetodo. I offer you escape,
but you must trust me, and we must act *now*. Are you
willing?"

For a moment, ci'Vliomani did nothing and Mahri

prepared to let himself drop back into his own body once more. Then the man gave the barest of nods, and Mahri struggled keep his awareness in the cell. He no longer dared to move; if he did, the connection would break and he would go tumbling back. *Yes. This is the way I saw it in the vision-bowl* ... "You can read?" he asked the man, who nodded again. "Good. Then we must hurry. Come here. Step into the space where I'm standing ..."

Too slowly for Mahri's comfort, ci'Vliomani stood and shuffled over toward him. He hesitated as he stood in front of Mahri, and Mahri thought that the man would change his mind. Then he took the final step, and Mahri's awareness doubled.

... What is this? What are you doing to me?

... Trust me ...

Mahri spoke the final word of the spell, and the world shifted. His viewpoint swung around; he was no longer looking through his own eyes, but ci'Vliomani's. He heard a wail and a cry, and a shimmering ghost fled from the room, a streak of fog blown by the winds of an unseen tornado.

The specter's scream faded into the night. ...

~

Karl ci'Vliomani

HE WAS SITTING on a grassy bank of the A'Sele with the rain pelting down on him. For a moment, that was enough, because there was no strength in him. He was utterly exhausted, as drained as if he had used the Scáth Cumhacht too much and must pay the steep price. Slowly, as if from a deep dream-fog, he allowed himself to come back to life.

Everything was wrong. Everything.

He could not see well. His vision was strangely flat; only his right eye seemed to be working. A strange odor hung around him, of spices and scents he could not identify. He brought up his hands, and the hands that emerged from black, tattered sleeves were not his hands at all. His breath was tight in his chest and when he turned his head, the flesh tugged hard at the left side of his face, resisting the movement. His probing tongue found empty gums and only a few teeth, and the taste in his mouth was sour and unpleasant. Glancing down, he saw a body encased in dark rags and tatters.

It was Mahri's body, he suddenly realized. Karl gasped, turning his head to look to the Bastida's tower, a hundred or more strides away. He saw a tiny figure there, standing on the high balcony of his cell: himself, his hands chained and bound, his head encased in the silencing mask. The figure stared down through the rain toward him, and as Karl watched, the snared hands lifted as if in salute and the captive turned to go back into the cell.

Karl tried to stand. He could not; the body would not obey. Muscles screamed and cramped; he felt as if he were trying to lift the weight of Nessantico itself. "What did you do to me!" he shouted, and the voice wasn't his: it was phlegm-racked and deeper than his own, the words slurred through the gap-toothed mouth. The sound of it echoing from the nearest buildings made him shut his mouth. The movement had sent a roll of oiled paper tumbling to the grass from his clothing. He reached to pick it up. *"Can you read?"* Mahri had asked. Karl unrolled the paper with clumsy fingers that were too stubby and too stiff-jointed, feeling panic running cold through him. The words set the blood pounding in his head.

Envoy ci'Vliomani—You are no doubt confused and afraid, and that is to be expected. I asked you to trust me, and I ask you to continue to do so. Trust me. If all goes to plan, you will not remain in this body for too long. If the plan fails, then your own body will be destroyed and me with it, but at least you will survive. We are all more than simply the bodies which we inhabit— remember that if the worst happens. Go to my rooms at 12 Rue a'Jeunesse; I will find you there in time, hopefully, and we can each return to the bodies we know best. Take care of my poor mortal cage as well as you can; I will try to do the same with yours.

Karl read the note twice. The rain splattered and beaded on the paper, blurring the ink despite the oil. He lifted his head to the clouds; the rain felt good on his face, as if it cooled a heat there. He glanced again at the Bastida; he saw only the stones and the dark hole of the opening to his cell. He wondered if Mahri were there, watching him.

He wondered if he were somehow dreaming all of this.

Karl tried to get to his/Mahri's feet again. This time, he managed it, but he swayed and nearly slid back down. He was the wrong height, and everything felt wrong. He took a tentative step, shuffling along slick, damp grass and bracing himself against the slope that led down to the swirling brown currents of the A'Sele. He nearly fell once more, but forced himself to take another step, then another, moving back toward the streets of Nessantico. Anyone who saw would have guessed that he was drunk. He glanced back again at the Bastida, shaking a head that felt too heavy.

As he walked, he saw people staring at him in disgust before looking away again. He continued on, staying to the shadows as Mahri himself once had, and making his way back to Oldtown and the address that was written on the scroll.

~

Ana cu'Seranta

THE CARRIAGE was there for her as she came out of the Archigos' Temple, as the Kraljiki had promised. A new insignia had been placed on the side of the vehicle, no longer the trumpet flower of the Kraljica, but a fist clad in studded mail. The carriage was drawn by a pair of white stallions. Their reflections shimmered in the puddles left by the afternoon's rain.

The Archigos came up alongside Ana as she stared at the carriage, as the driver jumped down from his seat to open the door. Kenne and the rest of the staff judiciously kept the congregation spilling out from the church away from the two of them. "I hope you know what you're doing, Ana," he said quietly. "Justi is not someone you can trifle with."

"I understand that," she told him. "It was you who set me on this course, remember? I promised the Kraljiki I would meet him for dinner."

His eyes searched hers. "We should not have lies between us."

Ana grimaced, her lips tightening. She nodded. *No, you won't abuse me as my vatarh did; you will only sell me to another.* "No, we should not," she told him. "Which is why I won't say more."

She thought he would protest, but the dwarf sighed and touched her hand. "Then be careful, Ana. And be safe." He gave her the sign of Cénzi, gathered his staff around him, and walked into the crowds, already talking to the waiting ca'-and-cu'. Ana went to the carriage and nodded to the driver, who helped her in and shut the door behind her. She sat on the leather cushions as the driver called to the horses and they moved away.

They did not go to the main entrance of the Grande Palais off the Avi a'Parete, but to one of the side entrances facing the gardens enclosed by the wings of the palais. Renard was waiting for her at the door as the driver helped her down. "The Kraljiki is in his outer chambers, O'Téni cu'Seranta," he said. Anything the man might be thinking was carefully veiled. He smiled neutrally; his gaze never staying long on her. He led her along carpeted back corridors vacant of servants to an unremarkable door. He knocked, turned the handle and opened it, gesturing to her. "If you please, O'Téni," he said. She approached, glancing inside. "You have only to knock on this door," Renard said as she glanced into the room beyond. His words were a whisper, private. "At any time. I will be here to escort you safely out, with no questions."

She glanced at him. His chin was lifted slightly, and there was open concern in his old eyes. "Thank you, Renard."

He nodded to her. "He waits for you."

She went in; Renard shut the door behind her.

The room in which she found herself was richly decorated. Heavy curtains shielded the windows and brought early night to the room, which was illuminated by several dozen candelabra set on the tables and above the mantel, and by a fire that flickered invitingly in the hearth. A table was set for two in the center of the room, with several covered plates and wine already in the goblets. She could not see anyone in the room, though an open doorway led away into other chambers. A log fell in the hearth with a fountaining of sparks, drawing Ana's gaze. She drew in her breath. Over the mantel, swathed in candlelight, was ci'Recroix's portrait of Kraljica Marguerite, eerily lifelike. She seemed to gaze back at Ana almost sadly, her mouth open as if she were about to speak.

"Startling, isn't it? I think it's the eyes that fascinate me most; you can almost see the firelight glinting in them."

With the sound of the high-pitched voice, Ana spun around to see the Kraljiki standing by the table. He was dressed casually, in a bashta of yellow silk. She tried to smile and failed. "That painting ... Kraljiki, it was ensorcelled and was responsible for your matarh's death. I'm certain of it. You can ask the Archigos if you don't believe me. This ... this was the instrument of your matarh's death."

The Kraljiki's shrug closed her mouth. "Perhaps," he answered in his high voice. "Or perhaps not. It changes nothing, though. The painting's exquisite, regardless. Ci'Recroix was a true genius, even if he was also an assassin."

"You'd keep the painting, knowing what I just told you?"

"Would I cast away the Kralji's ceremonial sword because it has killed before? It's not the sword that kills, but the person, Ana." She shivered at his use of her name. "I took the liberty of having our food served already. Sit—the lamb roast, the chef has assured me, is delightful and so moist it will dissolve in your mouth. And if the painting bothers you, then sit here, where the fire will warm your back ..." She heard the scrape of a chair on the floor, and turned away from the painting with a final, lingering glance. She allowed the Kraljiki to seat her. His hand lingered on her shoulder for a moment before he took his own seat across from her.

She thought then, for a time, that perhaps he *had* simply invited her to eat with him. As they ate, he spoke of Nessantico, of how he hoped to continue the growth of the Holdings, of how he intended to visit each of the nations within the Holdings as part of a Grand Tour to celebrate his coronation, to travel even to the Hellins across the Strettosei. He spoke of his devotion to Cénzi, how he believed that the Concénzia Faith was the bed-

rock of the Holdings, but how the Holdings must be prepared to allow within their borders those who had yet to
learn the truth of the Faith.

"The Archigos understands this, of course," Justi said,
breaking off a bit of bread, dipping it into the sauce
on his plate, and tucking it into his mouth. "He served
Matarh well, and I expect him to do the same for me
until such time as Cénzi calls for him. And after that . . .
well, he certainly speaks highly of you, and your skills.
Only six women have ever been Archigos. Perhaps it's
time for the seventh?"

Ana thought of her shaken faith, of her lost gift, of
her uncertainty, and shook her head as she sipped at the
wine. "You flatter me, Kraljiki, but I'm not ready for that
burden. I don't know that I'll ever be."

"You would rather have A'Téni ca'Cellibrecca ascend
to the title?"

"No, I wouldn't," she answered quickly, then realized
how blunt that sounded as Justi laughed.

"Your openness is charming," he said. "Most people
are afraid to speak their thoughts in front of me. But not
you . . ." He set his goblet down. "So tell me, Ana," he
said. "This Numetodo, Karl ci'Vliomani; does he satisfy
you as a lover?"

The shock of his question, so frank and direct, startled
her. Her goblet crashed against porcelain and silver as
she set it hurriedly down. "The envoy and I are not lovers, Kraljiki," she said, swallowing and forcing herself to
return his challenging, amused stare. "If this is the quality of the information Commandant ca'Rudka is giving
you, then I can understand why the Numetodo have
been unjustly detained."

"Oh, the commandant is very careful to only give me
verifiable facts." Justi's finger circled the gold-chased
rim of his goblet, the thin metal ringing. "I know you
were with him when he was arrested; I know you visited
him at the Bastida. I was making the natural inference."

"It would be better for the Holdings if the Kraljiki

made his decisions not from inferences but from certain knowledge."

She thought for a moment that she'd gone too far. His face darkened and lines furrowed the tall brow under his thinning hair. Then he smiled again. "You are undoubtedly correct, Ana," he said. "So give me that knowledge. You've gone to see ci'Vliomani alone, more than once. If you are not lovers in fact, then what is your interest in him, an interest so strong that you would come to me to intercede for him?" He paused, but before she could form a reply, he raised a hand. "No matter; I see it in your face. There *is* 'certain knowledge' in faces, if you know where to look, Ana, and I've had much practice with that over the years—and a harsh taskmaster in Matarh to school me. You might not be lovers, but there is an attraction there."

The words were harder to say than she thought they would be. "There is," she admitted. "But attraction doesn't mean there will be anything more."

" 'Love rarely respects the order of life, but love is not a prerequisite for marriage,' " Justi said. "That's a saying of Matarh's. She would drag that out whenever she ordered one of her nieces or nephews to marry for the sake of Nessantico. She used it with me when she arranged my own first marriage." He rose from his seat, the chair scraping against the parquet floor. Ana watched him come around the table to stand behind her chair. His hands stroked her neck, lifting her hair, and he leaned down to whisper in her ear. "The person I marry would have to understand that I would not be a faithful husband," she heard him say. "My appetite is . . . large, and while I would certainly continue to do my duty by my wife, I also know she would not be enough for me. But I'm not an unreasonable man. I would not expect faithfulness of her, either, were she to find solace in another's arms. Not as long as there was sufficient discretion so that no embarrassment came to me." His fingers trailed down, under the loose collar of her téni's robe to the nape and down to the slope of her breasts. She sucked in her breath at his touch. "Do you understand me, Ana?"

Ana stared blindly across the table to his empty seat. She realized her hands were clenched, that she was holding her breath, that she wanted to flee. *He is not your vatarh. You don't have to do this. This is* your *choice this time, not his.*

She nodded silently.

"Good," Justi said. His hands slid back up, cupping her face. His hands surprised her with their softness, and they held the odor of lavender oil. *I used to love that scent. . . .*

His hands left her and turned her chair abruptly. He lifted her up, his eyes on hers now. There was fire in his eyes, but no affection. His kiss was ungentle and quick, but she opened her mouth to his tongue as his hands went around her, pulling her to him. She could feel the hair of his mustache and beard, prickling her skin. She moved her face from his with a gasp, making her own arms go around him so that she rested her head on his shoulder. She could see the painting of Kraljica Marguerite over the fireplace; she seemed to gaze almost approvingly to her. The Kraljiki's hands slid down her back to her buttocks, pressing her against him so that she felt his arousal.

Is this what you want? There was no answer within her.

"I trust I won't be just a duty with you, Ana," Justi spoke in her ear. He released her, taking her hand. She followed him, her eyes on the picture rather than him. The Kraljica's gaze seemed to follow her as she left the outer room and went into the bedroom beyond.

Ana wondered what Renard was thinking as he led her down from the Kraljiki's apartments the next morning well after First Call. He said nothing, walking in front of her a few strides and never glancing back. He guided her through the back corridors and out through a door to the more public corridors of the palace.

Justi had left their bed much earlier, with a perfunctory kiss to the forehead. "The duty of the Holdings calls," he said. "Renard will be here in a turn of the glass for you. If you would like to break your fast here, tell him and he will arrange it. I may call for you later, perhaps." He seemed distracted, cool and distant.

She pulled the covers to herself and watched him leave and close the door behind him. Through the carved wooden panels, she heard servants entering the dressing chamber to assist him.

The normal bustle of the day had already begun, with the courtiers gathering near the door of the reception hall and the ca'-and-cu' who had business at the palace that day arriving in their carriages at the front entrance. "I took the liberty of having your servants send a carriage for you," Renard told Ana, stopping near the doors of the hall. "It's waiting for you now."

"Thank you, Renard," she told him. "I can find my way from here."

He bowed with clasped hands to forehead and left her. Ana took a breath, pulled the cowl of her robes over her head, and started toward the main entrance and the crowds there.

"O'Téni cu'Seranta!" She heard her name called, a feminine voice, and she saw Francesca ca'Cellibrecca just leaving the hall. She detached herself from a knot of courtiers with a word and came toward her. The woman seemed to be assessing her, her head slightly tilted.

"Vajiki ca'Cellibrecca," Ana said, clasping hands to forehead. "I wanted to tell you how sorry I am for the loss of your husband."

Francesca waved away the comment. Her lips pressed together before she spoke, as if she were suppressing a thought. "It's surprising to see you here at the palais so early," she said. "Weren't you with the Archigos at the temple for the First Call?"

"Normally I would have been, Vajica," Ana said. "But the Archigos sent me here to deliver a message."

"Ah ..." Francesca smiled. "The message must have been an important one to necessitate making his favorite o'téni an errand girl." She stopped. Sniffed the air. "Lavender," she said. "It's an exquisite scent, don't you think?" Her eyebrows arched with the question.

Ana felt herself color and hoped that the cowl shadowed her face sufficiently. "Indeed," she said. "I'm sorry, Vajica, I really must be getting back. I have a driver waiting."

She started to hurry past the woman, but ca'Cellibrecca reached out her hand and caught Ana's arm. Fingers dug into her biceps as Francesca drew her close. "You fuck him, don't you, O'Téni?" she whispered, and the raw obscenity snapped her head around to glare at the woman. "Yes, you do," Francesca purred, her voice sounding strangely satisfied. "Well, so do I. Interesting. Well, I knew I wouldn't be the only one to share his bed. I wonder which one of us he prefers, O'Téni?"

Ana pulled her arm away. Courtiers, chevarittai, and supplicants stared at them from down the hall, the ca'- and-cu' whispering and pointing. "I have nothing to say to you, Vajica," Ana said. "You don't know what you're talking about."

Francesca laughed, as if the two of them were sharing a joke. "Oh, we both know that I do, though I must admit that I'm a bit startled. It certainly can't be *beauty* he sees in you, only the possibility of gaining power—that's all he really wants from us, after all—the advantage we can give him. The fact that we'll spread our legs for him as if we were *grandes horizontales* is just an additional benefit."

Ana gasped as if the woman had slapped her across the face. "Vajica, I won't listen to this crudity." She started to walk away but Francesca's voice stopped her, nearly loud enough to be heard by the others watching them.

"You reek of him, O'Téni. I would suggest a long bath and strong perfume. It's what I do afterward. And if you haven't already taken precautions, I can recommend a good midwife who has potions you can take to avoid . . . consequences."

Ana half-turned to her. "We've nothing more say to each other, Vajica. I am done with this conversation."

"Then listen to this as a parting word," Francesca told her. "I won't be replaced by you, O'Téni. I won't."

"No one ever wishes to replace a pile of dung, Vajica. They only wish to get rid of it as quickly as possible." Francesca's eyes widened as Ana gave her the sign of Cénzi once more and strode away.

"I'm to meet the Kraljiki and my vatarh after lunch, O'Téni cu'Seranta," Francesca called after her—loudly now, so that all those in the hall heard her clearly. "I'll be certain to mention to him that you and I had a perfectly charming conversation."

Ana ignored her, continuing to walk toward the open doors of the palace. She could feel the stares of the courtiers and their whispered speculations at her back as she made her way to her carriage.

DECEPTIONS

Jan ca'Vörl
Ana cu'Seranta
Justi ca'Mazzak
Sergei ca'Rudka
Dhosti ca'Millac
Ana cu'Seranta
Mahri

Jan ca'Vörl

THE RIDER—an outrider scout, an e'offizier named ci'Baden—was mud-spattered and exhausted. He gratefully drank the flagon of water that Jan handed him, though he refused to take the seat that was offered. "My Hïrzg, I came as quickly as I could. I have seen a platoon of the Garde Civile. They are within our borders and moving in our general direction. They number thirty men; they also have a single war-téni with them, and several messenger birds in cages."

They were outside Jan's tent, in the early morning sun. Jan glanced over to Markell and Starkkapitän ca'Staunton; behind them, Allesandra sat on the stool of Jan's field desk, listening quietly with her tutor Georgi, O'Offizier ci'Arndt, at her side. The army was encamped in a steep-sloped valley of pastureland. Sheep and goats wandered the hillsides, grazing on the heather. Around them, the men were striking their tents in preparation for the day's march. "You know where they are now?"

The outrider nodded, gulping at the water. "I can find them again easily; they're less than a morning's ride away by now, following the Clario road."

"Good. Go now and get some food. The starkkapitän will make certain you're given a new horse and a troop of your own: ten men, to leave as soon as possible. E'Offizier ci'Baden, I want you to find that platoon of Garde Civile again. You will carry the standard of the Third Chevarittai and be dressed in armor with our colors prominent. Let them glimpse you and the banner.

Make no contact with them and don't get close enough to let any of the war-téni's spells reach you. As soon as you know you've been seen, turn and retreat back to here as if you're startled at finding them and are rushing back to report—not so quickly that they can't follow you; not so slowly that they realize you're leading them. You see that knoll there?" Jan pointed to a small rise in the valley, with a stand of oaks at its summit. Ci'Baden nodded. "I will wait for you there. Can you do that?"

Ci'Baden bowed to Jan, who nodded back perfunctorily. "Bring them back by evening, E'Offizier." Ci'Baden bowed again and rushed away as Jan turned to ca'Staunton. "Starkkapitän, take the army on through the pass at double-time and wait. Leave me a company of men here as well as U'Téni cu'Kohnle and two more of the war-téni—that should be far more than sufficient."

Allesandra tugged at the sleeve of Jan's bashta. "I will stay with you, Vatarh. I want to see."

"No," he told her firmly. "You'll go with the starkkapitän. O'Offizier ci'Arndt will accompany you, so you can continue studying." As he glanced at ci'Arndt, he saw disappointment spread visibly over the man's face. "Is there a problem, O'Offizier? You may speak freely," Jan said to the man.

"My Hïrzg, I would rather be with you, where my sword might be of help." Jan saw Allesandra's face light with that.

"And me also, Vatarh," she said.

His daughter's eagerness momentarily dissolved Jan's irritation—it reminded him of how he'd reacted, when his own vatarh had left him behind to go to war. He'd wanted more than anything to be with him.... "There will be time and opportunity for you, O'Offizier," he answered ci'Arndt. "I promise you. For now, take the A'Hïrzg up on the slopes of the pass so she can see the valley. Stay with her and answer her questions."

O'Offizier ci'Arndt saluted, Allesandra pouted. Starkkapitän ca'Staunton shifted his weight, chain mail rustling. "My Hïrzg, I would rather you allow me to leave one of my a'offiziers in charge here. You should stay with the army, where you can be protected."

Ca'Staunton's whining objection rekindled Jan's irritation. "You don't think I'm competent enough to be in command, Starkkapitän?"

Ca'Staunton's face blanched. "No, my Hïrzg. Of course not. I only—"

Jan cut him off with a slash of his hand through the cool air. "You'll do as I ordered, Starkkapitän," Jan snapped. "I suggest you go make certain that those orders are carried out. Now."

Ca'Staunton looked as if he were about to protest further. His eyes narrowed and his fingers tightened on the jeweled hilt of his sword of office. Then he bowed to Jan as curtly as politeness allowed and stalked off. Jan heard him bellowing orders as he went.

"The starkkapitän's offiziers are going to be unhappy," Markell commented. "He'll take out his frustration on them. It would seem the Kraljiki has heard rumors of your advance."

"It's probably my dear wife who sent the Kraljiki the warning," Jan answered. "And if I find out that's the case, I won't need an annulment from the Archigos to rid myself of her." Markell rolled his eyes toward Allesandra, and Jan sighed. "Allesandra, perhaps you should leave ..."

"I don't like Matarh either, Vatarh. I told you—I like Mara much better."

He might have chuckled at another time. Instead, he grimaced. "Go on," he told her, sternly. "And this time, no listening. O'Offizier ci'Arndt, if you'd go with her ..."

Allesandra sighed dramatically. She hopped down from the stool and left the tent with ci'Arndt behind her. Markell's face didn't change expression, but the way his shoulders had drawn back told Jan that he was thinking, as was Jan, of the Kraljiki's insulting arrogance in sending troops within Firenzcia's border. "I will make inquiries on my own regarding the Hïrgin and report back to you," Markell said. "The Téte of the Palais staff in Brezno may have something he can tell us. But if the Kraljiki has sent out the Garde Civile to verify the rumors of our advance, won't the silence from one of his offiziers confirm that? The messenger birds indicate that he expects regular reports."

"By the time the silence becomes critical, we will be on the Avi a'Firenzcia and nearly within sight of the city. He won't have time to react. Besides, Markell, who says that this offizier won't be reporting back to the Kraljiki as he's supposed to?" Jan grinned and slapped the thin man on the back. "It's a fine day, I think, for the first battle of this war. . . ."

The sun had descended nearly to the shoulders of the western ridge before Jan saw the riders: first the galloping horses of ci'Baden's small group tearing at the soft earth of the valley as the banner of Firenzcia fluttered in the hands of the lead rider. Behind them by a half mile or so, the platoon of Garde Civile, their chain mail draped in the blue and gold of Nessantico, rode quickly but more cautiously into the valley. Ci'Baden brought his troop thundering up the short slope to the top of the knoll where Jan, Markell, and U'Téni cu'Kohnle waited for them on their own horses. Jan was dressed in his battle armor: his cuirass chased with silver filigree and draped in the white and red of Firenzcia. He wore a thin, golden crown. "My Hïrzg," ci'Baden said, saluting and panting as he leaned forward in his saddle. "They come."

"As promised," Jan told him. "Good work, E'Offizier; you'll be rewarded for this, I promise. Now, if you and your men would stand with me . . ." The men turned their horses and they waited on the knoll, the nostrils of their horses blowing clouds of heated breath as they watched the intruders approach.

They were no more than a quarter mile away now.

Jan could see that the offizier in charge was troubled. He signaled his men to a halt, glancing from Jan on the knoll to the sides of the valley around them. Jan saw him converse rapidly with his men, and two horses turned and pounded away the way they'd come. They'd gone no more than a few hundred yards when a volley of arrows from the nearest copse of trees took down both riders and their horses. Jan could hear the scream of one of the crippled horses from the knoll until a second flurry of arrows stopped it.

The riders had turned at the sound as well, and now they drew their weapons: as the soldiers Jan had placed around the valley emerged from cover; as he nudged his horse into a slow walk down from the knoll, the others following.

The war-teni had begun chanting, but he was already too late: cu'Kohnle had begun his own spell as soon as Jan had begun to move, and now he released it. The ground erupted under the téni, a fountain of rock and earth that sent the man, broken and screaming, high into the air and then slammed him back down again, taking down a half-dozen of the riders next to him as well. One of the cages for the messenger birds broke open with the impact. A trio of white-and-tan pigeons fluttered up from the carnage; archers quickly brought them down. The offizier bellowed orders, but Jan's voice was far louder.

"Enough! Put your weapons down. Surrender and none of the rest of you need die."

"Surrender?" the offizier asked, his voice sounding weak compared to Jan's. He was bleeding from one of the rocks torn from the ground, the side of his face streaming red down his neck. "Is Firenzcia at war against the Holdings, then?"

"I would say that it appears Nessantico is at war with Firenzcia," Jan answered. "The Kraljiki sends the Garde Civile into my country, against the laws of the Holdings and Firenzcia both," Jan answered. "I am Hïrzg Jan ca'Vörl, and I rule here. Put your weapons down. You've been sent on a fool's errand and you have no chance here. None."

He could see the man hesitating, looking about as Jan's soldiers closed around them. With a look of disgust, he tossed his sword on the ground. "Weapons down and dismount!" he growled to his men. "Do it!"

Steel clattered on grass as the men descended from their horses. Jan raised his hand; cu'Kohnle ceased chanting a new spell. Markell gestured to the foot soldiers to pick up the surrendered weapons, to take the caged messenger birds, and to lead the horses away. Other men bound the hands of the captives. "That was wise," Jan said. He was close enough now that he could see the stripes of the man's rank on his shoulders. "Tell me, O'Offizier, who sent you here, and what were your orders? What were you looking for?"

"The order came from my a'offizier," the man answered. "Who gave him that order, I don't know. As for what we were to look for . . ." The man wiped at the blood on his face. "We seem to have found that."

Jan sniffed. "You have, indeed." He turned to ci'Baden. "I leave you in charge," he told the e'offizier. "These men are spies, who have trespassed into Firenzcia against our laws, the laws of the Holdings, and the law of the Divolonté. Execute them."

Ci'Baden's face blanched, but he saluted. The Nessantican o'offizier shrieked at the Hïrzg, breaking away from the soldier who had tied his hands and surging toward Jan. Ci'Baden leaped from his saddle and pushed the man back even as the o'offizier spat invectives at Jan. "No! You can't do this! Is this what the word of the Hïrzg is worth? The Kraljiki will put your head on a pike of the Pontica Kralji. You're a gutless coward and a liar!"

Ci'Baden stepped forward and slammed the hilt of his sword into the offizier's face. Jan heard teeth and bone crack as the man crumpled.

"Execute them," Jan said again to ci'Baden. "As the laws demand. All but the o'offizier; we'll need him alive for a bit. Markell—we will rejoin the starkkapitän and the A'Hïrzg, and perhaps we will send a bird back to Nessantico."

He turned his horse and rode away to the screams and curses of the Nessantico captives.

~

Ana cu'Seranta

"ANA!"
         Ana turned, startled both by the sound of the voice and the too-familiar use of her name. She could see Mahri, crouched at the corner of the building. The ragged beggar beckoned to her. "How dare you address me in such a manner," she snapped at him. "Leave here now or I'll call an utilino and have you arrested." She turned quickly to hurry on.

"Please," the cracked voice pleaded. His ruined, one-eyed face glanced around at the crowded plaza, as if he were about to flee if noticed. "I have news for you. Of Envoy ci'Vliomani."

Ana hesitated. She was coming from the Second Call services, hurrying to her apartments to change before going to meet the Kraljiki again. There were many people about in the plaza; if she shouted, they would hurry to her. She bit at her lip, uncertain, then went over to him, following him back a few steps between the side of the temple and the sacristy alongside. "Tell me quickly," she demanded. "I don't have much time. What of Envoy ci'Vliomani?"

Mahri's breathed wheezed in his lungs. He tapped his chest. "I . . ." he said. He stopped and swallowed. "I am not Mahri. I'm Karl. I'm Karl, Ana."

Ana could not stop the laugh of disbelief. "I don't know what game you're playing here, but I won't be part of it. Good day to you."

"No!" Mahri spat out. "Listen. You came to me in my cell in the Bastida. Commandant ca'Rudka brought you. He chained your hands together. You told me that you'd lost the ability to use the Scáth Cumhacht, the Ilmodo. You said that you'd lost your faith . . ."

"How do you know that?" Suspicion narrowed her eyes. "You have spies in the Bastida, or you can use the Ilmodo yourself . . ."

"He can, indeed," Mahri answered. "And more than you would think. Mahri sent his presence into my cell, somehow, and switched our places. He is the one who is in my body, Ana, sitting in the cell. And I'm trapped in his body."

Ana was shaking her head. "No one could do that. There's no spell that allows it. Cénzi Himself would not allow it . . ."

"I would have said much the same a few days ago. But it's the truth. I can prove it to you."

"How?" His assertion held her while common sense shouted at her to leave, to refuse to believe any of this, to stop listening to what had to be the blathering of a madman.

"Go to the Bastida. Have the commandant let you see me . . . him . . . again. Look at the person in the body that was once mine and ask *him* if it's true."

She was shaking her head already. She started to step away from him, and the pendant that the Archigos had given her swung on its chain. "I gave you a stone shell," Mahri said. "Have you stopped wearing it?" Ana put her hand over the jeweled broken globe the Archigos had given her. She took a step backward. "It *is* me, Ana," Mahri persisted.

Ana retreated again. He started to pursue her, but she scowled and that seemed to stop his advance. "What do you want of me?" she asked. "What are you after?"

"I want you to come with me. To Mahri's rooms in Oldtown."

"That won't happen."

"You wanted me to teach you how to use the Ilmodo again. I could begin that process. And there are things there that you should see. That we *both* need to see."

"You're not Karl. I don't believe that." *It can't be true. I don't want it to be true.* And she knew that it was not only because of the horror of thinking of Karl trapped in Mahri's body. It was because that meant that the sacrifice of her body to the Kraljiki had been unnecessary.

"It's true regardless," he told her. "But whether you can believe it or not, I can still help you. Let me try, Ana. Please."

Denial forced her another step backward. She was at the corner of the building, one hand on the marble seams. She could feel the sunlight at her back. Another step, and she could run. "12 Rue a'Jeunesse," Mahri told her. "I'll be there. Tonight."

"Not tonight," she told him. "It's not possible."

"Then tomorrow night," he insisted. "Ana, it's very important."

She didn't reply. She took another step backward, then turned and hurried away. She didn't look back to see if he pursued her, not until she was safely in the crowds of the plaza. When she looked, she could not see him at all.

At her apartment, she let Watha and Sunna help her change into a formal dress robe and comb and arrange her hair. She tried not to think of Mahri or of Karl as they fussed over her, as Beida came in to announce that the Kraljiki's carriage had arrived, as she was driven again over the Pontica a'Brezi Nippoli to his palace on the Isle A'Kralji, as Renard led her to the private back corridors and into the Kraljiki's apartment.

As she went to him and kissed him, as she knew he expected that. He had made it clear to her that he wished his lovers to be actively affectionate in private, that he gave no pretense of propriety and expected none. There was a sharp, faint odor lingering around him, and his response was perfunctory, a bare brush of lips. "Is something wrong, Justi?" Ana asked. *Francesca,* was her immediate suspicion. *She's done something, said something*... She been expecting this—following her meeting with Francesca outside the Reception Hall, she knew that the Vajica would not easily give up her relationship with Justi, and it was not a subject that she could broach with him. Not safely. Francesca's presence had been in the background of all their conversations since, but Justi had never directly mentioned her.

But Justi put his fingers on his temples, closing his eyes, and Ana realized that she was smelling the scent of cloves. "You've a headache?"

"A horrible one," he answered. "It feels as if a smithy were smashing his hammer on the inside of my skull. I can't seem to rid myself of it, and the healer's potions have been worse than useless. I'm sorry, Ana."

"Don't be," she told him. "Here, sit and let me rub your temples. I used to do that with Matarh when she had headaches, and she would do it for me." He allowed her to lead him to one of the chairs in the apartment, and she stood behind him, massaging his forehead and scalp. She expected him to be tense, but he seemed relaxed and comfortable.

"You're not chanting," he said after a few moments.

She stopped. "Kraljiki?"

"Ana, you and the Archigos came every night after the Gschnas to my matarh. You kept her alive when she should have died immediately after ci'Recroix did his despicable act—you, not the Archigos. Matarh told me once that you had the 'healing touch,' and we both know what she really meant by that."

"Kraljiki, the Divolonté..." Ana began. Her hands had fallen to her sides, and Justi turned in the chair to look at her.

"I understand what the Divolonté says. I also know

that the Archigos will sometimes look the other way when a téni uses that power. There's no one here but the two of us, Ana. Who would know?"

She trembled. She looked down at the floor rather than at him. Her stomach burned. The walls of the apartment seemed to loom impossibly close, trapping her. "I can't . . ."

His eyebrows raised, his already-prominent chin jutted forward even more. "You would refuse me that?"

You can't refuse. You have to try . . . "No, Justi . . . But . . . I'm so tired, and I don't know . . ."

"Try," he said, the single word burning in her ears. He turned away from her again, leaning back in his chair, obviously expecting her obedience.

Ana took a breath. She closed her eyes. *Cénzi, I pray to You to help me now. Please. I can't do this without You. I know that . . .* She spoke the calming, prepatory prayer that U'Téni cu'Dosteau had taught her so long ago, letting the phrases open her mind to the Ilmodo. She could feel the energy pulsing around her after she finished the prayer, but it seemed to linger just outside the touch of her mind, almost mocking her with its proximity. She ignored the gathering feeling of failure, the sense that Cénzi had abandoned her for interest in the Numetodo. She allowed herself to find the words of healing, the syllables in words she did not know, and her hands moved as she chanted, following the path the words of release demanded. The Ilmodo writhed and sparked around her, yet continued to elude her grasp. She started the chant again, almost sobbing with frustration. *Cénzi, I beg of You. I am sorry for my failures. I am weak, and ask You to forgive me my weakness and make me Your vessel again. . . .*

The Ilmodo slid around her again, and this time, this time she felt the cold shock of contact. She groaned aloud with relief, snatching at the Ilmodo with her mind before it could dance away once more. The words and her hands shaped the power. She took the Gift and moved her awareness to the man in front of her, she put her hands on his head again and let herself fall into him, searching for the pain in him and ready to release the Ilmodo to erase it . . .

Thank you, Cénzi.

. . . and she felt nothing. There was no pain in Justi's head. No throbbing of agony in his temples or his neck. She moved through his body, searching . . . There was a nagging stiffness in his knees and lower back from years of hard usage in the saddle and on the fencing arena, and a clustering of scar tissue on his side from injuries in one of the Garde Civile's campaigns in which he'd been wounded. Nothing else. The Ilmodo burned in her and she could not hold it any longer, so she released it: to his knees, the spine, the scars. As the energy rushed from her, she gasped and sagged to the floor, exhausted.

He has no headache . . . Cénzi, what have I done?

She felt more than saw his hands around her, too weak to resist him as he lifted her and took her into the bedroom and laid her down there. "Thank you, Ana," he said. "I'm feeling *much* better now. . . ."

~

Justi ca'Mazzak

"WELL, WAS I RIGHT, Justi?" Francesca asked. "Did the Archigos' little whore perform as I told you?"

He thought about lying to her, just to see how she'd respond, but he cupped one of her breasts in his hand and kissed the soft flesh there. "It was as you said," Justi answered. "She used the Ilmodo against the laws of the Divolonté." He saw her try to hide a smug, self-congratulatory smile and fail. *She's ruthless but predict-*

able. Those were, in Justi's opinion, good qualities for a Kraljiki's wife.

"It's as my *vatarh* said," Francesca corrected him gently. "That whore and the Archigos use the Ilmodo against the Divolonté. They both deserve to be cast out of the Faith. They deserve the fate you should also give the Numetodo who are in the Bastida. You know that's why she gave herself to you—to save her Numetodo lover. She's nothing more than a harlot."

And why did you give me your *body, when you were already married?* He toyed with the thought of asking her that, just for the enjoyment of watching her reaction. Instead, he pressed his lips together as if in thought. "That may be," he said, "but I confess that after Ana's ministrations I feel better than I have for the last few years. I can understand why Matarh thought she would be a good match for me."

As he'd known it would, that banished the smile from her painted lips. The tiny lines around the corners of her eyes deepened as her eyes narrowed, and her lips pressed together. Then she seemed to realize the transparency of her emotions and ran her hand down his chest and past his waist. She caressed him as she snuggled close to him in the bed. "I'm the better match for you, Justi," she said coquettishly. "I could prove that again, if you'd like."

"I'm certain you could," he told her, kissing her. He began to move on top of her, but a bell rang quietly in the outer room and both of them sighed.

"Don't go," she whispered to him, tightening her arms about him.

"Renard knows not to interrupt me without good reason," he told her. "This can wait." Reluctantly, he rolled from bed and donned a dressing gown and slippers. He went into the outer room, closing the door behind him. He sat in the chair nearest the fire and poured himself wine from the flagon on the side table. He took a long sip. "Enter," he called.

The door opened and Renard hurried in. "My apologies

for the intrusion, Kraljiki," he said, "but you asked me to come to you if there were news from Firenzcia. One of the message birds came a half-turn ago. This was attached to its leg." Renard held out a roll of paper to Justi.

The message was one of the phrases which Justi, Renard, and Sergei had agreed upon. *There is bright sun in Firenzcia.* "Then there's no threat from the Hïrzg's army," Justi said. He found that the news was almost disappointing.

"Except that there was an additional verification word that commandant ca'Rudka had told them to attach to the message. That word is missing. And the commandant had O'Offizier ce'Kalti write out all the phrases before he left so he could compare them to the writing on any messages we received. According to the Commandant, this is not written in O'Offizier ce'Kalti's hand."

"Perhaps ce'Kalti suffered an accident, or had the bird handler write out the message."

"Or perhaps this is not a genuine message, or someone other than ce'Kalti was responsible for it and intends to deceive us."

"Ahh . . ." Justi leaned back, staring at the parchment again. "Interesting, isn't it, that A'Téni ca'Cellibrecca strongly urged us not to send the Garde Civile into Firenzcia. He said he was convinced that the Hïrzg would not be so foolish as to bring his army within a day's march of the border."

He heard the click of the bedroom door and saw Francesca pad barefoot into the room, clad in another of his gowns.

"Vatarh knows the Hïrzg better than anyone in Nessantico," she said. "Brezno is his charge, after all, and he and the Hïrzg talked often. I think that Vatarh's opinion is well worth attention. Always." Renard acted as if her presence were entirely expected, responding to her as if she were dressed in a vajica's finery rather than wrapped in one of Justi's robes.

"The a'téni's opinion is indeed valued, Vajica ca'Cellibrecca," he answered, though Justi noticed that he kept his gaze on the parchment in Justi's hand rather than on Francesca. "But the Hïrzg is famous for his rash decisions. Look at what he did in the war with Tennshah—without the Hïrzg's provocation, the war might have ended with the Kraljica's negotiations at Jablunkov."

"The Hïrzg has cooperated with my vatarh in the past," Francesca persisted. "He listens to Vatarh, almost as if he were the Archigos." She placed herself behind Justi's chair. Her hand rested on his shoulder, possessively.

"Indeed, Vajica," Renard said. His gaze found her now. "The Kraljica was very familiar with the relationship between the Hïrzg and your vatarh. And its consequences."

Justi felt Francesca's grip tighten angrily on his shoulder. Justi pushed himself up from the chair before she could speak. "I will want to speak with Commandant ca'Rudka in a turn of the glass, Renard. Please make sure that he's here." He fingered the scroll once more. "And thank you for bringing this to my attention so quickly." Renard bowed low to Justi, then gave a far more abbreviated bow to Francesca. He strode quickly to the doors and out.

"That man is unbearably insolent," Francesca hissed before the doors had fully closed. "He was the Kraljica's servant, not yours. You should have rid yourself of him."

"He was indispensable to my matarh and, for the moment, to me," Justi told her. "So I would prefer that you avoid making an enemy of Renard, my dear. He would make a very bad enemy, I think; he has been here long enough to know where all the skeletons are buried and who put them there. It would do you well to remember that."

He watched her struggle to put away her anger, drinking the rest of the wine. He dropped the parchment to the table. "I pray that your vatarh is right about the Hïrzg. If he isn't, then I will be looking to him to support me against the Hïrzg and against his country."

"My vatarh would support his marriage-son unconditionally. And his marriage-son would give me what I ask for. Also unconditionally."

"You are extraordinarily unsubtle, Francesca."

"Am I?" she asked. She smiled. She opened her robe and allowed it to cascade from her shoulders to the floor. Her fingers brushed the fleece between her legs. "Do you really think so?"

He laughed. "Most charmingly so," he said, and went to her.

~

Sergei ca'Rudka

THE KRALJIKI'S DECISION troubled Sergei, but the man was adamant. *"By the way, Commandant,"* the Kraljiki had said, almost as an afterthought toward the end of their meeting. *"I think we need to demonstrate to the Holdings, and to Firenzcia, just how seriously we will take threats to our security. The Numetodo must confess their part in the assassination of Kraljica Marguerite. Those now in the Bastida, even if they're not directly involved, must be given the appropriate punishment according to the Divolonté to prevent them from misusing the Ilmodo ever again. The leaders, beginning with Envoy ci'Vliomani, will be prepared for public execution. Tomorrow."* A'Téni ca'Cellibrecca, seated at the table with Sergei and the Kraljiki, had nodded his agreement, and it was obvious that no argument Sergei could make would change this order.

Sergei wondered why it was A'Téni ca'Cellibrecca

and not the Archigos who had been invited to the meeting. He also knew enough not to ask.

"I will do whatever the Kraljiki orders," Sergei had replied, rubbing the polished metal of his nose, *"but it's my duty as commandant to remind the Kraljiki that the Numetodo are no threat to anyone while they are in the Bastida. It would seem far more important that our attention stays on the very real threat of the Hïrzg."*

But the Kraljiki, with ca'Cellibrecca nodding vigorously beside him, had insisted that there *was* no threat from Firenzcia, and it was obvious that the Kraljiki had already made his decision. Sergei's objections had gone nowhere. Sergei knew it was also the duty of the Commandant of the Garde Kralji, once the decision was made, to carry out the orders without hesitation or second thought.

He would do so. But he would talk to ci'Vliomani first, so the man knew what he faced and could prepare himself. He strode through the gates of the Bastida, saluted the gardai there, glanced up at the baleful head of the dragon, and went to Capitaine ci'Doulor's office.

"Capitaine, I've come to meet with the prisoner ci'Vliomani."

Sergei stopped in mid-sentence. Capitaine ci'Doulor blanched with Sergei's statement. His hand clutched at a sheet of paper on his desk, crumpling it and tipping the inkwell set on its corner. The man didn't seem to notice the mess. "Commandant ca'Rudka," the man stammered. "You must know . . ."

"Know *what*, Capitaine?"

The man's eyes widened. His mouth gaped like a river carp's. "I was just writing an urgent message to you. Only a turn ago, while you were at the palais . . . the prisoner . . . the Numetodo . . ."

Sergei didn't wait to hear more. He spun on his toes and ran out of the capitaine's office, with ci'Doulor in pursuit. He went across the courtyard under the glare of the stone dragon and into the tower, taking the winding, ancient stone stairs two at a time. There was a garda at the landing to ci'Vliomani's cell, but the door was open. There were spots of blood on the garda's shoulders. Breathing heavily from the climb, Sergei went into the room, spinning around.

The cell was empty.

He heard ci'Doulor's panting entry a few moments later. "Where is he?" Sergei spat angrily, the question seeming to strike ci'Doulor like a fist. The capitaine shook his head as if denying the reality of what Sergei was seeing here. The garda, his face averted, pressed his back to the wall of the landing.

"I don't know how to explain it, Commandant."

"I'd suggest you try, Capitaine," Sergei told him. "I suggest you try very hard, and immediately."

Rather than answer, Capitaine ci'Doulor's gaze went from Sergei to the garda. Sergei followed the motion. "You!" Sergei snapped. "Tell me what happened here."

The man saluted and came into the cell. He stood at attention before Sergei. His eyes were focused more on Sergei's silver nose than his eyes. "The prisoner hadn't eaten for two days, Commandant," he said. "Not since the night that we found E'Offizier ce'Naddia unconscious at his post."

Sergei frowned. "*What?* I wasn't told of that. Was Capitaine ci'Doulor aware of this event?"

The man nodded. "We told him, sir."

"Ce'Naddia fell asleep at his post, Commandant," ci'Doulor said. "That's all. He has been disciplined severely."

Sergei nodded. "Undoubtedly. You said ci'Vliomani wasn't eating?" he asked the garda.

"No sir, not since that night. The prisoner just sat there on his bed, his eyes closed. Wouldn't answer any question we asked of him, or respond if we . . . well, if we tried to get him to respond. Two days he was that way."

"What happened tonight?"

The garda glanced again at the capitaine, as if waiting for him to answer. He took a breath and continued. "About a turn ago, I noticed that it was cold here, as cold as the middle of winter. My teeth were chattering, sir, and I could hardly hold onto my sword when I drew it. I could see ci'Vliomani in the middle of the cell, and there was wind swirling around him, and a glow all around. I called for the gardai below to get the capitaine, and when he came ..."

Sergei glanced at the insignia on the man's uniform. "What's your name, E'Offizier?"

"Aubri ce'Ulcai, Commandant."

"E'Offizier ce'Ulcai, how long was it before Capitaine ci'Doulor arrived?" Sergei asked the man.

Ce'Ulcai gave a sidewise glance at the capitaine. "I'm certain he came as quickly as he could, Commandant."

"That's not what I asked."

The man pressed his lips together at Sergei's tone. "The gardai below told me the capitaine would be up as soon as he finished his supper. I don't know how long that was, sir. Not for certain."

Sergei nodded. "Capitaine?" Sergei said, and ci'Doulor's eyes returned to him. "What happened when you finally arrived?"

Ci'Doulor licked his lips. "I looked in, and I saw ci'Vliomani."

"As e'Offizier ce'Ulcai described?"

"Yes, Commandant. I felt the cold and the wind, and saw the glow."

"And you didn't immediately send for me, or for one of the téni?"

"I thought ... After all, the man was still in chains and silenced. No. No, sir. I didn't."

Sergei glanced back to ce'Ulcai. "You opened the cell door?"

"I didn't want to, Commandant," he said. "I told the capitaine so. But he ordered me to open it."

Sergei nodded. "You did as you should, then, E'Offizier. The capitaine went in? You saw what happened then?"

A nod. "The capitaine went in. He went up to the prisoner, shouting at him to stop. I saw him take his bludgeon and hit the man. As soon as he did, right at the moment the capitaine touched him ..." Ce'Ulcai shivered. "The cold became worse than anything I've ever felt, and the glow was so bright I couldn't see anything at all. I heard the capitaine scream, and I started into the cell myself, but the wind threw me back into the wall, right there where you see the marks." He pointed out of the cell to the landing, where a few of the stones showed light scrapes in the dark surface. He touched the back of his head, and Sergei saw blood on his fingertips when he brought them away. "I hit the wall hard. When I managed to get up again, the cold and light were gone, and the only person in the cell was the capitaine. The prisoner had vanished. I went to the balcony, thinking he'd jumped, but there was no body in the courtyard, and even Numetodo can't fly. None of the gardai below say they heard or saw anyone on the stairs." The man ducked his head. "I'm sorry, sir."

Sergei ignored the apology. "Capitaine, is this man's story true?"

Ci'Doulor nodded. "Yes, Commandant. There was sorcery here. Numetodo work."

"You had a guard rendered unconscious two days ago and since then the prisoner was unresponsive, and you didn't inform me. When you were told that there was something odd happening here earlier this evening, you decided that finishing your supper was more important. Seeing sorcery inside the cell, rather than inform me or someone in the Kraljiki's or Archigos' offices, you ordered this e'offizier to unlock the cell. You went inside. Alone. And now the prisoner is... gone. Are any of those facts substantially incorrect, Capitaine?"

Miserably, ci'Doulor shook his head. "It just wasn't possible for him to escape, Commandant. We both know that."

"Then he's still here, eh? I'm sure you're right. Then I'll leave you to search the cell thoroughly."

The sarcasm struck ci'Doulor like a lash to his head. "Commandant, I'm sorry. I should have . . ."

Sergei lifted his hand, shaking his head at the same time and silencing the capitaine. "No, Capitaine. This is entirely my fault and I'll accept the blame. It was my decision to leave you in charge of the Bastida when you were obviously not competent to perform that function. Therefore, *I* lost the prisoner, not you. But I can at least rectify my mistake so it won't be repeated. I relieve you of your command."

Sergei gestured to ce'Ulcai to leave ahead of him, then walked to the cell door. Ci'Doulor was still standing in the center of the room, his body slumped, and now he began to follow them. Sergei shut the door in the man's face. As ci'Doulor called out in alarm—"Commandant! What are you doing?"—he turned a key in the lock and closed the viewhole in the center of the door. There were muffled screams and cries from the cell and a pounding of fists on the door. Sergei handed the set of keys to ce'Ulcai.

"Your rank is now o'offizier," Sergei told him. "I'll have another of the Bastida gardai relieve you from your post immediately. Have the Bastida's healer look at the wound on your head; tomorrow morning after First Call, report directly to me at the office of the Garde Civile. I can use competence there."

Sergei gave the sign of Cénzi to the man and went back down the long staircase, wondering how he would tell the Kraljiki and A'Téni ca'Cellibrecca what had happened, and wondering why he felt more relieved than angry.

~

Dhosti ca'Millac

"YOU'RE CERTAIN OF THIS?" Dhosti asked Kenne. His secretary nodded.

"It came directly from our source in the Bastida, Archigos," Kenne had told him. "I just received the message."

So the Kraljiki has ordered the execution of the Nume-todo, despite Ana. And ci'Vliomani has vanished some-how. That will only inflame them further. I wonder if Ana knows yet . . . ? The beginnings of a headache throbbed on either side of his forehead, and his shoulders sagged. He suddenly felt very tired and very old.

"I'll have to speak with the Kraljiki," Dhosti said. "Immediately. I pray that it's not true, though if ci'Vliomani has truly escaped, I'm glad, though I doubt the poor man can evade Commandant ca'Rudka for long. Let me just finish this letter, and . . ."

He had no time to finish. Dhosti heard the commotion in his outer office: one of his staff member's loud voice protesting that the Archigos could not be disturbed. Then the tall, double doors pushed open and A'Téni ca'Cellibrecca strode through, his robes swirling. There was a quartet of gardai from the Garde Kralji with him. Dhosti's e'téni receptionist trailed after them, still protesting.

The expression on ca'Cellibrecca's face told Dhosti everything he needed to know.

"E'Téni," he said. "A'Téni ca'Cellibrecca is always welcome in my offices. Please return to your duties." He looked at Kenne, who was glaring angrily at ca'Cellibrecca. "Kenne, why don't you deliver the package I gave you earlier while A'Téni ca'Cellibrecca and I talk?"

Kenne's head snapped away from ca'Cellibrecca. "Archigos? You're certain? I can stay here, in case you might need me."

"Go on," he said. "You should deliver the package. Please. And tell the téni in the office that we should not be interrupted. For any reason."

Kenne's eyes widened, but he gave the sign of Cénzi to the Archigos and and—perfunctorily—to ca'Cellibrecca, closing the doors behind them. Dhosti placed the quill he'd been using back in its holder and stoppered the ink. He blotted the paper in front of him, then folded his hands on top. "Orlandi," he said. He deliberately didn't look at the soldiers. "This would seem to be more than a social visit. I hope you're not making a foolish mistake."

"The mistake was yours, Dhosti, when you deliberately ignored the Divolonté. Not even the Archigos can do that." Ca'Cellibrecca seemed unable to keep a smug half-smile from his face.

"You have proof of this? I would like to see it."

"And you will, when you are brought before the Guardians of the Faith and the Concord A'Téni."

"And you, as Téte of the Guardians, will no doubt endeavor to give me a fair trial."

Ca'Cellibrecca's smile broadened. "I assure you that I will follow the precepts of the Divolonté, as I have sworn to do."

"No doubt." Dhosti wondered how long he could stall here before he would have to submit to the inevitable. *You had the throne of the Archigos for nearly eighteen years, longer than many. Eighteen good years, and you helped the Kraljica become the Généra a'Pace, the great creator of peace. You knew when the Kraljica was murdered that this might be coming. . . .* "And no doubt you will take the throne as the new Archigos before the seat has even grown cold."

"That decision will be up to the Conclave, as it has always been."

"I'm an old man, Orlandi. All it would have required is patience on your part and you might have been the Archigos in a few years anyway. Perhaps less. Cénzi will be coming for me soon."

"You think I could wait while you maneuver your own heir into position?" Ca'Cellibrecca sniffed. "Surely you don't think me that stupid. Cénzi will send you to the Hags for your sins against Him, Archigos, and for your arrogance. Were I you, that would not be something I'd be anticipating with pleasure. But the Guardians will leave to Cénzi the decision of when you visit the Hags."

Dhosti had seen the sad ones convicted by the Guardians, the téni who had violated their vows and been cast out from the Concénzia Faith, their hands cut off and their tongues removed so that they could no longer use the Ilmodo. Their terrible wounds were always cauterized, so that they might not die of them. They might wander for years as visible warnings of what the Faith would do to those who betrayed it. Dhosti imagined himself in that state, and his bowels turned queasily. "Who accuses me, Orlandi? You? Your cronies within Concénzia? Are you *sure* you have enough of the a'téni in your pocket?"

"The Kraljiki himself makes the accusation, Archigos. Justi himself will testify to the Guardians against you and O'Téni cu'Seranta. I'm certain that when the a'téni hear the Kraljiki speak, those who have hesitated will be convinced. I've already spoken to ca'Fountaine and ca'Sevini; they agree with me that the Concord should be convened immediately."

The words came with the finality of a sword strike to a bare neck. *It's done, then. There is no hope.* "Honestly, I would prefer you kill me outright, Orlandi. Now, if you like. I would accept the blow. That would be kinder than what the Guardians will do, and we both know it. We've never been friends, but even you would acknowledge that I care about the Faith as much as you do. All that I've done, I've done because I truly believed my course to be the right one, and I would say the same of you, Orlandi, even though we disagree. Slay me now, if that's what it's to be. I won't beg, but I ask you to have that much pity on me."

Ca'Cellibrecca laughed. "You'd have *me* disobey the Divolonté? No, Dhosti. I've already called the Guardians to the chamber. You'll be taken first to the Bastida, where Commandant ca'Rudka will oversee that your confession is taken and any other names given to us so we may interrogate them. Afterward, you'll be brought before the Conclave A'Téni and the Guardians and the correct punishment will be meted out. Your disobedience to the laws will be made public, so everyone will know your shame when you are cast out from the Archigos' Temple without your tongue or hands."

A winter storm lodged in Dhosti's gut, howling and freezing. His face was solemn and pale as he rose from behind the desk. The gardai around ca'Cellibrecca came to quick alertness, their hands going to weapon hilts. He knew that if he started to call the Ilmodo, if he began to move his hands in the pattern of a spell, they would strike. For a moment he considered whether that would be better, but he suspected that he would only end up wounded, not dead. This battle could not realistically be won. He could not prevail here: not at this moment. Not with the Kraljiki as ca'Cellibrecca's ally.

No, there was only one feeble hope here and that was to flee so he could fight at a different time and place, when the odds might be better. The Kraljiki would realize soon enough that he'd placed a dangerous snake on the throne of the Archigos.

If Dhosti were to be there when that happened, he would have to go to ground now. He would have to hide himself with those who might remain sympathetic to him. He hoped he'd given Kenne enough time.

Dhosti spread his hands wide as he backed away from

the desk. *Once, you'd have been able to do this easily. Once, you wouldn't have even needed to think about it.*

But that had been so many years ago. Too many . . .

The floor-to-ceiling doors to his balcony were open to admit the breeze from the plaza below, three stories down. There were balconies studding the outer wall of the building below, and a pole that flew the broken globe banner of the Concénzia Faith set to the right, half a story below. He'd stood on his balcony over the years and seen the possibility that he envisioned now: *a running leap up onto the railing to get some speed, then a headfirst jump to the pole. Come in above it and catch it with reversed hands—let the momentum swing you around. Release just as you hit the banner—the fall from there would be somewhat blind because of the flag, but you should be able to reach the balcony directly below this one. Run out into the rooms there, into the main hallway and down the northeast stairway. They'll think you're heading for the plaza, but keep going down to the tunnels under the plaza. You mapped out an escape route from the tunnels months ago, one you hope that those following you won't know.*

You could do it. Once upon a time. You only have to do it this once more. Once more: for Ana, for Kenne, for the Kraljica, for those who believe as you do. But you can't hesitate. You must have faith. Faith, Dhosti.

He could feel the doubt—*you're too old, Dhosti, and even back then you used the Ilmodo, even if you didn't realize it. All that meditation before the performance you used to do, your hands moving through the routines . . .*

He forced the pessimism down and away.

He took a breath. He smiled at ca'Cellibrecca.

Then he turned and ran.

He heard the shouts behind him: as he jumped clumsily, grunting, to the marble rail around the balcony, as he bent his knees and tried not to look at the long fall to the flagstones below, as he narrowed his gaze so that all he saw was the pole below and to the side.

He leaped.

He'd forgotten the strange sense of freedom that came with falling, the feeling that he'd surrendered himself to the hands of Cénzi. The wind fluttered his robes, tore at the wispy strands of hair, teared his eyes. He seemed to move in slow motion—as he once had, his body remembering the necessary positions. He saw the pole and reached out, his tiny fingers snaring the cold metal, the shock of the impact trembling the flabby, ancient muscles of his arms. The weight of his body and the force of his motion ripped his right hand from the pole, his short legs flailing to one side. Dhosti gripped the pole desperately with his left hand, but now the skewed angle took his body sideways and out.

His fingers slipped. He reached desperately for the banner there and found cloth. He dug his fingers into it as he started to fall again.

He heard the sound of ripping, tearing fabric. He was still holding onto the banner, but the piece he held tore away. He could see the colors in his fisted hand and he was falling free.

He had time only to pray to Cénzi that he would not feel the pain for very long.

~

Ana cu'Seranta

"OUT OF MY WAY, woman!"

Ana heard the muffled shout from outside the doors as they rattled in their frames and were flung open. Kenne rushed in with Watha trailing him in wide-eyed panic. Kenne's face was flushed and his hair was tousled and windblown. He panted as he touched clasped hands to forehead. "O'Téni," he said, then had to stop for a breath. "You must leave. Now." The panic in Kenne's voice was palpable.

"Leave?" Ana frowned. "Kenne, what's happened?"

He shook his head. "There isn't time to explain. Ca'Cellibrecca just came with Garde Kralji to the Archigos' office. The Archigos spoke a . . ." Another pause, another hurried breath, a swallow. ". . . code phrase he'd given me not long ago, just in case. You have to leave, have to hide. So do I."

Ana blinked at the torrent of impossible words. "I'll go to the Kraljiki . . ." she began, but Kenne cut off her protest.

"Ca'Cellibrecca wouldn't move against the Archigos without the Kraljiki's knowledge. There's no hope there. Ana, they ordered all the Numetodo executed."

Ana's hand went to her neck, but the stone shell wasn't there, only Cénzi's globe. "Karl . . ." she husked.

"Ci'Vliomani's vanished," Kenne told her. "The Bastida's in an uproar. But ca'Cellibrecca's come to bring the Archigos before the Guardians of the Faith and the Conclave. Take what you can and flee, Ana. They'll be coming for us next. They're already coming. We don't have much time at all."

"Flee? To where?" Ana was rooted where she was. She stammered, wild thoughts chasing themselves in her head. *You could go to the Kraljiki. Surely this is a mistake. He promised you. You gave him your body.* "I need to talk to the Archigos."

"You *can't*." Kenne's hands gripped her shoulders. His face was very close to hers. "You can't, Ana," he repeated, softly. "They've taken the Archigos by now, or maybe he's somehow managed to get away. Either way, he's gone. He's given us a little time to save ourselves, and that's what we have to do."

"Where are you going?"

"To friends I know. Out of the city. I can't take you with me, Ana; it's dangerous enough for them to take me in. You'll have to find your own way—but whatever you do and wherever you go, you have to do it *now*." He released her. Over his shoulder, Ana saw Watha press her hands to her mouth and flee from the room. "I'm leaving, Ana. I promised the Archigos that I would warn you, and I have. Get out of here. Take only what you can grab. They'll be coming for you at any moment."

Ana had no answer. Kenne gave her Cénzi's sign, touched her shoulder again gently, and left. She listened to his hurrying footsteps. Somewhere in her apartments, someone was screaming in a high, thin voice. The sound jolted Ana from stasis. She ran to her room, shedding the green robe of the téni as she went. She dressed hurriedly in a plain tashta, and stuffed a carpetbag with some of her old clothing and a purse with a handful of silver siqils and a few gold solas. She could think of nothing else to take; everything in the apartment had been there when it had been given to her.

She left, taking the stairs to the rear of the apartment. None of her servants were to be seen. The thud of the wooden door seemed final, like a hammer nailing closed the lid of a coffin. At the bottom of the stairs, she opened the street door slightly and glanced out. The entrance led onto one of the smaller side streets to the east of the temple plaza; only a cat prowling in the central gutter for food looked at her as she slipped out and started walking quickly away. She could hear the sound of some great commotion in the plaza: shouts and loud cries, and at the end of the street she saw people running in that direction. The low, shuddering, and mournful wind-horns in the temple domes began to sound at the same moment, making Ana shiver. It was still a good two turns of the glass before Third Call, yet someone had set the téni to sounding them.

The sound frightened her, the spectral wail slithering around her.

She turned her back, fleeing from it.

As she half-ran, the bag bouncing against her legs, she

wondered where she was going. Not to her old house; she could not involve Matarh in this.

Mahri.... The name came to her as she hurried through the streets toward the Pontica a'Brezi Nippoli, watching for the Garde and ready to duck into a doorway if she caught a glimpse of green robes or any familiar faces. *All that insane talk of his being Karl, and yet ...*

There was nowhere else she knew to go. She would go to Oldtown. Its narrow, twisted streets would be as good a place to hide as any.

Twelve Rue a'Jeunesse was a narrow, thin, two-story building with a gloomy front courtyard. The building was wedged between larger structures on either side, which seemed to be all that held the flimsy, ancient structure together. A tavern occupied the lower floor; a set of rickety stairs led up over a narrow porch to an outside door on the second floor. Ana spoke a prayer of protection as she climbed the steps, a simple warding spell, but the touch of the Ilmodo comforted her.

As her foot touched the landing at the top of the stairs, the door opened. "Hurry!" a voice whispered, and in the candlelit darkness beyond, she glimpsed Mahri holding the door open for her.

"How did you know?"

"He knew. He felt you use the Ilmodo," Mahri husked in reply. "Get inside—before someone sees you who shouldn't."

She wondered who the "he" was that Mahri referred to, but she slid past him (a scent of old clothes and sweat) and into the room. Another person stood there in the shabby, tiny room. Ana gave a cry of delight; without thought, she dropped her bag to the floor and went to him, folding him into her arms. "Karl!"

The man chuckled grimly, and he did not hug her in return. "You mistake the wrapping for the gift," he said.

"Envoy ci'Vliomani is there." He pointed to Mahri. "At least for the moment," he added.

Ana stepped back. Mahri—or was it truly Karl?—had shut the door and was slouched against it, the scars on his face yellowed in the light of the candles, his single eye gleaming under the black hood of his cloak. "I told you," he said. "Mahri, can we do this now? Not that I'm not grateful to you . . ."

Karl—*Mahri?*—sniffed. "This will take a few minutes, and it will leave you disoriented. We'll both need to rest afterward." He took a long breath. "Sit there," he said, pointing to a chair near the window. "Be very still."

Karl closed his eyes; the cloaked figure of Mahri went to the chair. Karl's hands moved; he began to chant in a language that Ana did not know, though the cadence and accent were both strangely similar to the language of the Ilmodo. Karl's body began to glow a sickly yellow-green, and fingers of that light slipped away from him, like an ink droplet spreading through water, moving toward Mahri. When it touched him, his scar-distorted mouth opened and he moaned.

Karl spoke a final word and spread his hands wide. The light flared. Mahri moaned again and slumped sideways to the floor; Karl's knees buckled and he went down, Ana rushing forward to catch him before he fell completely.

"Karl . . ."

His eyes opened. "Ana," he said. A hand came up to feel his own face. "It's me. I'm back . . ."

~

Mahri

"YOU DIDN'T CARE for my body? I'm disappointed."

Ana and Karl's head turned toward him. He'd managed to rise to his feet, though the weariness dragged on him as if an anvil were laced around his shoulders. All the old pains were there; after a few days in ci'Vliomani's younger and far healthier body, he could imagine the relief the man must be feeling at his release.

You could have stayed. . . .

He almost smiled at the thought. That would have been more of a sacrifice than ci'Vliomani could have realized. "Thank you," ci'Vliomani said now. "I thought . . ."

"I know what you thought," Mahri told him. "And you'd have been wrong. I've no use for your form. I actually prefer this one." Mahri could see the disbelief pull at Ci'Vliomani's face, but otherwise the man said nothing. "After all," Mahri continued, "I'm not being hunted by the Garde Kralji for having escaped the Bastida. They were going to kill you. The order came from the Kraljiki."

"No," the woman said, shaking her head. "He wouldn't have. He promised me . . . I . . ." She stopped.

"Yes," Mahri said. He knew what caused her shoulders to slump, the tears to start in her eyes. The Capitaine had told him the rumors. *"The téni who came to see you, who kept asking about you? She's the Kraljiki's mistress now, I hear. Just another of the* grande *horizontales. I can't say that I blame her—her future's better with the Kraljiki than you, eh?"*

Mahri also suspected what the woman thought she was trading for her body. He hoped that ci'Vliomani would be able to appreciate that when he learned what she'd done. "The Kraljiki lied," Mahri said to her gently. "I suspect he's very well-skilled at that. You're not the only one he's deceived." He stopped. "A moment . . ."

There was a soft knock at the door. Ci'Vliomani stared, and cu'Seranta began to chant a spell, but Mahri shook his head to the o'téni. He went to the door, and spoke to the man there—one of the beggars who formed his information network. When he closed the door, he took a long breath before turning back to them.

"The news is worse than I had thought," he told them. "The Archigos is dead."

Cu'Seranta stifled a cry with her hands. She closed her eyes and made the sign of Cénzi. "How?" she asked.

"He fell from his balcony at his residence. Jumped, some say. Or was pushed, according to others. A'Téni ca'Cellibrecca was seen at the same balcony immediately afterward, it seems. The news is all over the city. The Conclave A'Téni has convened in emergency session already; ca'Cellibrecca has been named acting Archigos until all the a'téni have been informed and a formal vote can be taken—they will meet here in a month."

"And ca'Cellibrecca will be Archigos in fact at that time," ci'Vliomani said.

"He has the backing of the Kraljiki," Mahri answered calmly.

Ci'Vliomani snorted his derision. "And his daughter shares the Kraljiki's bed." Mahri saw cu'Seranta startle at that, turning to stare at the Numetodo.

"You knew that?" she asked him.

Ci'Vliomani nodded, pointing to Mahri. "He showed us," ci'Vliomani said. "While the Kraljica was alive, we might have been able to use the information. Once she died . . ." He sighed. "With ca'Cellibrecca as Archigos, he'll marry her. She's the obvious choice."

Mahri saw cu'Seranta's face color, and she went silent.

Yes, she was seduced, or allowed herself to be seduced, by the Kraljiki also. And ci'Vliomani . . . that frown tells me he's suspicious as well.

"There's more news, and worse," Mahri told them. "It would seem that several of the Archigos' staff fled just before his death. They are suspected of gross violations of the Divolonté, as well as complicity in the Archigos' death."

"That's not true!" cu'Seranta shouted, and Karl shook his head toward her, a finger near his lips in caution.

"True or not," Mahri continued, "the Garde Kralji and the Garde Civile have been told to find those téni who were on the former Archigos' staff and bring them before the Guardians to be judged."

"I can't stay here, then," cu'Seranta said. Weariness and fear whitened her face. "I have to find somewhere else."

"This is as good a place as any," Mahri told her. "No one can come here that I don't allow, and there are things I can teach you." He included ci'Vliomani in his nod. "That I can teach both of you."

He saw the disbelief, the uncertainty in both of them. It amused him. He took a long breath, letting his shoulders rise and his chest fill, letting himself settle fully into his familiar body once more. "But that's for later," he said to them. "For now, we all need food, and then some rest. The world outside will take care of itself. . . ."

SKIRMISHES

Jan ca'Vörl

Ana cu'Seranta

Sergei ca'Rudka

Gilles ce'Guischard

Justi ca'Mazzak

Francesca ca'Cellibrecca

Ana cu'Seranta

Jan ca'Vörl

"THE BATTLE WAS a complete rout." Stark-kapitän ca'Staunton's nostrils flared, his chest filled, and his chin lifted as he spoke. A'Offizier cu'Linnett, accompanying his immediate superior, smelled faintly of fire and ash; when Jan glanced at cu'Linnett, the offizier was staring intently toward the rear of the tent, looking not at the starkkapitän but the array of toy soldiers Allesandra had laid out on the rug, in preparation for a session with Georgi ci'Arndt. She'd stopped playing with them to listen to the starkkapitän's report.

"There were approximately five hundred troops of the Garde Civile holding the border above the Ville Colhem," ca'Staunton continued, "and they broke across the River Clario bridge in the first turn of the glass. They saw A'Offizier cu'Linnett's division and ran like frightened house beetles with their offiziers screaming at them to hold ranks. When the first barrage from the war-téni came, even the offiziers and the few chevarittai with them fled."

Jan glanced again at the offizier, still staring intently at Allesandra's soldiers. "I understand that A'Offizier cu'Linnett commanded the engaging troops?"

"He did, my Hïrzg."

Jan nodded. "How many casualties?" he asked the starkkapitän. He was seated behind his field desk, the thin panels of which were adorned with painted images of his great-vatarh and namesake, the Hïrzg Jan ca'Silanta, fighting the bamboo-armored hordes of East Magyaria. Jan folded his hands on his lap.

"Of our troops, very few, my Hïrzg. A'Offizier cu'Linnett was able to effectively use his war-téni and archers and thus inflicted most of the damage from a distance."

"How very convenient," Jan commented drolly. "And for the Nessantico Garde Civile?"

"At least a hundred and fifty dead, perhaps two hundred."

"So three hundred escaped. Perhaps more. Is that what you're saying to me, Starkkapitän?"

Jan heard Markell, standing just behind his chair, suck in a breath. Allesandra snickered. Ca'Staunton seemed to notice the tone of Jan's voice for the first time. His chest deflated as he exhaled, his chin dropped, and his shoulders drooped. "My Hïrzg—" he began, but Jan cut him off, abruptly.

"I wonder, Starkkapitän . . . Did I fail to make myself clear when I gave you my orders? Because I distinctly remember saying to you, after we captured the Kraljiki's spies, that it was vital—*vital*—for Nessantico to remain unaware that we have crossed the border. I recall telling you that I wanted Ville Colhelm and any Garde Civile posted there surrounded before we initiated any engagement, so that none could escape to take word back to the Kraljiki in Nessantico. Are you saying, Starkkapitän, that *three hundred or more* troops are now running toward that city with the news that Firenzcia's army is on its way—troops that include offiziers and chevarittai; troops we will most assuredly meet again, perhaps before the gates of Nessantico?"

Cu'Linnett stared ever harder at Allesandra's toy soldiers in their painted silver and black, his hands clasped behind his back. Starkkapitän ca'Staunton visibly paled. "My Hïrzg, it was of course my intention to do exactly as you'd ordered. The third division had already been sent to cross the Clario well below Ville Colhelm, but we came upon the Garde Civile troops unexpectedly and A'Offizier cu'Linnett had no choice but to engage immediately. There was no time to coordinate the attack."

"A'Offizier," Jan snapped, and cu'Linnett's head threatened to snap entirely from his neck as he jerked his head around to meet Jan's gaze. "You had no vanguard scouting the terrain ahead of your forces? You were surprised by the Garde Civile? They initiated the contact?"

"No, my Hïrzg," the man answered. His voice was firm and solid, and Jan caught the hint of a frown when his eyes flicked over toward ca'Staunton. "The starkkapitän was perhaps somewhat unclear in his assessment of our situation. Our vanguard reported to me that a force of perhaps a half a thousand Garde Civile held the bridge across the Clario at Ville Colhelm, under the command of A'Offizier and Chevaritt Elia ca'Montmorte."

"I know ca'Montmorte," Jan said. "One of the few competent chevarittai, in my opinion. What did you do when that report came to you, A'Offizier?"

"I immediately sent runners to the starkkapitän with the news."

"Ah," Jan said. "As you should have. And the starkkapitän's response?"

Allesandra's toy soldiers clinked dully as her hand swept over them, striking down a battalion. Cu'Linnett stiffened his gaze, keeping his eyes only on Jan. "I was ordered to engage the enemy since we had a far superior force. I obeyed those orders. I sent my war-téni ahead along the path of the Avi, supported by archers and infantry, and had two squadrons of chevarittai flank the Garde Civile east and west along the Clario to attempt to contain the enemy. Unfortunately, the Clario isn't fordable at that point, so the Garde Civile's forces were able to retreat across the bridge once their offiziers realized they they were outflanked and badly outnumbered—the starkkapitän had specifically ordered that the bridge was not to be destroyed."

"And ca'Montmorte?"

"He ordered the retreat, and was among those holding the bridge. He retreated himself only when it was obvious that he had lost. I pursued Chevaritt ca'Montmorte through Ville Colhelm but felt that to go farther would leave my men too exposed and isolated from our main forces. I called a halt, and remained in Ville Colhelm to hold the bridge and the town. Perhaps I should have questioned the starkkapitän's orders or asked for clarification on how he wished me to proceed, but I did not. If that was wrong, my Hïrzg, any blame is entirely mine and not that of my offiziers or men."

"So you take the entire responsibility for your tactics, A'Offizier?"

Jan could see the man swallow. "I do, my Hïrzg. Given the suddenness of the attack and the lay of the land, I did what I thought best."

"You performed your duty admirably. An offizier must always obey his superior, and I admire your willingness to accept responsibility for your actions." Jan nodded to the man, who relaxed visibly. Allesandra began setting up her soldiers again. Jan turned his attention back to ca'Staunton. "A lesson the starkkapitän himself should have learned," he added.

Ca'Staunton reddened further. "My Hïrzg, that's unfair," he answered, his jowls flapping as he spoke. "I have always endeavored to follow your orders to the best of my ability."

"It's your ability that is in question," Jan snapped back at him. "But not any longer. Markell?"

Markell stepped forward then, standing to the side of Jan's chair. He withdrew a scroll from the single side drawer of the table and handed it to ca'Staunton. His voice was formal and unemotional. "Ahren ca'Staunton, you have been found guilty of treason by the Court of Chevarittai Firenzcia for deliberate disobedience of the orders from your Hïrzg, and for endangering Firenzcia, her people, and the Hïrzg with your actions. Your titles of chevaritt and starkkapitän are hereby revoked. The Court's judgment is that you deserve to be executed for your crime, and that punishment is to be carried out immediately. The Court's order has been reviewed and signed by the Hïrzg; his seal is affixed, as you see."

"No!" Ca'Staunton's shout pushed Jan's spine against his chair. "You can't do this!" the man bellowed. "You— your vatarh always said to me that you were reckless and a fool." With one motion, he tossed the scroll aside and drew his sword—Jan heard the hiss of blade against scabbard, like a shrill wind through fir branches—and charged toward Jan.

He made only a single step. Cu'Linnett moved at the same time, drawing his sword and pivoting. The a'offizier's blade slashed across ca'Staunton's ample stomach, the starkkapitän's rush burying the edge deeply in his abdomen. Ca'Staunton doubled over at the point of impact, his eyes wide, and he grunted like an animal. Cu'Linnett completed his turn, ripping out his sword. Blood spattered in a gory, diagonal line across the tent fabric very near Allesandra, who stared, her mouth open and a painted soldier clutched in her hand. Ca'Staunton remained standing for a breath, hunched over, his sword still pointed threateningly at Jan.

The sword dropped from the man's hand. A surge of red poured from his mouth.

He fell.

Jan was still seated in his chair, his hands folded in his lap. Markell's own sword was drawn, the double-edged steel gleaming protectively in front of Jan. Markell sheathed the blade as Jan slowly rose and came around to the blood-spattered front of the field desk. Ca'Staunton's body twitched, his eyes wide and frightened, the blood still flowing from his mouth and nostrils as his hands tried to stuff pink loops back into the gaping wound. Cu'Linnett stood above him, his sword tip at ca'Staunton's neck, his foot on the starkkapitän's chest. "My Hïrzg?" he asked. "If I may? The man suffers."

Jan didn't answer at first. "Allesandra?" he asked, looking back at his daughter. She stared at the blood, but now her head turned to him. Her face was serious and pale.

"I'm fine, Vatarh," she said. She gulped audibly before speaking again. "He was a bad starkkapitän."

"Yes, he was," Jan told her. He nodded to cu'Linnett. The man's sword thrust and ca'Staunton went still. Jan bent down beside the body and tore ca'Staunton's insignia of rank from his uniform blouse, heedless of the blood that stained his hand. He spat on ca'Staunton's body as he hefted the silver-and-brass weight of the starkkapitän's eagle in his palm. Markell nodded once behind the desk, as if he guessed at Jan's thoughts. Allesandra watched him from the rug. He held out the insignia toward cu'Linnett.

"Starkkapitän ca'Linnett," and the doubled change in title and name brought the man's head up sharply. "I thank you for your defense of your Hïrzg. And I extend my congratulations on your victory today—may you have many more as starkkapitän. You have demonstrated that you are a fine example of the chevarittai of Firenzcia. As reward, I name you Comté of the town of Ville Colhelm. Direct your offiziers to take the army across the Clario, and secure your town; I will cross the Clario myself this evening and will meet you there so we can discuss our future strategy."

Jan extended his hand with the insignia toward the man, who finally sheathed his sword and took it. "You may leave us, Starkkapitän," Jan told him as the man stared at the eagle in his hand. "You've much more to do before the end of this day." Ca'Linnett glanced at the body of ca'Staunton. "You *should* look at him," Jan said. "Look well. Memorize what you see."

"My Hïrzg?"

"You may think that you did this, but you didn't. This was ca'Staunton's fate, no matter whose hand held the sword. This is what happens to those who can't meet my expectations, Starkkapitän. I trust you don't think me reckless and foolish."

Ca'Linnett swallowed visibly again. He saluted. "Good," Jan told him. "I'm glad we understand each other. Until this evening, then, Starkkapitän. Oh, and if you would send someone in to remove the carcass . . ."

Another salute, and ca'Linnett fled. Jan went to Allesandra and gathered her in his arms. Together, they looked down at the body. "Your desk is ruined, Vatarh," Allesandra said. Splashes of brown-red crusted the surface of Great-Vatarh Jan's painted face and dripped thickly from the desk front.

"It will clean up," he told her.

~

Ana cu'Seranta

ANA CRIED SILENTLY in the darkness, her face to the wall. At least she hoped she was silent. She didn't know where Mahri was—he'd left the apartment for the streets a few turns before and not returned, but Karl was curled up in a nest of blankets on the other side of the room, and she didn't want to wake him.

Not silent enough . . . She realized she could no longer hear Karl's soft snoring even as she heard his footsteps behind her, then felt the movement of the straw-stuffed mattress on which she lay. "Ana . . ." Karl's hand touched her shoulder with his whisper. "I'm sorry. For everything that's happened to you."

Ana wiped furtively at her eyes, grateful for the gloom. She did not trust herself to speak. She remained huddled there, silent, as if she could stopper up her grief for the past and her fears for her future by sheer force of will. She heard him speak a spell-word and a soft light blossomed, no more than a candle's worth. She could see her shadow on the wall in its steady light.

"I thought I heard you," Karl said. "I thought . . ." She felt him shift his weight. The hand moved from her shoulder to stroke her hair. "Do you want me to leave you alone?"

She shook her head. The light vanished, and she felt the warmth of him along her back as he lay down next to her. "You should know that your coming to me in the Bastida was what kept me alive and sane," he said. "I was afraid that I was going to die there, afraid that I'd never see you or Nessantico or the Isle of Paeti again. Never smell the ocean or feel a soft shower from a passing cloud while the sun still was shining on the meadow. Never feel the power of the Scáth Cumhacht in me again . . ." He stopped. His hand slid down her arm until he found her hand. He laced his fingers in hers. "But I could always remember *you,* long after you left. Ana, I don't know what you did to keep me alive and safe, and I don't care. It doesn't matter. I will always be in your debt."

She could not hold back the sobs anymore. The emotions rose within her, racking her until her shoulders heaved. His fingers tightened around hers. After a moment, she returned the pressure, and that calmed her somewhat. Karl released her hand to put his arms around her and cradle her into himself. He let her cry, saying nothing, just letting the grief and shame flow from her. His head snuggled into her neck; she felt his lips against her there, kissing her once softly.

"You're safe for now," he whispered. "That's all that matters."

She shook her head. "No," she told him. "The Archigos . . . Kenne . . ." She inhaled, the sound breaking. "What have I done to my matarh? What will happen to her now? It would be better if I'd died with the Archigos."

"No," he said fiercely into her ear. "You can't say that. I won't let you."

She turned in his arms so that she faced him. He was a shadow against the darker background of the room. "I lay with him," she said, the confession rushing out unbidden. "With the Kraljiki. That was the bargain I made for you, Karl. Even the Archigos pushed me toward the Kraljiki, saying he thought it's what I should do. The Kraljiki said he would keep you safe if I'd be his lover. He said that . . ." She had to stop. "He said that he might marry me, said that the Archigos' favorite would make a good match." She laughed once, bitterly. Karl said nothing. His hands had stopped moving. "That wasn't really a lie, I suppose. Not really, now that ca'Cellibrecca will be the Archigos."

"Francesca . . ." The word was a breath and a knife.

"Yes. Francesca."

His hand found her cheek. "He used you, Ana. He and Francesca both. They played you and used you until they got what they wanted."

"I was using him in return," she answered. "That makes me no better." She took a breath, and it was empty of the sadness. "I'd like you to go," she said to him. "Leave me alone."

"Ana . . ." He put his arm around her, started to draw her to him. She wanted to let it happen. She wanted to lose her thoughts in heat and his taste and smell, but afterward . . . She didn't know what either one of them would feel afterward, and she couldn't face another loss. She put her hand on his chest, pushing him back.

"No," she said, and the single word stopped him. For a breath, the tableau held. She could feel his breath so close to her lips before he rolled away from her and off the bed. In the darkness, she heard him walk across the room to the pile of blankets that served as his own bed.

She forced herself not to cry again. She prayed to Cénzi instead, and wondered if He could hear her, or if He would listen.

When Ana awoke the next morning, Mahri had returned. He was seated near the hearth, and a pot boiled on the crane over the fire. The fragrant, sharp smell of mint filled the room. Karl snored in his corner. "Tea?" Mahri asked. Ana nodded, then winced as he reached out and swiveled the crane away from the fire; the crane had to be burning hot to the touch, but Mahri didn't seem to react to the heat.

He plucked the pot from the crane and poured liquid into two cracked-lipped mugs, stirring a dollop of honey from a jar into each. Ana padded over to him, still wrapped in her blanket, and he handed her one of the mugs. The man's terrible, scarred face regarded her, his remaining eye staring. She dropped her gaze away quickly, blowing at the steaming liquid and taking a sip. The sweetness burned its way down her throat and the heat of the mug made her put it down on the edge of the table where Mahri sat, near the room's single window. "It's good," she said. "Thank you."

"There are rumors all over the city," Mahri said as if he hadn't heard her. His own mug sat untouched on the rickety, scratched tabletop. The shutters of the window were open, and she could hear people moving on the street outside and see the early morning light. First Call sounded, the wind-horns of Temple Park loudest of them. Ana closed her eyes and went to one knee, reciting the First Call prayers silently to herself, her lips moving with the familiar, comforting words.

"You believe? Still? After all this?"

Mahri's question brought her head up again. Ana nodded as she rose. "I do believe," she told him. "Again, after I thought I'd lost belief. And you, Mahri? Do you pray to anyone, or do you believe in no gods at all like Karl?"

"I believe that there are many ways to use the X'in Ka, which you call the Ilmodo. For us, like you, we call on our gods—but it would seem that the Numetodo have shown both of us another way." He might have smiled; with the disfigured face, it was difficult to tell. "Even my people have things to learn, things you or the

Numetodo can teach us. But I do believe, yes. Where I come from, we worship Axat, who lives in the moon, and Sakal, whose home is the sun. Your Cénzi we don't know at all."

"Where is home?"

"Far from here in the West," he answered. "But not so far that we haven't heard of Nessantico, though we've so far managed to avoid her armies. But that day will come."

"Why are you here?"

He did smile then. And didn't answer. He took a sip of his tea.

"The city is like a nervous dog ready to bite anyone who approaches," he said finally. "First the Kraljica's assassination, then the Archigos dead under suspicious circumstances. Now there is talk that Firenzcia's army is on the march—the Kraljiki has expanded Commandant ca'Rudka's duties to include the Garde Civile as well as the Garde Kralji, and the Commandant has called for all able-bodied men to enlist in the Garde Civile. Some say that conscription squads will be roaming through the city soon. The Kraljiki sent out riders to the north, south, and west last night, supposedly to summon the nearest Garde Civile garrisons to come here. There's been a request to the local farmers for hay and any wheat stores they may have. Archigos Orlandi has sent additional worker-téni to the smithies and forges."

Mahri glanced over at Karl. "The Numetodo still in the Bastida have been executed," he continued. "Their bodies—hands cut off and tongues removed—are hanging this morning from the Pontica Kralji. But there weren't nearly as many of them in their cells as there were supposed to be. Most of the Numetodo escaped somehow last night via some dark magic."

Even as she recoiled from the news, she noticed the weariness in Mahri's body: the way he propped his body on the table, the heaviness of the lid over his good eye. "That was *your* doing, the escapes?"

Again, he didn't answer directly. He inclined his head toward the sleeping Karl. "He will need support when he hears of this," he said. "Not all those in the Bastida escaped, and those were his comrades who were murdered."

"Why are you here?" she persisted. "Whose side are you on?"

"I'm not on any side." Mahri drained his still-steaming mug of tea. She touched her own mug; it was still too hot to hold comfortably. "I need to sleep now. It's been a long, tiring night. Have some more tea if you like. There's bread and cheese in the cupboard. If you'll excuse me . . ." He rose from the table.

"What if someone comes?" she asked him. "What should I do?"

"No one will come," he told her. "And as long as you stay here, you're safe, at least for this day. If you go out on the street . . ." The folds of his cloak shifted as his shoulders rose and fell. "Then I can't say. That would be in the hands of your Cénzi."

With that, he shuffled off to the far corner of the room, pulled his cloak tighter around himself, and sat. She could hear his breathing slowing and becoming louder almost immediately.

She sat in the chair and sipped her tea, looking out at the Rue a'Jeunesse and wondering what she would say to Karl when he woke.

~

Sergei ca'Rudka

A DOUBLE HAND OF Numetodo bodies swung on their gibbets on the lampposts of the Pontica Kralji. There should have been two double hands, enough to decorate the Pontica Mordei as well. That those bodies were missing both troubled and pleased Sergei.

It pleased him . . . because he was convinced that the Numetodo had nothing to do with the death of the Kraljica or the heretical treason of the Archigos and his staff. He had personally supervised the interrogations of the Numetodo who had remained in the Bastida and who were now hanging above him for the crows. He had listened to and watched enough men under torture to see and hear the difference between extracted truth and lying admissions screamed in hopes of stopping the torment. All of the Numetodo had eventually "confessed" before their execution; all of them, Sergei was certain, had only said what they hoped their captors had wanted to hear—their stories didn't connect, didn't make sense, didn't substantiate each other. He was glad that ci'Vliomani had escaped that torment and that humiliation, glad that so many others had escaped it as well. It didn't please him to see so much unnecessary death.

But the escapes troubled him . . . because it *was* magic that had been at work in the Bastida last night: the fog that had risen suddenly and thick from the A'Sele and wrapped around the Bastida; the gardai rendered unconscious; the disappearance of many of the prisoners before several téni arrived from the Archigos' Temple and dispersed the false mist with their own spells. By then, it had been too late, but he knew that if Kraljiki Justi or Archigos Orlandi decided that they needed a high-level scapegoat, they might look at Sergei. Had the Numetodo all escaped, that certainly would have been the case.

Yes, the escapes troubled him . . . because Sergei suspected that truth lay elsewhere, and that if he dared to speak his own suspicions, his would be the next body hanging on the Pontica after days of torture in the Bastida.

"Commandant?"

The query brought him out of his reverie. His boots squelched in the mud of the riverbank as he turned. "Yes, O'Offizier ce'Ulcai?"

The man handed ca'Rudka a sealed letter. His gaze flicked past ca'Rudka to the bodies swaying above them on the Pontica, then back. "Your aide said to give this to you immediately."

"Thank you," Sergei said. He examined the seal, then tucked his finger underneath the flap to break the red wax from the thick paper. He unfolded the letter and read it quickly.

Commandant—I have investigated the matter you requested me to look into. I apologize for the length of time it has taken me to reply, but my queries required both more travel and correspondence than I expected. Here are the facts, as I know them:

The artist Edouard ci'Recroix was born here in Il Trebbio in a village on the River Loi, near our border with Sforzia and Firenzcia. There is no evidence that he had Numetodo tendencies; in fact, in his youth he spent two years as a téni-apprentice under A'Téni ca'Sevini of Chivasso, though he did not receive his Marque. Still, by all appearances he was a devout member of Concénzia. His early paintings, before his time as téni-apprentice, are unremarkable; I have viewed several of them, and there is little indication of his later skill. But after his release from his studies by the a'téni, his reputation (and his skills, evidently) began to rise, and in that time he obtained commissions in several of the cities within the Holdings. The fact that he had téni-training undoubtedly led to the persistent rumors that he tapped the Ilmodo to gain the vivid likenesses in his later painting. A shame no one realized how true that was.

One oddity—which I admit I would not have noticed had you not alerted me to look for any strange connections—is that most of the subjects of his portraits, especially those considered to be his masterworks, are dead. At least three of them died within a few days of ci'Recroix's delivery of the finished painting, at which time ci'Recroix was generally gone from the city, not that any suspicion was ever cast on him at all. Given the distance between cities and the slowness of news passing between them, the fact that most of his subjects were elderly, and ci'Recroix's consistent wanderlust, no one seems to have found anything sinister in this. I hesitate to remark on it myself. This still may be nothing beyond a set of odd coincidences. There is no proof of a definite connection, especially since not all of the painter's subjects have died.

However, you did ask me to determine who hired ci'Recroix to do his portrait of the Kraljica. The contact with ci'Recroix was made here in Prajnoli by Chevaritt cu'Varisi, a diplomat connected to the Kraljica's office. It was he who signed the commission for the artist to paint the Kraljica's portrait. In the wake of the Kraljica's death, cu'Varisi has been removed from his duties and is on house arrest until the matter is cleared up. I spoke to the chevaritt; he said that his contact was within the Grand Palais: a Gilles ce'Guischard, who is connected to the palais staff of the A'Kralj. Chevaritt cu'Varisi conducted a brief inquiry into ci'Recroix's qualifications and background before tendering the commission; he knew of the Ilmodo rumors but discounted them, something he now regrets. He let me see his notes from that investigation, and he insists that he found no connection between ci'Recroix and the Numetodo heretics.

That is all I have for you at this time, Commandant. I will continue to look into this, and should I uncover more that I feel you should know, I will write again.

I remain your loyal and grateful servant,
A'Offizier Bernado cu'Montague, Garde Civile,
Chivasso, Il Trebbio.

Sergei sighed and folded the letter again, tucking it inside his uniform blouse. "I need you to report back to O'Offizier ce'Falla," he said to ce'Ulcai. "There are two orders I need you to relay to him, and another I want you to carry out personally. . . ."

It was evening before word came to him that all was done. Sergei came into the cell in the Bastida, holding a roll of canvas under his arm. He looked at the man seated on the backless stool in the center of the tiny room, hands and feet chained: Remy ce'Nimoni, the green-eyed retainer for the Chateau Pré a'Fleuve. The cell smelled of guttering torches and stale urine. Sergei nodded his head to the garda. "Leave us," he said. The garda saluted, leered once at the prisoner, and left.

"Commandant," the man began blubbering almost immediately. "Surely this is a mistake. After all, I was the one who told you where to find the body of the Numetodo painter who killed the Kraljica."

"Yes, you did, Vajiki ce'Nimoni," Sergei said. "You also put this around his neck before you brought me to him." Sergei opened the hand that supported the canvas roll and a necklace with the polished stone shell swung from his fingers. The man shook his head in denial, but Sergei ignored him.

Crouching down in front of the man, he laid the roll of canvas down on the floor of the cell and spread it out. Inside, several large metal instruments stained with old blood were cradled in cloth loops: pincers, shears, pokers with their tips black from fire, hammers, metal plates and loops that looked as if they might fasten around a head or limb. "Oh, Cénzi, nooooo . . ." ce'Nimoni moaned, the last word transforming into a shuddering wail. He swayed on the stool. He retched suddenly, and acrid vomit spilled on the floor near Sergei's feet. Sergei glanced at the grotesque puddle, but didn't move.

"There is truth in pain," Sergei told the man, words he'd said many times before. "That's what I was once taught. With enough pain, properly applied, the truth always comes. Few can resist the compulsion. Are you one, do you think . . . ?"

*   *   *

Less than a turn of the glass later, Sergei left ce'Nimoni's
cell, going to what had once been Capitaine ci'Doulor's
office. There, O'Offizier ce'Falla waited with another
man, dressed in the colors of the Kraljiki's staff. "Vajiki
ce'Guischard," Sergei said, nodding to the man. "Forgive me for not saluting, but . . ." He went to a basin behind the desk and poured water into it from the pitcher,
washing his arms clean of the blood that stained them
to the wrist.

Ce'Guischard stared as Sergei dried his hands on a
towel, and then, ostentatiously, gave ce'Guischard the
sign of Cénzi. "Thank you for coming," Sergei said as
he took the chair behind ci'Doulor's desk. O'Offizier
ce'Falla remained standing to ce'Guischard's left and
just behind him; the man kept glancing over his shoulder nervously. Sergei folded his hands on the desk, gazing at ce'Guischard.

He had seen Gilles ce'Guischard dozens of times over
the years, always in the background, one of the ubiquitous staff running errands for the a'Kralj or escorting the ca'-and-cu' through the labyrinthian maze that
comprised the protocols of the palais. Ce'Guischard was
thin, with a severely-trimmed mustache and beard that
mimicked that of the new Kraljiki, but his was flecked
with gray. The man's skin was sallow and studded with
the scars and craters of the Children's Pox. His eyes were
the color of a storm-blown sea, and would not remain
still. His hands twitched in his lap, plucking at his cloak
and pants legs as if searching for dropped crumbs.

"You seem nervous, Vajiki," Sergei commented.

"Ah," the man said. *Twitch. Shake.* "It's just that I've been
here for a turn of the glass, waiting, and this place . . ."
Shudder. "Forgive me, Commandant, but the Bastida is
hardly a place to make one feel comfortable."

"I suppose not." Sergei took in a long breath. He
scratched under the metal loop of his left nostril, where
the adhesive that held his nose to his face itched his skin.

"You must be wondering why I requested that you meet me here."

A nod. The man licked dry lips. Shifted his weight in the chair. Sergei reached into his belt pouch and produced the shell necklace. He laid it carefully on the desk, smoothing out the silver links. Ce'Guischard's eyes seemed snared by the motion. "Do you recognize this, Vajiki?" Sergei asked.

He hesitated just a breath too long. "No, Commandant," he said.

Sergei nodded as if he'd expected the answer. "It's something a Numetodo would wear. It was found around the neck of the painter ci'Recroix, the painter that I understand you personally requested Vajiki cu'Varisi of Prajnoli hire for the Kraljica's portrait."

Another lick of lips. "Commandant, the A'Kralj told me that it was my duty to hire a painter for the Kraljica's Jubilee portrait, and when I made inquiries within the community, ci'Recroix's name was always prominent among the recommendations. I had no idea the man was a dangerous Numetodo, Commandant. I have lived with the guilt ever since ..." He stopped. Continued. "Chevaritt cu'Varisi actually met with the man since Ci'Recroix was living in Prajnoli at the time. The chevaritt assured us that he had investigated the painter's reliability and found nothing suspicious. I trusted his word—he is cu', after all, and has served the Kraljica for decades."

"Ci'Recroix *wasn't* a Numetodo," Sergei told him. "At least I don't believe so. I believe the necklace was placed on him to blame them. Gilles—" The use of the man's name nearly made him jump in his chair. "—do you know the retainer for the Chateau Pré a'Fleuvc? Remy ce'Nimoni?"

His gaze remained on the necklace. "No ..." he said slowly. "I don't think so."

"Strange. He was just telling me how the Kraljiki—as the A'Kralj—often had you run errands for his good friend Chevaritt Bella ca'Nephri, the owner of the chateau. He also mentioned how well he knows you, how you came to the chateau the day after Gschnas and told him that he should go the banks of the A'Sele the following day, how he would find ci'Recroix there." Sergei paused. "And that you told ce'Nimoni that he was to kill the man and put this necklace on the body."

"He lies!" ce'Guischard spat indignantly. "I was at the Grand Palais, Commandant, attending to my duties, and couldn't have gone to the chateau—"

"No," Sergei interrupted. "I had Renard check the records of the palais staff, though he remembered quite well on his own. You were not there the day after Gschnas, Gilles. Not at all. You'd asked for leave to tend to your matarh. I've spoken to her also: your matarh somehow doesn't recall your visiting her at all, nor do any of her house servants."

Ce'Guischard squirmed. Smiled. "Ah, that. I'd . . . I'd forgotten, Commandant. It's . . . well, it's rather *embarrassing*, actually." He gave Sergei a quick, tentative smile. "I had asked to be released from my duties that day and used Matarh as an excuse. In truth, there was a woman I've been seeing, a married woman of cu' rank. You can surely appreciate how, umm, *delicate* that might be, Commandant. Her husband had been sent out of town on business for a few days, and . . . well . . ." Another smile, creasing the mustache and beard. His hands lifted and fell back. "But this retainer ce'Nimoni . . . I'm sure I've seen him in my visits to the chateau, Commandant, but I know nothing about . . . that." He waved his hand at the shell necklace. "You have my word that what I say is the truth."

"No doubt the vajica would also confirm your story for me. Privately."

"I'm certain she could be convinced to do so, Commandant, if that's truly necessary."

"It will be."

Sergei could see the man thinking desperately. "Then allow me to contact her first, so I can prepare her and assure her that there will be no scandal."

Sergei plucked the necklace from the desk and placed it back in his belt pouch. He rose from his chair. "Thank you for your time and cooperation, Vajiki. I'll expect to hear from you with the vajica's name, and I'll make arrangements to meet with her and confirm your story. Discreetly, of course."

Ce'Guischard gave a hurried sign of Cénzi to Sergei, then lifted his clasped hands quickly to his forehead for ce'Falla. He rushed from the office and away. Sergei smiled at ce'Falla, who stared at the door through which ce'Guischard had vanished. "Say it," Sergei said. "You can speak freely."

"The man's lying, Commandant," ce'Falla said. "He knows about ci'Recroix and the Kraljica's assassination. But you let him go."

"He was lying, and I did let him go," Sergei admitted. "And you want to know why?

A nod.

"Because sometimes there is too much pain in truth," Sergei answered. Ce'Falla frowned, shaking his head slightly. "You've done well, O'Offizier," Sergei told him. "Go get some food and rest; you've earned it. You're dismissed for the evening. Oh, and if you would dispose of this on the way out." He gestured to the basin of bloodied water. "Lamb's blood," Sergei told the man, seeing his stare. "From the kitchens. I'm not entirely the butcher I'm reputed to be."

Ce'Falla smiled slightly, saluted, then took the basin and left. Sergei went to the door of the office. He looked out onto the courtyard of the Bastida, where the dragon's head glared out at Nessantico, and watched ce'Falla salute the guards at the gate. Iron groaned and echoed in the evening as ce'Falla went out onto the brilliantly-lit Avi a'Parete and strode away in the crowds under the téni-created glow. Somewhere out there, Gilles ce'Guischard was also hurrying home—undoubtedly with fear nipping at his heels. If Sergei was correct in his assumption, then ce'Guischard would waste no time talking to the person who had given him his orders. *I actually feel sorry for poor Gilles. He was only following orders, and now he's dangerous. Probably too dangerous . . .*

If Sergei was correct in his assumptions, then he would soon find that this investigation was abruptly over, and that to continue to pry into the matter of ci'Recroix would be too dangerous for Sergei as well.

~

Gilles ce'Guischard

"*D*ON'T WORRY, GILLES. *I will take care of this . . .*"

Gilles turned the corner of the Rue a'Colombes onto the Rue a'Petit Marché, several blocks away from the hubbub of the Avi a'Parete. There, the market was just preparing for the day, the farmers setting up their tables and getting their produce and goods ready to display. A few shoppers were about, hoping to snare the best choices while the sun still remained low in the sky and before the morning crowds arrived. Gilles' breath frosted in front of him—it had been a long walk from the palais—but he was near his destination now. He glanced up at the side of the nearest building, looking for the street placard. Yes, there it was: Ruelle a'Chats . . .

"*Go to this address a turn of the glass after First Call tomorrow morning. There will be a woman there: Sylva cu'Pajoli. She is married, but she will understand what she needs to say to the commandant; I will send her a note tonight telling her to expect you. Explain to her everything you've already told him; she will work with you to make certain your stories match. Then go back to the*

*commandant and give him Vajica cu'Pajoli's name and
address so he can speak with her."*

It would all work out. He was safe. The tension in
Gilles' stomach loosened as he turned the corner of the
Ruelle a'Chats, an alley which ran between the backs of
houses facing the parallel streets. Gilles could see the
end of the ruelle a hundred strides away, though the
closeness of the houses made the alleyway itself dim
and murky.

"Ah, good morning to you, Vajiki," a man's voice
said, and Gilles saw an utilino push himself away from
the nearest wall, his watchman's prod dangling casually from its handstrap; his lantern, the téni-light extinguished, was sitting on the ground near where he'd been
standing. "You're right on time. You've been expected."

"You're to take me to Vajica cu'Pajoli?" Gilles
asked the man, who smiled broadly, displaying missing
front teeth. The utilino clapped his arm around Gilles'
shoulder.

"We were told to make certain you got to where
you're supposed to go," he answered.

"We? What do you mean ..." Gilles stuttered, suddenly no longer certain of the situation. Two more men
appeared, one from either end of the small lane. The
utilino's arm tightened around Gilles' shoulder as he
started to retreat, and he felt the man coming behind
him press the point of a dagger into his back.

"I wouldn't try to run, my friend," the man whispered.
"Won't do you no good. Let's go along with the good
utilino now, shall we?"

"You don't know who I am," Gilles protested, dragging his feet as they pulled him farther into the ruelle, as
the man from the far end approached. "You don't know
who I work for."

"Ah, but we do, Gilles ce'Guischard," the utilino said.
"Don't we now?"

Hearing his name spoken, Gilles felt true fear for the
first time. This wasn't a random attack; this wasn't robbery.

If they knew his name, if they'd been told to be here, then ... He started to scream for help, but the man behind clapped his hand over Gilles' mouth, pulling his head and neck back sharply. "Shh ..." the man said, the knife pressing harder into Gilles' back as he struggled against the hold. "Won't do none of us any good you being noisy, now will it?"

The man from the far end was now within a stride, and Gilles saw the fellow making the hand motions of a téni and he heard the words of chanting. The téni—if that's what he indeed was, since he didn't wear green robes—nodded as he performed a final wave of his hands, and the man with the knife moved his hand from Gilles's mouth. Gilles shouted. "Help! I need help!" but his words seemed strangely blunted, as if he were shouting with his face pressed against a pillow.

"You can shout all you want now," the spellcaster said. His voice sounded tired. "They can't hear you anymore." He nodded again to the utilino. "Hold him," he said, and began chanting again, his hands dancing in the murk of the alley. Gilles struggled to free himself, but the man with the dagger pressed it to the side of his neck.

"Keep moving, an' I'll use this. Is that what you want: a messy, choking death with your neck smiling with its new mouth carved in it? Be still, or, by Cénzi, I'll do it." Gilles stopped struggling. He sagged in the arms of his attackers. *It will be all right. He wouldn't have ordered me killed. Not after all I've done for him, all the help I've been to him. This is something else.* Gilles watched the téni complete the spell.

The téni's hands glowed; lightning crackled between the poles of his fingers. He stepped forward and put his hands on Gilles' chest. The touch of the man's hands was like nothing Gilles had ever felt before, as if a wild storm had flared into existence inside him, all lightning and hail and gale winds. He screamed at the touch. The téni withdrew his hands, but the storm continued, growing larger and more fierce so that his voice was lost against its thundering in his head. He felt the hands holding him let go, and he tried to take a step, but the wet flags of the Ruelle a'Chats rose up to meet him, and he thrashed on the ground, helpless. He could taste blood; he could see the paving stones in front of his eyes, but even that landscape was growing dark.

He could hear voices, growing ever fainter against the storm. "... dead by no hand but Cénzi's ... the utilino will swear that he fainted ..." but then the thunder came again and it took the voices and his sight and Gilles himself away with the racing storm front.

~

Justi ca'Mazzak

JUSTI STORMED INTO the Archigos' office like a tornado, the offizier from the Garde Civile and Commandant ca'Rudka racing to keep up with him. A few of the staff-téni rose to intercept this evidently-irate trio of intruders, then stopped in mid-stride and mid-spell when they recognized the Kraljiki. "Ca'Cellibrecca!" Justi roared. He flung open the doors to the Archigos' office with a crash, sending a picture flying from the wall as ca'Cellibrecca, behind his desk with several o'téni huddled around him, stared wide-eyed.

"Out!" Justi shouted at the o'téni, pointing to the door. "All of you. Now!"

They gathered papers and scrolls and fled past Justi. The commandant quietly closed the doors behind them. Ca'Cellibrecca remained seated behind his desk. Justi saw him glance appraisingly at the disheveled and unshaven offizier. "Krajiki," ca'Cellibrecca said soothingly, "you're obviously distraught. What's happened? How can I help you?"

The offizier glanced at ca'Rudka, who nodded. "Tell him," ca'Rudka said to the offizier. "Tell him what you just told me and the Kraljiki."

The man nodded. Justi saw ca'Cellibrecca taking in the soiled clothing, the mud spattering his boots, the weariness in the man's stance as he wiped uselessly at stubble on his face.

"I've come from Ville Colhelm on the border, riding hard and constant for a hand of days now with little sleep. I don't know how many mounts I've killed under me getting here this quickly . . ." He stopped. Licked his lips. "The army of Firenzcia has crossed the River Clario in force and overrun Ville Colhelm. They are even now moving toward Nessantico. The Garde Civile were routed at the bridge, far outnumbered. We lost a third of our men trying to hold the bridge before A'Offizier ca'Montmorte ordered the retreat. He sent me to give the Kraljiki the news; the rest of the troops with A'Offizer ca'Montmorte are falling back toward Passe a'Fiume, planning to stay there to await orders and reinforcements."

"You say the Hïrzg was with them?" Justi prompted the man. "And war-téni as well?"

"The division we met was flying the banner of the Hïrzg, my Kraljiki," the soldier answered. "We're certain he is with them, though we didn't see him during the battle. And they had many war-téni with them—they were devastating. We had nothing to counter them. Nothing."

Justi nodded. "I want to thank you greatly for your service," he told the man. "Go—get some food and rest. We'll need you later."

The man saluted both Justi and the commandant, then gave the sign of Cénzi to the Archigos. Ca'Rudka opened the door and closed it after the offizier. As the door closed, Justi turned back to ca'Cellibrecca. The Archigos' face was drained of color. He looked years older as he stared at Justi. "But the message birds we've received . . ."

"... were meant to deceive us, as the commandant suspected all along. If I hadn't ordered troops to the border—against your express advice, as you may recall, Archigos—then we might never have known what ca'Vörl intended until his army reached the A'Sele. So, Archigos ..." The anger burned in Justi, sullen.

It was ca'Rudka who spoke: quietly, saying the words that were in Justi's mind also. "I have to wonder, Archigos, how it is that the Hïrzg has war-téni with his army—war-téni who would have been trained in Brezno, in *your* temple, under *your* U'Téni cu'Kohnle."

"Commandant, you're not suggesting ..." Ca'Cellibrecca's voice trailed off and his gaze moved to Justi as if looking for support. Justi simply stared at the Archigos, whose hand pressed against the base of his throat as if trying to stop his words. The man blanched even more; his skin seemed to be the shade of the alabaster statues in the corridors. "Certainly I knew about the maneuvers, Commandant, Kraljiki," ca'Cellibrecca continued. "As did your matarh. But that is *all* they were supposed to be: maneuvers. I certainly didn't know the Hïrzg's intentions when I granted permission for the war-téni to accompany him. The war-téni should have returned to Brezno when it was apparent that the Hïrzg threatened the peace of the Holdings; to do otherwise was a blatant disobedience of standing orders, and U'Téni cu'Kohnle will be appropriately punished if it is true. Cu'Kohnle must have gone rogue, or perhaps worse has happened to him."

"Indeed," Justi said. "I would hate to believe that he was following orders you gave to him."

"Kraljiki ..." Ca'Cellibrecca rose now, calming himself visibly. Justi nearly snorted at the obviousness of it. The Archigos arranged himself in a pose of wounded pride, his right hand spread and pressed against his chest. "If you're accusing someone of treason, then I wonder why you aren't instead looking at the man beside you. It wasn't *me* who lost so many of the Numetodo enemies of the state, including their leader."

"Attempting to deflect attention, are we, Archigos?" ca'Rudka asked. The commandant's tone was offhand, his posture casual as he leaned against the wall next to the door. He rubbed at his sculpted, silver nose. "I've already made my apology to the Kraljiki and accepted the blame for my failure. But a few dozen heretics cowering in the shadows of Oldtown is hardly the equal of an army massing on Nessantico's doorstep."

"Shut up, both of you." Justi glowered at the two men: as ca'Rudka bowed his head; as ca'Cellibrecca sat once more. "Archigos, I've come here to ask you one simple question—do you stand with me?"

"If you don't," ca'Rudka interjected, "then perhaps the Archigos would enjoy one of the cells the Numetodo have so recently vacated."

"Commandant!" Justi snapped, and ca'Rudka shrugged. "Archigos, an answer, please."

Ca'Cellibrecca spread his hands as if in blessing. "I can assure the Kraljiki that he has my complete devotion." He seemed to attempt a conspiratorial smile; it failed utterly, collapsing into an uncertain frown. "After all, my Francesca . . ."

"Your daughter has nothing to do with this," Justi told him. "I'm certain she would as easily be persuaded to marry the Hïrzg as me. After all, ca'Vörl could have his present marriage annulled. The Archigos can grant such favors, can't he? At least that's what a certain trader in Oldtown whispers—Carlo cu'Belli, who has been to Brezno under the seal of A'Téni ca'Cellibrecca many times."

Justi saw the Archigos visibly flinch. "It's obvious that someone has been filling your ears with innuendo and lies, Kraljiki," he said. "I have done nothing, *nothing,* that hasn't been for the good of Nessantico, and for you especially, Kraljiki. I was Brezno's A'Téni for years, yes, and it's true that I know the Hïrzg well and have worked with him many times, but I am not a traitor: not to Concénzia, and not to the throne of the Kralji."

"Then I have your answer?" Ca'Cellibrecca nodded, with a quick glare at the lounging commandant. "Good," Justi said. "Then you will prepare to leave with me tonight."

"*Leave,* Kraljiki?"

"The Kraljiki has sent a request to the Hïrzg for parley," Commandant cu'Rudka said. "He intends to meet with ca'Vörl before their army reaches Passe a'Fiume. Along with the Garde Civile from the city, we will pick up the remnants of the Garde Civile from Ville Colhelm, as well as the garrisons of Passe a'Fiume, Ile Verte, and Chiari. I have conscription squads out in the city as we speak, and pages have gone to all the houses of the ca'-and-cu' to summon the chevarittai. You will arrange for the war-téni of the Garde Civile to accompany us. We will have a force capable of holding Passe a'Fiume, if it comes to that."

Ca'Cellibrecca gaped, then seemed to shake himself. "Kraljiki," ca'Cellibrecca protested, "it's not the role of the Faith to interfere in political affairs. That is your arena, as the nurturing of the faithful of Cénzi is mine. I would think I would better serve you *here,* where I could help to calm the fears of the populace and make certain that the Numctodo take no advantage of your absence. After all, I'm not a war-téni myself."

"And that way the Archigos can appear to have been a neutral party, just in case the Hïrzg prevails," ca'Rudka said laconically. Ca'Cellibrecca shot him another glance.

"Despite the commandant's rude insinuations, I will do as the Kraljiki wishes, of course," the Archigos said. "But I ask him to consider what happens if Hïrzg ca'Vörl chooses to ignore the rules of parley as he has ignored the laws of Nessantico, and decides to snatch up the Kraljiki, the new Commandant of the Garde Civile, *and* the Archigos of the Concénzia Faith, all at once. The power that would give him, the ransoms he could demand, the concessions he could force . . ."

"You wouldn't immediately declare him a heretic if he did that, Archigos?" Justi said. "You wouldn't cite the Divolonté to him? You wouldn't withdraw the favor of the Faith, or command his téni to no longer perform services for those of Firenzcia? You wouldn't tell the warténi with him that they can no longer call on Cénzi to perform their spells of destruction, and that if they do, you will cut off their hands and remove their tongues and send them from the Faith? In fact, all of that is exactly what I intend you to say to ca'Vörl when we meet: he must turn his army back; he must relinquish military command of the Holdings troops in Firenzcia, and, as surety, he will send his daughter Allesandra to Nessantico as a hostage. He will do that, or he will be declared an enemy of the Faith and of the Holdings, and he will suffer the consequences."

"Kraljiki . . ."

"I assume that I am sufficiently clear on this, Archigos," Justi barked, not giving the man time to protest. "I am not my matarh. I will not avoid confrontation by bandying marriage and alliances; I will not sit on the Sun Throne and weave spiderwebs of intrigue to tangle and confuse my enemies. No one will dub *me* 'Généri a'Pace,' and that bothers me not at all. When I am threatened, I *will* deal with the threat directly and with full, terrible force. I have played your little game regarding Archigos Dhosti and the Numetodo, and that has placed you in the position you so long coveted. Now it's time for you to return the favors I have granted you: in full, without reservation, and with full interest. If you *cannot* do that, Archigos, then—as I said—I will deal with that in a direct manner. I will consider your refusal to be a threat. We leave in three dozen turns of the glass, Archigos. I will see you with your carriage and any attendants you care to take with you at the walls of the Pontica Mordei at that time, as well as every warténi you can muster from within the city . . . or I will see you swinging from the Pontica as a warning to the new Archigos."

Ca'Cellibrecca blinked. Sat. His body slumped like a loaf of uncooked dough. "Kraljiki, you wound me to the core. I was only attempting to make certain that you've considered all aspects of the situation, as is the obligation of any good counselor. You have my entire loyalty. I will be there at your side, as you wish."

"It's not what I wish," Justi told him. "It's what I demand."

~

Francesca ca'Cellibrecca

"THREE DOZEN TURNS of the glass ... What is the man thinking? He can't possibly muster enough soldiers by then. Even with the armories running at full capacity, they won't have the quantities of swords or armor they'll need. He's impossibly impatient to have his war."

Francesca heard Vatarh's irritated muttering from the hallway as his secretary escorted her up to his rooms. The entire temple grounds were in a frantic uproar with rushed preparations, téni and staff scurrying around like a nest of disturbed hornets. "Archigos," his secretary said, clearing his throat, "Vajica Francesca ca'Cellibrecca is here, at your request."

"Ah ..." Orlandi looked over his shoulder. She had rarely seen him so obviously agitated and worried. The pouches of skin under his eyes were dark; his hair was disheveled; there were stains on the front of his robes. He waved his hands wildly at the servants. "Don't forget the new robes the tailor brought over this last Parladi," he told them. "I want them available to me. And make certain that the wine is packed carefully in straw. Oh, and we can't forget the sacristy articles. Francesca, no doubt you've heard . . ." He took his daughter by the arm and escorted her out onto the balcony of his apartments, closing the door on the chaos behind them. There, he embraced her.

"Vatarh, you're trembling." She released him, stepping back.

"I know, I know," he said. He went to the railing, looking down on the plaza, where dozens of people were readying the Archigos' train of carriages. The temple itself was ablaze with light. The line of the Avi a'Parete was a glittering row of pearls snaking through the city. "Francesca, I don't know what will happen. Kraljiki Justi . . . the man is forcing my hand before I'm ready. He knows. Somehow he knows that Hïrzg ca'Vörl and I have been in contact. He doesn't know the full extent of it, or we wouldn't be here talking, but the knowledge itself is dangerous."

For the first time, Francesca felt a burning of fear in her own stomach. Justi might be genuinely attracted to her, but if Vatarh were no longer needed as a political ally or if the Kraljiki perceived him as an active enemy, then his attraction to her would dissolve as well. Justi didn't desire people or objects that failed to either glorify or serve him, and he discarded such useless things without a thought or regret. The heretic Ana cu'Seranta had demonstrated that for Francesca all too well. It perhaps explained why Justi had been so distracted and rough during their lovemaking this afternoon. She could feel the bruises rising on her arms and breasts. "What will you do, Vatarh?"

"I don't know." It was nearly a moan. His eyes rolled from side to side in the reflection of the téni-light from the square. "I don't know. I am trapped between two forces."

"Vatarh, Justi would marry me. I can force the issue.

In fact, wouldn't making that commitment now allay his suspicions?"

"And what good would that do for either of us if Justi dies, or if he's cast down as Kraljiki?" He shook his head so fiercely that sweat-heavy strands of white hair moved. "No, my dear, we need to keep as many options in play as possible. I won't know more until we meet with the Hïrzg and I can see what the situation truly is, with my own eyes. In the meantime, you must leave Nessantico. As soon as I've left the city with the Kraljiki, go to the main temple at Prajnoli and wait there for word from me—I've already sent instructions to A'Téni ca'Marvolli and he's told his u'téni to expect you. It may be that you will need to leave Nessantico entirely, Francesca. You'd be able to reach the border of Firenzcia in two days from Prajnoli if you need to, or return to Nessantico. You have the code wheel I gave you? Keep it with you—you'll need it for any messages I send."

"Vatarh . . ."

He shook his head again. "I don't have anything better to offer you, Francesca. Not at this juncture. It is all in Cénzi's hands." He took his daughter's hands in his own. "I know this. Cénzi looks down on us with favor because I am the Defender of His Word and of the Divolonté. He will not desert me. He will not fail us, however this turns out."

~

Ana cu'Seranta

THE PROCESSION TRAILED off south over the
Pontica a'Brezi Nippoli and north to the gates of
the Avi a'Firenzcia. Ana could not guess at the number of the troops escorting the Kraljiki: several thousand or more—many of them forcibly enlisted in the
last few days as squads of Garde Civile moved through
the city snatching up able-bodied men. Oldtown particularly had been scoured; the tavern below Mahri's
rooms had been raided twice, though the squads had
somehow ignored their rooms above. The unison boot-
falls of the swelled ranks of the Garde Civile shuddered
the ground like an earthquake, their spears as thick as
marsh sawgrass above them. Ana huddled against Karl
on a rooftop across the Avi from the ancient city wall.
Mahri stood next to them, fidgeting with some contraption near the edge of the rooftop.

"That's Commandant ca'Rudka," Ana said. "There—
see him on the white charger? He looks our way, to the
rooftop . . ."

'He won't see us or recognize you," Mahri said. "Not
today. Not with me here." He spoke with utter confidence, and if Karl scowled uncertainly, Ana believed
Mahri without understanding why. She held Karl's arm,
watching the procession stream by and out of the city.

"Look, there's the Kraljiki," Karl said, and Ana hugged
his arm tighter as the Kraljiki's carriage appeared at the
north end of the Pontica. Blue-and-gold banners with
the clenched fist of the Kraljica holding Cénzi's broken
globe fluttered from the attendants around him and the

carriage itself, and the huge stone heads of ancient rulers at the gates rumbled and groaned as they turned to track the current Kraljiki's progress. Ana heard the chanting of téni and smelled perfume and saw the glow of téni-light around him, visible even in the sunlight. The ca'-and-cu' chevarittai pressed around him on their mounts, clad in armor draped with their family colors, the crests of their rank as offiziers of the Garde Civile on their surcoats. The crowd around them cheered at the sight, and the Kraljiki lifted his radiant, muscular arms to them, clad in ornate robes under which polished armor plate glinted. She saw his outthrust chin lift to the accolades, saw the tight satisfaction on his lips. Some of the court wives and *grande horizontales* were among the courtiers and pages accompanying the Kraljiki's train, but Francesca was nowhere to be seen—that was a small consolation. Ana wondered what had happened to the woman, and why she wasn't accompanying the Kraljiki.

"Here," said Mahri. He stepped away from the device he'd erected and gestured to Ana and Karl. "Come look into this. Put your eye here, Ana." He pointed to a small tube. Ana closed one eye and placed the other to the smooth bone lip of the tube. She saw glass set in the tube as she lowered her head.

There was the Kraljiki, so close to her that she could see the stubble on his face and the individual jewels sewn into the collar of his robe. As close as she was when she'd made love to him ... His eyes, the color of plowed earth, so close and so piercing that he might be standing next to her, the whole scene seeming to vibrate slightly, as if the booted thudding of Garde Civile were shaking the very world ...

She gasped and stumbled back. Mahri chuckled. "A spell?" she asked. Karl now pressed his eye to the device; he, too, stifled a cry and stepped away a moment later.

"Not a spell," Mahri said. "Only glass and metal. Look ..." He went to a pool of water on the rooftop and dipped his hand in. Holding out his other hand, he let a single drop fall from his fingertip onto his skin. "See how the drop magnifies the skin underneath? The glass in the tube there is shaped in the same manner; it bends the light and brings closer the vision of things that are far away. But that's not magic, not the X'in Ka or the Ilmodo. It's only a device that anyone can use—a 'verzehen,' it's called: a far-seer."

Karl put his eye to the optics again. "If I could get that close to him, without him knowing it ... I don't know how he can't feel my stare, like I'm standing just to the side of him." He straightened up again. "Ana, go ahead and take another look."

She shook her head at him. "I prefer this distance," she said, looking at the carriage from the rooftop: safely small and removed. She saw the Archigos' carriage appear on the far end of the Pontica, surrounded by green-robed téni. Seeing ca'Cellibrecca in the ornate, gilded brocades of the Archigos that Dhosti ca'Millac had worn so recently, the broken globe of Cénzi golden at his breast, made her lips twist into a scowl.

Mahri touched the device and it swung easily, the thicker end pointing toward the city gates. "Look here," he said. "Tell me what you see."

Ana bent over the verzehen again. As her eye adjusted to the circular world it revealed, she saw the stones of the mighty gate that had been formed from the massive stones of the ancient city wall. There, caught between the stones midway up the tall column to the south side of the gate, there was a cylinder that seemed to be formed of glass—she could see just one end of it, thrust deeply into a chink in the mortared cracks. "A vial," Ana said, "sealed with brown wax on one end. There's something inside—a red substance?—but I can't see it well."

"I put the vial there," Mahri said. "Like the verzehen, there's nothing magical about it. It holds two different chemicals, separated by a stopper of wax. Alone, those substances do nothing. But if that vial should break or the wax melt, and the chemicals come into contact . . . well, they are violently incompatible with each other. Each would seek to destroy the other and erupt like one of the great volcanoes of Il Trebbio, spewing flames and smoke and sending the stones of the gates crashing down on whomever was below."

Ana had straightened again. Out on the Avi, the Kraljiki's carriage moved slowly and inexorably toward the city gates. Mahri's single good eye held her. "But nothing will happen unless the vial breaks or is heated—something someone who knew the Ilmodo could do easily, I'm certain. All it would take is a few moments of chanting and the proper release, easily reachable from here." From the street, the cheering intensified as the Kraljiki's carriage rolled below their building and began to make the turn toward the gate. Mahri's eyebrow raised. The sun touched the scars of his face; to Ana, it appeared to be a stern mask. "The stones would crush those beneath utterly, and the panic that would follow would kill more. Such an event, properly timed, would end the life of the Kraljiki or the Archigos," he continued. "I've no doubt of that."

Ana tore her gaze away from Mahri. She stared at the Kraljiki, then down the street to ca'Cellibrecca, whose carries was now leaving the Pontica. "I'll do it," she heard Karl say, almost eagerly, but Mahri lifted a hand.

"No," he said. "You won't. I won't allow it. It's Ana's choice. Ana's alone."

"Who will be blamed?" Karl persisted. "The Numetodo. That's always the way it is with them. Why not make it the literal truth this time?"

"I won't allow it," Mahri repeated. "Ana?"

Why not? Either of them would take your life without remorse or regret. Justi never loved you, not one moment; he took what you offered and used you to betray the true Archigos. And ca'Cellibrecca would have done to you as he did to poor Dhosti. It was only Dhosti's warning that

*saved you at all. You would only be doing to them what
they would do to you, or to Karl, or to Mahri. . . .*

"Ana?"

The Kraljiki's carriage turned. The Garde Civile
around him were at the gate, the carriage itself close
now. *Why not? Can the Hïrzg be a worse ruler? Can he
hurt you more than the Kraljiki or ca'Cellibrecca already
has? Cénzi would forgive you—the Divolonté itself says
it: "Those who defy and subvert Cénzi's Will will be sent
to meet Him, and full justice will be given unto them."
You can make them pay for Dhosti, for the Numetodo
they've killed, for the torment they gave Karl, for the way
they treated you. It would only be fair. . . .*

The Kraljiki's carriage was nearly at the gate. All she
had to do was speak the words. A simple spell of fire—
something U'Téni cu'Dosteau had taught the class in
the first year. She mouthed the words of the Ilmodo, felt
her hands begin the shaping of the spell.

The carriage moved into the gate. The crowds pressed
around it, cheering and waving as the Kraljiki waved
back to them. They would wave and cheer the same way
if it were Hïrzg ca'Vörl riding through those gates, because cheering was safe. Pretending to be on the side of
the victor was safe, even when the victor was no better
than the person he replaced.

*The flame searing flesh, great boulders flying in the air,
the screams . . . Justi's death, or the Archigos', yes, but others would die with them, all those down there who are
cheering and shouting only to protect themselves, and
who haven't asked for any of this . . .*

Her mouth closed. Her hands stopped moving.

"I can't," she said.

"Ana," she heard Karl say, but she was looking at
Mahri's impassive face.

"I just . . . can't," she said again, not quite certain who
she was trying to tell. "Not like this. What happens if I
do it?" she asked the wind, the sun, the sky. "Do I help,

or do I just end up causing more hurt and confusion and death? I don't know . . ."

She lifted her hands, let them fall. The Kraljiki's carriage moved through the gates and past; the Archigos' carriage moved between. The crowds roared, a sound like the roaring breath of Cénzi Himself. Ana felt tears burn her eyes. "I can't do it. Not without knowing. Not without some hope that I'm changing things for the better."

Mahri simply nodded. She felt Karl's arms go around her from behind. "I understand," he whispered in her ear. "I do."

They watched the Archigos' carriage pass through the gate, following the Kraljiki out of Nessantico and onto the Avi a'Firenzcia and the waiting Hïrzg.

PARLEYS

Jan ca'Vörl
Ana cu'Seranta
Justi ca'Mazzak
Orlandi ca'Cellibrecca
Sergei ca'Rudka
Justi ca'Mazzak
Ana cu'Seranta

Jan ca'Võrl

"**I**THINK IT'S VERY pretty, Vatarh. It should be a painting."

"I wish I could see it with your eyes," Jan told his daughter. "All I see is a battlefield." He let his arm rest around her shoulders and hugged her.

The pine-studded arms of the Cavasian Range cradled Passe a'Fiume in their long, steep slopes. There, the River Clario poured white and fast in its descent from the Sigar Highlands of Nessantico's eastern reaches. The town was perched on the Clario's western bank; a wide bridge arched over the Clario from Passe a'Fiume's eastern gate: the Pontica Avi a'Firenzcia, the only safe place to cross the wild Clario for many miles in either direction, until the river settled itself and widened as it prepared to meet the great A'Sele.

The town knew its importance—the largest of the cities in eastern Nessantico, it still resided almost entirely within the three-century-old fortified walls that had been erected on the orders of Kraljiki Sveria I during the interminable Secession War, as Nessantico sought to bring Firenzcia fully under its control. The thick, granite walls had repelled a half-dozen sieges since the time of the Kraljiki Sveria.

Now the populace looked out from flower-boxed windows and crenellated towers and wondered whether they could survive a seventh assault.

"Can the war-téni really break those walls, Vatarh? They look so thick."

"They can. They will, if the Kraljiki doesn't submit to our terms."

"He won't," Allesandra said with certainty. "If he's like you, Vatarh, he won't submit."

He chuckled at that. The mirth sounded out of place.

Jan had arrayed the army on the slopes across the Clario—a few miles from the city but high on the ridges that faced the town. He knew the citizenry could see the tents and cook fires, the fluttering banners and the dark, writhing mass of the soldiery, covering the slopes like a horde of ravening insects about to descend and feed upon the town. They had seen the army assemble over the last two days; they could glimpse them through the wisps of morning fog even now. He knew the fear they would be feeling, and knew the forces the Kraljiki had brought with him would give them little solace.

Even if the Kraljiki could manage to hold the town, a siege would mean the deaths of many who lived there. A victory that costly would be hardly distinguishable from defeat.

From his vantage point, Jan could make out through the mist the parley tents set in the field just across the Clario from Passe a'Fiume: like white flowers set in the grass before the glowering city walls and the dirty brown-green ribbon of the river. The banner of the Kraljiki flew from the central post of the largest tent. There were a few hundred of the Garde Civile there, but the Kraljiki kept the bulk of his soldiers hidden behind the stern, gray, and impassive ramparts of the city walls. It didn't matter: Jan's spies, set out well ahead of the army, had reported their numbers to him.

Perhaps half of the forces that had been at Ville Colhelm under ca'Montmorte, a few thousand straggling in from Chiari and Prajnoli, perhaps five thousand who marched with the Kraljiki and the Archigos from Nessantico. Many of the citizens are fleeing from the eastern gates, desperate to leave the city, but the conscription squads are at work there, not letting the men leave.

The Kraljiki commanded a force smaller than the army at Jan's back but more than enough to make a siege of Passe a'Fiume difficult. However, there were movements underway that Jan doubted had touched the Kraljiki's awareness. As in a game of cards, knowing the hand your opponent has been dealt grants an enormous advantage in the bidding process. Jan smiled grimly as he stared down at the parley tents, waiting for the meeting this afternoon.

"The Kraljiki will make his stand here, but he's not certain of the outcome—that's why he wants to parley," Markell's voice said.

Jan chuckled again as he released his daughter to glance at Markell. His aide's stick-thin figure appeared strangely out of place in chain mail. Markell, too, was gazing out through the thin morning fog at Passe a'Fiume. "As usual, you know exactly what I'm thinking," Jan told him. "As does Allesandra. I would seem to be utterly transparent to both of you."

"It's my job to anticipate you, my Hïrzg," Markell answered somberly. "I know this isn't what we'd hoped for—former Starkkapitän ca'Staunton's stupidity at Ville Colhelm cost us an easy crossing of the Clario, and many lives if we have to take this city by force. Still, a siege of a week, quite possibly less, and you would have your surrender, I think. The Kraljiki is seeking a diplomatic solution, not a military one. As his matarh would."

Jan scowled. Markell's assessment was all too true: had ca'Staunton obeyed his orders at Ville Colhelm, the Kraljiki would still be in Nessantico and the Garde Civile in their garrisons, and the gates of Passe a'Fiume would already be open to Jan—as well as the road to Nessantico. Stupidity would need to be repaid in blood now. Much blood . . . "You sound certain, Markell. I'm afraid I'm not."

It was Allesandra who answered. "Kraljiki Justi has never met you in battle, Vatarh."

"I appreciate your confidence," Justi answered her with a smile, "but Markell's face is far too solemn. What is it, Markell?"

"U'Téni cu'Kohnle has requested an audience," Markell told Jan. "He's waiting in your tent. He says he is ... *concerned* about the war-téni, since we know the Archigos is with the Kraljiki in Passe a'Fiume."

Jan sighed audibly. He rubbed his arms against the morning chill. "Ah. I was expecting that. Do we have word from ca'Cellibrecca?"

"No, Hïrzg. Though in the Archigos' defense, it would be difficult for him to contact us at the moment."

Jan sniffed. "Ca'Cellibrecca can't straddle sides any longer. He'd best realize that. He'd be well-advised not to betray me, or if he does, he should pray to Cénzi that the Kraljiki prevails because I will have worse than his life if he stands in my way." He took a long breath and let it out abruptly.

"Yes, my Hïrzg," Markell said. "And U'Téni cu'Kohnle?"

"I'll talk with him. Come, walk with me and Allesandra back to the tent." Jan put his arm around his daughter again as he took a last glance at the field and the tents waiting outside the walls. . . .

"Semini," he said as he entered. "You wanted to see me."

Cu'Kohnle gave Jan the sign of Cénzi along with a deep bow that displayed the thick growth of gray-flecked, black hair on his skull. His cheeks and chin were stubbled with the same gray as his hair. Muscular arms flexed under the green robes, and Jan saw the steel links of mail underneath. The broken globe of Cénzi hung prominently around his neck. "My Hïrzg," he said. "Thank you for taking the time."

"I know what concerns you, Semini," Jan said. "Certainly you knew that it might come to this."

Cu'Kohnle smiled tight-lipped. "If you'll forgive me, the entire Strettosei spans the difference between 'might' and 'has,' my Hïrzg. It's no longer a case of 'might,' and because of that, many of the war-téni are troubled. I came to speak for them."

Jan was certain that there were other motives at work here. He knew cu'Kohnle enough to know that the man was fanatically devout; he also knew him well enough to know that his devotion was to Cénzi and not necessarily to those who claimed to speak for the God. There was raw ambition and ego in the man . . . and that meant he could be manipulated. Jan gestured to the table where the pages had placed wine and bread. "Please, help yourself," he said. "What of you, Semini? Are *you* troubled?"

"I'm as troubled as any person of faith would be," he answered. He took a piece of the bread and broke off a hunk from the end of the loaf. He turned it in his fingers. "The Concénzia Faith is what sustains us, and the Archigos is the person to whom we swear our allegiance. Not to the Kraljiki. Not even, with your pardon, the Hïrzg. So yes, I am troubled, because the Archigos is there in Passe a'Fiume and with the Kraljiki, and it's not a trivial consequence for a téni to be cast out from the Faith." He glanced down at his wiry hands, holding them up to Jan. "You know what happens to a téni who has been cast out, should he ever use the Ilmodo again."

There it is, then. Jan watched as cu'Kohnle tucked the bread carefully into his mouth, chewed a moment, and swallowed. "Continue, Semini. I'm listening."

"I'm a practical man, as you know, my Hïrzg. I was born in Firenzcia. Within the Faith, I served Archigos Orlandi for his entire tenure as A'Téni of Brezno. My loyalty was always more to him than to that dwarf Dhosti, and my loyalty was also always more to the Hïrzg than to Kraljica Marguerite, and certainly far more to you than to Kraljiki Justi. My sympathies are with the new Archigos' stated goals, as you know. I would gladly help drive the Numetodo from the Holdings and end their heresy. The Ilmodo must remain in the hands of Concénzia, for many reasons. I realize these are sentiments you share as well, and that is why you and the Archigos were so well-suited to each other. I also gave my word to serve you in your position as the leader of the Firenzcian army, as did the other war-téni here. I am Firenzcian. But . . ."

He tore another piece from the loaf. "If the Archigos declares that we war-téni who fight with you are in defiance of the Divolonté, then I don't know. Some will still fight; some will not. The same is true of the chevarittai and the soldiers: there are those who will be afraid to fight if they think doing so endangers their relationship with Cénzi."

Jan nodded. *And you wouldn't be saying this to me if you didn't already have your solution in mind, and if you weren't looking for something.* He poured wine into one of the goblets and held it out to cu'Kohnle, then poured himself a glass. "I appreciate your cautions and thoughts, Semini," he said. "It strikes me that, since poor Estraven ca'Cellibrecca never reached Brezno, the seat of A'Téni of Brezno lies vacant, and that as the person who leads my war-téni and as the confidant of the Archigos when he was at Brezno, you are now the highest ranking téni in all Firenzcia. I would suspect—and I only speculate here, Semini—that the Archigos could be persuaded, after we have prevailed, to name you as A'Téni of Brezno."

Jan saw small muscles twitch along cu'Kohnle's jaw line as the man pondered Jan's half-promise. *Yes. That was it!* "For that matter," Jan continued, "should the Archigos make the terrible mistake of betraying me here, a mistake he might well make, then after our victory I would be in a position to influence all the a'téni of the Faith to name a new Archigos, one whose loyalty was beyond question. I reward well those who stand with me, Semini. I reward them *very* well, especially if they demonstrate how effective a leader they can be. I assure you that the soldiers of Firenzcia will not fail to fight even if a false Archigos threatens their souls—because those who command them will not allow it. Because *I* will not allow it. Starkkapitän ca'Staunton failed to understand that, but Starkkapitän ca'Linnett seems to have grasped the concept. Do you take my meaning, Semini?"

The man nodded, slowly. "Yes. I believe I do, my Hïrzg."

Jan took a step toward him, close enough that he could see the hairs in the man's nostrils. "Then I ask you, U'Téni cu'Kohnle, as the commander of the war-téni, do you think that those in your charge would understand that an Archigos who has betrayed his word to me is a false Archigos who does not deserve his title? Do you think they would understand that such a man no longer speaks for Cénzi, no matter what title he might claim for the moment?"

The man's eyes narrowed. He was looking at Jan, but his gaze was somewhere else, wandering in his imagination. "I think I can persuade them to see your point of view, my Hïrzg, if it should become necessary. Yes."

Jan lifted his wine and tapped the rim of his goblet against that of cu'Kohnle. "Good," he said. "Then let us drink to our understanding."

～

Ana cu'Seranta

NESSANTICO BEREFT of a Kralji lurched like a boat without a hand on the tiller. Concénzia bereft of an Archigos in the temple stuttered and hesitated. The city held its collective breath and jumped at every strange noise and cowered with every cloud-shadow. Rumors flew through the city like dark, flapping bats, frightening and furious.

The Garde Kralji was especially skittish, and the

Bastida was crowded with people arrested for treason-
ous statements. The judicial system was quickly overwhelmed; judges offered many of those incarcerated the
chance to prove their loyalty (and regain their freedom)
by joining the Garde Civile; many did so. In addition, the
conscription squads of the Garde Civile roamed through
the city and the villages and farmlands around it daily,
taking any unwary men they found and depositing them
in the growing tent encampment outside the city walls
along the Avi a'Parete. There, ragged and uncertain
squads could be seen marching and training during the
day. Garrisons from Villembouchure and Vouziers arrived a few days after the Kraljiki's departure, swelling
the encampment so that the Avi north and west of the
city swarmed with them from the road to the banks of
the River Vaghian. Hundreds if not thousands of the soldiers flooded into the city at night: into the restaurants,
the bars and taverns, the brothels. Even during the day,
groups of sword-girt soldiers were seen in every public
square.

The crisis affected Concénzia as well. With the Archigos and the more adept lesser téni gone, the infrastruc-
ture of Nessantico faltered. The a'téni, most of whom
had remained behind to attend to the affairs of Concénzia in the Archigos' absence, were rumored to be
looking for excuses to return to their home cities and
planning their departures. The téni of the city were
poorly directed as a result, and worries and uncertainty
rendered their Ilmodo spells weak and ineffective. Sewage flowed untreated into the A'Sele, making it more of
a cesspool than usual, the stench reaching far out from
its banks. The nightly lighting of the Avi a'Parete was
erratic—sometimes long stretches of the Avi, especially
in east Oldtown, went dark only a few turns of the glass
after the lamps were set aglow. The foundries that ut-
lizied téni to power their great ovens and forges found
their Ilmodo-fires sometimes too weak to melt the ore
without using far more coal than usual. The téni-driven

carriages were a rare sight even for those within Concénzia, and since the growing army had taken most of the horses, people walked or stayed home. Of greatest concern was the lack of téni for the fire patrols, and there were worries that an errant spark could destroy blocks of houses, especially in Oldtown, before enough téni could be found to extinguish the flames.

The great stone heads at the various gates of the city no longer rotated with the sun; there were no téni available to lend them mobility. The wind-horns on the temples still sounded the calls and the services continued in the temples—the u'téni and o'téni who performed the rituals found more people in the seats than usual but fewer folias, siqils, and solas in the donation boxes.

War shadowed everyone's thoughts, everyone's activities. Nessantico herself hadn't experienced a siege or even a nearby battle in centuries. This was not a situation that had a counterpart for long generations of the families living within the long-sundered walls of the capital. War was something that took place on the edges and frontiers of the Holdings—in Tennshah, in Daritria, in Shenkurska or cold Boail or the far Westlands—always there, always easily available for those who sought glory and fame through its bloody auspices, but always held at a safe distance.

No more. War hovered just to the east, a thunderhead on the horizon, lightning crackling under black ramparts. The markets were crowded every day, but the stalls were thinned by the swelled ranks of the city and by all the produce diverted to feed the army, and the haggling was halfhearted and the conversation was not regarding the quality of the vegetables and meats, but what might happen if the Kraljiki's negotiations failed. On the South Bank, it became even more expensive to eat in the fashionable restaurants as supplies became short and menu prices rose in response. On the North Bank, for the poorer residents, bread prices that had been fixed for decades at a d'folia tripled overnight after the Kraljiki's departure and continued to rise; there were reports of sawdust mixed in with the flour, or of loaves rather smaller than the required minimum standards—both illegal practices but also unsurprising. Storekeepers opened their shutters each morning but fewer customers entered, and those who did wanted to talk about politics, not the goods on display. Those in the crafts found that the rich patrons who hired them to build or remodel, to plaster and decorate, to play music for their parties or paint their portraits, had few commissions. "The war, you know . . ." was always the answer, with a roll of the eyes to the east.

The war . . .

The war shadowed Ana as well. The conscription squads raided the tavern below Mahri's dwelling twice more in the week following the Kraljiki's departure. The uproar woke her and Karl from sleep late at night, though again the squads never came upstairs to their rooms, a fact that Ana no longer found quite so unusual. The third time they came, it began with the same muffled shouts heard through the floor of their apartment, shouts that disrupted, then banished, the dream she had of herself talking to Archigos Dhosti in the Old Temple. In the dream, the Archigos was telling her to heal her Matarh, but matarh seemed possessed, speaking in voices that were not hers, shouting loudly. . . .

"Ana?"

"I hear them." She opened her eyes. She could dimly see Karl in the bit of moonlight trickling from between the slats of the shutters. He was standing at one of the windows, holding the shutter slightly open to see the courtyard below. Mahri was gone. Ana heard the crash of glass below, and more shouts.

"There they go," Karl said from the window. "Dragging four poor bastards with them who won't be coming home to wives or family tonight or any time soon. They'll be down to taking children soon."

Ana rose from her blankets and went to him. Karl's

proximity felt good, a warmth along her side, and his arm came around her as they watched the conscription squad hauling the men away down the street. She felt Karl's arm lift from about her, heard him start to speak in his odd version of the Ilmodo-speech.

"You can't, Karl," she told him. "They'd know you were here, they'd take you back to the Bastida."

His hands stopped moving, his voice stilled. She could see other faces at the windows along the street—people wondering who had been taken this time. A woman came hurtling from one of the doorways, screaming and trying to pull one of the men away from the squad; they pushed her away. "Falina, I'll be back. Take care of Saddasi. I'll be back . . ." they heard the man calling as he was hauled along the street and down the next corner. The woman huddled on the street wailing as neighbors came out to comfort her.

Karl's arm tightened around Ana's shoulder. She leaned into the embrace.

"I hate this," she heard him say. "I hate all of it: the hiding, the constant fear, the way the whole city *feels.*"

"I know," she said. "I'm tired of it also."

"We should leave," he said. "Go somewhere else. Back to the Isle, maybe. There are things I would love to show you there, if you'd come with me."

Like the woman you left there with the promise of your betrothal? She was afraid to say it, afraid that there would be too much bitterness in her voice and too much vulnerability in her heart. "I can't leave," she said instead. "This is my home. Matarh is here, the Archigos' Temple is here, and any hope I have of ever defeating the lies that have been spread about me and Archigos Dhosti. If we run, Karl, everyone will think they were all true, and—" She stopped. Sniffed. "*Smoke,*" she said, her voice catching. "Something's burning." She turned, looking back into the room. She thought she could see a dark mist seeping in the twilight of the room, like a black fog seeping from the floorboards on the other side of the room. There was light as well, a ruddy glow penetrating the cracks between the worn blackwood planks.

"Fire," Ana breathed. "The tavern . . ."

"Come on," Karl said. He took her arm. "We have to get out of here. Quickly—"

They fled from the rooms and down the outside stairs. Flames were already licking at the shutters of the first floor and smoke boiled from the front of the building. The alarm was beginning to spread, with shouts and cries from the nearby buildings as neighbors alerted each other. "Find the utilino!" someone shouted. "We need the fire-téni or the whole block will go!"

Karl was tugging at Ana's arm as she stood in the center of the lane and stared at the building, the door of the tavern outlined in fire. "We have to leave. You can't be here when they come."

"They won't come in time," she protested. "You know that. We can put it out. I know the spell."

"I don't," Karl answered, "and that blaze would take a dozen fire-téni, Ana. The building's gone and so will be all the others around it; we can't stop this."

She shook away his hand on her arm. "Ana—"

She closed her eyes to his plea. She began to chant, trying to recall the words that U'Téni cu'Dosteau had taught her. *Larger gestures, this time; even bigger than before* . . . The words came slowly, but then she caught the rhythm of the chant and the words flowed easily, her hands shaping the power that she felt rising around her with the chant. The form that U'Teni cu'Dosteau had taught them was a truncated one, a small practice spell, but she improvised on it, letting her mind find pathways that expanded it. She thought of nothing, just letting her mind open to the Ilmodo, letting her hands move unconsciously. The power continued to build, an invisible storm of rain and wind around her that only she could feel, thrashing and bucking and fighting her. When it became so strong that she was afraid that she could not hold it back any longer, she stopped chanting, holding the release word in her mind: again, a word that she did not know, a word that Cénzi must have put in her head.

She opened her eyes and at arm's length cupped her hands around the tavern. She could see her fingers trembling, glowing with cold blue.

She spoke.

The very air answered her.

The spell rushed outward, an invisible, frigid explosion that sent the tavern doors and the shutters of the windows into splinters. The wind shrieked and howled, a scream that caused the people nearby to clap hands to ears. The smoke roiling from the building increased dramatically, but turned a strange pale white that seemed to glow in the moonlight, overpowering the ruddy flames. A quick *fa-WHOOMP* reverberated along the street, followed by silence.

The building sat: the first story blackened around the open holes of windows and door, wisps of smoke still trailing upward. But no flames were visible. Ana saw it, but then the weariness of the Ilmodo struck her, as strongly as she'd ever experienced it. Her knees buckled, and she felt Karl's hands go around her to support her, and she heard the crowd yelling, and a voice close to her saying "Ana, you are more dangerous than anyone thought." The voice was Mahri's, and she glimpsed his hooded, scarred face in the narrowed tunnel of her vision.

"Mahri," she said. "I had to . . ."

"No, you didn't, but I'm not surprised that you thought you did," he told her. "And now we have to get you out of here."

She felt herself being lifted—"Karl?"—and she saw the buildings moving around her and heard the people shouting around them . . . but it was easier to fall into sleep than to worry about it, and Karl and Mahri were there to keep her safe, so she allowed herself to fall away for a time.

*   *   *

She never quite reached unconsciousness. She was aware of movement, of voices, of being carried into somewhere. She must have slept a bit; she woke smelling warm bread and tea. She opened her eyes to daylight in a room she didn't recognize.

"It's about time," she heard Karl say. He came from the outer room with a plate and mug and set it down on the floor next to her mattress, then sat beside it himself. "Four full turns of the glass, I'd bet, if we had a glass to turn. It's morning." He smiled. "I have breakfast. I knew you'd be famished."

He handed her the bread, with a single thin dab of precious butter on it. The smell alone made her ravenous, and she took one of the slices and tore into it hungrily. "Mahri?" she manage to ask between bites.

"He brought us here, then vanished. Haven't seen him since around daybreak. The man must not sleep like normal people." She could feel his gaze on her as she reached for another slice and took a sip from the mug of steaming tea. "That was some impressive display of the Ilmodo," he said to her. "It almost made me want to believe in Cénzi. I think it impressed Mahri, too. He was mumbling to himself the whole time we were carrying you."

"The fire would have taken so many houses. All those people . . ."

"I know. I know why you didn't listen to me. I just don't understand how you did all that."

"I don't understand how you do what you do, either," she told him. "For a time, that made me doubt everything. Especially myself."

He smiled again. "Evidently you found yourself again." His hand stroked her cheek; the feel of it on her skin made her shiver.

"No," she told him, and he pulled his hand away.

"What's the matter?"

"What's her name?" Ana asked him. "The woman in Paeti. Your fiancée."

She wasn't certain why she said it; the words slipped out, as they had lurked there in her head, waiting. There was a long silence. Karl stared at her. "How did you know?"

"Does that make a difference?" she asked him. It bothered her that he seemed more irritated than ashamed. "What matters more to me is that you never told me about her. What's her name?"

She watched him take a breath, then another. "Kaitlin," he said at last. "Ana, I've been gone two years now. I don't know when I'll return, or if. Kaitlin and I . . . we said we'd be faithful. But I think we both knew that I might find someone else, or that she might . . ."

"*Has* it happened?"

He ducked his head. Nodded. "For me, it has," he said. "I think you know that."

"And for her?"

"I don't know."

"You *should* know, Karl."

He said nothing. The tea steamed in the mug in her hands. "Has it happened for *you?*" he asked finally. "With me?"

"Perhaps," she answered. "I don't know. Too much has happened and I'm not sure of anything now. But I don't know that I'm ready for what you want."

"Because of Kaitlin."

Ana couldn't decide whether that was a statement or a question. She nodded. "Yes. And . . . other things. Karl, I may never be ready."

Had he left then, had he simply nodded and accepted that, she knew that it would all be over between them. She knew that it would have killed whatever it was that had brought them together. It would have changed things between them forever.

He did not. He knelt in front of her and his hands went around hers as she held the mug.

"Then I can wait," he told her.

~

Justi ca'Mazzak

THE MORNING FOG had lifted several turns of the
glass ago, and the sky was crowded with gray clouds
drifting lethargically above them. Justi gestured, and the
great portcullis of Passe a'Fiume groaned and protested
as it was hauled up and the thick oaken gates of the
town swung open. Justi's entourage was small: no more
than twenty of the ca'-and-cu' chevarittai attending him,
Commandant ca'Rudka accompanied by two double-
hands of the Garde Civile, Archigos ca'Cellibrecca with
U'Téni cu'Bachiga of Passe a'Fiume and a half-dozen
war-téni from the Archigos' Temple.

Justi had watched from the walls of the town as Hïrzg
ca'Vörl's retinue entered the field conspicuously just beyond bowshot range of the walls (though not unreach-
able by war-téni). The archers remained arrayed on the
walls as Justi's small force advanced out from the gate
and onto the Clario bridge. A page in the livery of the
Kraljiki waited at the far side of the bridge, a scabbarded
sword cradled in his arms. He bowed low as Justi rode
slowly up to him.

"My Kraljiki, the Hïrzg Jan ca'Vörl has accepted your
sword from me and asked me to give you this in return,"
the page said. The young man's voice trembled slightly
as he presented the sword hilt-first. Justi leaned down
to take the sword as the page, still bowing, backed away.
The sword was plain but obviously well-used: the sword
of someone who used the weapon as a tool of war, not
in tedious ceremonies. The leather wrapping of the hilt
was stained, and the feel was solid. The Hïrzg's initials

were engraved in the pommel, the deep-cut, ornate lines filled with glittering lapis, the only touch of ostentation on the weapon. Justi drew the weapon; it was beautifully balanced in his hand, and the twin edges were polished and keen, with the slight curve that was the hallmark of the Firenzcian saber. The steel was satin and almost dark, and it sang a shimmering high note as it left the scabbard.

The sword was a message, he knew. The presentation sword Justi had given to ca'Vörl had been one of the ceremonial swords his matarh had commissioned as gifts for ambassadors and representatives: more show-piece than weapon, more jewelry than edge.

"Firenzcian steel," Commandant ca'Rudka commented, coming up alongside Justi. His silver nose gleamed in the sunlight; Justi could see his own distorted reflection in one nostril. "Beautiful, if you like deadly things." From ca'Rudka's raised eyebrows, Justi knew that the man understood the significance of the gift. Justi sheathed the weapon and hooked the loop of the scabbard to his belt, and gently nudged his horse forward again as the page stepped aside. The retinue began to move, hooves loud on the wooden planks of the bridge. Justi glanced up toward the tents farther down the Avi, their sides up to allow breezes to enter—and to allow Justi to see that there was no deception. He could see the Hïrzg's retinue in the shadows under the linen cloth.

"We'll know soon enough whether steel will be necessary," Justi told ca'Rudka.

"Do you think that's a possibility, Kraljiki?" Ca'Rudka was looking past the tents to the mountains and the army waiting there.

Justi was wondering the same, but he didn't answer and ca'Rudka didn't pursue the question. Justi gestured to the others, and they continued on toward the tents. Pages hurried forward as they reached the greensward: taking the reins of the horses; bringing steps to help Justi and the others alight from their mounts. Servants led the horses away to graze, and others came forward to offer drinks to the retinue. Justi waved them aside, not wanting to put anything in the burning pit that was his stomach. "This way, Kraljiki. The Hïrzg is waiting for you."

A long table had been set up in the middle of the tent, with two ornate chairs at either end. Less comfortable and ornate seating was arranged around the focus of the two ends so that the Kraljiki and the Hïrzg could each consult with their advisers at need. Two scribes stood by folding desks with parchment, quills, and fully-charged inkwells, prepared to document the proceedings. Pages and servants stood by along either side, ready to provide refreshment or to ferry documents from one end to the other, or simply to shoo away annoying insects.

As Justi strode into the cool twilight of the tent, Hïrzg ca'Vörl rose slowly and almost grudgingly from his chair at the end of the table, though his retinue was already standing. Justi recognized a few of them from his ceremonial trips to Brezno: the stick-figure of Markell, the Hïrzg's secretary and adviser; U'Téni cu'Kohnle, the head of Firenzcian war-téni. But the person wearing the starkkapitän's eagle wasn't Ahren ca'Staunton, but some younger offizier whose face was unknown to Justi.

All but ca'Vörl had bowed their heads reflexively as he approached the table with the Archigos and ca'Rudka to either side of him, but Justi could feel them staring as if they were trying to see inside him—all but ca'Vörl himself. The Hïrzg simply watched, as if slightly bored by the proceedings. Justi stood behind the chair and stared back, and finally ca'Vörl gave the barest motion of his head to Justi, the shadow of a nod.

"I had hoped to meet you again in more ... pleasurable circumstances, Hïrzg Jan," Justi said as a page pulled back the heavy chair for him and he sat. He nodded to the gathering; the Hïrzg seated himself across from Justi, and then there was the rustling of cloth and harsher groan of mail and plate as the others found their seats around them. Justi glanced at a thick leather portfolio placed on the table in front of him, stamped with the rampant stallion insignia of Firenzcia. "What is this?"

"Those are my terms for your surrender, Kraljiki," ca'Vörl answered easily. "Let me summarize them for you. You will abdicate your title in favor of me, and hand over control of the Garde Civile to Starkkapitän ca'Linnett. My army will continue through Passe a'Fiume to Nessantico City to retain order during the transition of government. Archigos ca'Cellibrecca will return with me; he would be permitted to retain his title as Archigos as long as I perceive that he is cooperating. For your part, Kraljiki, I will allow you to retain your ca' status, your title of chevaritt, and the lands of the ca'Ludovici estates in northern Nessantico, but you will absent yourself from all affairs of the Holdings on peril of your fortune and your life. There are, of course, many more details set out in the agreement, but those are the broad strokes. All I require is your signature and we are done here."

Justi glanced down once at the folio, resisting the urge to spit on it. *The man has always been arrogant, but this is beyond arrogance. . . .* Some of Hïrzg's retinue were carefully smiling, amused by Justi's discomfiture; his own people sat silent and stunned. *Did he know what I'd planned?* Justi gestured, and one of the pages scurried forward to place a portfolio in front of the Hïrzg.

"These are *my* terms," Justi told the Hïrzg. "Your army will immediately retreat beyond the Nessantico borders. Your starkkapitän and all a'offiziers of the army will surrender their arms and commissions to Commandant ca'Rudka. You, Hïrzg ca'Vörl, will be taken to Nessantico as my hostage until the ransom I demand is paid by your family, at which time you will exchange your daughter for yourself as hostage. Firenzcia will also pay damages to the town of Ville Colhelm and for your plundering of Nessantico's land. Those who disobey any of the decrees in these terms will be declared outlaw by the

Holdings, and also by the Archigos of the Concénzia Faith. Henceforth, Firenzcia will no longer have a Hïrzg, but will be under direct control of a representative of the Holdings."

The smiles were gone from the Hïrzg's retinue now, and Justi leaned back in his chair as he swept the Hïrzg's portfolio contemptuously to the floor and thrust out his famous chin even further. "All I require is your signature, Hïrzg ca'Vörl," he said deliberately. "And we are done here."

Ca'Vörl glowered and a deep flush covered his face. Justi thought that the man was about to go into a frothing rage, but instead ca'Vörl slapped his hands open-palmed on the portfolio and roared a laugh that was made louder by the silence around them. "Kraljiki Justi, I have underestimated you. When I've met you in the past ... well, I confess that I thought you entirely devoid of humor. I see that I was wrong." The grin vanished as quickly as it had come. His eyelids lowered, and he stared at Justi. "But that doesn't alter the fact that I have an army perched before Passe a'Fiume, which is the doorstep to Nessantico, and I don't believe that you have the forces or the will to stop me from walking through that door. The Garde Civile has been nothing but an adjunct to the Firenzcian army for two centuries now; it is Firenzcia who has fought the Holdings' battles for the Kralji, not the Garde Civile. So ... let us talk realities here, not dreams. We both know what each of us want; neither will get it without bloodshed." He picked up Justi's portfolio and dropped it on the grass next to his chair. "What do you really offer, Kraljiki?" he asked. "What is genuinely on the table for us to consider?"

Justi sniffed. He ached to draw the sword ca'Vörl had given him and strike the man dead—he could do that, he was certain, before the man could react or anyone could respond. He *wanted* the fight; he could feel it. It would feel good, better than this fencing with blunted words. It would ease the fury gathering in his chest and the fire in his belly. Matarh might have enjoyed this word-dancing, but he did not. *You have to continue ... You need more time to be ready, time you can buy here.*

"Let's define the true situation first," Justi said finally. He could hear ca'Rudka relax alongside him; the man had tensed, ready—Justi realized—to defend him. Ca'Cellibrecca gave an obvious sigh of relief. "Passe a'Fiume has never been taken in a siege when it has been guarded by a full complement of Garde Civile; it now has that full complement and more. You can't besiege the city without controlling the western gates on the other side of the Clario, and your army, no matter how strong, has no easy crossing of the river anywhere close. Should you somehow manage to make the crossing and continue your aggression in Nessantico, then Archigos ca'Cellibrecca will declare your troops and your war-téni in violation of the Divolonté. The Marque of all your téni will be immediately revoked and any services performed by them will be considered empty and void. The blessings of Cénzi will be withdrawn from your troops—those who die will find themselves in the hands of the death hags. Any war-téni who are captured will suffer the fate of those who use the Ilmodo against Cénzi's Will."

Justi paused and glanced sharply at ca'Cellibrecca. The man looked ill. He was staring somewhere beyond ca'Vörl. "Archigos," Justi snapped, and the man shivered, his jowls wiggling on either side of his jaw. He bowed and nodded, his gaze skittered past and around Justi's face.

"Yes," he said. "That's exactly so, Kraljiki."

Justi blinked angrily at the slowness of the reply and its lack of fire, but he could say nothing to ca'Cellibrecca, not here where they needed to present a unificd front. "I'm prepared to allow you and your army safe passage back to Firenzcia. I will permit you to retain your title as Hïrzg and your estates, but the tribute Firenzcia pays to Nessantico will be tripled for the next three years to pay for the damages you have caused. Command of the Firenzcian army garrisons will pass to Commandant ca'Rudka and offiziers to be named by me from among the Chevarittai of Nessantico. That's what is on the table for you, Hïrzg. That, or you may attempt to siege Passe a'Fiume and have your army break here."

Ca'Vörl yawned dramatically. "A fine, blustery performance, Kraljiki, but did you look out from the walls before you came here? Did you fail to see the number of cook fires or did Chevaritt ca'Montmorte and the Garde Civile who ran screaming form Ville Colhelm fail to tell you how well and fiercely my Firenzcians fight? Is the Kusah of Namarro sending troops to come to your aid, or the Fjath of Sforzia, or the Ta'Mila of Il Trebbio?—or are those rulers sending you empty pledges of support while they tremble on their own thrones and wait to see who finally takes the Sun Throne in Nessantico? Why, I don't see any of *their* banners flying above Passe a'Fiume . . . and I won't, will I? As to the Archigos . . ."

Justi saw the Hïrzg's gaze linger on ca'Cellibrecca for a breath. "In the Toustour," the Hïrzg continued, "it says that Cénzi listens to all those who pray to Him and that if their prayers are true and genuine, He will answer. I know we're both also familiar with the Divolonté. The Archigos might recall Admonitions, where it says: 'Kralji, be concerned with the lives of the faithful before death, for that is your role; Archigos, be concerned with the lives of the Faithful beyond death, for that is your task.' So, I will listen to the Archigos when he talks to me about my *Faith*, not about politics. In the meantime, I prefer to listen to Cénzi Himself, rather than those who claim to speak for Him. If Cénzi is displeased with me, then I call on Him to take away the power of the Ilmodo from my war-téni. I assume He is perfectly capable of doing exactly that. Otherwise . . ." The Hïrzg brought his shoulder toward his cheek. "Perhaps the Ilmodo will tell us whose prayers Cénzi prefers: those of the Archigos, or those of my war-téni."

Orlandi ca'Cellibrecca

"PERHAPS THE ILMODO will tell us whose prayers Cénzi prefers."

Ca'Vörl fixed Orlandi then with a stare that Orlandi could return only with great effort. He could feel the Kraljiki glaring at him from the side as well, and U'Téni cu'Kohnle also regarded him with an intensity that made Orlandi wonder how much the Hïrzg had promised the war-téni. Orlandi wanted to wipe away the beading sweat that was rising at the top of his forehead but didn't dare. He knew that the Kraljiki was waiting for him to respond to the Hïrzg's defiance; he also knew that ca'Vörl was warning him. The Hïrzg had no intention of bending to compromise here; the parley was already over. Orlandi knew it, whether Kraljiki Justi did or not.

He is telling you that you have to choose. You must make your decision. Cénzi, what must I do?

Cénzi didn't deign to answer in any manner that Orlandi could discern. He opened his mouth, and prayed that Cénzi would send him the words to say. "I am the Voice of Cénzi here in this world," he said, with all the firmness he could muster. "That is and always has been the role of the Archigos."

Ca'Vörl's lips curled in amusement; the Kraljiki grunted. "There. You have your answer, Hïrzg . . ." Justi was saying, but Orlandi wasn't truly listening. Not anymore. All his attention was on the thoughts battering against his skull.

He had seen the army on the mountainsides and

crawling along the Avi. He had looked out from the walls of Passe a'Fiume, and he had glimpsed the future. He thought of Francesca waiting in Prajnoli; he thought of the throne of the Archigos in Nessantico and how long he had coveted it and how it had become his and how he did not want to lose it, how it must be Cénzi's Will that Orlandi become the Archigos: now and for the rest of his life. He had felt the chill of the air and smelled the foul odor of fear that rose from the sewers of Passe a'Fiume, a scent that would only grow more ripe and more pungent and more urgent if the city were closed up and surrounded.

He did not want to be here if that occurred.

He especially did not want to die here.

It's the dwarf's fault. He brought in that woman cu'Seranta who nearly destroyed my plans for Francesca, then he died before I could bring him to trial and show everyone just how far from Cénzi's design he had taken Concénzia. Even in death he cheats me. . . .

It had all seemed simple when he'd spoken with the Hïrzg in Brezno so many months ago, when the Hïrzg had broached the idea of their alliance and of deposing the Kraljica. But the Archigos had claimed a favorite in cu'Seranta and awakened from his long slumber, the Numetodo had risen, the Kraljica had been assassinated, and everything had become murky and complicated.

He should not have been sitting here on this side of the table with the Kraljiki. He should have been entering Nessantico in triumph alongside the Hïrzg. Now he wasn't certain which side would win.

He truly didn't know, and Cénzi wouldn't tell him.

Orlandi lifted doleful eyes past the Hïrzg to the steep hillsides beyond the tent. The Hïrzg was talking again, replying to something Justi had said, but Orlandi heard none of it. As he gazed at the landscape, the clouds parted momentarily and shafts of bright sunlight sluiced over the Firenzcian encampment. Armor glinted and sparkled, the tents gleamed, the banners waved.

Not over the city, though, Orlandi realized as he glanced over his shoulder. The city remained in shadow. Then the clouds closed over the sun once more, and the gloom returned. Orlandi smiled.

Thank you, Cénzi.

Orlandi sat in his chair, feeling the relief and certainty fill him. He knew now what he must do. He knew. He would send word to Francesca tonight, and then he would act.

There was motion in front of him and he realized, belatedly that everyone was standing. He rose from his own chair, groaning with the effort. "I will send you my answer by tomorrow, Kraljiki," the Hïrzg was saying.

"Then I hope you come to the right decision, Hirzg. We both understand the consequences, either way."

"Indeed." The Hïrzg gave a slight bow, his clasped hands to his forehead; his attendants bowing lower behind him, and around Orlandi there was a rustling as the Kraljiki and those around him returned the gesture. Servants and pages ran for horses and cloaks as the parties left the tent in opposite directions.

Justi said nothing until they were riding back to Passe a'Fiume. He gestured to ca'Rudka to ride alongside him, and for Orlandi's carriage to pull abreast. "There will be war," he said without preamble. "We can expect the Hïrzg's answer in the form of an attack."

"I agree, Kraljiki," ca'Rudka said.

"We'll continue preparations inside the walls," Justi said. "I will send messenger birds to Prajnoli to empty the garrison there. Better to make our stand here than at Nessantico. Archigos, you will prepare your declaration against the Hïrzg, his war-téni, and those who fight with him."

Orlandi smiled and bowed his head from the carriage. The satisfaction continued to flow through him; nothing the Kraljiki said could upset him. "As you wish, Kraljiki."

"Good. The Hïrzg has overreached, and he will pay for his ambition. He has built his house, now let him live

in it." Justi glanced over his shoulder at the Hïrzg's entourage, moving up the Avi toward their encampment.
The hillsides were sullen with the gray clouds overhead,
but Orlandi didn't care.

He had seen the sun there. He had been given his
answer.

~

Sergei ca'Rudka

"THEY CAN'T TRULY SIEGE the town until
they have all western gates blocked. That means
the Hïrzg either has a hidden force approaching us from
Montbataille Pass—which wouldn't surprise me—or he
intends to have at least two battalions ford the Clario
north or south of the town. My bet would be south, since
the river's less wild there, but we can't rule out a northern crossing. We'll need forces here and here, and possibly here as well."

"Commandant?"

Sergei glanced up from the maps of Passe a'Fiume
and the surrounding area to see his aide ce'Falla at the
door. Ca'Montmorte and the other offiziers and chevarittai in the room continued to stare down at the maps.
"Did you fetch the Archigos for me, Aris?" he asked,
his index finger still pressed to the yellow parchment. "I
was beginning to wonder. We really need his input on
the war-téni."

"I can't find the Archigos, Commandant," ce'Falla
said. "I don't think . . ." He stopped. Swallowed. "I don't
think he's inside the town walls. None of the e'téni in his
retinue know where he is, and his u'téni are gone as well,
and there are reports that the temple gate in the outer
wall was found unlocked."

Sergei suddenly felt as if he'd swallowed a live coal. "Get others searching," he called to the others. "We need to know what's happened."

A turn of the glass later, it was apparent that ca'Cellibrecca had fled Passe a'Fiume, and Sergei reluctantly informed the Kraljiki. "The Archigos is probably with Hïrzg ca'Vörl now," Sergei said to the Kraljiki, who stared out into the night from a window, his thoughts unguessable. The Kraljiki had taken residence in the villa of Passe a'Fiume's Comté; from the tower that rose well above most of the buildings of the town, Sergei could glimpse the fires on the mountainside beyond the Kraljiki. A table in the middle of the room was spread with copies of the maps that decorated Sergei's office. "Those barricading the walls near the temple heard Ilmodo-chanting," Sergei continued, "and there were strange flashes of light from the windows—about a turn of the glass after supper, according to the servants."

"Trust ca'Cellibrecca not to miss his supper, even for treason," Justi muttered. Sergei couldn't see the scowl, but he could hear it. The Kraljiki shook his head. "He will never sit as Archigos in Nessantico again. I swear that. I don't care what I have to do—ca'Cellibrecca won't profit from this."

"I will help you make certain of that," Sergei told him.

"Will you?" Justi turned from the window. He stood over the desk in the middle of the room, littered with papers and maps. "And how will you accomplish that, Commandant? As much as I hate to admit it, we have lost one of the edges of our sword and the Hïrzg knows it. There's no hope now that he will accept my terms of parley."

"May I speak frankly, Kraljiki?"

The Kraljiki snorted. He lifted his hands in invitation. "Please."

Sergei paused, wondering if he truly wanted to do this. He took a long breath. "Kraljiki, I know who killed your matarh."

He watched the Kraljiki's face stiffen, then the man waved a hand. "Of course. The painter ci'Recroix . . ."

"I know who hired the painter, Kraljiki."

Justi's mouth closed audibly. "Go on, Commandant," he said. It was nearly a grunt. "But, were I you, I'd proceed very carefully."

"My loyalty, Kraljiki, is to Nessantico. Always. Not to any person, but to Nessantico herself: the empire. I see a Nessantico that one day will span the world from the mouth of the Great Eastern River in Tennshah to the far shores of the Westlands. I see a Nessantico whose citizens thrive, where wonders we can't even imagine are glimpsed every day. That's what I would like generations to come to experience. I'm also a realist, Kraljiki. I know that there's no easy path to that future, and I know that sometimes a tree must be pruned in order for it to continue to grow. The death of the Kraljica . . . well, I loved Kraljica Marguerite as much as anyone, and I served her as well and faithfully as I could. She brought peace to Nessantico for a long time, and we grew immeasurably under her reign. But . . ."

Sergei paused. He cocked his head slightly. *You'd better pray that you've judged the man correctly.* "I mourned her passing in gratitude for what she had done, but in truth, she was a dying branch and already what she had created was starting to crumble. She was sleeping on the Sun Throne, as Archigos Dhosti was sleeping in the temple. Nessantico needed a new, stronger hand—in that sense, the loss of the Kraljica was necessary."

Sergei waited. The Kraljiki said nothing. "I have done or ordered done many awful deeds in the Bastida as commandant," Sergei continued. "I have injured and maimed and killed; I have watched men and women scream in torment in front of me, and I have wondered at what Cénzi might think, of how He might judge me. But the torment was necessary. I did those misdeeds for the good of Nessantico. I think that's happened with the Kraljica as well: a misdeed done for the sake of the

greater good of Nessantico." He waited. The Kraljiki remained silent and staring. "Had the Kraljica not died,
she would be on the throne at this very moment, en-
joying her Jubilee, and we would have known *nothing*
of this." Sergei pointed to the window, to the flickering
of campfires on the mountainside, like stars fallen from
the night sky. "We would have known nothing of it until
the Hïrzg and his army were nearly at Nessantico's gates
and it was too late to stop him. The Hïrzg is not someone
I would ever wish to see sitting on the Sun Throne."

"And I am?" the Kraljiki asked suddenly. "Speaking
frankly, Commandant?"

"I admire those who know when to wait, when to act,
when to sacrifice, and when to retreat. You waited a long
time, Kraljiki." *And then you acted.* Sergei didn't say
that, but the words hung there in the air between them.

The Kraljiki took several breaths before speaking.
Sergei wondered what he was thinking, what he was
turning over in his mind. Muscles bunched along his
jawline, under the well-trimmed line of mustache and
beard. "You still haven't answered my question about
ca'Cellibrecca," he said finally.

Nor about you, Sergei thought. "I said that I admire
those who know when to sacrifice and retreat as well as
when to act," Sergei said. "You need to return to Nessantico, Kraljiki. You need to leave."

"And let Passe a'Fiume fall the next day? The Hïrzg's
troops would be at our feet as we run back to Nessantico. How is that a victory?"

Sergei was shaking his head. "I'm not saying that we
all must go back to Nessantico. Only *you,* Kraljiki. You
need to leave. I will stay here in Passe a'Fiume with half
the Garde Civile and we will hold the town for as long as
possible. You, the court, and most of the chevarittai must
return to the city. We will buy you as many days as possible: to order in the garrisons, to mobilize the countryside, to conscript every last able-bodied person. You'll
need to prepare for the battle, to name an Archigos in

Nessantico to replace the traitor so that any declarations ca'Cellibrecca makes have less weight. That's what you need to do, Kraljiki. And while you do that, let me hinder ca'Vörl's progress. Let me whittle down the size of his army for you. If he tries to cross at the bridge, the walls will hold him back. If he tries to ford the Clario north or south, we follow on this side and engage him. In the meantime, you prepare Nessantico."

"And you? What do you gain from this? I don't believe in altruism, Commandant. I especially don't believe in it from you."

Sergei smiled. "Assuming I survive—and I will make every effort to do so, Kraljiki—I would expect to be well rewarded for my services. I would expect to be permanently awarded the title of commandant of the Garde Civile and to retain my title as Chevaritt of Nessantico, and I will return the Garde Civile to what it once was: the true strong right arm of the Kraljiki. As commandant, *I* will also command the army of Firenzcia rather than the next Hïrzg, so I can ensure that this never happens again. You would name me Comté of Brezno. As the Archigos controls Concénzia, I would control the military, all for the glory of the Kraljiki and Nessantico." His smile widened. "No, Kraljiki, I'm not an altruist. I prefer the thought of rewards in this lifetime to the possibility of those in the next. May Cénzi forgive me for that."

The muscles in the Kraljiki's face relaxed. He smiled also, a careful gesture, and Sergei relaxed. *It may yet go the way you wanted it to go. At least on this side . . .*

"I take it you have specific tactics to go with this strategy of yours, Commandant?"

"I do."

The Kraljiki nodded. He walked over to his dressing table; the Hïrzg's sword had been placed there. The Kraljiki picked it up and pulled it halfway from its scabbard. He turned the blade, examining it closely in the light of the candles. He nodded, as if satisfied. "I'll credit the bastard with knowing his steel," he said. "This is a weapon that cries out to be used." He shoved the blade back into the scabbard, then tossed both sword and scabbard toward Sergei. Sergei caught it one-handed. "A pity. I'd have enjoyed using the sword, but I think you should keep it, Commandant. Use the Hïrzg's gift against him—I will take my pleasure in the irony."

Sergei bowed. "I'll do that, Kraljiki." Sergei took off his own sword and placed it on the table alongside the maps. "You may still yet need a blade, my Kraljiki," Sergei said. "It's not the equal of the Hïrzg's, but it will serve."

The Kraljiki nodded again and took the proffered weapon. "I'm certain it will. Now, Commandant, let's go over these tactics of yours in detail, and we'll see where we might be in agreement."

Sergei leaned over the maps as the Kraljiki came to stand beside him. "The Hïrzg will be expecting us to send troops south along the Avi to guard against a Firenzcian crossing," he said, his fingertip moving along the curves of the river. "My thought is that you and those of the court can ride out with them dressed as common soldiers. Once you're well south of Passe a'Fiume, you can continue on to Nessantico unseen. The Hïrzg will assume you're still here, which is what we want him to believe. Then, once you're back in Nessantico . . ."

~

Justi ca'Mazzak

THE CITY SHUDDERED with the news that the parley had failed, and that it was likely that Passe a'Fiume was already under siege. The city had merely been worried before; now it was truly frightened, a feeling heightened as Kraljiki Justi trebled the conscription squads, as the Garde Kralji patrolled the gates of the city so that none could leave without travel documents bearing the seal of the Kraljiki, as couriers carrying urgent orders from the Kraljiki went out from the city in all directions, as the encampment of the Garde Civile outside the walls continued to swell. The farmlands around Nessantico were scoured as if by a ravenous plague of locusts, all the food carried back to the city: if there was to be war, then there would be as little as possible for the Hïrzg's troops to plunder as they moved toward Nessantico.

Agents of the Garde Kralji also moved through Oldtown, asking blunt questions about the Numetodo and especially about the former O'Téni Ana cu'Seranta and the once Envoy Karl ci'Vliomani. Several of those questioned were taken away and did not return, though the Pontica remained devoid of new bodies to join the skeletal remains of the Numetodo already gibbeted there.

Worst of all was the news that the Archigos had betrayed the Kraljiki. The Kraljiki ordered those téni who had been closest to ca'Cellibrecca at the Archigos' Temple placed under arrest. A'Ténis ca'Marvolli, ca'Xana, ca'Miccord, and ca'Seiffel—those who had most vocally supported ca'Cellibrecca in the last few years—found themselves in residence in the Bastida, and the remaining a'téni were required to sign a declaration of obedience to the Kraljiki with their lives forfeit should they recant. Now truly headless, Concénzia reeled; the already erratic service of the téni in the city became even more stretched and ineffective.

Nessantico throbbed and quaked with fear, and Justi watched it from the colorful windows of the Hall of the Sun Throne in the Grande Palais. If he looked east more often than any other direction with a face strained with concern, he could hardly be blamed.

"They loved their Kraljica. They only *fear* you. That's why they're frightened."

Justi scowled and gave a guttural curse at the words. He tried to turn and draw his sword—Sergei's sword—from his scabbard, but he found it strangely difficult, as if the air had hardened around him. He stopped with the blade half-drawn.

He gaped.

The beggar known as Mahri was standing a few paces from him, on the dais where Justi stood near the Sun Throne. He could see the one-eyed, disfigured face under the cowl, splashed with color from the stained glass. But it wasn't the man's face that stopped Justi: the room behind the beggar was . . . *wrong*. The only things in motion were Mahri and himself. Nothing else moved. A fly hung in the air to his left. The dozen or so courtiers as well as the ca'-and-cu' supplicants sitting in small groups or clustered together talking, were stopped in mid-gesture. Servants were standing as if frozen while hurrying to their tasks. Silence wrapped all of them; the air was dead and still when a moment ago it had stirred with the breezes from the open balconies. It was as if he were looking at a painting of the throne room, with he and Mahri somehow inhabiting the canvas.

It reminded him uncomfortably of ci'Recroix.

"Mad Mahri . . . So you're one of the Numetodo," Justi said. His hand remained on his sword hilt. He wondered if he could draw it quickly enough in this half-solid air.

Mahri shook his head. He gave a grotesque smile marred by the white scars on his face. "No Numetodo could do this," he said, waving his hand at the motionless crowd around them. "And I can't continue it for very long, so I won't waste it with conversation, Kraljiki. You are looking for Ana cu'Seranta and Karl ci'Vliomani. I know where they are."

"And what do you want in return?" Justi asked. His own voice sounded hollow, as if the very air around them didn't want to move to allow the words to leave his mouth. His fingers loosened slightly on the sword hilt.

"I want nothing you can give me," Mahri answered.

"Wealth, then. A thousand solas . . ."

Mahri laughed. "Keep your money. Just have your Garde Kralji at Oldtown Center tomorrow at a turn of the glass after First Call. Look for me; both of those you seek will be with me. Your people will have to move quickly and with force; the o'téni especially is dangerous if she has the chance to use the Ilmodo." The air was shimmering between them; the figures around the room started to move. "After First Call, Oldtown Center," Mahri repeated.

The air flashed, as if lightning had struck between them, and Justi's sword seemed to leap from the scabbard of its own volition. The world seemed to jolt. Justi blinked involuntarily. When he could see again, the people around the room were once again in motion and the room was loud with their conversations. The courtiers were staring at him, standing beside the Sun Throne with his sword held threateningly in front of him.

The fly droned past him. Justi watched it strike a glass pane caught in strips of black lead, bounce back angrily, then find the opening between the windows and escape into the sunlight.

~

Ana cu'Seranta

MAHRI HAD PROMISED them that they would be safe. There was no reason not to believe him.

After the fire in the tavern, they had moved to another set of rooms deep in Oldtown, then a few days later to yet another. For Ana, it didn't matter. None of it mattered. She went through the days wrapped in a dark fog. Karl tried to lift her from the depression; as he had promised, he began to teach her some Numetodo spells. She found that some of the words were similar to the words she used herself, and she found that she could begin to learn to hold the spell in her head. It was a strange feeling, to have the Ilmodo contained and confined in her mind, an insistent presence that rattled against the spell-cage that restrained it, aching to be released.

Cénzi did not punish her for her learning. If anything, she found that she could reach the Second World easier than before.

On the fourth day, after First Call prayers and the necessary ablutions, Ana, Karl, and Mahri broke their fast with stale bread and weak tea. "There's nothing else here to eat," Mahri said. "As soon as you're ready, we'll go to Oldtown Center and the market there."

"All of us?" Karl asked. "The streets aren't safe, not for us. Ana should stay here. We know they're looking for her, especially after the fire."

Ana scoffed. "If anything, Karl, you should be the one staying here. Wouldn't the conscription squads love to get hold of you? I should go; they're not grabbing women off the street."

"We can all go," Mahri answered. "The air will do us all good, and no one will notice you who does not need to see you—I promise that."

Ana nodded emphatically, putting down the crust on which she'd been gnawing. "I'm tired of hiding away and not seeing the sun. I'll go mad if I have to stay in here much longer."

Karl frowned, but Mahri chuckled. "There's your answer. I'm told the farmers have brought in fresh produce; I've had one of them set some aside for us. And one of the bakers has promised me new-made loaves—without the sawdust: he lives close to the old rooms over the tavern, and he's grateful for what you did, Ana. And I know of a farmer who has brought in fresh butter to go with the bread."

Ana's mouth was already watering involuntarily

at the thought. The depression that bound her lifted slightly. "Then let's go now," she said, "before they sell everything."

They were quickly out of the rooms and moving through the early morning streets. The number of people on the streets steadily increased as they approached Oldtown Center and the market set around the open square, but the crowd was different than the crowds of months past. There were few males out, and those Ana saw were mostly elderly or visibly crippled. Mahri had kept his promise: Karl leaned heavily on a crutch Mahri had given him, and when Ana looked at his face, it was the lined visage of an elderly great-vatarh, with wisps of white hair like faint clouds above an age-spotted scalp. She wondered whether Mahri had done something similar to her face, as no one seemed to pay her any attention at all, the gazes of those they passed sliding away from her without curiosity.

The market bustled with activity, loud with haggling as buyers examined the offerings with critical eyes. The tables in front of the sellers were rather bare, and the produce on display looked either too early-harvested or limp and old. Still, the city was hungry, bargains were few, and Ana knew that everything offered would be sold. The sight of the market and the desperation she could feel there, dissipated any of the joy she felt at being outside again. Despite the sun, despite the warmth, she felt cold and ill, and she knew that the hunger that gnawed at her stomach was shared by most of those here.

"The bread, Mahri," she said. "Let's get the bread first. But one loaf only. The rest . . . let the baker sell it to them." She gestured with her chin at the people. "They need it as much as we do. More."

Mahri grunted. His single eye stared at her. "This way, then," he said, and they followed him across the square toward the buildings on the other side. As they approached the stalls and storefront there, Karl slowed down, his hand grasping for Ana's and pulling her back slightly. "Look," he husked.

Ahead of them was a squad of Garde Kralji, well-armed and obviously looking their way. An o'offizier, his uniform displaying the dragon-skull insignia of the Bastida, led the gardai. "Mahri," Ana said warningly, as quietly as she could.

He shook his head. "Don't worry," he told them. "I told you that you'd be safe. Do nothing to arouse suspicion. Nothing."

He continued walking directly toward them. Reluctantly, Ana followed. She smiled in their direction, as if wishing them a good day. The o'offizier smiled back. His hand made a short waving motion, and the gardai with him spread out, letting the trio pass. They moved between the gardai, Ana keeping her head down. She glanced over at Karl—and his face was Karl's again, the spell-mask gone. "Mahri—" she said in alarm, but it was already too late. Hands grabbed her, grabbed Karl, and though she tried to begin a chant, they held her too closely. She heard Karl speak a release word, and one of the gardai went down with a cry, but then the others bore him down to the ground, forcing a gag into his mouth. His eyes were wide and furious, and one of the gardai clubbed him with the pommel of his sword.

"Mahri!" Ana shouted in the grasp of the gardai, struggling as they held her arms, as they tried to shove a gag into her mouth as well. "What have you done?"

But Mahri wasn't there. He had vanished.

RETREATS

Sergei ca'Rudka
Ana cu'Seranta
Jan ca'Vörl
Mahri
Ana ca'Seranta
Sergei ca'Rudka
Jan ca'Vörl
Karl ci'Vliomani

Sergei ca'Rudka

THE BATTLE OF Passe a'Fiume began slowly. The same day that the Kraljiki quietly departed the town to return to Nessantico, the Hïrzg broke from his encampment on the mountainside, leading his army to the parley field. There, in full view of those watching from the city walls, they erected their tents: thousands of them, like thick mushrooms clustered in the grass. A force of a few dozen Firenzcian chevarittai, dressed in gilded armor and seated on black destriers, rode forward to the far end of the bridge, led by Starkkapitän ca'Linnett. Sergei, watching from the wall, saw one of the chevarittai ride forward from the group, his spear tipped with a white kerchief. He cantered his horse across the bridge until he was directly underneath Sergei. He brandished a scroll before dropping it in the dust of the road before the gate. The man saluted Sergei with clasped hands, then turned his horse and rode back across the bridge.

Sergei knew what it would say, even before it was delivered to him. The scroll called for an individual challenge: for the Kraljiki (who could not answer), and for Sergei, who could. "Do we ride out, Commandant?" Sergei could hear the eagerness in Elia ca'Montmorte's voice. "Or, if you don't wish to accept the challenge, I will go in your stead; I owe ca'Linnett for what he did to us at Ville Colhelm. It would give me nothing but pleasure to see the grass of Nessantico grow tall with his blood."

"You can't answer the challenge, Commandant."
Bahik cu'Garret, A'Offizier of the Garde Civile in Passe
a'Fiume—but only a vajiki, not a chevaritt—was shaking his head, as was U'Téni cu'Bachiga. "You can't
let the fate of Passe a'Fiume rest on a duel between
chevarittai."

"Why not?" ca'Montmorte snorted. "There's honor in
it. And Passe a'Fiume will still be standing afterward,
and with the banner of Nessantico flying over it."

"The chevarittai code has been abandoned for generations," cu'Bachiga answered. "Look at Jablunkov, or
the Battle of the Wastes, or the Riven Fields—there are
a dozen or more examples. Why should this be any different? It's posturing, and nothing more, and the Hïrzg
knows it. It's the chevarittai playing at war, and even
should you happen to prevail, Chevaritt ca'Montmorte,
the Hïrzg won't take his army away."

"Then he dishonors himself as a chevaritt," ca'Montmorte retorted.

"He is Hïrzg, and he wants to be Kraljiki," cu'Garret
scoffed. "You think your 'dishonor' worries him even
slightly?"

Sergei listened to the men argue, rubbing the smooth
metal of his nose. "Enough!" he said sharply. "Elia, I'm
afraid I agree with A'Offizier cu'Garret: no matter the
outcome of this challenge, the Hïrzg isn't likely to pull
back his army after coming this far. I think it's more
likely a ruse. Our task here is to delay the Hïrzg's advance to give the Kraljiki time to prepare the defense
of Nessantico—would you have me swing open the
gates of Passe a'Fiume because a chevarittai cham-
pion lost their challenge?" Ca'Montmorte scowled but
didn't answer. "I can't do that. Chevaritt, I would love
to ride out across the bridge with you and answer this
ca'Linnett's challenge in the name of the Kraljiki, but I
can't. I won't."

"Then you condemn Passe a'Fiume to slow torture, Commandant," ca'Montmorte answered. "I hope

A'Offizier cu'Garret and U'Téni cu'Bachiga fully understand that, because they'll be here with us to experience it, along with many innocents."

Sergei ended the conversation not long afterward, and directed one of the archers to wrap the challenge around the shaft of an arrow and shoot it over the bridge. Ca'Linnett himself rode forward to pluck the arrow from the ground and glance at Sergei's scrawled refusal. Hoots of laughter and derision cascaded from the Firenzcian chevarittai to assault the walls of Passe a'Fiume, but the jeers and taunts did not tear down the battlements.

Sergei was satisfied with that, if the chevarittai in the city were not.

Worse news came that night. Stragglers from the troops he'd set out along the north bank of the Clario came rushing back to the town in full retreat. Two battalions of Firenzcians, using war-téni to cover their crossing, had forded the Clario in darkness and attacked the Nessantico troops, overrunning their encampment. Sergei ordered all gates to the city closed; by predawn light, they could see from the walls the colors of Firenzcia surrounding Passe a'Fiume entirely.

By dawn of the next day, the assault had begun in earnest.

It began with the war-téni. A dozen great spheres of enchanted fire rose into the dawn, arcing across the sky like huge, roaring meteors. The téni of Passe a'Fiume, along with the war-téni left behind by Archigos ca'Cellibrecca, were waiting on the walls. Their chants began as soon as they saw the spell-fires flicker into life, their hands moved in counter-spells and return-spells, turning aside a hand of the spheres and sending them back to where they'd originated—their efforts were rewarded by faint screams and black smoke rising from the Firenzcian encampment. But far too many of the fireballs rushed past the walls in waves of blistering heat and blinding light, crashing into houses or onto the streets where they rolled and broke open and sent spatters of thick flame flying. Now the screams were close and frantic behind Sergei and those on the walls, as the townsfolk rushed to aid the injured, to put out the fires, and pull the dead from the rubble.

There was no time to rest. Siege engines in the Firenzcian encampment flung boulders toward the walls, their impacts shuddering the ground and tearing great chunks of rock from the ramparts and crenellations. Only a few strides away from where he stood, Sergei saw a soldier in the livery of the Garde Civile shriek as a huge rock tore his arm entirely from his body before the stone crashed into the street beyond, killing three men and a horse. Now came the rain of arrows from archers moving under cover of the barrage to the far bank of the Clario: as the siege engines continued to hammer at the walls, as more téni-fireballs flared overhead.

Through the smoke and noise of the assault, Sergei glimpsed movement: soldiers massing on the bridge and pushing a battering ram in its sling; others placing rafts in the river. "Archers!" he shouted, and arrows rained out from the walls, a furious and thick hailstorm. The Clario frothed with men falling into its waters, flailing in panic or motionless, dead before the water took them. The ram squad was better protected with their shields turtling over them—the ram continued steadily and slowly across the bridge, and more soldiers came behind it to replace the fallen.

"Chevarittai, to the gates!" Sergei called, and hurried down from the walls himself. His horse was there, stamping and nervous as the page held him. Sergei calmed the stallion as he put on his helm and adjusted his mail. The page helped to hoist him astride the destrier. Mounted, he pulled the Hïrzg's sword from its sheath as the other chevarittai gathered before the gates. The weight of the blade was heavy and comforting in his hand. "Drive them back across the bridge!" Sergei shouted. "O'Offizier ce'Ulcai, you will take a squadron of the Garde Civile and push that ram into the river once we have the bridge clear. Archers, make certain that the bridge *stays* clear. Understood?" There were salutes and shouts of agreement. "Open the gates!" Sergei called, and soldiers hurried to pull aside the great timbers that braced them, swinging open the thick wooden doors as they raised the portcullis.

Sergei thrust his sword high. "For the glory of Nessantico and the Kraljiki!"

The chevarittai and Garde Civile around him echoed the cry, a throaty challenge. They rode out in thunder.

The destriers, clad in armor and trained in close combat, cleaved through the front ranks of enemy soldiers boiling around the ram. Sergei swung his sword down at a thrusting spear, breaking the weapon in half and hearing the scream as his mount trampled the man underfoot. He cut again, and again, no longer thinking but only reacting to the bodies around him. He could hear screams and cries; he felt a spear tip jab through his mail to bite deep into his thigh, the shaft breaking off with the onward rush of his horse. He screamed himself then, taking the pain and anger and letting it flow through his arm.

"Back! Back!" he heard someone cry, and suddenly the Firenzcian soldiers were no longer holding their ground but fleeing, and Sergei was past the ram and across the bridge entirely, hacking at the retreating soldiers, running them down under the destrier's hooves. The other chevarittai surged around him, savage and relentless. Sergei pulled on his mount's reins, glancing back—on the bridge, soldiers in blue and gold were streaming out from the city and pushing at the ram. Arrows streaked overhead, so thick they seemed to dim the sun. His wounded thigh throbbed as he clamped his legs around the saddle, holding back his mount.

"Form up!" he called the chevarittai. "Hold here!" Most of them obeyed, though not all: a few continued beyond the bridge, chasing the soldiers. In the field

ahead, he could see the Firenzcian chevarittai readying
to charge: the Red Lancers. "Return to the city!" Sergei
ordered.

There were protests from the chevarittai, and Sergei
scowled. "I am commandant here. Inside! There will be
time enough for fighting. Inside!" He turned his horse;
reluctantly, they followed. The bridge had been cleared;
soldiers from the city were bringing in their own dead
and wounded.

Sergei slid from his destrier as he passed the gates, handing the reins to one of the waiting pages. His leg buckled
under him from the shock of hitting the ground; he forced
himself to stand, though he allowed the page who rushed
over to help to wrap a binding around his leg to staunch
the bleeding. He watched as the chevarittai passed, then
the remainder of the Garde Civile on the bridge. He gestured to those around the gate; the portcullis rang metallically as it slammed back down, the hinges groaned as the
men pushed the gates closed and replaced the bracing.
Sergei limped to the wall. Around the town was smoke
and destruction and bodies. Crows were already flapping
to the ground. A lone chevaritt rode forward to the far
end of the bridge, with a white flag on his spear.

"The Hïrzg asks for a brief truce to give us time to
recover our dead," he called up to Sergei.

"Tell the Hïrzg he has the Kraljiki's permission to do
so if he wishes," Sergei replied.

The chevaritt gave a salute and rode away. In time,
soldiers approached the walls from the encampment
with carts and began to haul away the dead. In both
Passe a'Fiume and in the fields outside, the flames of
pyres would light the evening sky.

The second day of the siege of Passe a'Fiume ended.

On the third day, the téni redoubled their assault on the
city, striking from all sides of the wall, not only from
beyond the Clario. The bulk of the téni-fire passed
through the defenses of the town's few and exhausted

war-téni, reaching even into the city center. There were few buildings left whose roofs were untouched or that didn't show some damage; the casualties, civilian and military, mounted quickly as the siege engines again began their merciless barrage, also from all sides. All five city gates were under assault, not just the Clario Gate, and Sergei directed the chevarittai in sallies against them, but they were spread too thin now, and the enemy rams battered at the gates. Arrows rained down on the besiegers; those war-téni who were still able cast their spells; heated oil cascaded down from the battlements and was set afire.

The smell of smoke and blood were thick in the air from morning until dusk.

When the day finally ended, the sun falling behind a hundred columns of smoke and ash, the city walls were pockmarked and gouged, the gates cracked, and fires burned unchecked, but the city had held.

Sergei knew she might not hold for another day under the ferocious assault.

"Two hundred or more dead of the Garde Civile; fully half the force injured so badly they can't fight." Ca'Montmorte read the tallies tonelessly as Sergei and U'Téni cu'Bachiga and A'Offizier cu'Garret listened. "Of the chevarittai, three double-hands have fallen, most are injured, and three quarters are unhorsed. I'm told that the wall of the west gate is nearly broken through. There are fires burning everywhere, and no one is able to say how many of the citizens of the city who remained behind have been killed or injured."

Sergei grimaced as he limped to the table to pour wine, his injured leg protesting. The leg had swelled, and blood seeped through the bandaging. "Passe a'Fiume has never been taken," cu'Garret said doggedly, and ca'Montmorte glanced at him with a look of distaste.

"Well, that might change tomorrow," ca'Montmorte answered. "Unless Cénzi grants us a miracle."

U'Téni cu'Bachiga glared at him and muttered

something, the only word of which Sergei caught was "blasphemy."

"Unfortunately, I have to agree with Chevaritt ca'Montmorte," Sergei said, sipping the wine. It tasted as if it had been dipped in greasy smoke, or perhaps it was just the air in the room. They were all filthy, their clothing stained with dirt and blood and worse, and the smell in the room was foul. Sergei set the goblet down and rubbed at his nose—it was cold and too hard. "The town may well fall tomorrow, and the Hïrzg realizes it. We've done all we can do here."

"So we must surrender and hope that the Hïrzg will show us mercy?" ca'Montmorte asked.

"That's an option we should consider," Sergei said. "We can send a chevaritt with a petition in the morning, surrender our arms to the Hïrzg, and he can release those he wishes and hold the rest of us for ransom."

"Or?"

"We stay and we fight until the walls collapse and the entire town burns, and we leave our corpses here as we return to Cénzi. We might be able to give the Kraljiki another day to ready Nessantico for the Hïrzg." Sergei shrugged. He glanced at each of their faces and saw the grim, weary fatalism there.

"Or," he added, "we remember that the deciding battle in this war won't be Passe a'Fiume but Nessantico, and acknowledge that is where we should go now. Those of us who wish to do so will ride out at first light, all of us who wish to attempt this. The Hïrzg's forces are thinnest near the southwest gate. We can try to break through his line to gain the Avi and retreat toward Nessantico—some of us may make it. Those who don't wish to join the foray can stay here to surrender the city to the Hïrzg and his mercy."

Ca'Montmorte was already nodding, his fist softly pounding his thigh. Cu'Garret stared at the table between them. Cu'Bachiga, in his green robes, wrung his hands. "I will lead the foray. As for the rest of you ... I don't care which choice you make," Sergei told them. "That is between you and Cénzi. We have done all we can here, and we have fulfilled our promise to the Kraljiki to hold as long as possible."

"Even if we can fight our way through, the Firenzcian army will follow us—and most will be on foot," cu'Garret said. "We'd be harried all the way to Nessantico."

Sergei shook his head. "If we can push through their ranks, I don't believe the Hïrzg will pursue; he'll need to move his full army across the Clario and reform them before they move on to Nessantico, and he won't believe that a few more chevarittai and Garde Civile at Nessantico will make a difference."

"You're wagering your life on that guess, and everyone else's."

Sergei managed to smile. "I am. But we all must die sometime. Why not now?" He gulped the last of the wine, wiping his lips with his sleeves and tossing the goblet across the room. The pottery shattered against the wall. "There's nothing more to discuss here," he told them. "A'Offizier ca'Montmorte, spread the word to all the chevarittai; A'Offizier cu'Garret, you'll do the same with the Garde Civile; U'Téni cu'Bachiga, if you or any of the war-téni wish to join us, your help will be appreciated. But remember, no one who chooses to stay and surrender with the city will be punished." He took a breath, going to the open window and staring down at the ruin of the town.

"I would suggest you rest as well as you can tonight," Sergei said. "And make your peace with Cénzi."

A'Offizier cu'Garret decided to remain in the city and negotiate the surrender. "Passe a'Fiume is my charge as Nessantico is yours," he told Sergei, "and I will see her through to the end." Sergei could only nod in understanding at that, and clap the man on the back. Nearly all the Garde Civile garrison of the city stayed with cu'Garret. Those chevarittai or Garde Civile too badly injured to ride or walk would by necessity remain behind, as would U'Téni cu'Bachiga and most of his téni.

At the southwest gate in the wan light of predawn, Sergei looked at the courtyard to see those grim-faced chevarittai who were still able to ride. Around them were the Garde Civile of the other garrisons, and a bare handful of the war-téni from Nessantico. Three hundred. Maybe less. Certainly fewer than he had hoped.

They waited, and Sergei knew that the tension was singing as loudly in each of their ears as it was in his. He checked that his injured leg was tied securely to the saddle, then gripped the Hïrzg's sword tightly in his hand and drew it from its scabbard. Around him, he heard the shimmering of well-used blades leaving leather scabbards as the others did the same.

He waited. Along the northwest quadrant of Passe a'Fiume's wall, at the gate of the Avi a'Firenzcia, téni-fire blossomed and arced outward. They could hear, faintly, the clatter of swords against shields and hoarse shouts, as if those gates were about to open and disgorge a sally force. Sergei glanced up to the broken summit of the wall. A man waved down to him. "The enemy is moving, Commandant," he said. "Away to the north."

Sergei nodded. He gestured to the men at the gate. The barricades had already been removed. Now the gates swung open and the portcullis was drawn up. Sergei kicked his mount into a gallop, the mounted chevarittai following him, and they galloped out from the city, the men on foot running after them.

The lines of the Firenczian besiegers were least thick here, where the ground was marshy and mosquito-infested. If the distraction had worked, many of the enemy soldiers would be moving toward the commotion at the next gate. A good number of the remainder would still be sleeping, waiting for the sun and their final attack on the town. The plan was for the chevarittai to act as a wedge to break through the Firenzcian line, then hold the break open so that the foot soldiers of the Garde

Civile could move through to the Avi, and finally act as
rear guard if the Firenzcians decided to pursue.

And if it fell apart, they would all die here.

They pounded across the loamy riverside earth, the
hooves of the destriers kicking up heavy clods. Already
Sergei could see the tents there, and a figure pointing
toward them and shouting alarm. Fireballs arced out from
a wagon carrying the war-téni, tearing into the Firenzcian
encampment. The commotion spread quickly along the
line, but by then Sergei and the chevarittai were already
among the tents. Sergei hacked at anything that moved,
not pausing but urging his mount on, always forcing his
way forward even as soldiers pressed against them. An
o'offizier, half-dressed and without armor, screamed as
he brandished his sword, and Sergei cut him down with
one stroke. To either side, he could hear the sound of battle and once the awful cry of a wounded destrier. Then
he and most of the other riders were through; there was
nothing but a ruined farmer's field between him and the
tree-lined Avi. The war-téni's cart rattled past, the horses
pulling it wide-eyed and frightened. Sergei pulled up on
the reins of his own mount, turning the horse to see the
Garde Civile hurrying through the gap the chevarittai
had made, a gap that was closing quickly.

"Move! Run!" he shouted to all of them. "Chevarittai, hold!" He galloped back, pushing against the Firenzcians, the Hïrzg's sword bloody and growing heavier
with each stroke until his muscles screamed. Most of the
Garde Civile was through, the first group with the war-
téni already on the road. There were banners of black
and silver rushing toward them, and the horns of Firenzcian chevarittai sounded alarm.

"Now!" Sergei shouted, and the chevarittai disen-
gaged. The gap in the Firenzcian line closed rapidly. Sergei held, waiting as the others rushed past him, waiting as
the Firenzcians threw their spears and pursued. He kicked
his horse's ribs with his good leg to urge it into a gallop
as the last of the chevarittai passed him: as arrows began

to fall around him, as téni-fire erupted in the midst of the fleeing Garde Civile in the field and a dozen men fell screaming. Sergei lagged behind the chevarittai as they galloped across the field toward the tree line, passing the last surviving stragglers of the Garde Civile.

Sergei was nearly to the field's edge when he felt arrows pummel his mailed back and fall away. He thought then that he was safe, but a sudden terrific stabbing blow to his neck nearly sent him from his seat despite the leather straps that bound his leg. He lifted a hand to his neck and felt the thick shaft of a crossbow bolt. He could feel hot blood pouring from the wound.

He heard the sinister *t-chunk* of crossbows again, and a bolt penetrated his armor near his spine, the force of the impact pushing him hard against the neck of his horse. He clung to the destrier desperately—as the branches of the trees lashed at him, as he heard the hooves of his mount break onto the hard-packed dirt of the Avi . . .

. . . as the world darkened around him even though the sun had finally touched the horizon . . .

. . . as he groaned and was lost in that darkness . . .

~

Ana cu'Seranta

"I'M SORRY it had to be this way, Ana."

Seated on the small bed in the cell, Ana's head turned at the sound of the tenor, familiar voice. Kraljiki Justi was standing at the door to her cell in the Bastida's tower—the same cell Karl had once inhabited. She was bound as he had been, with the vile silencer pressing into her mouth and her hands confined with chains, her hair matted and dirty and caught in the straps of the gag.

They had brought her here directly from Oldtown, in

a closed carriage that went careening through the city in a rush. She had no idea where Karl was, or Mahri who had betrayed them.

But she knew now who had wanted her. She wondered how long she had to live.

The Kraljiki glanced around the cell. "I'm told your Numetodo lover lived here, until his escape. Poor Capitaine ci'Doulor was here for a time, until he was moved to, ah, less palatial accommodations. And now you . . ." He stepped forward, with the easy, athletic grace she remembered. He sat down on the table in the room, regarding her.

"I don't admit mistakes easily, Ana," he said. "But I made one in aligning myself with ca'Cellibrecca and his serpent of a daughter, a mistake worse than I could have imagined, when the best choice for me—it pains me to admit—was the one my matarh had already suggested. I'm hoping it's not too late to rectify that." He gestured to the gardai outside the cell. "Remove her bonds," he said, and he watched as they unlocked her hands and undid the straps from the tongue-gag. The gardai moved back a step but, she noted, didn't leave. She rubbed at her wrists and worked her jaw.

"I'm sorry to have brought you bound like a condemned heretic, Ana," Justi said. "But would you have come if I'd simply asked?"

"No," she answered sharply, not caring about the impoliteness. "Where is Karl?"

"In the cell a floor below you. Unharmed."

She nodded. "You have me in front of you now, Kraljiki. What do you want?"

"It would seem," he said, "that I'm in need of an Archigos. Ca'Cellibrecca has abandoned Nessantico to be on the side of the Hïrzg; I will put a new head on the body of the Concénzia Faith, so that all will know that ca'Cellibrecca's voice is false."

"Choosing the Archigos isn't the role of the Kraljiki," Ana told him. "The Concord A'Téni must do that."

Justi gave her a smile that vanished in the next moment. "The a'téni are frightened of the army coming to Nessantico—those who are still here. Ca'Cellibrecca has left them bereft; they're afraid that ca'Cellibrecca will remain Archigos if the Hïrzg prevails, and they're just as frightened that he will fall with the Hïrzg. I've already spoken to the a'téni, and they ... well, let me just say that I've convinced them that as long as they remain in Nessantico, it's in their best interests to follow my preferences."

"And which of them have you chosen, and why should it matter to me?"

Justi smiled. It was a strange, apologetic smile. "I've chosen none of them," he said, the words thin and high. "I've decided that I will promote a young o'téni to the position."

It took a moment for the import of his words to register. Ana started to protest in shock and disbelief, but Justi waved her silent. "A moment," he said. "Choosing one of the existing a'téni simply won't have the symbolism and import that I require. Archigos Dhosti had picked you out, elevated, and obviously favored you. Your talent with the Ilmodo is undoubted. I can't bring the dwarf back, so I will choose his favorite, for the signal it will send to the rest of the Holdings."

"You can't be serious. I'm only an o'téni, and too young. And Concénzia has already cast me out."

"Too young?" The odd smile emerged again. "You're nearly the same age as my matarh was when she became Kraljica—if anything, I would say that enhances the symbolism, don't you think? And it was ca'Cellibrecca who cast you out—and he has already shown where his loyalty lies."

Ana was still shaking her head, but Justi continued speaking into her disbelief. "I offer you two choices, Ana. If you wish, you can remain here in the Bastida and you can watch from the balcony and see whether Nessantico falls to the Hïrzg and his pet Archigos; I would remind you that ca'Cellibrecca has already displayed his attitude toward you and the Numetodo. I daresay that he'd be pleased to find you and ci'Vliomani conveniently jailed so he can do what he loves to do with Numetodo. And if *I* should prevail, well, I will need to show the Holdings what I do to those who betray me. Even those who were once my lovers."

Ana felt nothing but loathing for the man. "Or?" she asked.

Justi gave a high bark of a laugh. "Or you may take my second choice: you can become Archigos and ca' rather than cu', and help me bury the man who would bury you. You can bring justice to the man who murdered Archigos Dhosti."

He was so smug, so certain. Ana rubbed at her wrists, chafed by the manacles. She wanted to spit at him, to refuse for the momentary satisfaction it would give her. But she didn't. Couldn't. "You plotted with ca'Cellibrecca against the Archigos, you and Francesca. You used me, Kraljiki, and now you want to use me again."

He waved a careless hand. "All true. Just as you tried to use me for ci'Vliomani's sake, and for Archigos Dhosti's as well. Well, neither of us got what we wanted, did we? So let us use each other again, Ana, this time to better effect. Do you still want a marriage to the Kraljiki? If you do, I will call an a'téni here immediately and have it done. I will become Justi ca'Seranta. Whatever you want. But I need an Archigos and I need one swiftly, and you're the best choice I have."

Ana scoffed. "Marry you? I'd sooner cut off my hands myself and tear out my own tongue than do that. I know what you do when those around you are no longer convenient. I watched the Kraljica die. I watched your matarh draw her last breath. Marry you?" She gave a single bark of harsh laughter. "I think not."

If he was offended, it didn't show on his handsome face. "I've come to believe that it's better to choose our own times than to wait, Ana. I chafed under my

matarh's thumb for decades, waiting and waiting for
mine, and I finally realized that I might wait forever,
that I might die before it came. I understood that Cénzi
wanted *me* to choose. So I did and I don't regret that.
This is *your* moment to choose, Ana. You don't like everything power brings you? Too bad. Cénzi has seen fit
to offer you, through me, the chance to take the globe
of the Archigos and use it. You can take what He offers,
or you can refuse and pray to Him as Nessantico falls
around us. What would Cénzi prefer you to do? What
would Archigos Dhosti tell you? What would Envoy
ci'Vliomani say?"

    She knew. She already knew, but she shook her head.
"I won't marry you, Kraljiki, and I won't necessarily do
what you ask. Understand that if I am Archigos, I *will be
Archigos*. Fully. Completely. You must realize that. Concénzia will interpret the Divolonté as *I* would interpret
it, as Archigos Dhosti would have interpreted it. I will be
your ally today, Kraljiki, but I won't consent to be your
pawn. I will be your ally today, but perhaps not tomorrow. I will speak with *my* voice, not yours."

    Justi inhaled. He nodded. "I would expect nothing dif-
ferent from you. I accept those conditions."

    Ana nodded. The fear in her was subsiding, but it
was replaced by a newer, darker one. *Let this be the
right choice, Cénzi. Let me not fail You.* "Then we will
go down and we will release Karl ci'Vliomani, Kraljiki.
Now. Any other Numetodo in the Bastida will also be
immediately released. When I see that has been done,
we can talk further."

    Another breath. Another nod. Justi waved in the
direction of the cell door. "After you, Archigos Ana
ca'Seranta," he said. "I took the liberty of ordering the
Concord A'Téni to meet, and they are anxiously waiting
for us."

~

Jan ca'Vörl

"WHERE IS GEORGI, Vatarh? I want him to show me how you besiege a city."

Her voice echoed in the expanse of the Comte's Palais of Passe a'Fiume. The open lobby under the broken, charred roof was littered with pallets of the wounded and dead, and what remained of the structure stank of blood and smoke. Jan regarded his daughter and sighed. He'd allowed her to enter Passe a'Fiume from the rear encampment this morning. It was safe enough now: U'Téni cu'Bachiga, A'Offizier cu'Garret, and those injured Chevarittai of Nessantico who had been unable to flee were incarcerated in the temple, which was one of the less-damaged buildings in the city. The executed bodies of some of the lesser offiziers of the Garde Civile—those whose families were unlikely to have enough wealth to make ransom likely or worthwhile— were gibbeted along the walls of the town. The war-téni, under ca'Cellibrecca's guidance, had briefly become fire-téni, putting out the flames their spells had caused. Despite their efforts, the town smoldered: the buildings were grave-shrouded in ribbons of gray, thin smoke; the walls were cracked and tumbling near the main gates. Crows feasted on the bodies left strewn in the streets or half-buried in rubble or sprawled on the fields outside, while soldiers monitored the citizens dragooned into removing the dead, stacking the corpses on flat-bedded carts, and taking them to the pyre built on the far side of the Clario. The dead-wagons fought against the constant influx of Firenzcian soldiers crossing into and through

Passe a'Fiume. Except for the laughter and howls from
the Firenzcian soldiers carousing in Passe a'Fiume's
still-open taverns and brothels, the city went about its
sad duties silently, in massive grief and shock.

Jan had hoped that this would be the worst Allesandra would need to see, but hope—as the Toustour said—
was a fickle mistress. Jan had studied the reports that
Markell had given him regarding their own losses. He
looked at his aide now, standing behind Allesandra with
his head bowed.

"That's why I asked Markell to bring you here," he
told her. "Come with me, love. I must show you something." He held out his hand to her. She took it, and he
marveled again at how smooth her hand was in his, and
how it was no longer quite so small in his grasp. They
walked down the main aisle between the pallets, with Jan
stopping occasionally to comfort one of the wounded
Firenzcian soldiers. Jan could see Allesandra's eyes widening, seeing the blood and the decaying flesh, the missing limbs and terrible, open wounds. Her breathing was
shallow and fast, and she clung hard to him.

They stopped, finally, before a pallet in the middle of
the room. "No . . ." Jan heard Allesandra breathe, then a
sob cracked in her voice and she tore her hand away from
Jan, kneeling down beside the pallet and the still, bloodied body laying there. She looked up at Jan with eyes
brimming. "This can't be," she said. "I won't let it be."

"I wish it were that easy, my little bird," he answered.
He crouched alongside her. "Allesandra, your Georgi
was a soldier. An o'offizier. He asked to participate in
the siege and he performed valiantly, but when the Nessantican chevarittai fled yesterday it was his encampment they went through. He fought to hold them back.
But he fell."

Jan reached for the blanket and started to pull it over
Georgi's head; Allesandra reached out and touched
his hand. "No," she said. "Let me, Vatarh. He was my
friend."

Jan let her take the blanket, and Allesandra gently pulled the folds over Georgi's face. She touched her hand to the o'offizer's hidden face.

"Allesandra," Jan said softly, "war might seem like a game, but a starkkapitän or a Hïrzg must realize that the pieces aren't lead and paint; they're flesh and blood, and once they fall, you can't pick them up again and put them back. Look around you; this is the reality of war, and you need to understand it if you are to be the Hïrzgin. Georgi was teaching you how to move the pieces; now he teaches you what it means to *be* one of those pieces."

Allesandra glanced back up at him and though her cheeks were stained with the tracks of moisture, her eyes were dry. "Tell me that we'll go to Nessantico now, Vatarh," she said, her voice tinged more with anger than sorrow. "Tell me that."

He crouched down and cradled her in his arms, and her anger returned again to tears. She sobbed against his chest, hard and inconsolable. He stroked her hair and pressed her against him.

"We will go to Nessantico, Allesandra," he told her. "I promise you that. You will walk its streets soon enough."

"Another week, perhaps a bit more, and this will be Nessantico's fate. Cénzi has indeed blessed us," ca'Cellibrecca said, his voice as raucous as one of the carrion crows. "What a wonderful victory, my Hïrzg!"

Jan turned from a broken window set high in a domed tower of the temple. He'd given Allesandra into Markell's care before going to find the Archigos. Ca'Cellibrecca was beaming at him, his corpulent face alight above the ornate robe of the Archigos. Jan scowled back.

"You're a fool, ca'Cellibrecca," he snarled. He pointed to the shattered window. Shards of colored glass were snared in the leaden frame, and the sill was blackened with smoke. "Is that *victory* you see out there?" he railed at the man, who cowered back in the doorframe as if searching for a retreat. "Will you tell me that Kraljiki Justi is among our prisoners? Was it the Kraljiki or even Commandant ca'Rudka who surrendered the city to us, or only some unimportant local offizier? Did you fail to notice how many men we lost here, or how many days we've wasted while Nessantico readied its defenses?" Jan spat out from the window, watching the gob of spittle arc in the air to fall on shattered roof tiles far below. He turned back to ca'Cellibrecca. "The Kraljiki played us here, ca'Cellibrecca, better than his matarh could have. He offered parley to gain days, then he fled and left his commandant here to hold us. Then the chevarritai fled themselves before they could be captured."

"I realize that," ca'Cellibrecca said. "Starkkapitän ca'Linnett should have ordered his men to pursue. I told the man so, but he wouldn't listen to me." Ca'Cellibrecca shook his head. "Now we'll have to contend with them at Nessantico. I've been thinking about this, my Hïrzg. If we take our troops, and divide them so that we come in from the north and west as well as the east . . ."

Jan interrupted the man with a snarl. "Come here a moment, Archigos—I need to show you something."

Ca'Cellibrecca walked across the room toward him; Jan stepped aside to let him stand before the window, his nose wrinkling at the smell of incense clinging to the man's robes. "What is it you want me to see?" ca'Cellibrecca asked, and Jan caught the man's green robes in his fists and pushed him forward hard. Ca'Cellibrecca squalled in fright but his hands flailed only at cold air. Jan could see shards of glass digging into the rolls of the man's waist. Overbalanced, ca'Cellibrecca was heavier than Jan had expected; he had to brace himself to keep from losing his grip entirely.

"Can you fly, Archigos?" Jan asked as the man shouted in alarm. "Can Cénzi give you wings like a bird?"

"My Hïrzg . . . Pull me back up!"

"Shut up," Jan told him. "You look more like a cow

than a bird to me, Archigos. That's what you are, Archigos: a cow. As long as you give me the milk of Cénzi, I
will keep you. If you can't be my cow, then I have U'Téni
cu'Kohnle to serve as such. Frankly, I don't really care
which one of you it is as long as you give me what I want
from you. I don't need you to be a bird and tell me about
bird matters unless you can demonstrate to me how well
you fly. I already have a starkkapitän, but maybe you
think you're a better strategist, eh? We can find out now.
So tell me, Archigos, because my arms are tired and I
can't hold you for much longer: are you a cow, or are
you a bird?"

He shook the man and heard the sound of cloth ripping. Ca'Cellibrecca screamed. "I'm a cow! A cow!" Jan
could see his arms flailing. People were looking up from
the ground and pointing to the Archigos.

"Louder," he called to the Archigos, shaking him
again. "I can't hear you. They can't hear you."

"I'm a cow!" the man screamed. He could hear the
bellowing reverberate in the streets below. "I am a cow,
my Hïrzg!"

"Moo for me then, Cow," Jan said. "Let us hear
you moo."

Ca'Cellibrecca gulped. He mooed, a plaintive wail
sounding over and over again, as if he were one of the
wind-horns of the temple. Jan could hear laughter in the
streets below.

"That will do," Jan said, and pulled the man back up.
The Archigos' hair was disheveled and blood stained
his robes where the glass had sliced through the cloth
into the flesh underneath. "I would advise you to attend
to your cow matters, Archigos. We will be leaving Passe
a'Fiume in the morning."

~

Mahri

THE LEATHER POUCH on his belt felt heavy
against Mahri's thigh, a glass ball the size of a child's
fist nestled within it. Placing the X'in Ka inside the ball
had cost him an entire night's sleep, but doubts still
plagued him.

*The signs aren't clear enough. They never are when
they concern her. . . .*

The wind-horns on the Temple of Cénzi sounded,
echoed by the horns on all the temples as well as the
bells of the Kraljiki's Palais. With the clamor, the new
Archigos appeared in the traditional middle tower
window to wave to the throngs of the faithful ...
though the throngs were far fewer than those which
usually greeted a new Archigos. Nessantico's population had been decimated: most men were away with
the army swelling beyond the eastern gates, and many
citizens had decided that visiting relatives in towns to
the west would be an excellent idea. The temple square
was full and cheers rose toward the new Archigos, but
the crowd didn't overflow out into the Avi a'Parete, the
cheers were less than deafening and more rehearsed
than authentic. The heralds had already announced
that, due to the current crisis, Archigos Ana the First
would forgo the traditional procession around the city;
after a few minutes and a blessing called out over the
onlookers in a thin, nervous voice, the crowd dispersed
quickly except for the ca'-and-cu' who filed into the
Archigos' Temple to witness Ana's initial service.

As the citizenry walked away toward home and businesses, the air was alive with gossip, and Mahri caught snatches of it as they passed him.

"... told me that she's already agreed to marry the Kraljiki. She might as well be one of the *grandes horizontals* ..."

"... seems that when the Kraljiki's wishes aren't followed he'll just create his own Concénzia ..."

"... that the Numetodo will be welcome in the city. From what I hear, ci'Vliomani's title of envoy has been restored ..."

Mahri smiled grimly. He touched the glass ball once more and wrapped his cloak around him. Sheltered against one of the buildings across the square, he invoked a quick spell, and the air shimmered around him as if he were enclosed in water. He walked across the courtyard and into the temple, knowing that casual eyes would only see a heat-shimmer if they glanced at him. Inside the temple, he found a dark niche to one side of the nave. There, he settled in to watch as Ana and a retinue of a' and u'téni went through the rituals of the High Worship. He listened to Ana's fledgling Admonition from the High Lectern. Her Admonition was largely a tribute to Archigos Dhosti's memory and a plea for tolerance.

"... remember that Archigos Dhosti realized that there are more things in the world than we can imagine, and that even Nessantico must change. With Kraljica Marguerite, we were lulled by peace for too long a time, and we woke to find that there were movements afoot that we had not seen because we didn't *want* to see them. We were afraid. We can no longer be afraid; we can no longer close our eyes and pretend that all is as we wish it to be. We must embrace those who can help us, because without their help, we cannot survive. My ..." Mahri heard the pause, saw the almost-amused grimace that accompanied the hesitation. "... predecessor as Archigos had a fondness for quoting the Divolonté. I tell you that I hold those laws in no less regard than he. Let me quote: *'As child grows to adult, so must the Divolonté grow.'* We have no choice but to accept such change now. The Concénzia Faith is emerging from a long, quiet childhood; from the sheltering arms of its parents into a world that is dangerous and uncomfortable. We are Nessantico. We are the Holdings, and we are great and we are vast, but there are those who would destroy our greatness with their petty, narrow concerns. I tell you this: to contend with the rest of the world, we must also be willing to learn from it."

There was silence in the temple when she finished speaking, then came a susurrus of whispers among the ca'-and-cu' gathered there. He saw them lean toward each other with faces grim and frowning; he could see the mouthed word "Numetodo" on their lips even if he could not hear it. If Ana had hoped to convince the ca'-and-cu', she'd not succeeded, not if their posture was any indication. Even the Kraljiki, in attendance in the royal alcove to the left of the High Lectern, seemed uncomfortable with her words, and none of the a'téni on the dais with her were smiling. Karl was in attendance also, in a rear alcove of the temple with people who Mahri knew to be among the remaining local Numetodo. They were also grim, watching the reaction.

The rest of the service went quickly. When Ana gave the Blessing of Cénzi to the attendants, they left the temple quickly while Ana and the a'téni went to the vestry at the rear of the building.

Mahri, in his niche, sighed and closed his eyes. His hand touched the glass ball in its pouch. She would want this now. He knew it. He hurried toward the vestry, stopping in the shadows at the edge of the nave. Several of the e' and o'téni attendants waited there for their superiors to emerge, talking softly among themselves. Ana and the other a'téni of the Conclave were inside the closed doors.

He could feel the X'in Ka swirling about him, and he let down the barriers of his mind to bring it in. He spoke softly so that the téni would not hear him; his hands swayed and turned and cupped the air. This spell was long and complicated, and it would utterly exhaust him later. It would also cost him a few years of his life. But again it was necessary, as it had been necessary in the past.

He knew the sacrifices that were demanded of him. He'd agreed to them long, long ago.

The world shifted around him. The very air hushed. The sound of the e' and o'téni's voices became low and almost unheard. He moved, and it was as if he were pushing his body through sand. Each step was a labor, and it seemed to take him days to reach the vestry doors a dozen strides away and slide past the living statues of the téni. It took nearly all his strength to push one of the doors open and shut it again.

Around him, Ana and the a'téni were frozen, caught in the midst of removing their gilded outer vestments from the service. The crown of the Archigos lay on the seat of the chair next to Ana; she was still leaning over, her hands open as if she had just laid down the golden band.

He went up to her and put his finger along the side of her neck. He took her presence in his mind, holding it. He felt her lurch into motion, heard her gasp.

"It's just my finger," Mahri said in his broken, raspy voice. "It might as easily have been a knife."

Ana straightened, taking a stumbling step back from him. She glanced quickly around the vestry, seeing the others snared in mid-motion. Her eyes narrowed, her lips pressed together. "You betrayed me, Mahri. You gave me to the Kraljiki."

"Yes," he answered calmly. "I gave you to the Kraljiki. And look at where you are now."

"You didn't know that would happen."

"It was by far the most likely scenario. Tell me, Ana, if I had advised you and Karl to surrender yourselves to the Kraljiki, would you have done it? You don't have to answer; I already know. And so do you."

She started to protest, but he spoke over her. The X'in Ka burned inside him as he held them both in the spell, searing him from the inside; he wanted to scream with the pain. He could almost feel the new scars rippling his already-savaged face. He had to release her, quickly, or the fire would begin to consume her as well. "Not much time," he said. "I came to give you this." He untied the pouch from his belt and handed it to her. It seemed heavier than before as he placed it in her palm. "Inside the ball is this very spell," he told her, gesturing at the unmoving people around them. "It takes you outside the constraints of time. Say my name when you hold the ball in your hand, and the spell will release."

"Why?" The single word hung there as she looked at the pouch, as she glanced at the glittering orb inside, shimmering with soft orange light.

"You will need it. Think, Ana: it could have been a knife at your throat and not my finger. I give you the same power—to hold time still and do whatever it is you need to do. I'll tell you this, also, a saying we have in the Westlands: a snake without its head cannot strike you."

She shook her head, but Mahri closed his eyes and released her from the spell. She froze in mid-protest, and he walked laboriously to the door, as rapidly as he could in the gelid air. As soon as he was out of the temple, he released the spell entirely, almost falling to the stone flags of the court as the X'in Ka flowed out from him and the world surged into motion again.

He hurried away toward Oldtown, toward the bed into which he would collapse for the next few days.

Ana ca'Seranta

" . . . A SNAKE WITHOUT its head cannot strike," Mahri said.

Ana shook her head. "I don't know what you mean," she started to say, but a sudden disorientation came over her in that moment, and Mahri vanished while the téni in the vestry with her lurched back to sudden life.

The disorientation felt oddly familiar. She couldn't quite decide why.

She was holding the pouch in her hand. The leather was supple and worn; the weight inside was heavy and she remembered the glow of it, the color of a dying sun behind clouds. She tucked it quickly into a pocket of her green robes. None of the a'téni noticed; none of them were looking at her. None of them had looked at her since she'd left the High Lectern. Colin ca'Cille, Alain ca'Fountaine, Joca ca'Sevini, all the others: they were old men, all of them. At least a few of them had harbored aspirations to be Archigos themselves, and they would all rather have been in their own cities than trapped here in Nessantico with the Hïrzg's army approaching. She could feel their resentment, palpable.

"You're all blind," she told them. They glanced at her now, startled. "You're so folded into yourselves that you can't see," she told them. Her hands were trembling, as if from the exhaustion of a spell. "I need all of you to leave me now. Send Kennc in to me as you go."

"Archigos," one of them said: ca'Sevini of Chivasso. From his expression, her title seemed to taste like fish oil. "You've already made a terrific mistake today with

the Admonition you gave the ca'-and-cu'. You're making
another now. The Kraljiki may have been able to force
your ascension on us in this terrible time, but if you have
any hope of ever being more than just Archigos in title,
then you need our cooperation. Showing arrogance isn't
the way to gain it—not when someone else still claims
the title of Archigos. You can't dismiss us as if we were
inconvenient e'téni."

Ana had no answer for him, or, rather, she had too
many. *People like you have been telling me what I must
do all my life, from my vatarh to the Kraljiki.* She wanted
to spit the bile back at him. But past the anger, she knew
he was at least partially right, no matter how much she
wanted to deny it. She could not be Archigos without
their support. She would not survive the coming battle
without them; she especially could not risk their defect-
ing to ca'Cellibrecca.

There will be a time to assert yourself. This isn't it. She
could almost imagine Dhosti's voice saying the words.

She managed, if not to smile, to at least not frown.
"You're right, and I apologize, A'Téni ca'Sevini. Cénzi
knows, I deserved your rebuke, and I thank you for having the courage to speak bluntly. Please, I ask all of you
for forgiveness: I know we must work together, especially now."

She didn't know if it mollified them. A few nodded;
ca'Sevini actually showed his few remaining teeth in a
brief smile. She put away the service vestments and left
the vestry as quickly as she could, calling Kenne—newly
returned to the city—to her. "You saw no one outside,
Kenne?" she asked. "Mahri?"

Kenne shook his head, a bit wide-eyed. "No, Archigos.
There was no one in the hall but us. Why?"

She shook her head. "Never mind. I need you to do
something for me. . . ."

Karl hugged her as soon as Kenne closed the door
behind him. "Are you sure it's a good thing for a Nu-

metodo to be seen coming to the Archigos' office?" he asked. "People might talk, especially after your Admonition today."

"At this point I'm beyond caring," she told him.

He laughed, throatily, and pulled her to him. She allowed herself to sink into the embrace. Karl's arms tightened around her, and she closed her eyes so that there was only that hug, that comfort, that moment. Karl finally pulled away, and she opened her eyes again to see him looking around the room: the huge desk behind which Dhosti had sat for many years, that ca'Cellibrecca had desecrated with his presence most recently; the throne-chair at one end of the large room where Dhosti had sat for formal receptions of visitors; the gilded images of the Moitidi carved into the cornices; the massive broken globe, gilded and ornate and held in puffs of wooden clouds, looming over the main doors.

"Impressive," he said. "Have you tried out the throne yet?"

She shook her head. "This isn't the time for jests, Karl," she told him. "Right now, I need you to be the Envoy for the Numetodo." She took his hands. "Mahri came to me, after the service."

Karl scowled. His hands squeezed hers. "Traitorous bastard. Handing us over like that ..."

She shook her head. She touched the leather pouch tied to the belt of her robes, and she could feel the throbbing of the Ilmodo trapped within it. But she didn't tell Karl about it or show him the small globe inside. She held back, and she wondered at that. "I'm not so certain. I thought the same after he handed us over to the gardai, but now ..." She shivered and stepped back from Karl. "I don't know what Mahri wants, or why he does what he does, but I think he knew that neither of us would be long imprisoned."

Karl moved his jaw as if remembering the ache of the silencer. "What did he want?"

Ana shrugged and dropped his hands. "I don't know,"

she said. "Not really. He ... gave me something, but what it does ..." She shook her head, catching her upper lip in her teeth momentarily. "I won't last as Archigos, Karl. I think Mahri knows that, and Kraljiki Justi, and ca'Cellibrecca and the rest of the a'téni. I've been given the title because none of the a'téni would take it right now, not with the strong possibility that ca'Cellibrecca might return as Archigos when this is all over. I'm just the False Archigos, the Kraljiki's Archigos."

"They can't all feel that way."

She nodded vigorously. "That's the way nearly all of them are thinking. Yes, there are some téni who support me: U'Téni Dosteau—and I must promote him; that would be a small help—Kenne, most of the e'téni and o'téni who were part of Archigos Dhosti's staff, even a few of the u'téni. But the a'téni ..." A breath. "At best, they will do no more than they absolutely must just in case the Kraljiki *does* win. They'll wait and see what happens when the Hïrzg's army comes. I have a title, Karl; that's all."

"And you want more than that."

A smile emerged momentarily. "You know me better than I thought. Yes. I want more."

"What can I do?"

"You started to teach me. I need you to show me all you can do, and I need you to bend the Divolonté with me. ..."

The war-téni had assembled, as ordered by their new Archigos, in the Stadia a'Sute. With one exception, none of the a'téni had been invited; in fact, those few who tried to enter were forcibly turned away by the Archigos' staff and the Garde Kraljiki, who patrolled all the entrances. The war-téni were seated at the north end of the stadia; on the athlete's field below, they could see a small stage erected on the grass and the Archigos' throne set to one side of it. When the wind-horns sounded Second Call, the doors to the stadia clanged shut even as the téni were saying their prayers. A few moments later, the Archigos herself emerged from one of the field doors, accompanied by the newly promoted A'Téni cu'Dosteau and a few others, one of them quickly recognizable to the téni who were from the city.

"That's Envoy ci'Vliomani, the Numetodo..." The gossip moved rapidly through the ranks of the war-téni as the Archigos bowed to them and gave the sign of Cénzi, then took her seat on the throne. She gestured, and ci'Vliomani and another man stepped onto the stage.

"One of your duties," Archigos Ana said, addressing the war-teni, "is to protect those around you from the spells of the war-téni of the false Archigos. What I'd like you to do now is show me how well you can do that. I think some of you have already recognized Envoy ci'Vliomani, who came to Nessantico to represent the Numetodo everywhere in the Holdings. I've asked him here today to play the role of the enemy. On my command, he will attack me—the spell itself will be harmless, I assure you, but your task will be to stop his attack from touching me at all. Let's see how well you perform. Each of you: I know you've been taught by A'Téni cu'Dosteau, as he once taught me. Go on—you may start your counter-spells now."

The war-téni glanced at each other, then several of them began to chant and move their hands, though they were obviously puzzled as the Archigos still made no command to Envoy ci'Vliomani to start his own spell. Finally, several breaths later, she turned to him. "Envoy," she said. "If you'll begin your attack ..."

What happened then stunned them all. Ci'Vliomani spoke a single guttural word that sounded like the language of the Ilmodo but was no spell-word they knew, and he gave a casual flick of his hand. The word boomed thunderously in the stadia. Impossibly, a fire brighter than the sun glared in his hand and flared through the air, arrowing straight toward the Archigos.

But a moment after ci'Vliomani had begun his inexplicably rapid spell, Archigos Ana also spoke: again, a single word of spell-speech as she held up her hand. The flare of light spattered and exploded, as if it had struck an invisible barrier. The brilliant fury caused many of the war-téni to raise their hands, and the ball of fire shrieked like a dying animal as it expired.

A stunned silence wrapped the stadia as the war-téni stood, their own counter-spells—perhaps three quarters completed—forgotten.

Too fast: the whole exchange had been far too fast.

"You were all late. You all would have failed in your duty." Archigos Ana spoke into the hush. She rose easily from her chair—neither ci'Vliomani nor the Archigos seemed unduly fatigued by the casting of their spells, and that was also strange—and walked onto the stage. "I know your thoughts," she said. "When I first saw what the Numetodo were capable of doing with the Ilmodo, it shook me all the way to the core of my being. For a time, in my loss of faith, Cénzi punished me and I lost my own path to the Ilmodo, until He spoke to me again." She smiled briefly. "Or, let me be honest, until I was willing to listen to Him. I will tell you now what I came to realize: the Ilmodo was created by Cénzi, yes, and our way to the Ilmodo remains the most powerful. I know in my heart that this is the way of Cénzi. I will tell you, and Envoy ci'Vliomani will agree with me: the Numetodo might have the advantage of speed, but not of force. None of the Numetodo can match what the least of you can do on the battlefield with your war-spells. But . . ." She stopped and paced for a moment. ". . . our way is not the *only* way Cénzi has created, and we are fools if we are not willing to learn from those other paths."

She strode forward until she stood at the front of the stage, leaning forward toward the war-téni in the stands. Her gaze moved across each of their faces. "I tell you this: *The Numetodo are a threat to Concénzia only if your own faith is lacking.*"

"That's not what Archigos Orlandi believes."

The challenge was loud, from a téni who stood abruptly in his seat. Several of the war-téni around the man also rose, placing their hands on the speaker. "No!" Ana shouted at them. "Let him talk!"

The anger in her voice loosened the hands that had grasped at the war-téni, and he shook them away. He pointed toward Ana, toward Karl. "*You're* the false Archigos," he said. "Look who you consort with. The Numetodo mock the Divolonté. They mock the Toustour. They deny Cénzi. How can you stand there and say that we must learn from *them?*"

"What is your name?" Ana asked.

"I am U'Téni Georgi cu'Vlanti."

"I know of your family, U'Téni. They're good people and devout, and I'm not surprised to find that at least one of them has chosen to serve Concénzia. If you think I'm the false Archigos, U'Téni cu'Vlanti, then it's your duty under Cénzi and the Divolonté to strike me down. I give you that opportunity now. Pray to Cénzi to guide your hands and strengthen your spell, as I will pray to Him to guide mine." Ana spread her arms wide. "Begin your spell," she told him. She looked around the stadia slowly, especially to those on the stage with her. "I promise you that no one here will stop you."

"Ana . . ." Karl began, and she shook her head at him.

"No one here will stop you," she repeated to both Karl and the war-téni. "The Divolonté is clear on this: *Rip out the tongues and crush the hands of those who falsely claim they speak with Cénzi's voice, for you risk your own soul if you listen.* I make that claim, U'Téni cu'Vlanti. I say that Cénzi is speaking through me, as He does through each Archigos. I say that the false Archigos is out there with the Hïrzg. But if you believe otherwise, then the Divolonté demands that you strike me. Do it, U'Téni. Do it if you think that Cénzi will fail to protect me. Do it if you believe that ca'Cellibrecca should wear the shattered globe around his neck and that Jan ca'Vörl of Firenzcia should sit on the Sun Throne and end the long rule of the ca'Ludovici lineage."

The man was standing silent, glaring at her with his hands at his sides. "*Do* it!" Ana barked, and he nearly jumped.

His hands began to move; he began to chant. A searing light flared between his hands. Ana did nothing, waiting, and the murmuring of the other war-téni rose. Cu'Vlanti finished the spell rapidly and spread his hands as Ana spoke a word and gestured—too late. Fire erupted on the stage, a raging, quick conflagration that submerged all gathered there in flame so that they couldn't be seen from the stands where the war-téni stood. They knew the damage a full war-spell would inflict, and there were shouts of alarm and surprise and horror from the téni in their seats.

War-fire left behind only the blackened husks of charred bodies.

The flames vanished, their fury expended. The planks of the stage smoldered with great blisters of black ash; the hangings above dripped sparks as charred fabric fell away. But where the Numetodo ci'Vliomani and the Archigos stood, the wood was untouched. Archigos Ana was standing with her hands extended in a shielding spell—cast with impossible speed.

Karl Ci'Vliomani suddenly broke the tableau as he jumped with a curse and started beating at the folds of his bashta on his left side. Smoke and tiny flames curled from where his hands struck. He looked reproachfully at Ana as he smothered the fire. "You were a little slow there, Archigos," he said. "And a little too sparing of your shield."

Someone out in the stands chuckled, and the laughter spread slowly, as Ana smiled herself. U'Téni cu'Vlanti had collapsed, exhausted, in his seat, but Ana stood as if the spell had cost her nothing.

"Cénzi has allowed me to do this," Ana said to the war-téni. "And the Numetodo have helped show me how. In this time, we can't afford to cast out those who offer to be our allies. I ask you to let the Numetodo stand with us. I ask you, like me, to learn from them what they can teach us."

There were no cheers. There was no audible response to her plea at all. But Ana glimpsed a few grudging nods among the faces of the war-téni.

It would have to be enough.

~

Sergei ca'Rudka

THE WORLD FLICKERED in and out, as if illuminated by lethargic, erratic strokes of lightning.

. . . someone (he thought it might be ca'Montmorte) helping him down from his horse with a hiss of concern. "Fetch a healer . . ." he heard ca'Montmorte say, and there were hands around him, and he screamed as they lifted him.

. . . waking to pain and firelight. A face passed through his field of vision. He tried to speak through cracked and dry lips. "Where . . . ?"

"On the Avi," he heard someone answer. "Maybe two days from Nessantico. Please don't try to move, Commandant."

He started to laugh at the thought of moving, but the laugh turned to a cough, and the cough took his breath from him and he left the world again.

. . . the insistent saltiness of meat broth on his tongue. The taste was so wonderful that his hands grabbed the hands holding the mug to his lips as he gulped at the soup. "Gently, Commandant," a voice said. "There's plenty for you. Take your time."

He tried to sit up, and found that he could do so only

with great difficulty. It seemed to be night. His body was bound tightly, and his skin pulled all along his back. His vision was blurry and he couldn't focus, but he could see the shifting light of a campfire close by and bodies sitting around it. Horses nickered quietly somewhere close. He felt chilled, his body shivering uncontrollably. "Careful," the voice said. "You're been hurt."

"So cold . . ."

"You're feverish, Commandant. Here, drink some more of the broth . . ."

He did, and he slept again.

. . . they were talking about him, as if he couldn't hear them. ". . . going to die?"

"That's in Cénzi's hands. I can't do any more for him. The infection has him."

"How long does he have?"

"Another day. Maybe two."

"We'll reach Nessantico in the morning. Perhaps someone there? The Kraljiki's healer?"

"He's beyond the skills of any healer, A'Offizier ca'Montmorte. There is only Cénzi's Will now."

Wait, Sergei wanted to shout. *There's something I have to tell the Kraljiki, something he must know . . .* but he couldn't open his eyes or force his mouth to open and even the effort of thinking about it sent him reeling into darkness.

. . . someone was chanting and he could feel hands touching his chest, his neck. The hands were cold, and the heat that burned him from the inside flowed toward his heart and those hands, rushing away from him. He took in a long, shuddering breath. Along his spine, needles stabbed at his skin, pulling as he arched his back shouting with the agony of it, but even the pain was rushing away toward those hands and the voice speaking in words he could not understand. His eyelids flew open, and he stared into Ana cu'Seranta's face. Her own eyes were closed, and it was her voice that he heard and her hands on his bare chest. Her presence was the only

refuge in a world that was on fire, and she was taking in the fire. Sergei gasped with the wonder of it, and he sighed when she pulled her hands away from him.

"Welcome back, Commandant," she said before her eyes rolled back and her knees collapsed under her. A man—Envoy ci'Vliomani, he realized—rushed forward to help her, placing her in a chair beside the bed. Sergei pushed himself up with his elbows: he could move, though his joints were stiff and protesting, and the skin of his back still pulled strangely, though no longer painfully. His wounded leg was splinted and wrapped as well. Another person—Renard—came forward to place a pillow behind him, so that he could sit comfortably. He had time to take in his surroundings: a large bedroom, the walls painted with frescoes of the Moitidi, above the large windows, stained glass shattering the light with the insignia of the Kraljiki.

"The Grande Palais . . ." he said.

"You're in one of the guest bedrooms," Renard said. "And if you'll excuse me, Commandant, the Kraljiki asked to be informed when you woke."

As Renard hurried off, Sergei turned to Ana. He saw the broken globe on the wide chain around her neck; it pleased him that the Kraljiki had followed at least one piece of his advice. "You're not worried that it might have been Cénzi's Will that I die, Archigos?" he asked.

Ana took a long breath, her eyes closed as Karl stroked her unbound, sweat-darkened hair. Slowly, the eyes opened and found him. "If Cénzi wanted you dead, Commandant," she told him, "He would have killed you before you came to me."

"Your predecessor would have you in the Bastida for exactly those sentiments."

"Where you would have tortured me to gain my full confession. Where you would have eventually executed me."

Sergei shrugged. He held her gaze, not flinching from it at all. "Yes," he told her. "That would have been my duty, and I would have performed it."

"The commandant always performs his duty." Kraljiki Justi's high-pitched voice was loud as he entered the bedroom and strode quickly to Sergei's bedside. Reluctantly, Sergei looked away from Ana to Justi. "As you did your duty in Passe a'Fiume," Justi finished. His bearded face seemed inordinately pleased. "I've just met with ca'Montmorte. He told me what happened there. We're as ready here as we can be, and you have our gratitude for that, Commandant." He glanced across the bed to Ana. "And we're grateful for your ... prayers for the commandant, Archigos. It seems Cénzi has listened to your entreaties."

Ana sniffed audibly. "I *healed* the man, Kraljiki. I healed him with the Ilmodo—just as I tried to heal your matarh but failed because I was weak then and too afraid. If that is against the Divolonté, then I will direct the Concord A'Téni to change the Divolonté, because I won't be silent and I won't lie. Not any longer."

The Kraljiki's chin seemed to thrust out even further, and his thin mustache was an arc over his scowl. "The Archigos is tired. She should rest."

"The Archigos isn't the Kraljiki's lap dog to be ordered around," Ana answered. Her fingers were laced with those of the envoy. "You chose me, Kraljiki Justi; now you live with your choice. Unless you prefer the Archigos who is out there." She pointed to the window, to the sun in the eastern sky. "I'm sure the Hïrzg will be happy to allow him back into Nessantico."

"Kraljiki, Archigos," Sergei said, and that brought their attention back to him. "There are enemies enough without making new ones here. Archigos, I am forever in your debt, and I won't forget that; Kraljiki, I would like to see the defenses here, as soon as I can."

"Yes," Justi said quickly. "We need your guidance to ensure victory."

Sergei shook his head. "Victory?" He shook his head. "I've fought them, Kraljiki, and I don't see victory. Passe a'Fiume had never fallen in all of Nessantico's history, yet

the Hïrzg walked through its broken gates in four days."
He grimaced, sitting up higher in the bed. "Hïrzg Jan is
already looking at Nessantico and considering it his," he
said. "I don't know that we can prove him wrong."

~

Jan ca'Vörl

"IT'S LIKE A JEWEL, Vatarh. Like something I
could wear. See—there's a necklace of lights. . . ."
Jan grinned indulgently at Allesandra. From behind,
he cuddled her against him, her body warm in the cool
night air. Ahead of them, far down the unseen line of the
Avi a'Firenzcia, the shimmering lights of the great city
glittered in the night, mocking the stars that dared to
peek between moon-silvered clouds. "And I will give it
to you," Jan told her. "You can wear that necklace soon,
my little bird, all for your very own."

"Don't be silly, Vatarh. I can't wear a whole city." She
reached out into the night and her forefinger and thumb
closed, as if she could pluck the lights from the landscape. "But it is pretty. When you're the Kraljiki, you
have to make sure that the téni still light the lamps."

"I'll make certain that Archigos ca'Cellibrecca fulfills
your request," he answered, chuckling.

They were camped on a hilltop outside Carrefour; tomorrow, Jan knew, they would have their first contact
with the defenders of Nessantico. His army was spread
wide over the landscape, the crescent of a scythe about to
strike the capital and remove its head from his throne.

Someone looking out from what remained of Nessantico's old walls would see *their* lights glimmering in
the dark, and they would not think them pretty at all.
The thought pleased Jan.

"How long will it take, Vatarh?" Allesandra asked. "U'Téni cu'Kohnle said that he thinks it will take less time than Passe a'Fiume. He said that you've already broken their will."

"I don't know, sweet one. How long do you think it will take?"

"One day," she said. "The war-téni will start their spells. They'll crush the soldiers and the chevarittai, and they'll scream as they die, and we'll all laugh at them. The rest of the chevarittai will go running like they did, then the rest of their soldiers will throw down their weapons and run away too, and this time it will be the Kraljiki who comes out from the city with the white flag."

"All that in one day?"

Her voice was nearly a growl. "That's what I would like—because of what they did to Georgi."

"I wish you were right, but I think both you and U'Téni cu'Kohnle are wrong. Do you remember the kitten you had, how it fought when the dogs trapped it in the corner?"

Allesandra nodded. "I remember. It was just a tiny thing, but it clawed Whitepaw's nose so badly that he ran away with his tail tucked, and there was blood everywhere and the healer had to sew Whitepaw's nose back together again. And the kitten made Skitters yelp and bleed, too, before Skitters finally got it and shook it to death." Allesandra looked at the jewel of the city set in the night landscape. "Oh," she said. "I understand what you mean, Vatarh," she said. "I do."

Karl ci'Vliomani

FROM THE BALCONY of the Archigos' residence, it was possible to believe that there was no war looming. From that vantage point, the lights of the Avi curled past the brilliantly-lit dome of the Archigos' Temple. The breeze was cool from the northwest, ruffling the edges of the ferns in their pots, and the Nessantico herself was strangely silent.

Karl knew the calm for the chimera it was. He'd been gathering together the Numetodo in Oldtown, and on the North Bank, where the first thrust of the Firenzcian assault would take place, there was no calm at all. From the outskirts of Oldtown, one could look out and see not only the campfires of the Garde Civile, but the more distant fires of the Hïrzg's army. There, the citizens were panicked, and it showed. Twice during the day, Karl had witnessed riots in the main streets, both violently put down by the Garde Kralji, as the citizenry stormed butcher shops and bakeries looking for food (and conveniently broke into any adjacent taverns as well). Heads were broken, the cobblestones grew slick with blood, and the mood turned uglier as the sun itself retreated to the west.

A constant stream of people and carts flooded the Avi a'Parete: soldiers, Garde Civile, various chevarittai and the occasional war-téni all heading east, and everyone else moving west. From what Karl had been told, both the Avi a'Nostrosei and Avi a'Certendi, as well as the Avi A'Sele, were packed with refugees from the city, carrying as much of their belongings as they could.

Only here, on the South Bank, did the city seem to retain any semblance of normalcy, and even that was the thinnest of veneers. Underneath the calm surface, there was a boiling, nervous energy.

Karl stood beside Ana as they both leaned on the balcony railing. He could feel her warmth against his side, but though he longed to do more, he did not. The ghost of Kaitlin stood between them as they stared out into the night. "I wish you would leave the city, Ana," he said.

"And I wish the same of you," she answered. "And you know neither of us can do that."

"Everything will change in the next few days. Six months ago, I would have left the city and not cared at all who lived or died here. Now it scares me, Ana—because of you. Because of us."

She gave a barely perceptible nod. She didn't answer otherwise, didn't move.

"There hasn't been enough time for your war-téni to learn enough. We can hope they'll be able to employ the Ilmodo a little faster than before. That's all."

"If they don't fail in their spells entirely, the way I did," Ana said. He felt her shiver. "I worry about that, too. This has shaken their faith. What good does speed do if they're no longer effective? I wonder if I've actually harmed the city's defenses rather than helped them."

"They have you as an example, and the Numetodo in the city will be there to help," he answered. "We'll do what we can to shield the war-téni, and they can always use the Ilmodo as they did before. Ana, stay with me tonight . . ." he began, but she turned to him and the look on her face stopped his words.

"No," she said. "I won't. You've made a promise to another; I won't help you break it."

"Then, after . . . I will write to her, tell her . . ." He realized he was deliberately avoiding saying Kaitlin's name aloud, and he wondered why.

"Don't talk of 'after,' Karl," she said. "We don't know that there will be an 'after.' There's only now. This moment, then the next and the next. That's all we have right now. If there's an after, we'll figure out then what that might mean for us, or if there even *is* an 'us.' For now, all I can think about is how to survive tomorrow."

She walked back into the apartments. Karl didn't follow her. He stood at the railing of the balcony, and listened to the city and to his conscience.

WAR

Sergei ca'Rudka
Jan ca'Vörl
Justi ca'Mazzak
Ana ca'Seranta
Orlandi ca'Cellibrecca
Sergei ca'Rudka
Jan ca'Vörl
Karl ci'Vliomani
Justi ca'Mazzak
Karl ci'Vliomani
Jan ca'Vörl
Mahri
Ana ca'Seranta
Allesandra ca'Vörl

Sergei ca'Rudka

THE BATTLE BEGAN with spell-fire and a sword thrust to the belly of the city.

All that morning the Firenzcian army approached: a steady advance that edged ever closer, a great arc slowly pressing down toward the forces Sergei had placed around the city from nearly Nortegate to the banks of the A'Sele.

The defensive line was dangerously thin. Sergei didn't have enough men; despite Sergei's persistent urgings, Kraljiki Justi had refused to allow the entirety of the Garde Civile and war-téni to move forward. Instead, the Kraljiki wrapped battalions of Garde Civile and his most loyal chevarittai around himself as a protective cocoon: inside the city walls. Sergei had been given orders by the Kraljiki not to engage unless necessary, and so the defending forces grudgingly gave ground to the advancing ranks. There were occasional skirmishes, brief flurries of combat punctuated with the challenges of the Firenzcian chevarittai. Some of the chevarittai of the city couldn't resist the challenge and went out to meet their cousins—a few ca'-and-cu' of both sides bloodied the ground prematurely as a result.

By Second Call, the tension had become nearly unbearable. The army of Firenzcia was a thunderhead looming near the city, like a silver-and-black cloud issuing tongues of lightning and growling with low thunder, the wind cold and vicious and rising.

The storm, inevitably, broke.

Sergei sat astride his horse on a small knoll a mile outside the old city walls, up the Avi a'Firenzcia along the River Vaghian. His leg ached, and his back was stiff, but he forced himself to ignore the nagging pains. Several flag-and-horn pages waited near him to relay orders and A'Offizier ca'Montmorte was at his side. From the knoll, Sergei could see the front ranks of the opposing force. The banner of the Hïrzg and the Red Lancers was being flown prominently: Jan ca'Vörl was out there, somewhere close. In front of Sergei, the two armies were separated by a muddy field, the once-ripening crop of wheat prematurely harvested and the remainder trampled under the hooves of the chevarittai and the boots of the Garde Civile and conscripts as they'd retreated to their present position in the western tree line.

Sergei had stopped the grudging retreat—if they backed any closer to the city, the fighting would be taking place among the houses and buildings that had grown up outside the original walls. Their spines were to Nessantico's outskirts; the offiziers had reformed the lines. Seeing them waiting, the Firenzcian army had halted, but Sergei didn't believe they would remain there for long.

The sun fell directly on the field. The light did nothing to warm them.

"If I were Hïrzg Jan, I would wait," ca'Montmorte said. "It's already past Second Call. He should establish his lines, call his offiziers together for consultation and settle the troops in for the night. I'd continue the advance at First Call tomorrow." Ca'Montmorte nodded at his own advice. "That would give us time to bring more conscripts from the city and have the Archigos send up the remainder of the war-téni. The Hïrzg doesn't know that we don't have the entire Garde Civile waiting in reserve."

Sergei shook his head. "I know the man, Elia. The Hïrzg is a decent tactician but a mediocre strategist—if there's any strategy here, it will be the starkkapitän's.

Ca'Vörl's most dangerous in the midst of a fight, but he has no patience. He also knows he has the advantage. No, this is what he wants and he will have it now. I'd wager that he intends to sleep tonight inside Nessantico, and we're in his way. He'll attack. He won't wait."

Ca'Montmorte shook his head. "That would be foolish."

"Wait," Sergei told him. "I know the man . . ."

They waited less than a quarter-turn of the glass. Without warning, a half-dozen fireballs bloomed, brilliant even in the sunlight. They rushed over the field, arcing no more than a half-dozen men's height from the ground, streaking from the far trees beyond the roving groups of Firenzcian chevarittai and the impassive lines of infantry. "Téni!" Sergei cried and the pages reached for flags and horns to sound the alarm, but the few war-téni with Sergei had already responded. Their counter-spells, Sergei realized gratefully, were curiously rapid—no doubt the Envoy ci'Vliomani, who along with a hand of Numetodo was with the war-téni, was responsible for that. Given the lack of warning, Sergei had expected the téni's response to be too late, but two of the onrushing suns fizzled and died before they reached the front ranks of the defenders, and two more went careening back toward the far side of the field to explode in front of the enemy ranks.

Cheers went up from the Garde Civile.

But the remaining fire-spells were untouched. They slammed hard into the ranks, exploding with gouts of the liquid fire, and cheers dissolved into screams. Those caught directly died instantly, their bodies torn apart; those nearby were enveloped in blue Ilmodo-fury that clung to their skin and clothes. They bellowed in agony, rolling on the ground, trying to smother the stubborn flames. Those who rushed to help their fellows found that the spell-fire adhered to their own hands. Where the war-fire blazed, the ranks shuddered and threatened to fall apart, the conscripts panicking, and Sergei shouted along with the other offiziers and chevarittai. "Hold!" he cried. "Damn it, make them hold!" The flag-pages waved yellow flags desperately; the horn-pages blasted an imperative two-note call on their cornets and zinkes.

More spell-fire came; again, most were countered and a few thrown back into the enemy, but not all could be stopped. The trees on the west side of the meadow were on fire now, and the panic was beginning to spread along the lines. The offiziers had swords out, keeping their men under control. The cornets of the pages seemed to be lost in the growing noise.

But the lines, tenuously, held together.

Sergei nodded—if the Hïrzg had intended to send him fleeing under the barrage of the war-téni, that plan had failed.

"The Archigos' war-téni deserve commendation," ca'Montmorte said. "Right now, we're holding our own, but if they keep up the barrage, we're going to have to give ground."

"The Hïrzg isn't that patient," Sergei repeated. "That will be the last volley of the war-téni. He'll bring in the chevarittai and the army now."

Again, they did not have to wait long. With a thousand-throated voice, the Firenzcians charged. The hooves of their chevarittai pummeled the ground; behind them, the infantry spread out like a horde of black ants. "Archers!" Sergei shouted: the pages dropped their yellow flags to pick up blue, the cornets shrilled, and the offiziers took up the cry. With a sibilant, wordless steam-kettle hiss, arrows crowded the sky, arcing up and down into the onrushing forces. There were counter-spells from the Firenzcian war-téni—arrows went to harmless ash in great puffs of cloud and arrowheads pattered like metal rain onto the mud—but some of the chevarittai and their horses went down, as did many soldiers. But there were far too many behind them, and more continued to flow out from the trees.

The charge hit the front line in a clash of metal. A frothing chaos spread, the angry foam of a storm-driven wave crashing into unyielding land.

Sergei had to force himself to stay back and not charge into the fray with his sword—the Hïrzg's sword—held high. But it was difficult enough with his healing wounds just to sit his horse, and it was not the commandant's role to fight.

Not yet. Not today. For a turn of the glass, perhaps more, the Nessantico line held, as Sergei directed his offiziers through the scurrying pages and the signals of flags and cornets.

But they couldn't hold forever.

The line sagged inward toward Sergei's position as the meadow filled with Firenzcian black and silver. The war-téni lobbed spells and counter-spells into the field and onto the rear ranks; fire burst in colorful sparks over the field, and the screams of the wounded and dying were muffled in drifting smoke and confusion.

Distantly, Sergei saw a portion of the northern end of the line give way entirely. Firenzcians poured through the gap, the banners of the chevarittai fluttering as they pushed deep into the Nessantico ranks. The flag-pages around Sergei glanced over nervously. He scowled down at the battlefield.

"It's over, Commandant," ca'Montmorte said. "They're through the defenses. We can't hold them here any longer."

Sergei hadn't expected to prevail, but he'd also not expected to be routed so quickly. "I know," he nearly shouted at ca'Montmorte. The angry words tasted like bitter, unripe sunberries in his mouth. "Tell the offiziers to fall back," he grunted, and the pages snatched red flags from the ground and began waving them frantically, the horns changed their call. The cry went up from around the field.

The Nessantico war-téni turned to different spells; now they covered the field with a thick, dense fog to

confuse the inflow of the Firenzcians and cover the retreat. The chevarittai reluctantly turned their mounts;
the foot soldiers gave way and the archers tried to slow
the enemy troops that filled the vacated space.

Faintly, Sergei heard the Firenzcian horns. He'd hoped
that the Hïrzg would let them retreat, so that the Hïrzg
could lick his own wounds and set the army for the final
thrust toward Nessantico. That was the way of polite
warfare: when the outcome of the battle was decided,
the the triumphant side allowed the loser to draw back,
perhaps to exchange prisoners and recover the bodies of
any important ca' or cu' who had fallen.

But the horns across the field weren't sounding halt,
but pursuit.

Ca'Montmorte spat onto the grass. "The bastard . . ."
Sergei shook his head. He pulled on the reins of his
horse.

"Regroup the chevarittai with the Kraljiki's troops
near the Fen Fields," he told ca'Montmorte. "Send a
runner to the Archigos; we'll need all the war-téni to
try to stop them there. Tell the Kraljiki to be ready. The
Hïrzg wants his city today."

Sergei glanced once more at the battlefield wreathed
in spell-fog. He shook his head and kicked at his destrier's sides.

~

Jan ca'Vörl

THE PAGES RUSHED ABOUT, carrying news
from the front lines and relaying orders from
Jan and Starkkapitän ca'Linnett as the attack began.
Well back from the front line and protected, Allesandra was with Jan, as were Archigos ca'Cellibrecca

and Starkkapitän ca'Linnett. From the cover of the trees, they watched as war-fire arced away from the téni toward the defenders of Nessantico. But the sense of destiny and power faded almost immediately. Jan cursed and Archigos ca'Cellibrecca gaped in shock as the spell-fires were countered, as the blazing suns were extinguished or—far, far worse—were sent back toward their own lines. There were cries of alarm from across the field of battle, but the overwhelming terror that Jan had been assured would be the result was lost. "They're using the Numetodo . . ." the Archigos muttered. He made the sign of Cénzi, as if to ward off evil.

Jan was merely furious. "Archigos, I'd remind you that both you and U'Téni cu'Kohnle assured me that our war-téni would send our enemies running back to the city. It seems to me that nothing of the sort has happened, and that, in fact, you've just caused the death of many of our own men."

"The counter-spells came impossibly quickly, my Hïrzg," ca'Cellibrecca answered nervously.

"Impossible, Archigos? I *saw* them. Or are you telling me that I'm mistaken?"

Ca'Cellibrecca bowed his head. "I'm sorry, my Hïrzg. But it's obvious the Kraljiki and the heretic cu'Seranta have made a pact with the Numetodo." Ca'Cellibrecca clenched his hands and made the sign of Cénzi. "They deserve everything Cénzi will bring them. Everything."

Allesandra answered him. "My *vatarh* brings the Kraljiki's fate to him," she said tartly, the emphasis in her statement obvious. Jan's anger didn't fade, but he smiled grimly at his daughter's admonition, as did ca'Linnett.

"We'll deal with this failure later, Archigos," Jan told him. "Numetodo or not, and despite the performance of your war-téni, we *will* prevail here. Starkkapitän, send our troops forward. Let us see how well the Garde Civile fares against true Firenzcian fury."

Ca'Linnett bowed and barked orders: cornets blared,

and with a great cry, the army surged out from the trees, the chevarittai leading the way with banners of black and silver flying.

But the resistance was stiff, far more tactically adroit than Jan had hoped. The flood of pages continued to come over the next turn of the glass, and the news was never what Jan wanted to hear. "That's ca'Rudka," Jan grumbled. "Ca'Montmorte hasn't this kind of flair. The bastard should never have been allowed to escape Passe a'Fiume."

With that, ca'Linnett glanced at Jan uneasily. "They're outnumbered, and your strategy has them spread along too long a line to defend well," the starkkapitän insisted. "We have more war-téni and more chevarittai. They won't be able to hold for much longer, my Hïrzg."

Jan raised his eyebrows. "They'd better not, Stark-kapitän," he said. "For your sake." At his side, Allesan-dra giggled at the face ca'Linnett made.

Jan prowled the tree line restlessly, glaring across the field, his hand on his sword. He ached to be out there, even if he knew it was not his place. The adrenaline of battle sang in his ears, and he could not stay still. Allesan-dra watched him as he paced, her gaze always on him.

But the starkkapitän proved to be prophetic. One of the pages came riding up, breathlessly, a grin on his stained face. "Their line's broken, my Hïrzg," he shouted. "We are behind them now." Even as the boy spoke, Jan heard Nessantico's horns on the far side of the meadow calling retreat and saw a spell-fog rise near the trees on the other side of the clearing.

"Excellent," Starkkapitän ca'Linnett nodded to the page. The relief was obvious on his face. "It was only a matter of persistence. Tell the offiziers to let them run. Have the horns call 'Halt' and . . ."

"No," Jan interrupted, striding up to them. "We pursue."

Jan watched ca'Linnett struggle not to let relief turn to irritation. Ca'Cellibrecca simply blustered. "My Hïrzg,"

ca'Cellibrecca said, "it's well past Second Call already
and this is an excellent location to consolidate our
forces. We should plan our final assault. We shouldn't be
reckless . . ."

"Reckless?" Jan interrupted, and ca'Cellibrecca's
mouth closed as if a fist had struck his lower jaw.
"Allesandra deserves her crown of lights tonight. We
will pursue." He tousled the girl's hair, and she smiled
up at him. "Starkkapitän ca'Linnett? I trust you have
confidence in the strength of our forces and your ability
to lead them, even if our Archigos does not?"

Cu'Linnett bowed low to Jan, hiding whatever expression might have crossed his face. "The Hïrzg has given
his orders," he told the page. "Send word to the offiziers
and have the horns call 'Pursuit.' "

Jan watched the page, his face serious and drawn,
ride away. He hugged Allesandra as the horns began to
blare. She beamed up at him. "We'll rest tonight inside
the walls of Nessantico," he told her.

~

Justi ca'Mazzak

THE COURTIERS, the sycophants, the chevarittai, the ca'-and-cu': they gathered about Justi. He
was surrounded by them while they cooed support and
encouragement. He swaddled himself in their comfort,
even though he glimpsed the uncertainty on their faces
when they thought he wasn't watching.

The pages had returned from the battlefields at three
separate points around the city; the word was not good
anywhere: the northern arm had been entirely routed and
the Firenzcian forces were nearing the sections of the city
outside the walls; the news was little better in the south,

though the fens and marshes along the river worked as their ally there. But there was one ray of hope: in the center, Commandant ca'Rudka had kept his men in order and was still holding back the main enemy force. It seemed that the Firenzcians could not break through him.

"Kraljiki," the courtiers crooned, "everyone knew that it would not be a swift battle, and the closer to Nessantico the Hïrzg comes, the less room he will have to maneuver and the more our resistance will stiffen. The commandant is already demonstrating this. Hïrzg ca'Vörl *can't* take the city, not while your arm holds your sword . . ."

If Justi noticed that the words were spiced with desperation, as if they were trying to convince themselves as much as him, he pretended not to notice. Instead, he nodded knowingly and gazed fiercely out from the wall at the Avi a'Firenzcia. Behind him, Nessantico seemed oddly quiet and deserted; ahead, the road and the fields beyond the last houses of the city swarmed with soldiers in blue and gold.

In their thousands, a bulwark against the Hïrzg, they comforted him.

"You have never been defeated, Kraljiki," Bella ca'Nephri said loudly, and the ca'-and-cu' murmured their agreement, all the chevarittai who had been his friends and cronies for decades now. "You *will* never be defeated."

But when I went to war, it was the Hïrzg's army I had behind me. I never rode against a force that was the equal of ours, and I had Firenzcian-trained offiziers directing the Garde Civile, and Firenzcian troops swelling the infantry, and Firenzcian war-téni . . . .

He closed his mind to the doubts. He frowned more fiercely and gripped the pommel of his sword more tightly. "We will never be defeated," he agreed. "Where is the Archigos?" he asked Renard, as always near his side. "I thought she would be here with me."

"She told me to inform you that she has moved forward with the remaining war-téni and the Numetodo, Kraljiki," Renard told him.

Justi frowned. "She did that without . . ." he began, but there was a disturbance near the gate, the ranks of the Garde Civile parting to let a rider through: a page, the boy covered in dust and his horse lathered with sweat. He half-fell from the horse and staggered over to Justi, dropping to his knees before him. "Kraljiki," he panted. "The commandant . . . Could not stop the Firenzcians . . . Falling back to the Fen Fields . . . Garde Civile must come . . . And the rest of the chevarittai . . ."

Justi stared at the boy. The whispers were already spreading through the crowd, racing back into the city. Ca'Nephri and the other ca'-and-cu' watched Justi, the masks momentarily struck from their faces. He could almost hear their thoughts. They were prepared to tell him whatever he wanted to hear, and they would be equally prepared to say whatever the Hïrzg might want to hear, should he take the Sun Throne from Justi.

There was less loyalty in them than in the palais dogs.

As long as they thought Justi would remain Kraljiki, they would do as he asked. But if they believed he were about to fall, they would be on him, snarling and vicious . . .

If you go out now, at least they will remember. At least they will say, "He died bravely."

Justi chuckled at the boy, as if his reports were amusing. "Renard, please give this boy some refreshment. He's had a hard ride and he's done his task well. It seems I will have to go rescue our commandant."

The sycophants laughed with him, their amusement edged with nervousness.

Justi drew his sword, and the crowd cheered. "We ride forward" he cried, "and we will show the Hïrzg what happens when he rouses the ire of Nessantico."

Their cheers rose as he urged his destrier forward,

and the chevarittai closed around him and the troops of the Garde Civile surged through the gates of Nessantico to the sound of blaring horns.

They cheered, and Justi showed them a stern face, and he wondered whether he would ever ride through these gates again.

~

Ana ca'Seranta

ANA HAD SENT the dozen or so most effective war-téni ahead with Commandant ca'Rudka and Karl. The others . . . she wasn't as certain about any of them—in more than one way.

The training with the Numetodo had been at best erratic. Ana found that she couldn't blame the war-téni, given the way she'd reacted to seeing the Numetodo spell-magic. Many of them had resisted the training, they'd scoffed and hesitated and argued with Karl, Mika, and the other Numetodo who tried to show them ways to speed their spells or to store them for future use. Several, like Ana, had found their faith tested enough that they'd become less rather than more effective.

Worse, she wondered whether when the time came— and she knew it would come—that ca'Cellibrecca called on them to obey him as Archigos rather than Ana, whether they would stay loyal to her at all.

But . . . a handful had taken to the training with enthusiasm. And many of the Numetodo had set aside their suspicions and recent history and pledged their support to Nessantico. "The better of two ills," Karl had said to her when he brought the news. "We know well how ca'Cellibrecca would treat us."

Is this what you want, Cénzi? Do You truly want me to

*defend a man who killed his own matarh and who would
sacrifice me without a thought if he believed it would
save him? Someone who used me in the same way Vatarh
used me? I know ca'Cellibrecca and the Hïrzg are no better and perhaps worse, but I could flee instead. I could
run away with Karl, perhaps to his home or beyond into
Mahri's Westlands. Are You truly asking me to die here?
Are You saying that I must be willing to shed Your blood
and the blood of the téni who follow You for this? Is this
is Your will? Is this why You brought me here? Please, I
beg You, tell me. . . .*

"Archigos!" Kenne's voice broke in on her prayer.
Ana, her head bowed and hands folded before her,
brought her head up. "Look!"

Perhaps a half mile beyond the old gates of the city, the
Avi a'Firenzcia made a turn eastward. Several buildings,
the outliers of the city, were set there, with fields around
them and the River Vaghian murmuring behind. The
fields had, only a century before, been a low mosquito-
infested swampland, frequently flooded when the rain-
swollen Vaghian left its bed. But during the Kraljica's
reign, the Vaghian had been tamed with mounds of
earthern banks, and the fens converted to farmland.

Ana had commandeered the second-story balcony of
an inn there, at the curve of the road. From her vantage
point, she could see out to where Kenne was pointing.
The fields, like all the farmland to the east of the city, had
been stripped and harvested early. The meadows were
now muddy encampments. At the eastern edge of the
camp, soldiers in the colors of Nessantico were pouring
from a small woods bordering the fields, and she could
hear distance-blurred shouting.

"The commandant's outer line must have broken,"
Kenne said, and Ana felt a stab of fear run through her
for Karl. "They're retreating. Yes, look, there are the chevarittai, and that's the commandant's personal banner."

Ana had already turned. Her hand brushed the hard,
heavy bulk of the glass ball Mahri had given her, in its

leather pouch tucked in a pocket of her green robes, and she felt the tingling of the power within it through the cloth. "Gather the war-téni," she said to Kenne. "We're going to them . . ."

The ride through the Nessantican troops seemed to take a turn of the glass, though she knew it was far less. The agitation was spreading through the gathered army: the conscripts and soldiers of the Garde Civile grabbed armor and weapons nervously, the offiziers were shouting and assembling them. Pages were rushing about, and cornets and zinkes were sounding their calls.

When they reached the banner of the commandant, the chaos was more ordered but no less frantic. "Archigos," ca'Rudka said, his voice almost sounding relieved. "I'm glad you're here. We need more war-téni. If you'll direct them—the téni banners are over there—you, Page, direct the Archigos."

"The envoy?" she asked, almost afraid to voice the question.

Ca'Rudka nodded indulgently even in the midst of the rush. "He's fine," he told her. "And he's amply demonstrated his worth. Go to the war-téni and you'll find him. I'll send word as to what we need you to do. Hurry, Archigos. There isn't much time. Check on the war-téni for me, then come back here. I need to meet with the a'offiziers."

She gave him the sign of Cénzi and followed the page south toward the Avi a'Firenczia, just behind the newly-coalescing lines. Among the trees and along the road, she could hear the sound of cornets and the call of offiziers with strange accents—the Firenzcians. A low rumble seemed to shake the earth.

She saw him. "Karl!" He turned. His face was streaked with soot and dirt, his clothes were filthy, and he looked exhausted. The war-téni with him looked no different. "I've brought the rest of the war-téni. You can rest, recover your strength."

He shook his head. "No time," he said. "They're on our

heels. Put them in position, but they have so many . . ."
He shrugged. "War-spells won't be enough."

"Then we must do something different," she told him.

~

Orlandi ca'Cellibrecca

"YOU WEREN'T THERE with us, Archigos,"
U'Téni cu'Kohnle said, the scorn far too obvious in his voice. They were riding quickly along the Avi a'Firenzcia just behind the Hïrzg's retinue, with the army an ocean around them, grim-faced. "I tell you that my war-téni did all we could, and more. There should have been no time for response to our first volley of spells, Archigos—no time. But they *did* respond, and it was strong. This false Archigos and her war-téni are using the Numetodo. It has to be. It's a shame, Archigos, that the Numetodo blight was not removed entirely in Nessantico, as the Hïrzg suggested to you."

Orlandi grimaced with the unsubtle rebuke, as much from the pounding his rear end was taking despite the cushioned seat of his carriage as from cu'Kohnle's words. "The false Archigos will be dealt with," he told cu'Kohnle, "as will the Numetodo: once I am seated back on the Archigos' Temple throne. I assure you of that, U'Téni."

He didn't care for the man's attitude, or the fact that cu'Kohnle seemed to consider himself a peer, or worse, a superior. *I don't take my orders from you, Archigos.* That's what the man's expression seemed to say—that, and the impatience with which he twitched at his horse's reins, ready to ride forward to the Hïrzg, as if talking to Orlandi was a waste of his time. More worrisome was that the Hïrzg seemed to admire the man; certainly Orlandi's suggestion that the Archigos rather than cu'Kohnle should direct the war-téni had met a stony refusal from the Hïrzg.

"U'Téni cu'Kohnle has served me very well thus far, and he understands both my tactics and my army. You don't,'Archigos."

Orlandi was beginning to fear that the only reason the Hïrzg was dragging him along was because of the title he held.

Well, he would show the Hïrzg once he was back on the throne. He would demonstrate to the man that Concénzia was separate from Nessantico and the Holdings, that *he* ruled Concénzia and not the Kraljiki. The Numetodo would be hanging from the bridges, as thick as pigeons, with the false Archigos among them. And U'Téni cu'Kohnle, with his arrogance, might just find himself serving in the Hellins. "*Phah* on the Numetodo," Orlandi told the man, spitting over the side of his carriage. "Our war-téni are stronger. *We* have Cénzi on our side."

Cu'Kohnle gave the sign of Cénzi at the mention of His name, but his long nose wrinkled at the same time. "My war-téni are half exhausted, Archigos. And we will be entirely so before the day is done, it seems. I get no rest bandying words here. You asked for my report; I've given it to you. Now I need to consult with the Hïrzg so he can direct the battle. With your leave, Archigos."

"A moment yet, U'Téni . . ." Orlandi began, but cu'Kohnle didn't wait or listen. He kicked his horse into a gallop, hooves tearing clods from the ruts of the Avi that splattered against the sides of his carriage and tossed muddy droplets on Orlandi's sleeve and shoulder.

The téni-driver of the carriage chanted, perhaps a bit too loudly. The e'téni walking along the road beside the carriage looked carefully down at the ground. Orlandi wiped at his soiled robes.

Orlandi sank back into his seat as the carriage jolted over a pothole in the Avi. Through a gap in the trees, he thought he could glimpse the roofs of the taller buildings on the North Bank. He began to imagine his revenge on everything and everyone who had put him in this position.

That revenge, in his imagination, was pleasantly slow, detailed and creative.

~

Sergei ca'Rudka

THE A'OFFIZIERS OF THE Garde Civile were huddled around Sergei. A broken door laid across two boulders served as a table, and a map was spread out on the raw, splintered wood. Sergei gave hurried orders. "Cu'Simone, I need you to take the river fields—keep them from following the A'Sele into the city. Cu'Baria, you will take your men north; the Hïrzg may try to send a few battalions around our main force; if that happens, hold them as well as you can and send a page for reinforcements. Cu'Helfier and cu'Malachi; you will spread out on either side of the Avi. Ahh, Archigos—you're back already? Good. Here's what I want you to do—put your war-téni in position with A'Offizier cu'Helfier's battalion; that's where we're expecting the main thrust to come. Envoy ci'Vliomani and his war-téni will be with A'Offizier cu'Malachi, though I suspect they're nearly exhausted from the first attack—is that the case, Archigos?"

"It is," the woman answered. "They won't be able to hold back many war-spells, Commandant, and those with me . . ." She shook her head. "I don't know how effective they'll be, either."

"They'd better be damned effective," Sergei told her. "We have no choice. If they don't, their war-téni will de-

stroy our lines before we ever have a chance to draw
swords again. They will overrun us."

"I understand," she told him. She pointed at the map.
"Where are you placing your main defenses, and where
would you expect their war-téni to be?"

"Here, and here," Sergei said, pointing. "Which is why
I want your war-téni with cu'Helfier."

But the Archigos was shaking her head. "No," she
said. "Hold the battalions back—here." She pointed farther west along the Avi, much closer to Nessantico. "And
the chevarittai, if they could be close to this bend in the
Avi . . ."

Sergei could not stop the laugh; his a'offiziers
chuckled also. If the battalions were placed where the
Archigos suggested, the Firenzcian army would own
the Fen Fields, and shortly thereafter, the gates of·
Nessantico. "With all due respect, Archigos," he said,
interrupting her, "you've no experience in battle or
with tactics, and you show it."

"With all due respect," she answered him, "you would
not be here at all, Commandant, with all your grand
experience, if I had not healed you. I would think you·
might give me the courtesy of hearing me out without
interruption, in gratitude."

She glared defiantly at him, and he sighed. "Quickly,
then," he said. "We haven't much time. And whatever
we do, it will be *my* decision."

"Agreed," she said. "Commandant, the Hïrzg has
more war-téni than we do, and they're better skilled in
their arts than those I have been able to muster. Would
you agree with that assessment?"

He shrugged. "Envoy ci'Vliomani did surprisingly
well," he said. "I wouldn't have believed it if I hadn't
seen it with my own eyes. But, yes, I agree."

"Then, as you've already suggested, we lose this battle
if we fight them as they expect."

"What else do you suggest, Archigos?" It was difficult
for Sergei to keep the condescension from his voice.

"Their war-téni have already used much of their strength in the first attack, and in that way they're no better than any other téni—if they use the Ilmodo, they will become exhausted. So I suggest we *let* them use their spells . . . but not on us."

Sergei's eyes narrowed, causing the skin to wrinkle around his false nose. A suspicion began to take shape in his mind. "And how do you suggest we can accomplish that?" he asked.

The Archigos shrugged. "You've already said it, Commandant: you believe what you see with your own eyes."

~

Jan ca'Vörl

THE HORNS SOUNDED "Halt," and a page came riding wildly down the line to Jan's carriage. "The Garde Civile holds the road and the fields ahead," the page said. "They're drawn up in battle formation, at least three full battalions."

"This far from the walls?" Jan said. "If I were the commandant, I would have taken them closer to the city. But . . ." He shrugged. "U'Téni cu'Kohnle! You'll ride forward with the starkkapitän and me to see this."

"My Hïrzg," ca'Cellibrecca called from his carriage behind Jan's. "I will go with you."

Ca'Cellibrecca was already struggling to rise from his seat, and Jan heard cu'Kohnle sigh. He nearly sighed with him. Jan waved at ca'Cellibrecca to remain. "Stay here, Archigos," Jan ordered. "You can . . . pray for the outcome of the battle."

"Vatarh, may I come also?" Allesandra asked. "I'd also like to see. How else can I learn, now that Georgi's gone?"

He nodded indulgently, stroking her hair. "Bring our horses forward," he called to his attendants. "We'll ride without banners."

The sun was heavily westering and the weather had deteriorated, with storm clouds gathering behind Nessantico. The light was dim, and an odd fog clung close to the ground—the Fen Fields were reputed to be haunted and fogs were common here, though generally not in the afternoon. They rode up a small rise toward the front of the Firenzcian column and paused to look down.

The line had halted at a bend in the Avi. There, beyond the long curve, was a field where thick lines of men in blue-and-gold livery waited. Spears hedged their ranks, and the banners of chevarittai fluttered just behind them, moving along the lines as if the chevarittai were impatient for the battle to start, ready to burst through. "There are more of them than before," Jan said. "The Kraljiki has emptied the city of troops. Good. That will make things easier. Semini, how are your war-téni?"

"Tired from the last attack, my Hïrzg, but we're ready," the u'téni answered. A small smile curled his lips under his beard. "Those Numetodo-tainted fools will be rather more exhausted than us, I would think."

Jan chuckled. "Starkkapitän?"

"Their troops are badly positioned, my Hïrzg," ca'Linnett said. "It's difficult to tell in this damned fog, but I don't think the lines are deep. They're too far out from the trees and the river will hem them in farther. Let the war-téni and archers take as many as they can, and concentrate on the middle of the line along the Avi. I'll loose the chevarittai there." He pointed north of the Avi, where the trees grew thickest. "They can move them into position while the war-téni attack. Then we'll drive our infantry straight at where we've weakened them—down the Avi—while the Red Lancers take the wing. Drive hard enough and fast enough, and we might still make the city gates before sunset. If ca'Rudka or the Kraljiki have any sense at all, they won't try to hold the entire North Bank of the city; they'll pull back near the ponticas."

"Allesandra?" he asked his daughter, seated in front of him. She tilted her head back to look up at him.

"Can I watch from here, Vatarh, where I can see it all?"

He tousled her curls. "We both will," he told her. "Starkkapitän, I leave it to you. Send my attendants and pages to me. U'Téni cu'Kohnle, you may start the attack when your war-téni are ready."

Ca'Linnett and cu'Kohnle bowed low and rushed away. Calls went out along the lines, horns blared and flags waved, and the Firenzcian line spread out slowly to either side of the road. Half a turn of the glass later, they heard the boom and thunder of fire-spells arcing out from just behind the front of the line, followed by the hissing of flights of arrows. The sputtering, roaring glares—a full dozen of them—traced smoky lines over the intervening yards between the armies. Jan watched them, waiting to see if the defensive spells of the Nessantico war-téni would take some of them, but they continued on without resistance, and the men shouted in triumph as the fireballs crashed into the opposing lines, tearing great holes through them. They could hear shrieks of alarm and pain, but except where the fireballs crashed into them, the Nessantico lines held.

"Vatarh?"

The war-téni loosed another barrage, larger than the first, and these also streamed unchallenged across the field to plow into the ranks on the other side. More men fell. The screams redoubled, but other men in yellow and blue slid into the gap. Jan frowned; the opposing war-téni might have been sapped, but he doubted that they had *no* ability left to counter the spells. Why were they waiting, when their people were dying? This was slaughter, not battle. He wondered how they could possibly hold . . .

"Vatarh!"

As a third volley of fire-spells sizzled across the land-

scape, Jan glanced down at Allesandra. "What, little
bird?"

"*Look* at them, Vatarh," she said. "Really *look* at them.
The ones next to where our spell-fire strikes; they're not
moving. Not at all."

As the next wave of destructive suns raced over the
field, he did watch—not to where they struck but to the
side. It was difficult to see through the smoke and fog,
through the gathering dark under thickening clouds,
but he saw that Allesandra was right. There was an un-
natural stiffness to the soldiers alongside the blasts of
the war-téni. They didn't flinch, didn't cower, didn't run.
They stood upright, always looking forward, their heads
not turning at all as their companions were consumed
in fire.

The spell-fire ripped through them as if they were
stones thrown through a painted canvas.

"We've been deceived . . ." he breathed, but it was already too late. The ranks of enemy Garde Civile shredded away entirely, like smoke driven by a gale. Fire-spells
came now from the Numetodo: not from the ghostly ranks
before them, but from the southern flank, fire-spells rak-
ing the Firenzcian lines. Not far distant came the clashing
of arms and the pounding of hooves, and Jan saw the Nessantico chevarittai leading a charge, soldiers in yellow and
blue pouring in from the river side of the Avi. "There!"
he shouted to his aides, pointing. "Sound the horns!
Quickly!"

As the horns began to shriek, as the battle clamor rose
below him, he set Allesandra down from his horse. "Go
back to the Archigos," he told her. "Hurry! You, Page,
take her!"

He drew sword then, without looking back, and kicked
his destrier into motion.

~

Karl ci'Vliomani

KARL FELT ANA shivering with the effort and exhaustion. "Let it go," he told her. "You can let it go now . . ." With a gasp and cry, Ana collapsed into his arms. He held her tightly. Around her, the ground was littered with the prone bodies of men and women in green robes—those who had helped her, who had taken the Ilmodo and fed it to her to create the illusion she'd woven.

He'd seen nothing like this, ever before. He hadn't even realized it was possible. He suspected Ana hadn't either.

"Now," Karl called to the remaining war-téni. "Start the attack!"

He heard the quick chanting, and false suns bloomed above them to go shrieking off toward the Firenzcians. Around them, the Garde Civile gave a whooping cry and surged forward. A knot of chevarittai pounded up the Avi on their destriers, calling out a challenge to the Firenzcian chevarittai. As the hiss and boom of war-fire subsided, the clamor of steel on steel began to rise.

"Karl?" Ana whispered. Her eyes were closed. "Did it work?"

"It did," he told her. "I don't know how, but it worked."

"Good . . ." The word was mostly a sigh. "I need to sleep . . ."

"Sleep, then. You deserve it." He brushed the hair back from her head and kissed her forehead, laying her down on the ground. Another flurry of war-fire erupted above them to go shrieking off toward the Firenzcian line, lighting the meadow in a furious yellow glare, but it would be the last, he saw: both the war-téni and the Numetodo were exhausted. They would all need time to recover; the battle would be decided by steel now, not spells.

Karl motioned to Kenne. "Take care of your Archigos," he said. "I need to go to the commandant."

He brushed Ana's cheek a last time and swung up on the horse that one of the e'téni was holding. As he rode away, he thought of what he'd seen, still marveling.

"I need all of you to do the Opening chant," Ana had said, gathering several of the e' and o'téni from the Archigos' Temple around her while the war-téni and Karl's fellow Numetodo watched. *"Just as you were all taught in your first lessons: open yourself to the Ilmodo but don't shape it. That's all you need to do. Now!"*

They'd done as she asked, as Ana chanted herself. Karl could feel the power rising around them. He thought he could almost see it, like a mist caught in the side of his gaze that vanished if he tried to look directly at it.

Several of the téni cried out as Ana continued to chant, as she gathered the power they'd opened to herself. "No!" she called to them. "Leave the Ilmodo open. Let me take it from you . . ."

And she did. Already, they could see the illusion forming out in the fields and across the Avi in front of them: ghostly men in the garb of the Garde Civile, wreathed in fog and mist that the freshening wind didn't touch, facing out toward where the Firenzcian army would appear. They stood there: motionless, waiting.

He could see Ana: her hands and lips moving as she controlled the spell she wove, the words lost in the cry of surprise that rose from all those around. Sergei, watching, had laughed. "The Archigos has done her part," he called to the offiziers and the chevarittai. "Now, let's do ours . . ." Calling out orders, he had ridden away.

Ana had continued to chant, and the ghost soldiers so-

lidified and became more numerous as she continued to pull the energy from the other téni. It was marvelous to watch. It nearly made him want to believe as she did, if faith in Cénzi could lend her this much power.

For the first time, Karl had dared to think that this would work. . . .

A shrill of bright horns brought him out of his reverie. He could see the banner of the commandant ahead of him in the press of men, but the cornets were sounding from *behind* him, and they were blaring the call of the Kraljiki.

Justi, unannounced and unasked for, had entered the field.

~

Justi ca'Mazzak

"KRALJIKI!" ca'Rudka bowed perfunctorily to him. "I thought you intended to remain in the city." Justi thought he saw irritation in the man's scarred face, in the way his skin folded around the silver nose glued to his skin. Justi saw the Numetodo envoy standing next to ca'Rudka along with A'Offizier ca'Montmorte. The Archigos was nowhere visible, and he wondered where she was.

"The battle is here," Justi said to the commandant, "and I intend to fight this time. Word came to me that you were retreating. I will *not* have us retreat, Commandant."

"I fell back at need, Kraljiki," ca'Rudka answered, making no pretense to hide his scowl now. "But we've turned again."

"Then we waste our time here, Commandant. I have brought the chevarittai with me, and they are ready."

The riders with him shouted agreement, their horses stamping impatiently.

"Kraljiki, you should remain here, so that we can place your men where they will do the most good. The pages will bring us news."

"News?" Justi howled. "You'd have me wait here like a doddering matron? I sent you forward to stop the Hïrzg; you have not. Now I will do it myself."

"Kraljiki . . ."

"No!" Justi shouted. The man denied him his moment, and he would not have that. *Better to die on the battle-field than in the Bastida. Better to die as Kraljiki than as a prisoner.* "You can remain here if you wish, Commandant, but I go forward to lead my men in defense of their city. I listened to you at Passe a'Fiume, and you gave up that city quickly. If you have courage, then join me; otherwise, stay here. Who is in command here?"

"You are, Kraljiki," the commandant said. At the mention of Passe a'Fiume, his face had gone ruddy, and a scowl had twisted the mouth under the silver nose. Justi saw ca'Rudka glance at the ca'Montmorte, at the Numetodo, at the offiziers and pages around them. "Bring my horse," the commandant said. "We ride with the Kraljiki."

Justi nodded, grim-faced. He drew his sword and gestured up the Avi, to where the sound of battle was loudest. "Ride, then!" he cried. "Ride!"

They pounded away, the chevarittai around him, the banner of the Kraljiki snapping angrily in the wind, not waiting for the commandant and the others. The Garde Civile shouted encouragement as they galloped past their ranks, and their cheers drove Justi forward harder. Ahead, he could see the melee of the spreading front line, and he and the chevarittai plunged into it, breaking the line of infantry and plowing through into the ranks beyond.

The fury of battle banished any other thoughts.

Justi hacked at a spear thrust toward him, hewing off

the hand that held the weapon, and the man's lifeblood spurted out as he screamed and fell under the hooves of Justi's horse. Justi began to strike blindly, at anything that moved wearing silver and black. Around him, his chevarittai tore through the Firenzcians like a plow through earth, blood and death in their trail. They were deep behind the lines now, and the Firenzcian cheva-rittai had noticed the banner of the Kraljiki and were pushing toward them. "Kraljiki!" Justi heard Sergei shout from behind him. "You're too isolated here! We must fall back to our own line!"

"No!" Justi shouted over his shoulder. "I will not be called a coward!"

He struck at the nearest man, heard a howl as glittering red spattered his sword arm. He pushed forward. He heard the challenge of the enemy chevarittai, and he shouted back at them defiantly.

They came.

Justi managed to take down the first chevaritt who reached him—a man whose face was vaguely familiar, a ca' who had perhaps once been at the court or to whom Justi had been introduced on one of his sojourns to Brezno. He didn't know the man's name, only knew that his own sword was growing heavier even as their blades met and he thrust hard into the space between helm and chestplate, finding flesh above the collar of the man's surcoat. Justi tried to pull his sword back as gore splashed over the surcoat's embroidered crest, but his blade was snagged on bone or armor. There was no time to think; another chevaritt was on him and he could not defend himself. He let go of the sword (the cheva-ritt tumbling from his saddle) and brought up a hopeless arm, hoping the steel of the vambrace could deflect the blow . . . but ca'Rudka's horse slammed hard into Justi's attacker, the commandant's sword slicing through the Firenzcian's hauberk. The chevaritt slid to the ground under their destriers with a scream.

"Kraljiki—" Sergei started to say, but there was no

time. They were caught, snared in the press of foot soldiers and chevarittai. The young chevaritt holding Justi's banner was down. To his left, Justi saw ca'Montmorte borne under, skewered on a spear, his surcoat and hauberk feathered with arrows. Near ca'Montmorte, the Numetodo ci'Vliomani gestured and fire exploded, but his war-fire was pale and ineffective. Everything was chaos: screaming and shouting and movement. Pain lanced Justi's right leg and he cried out in shock, glancing down to see his greave rent and blood streaming from the gash in the metal. Hands clutching at him, threatening to pull him down.

Justi knew that he was about to be captured, if not slain outright. If either happened, this war was over. Any parley for his release would include his abdication. He struck at the hands with a dagger pulled from his belt, kicking at his destier's side. But the destrier was hemmed in and though he saw Sergei still fighting desperately at his side, they were surrounded now in a sea of black and silver.

Justi screamed in fury.

~

Karl ci'Vliomani

HE HAD NOTHING LEFT. The spells he had prepared so carefully before the battle were gone, and it would take too long and he was far too exhausted to call up new ones. His arm was already exhausted from using his sword—and swordplay was hardly his strength, in any case.

He wondered what death was going to feel like. He wondered—briefly—what he might say to Cénzi if He were there in the afterlife.

He heard the Kraljiki scream and saw the man surrounded, about to be borne down.

But the earth answered the Kraljiki's scream.

The ground erupted as if some demon of the Moitidi had risen from the depths: an explosion of mud and trampled wheat tossed away from them anyone in black and silver, though it left the Kraljiki, the commandant, and the remaining chevarittai of Nessantico untouched.

And Karl.

For a moment, there was silence.

That was a spell. Ana? Where did she find the strength?

Karl saw the commandant grab for the reins of the Kraljiki's horse; the Kraljiki himself swayed in the saddle, clutching at his leg. "Retreat!" ca'Rudka shouted to the others. "Retreat while we have the chance!"

Ca'Rudka yanked at the reins of the Kraljiki's mount. Karl kicked his own horse into movement, dropping the useless sword to better hold the reins. They galloped back toward the Nessantico lines through the tumbled bodies.

Black and silver merged into blue and gold: they were through and behind the lines as the sounds of battle arose anew behind them. "We need a healer!" Sergei shouted to a page as they halted. The commandant was helping the Kraljiki down from his saddle; Sergei slid from his own horse to aid him, but the commandant nearly fell himself with his own wounded leg. The Kraljiki was moaning and fighting their hands; Sergei saw blood pulsing from the wound in the man's thigh. He and ca'Rudka looked at each other as they lay the Kraljiki on the grass and mud. Sergei was already stripping off his coverlet, ripping the cloth and stuffing it into the wound. "Get his greave off so we can bind the wound," he said to Karl. "Quickly."

Karl cut the straps of the plate mail with his dagger and pulled it free of the torn links of the mail leggings underneath. More blood gushed over his hands. The

spear, he saw, had come in at the top of the plate and
pierced deep into the muscle. He glimpsed white bone
before Sergei packed the wound and bound another
strip above the gash. The flow of blood slowly subsided,
though the Kraljiki's face was pale and he'd lapsed into
unconsciousness.

"He may lose that leg, if not his life," the commandant
said to Karl as the healer arrived, and ca'Rudka stood
up, watching as the healer fussed over Justi. "This was
so unnecessary. The Archigos, though, she might be able
to help."

Karl shook his head. "Ana has no strength left. The
Kraljiki is in the hands of the healers for now."

A nod. The commandant was looking back, toward
the line of battle. The gloom of twilight was beginning
to deepen, aided by the dark fan of a storm front. A few
large drops of rain were beginning to fall and the wind
had picked up. "We've done all we can do," the commandant said, glancing up. "The city is safe for another
day, at least." He gestured to a nearby page. "Find the
horns. Have them call 'Disengage.' Tell the a'offiziers to
fall back toward the city. I doubt the Hïrzg will follow
this time."

He looked down again at the Kraljiki. Karl watched
him shake his head.

~

Jan ca'Vörl

"THEY'RE PULLING BACK all along the line,"
ca'Linnett said to Jan. The starkkapitän's face,
like Jan's own, was spattered with mud and blood
smeared by the driving rain, and the edge of his sword

was badly nicked. "If we press, they will turn and fight; if we allow them, they'll retreat."

Jan grunted. He wiped at sodden eyes. He was surprised that the rain did not hiss like water dropped on heated steel as it struck him, the anger burned in him so hot.

The carriages had come forward as the line of battle had pushed on toward the city. Allesandra, wrapped in an oilcloth against the wet, was at his side again, looking up at him as ca'Linnett gave his report. U'Téni cu'Kohnle stood by ca'Linnett, his hair plastered to his skull and dripping with the rain; he looked as if he'd not slept in a week, drained by the efforts of his spells. Ca'Cellibrecca was present as well—unsoiled, untouched, protected from the rain by a large umbrella held by an e'téni, yet somehow managing to look as if he'd suffered worst of all.

This was not a victory. At best this was a draw. Jan stared at the men in black and silver lying unmoving in the field as the rain pummeled them. This was a defeat. He knew it. The Numetodo illusion had wasted their war-téni's efforts, and they'd been unable to counter the war-fire that had been sent after them. The Garde Civile had fought like madmen rather than halfhearted conscripts, and the chevarittai of Nessantico had shown their worth. Jan had felt some hope when he'd glimpsed the Kraljiki's foolish advance beyond his own lines, but another unusual spell—was it the Numetodo again, or the false Archigos?—had saved the idiot.

Now darkness threatened and the rain poured down on them.

"Pursue," he said, furious. "I don't care. I will rest tonight inside the walls.

"Hïrzg," ca'Linnett persisted, "they're not fleeing in panic. Their retreat is orderly and slow, and they *will* fight all the way back if we press them, on ground they know better than we do. Who knows what these Numetodo can still do? Our war-téni need to rest, and we could use the time to prepare our siege engines."

Jan was shaking his head at the argument. "Hïrzg," cu'Kohnle broke in, "the starkkapitän is right. My war-téni are exhausted; we have nothing left. Give us the night, though, and we'll be ready for a final assault in the morning."

"Are you not *listening* to me?" Jan spat at them. "I want this city. I will have it. If you won't help me take it, then I will find offiziers and téni who will." He glared at them, and was gratified when both ca'Linnett and cu'Kohnle bowed their heads. Ca'Cellibrecca, in his ornate robes under the umbrella, was looking away, as if fascinated by the Avi behind them.

"Vatarh." Allesandra tugged at his cloak. He glanced down at her serious face, blinking against the raindrops pelting them. "The starkkapitän and the u'téni are right. They'll do as you tell them to do because they respect you, but they're right. I know you want the city, and I know you'll give it to me as you promised. But not tonight, Vatarh. Tomorrow." She smiled at him, and the fury inside him cooled somewhat. "Or even the next day," she said. "It doesn't matter. The Firenzcian army is strong, and you are their leader. You will take the city, but it doesn't need to be *this* day."

"I promised you, Allesandra," Jan said. With his forefinger, he brushed dampened curls back from her cheeks.

"I can wait, Vatarh," she answered. "I can wear the lights of the city for the rest of my life. Another day won't matter. I can wait."

He took a breath. Thunder grumbled overhead, but the rain was lessening, and the lightning was flickering east of them, toward Firenzcia.

"We'll make camp here," he said. "U'Téni cu'Kohnle, make certain that the war-téni sleep and are ready for tomorrow. Starkkapitän, you'll prepare your offiziers and troops for the final assault, and I will meet with both of you later this evening. We'll move at first light tomorrow."

He hugged Allesandra to him. "And you shall have your jeweled city tomorrow," he told her.

~

Mahri

ANA WAS DOZING in her chair, but she must have sensed his presence. Her eyes fluttered open. If she was surprised to see him standing in her apartments near the Archigos' Temple, she didn't show it.

"You don't agree to my advice?" he asked her, chiding her gently. "You won't use the gift I gave you?"

He saw Ana touch her robe at her right side. He could see how the cloth rounded there over the enchanted glass he'd given her. She said nothing. "I heard the gossip in the city, Archigos. They say that you saved the Kraljiki's life with a spell," he continued.

"It wasn't me," she said. "I don't know . . ." Then her eyes widened a bit.

"Yes," he told her. "I shouldn't have interfered, but if I hadn't, my gift to you would have been wasted."

She stirred, sitting up in the chair in which she'd fallen asleep. Her hand brought out the ball. He could see the glowing colors within it; he could feel the power he'd placed within the glass for her. "Here, then," she said. "I give it back to you. Use it yourself if you're so certain."

"I can't." He kept his hands at his sides, refusing to take it. After a moment, she placed it on the stand next to the chair, on her untouched dinner tray.

"Why not?"

In answer, he brought a shallow brass bowl from the bag he wore under his cloak, the rim decorated with ornate filigrees of colored enamel. He went to the desk and set the bowl there, pouring water into it from a pitcher the servants had left there. From a leather pouch, he sprinkled a dark powder into the water and stirred it, chanting words in the Westspeech. He could see her watching him, her head cocked to one side as she listened, and he knew that she heard the similarity between Westspeech and the language of the Ilmodo: the same cadences and rhythms, the same sibilance and breathy vowels. A mist rose above the bowl.

"Look into it," he said.

She gave him a long, appraising look. Then, finally, she rose from her chair (he could see her weariness in the grimaces and the way she stretched her limbs) and—on the far side of the desk from him—stood over the bowl. She looked down.

He knew what she saw, knew because he'd glimpsed it himself a dozen or more times over the last few months.

In the mists, Ana's face, and the figure of Jan ca'Vörl. She holds a knife, and the blade is bloodied. The mists roil, and there is ca'Cellibrecca, sprawled on the ground alongside the Hïrzg, blood spread across his chest, his chest unmoving. Ana's face is a mask as she stares, her eyes cold and hard. The knife drops from her hand, and the mists swirl again, and there is Nessantico, untouched, and on the Sun Throne is Justi . . .

He knew what she saw. He stretched his scarred hand between Ana's rapt face and the bowl, sweeping away the mist.

He would not let her see what came afterward. That was only for him.

Ana looked up at him, her hands fisted on the desktop. "This is the future?" she asked.

He nodded. "It is a glimpse of one path the future can take," he said. "A path that's uncertain and hard to decipher sometimes. But when I see the Hïrzg's death, when I see Nessantico saved and Justi on the throne, it is always *you* who do this deed, Ana. Not me. That's why I gave you the spelled glass—because I know that if *I* kill them, Nessantico still falls. Inevitably."

He wondered if she could hear the half-lie.

"I can't," she said. "To murder people while they're helpless . . ."

He smiled, and saw her recoil from his expression. "How better to do it?" he said. "My people have a saying: 'In time of war, all laws are silent.' How many have died today—unnecessarily—because you *didn't* do what I suggested?"

Her gaze hardened then, and he realized he'd pushed her too far. "You blame *me?*"

Mahri hurried to answer, shaking his head. He could not give her time to think, or it would be too late. "No, Ana. I don't blame you—if anything, the blame is mine for not making it clear enough. You can play by the rules of 'civilized' war if you wish, Ana, but you will lose if you do so—ask Commandant ca'Rudka if he truly thinks you will prevail against Hïrzg Jan; ask your war-téni if they believe they are stronger than those on the other side. You've already bent the rules of your Faith and your Divolonté. Bend them further. You have tonight to do this. Tonight only. Tomorrow, it will be too late, because the Hïrzg will be dining in the palais and ca'Cellibrecca will be standing where you're standing right now. Both you and Justi will be dead, or worse."

"Why?" she asked him. "Why do *you* care who is Kraljiki or Archigos?"

"I don't," he told her. "I care for what is best for my people, as you do. And so I want Justi as Kraljiki and you as the Archigos."

"You saw that here?" she asked, pointing at the bowl.

For a moment he wondered if she had guessed, or if she'd seen more in the bowl than he'd intended for her to see. "Yes," he told her tentatively. "Glimpses, as you saw. And I hope that they're right."

He was relieved when she nodded. He plucked the glass ball from the dinner tray. "Tonight," he repeated, holding the ball. "It's your only chance."

She stared at him. He was afraid she was going to refuse, afraid that what he'd seen in the bowl would be forever shattered and lost. But finally her hands came up from her sides, palms up.

He placed the ball in her hands and closed her fingers around the glow.

~

Ana ca'Seranta

ANA WAS MORE FRIGHTENED than she could remember. Her hands were shaking, and she felt impossibly cold.

Kenne brought the carriage, driven by a trusted e'téni. When she told him that she wanted to leave the city along the Avi a'Firenzcia, that she wanted to come as close as she could come to where the Hïrzg's army was camped (trying desperately to keep her voice from shaking), he nodded as if she'd asked him to take her on a promenade around the Avi a'Parete. "And Envoy ci'Vliomani? Will we be picking him up also?"

"Let Karl sleep," she'd told him. "This is something I must do on my own—but I need your help."

Kenne had nodded and kept any thoughts he might have had to himself. That gratified Ana; she didn't know if she would have been able to answer his questions.

She stared out from the curtains as they rattled through the city. The Avi a'Parete was strangely dark, the téni-lamps unlit for the first time in generations. The storm front had passed on eastward, leaving moon-silver puddles on the flags of the courtyards and the Avi. The streets were deserted except for Garde Civile (though the taverns they passed were both crowded and noisy), and it was only the cracked globe of Cénzi on their carriage that saved them from being stopped and questioned several times. The A'Sele flowed dark and forbidding under the Pontica Mordei, and the heads on either side of the gates of the Avi a'Firenzcia were black and still, frozen as they stared outward into the night, gazing blindly to where the army of Firenzcia slept.

The carriage was hailed as they came to the barricades at the gate; Kenne leaned out from the carriage and answered the challenge. At his insistence that they were on the Archigos' business, they were permitted through. They passed between uncounted tents of the Garde Civile along the Avi.

The world seemed calm, despite the cataclysm that had come to Nessantico, despite Ana's own apprehensions. She cradled the glass ball nestled in her pocket, letting the Ilmodo energy captured within it tingle her fingers and praying to Cénzi to tell her that she was doing the right thing.

There was no answer. Only an aching uncertainty in her heart and the fear of what she was setting out to do.

She felt the carriage come to a halt as the driver stopped chanting. "Archigos," she heard the driver say. "I can't go farther . . ."

Kenne opened the carriage door and Ana peered out. Ahead, the Avi was entirely blocked: the rear defensive line of Nessantico troops. A squad of the Garde Civile were approaching the carriage; as they saw Ana and Kenne step from the carriage, they all hurriedly gave the sign of Cénzi. "Archigos, U'Téni," the e'offizer with them said. "I'll send word to Commandant ca'Rudka that you've come." He started to gesture to one of his men, but she stopped him.

"No, E'Offizier. Let the commandant have his rest. I've come to look at the lines, that's all. I couldn't sleep, so I thought I'd see where we should place the war-téni."

He nodded, with a quick, almost shy smile. "I understand. Right now, though, things are quiet."

"Where are the Firenzcian troops?"

The man pointed up the road. "No more than a quarter mile past our lines. You can glimpse their campfires through the trees."

"I'd like to see."

"We'll take you . . ."

Ana walked with Kenne, the e'offizer, and his squad through the quiet lines, where most of the Garde Civile were sleeping on the ground or packed into small tents, getting what rest they could before the sun and inevitable battle came. The Avi itself was blocked by a barrier of quickly-felled trees, but there was nothing but field, trees, and the occasional abandoned farmhouse between the two forces on either side of the road. The e'offizier led them to one side of the Avi, to a small stand of apple trees. She could see a few lookouts stationed along the line, but otherwise there was no one near them. "This is as far as we should go," the e'offizier said. "Any farther out from cover and it would be too dangerous." Yellow flames blinked like distant fireflies in a rough line ahead of her, flickering through the swaying foliage of trees and brush. She stared out into the dark.

"You saved us earlier, Archigos," the e'offizier said behind her. "I want you to know that we appreciate that, all of us."

She nodded. "Thank you, E'Offizier. Now, if you would leave us alone for a bit, please," she said. "To pray . . ."

He gave her the sign of Cénzi once more. He gestured to the squad and they strode away, leaving Ana and Kenne standing alone in the little grove. She pulled out Mahri's gift. She cupped it in her hand. "Archigos?" Kenne said, looking at the ruddy fire in her hand.

"I need you to hide me, Kenne," she told him. "A

shielding spell so no one sees or hears me moving in the night. I need to get as close as I can."

She thought she saw Kenne's eyebrows lift in the moonlight, but he nodded. He began to chant, his hands swaying in the moonlight. The air shimmered around her—she was not invisible, but unless one looked carefully they might mistake her form for a tree's shadow or a cloud over the moon.

It was the best she could hope for.

Ana took a long breath, then stepped forward from the sheltering trees and into the open field. She waited, half expecting to hear the hiss of arrows or a call of alarm. Yett she heard nothing but Kenne's chanting behind her. She continued to walk: a step, another, with each step fighting the temptation to run.

She was nearly across to the line of trees and the campfire among them when the shimmering of air began to lessen: Kenne was tiring. She lifted the glass ball in her hand.

Speak my name, he'd said. "Mahri," she whispered, and she felt the power within the glass well up. In her mind, it spread around her and she saw the shape of the spell that contained it in the pattern of the Ilmodo. She marveled at the spell's complexity, wondering if she could have crafted something like this herself. But she had little time—she remembered how Mahri had said that the spell was difficult to hold, and she could already feel the wildness of it in her mind.

She looked about. In the sky, the fast-moving clouds had stopped. There was no sound but the roaring of the power in her mind. A night swallow hovered high above her, captured in mid-turn, its wings locked in mid-beat.

Ana began to walk as quickly as she could toward the campfires—but now she found movement difficult and slow. She felt as if she were wading through deep water. As she reached the enemy lines, her heart pounded, seeing a man staring directly at her as he stood beside the nearest tree. She gathered herself—to run or to ready

a spell—but then she realized that he was as unresponsive as a sculpture, and that the flames of the campfire
against whose light he was outlined appeared painted
on the air.

She hurried past the soldier, feeling a chill as he stood
there, still staring outward. *Kill the head and the snake
dies....*

It was easy to locate the Hïrzg's tent, with his banner
caught in mid-flutter above. She walked unchallenged
through the encampment and past the gardai outside.
She lifted the flap—the canvas as stiff and unyielding as
if it were frozen—and stepped inside.

She stopped, breathing heavily with the exertion of
simply walking in this gelid air. The interior of the tent
was ornate: a thick rug covered the ground, a wooden
field desk stood on its stand to one side, a brazier trailed
an unmoving wisp of incense, and téni-lights had been lit
to brighten the room. There were several people in the
tent, gathered around a table set with food: ca'Cellibrecca
she recognized instantly, his hand lifting a forkful of
meat toward his gaping mouth. There was another man
in black and silver with the insignia of the starkkapitän
on his sleeves; a thin man who was seated at the middle
of the table; a green-robed téni with the slashes of an
u'téni—that could only be cu'Kohnle.

The Hïrzg sat at the head of the table ... and on his
lap, unexpectedly, was a young girl. The sight puzzled
Ana for a moment, then she realized: it was the Hïrzg's
daughter Allesandra. It had to be her; she could see the
similarity in their faces.

They were all statues crafted by a flawless artist. The
power snarling in her head, she went to the Hïrzg. She
pulled the knife from its scabbard.

*So easy ... Draw it hard and deep, and he will die, and
then do the same to ca'Cellibrecca and cu'Kohnle, and
the starkkapitän as well....*

But she stood there, staring at the tableau, the power
within Mahri's spell buzzing insistently in her ears.

Allesandra was gazing up at her vatarh, her mouth half-open, and there was such deep love and affection in her gaze that it stopped Ana's hand.

Once it was that way for me, before Matarh became sick. Vatarh loved me, and I loved him in return, and he would hold me on his knees and play with me and I never, never wanted to leave....

She almost heard the girl's chuckle. She saw the Hïrzg's hand, ready to brush away an errant curl from her forehead, and in his eyes was the same affection, the same love.

Ana's hand trembled. The tip of the knife wavered just above the Hïrzg's flesh. The Ilmodo seethed and crackled around her, as if Cénzi Himself were laughing.

You don't have time. Mahri told you. Kill him. Leave ...
She imagined the aftermath and how it would be for the girl: one moment laughing with her father, then a breath, a waver, and the blood would be pouring from him and her vatarh would collapse on her, dead in an instant. Impossibly taken.

A breath, a waver ... A brief instant of disorientation and reality dissolving around her. As Ana had felt when Mahri came to her with the glass ball. "It's just my finger. It might as easily have been a knife ..."

The brief instant of disorientation ...

The dissolution of reality ...

So familiar ...

Ana gasped.

She knew. All in that instant, she knew. This was what *Mahri* needed. Not what she needed.

She glimpsed another way. A better way, she hoped.

There was little time left. The Ilmodo screamed in her mind, a rising wail, and she could not hold the spell together for much longer. She slid the knife back in its scabbard and went to the field desk, spreading out a piece of thick paper that seemed to fight her hand, taking a quill and dipping the end into the inkwell.

Even writing was a struggle, as if the ink itself were

fighting her. She wrote a brief, scrawling note and signed
it. Returning to the table, she tugged the Hïrzg's arms
away from Allesandra—they moved reluctantly, as if he
were loath to allow this. She tucked the note in his hand
and closed his fist around it.

Finally, she took the unaware girl in her arms.

Hoping she could make her way from the encampment before she could no longer hold the spell together,
she fled. Carrying the stiff body of Allesandra, it was as
if Ana were fighting her way upstream against a rushing,
white-watered current. She stumbled from the encampment with the burden of the young girl, past the campfire and beyond the line of guards, and out into the open
field between the two armies, pausing a few times to rest
and recover her breath.

The campfires of the Nessantico defenders edged
closer.

There was a man standing between herself and the
campfires, though, and he stood where there had been
no one before. "Kenne?" she breathed, hoping somehow it was true and knowing it was not. "Karl?"

"No," the apparition answered, and the shock of his
speech was enough to tear away the remnants of the spell.
The world returned to motion around Ana, the impact of
it causing Ana to drop Allesandra to the ground.

"It was you, wasn't it, Mahri?" Ana said.

~

Allesandra ca'Vörl

"**YOU ARE MY LITTLE BIRD**, and I love—" her vatarh said, but then the world lurched around her and she wasn't there on his lap anymore but somehow lying on the cold, wet ground in the night. Someone—a woman's voice—was growling at a black figure in the middle of a meadow. Allesandra tried to get up, but she was disoriented and could only struggle to her knees.

"It was you, wasn't it, Mahri? The Kraljica didn't die because of ci'Recroix's spell—it was you who killed her."

Dizzy, feeling nauseous from the strangeness, Allesandra stared at the speaker. It was hard to see in the dim, fleeting moonlight, but the woman was dressed in a téni's robes—robes that looked similar to those the fat Archigos wore. She was speaking to a man: he was little more than a beggar. His face, when the moonlight caught it under the hood of his cloak, was horrid: all twisted and scarred with one eye missing, and the smile he gave the woman was hideous.

"Yes, it was me," he admitted. "This won't do, Ana. I can't have you take the girl back to be ransomed. That would leave the Hïrzg alive . . ." He smiled again, and the coldness of the expression made Allesandra shiver. She would have cried out, but they were both ignoring her. She remained still, but her fingers crept to where her vatarh's knife was tucked under her tashta. "But I can remedy that problem. After all, finding you out here with the girl's body will tell everyone who killed the

Hïrzg—that will work nearly as well for my purposes, I think. There's still time. In fact, there's all the time I need."

He lifted a hand; in it was a small glass ball. He closed his eyes and spoke a word; but the woman had done the same—gesturing sharply with one hand and speaking a phrase that boomed loudly in the night air. The glass ball shattered in the man's hand. Green-and-yellow light shot through the air, sending shadows racing over the ground. The man shouted and staggered backward.

"I didn't come entirely unprepared, Mahri," the woman—could she really be Ana, the false Archigos?—said to the man. "And I've learned from Karl, too."

"You've not learned enough," the cloaked man told her, cradling his arm. "Not enough . . ."

He lifted both his hands, sweeping them through the air, and speaking a sequence of words in a strange tongue. The attack came so quickly that Allesandra was certain that the woman would be consumed by it: crackling blue fire streamed from the gesturing man to envelop the woman. But Ana had raised her own hands at the same moment and the blue fire split into two streams just in front of her, hissing and fuming as they struck the ground on either side of the Archigos.

But the firestream continued to pour toward her, and Allesandra heard the woman gasp as she held her shielding hands before her. Her mouth was moving, but the words were unheard over the fury of the spell; her eyes were closed and lines of effort creased her face. The sundered firestreams began to close, threatening to drown her in the blue flames.

Allesandra wanted to believe this was a nightmare, that she had simply fallen asleep suddenly in her vatarh's lap, but it couldn't be a dream. And she knew that when the cloaked man killed Ana, he would look next at her. . . .

Georgi had told her that a starkkapitän must know when to make alliances, even with those who might the next day be your enemy. Vatarh had shown her the same.

Allesandra closed her fingers around the knife Vatarh had given her. She pulled the blade free of the scabbard. Gathering all her strength, pushing away the dizziness, she rushed toward the man, screaming. His gaze shifted to her and the firestreams began to curl, but she was already beside him and she thrust the blade into his cloak blindly.

The firestream nearly touched her, but in the instant she thought she would feel its touch, the blaze shifted as if someone had taken hold of it, and the flames instead wrapped around Mahri himself. He screamed, and Allesandra flung herself away from him, dropping the knife. She struck the ground hard, the breath taken from her. As she tried to breathe, to move, she saw the firestreams crackle and flare, covering the man's entire body and flinging him a dozen feet away. The spell-fire vanished then, but real flames—yellow and pale in comparison—sputtered on his clothing.

He did not move.

Allesandra could hear people shouting nearby, calling alarm. Téni-fire was beginning to glow to both sides of them.

Ana was on her knees in the mud, breathing heavily. Allesandra saw the woman rise, and she tried to get up herself to run away, but she didn't know which way to go, she was frightened and sore, and Ana already stood over her. "Are you all right?" Ana's voice was hoarse and cracked and tired.

Allesandra nodded silently, sniffing away the tears that threatened, and when Ana stretched a hand toward her, she took it. "We have to hurry," Ana said.

"I want to go back to my vatarh."

Ana nodded. "You will," she said. "I promise you. In time, you will."

There were men approaching them, and they wore blue and gold rather than black and silver. Allesandra whimpered in alarm and tried to break free from the older woman, but Ana hugged her tightly. "They won't hurt you," she whispered to Allesandra. "I promise you. They won't hurt you. I won't let them."

"Vatarh promised me the city," Allesandra told her.

"And I will show it to you," Ana said. "But Nessantico belongs to itself."

Epilogue: Nessantico

EBB AND FLOW . . .
Nessantico breathed a collective sigh as the army of Firenzcia melted away like a spring ice storm, the Hïrzg returning to Firenzcia and his throne in Brezno, returning to his wife who was, after all, a relative of the Kraljiki and therefore still useful.

The Hírzg's daughter Allesandra remained behind, in palatial imprisonment in the Archigos' Temple where she waited for the ransom to be paid for her release— she would wait much longer than she imagined. Hïrzgin Greta would produce a healthy son for the Hïrzg not long after his return to Brezno; having a new heir in hand would make the Hïrzg slow to pay the ransom.

A descendant of the ca'Ludovici line held the Sun Throne and ruled as Kraljiki—but Justi the One-Legged would not rule anywhere near as long as his matarh had, nor would his reign be remembered as anything but a disaster.

Archigos Ana the First ruled in the temple, though another claiming the title of Archigos dwelled in Brezno. The Concénzia Faith, for the first time, was sundered, and some gave their allegiance to Nessantico and others to Brezno. The two branches of the Faith would drift farther and farther apart in both belief and temperament.

In Nessantico, the Numetodo gained acceptance and even some prominence, and those professing to be in their ranks would eventually be among the ca'-and-cu'.

There were even rumors that the Archigos took one of them as a lover, though she would never marry.

The other countries of the Holdings would remember how Firenzcia had nearly thrown off the yoke of Nessantico, and they would wonder if perhaps they could succeed where Firenzcia had failed. None would try, however.

Not yet.

Ebb and flow . . .

Nessantico: the city, the woman.

Once there had been no city who could rival her. She wondered now if that would always be true. She had escaped the rape of invaders, but the reverberations of the attack shook the empire from her center to the far borders, and their echoes would linger for decades.

She knew that with age and prominence inevitably come jealousy and risk. She was no longer invulnerable, and there were rivals in the world who wanted what she had always had.

There was darkness, and forces gathered in that gloom: in the west, she saw, as well as in the east . . .

After twilight, there would inevitably come nightfall. She could not hold it back forever.

Appendices

VIEWPOINT CHARACTERS
(alphabetical order by family name)

Orlandi ca'Cellibrecca *[Orh-LAHN-dee Kah-sell-eh-BREK-ah]*
One of the a'teni, and the chief traditionalist among
them

Marguerite ca'Ludovici *[Marhg-u-REET
Kah-loo-doh-VEE-kee]*
The current Kraljica of Nessantico

Justi ca'Mazzak *[JUSS-tee Kah-MAH-zak]*
(nee ca'Ludovici) The A'Kralj (Heir Apparent) to
the Kraljica, the only surviving child of Marguerite
ca'Ludovici

Dhosti ca'Millac *[DOST-ee Kah-MEE-lok]*
The Archigos of the Concénzia Faith; a dwarf

Sergei ca'Rudka *[SARE-zhay Kah-ROOD-kah]*
The Kraljica's head of security

Allesandra ca'Vörl *[Ahl-ah-SAHN-drah Kah-VOORL]*
First daughter of Jan ca'Vörl

Jan ca'Vörl *[Yahn Kah-VOORL]*
(nee ca'Belgradin) Hïrzg (King) of Firenzcia

Karl ci'Vliomani *[Kurhl Kee-vlee-oh-MAHN-ee]*
A Numetodo sent from the Isle of Paeti to
Nessantico

Ana cu'Seranta *[AHN-ah Koo-sir-AHN-tah]*
Daughter of Abini and Tomas cu'Seranta

Mahri *[MAH-ree]*
A beggar in Nessantico

SUPPORTING CAST
(alphabetical order by family name)

Ludwig ca'Belgradin *[LOOD-vigh Kah-bell-GRAH-deen]*
Jan's older brother; died of Southern Fever

Karin ca'Belgradin *[KAH-reen Kah-bell-GRAH-deen]*
Jan's vatarh, the previous Hïrzg of Firenzcia; died of
Southern Fever

Estraven ca'Cellibrecca *[Ess-TRAY-vehn
Kah-sell-ee-BREK-ah]*
(nee ca'Seurfoi) Husband of Francesca ca'Cellibrecca; u'téni of the Old Temple in Nessantico

Francesca ca'Cellibrecca *[Frahn-SESS-ka
Kah-sell-ee-BREK-ah]*
Justi ca'Mazzak's lover

Colin ca'Cille *[CALL-inn Kah-KEEL]*
A'Téni of An Uaimth on the Isle of Paeti, an ally of
Archigos Dhosti

Alain ca'Fountaine *[ah-LAIN Kah-fhon-TANE]*
A'Téni of Belcanto, Sforzia; an ally of Archigos Dhosti

Marcus ca'Gerodi *[MARH-kuss Kah-ger-OH-dee]*
A relative of the Kraljica imprisoned in the Bastida
for a time

ca'Marvolli *[Kah-mar-VOH-lee]*
A'Téni of the city of Prajnoli in Nessantico; an ally
of A'Téni ca'Cellibrecca

Hannah ca'Mazzak *[HAHN-ahh Kah-MAH-zak]*
Justi's deceased wife

Henri ca'Mazzak *[OHN-ree Kah-MAH-zak]*
Son of Hannah and Justi; deceased

Marguerite ca'Mazzak *[Marhg-u-REET Kah-MAH-zak]*
Daughter of Hannah and Justi; deceased

ca'Miccord *[Kah-me-CORD]*
A'Téni of Kishkoros; an ally of A'Téni ca'Cellibrecca

Safina ca'Millac *[Sah-FEE-nah Kah-MEE-lok]*
The Archigos' niece, and an acolyte in Ana's class

Elia ca'Montmorte *[Kah-mohnt-MOHRT]*
A'Offizier and chevaritt who led the Nessantico
troops at Ville Colhelm

Bella ca'Nephri *[BELL-lah Kah-NEFF-free]*
A chevaritt and confidant of Justi; owner of the
Chateau Pré a'Fleuve

ca'Seiffel *[Kah-SIGH-fell]*
A'Téni of Karnmor; an ally of A'Téni ca'Cellibrecca

Joca ca'Sevini *[ZHAK-ah Kah-she-VEEN-ee]*
A'Téni of Chivasso in Il Trebbio; an ally of Archigos
Dhosti

Ahren ca'Staunton *[AHH-Rhen Kah-STAHN-tun]*
Starkkapitän of the Firenzcian army

Greta ca'Vörl *[GREH-tah Kah-VOORL]*
Wife of Jan ca'Vörl, Hïrzgin (Queen) of Firenzcia,
great-grand niece of the Kraljica

Toma ca'Vörl *[TOH-ma Kah-VOORL]*
Son of Jan and Greta. Two years older than
Allesandra; deceased

ca'Xana *[Kah-ZAHN-ah]*
The A'Téni of Malacki; an ally of A'Téni ca'Cellibrecca

Dhaspi ce'Coeni *[DHAS-pee Keh-KOHN-ee]* .
A Numetodo and would-be assassin

ce'Falla *[Keh-FAH-lah]*
Sergei ca'Rudka's aide; an o'offizier

Mika ce'Gilan *[MEE-kah Keh-GHEE-ahn]*
A Numetodo serving with Karl ci'Vliomani

Gilles ce'Guischard *[Gheeel Keh-goo-SHARD]*
A person on Renard's staff within the palais

ce'Naddia *[Keh-NAH-dee-ah]*
An e'offizier with the Garde Bastida

Remy ce'Nimoni *[RAY-mee Keh-nee-MOHN-ee]*
Retainer of the Chateau Pré a'Fleuve

Aubri ce'Ulcai *[AHH-bree Keh-UHL-kie]*
A guard in the Bastida

Georgi ci'Arndt *[Jhor-JHEE Kee-ARHN-t]*
An o'offizier in the Firenzcian army; Allesandra's
tutor in the art of war

Parta ci'Doulor *[PHAR-tah Kee-DOHL-orh]*
Capitaine of the Bastida

Kenne ci'Fionta *[KENN-ah Kee-fee-ON-tah]*
An o'teni on the Archigos' staff; the Archigos'
personal secretary

ci'Narsa *[Kee-NAR-sah]*
An o'téni who is the Hïrzgin's personal téni

Edouard ci'Recroix *[EDD-ward Kee-reh-KROI]*
A famous artist

cu'Bachiga *[Koo-bah-SHE-gah]*
U'Téni of Passe a'Fiume

cu'Baria *[Koo-BAR-ree-ahh]*
An a'offizier of the Garde Civile

Carlo cu'Belli *[KAR-loh Koo-BEHL-ee]*
An agent of a'Teni ca'Cellibrecca

Renard cu'Bellona *[Rehn-ARD Koo-behl-OH-nah]*
The Kraljica's aide

Bertran cu'Dosteau *[BUR-trawn Koo-dhos-TOE]*
The u'téni in charge of teaching acolytes to use the
Ilmodo; Ana's mentor, and also the person who
found Dhosti ca'Millac

Bahik cu'Garret *[Bah-HEEK Koo-GAIR-et]*
Head of the Garde Civile in Passe a'Fiume

cu'Helfier *[Koo-HELL-fear]*
An a'offizier of the Garde Civile

Semini cu'Kohnle *[SEH-meen-eh Koo-KOHN-lee]*
U'Téni, the leader of the war-téni with the Hïrzg

cu'Linnett *[Koo-Lihn-AA]*
An a'offizier in the Firenzcia army

cu'Malachi *[Koo-Mah-LAH-kee]*
An a'offizier of the Garde Civile

cu'Meridi *[Koo-Mah-REE-dee]*
A family friendly with the cu'Seranta family

Markell cu'Minpali *[Mahr-KEHL Kee-min-PAHL-ee]*
Hïrzg ca'Vörl's aide and confidant

Bernado cu'Montague *[Bur-NARH-doh Koo-Mon-TAHG]*
An a'offizier in the Garde Civile who once served
under Sergei ca'Rudka

Mara cu'Paile *[MAH-rah Koo-PAHL]*
Mistress of Jan ca'Vörl

Abini cu'Seranta *[Ahh-BEE-nee Koo-sir-AHN-tah]*
Matarh (mother) of Ana cu'Seranta

Tomas cu'Seranta *[TOH-mas Koo-sir-AHN-tah]*
(nee cu'Barith) Vatarh (father) of Ana cu'Seranta

cu'Simone *[Koo-see-MOHN]*
An a'offizier of the Garde Civile

Ammon cu'Varisi *[EH-monn Koo-vah-REE-see]*
Chevaritt and diplomat based in Prajnoli

Georgi cu'Vlanti *[JOR-gi Koo-VHLAN-tee]*
An u'téni who is also a war-téni in Nessantico

Sunna Hathiga *[SOON-ahh HAH-the-gah]*
One of Ana's servants in the temple complex, and
Watha's matarh

Watha Hathiga *[WAH-thah HAH-the-gah]*
One of Ana's servants in the temple complex, and
Sunna's daughter

Kaitlin Mallaghan *[KAIT-linn MAHL-ahg-inn]*
Karl ci'Vliomani's betrothed

Naniaj *[NAHN-ee-ahzj]*
Allesandra's maidservant/nursemaid

Beida *[BEE-dah]*
One of Ana's servants in the temple complex

Cassie *[KASS-ee]*
A servant in Francesca's household

Darkmavis *[Dark-MAY-viss]*
A well-known composer

Falla *[FAH-lah]*
A servant in Francesca's household

Jacques *[Zhawk]*
A servant in Abini cu'Seranta's household

Sala *[SAH-lah]*
A servant of the cu'Seranta family

Stenonis *[STEH-no-niss]*
A Numetodo scientist who lives in Wolhusen,
Graubundi

Tari *[TAH-ree]*
A servant of the cu'Seranta family

Varina *[Vah-REE-nah]*
A Numetodo acolyte

DICTIONARY

A'Sele *[Ah-SEEL]*
The river that divides the city of Nessantico.

Archigos *[ARR-chee-ghos]*
The leader of the Concénzia Faith; the plural is
"Archigi."

Avi a'Parete *[Ahh-VEE Ah-pah-REET]*
The wide boulevard that forms a circle within the
city of Nessantico, and also serves as a focus for city
events.

Axat *[Ahh-SKIAT]*
The moon-god of Mahri's people.

Bashta *[BARSH-tah]*
A one-piece blouse and pants, usually tied with
a wide belt around the waist, and generally loose
and flowing elsewhere. Bashtas are usually worn by
males, though there are female versions, and can be
either plain or extravagantly ornate, depending on
the person's status and the situation.

Bastida a'Drago *[Bahs-TEE-dah Ah-DRAH-goh]*
The "Fortress of the Dragon," an ancient tower
that now serves as a state prison for Nessantico.
Originally built by Kraljiki Selida II.

The "ca'-and-cu' " *[Caw-and-Coo]*
The term for the high status families in the Holdings;
the rich.

The "Calls"

In the Concénzia Faith, there are Three Calls during the day for prayer. First Call is in the morning, when the sun has risen above the horizon the distance of a fist held at arm's length. Second Call is when the sun is at zenith. Third Call is when the sun is a fist's length above the horizon at sunset.

Cénzi *[SEHN-zee]*

Main god of the Nessantico pantheon, and the patron of the Concénzia Faith.

Chevaritt *[Sheh-vah-REE]*

Chevarittai *[Sheh-vah-REE-tie]*

The "knights" of Nessantico—men of the ca' and cu' families. The title of "chevaritt" is bestowed by the Kraljiki or Kraljica, or by the appointed ruler of the various countries within the Holdings; in times of genuine war, the chevarittai (the plural form of the word) are called upon to prove their loyalty and courage. The chevarittai will follow (usually) the order of the Commandant of the Garde Civile, but not particularly those of the common offiziers of the Garde Civile. Their internal status is largely based on familial rank. In the past, occasional conflicts have been decided by honorable battle between chevarittai while the armies watched.

Coinage

There are three primary coinages in use in Nessantico: the bronze "folia" in tenth (d'folia), half (se'folia), and full (folia) denominations; the silver "siqil" in half (se'siqil) and full denominations; the gold "sola" in half (se'sola) and full denominations. Twenty folias equal a se'siqil; fifty siqils (or two thousand folias) equal a se'sola. The daily wage for a simple laborer is generally around a folia; a competent craftsperson might command four or five folias a day or a se'siqil a week. The price (and size)

of a loaf of common brown bread in Nessantico is
fixed at a d'folia.

Colors

Each of the various countries within the Holdings
retained their colors and flags. Here are the basic
banner structures:

East Magyaria: horizontal stripes of red, green, and
   orange
Firenzcia: alternating vertical stripes of black and
   silver
Graubundi: a field of yellow with black stars
Hellin: red-and-black fields divided diagonally
Il Trebbio: a yellow sun on a blue field
Miscoli: a single white star on a field of midnight
   blue
Namarro: a red crescent moon on a field of yellow
Nessantico: blue-and-gold fields divided diagonally;
   used by both North and South Nessantico
Paeti: vertical stripes of green, white, and orange
Sesemora: a field of silver with a mailed fist in the
   center
Sforzia: a field of white with a diagonal blue bar
West Magyaria: horizontal stripes of orange, red, and
   blue

Comté *[KOM-tay]*

The head of a town or city, usually a ca' and a
chevaritt.

Concénzia *[Kon-SEHN-zee-ah]*

The primary theology within Nessantico, whose
primary deity is Cénzi, though Cénzi is simply the
chief god of a pantheon.

Concord A'Téni

The gathering of all a'téni within Concénzia—a
Concord A'Téni is called to elect a new Archigos or
to make changes to the Divolonté.

Cornet

A straight wind instrument made of wood or brass, and played like a trumpet.

Days of the Week

The six days of the week in Nessantico are named after major deities in the Toustour. The week begins with Cénzidi (Cénzi's Day), and follows with Vuctadi, Mizzkdi, Gostidi, Draiordi, and Parladi.

Divolonté *[Dee-voh-LOHN-tay]*

"God's Will"—the rules and regulations that make up the tenets followed by those of the Concénzia Faith.

Family Names

Within Nessantico and most of the Holdings, the family names follow the female line. A man will (except in rare cases) upon marriage take his wife's family name, and all children (without exception) take the family name of the matarh. In the event of the death of a wife, the widower will usually retain his wife's family name until remarried.

Fjath *[Phiy-AHTH]*

The title for the ruler of Sforzia.

Garda

"Guard" or "soldier" (used interchangeably). The plural is gardai.

Garde Brezno *[GAR-duh BREHZ-noh]*

The city guard of Brezno in Firenzcia.

Garde Civile *[GAR-duh Sih-VEEL]*

The army of the country of Nessantico. Not the largest force (that's the army of Firenzcia), but the Garde Civile directs all the armies of the Holdings in war situations.

Garde Kralji *[GAR-duh KRAHL-jee]*

The city guard of Nessantico. Based in the Bastida,

their insignia is a bronze dragon's skull. The common ranks are "gardai" (ranging from a prefix of e' to a'), the officers are "offizier" (also ranging from a prefix of e' to a'). The highest rank in the Garde Kralji is commandant.

Gardes a'Liste *[GAR-dess Ah-LEEST]*
The bureaucratic organization responsible for maintaining the rolls of family names, and for assigning the official prefixes of rank to them.

Généra a'Pace *[Jhen-AH-rah Ah-pah-SAY]*
"Creator of Peace"—the popular title for the Kraljica. For three decades under her rule, there were no major wars within the Holdings.

Grandes Horizontales *[GRAHN-days Hor-eh-ZHON-tah-leh]*
The term for the high-class courtesans with ca' and cu' patrons.

Greaves
Leg armor.

Gschnas *[Guh-SHWAZ]*
The "False World" Ball—takes place every year in Nessantico.

Hauberk
A short chain mail coat.

Hïrz *[HAIRZG (almost two syllables)]*
The title for the ruler of Firenzcia. "Hïrzgin" is the feminine form, and "A'Hïrzg" is the term for either the female or male heir.

Ilmodo *[Eel-MOH-doh]*
"The Way." The Ilmodo is a pervasive energy that can be shaped through the use of ritualized chants, perfected and codified by the Concénzia Faith. The Numetodo call the Ilmodo "Scáth Cumhacht." Other cultures that are aware of it will have their own name. Mahri's people call it "X'in Ka."

Instruttorei *[Inn-struh-TORR-ay]*
Instructor.

Kraljica *[Krahl-JEE-kah]*
Title most similar to "Empress." The masculine form
is "Kraljiki" [Kralh-jee-kee]. To refer to a ruler non-
gender-specifically, "Kralji" is generally used, which
is also the plural.

Kusah *[KOO-sah]*
The title for the ruler of Namarro.

Marque
The document given to an acolyte who is to be taken
into the Order of Téni and placed in the service of
the Concénzia Faith

Matarh *[MAH-tarr]*
"Mother."

Moitidi *[Moy-TEE-dee]*
The "half-gods"—the demigods created by Cénzi,
who in turn created all living things.

Montbataille *[Mont-bah-TEEL]*
A city set on the long slopes of a mountain in the
east of North Nessantico; also the site of a famous
battle between Nessantico and the province of
Firenzcia, and the only good pass through the
mountains between the Rivers Clario and Loi.

Namarro *[Nah-MARR-oh]*
The southernmost province of the Holdings of
Nessantico.

Nessantico *[Ness-ANN-tee-ko]*
The capital city of the Holdings, ruled by the
Kraljica.

Note of Severance
A document that releases an acolyte from his or her

instruction toward being in the Order of Téni.
Typically 10 percent or less of acolytes complete
their training and are accepted into the Order. The
vast majority will receive a note.

Numetodo
A sect that believes that the manipulation of
magical energy in the world does not come from
Cénzi or any god, but instead only requires a
"formula" to manipulate. They explain the world in
humanistic terms, and are considered both heretical
and dangerous by the Concénzia Faith.

Offizier *[OFF-ih-zeer]*
"Officer"—the various ranks of offizier follow the
ranks of téni. In ascending order: e'offizier, o'offizier,
u'offizier, a'offizier. Often, an offizier in one of the
armies also is a chevaritt.

Passe a'Fiume *[PASS-eh ah-fee-UHM]*
The city that sits on the main river crossing of the
Clario in eastern Nessantico.

Pontica a'Brezi Nippoli *[Phon-TEE-kah Ah-BREHZ-ee
Nee-POHL-ee]*
One of the Four Bridges of Nessantico.

Pontica a'Brezi Veste *[Phon-TEE-kah Ah-BREHZ-ee
VESS-tee]*
One of the Four Bridges of Nessantico.

Pontica Kralji *[Phon-TEE-kah KRAWL-jee]*
One of the Four Bridges of Nessantico.

Pontica Mordei *[Phon-TEE-kah MHOR-dee]*
One of the Four Bridges of Nessantico.

Quibela *[Qwee-BELL-ah]*
A city in the province of Namarro.

Sakal *[Sah-KHAL]*
The sun god of Mahri's people.

Sapnut
  The fruit of the sapnut tree, from which a rich yellow
  dye is made.

Scarlet Pox
  A childhood illness, often deadly.

Scáth Cumhacht *[Skawth Koo-MOCKED]*
  The Numetodo term for the Ilmodo.

Second World
  In the Concénzia Faith, an invisible "world" that
  surrounds that of Nessantico, from which magical
  energy emanates.

Sesemora *[Say-seh-MOHR-ah]*
  A province in the northeast of the Holdings of
  Nessantico.

Southern Fever
  An affliction that kills a high percentage of those
  affected—the fever causes the brain to swell,
  bringing on dementia and/or coma, while the lungs
  fill with liquid from the infection, causing
  pneumonia-like symptoms. Often, even if the
  victim recovers from the coughing, they are left
  brain-damaged.

Starkkapitän *[Starkh-KAHP-ee-tahn]*
  "High Captain"—the title for the commander of
  Firenzcian troops.

Strettosei *[STRETT-oh-see]*
  The ocean to the west of Nessantico.

T'Sha *[Ti-SHAH]*
  The ruler of Tennshah.

Ta'Mila *[Tah-MEE-ah]*
  The ruler of Il Trebbio.

Tashta *[TAWSH-tah]*
  A robelike garment in fashion in Nessantico.

Téni *[TEHN-ee]*

"Priest." Those of the Concénzia who have been tested for their mastery of the Ilmodo, have taken their vows, and are in the service of the temple. The téni priesthood also uses a ranking similar to the Families of Nessantico. In ascending order, the ranks are e'Téni, o'Téni, u'Téni, and a'Téni.

Téte *[teh-TAY]*

"Head"—a title for the leaders of an organization, such as the Guardians of the Faith.

Toustour *[TOOS-toor]*

The "All-Tale"—the bible for the Concénzia Faith.

Turn of the glass

An hour.

Utilino *[Oo-teh-LEE-noh]*

A combination concierge and watchman who patrols a small area (no more than a block each) of the city. The utilino—who is also a téni of the Concénzia Faith—is there to run errands (for a fee) as well as to keep order, and is considered to be part of the Garde Kralji.

Vajica *[Vah-JEE-kah]*

Title most similar to "Madam," used in polite address with adults who have no other title, or where the title is unknown. The masculine form is "Vajiki." The plurals are "Vajicai" and "Vajik."

Vambrace

Armor protecting the lower arm.

Vatarh *[VAH-ter]*

"Father."

Verzehen *[Ver-ZAY-hehn]*

Foreign term for a telescope.

Ville Colhelm *[VEE-ah KOHL-helm]*

A town on the border of Nessantico and Firenzcia, at the River Clario.

War-téni
> Téni whose skills in Ilmodo have been honed for warfare.

Zinke
> A wind instrument similar to a cornet, but curved rather than straight.

HISTORICAL PERSONAGES

Falwin (I) *[FAHL-win]*
> Hïrzg Falwin of Firenzcia led a brief, unsuccessful revolt against Kraljiki Henri VI, which was quickly and brutally put down.

Henri VI *[OHN-ree]*
> First Kralji of the ca'Ludovici line, from whom Marguerite I was descended.

Kalima III *[Kah-LEE-mah]*
> Archigos from 215–243.

Levo ca'Niomi *[LEHV-oh Kah-nee-OH-mee]*
> Led a coup in 383 and was Kraljiki for three days. Forcibly removed, he would be imprisoned for almost two decades in the Bastída, and there would write poetry that would long survive his death.

Maria III
> Kraljica of Nessantico from 219–237.

Pellin I *[PEH-Lihn]*
> Archigos of the Faith from 114–122.

Selida II *[Seh-LEE-dah]*
> Kraljiki of Nessantico. Finished building the city walls and the Bastída a'Drago.

Sveria I *[seh-VERH-ee-ah]*
> Kraljiki of Nessantico 179–211. The Secession War

occupied nearly all his reign. He finally brought
Firenzcia fully into the Holdings

SNIPPETS FROM THE *NESSANTICO CONCORDIA*
(4th Edition, Year 642)

Family Names in the Holdings:

Within Nessantico, lineage follows the matrilineal
line. A husband might, in rare cases, retain his own
family name (especially if it were considered higher
in status than his wife's), but the wife can never take
his name. In the vast majority of cases, however, the
husband will legally take on his wife's family name,
thus becoming a member of that family in the eyes of
Nessantico law—the husband will continue to bear
that name and be considered to be part of that family
even upon the death of his spouse, unless and until he
remarries and thus acquires his new wife's name.
(Divorces and annulments are rare in Nessantico,
requiring the signature of the Archigos, and each
divorce is a special situation where the rules are
sometimes fluid.) Children are, without exception,
given the mother's family name: "One always is certain
of the mother," as the saying goes in Nessantico.

The prefix to a family name can change, depending on
the relative status of the immediate family within
Nessantico society. The prefixes, in order of rising
status, are:

- none
- ce' (keh)
- ci' (kee)
- cu' (koo)
- ca' (kah)

One of the functionary roles of the Kralji was to sign
the official family rolls every three years wherein the

prefixes are recorded, though the Kraljiki or Kraljica
rarely determined any changes personally; that was the
role of the bureaucracy within Nessantico known as the
Gardes a'Liste.

Thus, it is possible that the husband or wife of the
ci'Smith family might gain status in some manner and
be awarded a new prefix by the Gardes a'Liste.
Husband, wife, their children and any surviving maternal
parents thus become cu'Smith, but brothers, sisters, and
any cousins would remain ci'Smith.

Royalty Succession Within the Holdings:
   Various countries within the Holdings, not surprisingly given the variance of customs, have various rules
of succession within their societies. This is especially
true when those countries are independently ruled. For
instance, in East Magyaria, the closest male relative
of the previous ruler who is also not a direct child of
that ruler is named as the successor. However, with
the ascension of Nessantico and the Holdings, those
countries within Nessantico's influence tend to follow
the lead of the Kralji.

   For the royal families of Nessantico, title succession
is normally to the Kralji's children by birth order
regardless of gender. However, it is possible for the
Kralji to legally designate a favorite child as the heir
and bypass earlier-born children, if the Kralji deems
them unfit to rule or if for some reason they fall out of
favor. This is an uncommon occurrence, though hardly
rare throughout history. For the Kralji, it means that his
or her children will tend to curry favor so as to remain
in good graces or perhaps to unseat one of their
brothers or sisters from being named the a'Kralj.

The Ilmodo and Spellcasting:
   Some people have the ability to sense the power that
exists all around us: the invisible potent energy of the
Second World that surrounds us. In the Nessantico-

controlled regions of the world, usage of magic has always been linked to religious faith, all the way back into prehistory. The myth of Cénzi extends deep into the historical mist, and it is the followers of Cenzi who have always possessed the power to manipulate the "Ilmodo" through chants and hand motions.

The chanting that binds the power of the Ilmodo is the "Ilmodo language" that all acolyte téni are taught. The Ilmodo language actually has its linguistic roots in the speech of the Westlands, though neither those of the Concénzia Faith nor the Numetodo realized that for centuries. Those of the Westlands also take power from the Second World via the instrument of religion, though through a different god and mythology, and they have their own name for the Ilmodo: X'in Ka.

The Numetodo have taken the most recent path to this power: not through faith at all, but essentially by making a "science" of magic. The cult of the Numetodo first arose in the late 400s, originally from the Isle of Paeti, and spread mostly west and south from there, sometimes reacting violently with the culture of Nessantico and the Concénzia Faith.

However the power is gained, there is a necessary "payment" for spell use: using spells costs the wielder physically; the greater the effect, the higher the cost in exhaustion and weariness for the caster.

Different paths have resulted in different abilities—for Concénzian téni, there is no "storage" of spells—their spells take time to cast and once prepared, they must be cast or they are lost. However, the téni of the Faith have the advantage of being able to cast spells that linger for some time after the casting (see "The Lights of Nessantico" or "The Sun Throne of the Kralji"). Téni who cast spells quickly and effectively are unusual, and have in historical times been suspected of heresy.

The Numetodo, in contrast, have found a way to cast their spells several turns of the glass earlier (though such spells can't be stored indefinitely). Like all users of this power, they "pay" for it with exhaustion but hold the power with their minds to be released with a single gesture and word. Their spells are generally longer and more arduous to create (even more so than those of the téni), but do not require "faith"—as is required by both the path of Concénzia and the Westlanders. All they require is that the spellcaster follows a "formula." However, any variation from the formula, even small, will generally ruin the spell.

The Westlanders, following what they call X'in Ka, must perform the chants and hand gestures much like the téni, but they can also "enchant" an object with a spell (something neither téni nor Numetodo can do), so that the object (e.g.: a walking stick) manipulated in a particular way (e.g.: striking someone) can release a spell (e.g.: a shocking jolt that renders the struck person unconscious).

In all cases and whatever the path of the spellcaster, the spells of the Second World tend to be linked to elementals in our world: fire, earth, air, and water. Most spellcasters have an ability sharply stronger in one element and much weaker in the others. Rarely does a spellcaster have the ability to handle two or more elements with any skill; even more rare are those who can move easily between any of the elements.

The Ranks of Téni in the Concénzia Faith:

The téni are ranked in the following order, from lowest to highest:

- **Acolyte**—those who are receiving instruction to become one of the téni—generally, the instructions requires tuition be paid to Concénzia by the students' families. The Concénzia Faith brings in both male and female students to become téni, though realistically the classes tend to be largely male, and there are fewer women than men represented in the higher ranks of the téni. (There have been only six female Archigi in the long history of the Faith.) During the acolyte period (typically three years), the students serve within the Faith, doing menial tasks for the téni, and also begin to learn the chants and mental discipline necessary for Ilmodo, the manipulation of the universe-energy. Typically, only 10 percent or less of the acolytes receive the Marque of the Téni. There are schools for acolytes in all the major cities of Nessantico, each presided over by the a'téni of the region.

- **E'Téni**—the lowest téni rank for those brought into the service of the Faith. The acolytes who receive their Marque are, with exceedingly few exceptions, awarded this rank, which denotes that they have some small skill with the Ilmodo. At this point, they are generally tasked with menial labor that requires the magic of Cénzi, such as lighting the city lamps, and expected to increase their skill and demonstrate their continuing mastery of the Ilmodo.

- **O'Téni**—an e'téni will be awarded this rank generally after one to five years of service, at which point they are either put in service of one of the temples, administering to the needs of the community, or they are placed in charge of one of the téni-powered industries within the city. This is where most téni will end their careers. Only a select few will pass this rank to become u'téni.

- **U'Téni**—u'teni serve directly under the a'teni of the region. An u'téni is generally responsible for maintaining one of the temples of the city, and overseeing the activities of the o'téni attached to that temple.

- **A'Téni**—the highest rank within the Faith with the exception of that of Archigos. The a'téni each are in charge of a region centered around one of the large cities of the Holdings. There, they generally

wield enormous power and influence with the
political leaders and over the citizenry. At times
this can be a contentious relationship; most often,
however, it is neutral or mutually beneficial. In the
year of Kraljica Marguerite's Jubilee, there are
twenty-three a'téni in the Faith, an increase of three
from the time she ascended the throne. Generally,
the larger and more influential the city where they
are based, the more influence the a'téni has within
the Faith.

- **Archigos**—the head of the Faith. This is not
  necessarily an elective office. Often, the Archigos
  designates his or her own successor from among
  the a'téni or even potentially a favorite u'téni.
  However, in practice, there have been "coups"
  within Concénzia where either the Archigos died
  before naming a successor, or where the right of
  the successor to ascend to the position has been
  disputed, sometimes violently. When that happens,
  those a'téni who aspire to the seat of the Archigos
  are locked in a special room within the Archigos'
  Temple for the Concord A'Téni. What happens
  there is a matter of great speculation and debate.
  One will, however, emerge as Archigos.

The Creation of Cénzi:

*At the start of all things, there was only Vucta, the
Great Night, the eyeless female essence who had always
existed, wandering alone through the nothingness of the
universe. Though Vucta could not see the stars, she could
feel their heat, and when she was cold she would come
to them and stay for a time. It was near one star that she
found something she had never experienced before: a
world—a place of rocks and water, and she stayed there
for a time, wondering and dreaming as she walked in
this strange place, touching everything to feel its shape
and listening to the wind and the surf, feeling the rain
and the snow and the touch of the clouds. She hoped*

*that here, in this strange place near the star, there might
be another like her, but there were no animals here yet,
nor trees, nor anything living.*

*As Vucta walked the world, wisps of her dream-
thoughts gathered around her like a mist, coalescing and
hardening and finally growing heavy from their sheer
volume. The dream-thoughts began to shape themselves,
a white shroud around Vucta that grew longer and more
substantial as she walked, heavier and heavier with each
step until the weightiest part of it drooped to the ground
and snagged on a rock. Eyeless, Vucta could not see that.
She continued her walking and her thinking, and her
dream-thoughts poured from her, but now they lay solid
where they had fallen, stretching and thinning as she
strode away from where they were caught. Vucta, in truth
was already growing tired of this place and her search,
and she desired the heat of another sun, so she leaped
away from the world and the shroud of her dream-
thoughts snapped as she flew.*

*Vucta's dream-thoughts lay there, all of them
coalescing, and when the sun shone on the first day after
Vucta's departure, there was a form like hers curled on
the ground. On the second day, the sun's light made the
dream-thoughts stir, and the form moved arms and legs,
though it did not know itself. The dream-thoughts that
were the yearning of Vucta gathered in its head, and
from Vucta's desire to know the place where she walked,
they made eyes in the face.*

*On the third day, when the sun touched it once more,
it opened those eyes and it saw the world. "I am Cénzi,"
the creature said, "and this place is mine." And he rose
then and began to walk about. . . .*

That is the opening of the Toustour, the All-Tale.
In time, as the creation tale continues, Cénzi would
become lonely and he would create companions—the
Moitidi—fashioning them from the breath of his body,
which still contained Vucta's strong power. Those

companions, in turn, would imitate their creator and fashion all the living creatures of the earth: plant and animal, including the humans. The Moitidi's own breaths were weak, and thus those they created were correspondingly more flawed. But it was Cénzi's breath and the weaker breaths of the Moitidi that permeated the atmosphere of the world and would become the Ilmodo, which humans through prayer, devotion to Cénzi, and intense study could learn to shape.

But the relationship between Cénzi and his offspring would always be contentious, marred by strife and jealousy. Cénzi had given his creations laws that they were to follow, but in time, they began to change and ignore those laws, flaunting themselves over Cénzi. Cénzi would become angry with his creations for their attitudes, but they were unrepentant, and so they began to war openly against Cénzi. It was a long and brutal conflict, and few of the living creatures would survive it, for in that past there had been many types of creatures who could speak and think. Cénzi's throwing down of the Moitidi as they wrestled and fought would cause mountains to rise up and valleys to form, shaping the world which had until then been flat, with but one great ocean. The final blow that destroyed most of the Moitidi would fracture the very earth, tear apart the land, and create the deep rift into which the Strettosei would flow.

After that immense blow that shook the entire world, those few Moitidi who remained fled and hid and cowered. Cénzi, though, was haunted by what had happened, and he wished to find Vucta and speak with her, whose dream-thoughts had made him. Only a single speaking and thinking species were left of all of Cénzi's grandchildren, and he made this promise to them, our own ancestors: that if they remained faithful to him, he would always listen to them and send his power back to them, and that one day, he would return here and be with them forever.

With that promise, he left the world to wander the night between the stars.

In the view of the Concénzia Faith, Cénzi is the only God worthy of worship (Vucta being considered by the Concénzian scholars to be more an all-pervading spirit rather than an entity), and it is His laws, given to the Moitidi, that the Faith has codified and now follows. The gods worshipped by other religions within and without the Holdings are those cowardly Moitidi who came out of hiding when Cénzi left and have deceived their followers into thinking they are true gods. The surviving Moitidi remain in mortal fear of Cénzi's return and flee whenever Cénzi's thoughts turn back to this world, as they do, reputedly, when the faithful pray strongly enough.

The truth of this is shown in that the laws of human-kind, wherever they may live and whomever they may claim to worship, have a similarity at the core—because they all derive from the original tenets of Cénzi.

The Divolonté:

The Divolonté is a loose collection of rules and regulations by which the Concénzia Faith is governed, the majority of which derive from the Toustour. However, the Divolonté is secular in origin, created and added to by the various Archigi and a'téni through the centuries, while the Toustour is considered to be derived from Cénzi's own words. The Divolonté is also a dynamic document, undergoing slow, continual evolution through the auspices of the Archigos and the a'téni. Many of its precepts and commands are somewhat archaic, and are ignored or even flaunted by the current Faith. It is, however, the Divolonté that the conservative element within the Faith quotes when they look at the threat of other faiths, such as that of the Numetodo.

Allesandra ca'Vörl

HER VATARH HAD BEEN THE SUN around which she had orbited for as long as she could remember. Now that sun, at long last, was setting.

The message had arrived from Brezno by fast-rider, and she stared at the words scrawled by a hasty, fair hand. *"Your vatarh is dying. If you want to see him, hurry."* That was the entire message. It was signed by Archigos Semini of Brezno and sealed with his signet.

Vatarh is dying . . . The great Hïrzg Jan of Firenzcia, after whom she had named her only child, was passing. The words set alight a sour fire in her belly; the words swam on the page with the salt tears that welled unbidden in her eyes. She sat there—at her fine desk, in her opulent offices near the Gyula's palais in Malacki—and she saw a droplet hit the paper to smudge the inked words.

She hated that Vatarh could still affect her so strongly; she hated that she cared. She should have hated him, but she couldn't. No matter how hard she'd tried over the years, she couldn't.

One might curse the sun for its scorching heat or its absence, but without the sun there was no life.

"I hate him," she declared to Archigos Ana. It had been two years since Ana had snatched her away from her vatarh to hold her as hostage. Two years, and he still hadn't paid the ransom to bring her back. She was thirteen, on the cusp of her menarche, and he had abandoned her. What had originally been anxiety and disappointment had slowly transformed inside her into anger. At least that's what she believed.

"No, you don't," Ana said quietly, stroking her hair. They were standing on the balcony of her apartments in the Temple complex in Nessantico, staring down to where knots of green-clad téni hurried to their duties. "Not really. If he paid the ransom tomorrow, you would be glowing and ready to run back to him. Look inside yourself, Allesandra. Look honestly. Isn't that true?"

"Well, he must hate me," she retorted, "or he'd have paid."

Ana had hugged her tightly then. "He will," she told Allesandra. "He will. It's just . . . Allesandra, your vatarh wished to sit on the Sun Throne. He has always been a proud man, and because I took you away, he was never able to realize his dream. You remind him of all he lost . . . And that's my fault. Not yours. It's not yours at all."

*   *   *

Vatarh hadn't paid. Not for ten long years. It had been Fynn, the new son her matarh Greta had given the Hïrzg, who basked in Vatarh's affections, who was taught the ways of war, who was named as the new A'Hïrzg—the title that should have been hers. Instead of her vatarh and her matarh, it was Archigos Ana who become her surrogate parent, shepherding her through puberty and adolescence, comforting Allesandra through her first crushes and infatuations, teaching her the ways of ca'-and-cu' society, escorting her to dances and parties, treating her not as a captive but as a niece it had become her responsibility to raise.

"I love you, Tantzia," Allesandra said to Ana. She'd taken to calling the Archigos 'aunt.' The news had come to Kraljiki Justi that a treaty between the Holdings and the Firenzcian "Coalition" was to be signed in Passe a'Fiume, and as part of the negotiations, Hïrzg Jan had finally paid the ransom for his daughter. She'd been a decade in Nessantico, nearly half her life. Now, at 21, she was to return to the life she'd lost so long ago and she was frightened by the prospect. Once, this had been all she'd wanted.

Now . . .

Part of her wanted to stay here. Here, where she knew she was loved.

Ana folded her in her arms. Allesandra was taller than the Archigos now, and Ana had to raise up on tiptoes to kiss her forehead. "I love you too, Allesandra. I'll miss you, but it's time for you to go home. Just know that I will always be here for you. Always. You are part of my heart, my dear. Forever. . . ."

Allesandra had hoped that she could bask in the sun of her vatarh's love again. Yes, she'd heard all about how the new A'Hïrzg Fynn was the child Hïrzg Jan had always desired: skilled at riding, at the sword, at diplomacy. She'd heard how he was being groomed already for a career in the Garde Firenzcia. But she had once been the pride of her vatarh, too. Surely she could become so again.

But she knew as soon as he looked at her, across the parley tent there at Passe a'Fiume, that it was not to be. In his hawkish eyes, there had been a smoldering distaste. He'd glanced at her appraisingly, as he might at a stranger—and indeed, she was a stranger to him: a young woman now, no longer the girl he'd lost. He'd taken her hands and accepted her curtsy as he might have any ca'-and-cu' and passed her off to Archigos Semini a moment later.

Fynn had been at his side—the age now that she'd been when she'd been taken—and he looked appraisingly at his older sister as he might have at some rival. Allesandra had sought Ana's gaze from across the tent, and the woman had smiled sadly toward her and raised her hand in farewell. There had been tears in Ana's eyes, sparkling in the sun that beat through the thin canvas of the tent. Ana, at least, had been true to her word. She had written Allesandra regularly. She had negotiated with her vatarh to be allowed to attend Allesandra's marriage to Pauli ca'Xielt, the son of the Gyula of West Magyaria and thus a politically-advantageous marriage for the Hïrzg, and a loveless one for Allesandra.

Ana had even, surreptitiously, been present at the birth of Allesandra's son, nearly sixteen years ago now. Archigos Ana—the heretical and false Archigos according to Firenzcia, whom Allesandra was obliged to hate as a good citizen of the Coalition—had blessed the child and pronounced the name that Allesandra had given him: Jan. She'd done so without rebuke and without comment. She'd done so with a gentle smile and a kiss.

Even naming her child for her vatarh had changed nothing. It had not brought him closer to Allesandra—Hïrzg Jan had mostly ignored his great-son and namesake. Jan was in the company of Hïrzg Jan perhaps twice a year, when he and Allesandra visited for state occasions, and only rarely did the Hïrzg speak directly to his great-son.

Now ... Now her vatarh was dying and she couldn't help crying for him. Or perhaps it was that she couldn't help crying for herself. Angrily, she wiped at the dampness on her cheeks with her sleeve. "Aeri!" she called to her secretary. "Come in here! I have to go to Brezno ..."

Allesandra strode into the Hïrzg's bedchamber tossing aside her travel-stained cloak, her hair wind-tossed and the smell of horse on her clothes. She pushed past the servants who tried to assist her and went to the bed. The chevarittai and various relatives gathered there moved aside to let her approach; she could feel their appraising stares on her back. She stared at the wizened, dried-apple face on the pillow and barely recognized him.

"Is he ... ?" she asked brusquely, but then she heard the phlegm-wracked rattle of his breath and saw the slow movement of his chest under the blankets. The room stank of sickness despite the perfumed candles. "Out!" she told them all, gesturing. "Tell Fynn I've come, but leave me alone with my vatarh. Out!"

They scattered, as she knew they would. None of them attempted to protest, though the Healers frowned at her from under carefully-lowered brows, and she could hear the whispers even as they fled. *"It's no wonder her husband stays away from her ... A goat has better manners ... She has the arrogance of Nessantico ... "*

She slammed the door in their faces.

Then, staring down at her vatarh's gray, sunken face, she finally allowed herself to cry, kneeling alongside his bed and holding his cold, withered hands. "I loved you, Vatarh," she told him. Alone with him, there could be truth. "I did. Even after you abandoned me, even after you gave Fynn all the affection I wanted, I still loved you. I could have been the heir you deserved. I will *still* be that, if I have the chance." She heard the scrape of bootsteps at the door and rose to her feet, wiping at her eyes with the sleeve of her tashta, and sniffing once as Fynn pushed the door open. He strode into the chamber—

Fynn never simply walked into a room. "Sister," he said. "I see the news reached you."

Allesandra stood, arms folded. She would not let him realize how deeply seeing her vatarh on his deathbed had affected her. She shrugged. "I still have sources here in Brezno, even when my brother fails to send a messenger."

"It slipped my mind," he said. "But I figured you would hear anyway." The smile he gave her was more sneer, twisted by the long, puckered scar that ran from the corner of his right eye and across his lip to the chin: the mark of a Tennshah scimitar. Fynn, at twenty-four, had the hard, lean body of a professional soldier, a figure that suited the loose pants and shirt that he wore. Such Tennshah clothing had become fashionable in Firenzcia since the border wars six years before, where Fynn had engaged the T'Sha's forces and pushed Firenzcia's borders nearly a hundred miles eastward, and where he had acquired the long scar that marred his handsome face.

It was during that war that Fynn had won their vatarh's affection entirely and ended any lingering hope of Allesandra's that she might become Hïrzgin.

"The Healers say the end will come sometime today, or possibly tonight if he continues to fight—Vatarh never did give up easily, did he? But the soul shredders will come for him this time. There's no longer any doubt of that." Fynn glanced down at the figure on the bed as the Hïrzg took another long, shuddering breath. The young man's gaze was affectionate and sad, and yet somehow appraising at the same time, as if he were gauging how long it might be before he could slip the signet ring from the folded hands and put it on his own finger; how soon he could place the golden crown-band of the Hïrzg on the curls of his own head. "There's nothing you or I can do, Sister," he said, "other than pray that Cénzi receives Vatarh's soul kindly. Beyond that . . ." He shrugged. "How is my nephew Jan?" he asked.

"You'll see soon enough," Allesandra told him. "He's

on his way to Brezno behind me and should arrive tomorrow."

"And your husband? The dear Pauli?"

Allesandra sniffed. "If you're trying to goad me, Fynn, it won't work. I've suggested to Pauli that he remain in Malacki and attend to state business. What of yourself? Have you found someone to marry yet, or do you still prefer the company of soldiers and horses?"

The smile was slow in coming and uncertain when it appeared. "Now who goads whom?" he asked. "Vatarh and I had made no decisions on that yet, and now it seems that the decision will be mine alone—though I'll certainly listen to any suggestions you might have." He opened his arms, and she reluctantly allowed him to embrace her. Neither one of them tightened their arms but only encircled the other as if hugging a thorn bush, and the gesture ended after a single breath. "Allesandra, I know there's always been a distance between us, but I hope that we can work as one when . . ." He hesitated, and she watched his chest rise with a long inhalation. ". . . when I am the Hïrzg. I will need your counsel, Sister."

"And I will give it to you," she told him. She leaned forward and kissed the air a careful finger's width from his scarred cheek. "Little brother."

"I wish we could have truly been little brother and big sister," he answered. "I wish I could have known you then."

"As do I," she told him. *And I wish those were more than just empty, polite words we both say because we know they're demanded by etiquette.* "Stay here with me now? Let Vatarh feel us together for once."

She felt his hesitation and wondered whether he'd refuse. But after a breath, he lifted one shoulder. "For a turn of the glass or so," he said. "We can pray for him. Together."

He pulled two chairs to the side of the bed, placing them an arm's length apart. They sat, they watched the faltering rise and fall of their vatarh's chest, and they said nothing more.

~

Jan ca'Vörl

"I HAVE TO RIDE as quickly as I can to Brezno,"
his matarh had told him. "I've instructed the servants to pack up our rooms for travel. I want you to follow along as soon as they have the carriages ready. And
Jan, see if you can convince your vatarh to come with
you." She kissed his forehead then, more urgently than
she had in years, and pulled him to her. "I love you," she
whispered. "I hope you know that."

"I do," he'd told her, pulling away and grinning at her.
"And I hope *you* know that."

She'd smiled, hugging him a final time before she
swung herself onto the horse held by the two chevarittai
who would accompany her. He watched the trio clatter
away down the road of their estate at a gallop.

That had been two days ago. His matarh should have
made Brezno yesterday. Jan leaned his head back against
the cushions of the carriage, watching the landscape of
southern Firenzcia pass by in the green-gold light of late
afternoon. The driver had told him that they would be
stopping at the next village for the evening, and arrive
in Brezno by midday tomorrow. He wondered what he'd
find there.

He was alone in his carriage.

He'd asked his vatarh Pauli to come with him, as his
matarh had requested. The servants had told him that
Pauli was in his apartments at the estate—in a separate
wing from those of Allesandra—and Pauli's chief aide
had gone in to announce Jan. The aide had returned
with arched eyebrows. "Your vatarh says he can spare a

few moments," he'd said, escorting Jan to one of the reception rooms off the main corridor. Jan could hear the muffled giggling of two women from a bedroom leading from the room. The door opened in the middle of a man's coarse laugh. His vatarh was in a robe, his hair was tousled and unkempt, and his beard untrimmed. He smelled of perfume and wine. "A moment," he'd said to Jan, touching a finger to his lips before half-staggering to the door leading to the bedroom and opening it slightly. "Shh!" he said loudly. "I am trying to conduct a conversation about my wife with my son," he said. That was greeted by shrill laughter.

"Tell the boy to join us," Jan heard one of them call out. He felt his face flush at the comment as Pauli waggled his forefinger toward the unseen woman.

"The two of you are delightfully wicked," Pauli told them. Jan imagined the women: rouged, bewigged, half-clothed, or perhaps entirely nude, like one of the portraits of the Moitidi goddesses that adorned the halls. He felt himself responding to the image and forced it out of his mind. "I'll be there in a moment," Pauli continued. "You ladies have more wine."

He closed the door and leaned heavily against it. "Sorry," he told Jan. "I have ... company. Now, what did the bitch want? Oh—you may tell your matarh for me that the a'Gyula of West Magyaria has better things to do than ride to Brezno because someone may or may not be dying. When the old bastard finally does breathe his last, I'll undoubtedly be sent to the funeral as our representative, and that'll be soon enough." His words were slurred. He blinked slowly and belched. "You don't need to go either, boy. Stay here, why don't you? The two of us could have some fun, eh? I'm sure these ladies have friends ..."

Jan shook his head. "I promised Matarh that I'd ask you to come, and I have. I'm leaving tonight; the servants have nearly finished packing the carriages."

"Ah, yes," Pauli said. "You're such a good, obedient

child, aren't you? Your matarh's pride and joy." He pushed himself from the door and stood unsteadily, pointing at Jan with a fingertip that drifted from one side to another. "You don't want to be like her," he said. "She won't be satisfied until she's running the whole world. She's an ambitious whore with a heart carved from flint."

He'd heard Pauli insult his matarh a thousand times, more with each passing year. He'd always gritted his teeth before, had pretended not to hear or mumbled a protest that Pauli would ignore. This time . . . The nascent flush in Jan's face went lava-red. He took three swift steps across the carpeted room, drew his hand back, and slapped his vatarh across the face. Pauli reeled, staggering back against the door, which opened and toppled him onto a braided rug there. Jan saw the two women inside—half-clothed, indeed, and in his vatarh's bed. They covered their breasts with the sheets, screaming. Pauli lifted an unbelieving hand to his face; over the thin beard, Jan could see the imprint of his fingers on his vatarh's cheek.

He wondered for a moment what he'd do if Pauli got up, but his vatarh only blinked again and laughed as if startled.

"Well, you didn't need to do *that*," he said.

"You may have whatever opinion you want of Matarh," Jan told him. "I don't care. But from now on, Vatarh, keep it to yourself or we will have more than words." With that, before Pauli could rise from the carpet or answer, Jan turned and rushed from the room.